D1239289

Short Stories International

Short Stories International

E. W. JOHNSON
Western Illinois University

HOUGHTON MIFFLIN COMPANY
BOSTON

New York
Atlanta
Geneva, Illinois
Dallas
Palo Alto

"Hills Like White Elephants" is reprinted
with the permission of Charles Scribner's Sons
from Men without Women by Ernest Hemingway.
Copyright 1927 Charles Scribner's Sons;
renewal copyright © 1955 Ernest Hemingway.

Copyright © 1969 by E. W. Johnson.
The selections reprinted in this book are
used by permission of and special arrangement with the proprietors of their re-
spective copyrights. All rights reserved.
No part of this work may be reproduced or
transmitted in any form or by any means,
electronic or mechanical, including photo-
copying and recording, or by any information
storage or retrieval system, without permission in writing from the publisher.

Printed in the U. S. A.

For Dr. John W. Eaton and David S. Rowe

To originate is carefully, patiently,
and understandingly to combine.
EDGAR ALLAN POE

E. W. Johnson *was born an Aries in*
1941 and has worked as a professional
gambler, sales promoter, writers' conference
director, and university instructor. He
earned a bachelor's degree from Florida
State University and a Master of Fine Arts
from the Writers' Workshop at the
University of Iowa; he has published two
books of art criticism (Sinclair,
Geoffrey: Power and the Image)
and a textbook (Contemporary American
Thought) *and, under a pseudonym,*
has written two erotic novels. E. W. lives
in a large squat crumbling Gothic country
house with his dog, Samantha. He teaches
creative writing at Western Illinois Uni-
versity and is completing a musical
comedy, a novel about race track
betting, and a book-length study of the
new nonfiction, co-edited by Tom Wolfe.

Preface

The fiction included in this collection spotlights the short story as a world-wide literary form. Although each individual selection is structurally unique, the short story has proven adaptable to nearly every culture in the world. This collection is perhaps a first attempt to gather representative contemporary stories by eminent native craftsmen. Indeed, many of these stories have never before been anthologized and are little-known in the English-speaking world.

The following thirty-one short stories offer a variety of literary techniques and cultural definitions; yet they form an artistically cohesive group of readings. They ask the basic questions: Who am I? Where do I come from? Where am I going? What should I do on the way? The latter half of the twentieth century is widely accused of struggling in disenchantment and confusion; but these stories do not negate the dignity of the human experience. Mankind—isolated, angry, absurd, frightened, guilty, and occasionally proud—is united here by a common vitality and a persevering spirit.

E. W. J.

Carthage, Illinois

FREDERIC WILL *is a poet, translator, classics scholar, and failed violinist. He publishes and edits an international poetry magazine,* Micromegas, *and is Professor of English and Director of the University of Iowa's Translation Workshop. Mr. Will, a marathon walker, world-wanderer, bicyclist, and beetle collector, earned a* B.A. *degree from Indiana University and a* Ph.D *from Yale. He has written six books of poetry, two translations of Greek* (The King's Flute, The Twelve Words of the Gypsy), *eight books of literary criticism, a travel book* (From a Year in Greece), *and a philosophical study* (The Argument of Water). *Fred lives in Iowa City with his wife, children, and two Corgi dogs, Chubbigh and Bendigh.*

A Note on the Translated Stories

Many translators would say that they never overcome the profound differences betwen the language of the original work and the language they're working into. Many would say they don't even try to overcome these differences, that they are satisfied with trying to make something linguistically new; they accept their own limitations as part of the business.

When these translators interpret their efforts, they may be partially wrong. They may be echoing a commonplace view of their craft. Whether the translator tries to equal what he translates, or to improve it, or to set up a balance in his own language, he is at least questioning the decisiveness of the difference between languages. His effort is based on an assumption that the peculiar genius of a specific language is a fact no more important than the general human content, the rendering of the human situation, that the language is capable of containing. That assumption underlies his willingness to throw himself and his own language against the cliffs of a foreign language; he is not simply committing suicide.

There is a better chance of overcoming the inherent difficulties of translating some of the stories in this collection than of others. Take Borges' "The Shape of the Sword" or Sartre's "The Room." Each story has a salient human content; it brings out discernible and describable patterns of human psychology. What is most important about Borges' story is what it says about a kind of pride and a kind of compensation for humiliation. This much of the story belongs almost accidentally to the Spanish in which it is embodied. Sartre, too, deals with fairly gross issues of psychopathology: morbidity, self-destructiveness, child-parent hatreds. The firmest part of his story also can well survive transplanting. When these stories are translated, we are still able to confront fully the issues they present.

Other stories lose a good deal more in translation, as do Robbe-Grillet's "The Secret Room," Gascar's "The Cat," and Landolfi's "Gogol's Wife." These stories depend heavily on atmosphere, on word-music, on harmonies of sound and sense, and on the distinctive cultural auras surrounding the languages in which they were written. It is possible to translate them well, as the faithful and lively English versions in this collection prove. But I believe it must have been harder to translate them, than it was to translate the two stories mentioned above, into an English which brings out their proportion of uniqueness and universality. A great deal of labor lies behind what we see here on the translated page.

The stories in this collection are readable, spirited, and creatively English. They have been drawn from many languages and cultures: Greek, Icelandic, French, German, Spanish, Russian, Italian. Inevitably, they have lost qualities found in all those languages and cultures, but being joined to one another gives them a distinctive flavor. Collectively they form an imaginary museum, a mosaic, a tapestry to which the individual stories contribute pictures of various parts of our world today.

The new tapestry which these stories form in English looks different from any of the particular threads of which it is woven. It looks very different from the tapestry which would have been made had all these stories been woven together in their original forms: German with French with Italian, etc. But that's the way with new tapestries! It is possible that they will be improvements, and it is likely that they will at least present things freshly.

To the extent that universal themes fill these stories and can cross language barriers relatively unchanged, there is an obvious value in placing these stories side by side in a single language, where themes can be seen as clearly and as saliently as possible. (How better, really, could we confront the sense of horror and grotesquerie than by having the Gascar and Landolfi and Mrozek stories juxtaposed in this way?) But this is to speak of the most translatable threads in the tapestry. The least universal, the most locally colored threads will be more changed. They will, for all the translator's skill, be far more homogeneous and monochromatic in the new weaving than they had been before. French and Icelandic will, through English, come to sound, feel, and smell more alike than they in fact are.

To enjoy this change, rather than only to take it as part of our linguistic limitation, we need to think that in this reweaving English is itself made richer. Our own experience, even through the atmospheres and the tones of different languages, is extended beyond its usual range. All we need to do is to experiment with thinking in this way and, with the help of a collection like this one, we find out how much more English has become to us. We can even feel tempted to speak aggressively of translation, to turn our losses upside down and consider them winnings.

FREDERIC WILL

Iowa City, Iowa

Contents

Jorge Luis Borges was born in Buenos Aires in 1899 and was educated in Geneva and Spain. At first he wrote poetry but gradually turned his attention to the essay and the short story; in the thirties he began to conceive an original genre, "the fiction," a metaphysical fantasy resembling the adventure story.

"The Shape of the Sword" depends on a surprise ending. Had we known the truth at the beginning of the story, it would seem a story hardly worth retelling; but perhaps the surprise ending is more than a mere gimmick. Might there be some point to our confusion of the identity of coward and hero, betrayer and betrayed? Is that half-moon scar perhaps symbolic of a more fundamental scar? Is it true that "whatever one man does, it is as if all men did it"? Further Reading: Labyrinths (1962), Dreamtigers, (1964).

ARGENTINA

The Shape
of the Sword

JORGE LUIS BORGES

A spiteful scar crossed his face: an ash-colored and nearly perfect arc that creased his temple at one tip and his cheek at the other. His real name is of no importance; everyone in Tacuarembó called him the "Englishman from La Colorada." Cardoso, the owner of those fields, refused to sell them: I understand that the Englishman resorted to an unexpected argument: he confided to Cardoso the secret of the scar. The Englishman came from the border, from Río Grande del Sur; there are many who say that in Brazil he had been a smuggler. The fields were overgrown with grass, the waterholes brack-

Jorge Luis Borges, *Labyrinths.* © 1962 by New Directions. Reprinted by permission of New Directions Publishing Corporation. Translated by Donald A. Yates.

ish; the Englishman, in order to correct those deficiencies, worked fully as hard as his laborers. They say that he was severe to the point of cruelty, but scrupulously just. They say also that he drank: a few times a year he locked himself into an upper room, not to emerge until two or three days later as if from a battle or from vertigo, pale, trembling, confused and as authoritarian as ever. I remember the glacial eyes, the energetic leanness, the gray mustache. He had no dealings with anyone; it is a fact that his Spanish was rudimentary and cluttered with Brazilian. Aside from a business letter or some pamphlet, he received no mail.

The last time I passed through the northern provinces, a sudden overflowing of the Caraguatá stream compelled me to spend the night at La Colorada. Within a few moments, I seemed to sense that my appearance was inopportune; I tried to ingratiate myself with the Englishman; I resorted to the least discerning of passions: patriotism. I claimed as invincible a country with such spirit as England's. My companion agreed, but added with a smile that he was not English. He was Irish, from Dungarvan. Having said this, he stopped short, as if he had revealed a secret.

After dinner we went outside to look at the sky. It had cleared up, but beyond the low hills the southern sky, streaked and gashed by lightning, was conceiving another storm. Into the cleared up dining room the boy who had served dinner brought a bottle of rum. We drank for some time, in silence.

I don't know what time it must have been when I observed that I was drunk; I don't know what inspiration or what exultation or tedium made me mention the scar. The Englishman's face changed its expression; for a few seconds I thought he was going to throw me out of the house. At length he said in his normal voice:

"I'll tell you the history of my scar under one condition: that of not mitigating one bit of the opprobrium, of the infamous circumstances."

I agreed. This is the story that he told me, mixing his English with Spanish, and even with Portuguese:

"Around 1922, in one of the cities of Connaught, I was one of the many who were conspiring for the independence of Ireland. Of my comrades, some are still living, dedicated to peaceful pursuits; others, paradoxically, are fighting on desert and sea under the English flag; another, the most worthy, died in the courtyard of a barracks, at dawn, shot by men filled with sleep; still others (not the most unfortunate) met their destiny in the anonymous and almost secret battles of the civil war. We were Republicans, Catholics; we were, I suspect, Romantics. Ireland was for us not only the utopian future and the intolerable present; it was a bitter and cherished mythology, it was the circular towers and the red marshes, it was the repudiation of Parnell and the enormous epic poems which sang of the robbing of bulls which in another incarnation were heroes and in others fish and mountains . . . One afternoon I will never forget, an affiliate from Munster joined us: one John Vincent Moon.

"He was scarcely twenty years old. He was slender and flaccid at the same time; he gave the uncomfortable impression of being invertebrate. He had studied with fervor and with vanity nearly every page of Lord knows what Communist manual; he made use of dialectical materialism to put an end to any discussion whatever. The reasons one can have for hating another man, or for loving him, are infinite: Moon reduced the history of the universe to a sordid economic conflict. He affirmed that the revolution was predestined to succeed. I told him that for a gentleman only lost causes should be attractive . . . Night had already fallen; we continued our disagreement in the hall, on the stairs, then along the vague streets. The judgments Moon emitted impressed me less than his irrefutable, apodictic note. The new comrade did not discuss: he dictated opinions with scorn and with a certain anger.

"As we were arriving at the outlying houses, a sudden burst of gunfire stunned us. (Either before or afterwards we skirted the blank wall of a factory or barracks.) We moved into an unpaved street; a soldier, huge in the firelight, came out of a burning hut. Crying out, he ordered us to stop. I quickened my pace; my companion did not follow. I turned around: John Vincent Moon was motionless, fascinated, as if eternized by fear. I then ran back and knocked the soldier to the ground with one blow, shook Vincent Moon, insulted him and ordered him to follow. I had to take him by the arm; the passion of fear had rendered him helpless. We fled, into the night pierced by flames. A rifle volley reached out for us, and a bullet nicked Moon's right shoulder; as we were fleeing amid pines, he broke out in weak sobbing.

"In that fall of 1923 I had taken shelter in General Berkeley's country house. The general (whom I had never seen) was carrying out some administrative assignment or other in Bengal; the house was less than a century old, but it was decayed and shadowy and flourished in puzzling corridors and in pointless antechambers. The museum and the huge library usurped the first floor: controversial and uncongenial books which in some manner are the history of the nineteenth century; scimitars from Nishapur, along whose captured arcs there seemed to persist still the wind and violence of battle. We entered (I seem to recall) through the rear. Moon, trembling, his mouth parched, murmured that the events of the night were interesting; I dressed his wound and brought him a cup of tea; I was able to determine that his 'wound' was superficial. Suddenly he stammered in bewilderment:

" 'You know, you ran a terrible risk.'

"I told him not to worry about it. (The habit of the civil war had incited me to act as I did; besides, the capture of a single member could endanger our cause.)

"By the following day Moon had recovered his poise. He accepted a cigarette and subjected me to a severe interrogation on the 'economic resources of our revolutionary party.' His questions were very lucid; I told him (truthfully) that the situation was serious. Deep burst of rifle fire agitated the south. I told Moon our comrades were waiting for us. My overcoat and my revolver were in my room; when I returned, I found Moon stretched out on the sofa, his eyes closed. He imagined he had a fever; he invoked a painful spasm in his shoulder.

"At that moment I understood that his cowardice was irreparable. I clumsily entreated him to take care of himself and went out. This frightened man mortified me, as if I were the coward, not Vincent Moon. Whatever one man does, it is as if all men did it. For that reason it is not unfair that one disobedience in a garden should contaminate all humanity; for that reason it is not unjust that the crucifixion of a single Jew should be sufficient to save it. Perhaps Schopenhauer was right: I am all other men, any man is all men, Shakespeare is in some manner the miserable John Vincent Moon.

"Nine days we spent in the general's enormous house. Of the agonies and the successes of the war I shall not speak: I propose to relate the history of the scar that insults me. In my memory, those nine days form only a single day, save for the next to the last, when our men broke into a barracks and we were able to avenge precisely the sixteen comrades who had been machinegunned in Elphin. I slipped out of the house towards dawn, in the confusion of daybreak. At nightfall I was back. My companion was waiting for me upstairs: his would did not permit him to descend to the ground floor. I recall him having some volume of strategy in his hand, F. N. Maude or Clausewitz. 'The weapon I prefer is the artillery,' he confessed to me one night. He inquired into our plans; he liked to censure them or revise them. He also was accustomed to denouncing 'our deplorable economic basis'; dogmatic and gloomy, he predicted the disastrous end. *'C'est une affaire flambée,'* he murmured. In order to show that he was indifferent to being a physical coward, he magnified his mental arrogance. In this way, for good or for bad, nine days elapsed.

"On the tenth day the city fell definitely to the Black and Tans. Tall, silent horsemen patrolled the roads; ashes and smoke rode on the wind; on the corner I saw a corpse thrown to the ground, an impression less firm in my memory than that of a dummy on which the soldiers endlessly practiced their marksmanship, in the middle of the square . . . I had left when dawn was in the sky; before noon I returned. Moon, in the library, was speaking with someone; the tone of his voice told me he was talking on the telephone. Then I heard my name; then, that I would return at seven; then, the suggestion that they should arrest me as I was crossing the garden. My reasonable friend was reasonably selling me out. I heard him demand guarantees of personal safety.

"Here my story is confused and becomes lost. I know that I pursued the informer along the black, nightmarish halls and along deep stairways of dizzyness. Moon knew the house very well, much better than I. One or two times I lost him. I cornered him before the soldiers stopped me. From one of the general's collections of arms I tore a cutlass: with that half moon I carved into his face forever a half moon of blood. Borges, to you, a stranger, I have made this confession. Your contempt does not grieve me so much."

Here the narrator stopped. I noticed that his hands were shaking.

"And Moon?" I asked him.

"He collected his Judas money and fled to Brazil. That afternoon, in the square, he saw a dummy shot up by some drunken men."

I waited in vain for the rest of the story. Finally I told him to go on.

Then a sob went through his body; and with a weak gentleness he pointed to the whitish curved scar.

"You don't believe me?" he stammered. "Don't you see that I carry written on my face the mark of my infamy? I have told you the story thus so that you would hear me to the end. I denounced the man who protected me: I am Vincent Moon. Now despise me."

Soul of Wood and Other Stories, *Jakov
Lind's first collection of short stories, appeared in 1962 when the author was thirty-
five. Lind was born in Vienna, retreated to
Holland in 1938, lived in Germany with
forged papers from 1943 to 1945, then returned to Vienna for two years' study at the
Max Reinhart Academy of Dramatic Arts.
These years (many of which were spent on
the run, often in hiding and in fear) influenced Lind's later writing—writing which
often relies upon the Nazi scourge as a
metaphor of human experience.*

*Night journeys frequently serve to sym-
bolize a passage from one sort of life to another, a kind of descent into the underworld
prefatory to a rebirth. Jakov Lind has written
a modern version of that same symbolic trip.
Sharing a compartment on the train to Paris
with a cannibal, the narrator learns something: despite the reasonableness of the
cannibal's argument, the narrator discovers
that he wants to live, if only to take a walk
in Paris. The story is a rather savage but not
completely pessimistic comment on contemporary life. The narrator is surprisingly
matter-of-fact about sharing a compartment
with a cannibal. His reasons for living are
modest, and his descision to pull the cord
seems uncertainly motivated. What do
these aspects of the story suggest about the
modern world? Further Reading:* Soul of
Wood (1964), Landscape in Concrete
(1966).

AUSTRIA

Journey through the Night

JAKOV LIND

What do you see when you look back?
Not a thing. And when you look ahead?
Even less. That's right. That's how it is.

Reprinted by permission of Grove Press, Inc.
Copyright © 1964 by Jonathan Cape Ltd.,
London, and Grove Press, Inc., New York.
Translated by Ralph Manheim.

It was three o'clock in the morning and raining. The train didn't stop anywhere. There were lights somewhere in the countryside, but you couldn't be sure if they were windows or stars.

The tracks were tracks—but why shouldn't there be tracks in the clouds?

Paris was somewhere at the end of the trip. Which Paris? The earthly Paris—with cafés, green buses, fountains, and grimy white-washed walls? Or, the heavenly Paris? Carpeted bathrooms with a view of the Bois de Boulogne?

The fellow-passenger looked still paler in the bluish light. His nose was straight, his lips thin, his teeth uncommonly small. He had slick hair like a seal. A moustache, that's what he needs. He could do a balancing act on his nose. Under his clothes he is wet. Why doesn't he show his tusks?

After "that's how it is" he said nothing. That settled everything. Now he is smoking.

His skin is gray, that's obvious—it's taut, too. If he scratches himself it will tear. What else is there to look at? He has only one face and his suitcase. What has he got in the suitcase? Tools? Saw, hammer and chisel? Maybe a drill? What does he need a drill for? To bore holes in skulls? Some people drink beer that way. When empty, they can be painted. Will he paint my face? What colors? Water-color or oil? And what for? Children at Eastertime play with empty eggshells. His play with skulls.

Well, he said non-committally, putting out his cigarette. He crushed it against the aluminum, making a scratching sound. Well, how about it?

I don't know, I said. I can't make up my mind. Doesn't the fellow understand a joke?

Maybe you need a little more spunk, he said. Now's the time to make up your mind; in half an hour you'll be asleep anyway, then I'll do what I want with you.

I won't sleep tonight, I said. You've given me fair warning.

Warning won't do you any good, he said. Between three and four everybody falls into a dead sleep. You're educated, you should know that.

Yes, I know. But I got self-control.

Between three and four, said the man, rubbing the moustache that was yet to grow, all of us get locked away in our little cubicles, don't hear nothing, don't see nothing. We die, every last one of us. Dying restores us, after four we wake up and life goes on. Without that people couldn't stick it out so long.

I don't believe a word of it. You can't saw me up.

I can't eat you as you are, he said. Sawing's the only way. First the legs, then the arms, then the head. Everything in its proper order.

What do you do with the eyes?

Suck 'em.

Can the ears be digested or have they got bones in them?

No bones, but they're tough. Anyway, I don't eat everything, do you think I'm a pig?

A seal is what I thought.

That's more like it. So he admitted it. A seal, I knew it. How come he speaks German? Seals speak Danish and nobody can understand them.

How is it you don't speak Danish?

I was born in Sankt Pölten, he said. We didn't speak Danish in our family. He's being evasive. What would you expect? But maybe he is from Sankt Pölten; I've heard there are such people in the region.

And you live in France?

What's it to you? In half an hour you'll be gone. It's useful to know things when you've a future ahead of you, but in your situation . . .

Of course he's insane, but what can I do? He has locked the compartment (where did he get the keys?), Paris will never come. He's picked the right kind of weather. You can't see a thing and it's raining; of course he can kill me. When you're scared you've got to talk fast. Would you kindly describe it again. Kindly will flatter his vanity. Murderers are sick. Sick people are vain. The kindly is getting results.

Well, first comes the wooden mallet, he said, exactly like a schoolteacher . . . you always have to explain everything twice to stupid pupils; stupidity is a kind of fear, teachers give out cuffs or marks.

. . . then after the mallet comes the razor, you've got to let the blood out, most of it at least, even so you always mess up your chin on the liver; well, and then, as we were saying, comes the saw.

Do you take off the leg at the hip or the knee?

Usually at the hip, sometimes the knee. At the knee when I have time.

And the arms?

The arms? Never, at the elbow, always at the shoulder.

Why?

Maybe it's just a habit, don't ask me. There isn't much meat on the forearm, in your case there's none at all, but when it's attached, it looks like something. How do you eat the leg of a roast chicken?

He was right.

If you want pointers about eating people, ask a cannibal.

Do you use spices?

Only salt. Human flesh is sweet, you know that yourself. Who likes sweet meat?

He opened the suitcase. No, I screamed, I'm not asleep yet.

Don't be afraid, you scarecat, I just wanted to show you I wasn't kidding. He fished about among the tools. There were only five implements in the suitcase, but they were lying around loose. It was a small suitcase, rather like a doctor's bag. But a doctor's instruments are strapped to the velvet lid. Here they were lying around loose. Hammer, saw, drill, chisel and pliers. Ordinary carpenter's tools. There was also a rag. Wrapped in the rag was the salt-cellar. A common glass salt-cellar such as you find on the tables in cheap restaurants. He's stolen it somewhere, I said to myself. He's a thief.

He held the salt-cellar under my nose. There was salt in it. He shook some out on my hand. Taste it, he said, first-class salt. He saw the rage in my face, I was speechless. He laughed. Those little teeth revolted me.

Yes, he said and laughed again, I bet you'd rather be salted alive than eaten dead.

He shut the suitcase and lit another cigarette. It was half past three. The train was flying over the rails, but there won't be any Paris at the end. Neither earthly nor heavenly. I was in a trap. Death comes to every man. Does it really matter how you die? You can get run over, you can get shot by accident, at a certain age your heart is likely to give out, or you can die of lung cancer, which is very common nowadays. One way or another you kick the bucket. Why not be eaten by a madman in the Nice–Paris express?

All is vanity, what else. You've got to die, only you don't want to. You don't have to live, but you want to. Only necessary things are important. Big fish eat little ones, the lark eats the worm and yet how sweetly he sings, cats eat mice and no one ever killed a cat for it—every animal eats every other just to stay alive, men eat men, what's unnatural about that? Is it more natural to eat pigs or calves? Does it hurt more when you can say "it hurts"? Animals don't cry, human beings cry when a relative dies, but how can anybody cry over his own death? Am I so fond of myself? So it must be vanity. Nobody's heart breaks over his own death. That's the way it is.

A feeling of warmth and well-being came over me. Here is a madman, he wants to eat me. But at least he wants something. What do I want? Not to eat anybody. Is that so noble? What's left when you don't want to do what you certainly ought to do?

If you don't do that which disgusts you, what becomes of your disgust? It sticks in your throat. Nothing sticks in the throat of the man from Sankt Pölten. He swallows all.

A voice spoke very softly, it sounded almost affectionate: There, you see you're getting sleepy, that comes from thinking. What have you got to look forward to in Paris? Paris is only a city. Whom do you need anyway, and who needs you? You're going to Paris. Well, what of it? Sex and drinking won't make you any happier. And certainly working won't. Money won't do you a particle of good. What are you getting out of life? Just go to sleep. You won't wake up, I can promise you.

But I don't want to die, I whispered. Not yet. I want . . . to go for a walk in Paris.

Go for a walk in Paris? Big deal. It will only make you tired. There are enough people taking walks and looking at the shop windows. The restaurants are overcrowded. So are the whore-houses. Nobody needs you in Paris. Just do me a favor, go to sleep. The night won't go on forever; I'll have to gobble everything down so fast you'll give me a bellyache.

I've got to eat you. In the first place I'm hungry, and in the second place I like you. I told you right off that I liked you and you thought, the guy is a queer. But now you know. I'm a simple cannibal. It's not a profession, it's a need. Good Lord, man, try to understand: now you've got an aim in life. Your life has purpose, thanks to me. You think it was by accident you came into my compartment? There's no such thing as an accident. I watched you all along the platform in Nice. And then you came into my compartment. Why mine and not someone else's? Because I'm so good-looking? Don't make me laugh. Is a seal good-looking? You came in here because you knew there'd be something doing.

Very slowly he opened the little suitcase. He took out the mallet and closed the suitcase. He held the mallet in his hand.

Well, how about it? he said.

Just a minute, I said. Just a minute. And suddenly I stood up. God only knows how I did it, but I stood up on my two feet and stretched out my hand. The little wire snapped, the lead seal fell, the train hissed and screeched. Screams came from next door. Then the train stopped. The man from Sankt Pölten stowed the mallet quickly in his suitcase and took his coat; he was at the door in a flash. He opened the door and looked around: I pity you, he said. This bit of foolishness is going to cost you a ten-thousand-franc fine, you nitwit, now you'll have to take your walk in Paris.

People crowded into the compartment, a conductor and a policeman appeared. Two soldiers and a pregnant woman shook their fists at me.

Already the seal from Sankt Pölten was outside, right under my window. He shouted something. I opened the window: See, he shouted, you've made an ass of yourself for life. Look who wants to live. He spat and shrugged his shoulders. Carrying his suitcase in his right hand, he stepped cautiously down the embankment and vanished in the dark. Like a country doctor on his way to deliver a baby.

The title of this story underscores the fairy-tale quality of "The Sailor-Boy's Tale", but it also emphasizes that the story deals with a boy. Isak Dinesen writes of a boy's initiation into manhood. In almost all cultures the celebration of this event involves certain mythic patterns of death and sex: the child dies, and the man emerges, a man in the biological sense that at puberty he is capable of reproducing his kind. The initiation might involve the slaughter of a giant or an animal; it might involve the transmutation of magical creatures between animal and human form. "Here he was," says the narrator of the tale, "he had killed a man, and had kissed a girl . . . He was Simon, a man like the men around him. . . ." This story, with its mythic overtones, dramatically illustrates the universality and timelessness of the event.

Isak Dinesen (pseudonym of the Baronesse Karen Blixen) was born in 1885 and studied painting in Copenhagen, Paris, and Rome. She always ignored the current literary climate; her work exists apart from time and fashion. Her first successful book of stories, Seven Gothic Tales, *was published in 1934, and she continued to write eerie, diabolic tales until her death in 1962. Further Reading:* Seven Gothic Tales (1934), Winter's Tales (1942), The Angelic Avengers (1947).

DENMARK

The Sailor-Boy's Tale

ISAK DINESEN

The barque *Charlotte* was on her way from Marseilles to Athens, in grey weather, on a high sea, after three days' heavy gale. A small sailor-boy, named

From *Winter's Tales,* by Isak Dinesen. Copyright 1942 by Random House, Inc. Reprinted by permission. Also published by Putnam & Company Ltd., London, and reprinted with their permission.

Simon, stood on the wet, swinging deck, held on to a shroud, and looked up towards the drifting clouds, and to the upper top-gallant yard of the main-mast.

A bird, that had sought refuge upon the mast had got her feet entangled in some loose tackle-yarn of the halliard, and, high up there, struggled to get free. The boy on the deck could see her wings flapping and her head turning from side to side.

Through his own experience of life he had come to the conviction that in this world everyone must look after himself, and expect no help from others. But the mute, deadly fight kept him fascinated for more than an hour. He wondered what kind of bird it would be. These last days a number of birds had come to settle in the barque's rigging: swallows, quails, and a pair of peregrine falcons; he believed that this bird was a peregrine falcon. He remembered how, many years ago, in his own country and near his home, he had once seen a peregrine falcon quite close, sitting on a stone and flying straight up from it. Perhaps this was the same bird. He thought: "That bird is like me. Then she was there, and now she is here."

At that a fellow-feeling rose in him, a sense of common tragedy; he stood looking at the bird with his heart in his mouth. There were none of the sailors about to make fun of him; he began to think out how he might go up by the shrouds to help the falcon out. He brushed his hair back and pulled up his sleeves, gave the deck round him a great glance, and climbed up. He had to stop a couple of times in the swaying rigging.

It was indeed, he found when he got to the top of the mast, a peregrine falcon. As his head was on a level with hers, she gave up her struggle, and looked at him with a pair of angry, desperate yellow eyes. He had to take hold of her with one hand while he got his knife out, and cut off the tackle-yarn. He was scared as he looked down, but at the same time he felt that he had been ordered up by nobody, but that this was his own venture, and this gave him a proud, steadying sensation, as if the sea and the sky, the ship, the bird and himself were all one. Just as he had freed the falcon, she hacked him in the thumb, so that the blood ran, and he nearly let her go. He grew angry with her, and gave her a clout on the head, then he put her inside his jacket, and climbed down again.

When he reached the deck the mate and the cook were standing there, looking up; they roared to him to ask what he had had to do in the mast. He was so tired that the tears were in his eyes. He took the falcon out and showed her to them, and she kept still within his hands. They laughed and walked off. Simon set the falcon down, stood back and watched her. After a while he reflected that she might not be able to get up from the slippery deck, so he caught her once more, walked away with her and placed her upon a bolt of canvas. A little after she began to trim her feathers, made two or three sharp jerks forward, and then suddenly flew off. The boy could follow her flight above the troughs of the grey sea. He thought: "There flies my falcon."

When the *Charlotte* came home, Simon signed aboard another ship, and two years later he was a light hand on the schooner *Hebe* lying at Bodø, high up on the coast of Norway, to buy herrings.

To the great herring-markets of Bodø ships came together from all corners of the world; here were Swedish, Finnish and Russian boats, a forest of masts, and on shore a turbulent, irregular display of life, with many languages spoken, and mighty fists. On the shore booths had been set up, and the Lapps, small yellow people, noiseless in their movements, with watchful eyes, whom Simon had never seen before, came down to sell bead-embroidered leather-goods. It was April, the sky and the sea were so clear that it was difficult to hold one's eyes up against them—salt, infinitely wide and filled with bird-shrieks—as if someone were incessantly whetting invisible knives, on all sides, high up in Heaven.

Simon was amazed at the lightness of these April evenings. He knew no geography, and did not assign it to the latitude, but he took it as a sign of an unwonted good-will in the Universe, a favor. Simon had been small for his age all his life, but this last winter he had grown, and had become strong of limb. That good luck, he felt, must spring from the very same source as the sweetness of the weather, from a new benevolence in the world. He had been in need of such encouragement, for he was timid by nature; now he asked for no more. The rest he felt to be his own affair. He went about slowly, and proudly.

One evening he was ashore with land-leave, and walked up to the booth of a small Russian trader, a Jew who sold gold watches. All the sailors knew that his watches were made from bad metal, and would not go, still they bought them, and paraded them about. Simon looked at these watches for a long time, but did not buy. The old Jew had divers goods in his shop, and amongst others a case of oranges. Simon had tasted oranges on his journeys; he bought one and took it with him. He meant to go up on a hill, from where he could see the sea, and suck it there.

As he walked on, and had got to the outskirts of the place, he saw a little girl in a blue frock, standing at the other side of a fence and looking at him. She was thirteen or fourteen years old, as slim as an eel, but with a round, clear, freckled face, and a pair of long plaits. The two looked at one another.

"Who are you looking out for?" Simon asked, to say something. The girl's face broke into an ecstatic, presumptuous smile. "For the man I am going to marry, of course," she said. Something in her countenance made the boy confident and happy; he grinned a little at her. "That will perhaps be me," he said. "Ha, ha," said the girl, "he is a few years older than you, I can tell you." "Why," said Simon, "you are not grown up yourself." The little girl shook her head solemnly. "Nay," she said, "but when I grow up I will be exceedingly beautiful, and wear brown shoes with heels, and a hat." "Will you have an orange?" asked Simon, who could give her none of the things she had named. She looked at the orange and at him. "They are very good to eat," said he. "Why do you not eat it yourself then?" she asked. "I have eaten so many already," said he, "when I was in Athens. Here I had to pay a mark for it." "What is your name?" asked she. "My name in Simon," said he. "What is yours?" "Nora," said the girl. "What do you want for your orange now, Simon?"

When he heard his name in her mouth Simon grew bold. "Will you give me a kiss for the orange?" he asked. Nora looked at him gravely for a moment. "Yes," she said, "I should not mind giving you a kiss." He grew as warm as if he had been running quickly. When she stretched out her hand for the orange he took hold of it. At that moment somebody in the house called out for her. "That is my father," said she, and tried to give him back the orange, but he would not take it. "Then come again tomorrow," she said quickly, "then I will give you a kiss." At that she slipped off. He stood and looked after her, and a little later went back to his ship.

Simon was not in the habit of making plans for the future, and now he did not know whether he would be going back to her or not.

The following evening he had to stay aboard, as the other sailors were going ashore, and he did not mind that either. He meant to sit on the deck with the ship's dog, Balthasar, and to practise upon a concertina that he had purchased some time ago. The pale evening was all round him, the sky was faintly roseate, the sea was quite calm, like milk-and-water, only in the wake of the boats going inshore it broke into streaks of vivid indigo. Simon sat and played; after a while his own music began to speak to him so strongly that he stopped, got up and looked upwards. Then he saw that the full moon was sitting high on the sky.

The sky was so light that she hardly seemed needed there; it was as if she had turned up by a caprice of her own. She was round, demure and presumptuous. At that he knew that he must go ashore, whatever it was to cost him. But he did not know how to get away, since the others had taken the yawl with them. He stood on the deck for a long time, a small lonely figure of a sailor-boy on a boat, when he caught sight of a yawl coming in from a ship farther out, and hailed her. He found that it was the Russian crew from a boat named *Anna*, going ashore. When he could make himself understood to them, they took him with them; they first asked him for money for his fare, then, laughing, gave it back to him. He thought: "These people will be believing that I am going to town, wenching." And then he felt, with some pride, that they were right, although at the same time they were infinitely wrong, and knew nothing about anything.

When they came ashore they invited him to come in and drink in their company, and he would not refuse, because they had helped him. One of the Russians was a giant, as big as a bear; he told Simon that his name was Ivan. He got drunk at once, and then fell upon the boy with a bear-like affection, pawed him, smiled and laughed into his face, made him a present of a gold watch-chain, and kissed him on both cheeks. At that Simon reflected that he also ought to give Nora a present when they met again, and as soon as he could get away from the Russians he walked up to a booth that he knew of, and bought a small blue silk handkerchief, the same colour as her eyes.

It was Saturday evening, and there were many people amongst the houses; they came in long rows, some of them singing, all keen to have some fun that night. Simon, in the midst of this rich, bawling life under the clear moon, felt his head light with the flight from the ship and the strong drinks. He crammed the handkerchief in his pocket; it was silk, which he had never touched before, a present for his girl.

He could not remember the path up to Nora's house, lost his way, and came back to where he had started. Then he grew deadly afraid that he should be too late, and began to run. In a small passage between two wooden huts he ran straight into a big man, and found that it was Ivan once more. The Russian folded his arms round him and held him. "Good! Good!" he cried in high glee, "I have found you, my little chicken. I have looked for you everywhere, and poor Ivan has wept because he lost his friend." "Let me go, Ivan," cried Simon. "Oho," said Ivan, "I shall go with you and get you what you want. My heart and my money are all yours, all yours; I have been seventeen years old myself, a little lamb of God, and I want to be so again tonight." "Let me go," cried Simon, "I am in a hurry." Ivan held him so that it hurt, and patted him with his other hand. "I feel it, I feel it," he said. "Now trust to me, my little friend. Nothing shall part you and me. I hear the others coming; we will have such a night together as you will remember when you are an old grandpapa."

Suddenly he crushed the boy to him, like a bear that carries off a sheep. The odious sensation of male bodily warmth and the bulk of a man close to him made the lean boy mad. He thought of Nora waiting, like a slender ship in the dim air, and of himself, here, in the hot embrace of a hairy animal. He struck Ivan with all his might. "I shall kill you, Ivan," he cried out, "if you do not let me go." "Oh, you will be thankful to me later on," said Ivan, and began to sing. Simon fumbled in his pocket for his knife, got it open. He could not lift his hand, but he drove the knife, furiously in under the big man's arm. Almost immediately he felt the blood spouting out, and running down in his sleeve. Ivan stopped short in the song, let go his hold of the boy and gave two long deep grunts. The next second he tumbled down on his knees. "Poor Ivan, poor Ivan," he groaned. He fell straight on his face. At that moment Simon heard the other sailors coming along, singing, in the by-street.

He stood still for a minute, wiped his knife, and watched the blood spread into a dark pool underneath the big body. Then he ran. As he stopped for a second to choose his way, he heard the sailors behind him scream over their dead comrade. He thought: "I must get down to the sea, where I can wash my hand." But at the same time he ran the other way. After a little while he found himself on the path that he had walked on the day before, and it seemed as familiar to him, as if he had walked it many hundred times in his life.

He slackened his pace to look round, and suddenly saw Nora standing on the other side of the fence; she was quite close to him when he caught sight of her in the moonlight. Wavering and out of breath he sank down on his knees. For a moment he could not speak. The little girl looked down at him. "Good evening, Simon," she said in her small coy voice. "I have waited for you a long time," and after a moment she added: "I have eaten your orange."

"Oh, Nora," cried the boy. "I have killed a man." She stared at him, but did not move. "Why did you kill a man?" she asked after a moment. "To get here," said Simon. "Because he tried to stop me. But he was my friend." Slowly he got on to his feet. "He loved me!" the boy cried out, and at that burst into tears. "Yes," said she slowly and thoughtfully. "Yes, because you must be here in time." "Can you hide me?" he asked. "For they are after me." "Nay," said Nora, "I cannot hide you. For my father is the parson here at Bodø, and he would be sure to hand you over to them, if he knew that you had killed a man. "Then," said Simon, "give me something to wipe my hands on." "What is the matter with your hands?" she asked, and took a little step forward. He stretched out his hands to her. "Is that your own blood?" she asked. "No," said he, "it is his." She took the step back again. "Do you hate me now?" he asked. "No, I do not hate you," said she. "But do put your hands at your back."

As he did so she came up close to him, at the other side of the fence, and clasped her arms around his neck. She pressed her young body to his, and kissed him tenderly. He felt her face, cool as the moonlight, upon his own, and when she released him, his head swam, and he did not know if the kiss had lasted a second or an hour. Nora stood up straight, her eyes wide open. "Now," she said slowly and proudly, "I promise you that I will never marry anybody, as long as I live." They boy kept standing with his hands on his back, as if she had tied them there. "And now," she said, "you must run, for they are coming." They looked at one another. "Do not forget Nora," said she. He turned and ran.

He leapt over a fence, and when he was down amongst the houses he walked. He did not know at all where to go. As he came to a house, from where music and noise streamed out, he slowly went through the door. The room was full of people; they were dancing in here. A lamp hung from the ceiling, and shone down on them, the air was thick and brown with the dust rising from the floor. There were some women in the room, but many of the men danced with each other, and gravely or laughingly stamped the floor. A moment after Simon had come in the crowd withdrew to the walls to clear the floor for two sailors, who were showing a dance from their own country.

Simon thought: "Now, very soon, the men from the boat will come round to look for their comrade's murderer, and from my hands they will know that I have done it." These five minutes during which he stood by the wall of the dancing-room, in the midst of the gay, sweating dancers, were of great significance to the boy. He himself felt it, as if during this time he grew up, and became like other people. He did not entreat his destiny, nor complain. Here he was, he had killed a man, and had kissed a girl. He did not demand any more from life, nor did life now demand more from him. He was Simon, a man like the men round him, and going to die, as all men are going to die.

He only became aware of what was going on outside him, when he saw a woman had come in, and was standing in the midst of the cleared floor, looking round her. She was a short, broad old woman, in the clothes of the Lapps, and she took her stand with such majesty and fierceness as if she owned the whole place. It was obvious that most of the people knew her, and were a little afraid of her, although a few laughed; the din of the dancing-room stopped when she spoke.

"Where is my son?" she asked in a high shrill voice, like a bird's. The next moment her eyes fell on Simon himself, and she steered through the crowd, which opened up before her, stretched out her old skinny, dark hand, and took him by the elbow. "Come home with me now," she said. "You need not dance here tonight. You may be dancing a high enough dance soon."

Simon drew back, for he thought that she was drunk. But as she looked him straight in the face with her yellow eyes, it seemed to him that he had met her before, and that he might do well in listening to her. The old woman pulled him with her across the floor, and he followed her without a word. "Do not birch your boy too badly, Sunniva," one of the men in the room cried to her. "He has done no harm, he only wanted to look at the dance."

At the same moment as they came out through the door, there was an alarm in the street, a flock of people came running down it, and one of them, as he turned into the house, knocked against Simon, looked at him and the old woman, and ran on.

While the two walked along the street, the old woman lifted up her skirt, and put the hem of it into the boys' hand. "Wipe your hand on my skirt," she said. They had not gone far before they came to a small wooden house, and stopped; the door to it was so low that they must bend to get through it. As the Lapp-woman went in before Simon, still holding on to his arm, the boy looked up for a moment. The night had grown misty; there was a wide ring round the moon.

The old woman's room was narrow and dark, with but one small window to it; a lantern stood on the floor and lighted it up dimly. It was all filled with reindeer skins and wolf skins, and with reindeer horn, such as the Lapps use to make their carved buttons and knife-handles, and the air in here was rank and stifling. As soon as they were in, the woman turned to Simon, took hold of his head, and with her crooked fingers parted his hair and combed it down in Lapp fashion. She clapped a Lapp cap on him and stood back to glance at him. "Sit down on my stool, now," she said. "But first take out your knife." She was so commanding in voice and manner that the boy could not but choose to do as she told him; he sat down on the stool, and he could not take his eyes off her face, which was flat and brown, and as if smeared with dirt in its net of fine wrinkles. As he sat there he heard many people come along outside, and stop by the house; then someone knocked at the door, waited a moment and knocked again. The old woman stood and listened, as still as a mouse.

"Nay," said the boy and got up. "This is no good, for it is me that they are after. It will be better for you to let me go out to them." "Give me your knife," said she. When he handed it to her, she stuck it straight into her thumb, so that the blood spouted out, and she let it drip all over her skirt. "Come in, then," she cried.

The door opened, and two of the Russian sailors came and stood in the opening; there were more people outside. "Has anybody come in here?" they asked. "We are after a man who has killed our mate, but he has run away from us. Have you seen or heard anybody this way?" The old Lapp-woman turned upon them, and her eyes shone like gold in the lamplight. "Have I seen or heard anyone?" she cried. "I have heard you shriek murder all over the town. You frightened me, and my poor silly boy there, so that I cut my thumb as I was ripping the skin-rug that I sew. The boy is too scared to help me, and the rug is all ruined. I shall make you pay me for that. If you are looking for a murderer, come in and search my house for me, and I shall know you when we meet again." She was so furious that she danced where she stood, and jerked her head like an angry bird of prey.

The Russian came in, looked round the room, and at her and her blood-stained hand and skirt. "Do not put a curse on us now, Sunniva," he said timidly. "We know that you can do many things when you like. Here is a mark to pay you for the blood you have spilled." She stretched out her hand, and he placed a piece of money in it. She spat on it. "Then go, and there shall be no bad blood between us," said Sunniva, and shut the door after them. She stuck her thumb in her mouth, and chuckled a little.

The boy got up from his stool, stood straight up before her and stared into her face. He felt as if he were swaying high up in the air, with but a small hold. "Why have you helped me?" he asked her. "Do you not know?" she answered. "Have you not recognized me yet? But you will remember the peregrine falcon which was caught in the tackle-yarn of your boat, the *Charlotte*, as she sailed in the Mediterranean. That day you climbed up by the shrouds of the top-gallant-mast to help her out, in a stiff wind, and with a high sea. That falcon was me. We Lapps often fly in such a manner, to see the world. When I first met you I was on my way to Africa, to see my younger sister and her children. She is a falcon too, when she chooses. By that time she was living at Takaunga, within an old ruined tower, which down there they call a minaret." She swathed a corner of her skirt round her thumb, and bit at it. "We do not forget," she said. "I hacked your thumb, when you took hold of me; it is only fair that I should cut my thumb for you tonight."

She came close to him, and gently rubbed her two brown, clawlike fingers against his forehead. "So you are a boy," she said, "who will kill a man rather than be late to meet your sweetheart? We hold together, the females of this earth. I shall mark your forehead now, so that the girls will know of that, when they look at you, and they will like you for it." She played with the boy's hair, and twisted it round her finger.

"Listen now, my little bird," said she. "My great grand-son's brother-in-law is lying with his boat by the landing-place at this moment; he is to take a consignment of skins out to a Danish boat. He will bring you back to your boat, in time, before your mate comes. The *Hebe* is sailing tomorrow morning, is it not so? But when you are aboard, give him back my cap for me." She took up his knife, wiped it in her skirt and handed it to him. "Here is your knife," she said. "You will stick it into no more men; you will not need to, for from now you will sail the seas like a faithful seaman. We have enough trouble with our sons as it is."

The bewildered boy began to stammer his thanks to her. "Wait," said she, "I shall make you a cup of coffee, to bring back your wits, while I wash your jacket." She went and rattled an old copper kettle upon the fireplace. After a while she handed him a hot, strong, black drink in a cup without a handle to it. "You have drunk with Sunniva now," she said; "you have drunk down a little wisdom, so that in the future all your thoughts shall not fall like raindrops into the salt sea."

When he had finished and set down the cup, she led him to the door and opened it for him. He was surprised to see that it was almost clear morning. The house was so high up that the boy could see the sea from it, and a milky mist about it. He gave her his hand to say good-bye.

She stared into his face. "We do not forget," she said. "And you, you knocked me on the head there, high up in the mast. I shall give you that blow back." With that she smacked him on the ear as hard as she could, so that his head swam. "Now we are quits," she said, gave him a great, mischievous, shining glance, and a little push down the doorstep, and nodded to him.

In this way the sailor-boy got back to his ship, which was to sail the next morning, and lived to tell the story.

*Graham Greene was born in Hertfordshire
in 1904 and was educated at Balliol College, Oxford. He has written short stories,
novels, "entertainments" (a form akin to
the "novel of suspense"), essays, criticism,
poetry, juvenile fiction, and plays. John
Buchan (a creator of spy-thrillers) and
François Mauriac have influenced his writing. Greene has worked as an editor* (London Times), *a film critic* (The Spectator),
and a war correspondent in Indo-China
(The New Republic). *His literary career
began in 1929 with* The Man Within.

*Greene has achieved both popular and
critical success. His characters are usually
motivated by guilt and fear; his fiction often
examines the question of salvation (man's
relationship to God, sin, and redemption).
Does the following story imply a nostalgia
for an irretrievable spiritual innocence? Or
does it suggest that the innocence of youth
is but an illusion of retrospective maturity?
Further Reading:* The Heart of the Matter
(1948), Nineteen Stories (1949), Twenty-
One Stories (1954).

ENGLAND

The Innocent

GRAHAM GREENE

It was a mistake to take Lola there, I
knew it the moment we alighted from
the train at the small country station. On
an autumn evening one remembers more
of childhood than at any other time of
year, and her bright veneered face, the
small bag which hardly pretended to contain our "things" for the night, simply
didn't go with the old grain warehouse
across the small canal, the few lights up
the hill, the posters of an ancient film.
But she said, "Let's go into the country,"
and Bishop's Hendron was, of course, the

From *Twenty-One Stories* by Graham Greene.
Copyright 1946 by Graham Greene. Reprinted
by permission of The Viking Press, Inc., and
William Heinemann Ltd.

first name which came into my head. Nobody would know me there now, and it hadn't occurred to me that it would be I who remembered.

Even the old porter touched a chord. I said, "There'll be a four-wheeler at the entrance," and there was, though at first I didn't notice it, seeing the two taxis and thinking. "The old place is coming on." It was very dark, and the thin autumn mist, the smell of wet leaves and canal water were deeply familiar.

Lola said, "But why did you choose this place? It's grim." It was no use explaining to her why it wasn't grim to me, that that sand heap by the canal had always been there (when I was three I remember thinking it was what other people meant by the seaside). I took the bag (I've said it was light; it was simply a forged passport of respectability) and said we'd walk. We came up over the little hump-backed bridge and passed the almshouses. When I was five I saw a middle-aged man run into one to commit suicide; he carried a knife, and all the neighbours pursued him up the stairs. She said, "I never thought the country was like *this*." They were ugly almshouses, little grey stone boxes, but I knew them as I knew nothing else. It was like listening to music, all that walk.

But I had to say something to Lola. It wasn't her fault that she didn't belong here. We passed the school, the church, and came round into the old wide High Street and the sense of the first twelve years of life. If I hadn't come, I shouldn't have known that sense would be so strong, because those years hadn't been particularly happy or particularly miserable: they had been ordinary years, but now with the smell of wood fires, of the cold striking up from the dark damp paving stones, I thought I knew what it was that held me. It was the smell of innocence.

I said to Lola, "It's a good inn, and there'll be nothing here, you'll see, to keep us up. We'll have dinner and drinks and go to bed." But the worst of it was that I couldn't help wishing that I were alone. I hadn't been back all these years; I hadn't realized how well I remembered the place. Things I'd quite forgotten, like that sand heap, were coming back with an effect of pathos and nostalgia. I could have been very happy that night in a melancholy, autumnal way wandering about the little town, picking up clues to that time of life when, however miserable we are, we have expectations. It wouldn't be the same if I came back again, for then there would be the memories of Lola, and Lola meant just nothing at all. We had happened to pick each other up at a bar the day before and liked each other. Lola was all right, there was no one I would rather spend the night with, but she didn't fit in with *these* memories. We ought to have gone to Maidenhead. That's country too.

The inn was not quite where I remembered it. There was the Town Hall, but they had built a new cinema with a Moorish dome and a café, and there was a garage which hadn't existed in my time. I had forgotten too the turning to the left up a steep, villaed hill.

"I don't believe that road was there in my day," I said.

"Your day?" Lola asked.

"Didn't I tell you? I was born here."

"You must get a kick out of bringing me here," Lola said. "I suppose you used to think of nights like this when you were a boy."

"Yes," I said, because it wasn't her fault. She was all right. I liked her scent. She used a good shade of lipstick. It was costing me a lot, a fiver for Lola and then all the bills and fares and drinks, but I'd have thought it money well spent anywhere else in the world.

I lingered at the bottom of that road. Something was stirring in the mind, but I don't think I should have remembered what, if a crowd of children hadn't come down the hill at that moment into the frosty lamplight, their voices sharp and shrill, their breath fuming as they passed under the lamps. They all carried linen bags, and some of the bags were embroidered with initials. They were in their best clothes and a little self-conscious. The small girls kept to themselves in a kind of compact, beleaguered group, and one thought of hair ribbons and shining shoes and the sedate tinkle of a piano. It all came back to me: they had been to a dancing lesson, just as I used to go, to a small square house with a drive of rhododendrons halfway up the hill. More than ever I wished that Lola were not with me, less than ever did she fit, as I thought "something's missing from the picture," and a sense of pain glowed dully at the bottom of my brain.

We had several drinks at the bar, but there was half an hour before they would agree to serve dinner. I said to Lola, "You don't want to drag round this town. If you don't mind, I'll just slip out for ten minutes and look at a place I used to know." She didn't mind. There was a local man, perhaps a schoolmaster, at the bar simply longing to stand her a drink: I could see how he envied me, coming down with her like this from town just for a night.

I walked up the hill. The first houses were all new. I resented them. They hid things like fields and gates I might have remembered. It was like a map which had got wet in the pocket and pieces had stuck together; when you opened it there were whole patches hidden. But halfway up, there the house really was, the drive; perhaps the same old lady was giving lessons. Children exaggerate age. She may not in those days have been more than thirty-five. I could hear the piano. She was following the same routine. Children under eight, 6–7 P.M. Children eight to thirteen, 7–8. I opened the gate and went in a little way. I was trying to remember.

I don't know what brought it back. I think it was simply the autumn, the cold, the wet frosting leaves, rather than the piano, which had played different tunes in those days. I remembered the small girl as well as one remembers anyone without a photograph to refer to. She was a year older than I was: she must have been just on the point of eight. I loved her with an intensity I have never felt since, I believe, for anyone. At least I have never made the mistake of laughing at children's love. It has a terrible inevitability of separation because there *can* be no satisfaction. Of course one invents tales of houses on fire, of war and forlorn charges which prove one's courage in her eyes, but never of marriage. One knows without being told that that can't happen, but the knowledge doesn't mean that one suffers less. I remembered all the games of blind-man's-buff at birthday parties when I vainly hoped to catch her, so that I might have the excuse to touch and hold her, but I never caught her; she always kept out of my way.

But once a week for two winters I had my chance: I danced with her. That made it worse (it was cutting off our only contact) when she told me during one of the last lessons of the winter that next year she would join the older class. She liked me too, I knew it, but we had no way of expressing it. I used to go to her birthday parties and she would come to mine, but we never even ran home together after the dancing class. It would have seemed odd; I don't think it occurred to us. I had to join my own boisterous teasing male companions, and she the besieged, the hustled, the shrilly indignant sex on the way down the hill.

I shivered there in the mist and turned my coat collar up. The piano was playing a dance from an old C. B. Cochran revue. It seemed a long journey to have taken to find only Lola at the end of it. There *is* something about innocence one is never quite resigned to lose. Now when I am unhappy about a girl, I can simply go and buy another one. Then the best I could think of was to write some passionate message and slip it into a hole (it was extraordinary how I began to remember everything) in the woodwork of the gate. I had once told her about the hole, and sooner or later I was sure she would put in her fingers and find the message. I wondered what the message could have been. One wasn't able to express much, I thought, in those days; but because the expression was inadequate, it didn't mean that the pain was shallower than what one sometimes suffered now. I remembered how for days I had felt in the hole and always found the message there. Then the dancing lessons stopped. Probably by the next winter I had forgotten.

As I went out of the gate I looked to see if the hole existed. It was there. I put in my finger, and, in its safe shelter from the seasons and the years, the scrap of paper rested yet. I pulled it out and opened it. Then I struck a match, a tiny glow of heat in the mist and dark. It was a shock to see by its diminutive flame a picture of crude obscenity. There could be no mistake; there were my initials below the childish, inaccurate sketch of a man and woman. But it woke fewer memories than the fume of breath, the linen bags, a damp leaf, or the pile of sand. I didn't recognize it; it might have been drawn by a dirty-minded stranger on a lavatory wall. All I could remember was the purity, the intensity, the pain of that passion.

I felt at first as if I had been betrayed, "After all," I told myself, "Lola's not so much out of place here." But later that night, when Lola turned away from me and fell asleep, I began to realize the deep innocence of that drawing. I had believed I was drawing something with a meaning unique and beautiful; it was only now after thirty years of life that the picture seemed obscene.

Men "exist on a frail web of friendship—
alone," V. S. Pritchett once explained. His
characters are usually ambivalent, vacillating
between private and social lives. Their virtues are often negative; their lives are both
absurd and dreadful. Can these characteristics be applied to the people in the following story? What parts do death, money,
love, passion, and a sense of humor play in
this story? What are the connections drawn
among them?

Victor Sawdon Pritchett is noted in the
United States primarily as a literary critic;
in England he is known also for his novels,
four collections of short stories, and several
works of nonfiction. Pritchett was born in
Ipswich in 1900 and began his literary
career in 1929 with the publication of Claire
Drummer and Marching Spain. A world
traveller and onetime literary editor of New
Statesman and Nation, Pritchett now con-
centrates on writing fiction which dramatizes the lives of characters who are alienated, frustrated, and bewildered. Further
Reading: The Spanish Virgin, and Other
Stories (1932), You Make Your Own Life
(1938), It May Never Happen, and Other
Stories (1947).

ENGLAND

Sense of Humour

V. S. PRITCHETT

It started one Saturday. I was working
new ground and I decided I'd stay at the
hotel the weekend and put in an appearance at church.

"All alone?" asked the girl at the cash-
desk.

It had been raining since ten o'clock.

"Mr. Good has gone," she said. "And
Mr. Straker. He usually stays with us. But
he's gone."

Reprinted by permission of A. D. Peters & Co.

That's where they make their mistake," I said. "They think they
know everything because they've been on the road all their lives."

"You're a stranger here, aren't you?" she said.

"I am," I said. "And so are you."

"How do you know that?"

"Obvious," I said, "Way you speak."

"Let's have a light," she said.

"So's I can see you," I said.

That was how it started. The rain was pouring down on the glass
roof of the office.

She'd a cup of tea steaming on the register. I said I'd have one,
too. What's it going to be and I'll tell them, she said, but I said just
a cup of tea.

"I'm T.T.," I said. "Too many soakers on the road as it is."

I was staying there the weekend so as to be sharp on the job on
Monday morning. What's more it pays in these small towns to turn
up at church on Sundays, Presbyterians in the morning, Methodists
in the evening. Say "Good morning" and "Good evening" to them.
"Ah!" they say. "Churchgoer! Pleased to see that! T.T., too." Makes
them have a second look at your lines in the morning. "Did you like
our service, Mr.— er—er?" "Humphrey's my name." "Mr. Humphrey." See? It pays.

"Come into the office, Mr. Humphrey," she said, bringing me a
cup. "Listen to that rain."

I went inside.

"Sugar?" she said.

"Three," I said. We settled to a very pleasant chat. She told me all
about herself, and we got on next to families.

"My father was on the railway," she said.

" 'The engine gave a squeal,' " I said. " 'The driver took out his
pocket-knife and scraped him off the wheel.' "

'That's it," she said. "And what is your father's business? You said
he had a business."

"Undertaker," I said.

"Undertaker?" she said.

"Why not?" I said. "Good business. Seasonable like everything
else. High-class undertaker," I said.

She was looking at me all the time wondering what to say, and suddenly she went into fits of laughter.

"Undertaker," she said, covering her face with her hands and went
on laughing.

"Here," I said, "what's up?"

"Undertaker!" She laughed and laughed. Struck me as being a
pretty thin joke.

"Don't mind me," she said. "I'm Irish."

"Oh, I see," I said. "That's it, is it? Got a sense of humour."

Then the bell rang and a woman called out "Muriel! Muriel!" and there was a motor bike making a row at the front door.

"All right," the girl called out. "Excuse me a moment, Mr. Humphrey," she said. "Don't think me rude. That's my boy friend. He wants the bird turning up like this."

She went out, but there was her boy friend looking over the window ledge into the office. He had come in. He had a cape on, soaked with rain, and the rain was in beads in his hair. It was fair hair. It stood up on end. He'd been economizing on the brilliantine. He didn't wear a hat. He gave me a look and I gave him a look. I didn't like the look of him. And he didn't like the look of me. A smell of oil and petrol and rain and mackintosh came off him. He had a big mouth with thick lips. They were very red. I recognized him at once as the son of the man who ran the Kounty Garage. I saw this chap when I put my car away. The firm's car. Locked up, because of the samples. Took me ten minutes to ram the idea into his head. He looked as though he'd never heard of samples. Slow—you know the way they are in the provinces. Slow on the job.

"Oh, Colin," says she. "What do you want?"

"Nothing," the chap said. "I came in to see you."

"To see me?"

"Just to see you."

"You came in this morning."

"That's right," he said. He went red. "You was busy," he said.

"Well, I'm busy now," she said.

He bit his tongue and licked his big lips over and took a look at me. Then he started grinning.

"I got the new bike, Muriel," he said. "I've got it outside. It's just come down from the works," he said.

"The laddie wants you to look at his bike," I said. So she went out and had a look at it.

When she came back she had got rid of him.

"Listen to that rain," she said. "Lord, I'm fed up with this line," she said.

"What line?" I said. "The hotel line?"

"Yes," she said. "I'm fed right up to the back teeth with it."

"And you've got good teeth," I said.

"There's not the class of person there used to be in it," she said. "All our family have got good teeth."

"Not the class?"

"I've been in it five years and there's not the same class at all. You never meet any fellows."

"Well," said I, "if they're like that half-wit at the garage, they're nothing to be stuck on. And you've met me."

I said it to her like that.

"Oh," says she. "It isn't as bad as that yet."

It was cold in the office. She used to sit all day in her overcoat. She was a smart girl with a big friendly chin and a second one coming, and her forehead and nose were covered with freckles. She had copper-coloured hair too. She got her shoes through the trade from Duke's traveller and her clothes, too, off the Hollenborough mantle man. I told her I could do her better stockings than the ones she'd go on. She got a good reduction on everything. Twenty-five or thirty-three and a third. She had her expenses cut right back. I took her to the pictures that night in the car. I made Colin get the car out for me.

"That boy wanted me to go on the back of his bike. On a night like this," she said.

"Oh," she said, when we got to the pictures. "Two shillings's too much. Let's go into the one-and-sixes at the side and we can nip across into the two-shillings when the lights go down."

"Fancy your father being an undertaker," she said in the middle of the show. And she started laughing as she had laughed before.

She had her head screwed on all right. She said:

"Some girls have no pride once the lights go down."

Every time I went to that town I took a box of something. Samples, mostly, they didn't cost me anything.

"Don't thank me," I said. "Thank the firm."

Every time I took her out I pulled the blinds in the back seat of the car to hide the samples. That chap Colin used to give us oil and petrol. He used to give me a funny look. Fishy sort of small eyes he'd got. Always looking miserable. Then we would go off. Sunday was her free day. Not that driving's any holiday for me. And, of course, the firm paid. She used to take me down to see her family for the day. Start in the morning, and taking it you had dinner and tea there, a day's outing cost us nothing. Her father was something on the railway, retired. He had a long stocking, somewhere, but her sister, the one that was married, had had her share already.

He had a tumour after his wife died and they just played upon the old man's feelings. It wasn't right. She wouldn't go near her sister and I don't blame her, taking the money like that. Just played upon the old man's feelings.

Every time I was up there Colin used to come in looking for her.

"Oh, Colin," I used to say. "Done my car yet?" He knew where he got off with me.

"No, now, I can't, Colin. I tell you I'm going out with Mr. Humphrey," she used to say to him. I heard her.

"He keeps on badgering me," she said to me.

"You leave him to me," I said.

"No, he's all right," she said.

"You let me know if there's any trouble with Colin," I said. "Seems to be a harum-scarum sort of half-wit to me," I said.

"And he spends every penny he makes," she said.

Well, we know that sort of thing is all right while it lasts, I told her, but the trouble is that it doesn't last.

We were always meeting Colin on the road. I took no notice of it first of all and then I grew suspicious and awkward at always meeting him. He had a new motor bicycle. It was an Indian, a scarlet thing that he used to fly over the moor with, flat out. Muriel and I used to go out over the moor to Ingley Wood in the firm's Morris—I had a customer out that way.

"May as well do a bit of business while you're about it," I said.

"About what?" she said.

"Ah ha!" I said. "That's what Colin wants to know," I said.

Sure enough, coming back we'd hear him popping and backfiring close behind us, and I put out my hand to stop him and keep him following us, biting our dirt.

"I see his little game," I said. "Following us."

So I saw to it that he did follow. We could hear him banging away behind us, and the traffic is thick on the Ingley road in the afternoon.

"Oh, let him pass," Muriel said. "I can't stand those dirty things banging in my ears."

I waved him on and past he flew with his scarf flying out, blazing red into the traffic. "We're doing fifty-eight ourselves," she said, leaning across to look.

"Powerful buses those," I said. "Any fool can do it if he's got the power. Watch me step on it."

But we did not catch Colin. Half an hour later he passed us coming back. Cut right in between us and a lorry—I had to brake hard. I damn nearly killed him. His ears were red with the wind. He didn't wear a hat. I got after him as soon as I could, but I couldn't touch him.

Nearly every weekend I was in that town seeing my girl, that fellow was hanging around. He came into the bar on Saturday nights, he poked his head into the office on Sunday mornings. It was a sure bet that if we went out in the car he would pass us on the road. Every time we would hear that scarlet thing roar by like a horse-stinger. It didn't matter where we were. He passed us on the main road, he met us down the side roads. There was a little cliff under oak trees at May Ponds, she said, where the view was pretty. And there, soon after we got there, was Colin on the other side of the water, watching us. Once we found him sitting on his bike, just as though he were waiting for us.

"You been here in a car?" I said.

"No, motor bike," she said, and blushed. "Cars can't follow in these tracks."

She knew a lot of places in that country. Some of the roads weren't roads at all and were bad for tires and I didn't want the firm's car scratched by bushes, but you would have thought Colin could read what was in her mind. For nine times out of ten he was there. It got on my nerves. It was a red, roaring, powerful thing and he opened it full out.

"I'm going to speak to Colin," I said. "I won't have him annoying you."

"He's not annoying me," she said. "I've got a sense of humour."

"Here, Colin," I said one evening when I put the car away. "What's the idea?"

He was taking off his overalls. He pretended he did not know what I was talking about. He had a way of rolling his eyeballs, as if they had got wet and loose in his head, while he was speaking to me, and you never knew if it was sweat or oil on his face. It was always pale, with high colour on his cheeks and very red lips.

"Miss MacFarlane doesn't like being followed," I said.

He dropped his jaw and gaped at me. I could not tell whether he was being very surprised or very sly. I used to call him "Marbles" because when he spoke he seemed to have a lot of marbles in his mouth.

Then he said he never went to the places we went to, except by accident. He wasn't following us, he said, but we were following him. We never let him alone, he said. Everywhere he went, he said, we were there. Take last Saturday, he said, we were following him for miles down the by-pass, he said. "But you passed us first and then sat down in front," I said. "I went to Ingley Wood," he said. "And you followed me there." No, we didn't, I said, Miss MacFarlane decided to go there.

He said he did not want to complain, but fair was fair. "I suppose you know," he said, "that you have taken my girl off me. Well, you can leave *me* alone, can't you?"

"Here," I said. "One minute! Not so fast! You said I've taken Miss MacFarlane from you. Well, she was never your girl. She only knew you in a friendly way."

"She was my girl," was all he said.

He was pouring oil into my engine. He had some cotton wool in one hand and the can in the other. He wiped up the green oil that had overflowed, screwed on the cap, pulled down the bonnet, and whistled to himself.

I went back to Muriel and told her what Colin had said.

"I don't like trouble," I said.

"Don't you worry," she said. "I had to have someone to go to all these places with before you came. Couldn't stick in here all day Sunday."

"Ah," I said. "That's it, is it? You've been to all these places with him?"

"Yes," she said. "And he keeps on going to them. He's sloppy about me."

Good God," I said. "Sentimental memories."

I felt sorry for that fellow. He knew it would be hopeless, but he loved her. I suppose he couldn't help himself. Well, it takes all sorts to make a world, as my old mother used to say. If we were all alike it wouldn't do. Some men can't save money. It just runs through their fingers. He couldn't save money, so he lost her. I suppose all he thought of was love.

I could have been friends with that fellow. As it was, I put a lot of business his way. I didn't want him to get the wrong idea about me. We're all human after all.

We didn't have any more trouble with Colin after this until bank holiday. I was going to take her down to see my family. The old man's getting a bit past it now and has given up living over the shop. He's living out on the Barnum Road, beyond the tram stop. We were going down in the firm's car, as per usual, but something went wrong with the mag and Colin had not got it right for the holiday. I was wild about this. What's the use of a garage who can't do a rush job for the holidays! What's the use of being an old customer if they're going to let you down! I went for Colin bald-headed.

"You knew I wanted it," I said. "It's no use trying to put me off with a tale about the stuff not coming down from the works. I've heard that one before."

I told him he'd got to let me have another car, because he'd let me down. I told him I wouldn't pay his account. I said I'd take my business away from him. But there wasn't a car to be had in the town because of the holiday. I could have knocked the fellow down. After the way I'd sent business to him.

Then I saw through his little game. He knew Muriel and I were going to my people and he had done this to stop it. The moment I saw this I let him know that it would take more than him to stop me doing what I wanted.

I said: "Right. I shall take the amount of Miss MacFarlane's train fare and my own from the account at the end of the month."

I said: "You may run a garage, but you don't run the railway service."

I was damned angry going by train. I felt quite lost on the railway after having a car. It was crowded with trippers too. It was slow—stopping at all the stations. The people come in, they tread all over your feet, they make you squeeze up till you're crammed against the window, and the women stick out their elbows and fidget. And then the expense! a return for two runs you into just over a couple of quid. I could have murdered Colin.

We got there at last. We walked up from the tram stop. Mother was at the window and let us in.

"This is Miss MacFarlane," I said.

And mother said: "Oh, pleased to meet you. We've heard a lot about you.

"Oh," Mother said to me, giving me a kiss, "are you tired? You haven't had your tea, have you? Sit down. Have this chair, dear. It's more comfortable."

"Well, my boy," my father said.

"Want a wash," my father said. "We've got a wash-basin downstairs," he said. "I used not to mind about washing upstairs before. Now I couldn't do without it. Funny how your ideas change as you get older."

"How's business?" he said.

"Mustn't grumble," I said. "How's yours?"

"You knew," he said, "we took off the horses: except for one or two of the older families we have got motors now."

But he'd told me that the last time I was there. I'd been at him for years about motor hearses.

"You've forgotten I used to drive them," I said.

"Bless me, so you did," he said.

He took me up to my room. He showed me everything he had done to the house. "Your mother likes it," he said. "The traffic's company for her. You know what your mother is for company."

Then he gives me a funny look.

"Who's the girl?" he says.

My mother came in then and said: "She's pretty, Arthur."

"Of course she's pretty," I said. "She's Irish."

"Oh," said the old man. "Irish! Got a sense of humour, eh?"

"She wouldn't be marrying me if she hadn't," I said. And then I gave *them* a look.

"Marrying her, did you say?" exclaimed my father.

"Any objection?" I said.

"Now, Ernest dear," said my mother. "Leave the boy alone. Come down while I pop the kettle on."

She was terribly excited.

"Miss MacFarlane," the old man said.

"No sugar, thank you, Mrs. Humphrey. I beg your pardon, Mr. Humphrey?"

"The Glen Hotel at Swansea, I don't suppose you know that?" my father said. "I wondered if you did, being in the catering line."

"It doesn't follow she knows every hotel," my mother said.

"Forty years ago," the old man said. "I was staying at the Glen in Swansea and the head waiter—"

"Oh no, not that one. I'm sure Miss MacFarlane doesn't want to hear that one," my mother said.

"How's business with you, Mr. Humphrey?" said Muriel. "We passed a large cemetery near the station."

"Dad's ledger," I said.

"The whole business has changed so that you wouldn't know it, in my life time," said my father. "Silver fittings have gone clean out. Everyone wants simplicity nowadays. Restraint. Dignity," my father said.

"Prices did it," my father said.

"The war," he said.

"You couldn't get the wood," he said.

"Take ordinary mahogany, just an ordinary piece of mahogany. Or teak," he said. "Take teak. Or walnut."

"You can certainly see the world go by in this room," I said to my mother.

"It never stops," she said.

Now it was all bicycles over the new concrete road from the gun factory. Then traction engines and cars. They came up over the hill where the A.A. man stands and choked up round the tram stop. It was mostly holiday traffic. Everything with a wheel on it was out.

"On this stretch," my father told me, "they get three accidents a week." There was an ambulance station at the crossroads.

We had hardly finished talking about this—in fact, the old man was still saying that something ought to be done—when the telephone rang.

"Name of MacFarlane?" the voice said on the wire.

"No. Humphrey," my father said. "There is a Miss MacFarlane here."

"There's a man named Colin Mitchell lying seriously injured in an accident at the Cottage Hospital, gave me the name of MacFarlane as his nearest relative."

That was the Police. On to it at once. That fellow Colin had followed us down by road.

Cry, I never heard a girl cry as Muriel cried when we came back from the hospital. He had died in the ambulance. Cutting in, the old game he used to play on me. Clean off the saddle and under the Birmingham bus. The blood was everywhere, they said. People were still looking at it when we went by. Head on. What a mess! Don't let's talk about it.

She wanted to see him, but they said "No." There wasn't anything recognizable to see. She put her arms round my neck and cried: "Colin, Colin," as if I were Colin, and clung to me. I was feeling sick myself. I held her tight and I kissed her and I thought: "Holiday ruined."

"Damn fool man," I thought. "Poor devil," I thought.

"I knew he'd do something like this."

"There, there," I said to her. "Don't think about Colin." Didn't she love me, I said, and not Colin? Hadn't she got me? She said, yes, she had. And she loved me. But, "Oh, Colin! Oh, Colin!" she cried.

"And Colin's mother," she cried. "Oh, it's terrible." She cried and cried.

We put her to bed and I sat with her, and my mother kept coming in.

"Leave her to me," I said. "I understand her."

Before they went to bed they both came in and looked at her. She lay sobbing with her head in the pillow.

I could quite understand her being upset. Colin was a decent fellow. He was always doing things for her. He mended her electric lamp and riveted the stem of a wineglass so that you couldn't see the break. He used to make things for her. He was very good with his hands.

She lay on her side with her face burning and feverish with misery and crying, scalded by the salt, and her lips shrivelled up. I put my arm under her neck and I stroked her forehead. She groaned. Sometimes she shivered and sometimes she clung to me, crying: "Oh, Colin! Colin!"

My arm ached with the cramp and I had a crick in my back, sitting in the awkward way I was on the bed. It was late. There was nothing to do but to ache and sit watching her and thinking. It is funny the way your mind drifts. When I was kissing her and watching her I was thinking out who I'd show our new Autumn range to first. Her hand held my wrist tight, and when I kissed her I got her tears on my lips. They burned and stung. Her neck and shoulders were soft and I could feel her breath hot out of her nostrils on the back of my hand. Ever noticed how hot a woman's breath gets when she's crying? I drew out my hand and lay down beside her and "Oh, Colin, Colin," she sobbed, turning over and clinging to me. And so I lay there, listening to the traffic, staring at the ceiling, and shivering whenever the picture of Colin shooting right off that damned red thing into the bus came into my mind—until I did not hear the traffic any more, or see the ceiling any more, or think any more, but a change happened —I don't know when. This Colin thing seemed to have knocked the bottom out of everything and I had a funny feeling we were going down and down and down in a lift. And the further we went, the hotter and softer she got. Perhaps it was when I found with my hands that she had very big breasts. But it was like being on the mail steamer and feeling engines start under your feet, thumping louder and louder. You can feel it in every vein of your body. Her mouth opened and her tears dried. Her breath came through her open mouth and her voice was blind and husky. Colin, Colin, Colin, she said, and her fingers were hooked into me. I got out and turned the key in the door.

In the morning I left her sleeping. It did not matter to me what my father might have heard in the night, but still I wondered. She would hardly let me touch her before that. I told her I was sorry, but she shut me up. I was afraid of her. I was afraid of mentioning Colin. I wanted to go out of the house there and then and tell someone everything. Did she love Colin all the time? Did she think I was Colin? And every time I thought of that poor devil covered over with a white sheet in the hospital mortuary, a kind of picture of her and me under the sheets with love came into my mind. I couldn't separate the two things. Just as though it had all come from Colin.

I'd rather not talk any more about that. I never talked to Muriel about it. I waited for her to say something, but she didn't. She didn't say a word.

The next day was a bad day. It was grey and hot and the air smelled of oil fumes from the road. There's always a mess to clear up when things like this happen. I had to see to it. I had the job of ringing up the boy's mother. But I got round that, thank God, by ringing up the garage and getting them to go round and see the old lady. My father is useless when things are like this. I was the whole morning on the phone: to the hospital, the police, the coroner—and he stood fussing beside me, jerking up and down like a fat indiarubber ball.

I found my mother washing up at the sink and she said: "That poor boy's mother! I can't stop thinking of her."

Then my father comes in and says—just as though I was a customer: "Of course if Mrs. Mitchell desires it we can have the remains of the deceased conveyed to his house by one of our new specially sprung motor hearses and can, if necessary, make all the funeral arrangements."

I could have hit him because Muriel came into the room when he was saying this. But she stood there as if nothing had happened.

"It's the least we can do for poor Mrs. Mitchell," she said. There were small creases of shadow under her eyes, which shone with a soft strong light I had never seen before. She walked as if she were really still in that room with me, asleep. God, I loved that girl! God, I wanted to get all this over, this damned Colin business that had come right into the middle of everything like this, and I wanted to get married right away. I wanted to be alone with her. That's what Colin did for me.

"Yes," I said. "We must do the right thing by Colin."

"We are sometimes asked for long-distance estimates," my father said.

"It will be a little something," my mother said.

"Dad and I will talk it over," I said.

"Come into the office," my father said. "It occurred to me that it would be nice to do the right thing by this friend of yours."

We talked it over. We went into the cost of it. There was the return journey to reckon. We worked it out that it would come no dearer to old Mrs. Mitchell than if she took the train and buried the boy here. That is to say, my father said, if I drove it.

"It would look nice," my father said. "Saves money and it would look a bit friendly," my father said. "You've done it before."

"Well," I said. "I suppose I can get a refund on my return ticket from the railway."

But it was not as simple as it looked, because Muriel wanted to come. She wanted to drive back with me and the hearse. My mother was very worried about this. It might upset Muriel, she thought. Father thought it might not look nice to see a young girl sitting by the coffin of a grown man.

"It must be dignified," my father said. "You see, if she was there, it might look as though she were just doing it for the ride—like these young women on bakers' vans."

My father took me out into the hall to tell me this because he did not want her to hear. But she would not have it. She wanted to come back with Colin.

"Colin loved me. It is my duty to him," she said. "Besides," she said, suddenly, in her full open voice—it had seemed to be closed and carved and broken and small—"I've never been in a hearse before."

"And it will save her fare too," I said to my father.

That night I went again to her room. She was awake. I said I was sorry to disturb her, but I would go at once only I wanted to see if she was all right. She said, in the closed voice again, that she was all right.

"Are you sure?" I said.

She did not answer. I was worried. I went over to the bed.

"What is the matter? Tell me what is the matter," I said.

For a long time she was silent. I held her hand, I stroked her head. She was lying stiff in the bed. She would not answer. I dropped my hand to her small white shoulder. She stirred and drew up her legs and half turned and said, "I was thinking of Colin. Where is he?" she asked.

"They've brought him round. He's lying downstairs."

"In the front room?"

"Yes, ready for the morning. Now be a sensible girl and go back by train."

"No, no," she said. "I want to go with Colin. Poor Colin. He loved me and I didn't love him." And she drew my hands down to her breasts.

"Colin loved me," she whispered.

"Not like this," I whispered.

It was a warm grey morning like all the others when we took Colin back. They had fixed the coffin in before Muriel came out. She came down wearing the bright blue hat she had got off Dormer's millinery man and she kissed my mother and father good-bye. They were very sorry for her. "Look after her, Arthur," my mother said. Muriel got in beside me without a glance behind her at the coffin. I started the engine. They smiled at us. My father raised his hat, but whether it was to Muriel and me or to Colin, or to the three of us, I do not know. He was not, you see, wearing his top hat. I'll say this for the old boy, thirty years in the trade have taught him tact.

After leaving my father's house you have to go down to the tram terminus before you get on the by-pass. There was always one or two drivers, conductors, or inspectors there, doing up their tickets, or changing over the trolley arms. When we passed I saw two of them drop their jaws, stick their pencils in their ears, and raise their hats. I was so surprised by this that I nearly raised mine in acknowledgment, forgetting that we had the coffin behind. I had not driven one of my father's hearses for years.

Hearses are funny things to drive. They are well-sprung, smooth-running cars, with quiet engines, and, if you are used to driving a smaller car, before you know where you are, you are speeding. You know you ought to go slow, say twenty-five to thirty maximum, and it's hard to keep it down. You can return empty at seventy if you like. It's like driving a fire engine. Go fast out and come back slow—only the other way round. Open out in the country, but slow down past houses. That's what it means. My father was very particular about this.

Muriel and I didn't speak very much at first. We sat listening to the engine and the occasional jerk of the coffin behind when we went over a pot-hole. We passed the place where poor Colin—but I didn't say anything to Muriel, and she, if she noticed—which I doubt—did not say anything to me. We went through Cox Hill, Wammering, and Yodley Mount, flat country, don't care for it myself. "There's a wonderful lot of building going on," Muriel said at last.

"You won't know these places in five years," I said.

But my mind kept drifting away from the road and the green fields and the dullness, and back to Colin—five days before, he had come down this way. I expected to see that Indian coming flying straight out of every corner. But it was all bent and bust up properly now. I saw the damned thing.

He had been up to his old game, following us, and that had put the end to following. But not quite; he was following us now, behind us in the coffin. Then my mind drifted off that and I thought of those nights at my parents' house, and Muriel. You never know what a woman is going to be like. I thought, too, that it had put my calculations out. I mean, supposing she had a baby. You see I had reckoned on waiting eighteen months or so. I would have eight hundred then. But if we had to get married at once, we should have to cut right down. Then I kept thinking it was funny her saying "Colin!" like that in the night; it was funny it made her feel that way with me, and how it made me feel when she called me Colin. I'd never thought of her in that way, in what you might call the "Colin" way.

I looked at her and she looked at me and she smiled but still we did not say very much, but the smiles kept coming to both of us. The light-railway bridge at Dootheby took me by surprise and I thought the coffin gave a jump as we took it.

"Colin's still watching us," I nearly said.

There were tears in her eyes.

"What was the matter with Colin?" I said. "Nice chap, I thought. Why didn't you marry him?"

"Yes," she said. "He was a nice boy. But he'd no sense of humour.

"And I wanted to get out of that town," she said.

"I'm not going to stay there, at that hotel," she said.

"I want to get away," she said. "I've had enough."

She had a way of getting angry with the air, like that. "You've got to take me away," she said. We were passing slowly into Muster, there was a tram ahead and people thick on the narrow pavements, dodging out into the road. But when we got into the Market Square, where they were standing around, they saw the coffin. They began to raise their hats. Suddenly she laughed. "It's like being the King and Queen," she said.

"They're raising their hats," she said.

"Not all of them," I said.

She squeezed my hand and I had to keep her from jumping about like a child on the seat as we went through.

"There they go."

"Boys always do," I said.

"And another.

"Let's see what the policeman does."

She started to laugh, but I shut her up. "Keep your sense of humour to yourself," I said.

Through all those towns that run into one another as you might say, we caught it. We went through, as she said, like royalty. So many years since I drove a hearse, I'd forgotten what it was like.

I was proud of her. I was proud of Colin, and I was proud of myself. And after what had happened, I mean on the last two nights, it was like a wedding. And although we knew it was for Colin, it was for us too, because Colin was with both of us. It was like this all the way.

"Look at that man there. Why doesn't he raise his hat? People ought to show respect for the dead," she said.

"The Loneliness of the Long-Distance Runner" describes personal integrity in the face of social sterility and records the triumph of an individual over a deadening social order. How is the narrator's violation of social norms relevant to the twentieth-century condition and, more specifically, to the mood of the 1960's? The final paragraph explains the narrator's conditions for publication; what are the implications of the fact that the story has indeed been published? The dialogue mirrors the Cockney dialect of England's lower class. How is this reflection accomplished? Is the narrative tone always consistent?

Alan Sillitoe was born in Nottingham in 1929 and left school at the age of fourteen to work in a bicycle factory. He was encouraged by poet Robert Graves to write fiction, and he published his first novel, Saturday Night and Sunday Morning, *in 1958. Since that time Sillitoe has written short stories, novels, and poetry. Further Reading:* Saturday Night and Sunday Morning (1958), The Loneliness of the Long-Distance Runner (1959).

ENGLAND

The Loneliness of the Long-Distance Runner

ALAN SILLITOE

As soon as I got to Borstal they made me a long-distance cross-country runner. I suppose they thought I was just the build for it because I was long and skinny for my age (and still am) and in any case I didn't mind it much, to tell you the truth, be-

From *The Loneliness of the Long-Distance Runner*, by Alan Sillitoe. © Copyright 1959 by Alan Sillitoe. Reprinted by permission of Alfred A. Knopf, Inc. and W. H. Allen & Company, London.

cause running had always been made much of in our family, especially running away from the police. I've always been a good runner, quick and with a big stride as well, the only trouble being that no matter how fast I run, and I did a very fair lick even though I do say so myself, it didn't stop me getting caught by the cops after that bakery job.

You might think it a bit rare, having long-distance cross-country runners in Borstal, thinking that the first thing a long-distance runner would do when they set him loose at them fields and woods would be to run as far away from the place as he could get on a bellyful of Borstal slumgullion—but you're wrong, and I'll tell you why. The first thing is that them bastards over us aren't as daft as they most of the time look, and for another thing I am not so daft as I would look if I tried to make a break for it on my long-distance running, because to abscond and then get caught is nothing but a mug's game, and I'm not falling for it. Cunning is what counts in this life, and even that you've got to use in the slyest way you can; I'm telling you straight: they're cunning, and I'm cunning. If only 'them' and 'us' had the same ideas we'd get on like a house on fire, but they don't see eye to eye with us and we don't see eye to eye with them, so that's how it stands and how it will always stand. The one fact is that all of us are cunning, and because of this there's no love lost between us. So the thing is that they know I won't try to get away from them: they sit there like spiders in that crumbly manor house, perched like jumped-up jackdaws on the roof, watching out over the drives and fields like German generals from the tops of tanks. And even when I jog-trot on behind a wood and they can't see me anymore they know my sweeping-brush head will bob along that hedge-top in an hour's time and that I'll report to the bloke on the gate. Because when on a raw and frosty morning I get up at five o'clock and stand shivering my belly off on the stone floor and all the rest still have another hour to snooze before the bells go, I slink downstairs through all the corridors to the big outside door with a permit running-card in my fist, I feel like the first and last man on the world, both at once, if you can believe what I'm trying to say. I feel like the first man because I've hardly got a stitch on and am sent against the frozen fields in a shimmy and shorts—even the first poor bastard dropped on to the earth in midwinter knew how to make a suit of leaves, or how to skin a pterodactyl for a topcoat. But there I am, frozen stiff, with nothing to get me warm except a couple of hours' long-distance running before breakfast, not even a slice of bread-and-sheepdip. They're training me up fine for the big sports day when all the pig-faced snotty-nosed dukes and ladies—who can't add two and two together and would mess themselves like loonies if they didn't have slavies to beck-and-call—come and make speeches to us about sports being just the thing to get us leading an honest life and keep our itching finger-ends off them shop locks and safe handles and hairgrips to open gas meters. They give us a bit of blue ribbon and a cup for a prize after we've shagged ourselves out running or jumping, like race horses, only we don't get so well looked after as race horses, that's the only thing.

So there I am, standing in the doorway in shimmy and shorts, not even a dry crust in my guts, looking out at frosty flowers on the ground. I suppose you think this is enough to make me cry? Not likely. Just because I feel like the first bloke in the world wouldn't make me bawl. It makes me feel fifty times better than when I'm cooped up in that dormitory with three hundred others. No, it's sometimes when I stand there feeling like the *last* man in the world that I don't feel so good. I feel like the last man in the world because I think that all those three hundred sleepers behind me are dead. They sleep so well I think that every scruffy head's kicked the bucket in the night and I'm the only one left, and when I look out into the bushes and frozen ponds I have the feeling that it's going to get colder and colder until everything I can see, meaning my red arms as well, is going to be covered with a thousand miles of ice, all the earth, right up to the sky and over every bit of land and sea. So I try to kick this feeling out and act like I'm the first man on earth. And that makes me feel good, so as soon as I'm steamed up enough to get this feeling in me, I take a flying leap out of the doorway, and off I trot.

I'm in Essex. It's supposed to be a good Borstal, at least that's what the governor said to me when I got here from Nottingham. "We want to trust you while you are in this establishment," he said, smoothing out his newspaper with lily-white workless hands, while I read the big words upside down: *Daily Telegraph*. "If you play ball with us, we'll play ball with you." (Honest to God, you'd have thought it was going to be one long tennis match.) "We want hard honest work and we want good athletics," he said as well. "And if you give us both these things you can be sure we'll do right by you and send you back into the world an honest man." Well, I could have died laughing, especially when straight after this I hear the barking sergeant-major's voice calling me and two others to attention and marching us off like we was Grenadier Guards. And when the governor kept saying how 'we' wanted you to do this, and 'we' wanted you to do that, I kept looking round for the other blokes, wondering how many of them there was. Of course, I knew there were thousands of them, but as far as I knew only one was in the room. And there *are* thousands of them, all over the poxeaten country, in shops, offices, railway stations, cars, houses, pubs—In-law blokes like you and them, all on the watch for Out-law blokes like me and us—and waiting to 'phone for the coppers as soon as we make a false move. And it'll always be there, I'll tell you that now, because I haven't finished making all my false moves yet, and I dare say I won't until

I kick the bucket. If the In-laws are hoping to stop me making false moves they're wasting their time. They might as well stand me up against a wall and let fly with a dozen rifles. That's the only way they'll stop me, and a few million others. Because I've been doing a lot of thinking since coming here. They can spy on us all day to see if we're pulling our puddings and if we're working good or doing our 'athletics' but they can't make an X-ray of our guts to find out what we're telling ourselves. I've been asking myself all sorts of questions, and thinking about my life up to now. And I like doing all this. It's a treat. It passes the time away and don't make Borstal seem half so bad as the boys in our street used to say it was. And this long-distance running lark is the best of all, because it makes me think so good that I learn things even better than when I'm on my bed at night. And apart from that, what with thinking so much while I'm running I'm getting to be one of the best runners in the Borstal. I can go my five miles round better than anybody else I know.

So as soon as I tell myself I'm the first man ever to be dropped into the world, and as soon as I take that first flying leap out into the frosty grass of an early morning when even birds haven't the heart to whistle, I get to thinking, and that's what I like. I go my rounds in a dream, turning at lane or footpath corners without knowing I'm turning, leaping brooks without knowing they're there, and shouting good morning to the early cow-milker without seeing him. It's a treat, being a long-distance runner, out in the world by yourself with not a soul to make you bad-tempered or tell you what to do or that there's a shop to break and enter a bit back from the next street. Sometimes I think that I've never been so free as during that couple of hours when I'm trotting up the path out of the gates and turning by that bare-faced, big-bellied oak tree at the lane end. Everything's dead, but good, because it's dead before coming alive, not dead after being alive. That's how I look at it. Mind you, I often feel frozen stiff at first. I can't feel my hands or feet or flesh at all, like I'm a ghost who wouldn't know the earth was under him if he didn't see it now and again through the mist. But even though some people would call this frost-pain suffering if they wrote about it to their mams in a letter, I don't, because I know that in half an hour I'm going to be warm, that by the time I get to the main road and am turning on to the wheat-field footpath by the bus stop I'm going to feel as hot as a potbellied stove and as happy as a dog with a tin tail.

It's a good life, I'm saying to myself, if you don't give in to coppers and Borstal bosses and the rest of them bastard-faced In-laws. Trot-trot-trot. Puff-puff-puff. Slap-slap-slap go my feet on the hard soil. Swish-swish-swish as my arms and side catch the bare branches of a bush. For I'm seventeen now, and when they let me out of this— if I don't make a break and see that things turn out otherwise— they'll try to get me in the army, and what's the difference between

the army and this place I'm in now? They can't kid me, the bastards.
I've seen the barracks near where I live, and if there weren't swaddies
on guard outside with rifles you wouldn't know the difference between their high walls and the place I'm in now. Even though the
swaddies come out at odd times a week for a pint of ale, so what?
Don't I come out three mornings a week on my long-distance running, which is fifty times better than boozing. When they first said
that I was to do my long-distance running without a guard pedalling
beside me on a bike I couldn't believe it; but they called it a progressive and modern place, though they can't kid me because I know it's
just like any other Borstal, going by the stories I've heard, except
that they let me trot about like this. Borstal's Borstal no matter what
they do; but anyway I moaned about it being a bit thick sending me
out so early to run five miles on an empty stomach, until they talked
me round to thinking it wasn't so bad—which I knew all the time—
until they called me a good sport and patted me on the back when
I said I'd do it and that I'd try to win them the Borstal Blue Ribbon
Prize Cup For Long-Distance Cross-Country Running (All England). And now the governor talks to me when he comes on his
rounds, almost as he'd talk to his prize race horse, if he had one.

"All right, Smith?" he asks.

"Yes, sir," I answer.

He flicks his grey moustache: "How's the running coming along?"

"I've set myself to trot round the grounds after dinner just to keep
my hand in, sir," I tell him.

The pot-bellied pop-eyed bastard gets pleased at this: "Good show.
I know you'll get us that cup," he says.

And I swear under my breath: "Like boggery, I will." No, I won't
get them that cup, even though the stupid tash-twitching bastard
has all his hopes in me. Because what does his barmy hope mean? I
ask myself. Trot-trot-trot, slap-slap-slap, over the stream and into the
wood where it's almost dark and frosty-dew twigs sting my legs. It
don't mean a bloody thing to me, only to him, and it means as much
to him as it would mean to me if I picked up the racing paper and
put my bet on a hoss I didn't know, had never seen, and didn't care
a sod if I ever did see. That's what it means to him. And I'll lose
that race, because I'm not a race horse at all, and I'll let him know it
when I'm about to get out—if I don't sling my hook even before the
race. By Christ I will. I'm a human being and I've got thoughts and
secrets and bloody life inside me that he doesn't know is there, and
he'll never know what's there because he's stupid. I suppose you'll
laugh at this, me saying the governor's a stupid bastard when I know
hardly how to write and he can read and write and add-up like a
professor. But what I say is true right enough. He's stupid, and I'm
not, because I can see further into the likes of him than he can see
into the likes of me. Admitted, we're both cunning, but I'm more

cunning and I'll win in the end even if I die in gaol at eighty-two, because I'll have more fun and fire out of my life than he'll ever get out of his. He's read a thousand books I suppose, and for all I know he might even have written a few, but I know for a dead cert, as sure as I'm sitting here, that what I'm scribbling down is worth a million to what he could ever scribble down. I don't care what anybody says, but that's the truth and can't be denied. I know when he talks to me and I look into his army mug that I'm alive and he's dead. He's as dead as a doornail. If he ran ten yards he'd drop dead. If he got ten yards into what goes on in my guts he'd drop dead as well—with surprise. At the moment it's dead blokes like him as have the whip-hand over blokes like me, and I'm almost dead sure it'll always be like that, but even so, by Christ, I'd rather be like I am— always on the run and breaking into shops for a packet of fags and a jar of jam—than have the whip-hand over somebody else and be dead from the toenails up. Maybe as soon as you get the whip-hand over somebody you do go dead. By God, to say that last sentence has needed a few hundred miles of long-distance running. I could no more have said that at first than I could have took a million- pound note from my back pocket. But it's true, you know, now I think of it again, and has always been true, and always will be true, and I'm surer of it every time I see the governor open that door and say Goodmorning lads.

As I run and see my smoky breath going out into the air as if I had ten cigars stuck in different parts of my body I think more on the little speech the governor made when I first came. Honesty. Be honest. I laughed so much one morning I went ten minutes down in my timing because I had to stop and get rid of the stitch in my side. The governor was so worried when I got back late that he sent me to the doctor's for an X-ray and heart check. Be honest. It's like saying: Be dead, like me, and then you'll have no more pain of leaving your nice slummy house for Borstal or prison. Be honest and settle down in a cosy six pounds a week job. Well, even with all this long-distance running I haven't yet been able to decide what he means by this, although I'm just about beginning to—and I don't like what it means. Because after all my thinking I found that it adds up to something that can't be true about me, being born and brought up as I was. Because another thing people like the governor will never understand is that I *am* honest, that I've never been anything else but honest, and that I'll always be honest. Sounds funny. But it's true because I know what honest means according to me and he only knows what it means according to him. I think my honesty is the only sort in the world, and he thinks his is the only sort in the world as well. That's why this dirty great walled-up and fenced-up manor house in the middle of nowhere has been used to coop-up blokes like me. And if I had the whip-hand I wouldn't even bother to build a place like this to put all the cops, governors, posh whores, penpushers, army officers, Members of Parliament in; no, I'd stick them up against a wall and let them have it, like they'd have done with blokes like us years ago, that is, if they'd ever known what it means to be honest, which they don't and never will so help me God Almighty.

I was nearly eighteen months in Borstal before I thought about getting out. I can't tell you much about what it was like there because I haven't got the hang of describing buildings or saying how many crumby chairs and slatted windows make a room. Neither can I do much complaining, because to tell you the truth I didn't suffer in Borstal at all. I gave the same answer a pal of mine gave when someone asked him how much he hated it in the army. "I didn't hate it," he said. "They fed me, gave me a suit, and pocket-money, which was a bloody sight more than I ever got before, unless I worked myself to death for it, and most of the time they wouldn't let me work but sent me to the dole office twice a week." Well, that's more or less what I say. Borstal didn't hurt me in that respect, so since I've got no complaints I don't have to describe what they gave us to eat, what the dorms were like, or how they treated us. But in another way Borstal does something to me. No, it doesn't get my back up, because it's always been up, right from when I was born. What it does do is show me what they've been trying to frighten me with. They've got other things as well, like prison and, in the end, the rope. It's like me rushing up to thump a man and snatch the coat off his back when, suddenly, I pull up because he whips out a knife and lifts it to stick me like a pig if I come too close. That knife is Borstal, clink, the rope. But once you've seen the knife you learn a bit of unarmed combat. You have to, because you'll never get that sort of knife in your own hands, and this unarmed combat doesn't amount to much. Still, there it is, and you keep on rushing up to this man, knife or not, hoping to get one of your hands on his wrist and the other on his elbow both at the same time, and press back until he drops the knife.

You see, by sending me to Borstal they've shown me the knife, and from now on I know something I didn't know before: that it's war between me and them. I always knew this, naturally, because I was in Remand Homes as well and the boys there told me a lot about their brothers in Borstal, but it was only touch and go then, like kittens, like boxing-gloves, like dobbie. But now that they've shown me the knife, whether I ever pinch another thing in my life again or not, I know who my enemies are and what war is. They can drop all the atom bombs they like for all I care: I'll never call it war and wear a soldier's uniform, because I'm in a different sort of war, that they think is child's play. The war they think is war is suicide, and those that go and get killed in war should be put in clink for attempted suicide because that's the feeling in blokes' minds when they rush to join up or let themselves be called up. I know, because

I've thought how good it would be sometimes to do myself in and the easiest way to do it, it occurred to me, was to hope for a big war so's I could join up and get killed. But I got past that when I knew I already was in a war of my own, that I was born into one, that I grew up hearing the sound of 'old soldiers' who'd been over the top at Dartmoor, half-killed at Lincoln, trapped in no-man's-land at Borstal, that sounded louder than any Jerry bombs. Government wars aren't my wars; they've got nowt to do with me, because my own war's all that I'll ever be bothered about. I remember when I was fourteen and I went out into the country with three of my cousins, all about the same age, who later went to different Borstals, and then to different regiments, from which they soon deserted, and then to different gaols where they still are as far as I know. But anyway, we were all kids then, and wanted to go out to the woods for a change, to get away from the roads of stinking hot tar one summer. We climbed over fences and went through fields, scrumping a few sour apples on our way, until we saw the wood about a mile off. Up Colliers' Pad we heard another lot of kids talking in high-school voices behind a hedge. We crept up on them and peeped through the brambles, and saw they were eating a picnic, a real posh spread out of baskets and flasks and towels. There must have been about seven of them, lads and girls sent out by their mams and dads for the afternoon. So we went on our bellies through the hedge like crocodiles and surrounded then, and then dashed into the middle, scattering the fire and batting their tabs and snatching up all there was to eat, then running off over Cherry Orchard fields into the wood, with a man chasing us who'd come up while we were ransacking their picnic. We got away all right, and had a good feed into the bargain, because we'd been clambed to death and couldn't wait long enough to get our chops ripping into them thin lettuce and ham sandwiches and creamy cakes.

Well, I'll always feel during every bit of my life like those daft kids should have felt before we broke them up. But they never dreamed that what happened was going to happen, just like the governor of this Borstal who spouts to us about honesty and all that wappy stuff don't know a bloody thing, while I know every minute of my life that a big boot is always likely to smash any nice picnic I might be barmy and dishonest enough to make for myself. I admit that there've been times when I've thought of telling the governor all this so as to put him on his guard, but when I've got as close as seeing him I've changed my mind, thinking to let him either find out for himself or go through the same mill as I've gone through. I'm not hard-hearted (in fact I've helped a few blokes in my time with the odd quid, lie, fag, or shelter from the rain when they've been on the run) but I'm boggered if I'm going to risk being put in the cells just for trying to give the governor a bit of advice he don't deserve. If my heart's soft I know the sort of people I'm going to save it for. And any advice I'd give the governor wouldn't do him the least bit of good; it'd only trip him up sooner than if he wasn't told at all, which I suppose is what I want to happen. But for the time being I'll let things go on as they are, which is something else I've learned in the last year or two. (It's a good job I can only think of these things as fast as I can write with this stub of pencil that's clutched in my paw, otherwise I'd have dropped the whole thing weeks ago.)

By the time I'm half-way through my morning course, when after a frost-bitten dawn I can see a phlegmy bit of sunlight hanging from the bare twigs of beech and sycamore, and when I've measured my half-way mark by the short-cut scrimmage down the steep bush-covered bank and into the sunken lane, when still there's not a soul in sight and not a sound except the neighing of a piebald foal in a cottage stable that I can't see, I get to thinking the deepest and daftest of all. The governor would have a fit if he could see me sliding down the bank because I could break my neck or ankle, but I can't not do it because it's the only risk I take and the only excitement I ever get, flying flat-out like one of them pterodactyls from the 'Lost World' I once heard on the wireless, crazy like a cut-balled cockerel, scratching myself to bits and almost letting myself go but not quite. It's the most wonderful minute because there's not one thought or word or picture of anything in my head while I'm going down. I'm empty, as empty as I was before I was born, and I don't let myself go, I suppose, because whatever it is that's farthest down inside me don't want me to die or hurt myself bad. And it's daft to think deep, you know, because it gets you nowhere, though deep is what I am when I've passed this half-way mark because the long-distance run of an early morning makes me think that every run like this is a life—a little life, I know—but a life as full of misery and happiness and things happening as you can ever get really around yourself—and I remember that after a lot of these runs I thought that it didn't need much know-how to tell how a life was going to end once it had got well started. But as usual I was wrong, caught first by the cops and then by my own bad brain, I could never trust myself to fly scot-free over these traps, was always tripped up sooner or later no matter how many I got over to the good without even knowing it. Looking back I suppose them big trees put their branches to their snouts and gave each other the wink, and there I was whizzing down the bank and not seeing a bloody thing.

II

I don't say to myself: "You shouldn't have done the job and then you'd have stayed away from Borstal"; no, what I ram into my runner-brain is that my luck had no right to scram just when I was on my way to making the coppers think I hadn't done the job after all.

The time was autumn and the night foggy enough to set me and my mate Mike roaming the streets when we should have been rooted in front of the telly or stuck into a plush posh seat at the pictures, but I was restless after six weeks away from any sort of work, and well you might ask me why I'd been bone-idle for so long because normally I sweated my thin guts out on a milling-machine with the rest of them, but you see, my dad died from cancer of the throat, and mam collected a cool five hundred in insurance and benefits from the factory where he'd worked, "for your bereavement," they said, or words like that.

Now I believe, and my mam must have thought the same, that a wad of crisp blue-back fivers ain't a sight of good to a living soul unless they're flying out of your hand into some shopkeeper's till, and the shopkeeper is passing you tip-top things in exchange over the counter, so as soon as she got the money, mam took me and my five brothers and sisters out of town and got us dolled-up in new clothes. Then she ordered a twenty-one-inch telly, a new carpet because the old one was covered with blood from dad's dying and wouldn't wash out, and took a taxi home with bags of grub and a new fur coat. And do you know—you wain't believe me when I tell you— she'd still near three hundred left in her bulging handbag the next day, so how could any of us go to work after that? Poor old dad, he didn't get a look in, and he was the one who'd done the suffering and dying for such a lot of lolly.

Night after night we sat in front of the telly with a ham sandwich in one hand, a bar of chocolate in the other, and a bottle of lemonade between our boots, while mam was with some fancy-man upstairs on the new bed she'd ordered, and I'd never known a family as happy as ours was in that couple of months when we'd got all the money we needed. And when the dough ran out I didn't think about anything much, but just roamed the streets—looking for another job, I told mam—hoping I suppose to get my hands on another five hundred nicker so's the nice life we'd got used to could go on and on for ever. Because it's surprising how quick you can get used to a different life. To begin with, the adverts on the telly had shown us how much more there was in the world to buy than we'd ever dreamed of when we'd looked into shop windows but hadn't seen all there was to see because we didn't have the money to buy it with anyway. And the telly made all these things seem twenty times better than we'd ever thought they were. Even adverts at the cinema were cool and tame, because now we were seeing them in private at home. We used to cock our noses up at things in shops that didn't move, but suddenly we saw their real value because they jumped and glittered around the screen and had some pasty-faced tart going head over heels to get her nail-polished grabbers on to them or her lipstick lips over them, not like the crumby adverts you saw on posters or in newspapers as dead as doornails; these were flickering around loose, half-open packets and tins, making you think that all you had to do was finish opening them before they were yours, like seeing an unlocked safe through a shop window with the man gone away for a cup of tea without thinking to guard his lolly. The films they showed were good as well, in that way, because we couldn't get our eyes unglued from the cops chasing the robbers who had satchel-bags crammed with cash and looked like getting away to spend it—until the last moment. I always hoped they would end up free to blow the lot, and could never stop wanting to put my hand out, smash into the screen (it only looked a bit of rag-screen like at the pictures) and get the copper in a half-nelson so's he'd stop following the bloke with the money-bags. Even when he'd knocked off a couple of bank clerks I hoped he wouldn't get nabbed. In fact then I wished more than ever he wouldn't because it meant the hot-chair if he did, and I wouldn't wish that on anybody no matter what they'd done, because I'd read in a book where the hot-chair worn't a quick death at all, but that you just sat there scorching to death until you were dead. And it was when these cops were chasing the crooks that we played some good tricks with the telly, because when one of them opened his big gob to spout about getting their man I'd turn the sound down and see his mouth move like a goldfish or mackerel or a minnow mimicking what they were supposed to be acting—it was so funny the whole family nearly went into fits on the brand-new carpet that hadn't yet found its way to the bedroom. It was the best of all though when we did it to some Tory telling up about how good his government was going to be if we kept on voting for them—their slack chops rolling, opening and bumbling, hands lifted to twitch moustaches and touching their buttonholes to make sure the flower hadn't wilted, so that you could see they didn't mean a word they said, especially with not a murmur coming out because we'd cut off the sound. When the governor of the Borstal first talked to me I was reminded of those times so much that I nearly killed myself trying not to laugh. Yes, we played so many good stunts on the box of tricks that mam used to call us the Telly Boys, we got so clever at it.

My pal Mike got let off with probation because it was his first job —anyway the first they ever knew about—and because they said he would never have done it if it hadn't been for me talking him into it. They said I was a menace to honest lads like Mike—hands in his pockets so that they looked stone-empty, head bent forward as if looking for half-crowns to fill 'em with, a ripped jersey on and his hair falling into his eyes so that he could go up to women and ask them for a shilling because he was hungry—and that I was the brains behind the job, the guiding light when it came to making up anybody's mind, but I swear to God I worn't owt like that because really I ain't got no more brains than a gnat after hiding the money in the place I did. And I—being cranky like I am—got sent to Borstal because to tell you the honest truth I'd been to Remand Homes before —though that's another story and I suppose if ever I tell it it'll be just as boring as this one is. I was glad though that Mike got away with it, and I only hope he always will, not like silly bastard me.

So on this foggy night we tore ourselves away from the telly and slammed the front door behind us, setting off up our wide street like slow tugs on a river that'd broken their hooters, for we didn't know where the housefronts began what with the perishing cold mist all around, I was snatched to death without an overcoat: mam had forgotten to buy me one in the scrummage of shopping, and by the time I thought to remind her of it the dough was all gone. So we whistled: The Teddy Boys' Picnic to keep us warm, and I told myself that I'd get a coat soon if it was the last thing I did. Mike said he thought the same about himself, adding that he'd also get some brand-new glasses with gold rims, to wear instead of the wire frames they'd given him at the school clinic years ago. He didn't twig it was foggy at first and cleaned his glasses every time I pulled him back from a lamp-post or car, but when he saw the lights on Alfreton Road looking like octopus eyes he put them in his pocket and didn't wear them again until we did the job. We hadn't got two ha-pennies between us, and though we weren't hungry we wished we'd get a bob or two when we passed the fish and chip shops because the delicious sniffs of salt and vinegar and frying fat made our mouths water. I don't mind telling you we walked the town from one end to the other and if our eyes worn't glued to the ground looking for lost wallets and watches they was swivelling around house windows and shop doors in case we saw something easy and worth nipping into.

Neither of us said as much as this to each other, but I know for a fact that that was what we was thinking. What I don't know—and as sure as I sit here I know I'll never know—is which of us was the first bastard to latch his peepers on to that baker's backyard. Oh yes, it's all right me telling myself it was me, but the truth is that I've never known whether it was Mike or not, because I do know that I didn't see the open window until he stabbed me in the ribs and pointed it out. "See it?" he said.

"Yes," I told him, "so let's get cracking."

But what about the wall though?" he whispered, looking a bit closer.

"On your shoulders," I chipped in.

His eyes were already up there: "Will you be able to reach?" It was the only time he ever showed any life.

"Leave it to me," I said, ever-ready. "I can reach anywhere from your ham-hock shoulders."

Mike was a nipper compared to me, but underneath the scruffy draught-board jersey he wore were muscles as hard as iron, and you

wouldn't think to see him walking down the street with glasses on
and hands in pockets that he'd harm a fly, but I never liked to get
on the wrong side of him in a fight because he's the sort that don't
say a word for weeks on end—sits plugged in front of the telly, or
reads a cowboy book, or just sleeps—when suddenly BIFF—half
kills somebody for almost nothing at all, such as beating him in a
race for the last Football Post on a Saturday night, pushing in before
him at a bus stop, or bumping into him when he was day-dreaming
about Dolly-on-the-Tub next door. I saw him set on a bloke once for
no more than fixing him in a funny way with his eyes, and it turned
out that the bloke was cock-eyed but nobody knew it because he'd
just that day come to live in our street. At other times none of these
things would matter a bit, and I suppose the only reason why I was
pals with him was because I didn't say much from one month's end
to another either.

He puts his hands up in the air like he was being covered with a
Gatling-Gun, and moved to the wall like he was going to be mowed
down, and I climbed up him like he was a stile or step-ladder, and
there he stood, the palms of his upshot maulers flat and turned out
so's I could step on 'em like they was the adjustable jack-spanner
under a car, not a sound of a breath nor the shiver of a flinch coming
from him. I lost no time in any case, took my coat from between my
teeth, chucked it up to the glass-topped wall (where the glass worn't
too sharp because the jags had been worn down by years of accidental
stones) and was sitting astraddle before I knew where I was. Then
down the other side, with my legs rammed up into my throat when
I hit the ground, the crack coming about as hard as when you fall
after a high parachute drop, that one of my mates told me was like
jumping off a twelve-foot wall, which this must have been. Then I
picked up my bits and pieces and opened the gate for Mike, who was
still grinning and full of life because the hardest part of the job was
already done. "I came, I broke, I entered," like that clever-dick Borstal
song.

I didn't think about anything at all, as usual, because I never do
when I'm busy, when I'm draining pipes, looting sacks, yaling locks,
lifting latches, forcing my bony hands and lanky legs into making
something move, hardly feeling my lungs going in-whiff and out-
whaff, not realizing whether my mouth is clamped tight or gaping,
whether I'm hungry, itching from scabies, or whether my flies are
open and flashing dirty words like muck and spit into the late-night
final fog. And when I don't know anything about all this then how
can I honest-to-God say I think of anything at such times? When I'm
wondering what's the best way to get a window open or how to force
a door, how can I be thinking or have anything on my mind? That's
what the four-eyed white-smocked bloke with the note-book couldn't
understand when he asked me questions for days and days after I

got to Borstal; and I couldn't explain it to him then like I'm writing it down now; and even if I'd been able to maybe he still wouldn't have caught on because I don't know whether I can understand it myself even at this moment, though I'm doing my best you can bet.

So before I knew where I was I was inside the baker's office watching Mike picking up that cash box after he'd struck a match to see where it was, wearing a tailor-made fifty-shilling grin on his square crew-cut nut as his paws closed over the box like he'd squash it to nothing. "Out," he suddenly said, shaking it so's it rattled. "Let's scram."

"Maybe there's some more," I said, pulling half a dozen drawers out of a rollertop desk.

"No," he said, like he'd already been twenty years in the game, "this is the lot," patting his tin box, "this is it."

I pulled out another few drawers, full of bills, books and letters. "How do you know, you loony sod?"

He barged past me like a bull at a gate. "Because I do."

Right or wrong, we'd both got to stick together and do the same thing. I looked at an ever-loving babe of a brand-new typewriter, but knew it was too traceable, so blew it a kiss, and went out after him. "Hang on," I said, pulling the door to, "we're in no hurry."

"Not much we aren't," he says, over his shoulder.

"We've got months to splash the lolly," I whispered as we crossed the yard, "only don't let that gate creak too much or you'll have the narks tuning-in."

"You think I'm barmy?" he said, creaking the gate so that the whole street heard.

I don't know about Mike, but now I started to think of how we'd get back safe through the streets with that money-box up my jumper. Because he'd clapped it into my hand as soon as we'd got to the main road, which might have meant that he'd started thinking as well, which only goes to show how you don't know what's in anybody else's mind unless you think about things yourself. But as far as my thinking went at that moment it wasn't up to much, only a bit of fright that wouldn't budge not even with a hot blow-lamp, about what we'd say if a copper asked us where we were off to with that hump in my guts.

"What is it?" he'd ask, and I'd say: "A growth." "What do you mean, a growth, my lad?" he'd say back, narky like. I'd cough and clutch myself like I was in the most tripe-twisting pain in the world, and screw my eyes up like I was on my way to the hospital, and Mike would take my arm like he was the best pal Id got. "Cancer," I'd manage to say to Narker, which would make his slow punch-drunk brain suspect a thing or two. "A lad of your age?" So I'd groan again, and hope to make him feel a real bully of a bastard, which would be impossible, but anyway: "It's in the family. Dad died of it last

month, and I'll die of it next month by the feel of it." "What, did
he have it in the guts?" "No, in the throat. But it's got me in the
stomach." Groan and cough. "Well, you shouldn't be out like this
if you've got cancer, you should be in the hospital." I'd get ratty now:
"That's where I'm trying to go if only you'd let me and stop asking
so many questions. Aren't I, Mike?" Grunt from Mike as he unslung
his cosh. Then just in time the copper would tell us to get on our
way, kind and considerate all of a sudden, saying that the outpatient
department of the hospital closes at twelve, so hadn't he better call
us a taxi? He would if we liked, he says, and he'd pay for it as well.
But we tell him not to bother, that he's a good bloke even if he is
a copper, that we know a short cut anyway. Then just as we're turning a corner he gets it into his big batchy head that we're going the
opposite way to the hospital, and calls us back. So we'd start to run
. . . if you can call all that thinking.

Up in my room Mike rips open that money-box with a hammer
and chisel, and before we know where we are we've got seventy-eight
pounds fifteen and fourpence ha'penny *each* lying all over my bed
like tea spread out on Christmas Day: cake and trifle, salad and sandwiches, jam tarts and bars of chocolate: all shared and shared alike
between Mike and me because we believed in equal work and equal
pay, just like the comrades my dad was in until he couldn't do a stroke
anymore and had no breath left to argue with. I thought how good
it was that blokes like that poor baker didn't stash all his cash in one
of the big marble-fronted banks that take up every corner of the
town, how lucky for us that he didn't trust them no matter how
many millions of tons of concrete or how many iron bars and boxes
they were made of, or how many coppers kept their blue pop-eyed
peepers glued on to them, how smashing it was that he believed in
money-boxes when so many shopkeepers thought it old-fashioned and
tried to be modern by using a bank, which wouldn't give a couple of
sincere, honest, hardworking, conscientious blokes like Mike and me
a chance.

Now you'd think, and I'd think, and anybody with a bit of imagination would think, that we'd done as clean a job as could ever be done,
that, with the baker's shop being at least a mile from where we lived,
and with not a soul having seen us, and what with the fog and the
fact that we weren't more than five minutes in the place, that the
coppers should never have been able to trace us. But then, you'd be
wrong, I'd be wrong, and everybody else would be wrong, no matter
how much imagination was diced out between us.

Even so, Mike and I didn't splash the money about, because that
would have made people think straightaway that we'd latched on to
something that didn't belong to us. Which wouldn't do at all, because even in a street like ours there are people who love to do a good
turn for the coppers, though I never know why they do. Some people

are so mean-gutted that even if they've only got tuppence more than you and they think you're the sort that would take it if you have half the chance, they'd get you put inside if they saw you ripping lead out of a lavatory, even if it weren't their lavatory—just to keep their tuppence out of your reach. And so we didn't do anything to let on about how rich we were, nothing like going down town and coming back dressed in brand-new Teddy boy suits and carrying a set of skiffle-drums like another pal of ours who'd done a factory office about six months before. No, we took the odd bobs and pennies out and folded the notes into bundles and stuffed them up the drainpipe outside the door in the backyard. "Nobody'll ever think of looking for it there," I said to Mike. "We'll keep it doggo for a week or two, then take a few quid a week out till it's all gone. We might be thieving bastards, but we're not green."

Some days later a plain-clothes dick knocked at the door. And asked for me. I was still in bed, at eleven o'clock, and had to unroll myself from the comfortable black sheets when I heard mam calling me. "A man to see you," she said. "Hurry up, or he'll be gone."

I could hear her keeping him at the back door, nattering about how fine it had been but how it looked like rain since early this morning—and he didn't answer her except to snap out a snotty yes or no. I scrambled into my trousers and wondered why he'd come—knowing it was a copper because 'a man to see you' always meant just that in our house—and if I'd had any idea that one had gone to Mike's house as well at the same time I'd have twigged it to be because of that hundred and fifty quid's worth of paper stuffed up the drainpipe outside the back door about ten inches away from that plain-clothed copper's boot, where mam still talked to him thinking she was doing me a favour, and I wishing to God she'd ask him in, though on second thoughts realizing that that would seem more suspicious than keeping him outside, because they know we hate their guts and smell a rat if they think we're trying to be nice to them. Mam wasn't born yesterday, I thought, thumping my way down the creaking stairs.

I'd seen him before: Borstal Bernard in nicky-hat, Remand Home Ronald in rowing-boat boots, Probation Pete in a pit-prop mackintosh, three-months clink in collar and tie (all this out of a Borstal skiffle-ballad that my new mate made up, and I'd tell you it in full but it doesn't belong in this story), a 'tec, who'd never had as much in his pockets as that drainpipe had up its jackses. He was like Hitler in the face, right down to the paint-brush tash, except that being six-foot tall made him seem worse. But I straightened my shoulders to look into his illiterate blue eyes—like I always do with any copper.

Then he started asking me questions, and my mother from behind said: "He's never left that television set for the last three months, so you've got nowt on him, mate. You might as well look for somebody else, because you're wasting the rates you get out of my rent and the

income-tax that comes out of my pay-packet standing there like that"
—which was a laugh because she'd never paid either to my knowledge, and never would, I hoped.

"Well, you know where Papplewick Street is, don't you?" the copper asked me, taking no notice of mam.

"Ain't it off Alfreton Road?" I asked him back, helpful and bright.

"You know there's a baker's half-way down on the left-hand side,
don't you?"

"Ain't it next door to a pub, then?" I wanted to know.

He answered me sharp: "No, it bloody well ain't." Coppers always
lose their tempers as quick as this, and more often than not they
gain nothing by it. "Then I don't know it," I told him, saved by the
bell.

He slid his big boot round and round on the doorstep. "Where
were you last Friday night?" Back in the ring, but this was worse
than a boxing match.

I didn't like him trying to accuse me of something he wasn't sure
I'd done. "Was I at that baker's you mentioned? Or in the pub next
door?"

"You'll get five years in Borstal if you don't give me a straight answer," he said, unbuttoning his mac even though it was cold where
he was standing.

"I was glued to the telly, like mam says," I swore blind. But he
went on and on with his loony questions: "Have you got a television?"

The things he asked wouldn't have taken in a kid of two, and what
else could I say to the last one except: "Has the aerial fell down?
Or would you like to come in and see it?"

He was liking me even less for saying that. "We know you weren't
listening to the television set last Friday, and so do you, don't you?"

"P'raps not, but I was *looking* at it, because sometimes we turn
the sound down for a bit of fun." I could hear mam laughing from
the kitchen, and I hoped Mike's man was doing the same if the cops
had gone to him as well.

"We know you weren't in the house," he said, starting up again,
cranking himself with the handle. They always say 'We' 'We', never
'I' 'I'—as if they feel braver and righter knowing there's a lot of them
against only one.

"I've got witnesses," I said to him. "Mam for one. Her fancy-man,
for two. Ain't that enough? I can get you a dozen more, or thirteen
altogether, if it was a baker's that got robbed."

"I don't want no lies," he said, not catching on about the baker's
dozen. Where do they scrape cops up from anyway? "All I want is
to get from you where you put that money."

Don't get mad, I kept saying to myself, don't get mad—hearing
mam setting out cups and saucers and putting the pan on the stove

for bacon. I stood back and waved him inside like I was a butler. "Come and search the house. If you've got a warrant."

"Listen, my lad," he said, like the dirty bullying jumped-up bastard he was, "I don't want too much of your lip, because if we get you down to the Guildhall you'll get a few bruises and black-eyes for your trouble." And I knew he wasn't kidding either, because I'd heard about all them sort of tricks. I hoped one day though that him and all his pals would be the ones to get the black-eyes and kicks; you never knew. It might come sooner than anybody thinks, like in Hungary. "Tell me where the money is, and I'll get you off with probation."

"What money?" I asked him, because I'd heard that one before as well.

"You know what money."

"Do I look as though I'd know owt about money?" I said, pushing my fist through a hole in my shirt.

"The money that was pinched, that you know all about," he said. "You can't trick me, so it's no use trying."

"Was it three-and-eightpence ha'penny?" I asked.

"You thieving young bastard. We'll teach you to steal money that doesn't belong to you."

I turned my head around: "Mam," I called out, "get my lawyer on the blower, will you?"

"Clever, aren't you?" he said in a very unfriendly way, "but we won't rest until we clear all this up."

"Look," I pleaded, as if about to sob my socks off because he'd got me wrong, "it's all very well us talking like this, it's like a game almost, but I wish you'd tell me what it's all about, because honest-to-God I've just got out of bed and here you are at the door talking about me having pinched a lot of money, money that I don't know anything about."

He swung around now as if he'd trapped me, though I couldn't see why he might think so. "Who said anything about money? I didn't. What made you bring money into this little talk we're having?"

"It's you," I answered, thinking he was going barmy and about to start foaming at the chops, "you've got money on the brain, like all policemen. Baker's shops as well."

He screwed his face up. "I want an answer from you: where's that money?"

But I was getting fed-up with all this. "I'll do a deal."

Judging by his flash-bulb face he thought he was suddenly on to a good thing. "What sort of a deal?"

So I told him: "I'll give you all the money I've got, one and fourpence ha'penny, if you stop this third-degree and let me go in and get my breakfast. Honest, I'm clambed to death. I ain't had a bite since yesterday. Can't you hear my guts rollin'?"

His jaw dropped, but on he went, pumping me for another half hour. A routine check-up, as they say on the pictures. But I knew I was winning on points.

Then he left, but came back in the afternoon to search the house. He didn't find a thing, not a French farthing. He asked me questions again and I didn't tell him anything except lies, lies, lies, because I can go on doing that forever without batting an eyelid. He'd got nothing on me and we both of us knew it, otherwise I'd have been down at the Guildhall in no time, but he kept on keeping on because I'd been in a Remand Home for a high-wall job before; and Mike was put through the same mill because all the local cops knew he was my best pal.

When it got dark me and Mike were in our parlour with a low light on and the telly off, Mike taking it easy in the rocking chair and me slouched out on the settee, both of us puffing a packet of Woods. With the door bolted and curtains drawn we talked about the dough we'd crammed up the drainpipe. Mike thought we should take it out and both of us do a bunk to Skegness or Cleethorpes for a good time in the arcades, living like lords in a boarding house near the pier, then at least we'd both have had a big beano before getting sent down.

"Listen, you daft bleeder," I said, "we aren't going to get caught at all, *and* we'll have a good time, later." We were so clever we didn't even go out to the pictures, though we wanted to.

In the morning old Hitler-face questioned me again, with one of his pals this time, and the next day they came, trying as hard as they could to get something out of me, but I didn't budge an inch. I know I'm showing off when I say this, but in me he'd met his match, and I'd never give in to questions no matter how long it was kept up. They searched the house a couple of times as well, which made me think they thought they really had something to go by, but I know now that they hadn't, and that it was all buckshee speculation. They turned the house upside down and inside out like an old sock, went from top to bottom and front to back but naturally didn't find a thing. The copper even poked his face up the front-room chimney (that hadn't been used or swept for years) and came down looking like Al Jolson so that he had to swill himself clean at the scullery sink. They kept tapping and pottering around the big aspidistra plant that grandma had left to mam, lifting it up from the table to look under the cloth, putting it aside so's they could move the table and get at the boards under the rug—but the big headed stupid ignorant bastards never once thought of emptying the soil out of the plant pot, where they'd have found the crumpled-up money-box that we'd buried the night we did the job. I suppose it's still there, now I think about it, and I suppose mam wonders now and again why the plant don't prosper like it used to—as if it could with a fistful of thick black tin lapped around its guts.

The last time he knocked at our door was one wet morning at five minutes to nine and I was sleep-logged in my crumby bed as usual. Mam had gone to work that day so I shouted for him to hold on a bit, and then went down to see who it was. There he stood, six-feet tall and sopping wet, and for the first time in my life I did a spiteful thing I'll never forgive myself for: I didn't ask him to come in out of the rain, because I wanted him to get double pneumonia and die. I suppose he could have pushed by me and come in if he'd wanted, but maybe he'd got used to asking questions on the doorstep and didn't want to be put off by changing his ground even though it was raining. Not that I don't like being spiteful because of any barmy principle I've got, but this bit of spite, as it turned out, did me no good at all. I should have treated him as a brother I hadn't seen for twenty years and dragged him in for a cup of tea and a fag, told him about the picture I hadn't seen the night before, asked him how his wife was after her operation and whether they'd shaved her moustache off to make it, and then sent him happy and satisfied out by the front door. But no, I thought, let's see what he's got to say for himself now.

He stood a little to one side of the door, either because it was less wet there, or because he wanted to see me from a different angle, perhaps having found it monotonous to watch a bloke's face always telling lies from the same side. "You've been identified," he said, twitching raindrops from his tash. "A woman saw you and your mate yesterday and she swears blind you are the same chaps she saw going into that bakery."

I was dead sure he was still bluffing, because Mike and I hadn't even seen each other the day before, but I looked worried. "She's a menace then to innocent people, whoever she is, because the only bakery I've been in lately is the one up our street to get some cut-bread on tick for mam."

He didn't bite on this. "So now I want to know where the money is"—as if I hadn't answered him at all.

"I think mam took it to work this morning to get herself some tea in the canteen." Rain was splashing down so hard I thought he'd get washed away if he didn't come inside. But I wasn't much bothered, and went on: "I remember I put it in the telly-vase last night—it was my only one-and-three and I was saving it for a packet of tips this morning—and I nearly had a jibbering black fit just now when I saw it had gone. I was reckoning on it for getting me through today because I don't think life's worth living without a fag, do you?"

I was getting into my stride and began to feel good, twigging that this would be my last pack of lies, and that if I kept it up for long enough this time I'd have the bastards beat: Mike and me would be off to the coast in a few weeks time having the fun of our lives, playing at penny football and latching on to a couple of tarts that would give us all they were good for. "And this weather's no good for picking-up fag-ends in the street," I said, "because they'd be sopping wet. Course, I know you could dry 'em out near the fire, but it don't taste the same you know, all said and done. Rainwater does summat to 'em that don't bear thinkin' about: it turns 'em back into hoss-tods without the taste though."

I began to wonder, at the back of my brainless eyes, why old copper-lugs didn't pull me up sharp and say he hadn't got time to listen to all this, but he wasn't looking at me anymore, and all my thoughts about Skegness went bursting to smithereens in my sludgy loaf. I could have dropped into the earth when I saw what he'd fixed his eyes on.

He was looking at *it*, an ever-loving fiver, and I could only jabber: "The one thing is to have some real fags because new hoss-tods is always better than stuff that's been rained on and dried, and I know how you feel about not being able to find money because one-and-three's one-and-three in anybody's pocket, and naturally if I see it knocking around I'll get you on the blower tomorrow straightaway and tell you where you can find it."

I thought I'd go down in a fit: three green-backs as well had been washed down by the water, and more were following, lying flat at first after their fall, then getting tilted at the corners by wind and rain-spots as if they were alive and wanted to get back into the dry snug drainpipe out of the terrible weather, and you can't imagine how I wished they'd be able to. Old Hitler-face didn't know what to make of it but just kept staring down and down, and I thought I'd better keep on talking, though I knew it wasn't much good now.

"It's a fact, I know, that money's hard to come by and half-crowns don't get found on bus seats or in dustbins, and I didn't see any in bed last night because I'd 'ave known about it, wouldn't I? You can't sleep with things like that in the bed because they're too hard, and anyway at first they're . . ." It took Hitler-boy a long time to catch on; they were beginning to spread over the yard a bit, reinforced by the third colour of a ten-bob note, before his hand clamped itself on to my shoulder.

III

The pop-eyed potbellied governor said to a pop-eyed potbellied Member of Parliament who sat next to his pop-eyed potbellied whore of a wife that I was his only hope for getting the Borstal Blue Ribbon Prize Cup For Long-Distance Cross-Country Running (all England), which I was, and it set me laughing to myself inside, and I didn't say a word to any potbellied pop-eyed bastard that might give them real hope, though I knew the governor anyway took my quiet-ness to mean he'd got that cup already stuck on the bookshelf in his office among the few other mildewed trophies.

"He might take up running in a sort of professional way when he gets out," and it wasn't until he'd said this and I'd heard it with my own flap-tabs that I realized it might be possible to do such a thing, run for money, trot for wages on piece work at a bob a puff rising bit by bit to a guinea a gasp and retiring through old age at thirty-two because of lace-curtain lungs, a football heart, and legs like varicose beanstalks. But I'd have a wife and car and get my grinning long-distance clock in the papers and have a smashing secretary to answer piles of letters sent by tarts who'd mob me when they saw who I was as I pushed my way into Woolworth's for a packet of razor blades and a cup of tea. It was something to think about all right, and sure enough the governor knew he'd got me when he said, turning to me as if I would at any rate have to be consulted about it all: "How does this matter strike you, then, Smith, my lad?"

A line of potbellied pop-eyes gleamed at me and a row of goldfish mouths opened and wiggled gold teeth at me, so I gave them the answer they wanted because I'd hold my trump card until later. "It'd suit me fine, sir," I said.

"Good lad. Good show. Right spirit. Splendid."

"Well," the governor said "get that cup for us today and I'll do all I can for you. I'll get you trained so that you whack every man in the Free World." And I had a picture in my brain of me running and beating everybody in the world, leaving them all behind until only I was trot-trotting across a big wide moor alone, doing a marvellous speed as I ripped between boulders and reedclumps, when suddenly: CRACK! CRACK!—bullets that can go faster than any man running, coming from a copper's rifle planted in a tree, winged me and split my gizzard in spite of my perfect running, and down I fell.

The potbellies expected me to say something else. "Thank you, sir," I said.

Told to go, I trotted down the pavilion steps, out on to the field because the big cross-country was about to begin and the two entries from Gunthorpe had fixed themselves early at the starting line and were ready to move off like white kangaroos. The sports ground looked a treat: with big tea-tents all round and flags flying and seats for families—empty because no mam or dad had known what opening day meant—and boys still running heats for the hundred yards, and lords and ladies walking from stall to stall, and the Borstal Boys Brass Band in blue uniforms; and up on the stands the brown jackets of Hucknall as well as our own grey blazers, and then the Gunthorpe lot with shirt sleeves rolled. The blue sky was full of sunshine and it couldn't have been a better day, and all of the big show was like something out of Ivanhoe that we'd seen on the pictures a few days before.

"Come on, Smith," Roach the sports master called to me, "we don't want you to be late for the big race, eh? Although I dare say you'd catch them up if you were." The others cat-called and grunted at this, but I took no notice and placed myself between Gunthorpe and one of the Aylesham trusties, dropped on my knees and plucked a few grass blades to suck on the way round. So the big race it was, for them, watching from the grandstand under a fluttering Union Jack, a race for the governor, that he had been waiting for, and I hoped he and all the rest of his pop-eyed gang were busy placing big bets on me, hundred to one to win, all the money they had in their pockets, all the wages they were going to get for the next five years, and the more they placed the happier I'd be. Because here was a dead cert going to die on the big name they'd built for him, going to go down dying with laughter whether it choked him or not. My knees felt the cool soil pressing into them, and out of my eye's corner I saw Roach lift his hand. The Gunthorpe boy twitched before the signal was given; somebody cheered too soon; Medway bent forward; then the gun went, and I was away.

We went once around the field and then along a half-mile drive of elms, being cheered all the way, and I seemed to feel I was in the lead as we went out by the gate and into the lane, though I wasn't interested enough to find out. The five-mile course was marked by splashes of whitewash gleaming on gateposts and trunks and stiles and stones, and a boy with a waterbottle and bandage-box stood every half-mile waiting for those that dropped out or fainted. Over the first stile, without trying, I was still nearly in the lead but one; and if any of you want tips about running; never be in a hurry, and never let any of the other runners know you are in a hurry even if you are. You can always overtake on long-distance running without letting the others smell the hurry in you; and when you've used your craft like this to reach the two or three up front then you can do a big dash later that puts everybody else's hurry in the shade because you've not had to make haste up till then. I ran to a steady jog-trot rhythm, and soon it was so smooth that I forgot I was running, and I was hardly able to know that my legs were lifting and falling and my arms going in and out, and my lungs didn't seem to be working at all, and my heart stopped that wicked thumping I always get at the beginning of a run. Because you see I never race at all; I just run, and somehow I know that if I forget I'm racing and only jog-trot along until I don't know I'm running I always win the race. For when my eyes recognize that I'm getting near the end of the course—by seeing a stile or cottage corner—I put on a spurt, and such a fast big spurt it is because I feel that up till then I haven't been running and that I've used up no energy at all. And I've been able to do this because I've been thinking; and I wonder if I'm the only one in the running business with this system of forgetting that I'm running because I'm too busy thinking; and I wonder if any of the other lads are on to the same lark, though I know for a fact that they aren't. Off like the wind along the cobbled footpath and rutted lane, smoother than the flat grass track on the field and better for thinking because it's not too smooth, and I was in my element that afternoon knowing that nobody could beat me at running but intending to beat myself before the day was over. For when the governor talked to me of being honest when I first came in he didn't know what the word meant or he wouldn't have had me here in this race, trotting along in shimmy and shorts and sunshine. He'd have had me where I'd have had him if I'd been in his place: in a quarry breaking rocks until he broke his back. At least old Hitler-face the plain-clothes dick was honester than the governor, because he at any rate had had it in for me and I for him, and when my case was coming up in court a copper knocked at our front door at four o'clock in the morning and got my mother out of bed when she was paralytic tired, reminding her she had to be in court at dead on half past nine. It was the finest bit of spite I've ever heard of, but I would call it honest, the same as my mam's words were honest when she really told that copper what she thought of him and called him all the dirty names she'd ever heard of, which took her half an hour and woke the terrace up.

I trotted on along the edge of a field bordered by the sunken lane, smelling green grass and honeysuckle, and I felt as though I came from a long line of whippets trained to run on two legs, only I couldn't see a toy rabbit in front and there wasn't a collier's cosh behind to make me keep up the pace. I passed the Gunthorpe runner whose shimmy was already black with sweat and I could just see the corner of the fenced-up copse in front where the only man I had to pass to win the race was going all out to gain the half-way mark. Then he turned into a tongue of trees and bushes where I couldn't see him anymore, and I couldn't see anybody, and I knew what the loneliness of the long-distance runner running across country felt like, realizing that as far as I was concerned this feeling was the only honesty and realness there was in the world and I knowing it would be no different ever, no matter what I felt at odd times, and no matter what anybody else tried to tell me. The runner behind me must have been a long way off because it was so quiet, and there was even less noise and movement than there had been at five o'clock of a frosty winter morning. It was hard to understand, and all I knew was that you had to run, run, run, without knowing why you were running, but on you went through fields you didn't understand and into woods that made you afraid, over hills without knowing you'd been up and down, and shooting across streams that would have cut the heart out of you had you fallen into them. And the winning post was no end to it, even though crowds might be cheering you in, because on you had to go before you got your breath back, and the only time you stopped really was when you tripped over a tree trunk and broke your neck or fell into a disused well and stayed dead in the darkness forever. So I thought: they aren't going to get me on this racing lark, this running and trying to win, this jog-trotting for a bit of blue ribbon, because it's not the way to go on at all, though they swear blind that it is. You should think about nobody and go your own way, not on a course marked out for you by people holding mugs of water and bottles of iodine in case you fall and cut yourself so that they can pick you up —even if you want to stay where you are—and get you moving again.

On I went, out of the wood, passing the man leading without knowing I was going to do so. Flip-flap, flip-flap, jog-trot, jog-trot, crunchslap-crunchslap, across the middle of a broad field again, rhythmically running in my greyhound effortless fashion, knowing I had won the race though it wasn't half over, won it if I wanted it, could go on for ten or fifteen or twenty miles if I had to and drop dead at the finish of it, which would be the same, in the end, as living an honest life like the governor wanted me to. It amounted to: win the race and be honest, and on trot-trotting I went, having the time of my life, loving my progress because it did me good and set me thinking which by now I liked to do, but not caring at all when I remembered that I had to win this race as well as run it. One of the two, I had to win the race or run it, and I knew I could do both because my legs had carried me well in front—now coming to the short cut down the bramble bank and over the sunken road—and would carry me further because they seemed made of electric cable and easily alive to keep on slapping at those ruts and roots, but I'm not going to win because the only way I'd see I came in first would be if winning meant that I was going to escape the coppers after doing the biggest bank job of my life, but winning means the exact opposite, no matter how they try to kill or kid me, means running right into their white-gloved wall-barred hands and grinning mugs and staying there for the rest of my natural long life of stone-breaking anyway, but stone-breaking in the way I want to do it and not in the way they tell me.

Another honest thought that comes is that I could swing left at the next hedge of the field, and under its cover beat my slow retreat away from the sports ground winning post. I could do three or six or a dozen miles across the turf like this and cut a few main roads behind me so's they'd never know which one I'd taken; and maybe on the last one when it got dark I could thumb a lorry-lift and get a free ride north with somebody who might not give me away. But no, I said I wasn't daft didn't I? I won't pull out with only six months left, and besides there's nothing I want to dodge and run away from; I only want a bit of my own back on the In-laws and Potbellies by letting them sit up there on their big posh seats and watch me lose this race, though as sure as God made me I know that when I do lose I'll get the dirtiest crap and kitchen jobs in the months to go before my time is up. I won't be worth a threpp'ny-bit to anybody here, which will be all the thanks I get for being honest in the only way I know. For when the governor told me to be honest it was meant to be in his way not mine, and if I kept on being honest in the way he wanted and won my race for him he'd see I got the cushiest six months still left to run; but in my own way, well, it's not allowed, and if I find a way of doing it such as I've got now then I'll get what-for in every mean trick he can set his mind to. And if you look at it in my way, who can blame him? For this is war—and ain't I said so? —and when I hit him in the only place he knows he'll be sure to get his own back on me for not collaring that cup when his heart's been set for ages on seeing himself standing up at the end of the afternoon to clap me on the back as I take the cup from Lord Earwig or some such chinless wonder with a name like that. And so I'll hit him where it hurts a lot, and he'll do all he can to get his own back, tit for tat, though I'll enjoy it most because I'm hitting first, and because I planned it longer. I don't know why I think these thoughts are better than any I've ever had, but I do, and I don't care why. I suppose it took me a long time to get going on all this because I've had no time and peace in all my bandit life, and now my thoughts are coming pat and the only trouble is I often can't stop, even when my brain feels as if it's got cramp, frostbite and creeping paralysis all rolled into one and I have to give it a rest by slap-dashing down through the brambles of the sunken lane. And all this is another uppercut I'm getting in first at people like the governor, to show how—if I can—his races are never won even though some bloke always comes unknowingly in first, how in the end the governor is going to be doomed while blokes like me will take the pickings of his roasted bones and dance like maniacs around his Borstal's ruins. And so this story's like the race and once again I won't bring off a winner to suit the governor; no, I'm being honest like he told me to, without him knowing what he means, though I don't suppose he'll ever come in with a story of his own, even if he reads this one of mine and knows who I'm talking about.

I've just come up out of the sunken lane, kneed and elbowed, thumped and bramble-scratched, and the race is two-thirds over, and a voice is going like a wireless in my mind saying that when you've had enough of feeling good like the first man on earth of a frosty morning, and you've known how it is to be taken bad like the last man on earth on a summer's afternoon, then you get at last to being like the only man on earth and don't give a bogger about either good or bad, but just trot on with your slippers slapping the good dry soil that at least would never do you a bad turn. Now the words are like coming from a crystal-set that's broken down, and something's happening inside the shell-case of my guts that bothers me and I don't know why or what to blame it on, a grinding near my ticker as though a bag of rusty screws is loose inside me and I shake them up every time I trot forward. Now and again I break my rhythm to feel my left shoulder-blade by swinging a right hand across my chest as if to rub

the knife away that has somehow got stuck there. But I know it's
nothing to bother about, that more likely it's caused by too much
thinking that now and again I take for worry. For sometimes I'm
the greatest worrier in the world I think (as you twigged I'll bet
from me having got this story out) which is funny anyway because
my mam don't know the meaning of the word so I don't take after
her; though dad had a hard time of worry all his life up to when he
filled his bedroom with hot blood and kicked the bucket that morning
when nobody was in the house. I'll never forget it, straight I won't,
because I was the one that found him and I often wished I hadn't.
Back from a session on the fruit-machines at the fish-and-chip shop,
jingling my three-lemon loot to a nail-dead house, as soon as I got
in I knew something was wrong, stood leaning my head against the
cold mirror above the mantelpiece trying not to open my eyes and
see my stone-cold clock—because I knew I'd gone as white as a piece
of chalk since coming in as if I'd been got at by a Dracula-vampire
and even my penny-pocket winnings kept quiet on purpose.

Gunthorpe nearly caught me up. Birds were singing from the briar
hedge, and a couple of thrushies flew like lightning into some thorny
bushes. Corn had grown high in the next field and would be cut down
soon with scythes and mowers; but I never wanted to notice much
while running in case it put me off my stroke, so by the haystack I
decided to leave it all behind and put on such a spurt, in spite of nails
in my guts, that before long I'd left both Gunthorpe and the birds a
good way off; I wasn't far now from going into that last mile and a
half like a knife through margarine, but the quietness I suddenly
trotted into between two pickets was like opening my eyes underwater and looking at the pebbles on a stream bottom, reminding me
again of going back that morning to the house in which my old man
had croaked, which is funny because I hadn't thought about it at all
since it happened and even then I didn't brood much on it. I wonder
why? I suppose that since I started to think on these long-distance
runs I'm liable to have anything crop up and pester at my tripes and
innards, and now that I see my bloody dad behind each grass-blade
in my barmy runner-brain I'm not so sure I like to think and that
it's such a good thing after all. I choke my phlegm and keep on
running anyway and curse the Borstal-builders and their athletics
—flappity-flap, slop-slop, crunchslap-crunchslap-crunchslap—who've
maybe got their own back on me from the bright beginning by sliding
magic-lantern slides into my head that never stood a chance before.
Only if I take whatever comes like this in my runner's stride can I
keep on keeping on like my old self and beat them back; and now
I've thought on this far I know I'll win, in the crunchslap end. So
anyway after a bit I went upstairs one step at a time not thinking
anything about how I should find dad and what I'd do when I did.
But now I'm making up for it by going over the rotten life mam led

him ever since I can remember, knocking-on with different men even when he was alive and fit and she not caring whether he knew it or not, and most of the time he wasn't so blind as she thought and cursed and roared and threatened to punch her tab, and I had to stand up to stop him even though I knew she deserved it. What a life for all of us. Well, I'm not grumbling, because if I did I might just as well win this bleeding race, which I'm not going to do, though if I don't lose speed I'll win it before I know where I am, and then where would I be?

Now I can hear the sportsground noise and music as I head back for the flags and the lead-in drive, the fresh new feel of underfoot gravel going against the iron muscles of my legs. I'm nowhere near puffed despite that bag of nails that rattles as much as ever, and I can still give a big last leap like gale-force wind if I want to, but everything is under control and I know now that there ain't another long-distance cross-country running runner in England to touch my speed and style. Our doddering bastard of a governor, our half-dead gangrened gaffer is hollow like an empty petrol drum, and he wants me and my running life to give him glory, to put in him blood and throbbing veins he never had, wants his potbellied pals to be his witnesses as I gasp and stagger up to his winning post so's he can say: "My Borstal gets that cup, you see. I win my bet, because it pays to be honest and try to gain the prizes I offer to my lads, and they know it, have known it all along. They'll always be honest now, because I made them so." And his pals will think: "He trains his lads to live right, after all; he deserves a medal but we'll get him made a Sir"— and at this very moment as the birds come back to whistling I can tell myself I'll never care a sod what any of the chinless spineless In-laws think or say. They've seen me and they're cheering now and loud-speakers set around the field like elephant's ears are spreading out the big news that I'm well in the lead, and can't do anything else but stay there. But I'm still thinking of the Out-law death my dad died, telling the doctors to scat from the house when they wanted him to finish up in hospital (like a bleeding guinea-pig, he raved at them). He got up in bed to throw them out and even followed them down the stairs in his shirt though he was no more than skin and stick. They tried to tell him he'd want some drugs but he didn't fall for it, and only took the pain-killer that mam and I got from a herb-seller in the next street. It's not till now that I know what guts he had, and when I went into the room that morning he was lying on his stomach with the clothes thrown back, looking like a skinned rabbit, his grey head resting just on the edge of the bed, and on the floor must have been all the blood he'd had in his body, right from his toenails up, for nearly all of the lino and carpet was covered in it, thin and pink.

And down the drive I went, carrying a heart blocked up like Boulder Dam across my arteries, the nail-bag clamped down tighter and tighter as though in a woodwork vice, yet with my feet like bird-wings and arms like talons ready to fly across the field except that I didn't want to give anybody that much of a show, or win the race by accident. I smell the hot dry day now as I run towards the end, passing a mountain-heap of grass emptied from cans hooked on to the fronts of lawnmowers pushed by my pals; I rip a piece of tree-bark with my fingers and stuff it in my mouth, chewing wood and dust and maybe maggots as I run until I'm nearly sick, yet swallowing what I can of it just the same because a little birdie whistled to me that I've got to go on living for at least a bloody sight longer yet but that for six months I'm not going to smell that grass or taste that dusty bark or trot this lovely path. I hate to have to say this but something bloody-well made me cry, and crying is a thing I haven't bloody-well done since I was a kid of two or three. Because I'm slowing down now for Gunthorpe to catch me up, and I'm doing it in a place just where the drive turns in to the sportsfield—where they can see what I'm doing, especially the governor and his gang from the grandstand, and I'm going so slow I'm almost marking time. Those on the nearest seats haven't caught on yet to what's happening and are still cheering like mad ready for when I make that mark, and I keep on wondering when the bleeding hell Gunthorpe behind me is going to nip by on to the field because I can't hold this up all day, and I think Oh Christ it's just my rotten luck that Gunthorpe's dropped out and that I'll be here for half an hour before the next bloke comes up, but even so, I say, I won't budge, I won't go for that last hundred yards if I have to sit down cross-legged on the grass and have the governor and his chinless wonders pick me up and carry me there, which is against their rules so you can bet they'd never do it because they're not clever enough to break the rules—like I would be in their place—even though they are their own. No, I'll show him what honesty means if it's the last thing I do, though I'm sure he'll never understand because if he and all them like him did it'd mean they'd be on my side which is impossible. By God I'll stick this out like my dad stuck out his pain and kicked them doctors down the stairs: if he had guts for that then I've got guts for this and here I stay waiting for Gunthorpe or Aylesham to bash that turf and go right slap-up against that bit of clothes-line stretched across the winning post. As for me, the only time I'll hit that clothes-line will be when I'm dead and a comfortable coffin's been got ready on the other side. Until then I'm a long-distance runner, crossing country all on my own no matter how bad it feels.

The Essex boys were shouting themselves blue in the face telling me to get a move on, waving their arms, standing up and making as if to run at that rope themselves because they were only a few yards to the side of it. You cranky lot, I thought, stuck at that winning post, and yet I knew they didn't mean what they were shouting, were really on my side and always would be, not able to keep their maulers to themselves, in and out of copshops and clink. And there they were now having the time of their lives letting themselves go in cheering me which made the governor think they were heart and soul on his side when he wouldn't have thought any such thing if he'd had a grain of sense. And I could hear the lords and ladies now from the grandstand, and could see them standing up to wave me in: "Run!" they were shouting in their posh voices. "Run!" But I was deaf, daft and blind, and stood where I was, still tasting the bark in my mouth and still blubbing like a baby, blubbing now out of gladness that I'd got them beat at last.

Because I heard a roar and saw the Gunthorpe gang throwing their coats up in the air and I felt the pat-pat of feet on the drive behind me getting closer and closer and suddenly a smell of sweat and a pair of lungs on their last gasp passed me by and went swinging on towards that rope, all shagged out and rocking from side to side, grunting like a Zulu that didn't know any better, like the ghost of me at ninety when I'm heading for that fat upholstered coffin. I could have cheered him myself: "Go on, go on, get cracking. Knot yourself up on that piece of tape." But he was already there, and so I went on, trot-trotting after him until I got to the rope, and collapsed, with a murderous sounding roar going up through my ears while I was still on the wrong side of it.

It's about time to stop; though don't think I'm not still running, because I am, one way or another. The governor at Borstal proved me right; he didn't respect my honesty at all; not that I expected him to, or tried to explain it to him, but if he's supposed to be educated then he should have more or less twigged it. He got his own back right enough, or thought he did, because he had me carting dustbins about every morning from the big full-working kitchen to the garden-bottoms where I had to empty them; and in the afternoon I spread out slops over spuds and carrots growing in the allotments. In the evenings I scrubbed floors, miles and miles of them. But it wasn't a bad life for six months, which was another thing he could never understand and would have made it grimmer if he could, and it was worth it when I look back on it, considering all the thinking I did, and the fact that the boys caught on to me losing the race on purpose and never had enough good words to say about me, or curses to throw out (to themselves) at the governor.

The work didn't break me; if anything it made me stronger in many ways, and the governor knew, when I left, that his spite had got him nowhere. For since leaving Borstal they tried to get me in the army, but I didn't pass the medical and I'll tell you why. No sooner was I out, after that final run and six-months hard, than I went down with pleurisy, which means as far as I'm concerned that I lost the governor's race all right, and won my own twice over, because I know for certain that if I hadn't raced my race I wouldn't have got this pleurisy, which keeps me out of khaki but doesn't stop me doing the sort of work my itchy fingers want to do.

I'm out now and the heat's switched on again, but the rats haven't got me for the last big thing I pulled. I counted six hundred and twenty-eight pounds and am still living off it because I did the job all on my own, and after it I had the peace to write all this, and it'll be money enough to keep me going until I finish my plans for doing an even bigger snatch, something up my sleeve I wouldn't tell to a living soul. I worked out my systems and hiding-places while pushing scrubbing-brushes around them Borstal floors, planned my outward life of innocence and honest work, yet at the same time grew perfect in the razor-edges of my craft for what I knew I had to do once free; and what I'll do again if netted by the poaching coppers.

In the meantime (as they say in one or two books I've read since, useless though because all of them ended on a winning post and didn't teach me a thing) I'm going to give this story to a pal of mine and tell him that if I do get captured again by the coppers he can try and get it put into a book or something, because I'd like to see the governor's face when he reads it, if he does, which I don't suppose he will; even if he did read it though I don't think he'd know what it was all about. And if I don't get caught the bloke I give this story to will never give me away; he's lived in our terrace for as long as I can remember, and he's my pal. That I do know.

The narrative point of view in "The Tree of Dreams" is unusual, for the story is addressed not to the reader, but to the narrator's mistress. The effect is entirely dramatic: it is as if the reader were eavesdropping on a conversation or reading someone else's mail. We learn the nature of the narrator as we learn the events of the story, and we are forced to evaluate his credibility, as well as the events he describes, without any external interpretation. We must react to him as we do to actual people and events in our own lives. The "tree of dreams" is surely the cranberry tree which springs often out of loathsomeness and corruption. Why does the narrator catch its fragrance at the moment when "everything was over"? What is the relationship between Marvi and "you"?

Mika Waltari was born in 1908 in Helsinki. He studied theology and at seventeen published a collection of short stories. Thereafter, he attempted to write one or two books a year and by 1938 had become a full-time free lance writer. Further Reading: The Egyptian (1949), A Nail Merchant at Nightfall (1954), The Tree of Dreams and Other Stories (1965).

FINLAND

The Tree of Dreams

MIKA WALTARI

1

Midsummer Day was raw and rainy, and we were all sitting in the kitchen that afternoon. The children were washing the dishes for once. My wife was playing solitaire at the cleared table and you sat by the window, silent. I tried not to look at you too often lest my glances disturb

Reprinted by permission of G. P. Putnam's Sons from *The Tree of Dreams and Other Stories,* by Mika Waltari. © 1965 by Mika Waltari. Translated by Lily Leino.

you. Perhaps also because of the others. We were speaking of love. I suppose I really began it, to amuse you or to make you aware of me.

"Love beautifies a woman amazingly," I said. "I know that from experience. I once loved a girl. It was a long time ago and only for a short while, but she had such a crush on me that she swore she didn't know how she had lived without me. She was so infatuated, in fact, that she compared me to a god."

"Oh, that was your childhood friend," my wife remarked, slapping cards onto the table. "No, I'm not going to win this game either. I'm cold. What a midsummer!"

"I'm not saying this in any conceit," I maintained. "Quite the contrary. I know only too well what I am." But that was not the truth. How should I know what I am? Because my whole body began to tremble at the mere sight of you from the attic window, knowing that you actually had come with the others, and recognizing you as you all waited for the rowboat on the other side of the river.

"I mention this only as an example," I assured them, "because she visibly grew more beautiful. Her eyes sparkled and even her skin became clearer. And all because she was in love. I don't doubt that she really did love me sincerely, but just the same, scarcely a month after telling me all this, she was married to another man."

"But—" you began breathlessly. I loved your air of breathlessness. With a flip of my hand I stopped you. You didn't have to say anything.

"There was nothing illogical, false or wrong in it," I said defensively. "You see, before that she hadn't attracted any attention where she worked. Of course, she was pretty enough to have some of the men walk her home, and she would go out now and then, but it was love that made her sparkle. One of the directors noticed her then. It was wartime, and the man was on work leave but could be sent elsewhere any day. He proposed and wanted an immediate wedding. That was easily arranged in those days. Naturally the girl wanted to get married, just as every woman does. In her defense, I must confess that she frankly sought my advice."

"And you?" you asked. Because of the rain the dusk had come early. I saw how the pupils of your eyes expanded with the darkness, until your eyes seemed black. It made me catch my breath.

"I?" I continued, although it was difficult for me to speak. "Naturally I said, 'By all means get married now that you have the opportunity. The very fact that you're asking me proves that you've already made your choice. But let's not meet anymore, at least not like this.' That's what I told her with a feeling of relief. Nothing would have come of our affair anyway, except unpleasantness and guilt."

One of the girls hung up her dish towel and said sagaciously, "That's how women are."

"No," I replied, "that's how love is." My throat was tight, I had difficulty in breathing and I couldn't look at you.

You said nothing. But from some depth a memory rose to the surface and I felt a compulsion to continue. "Whenever I remember her, I remember the cranberry tree."

"They grow beside outhouses," someone remarked in disgust. "Filthy things. Backyard love." That, too, was true.

My wife swept up the cards and rose abruptly. "Let's go outside, girls," she said. "It's not raining so hard anymore. It's stifling in here."

You rose obediently, for you were our guest in the country for the first time. And the last, although neither of us probably suspected that then. You were still somewhat shy with us. You tried to smile and I detained you. "Don't go yet." To the others I said, "You all go ahead. We'll come along after a while."

The rain had turned into soft mist. The kitchen had grown dark and your eyes were black as you looked at me. You must have been afraid of me, but you sat down obediently nevertheless.

"You must never think of me as an evil and cynical person." I said quietly. "I merely mentioned that experience because it popped into my mind. Because I wanted to tell it to you, too. Especially to you. One occasionally has such impulses. But it was all true. Of course, it could have been told another and perhaps a prettier way."

I rose and stepped across the floor in the darkening room to the table. The walk was years long. Frightening steps.

I sat beside you at the table, near you but separated by a chair.

"It could be told another way," I repeated. "She actually was a childhood friend—if a fifteen-year-old boy can be called a child. And she was fourteen when we first met. As the adage has it, a person always returns to his first loves. It's true, too. Whenever something remains unfulfilled, it must be fulfilled later in life. If one happens to meet again, and has matured meanwhile, and is receptive at that particular moment."

The dusk deepened on that raw midsummer night. You turned your head. "Why did you use the plural?" you asked. "Have you really been in love so many times?" There was no sarcasm in your words. You spoke like a child, in amazement.

"What about you?" I demanded. "Why should you say that to me —you of all people? You're not even thirty and already you've been divorced twice."

I wounded you deliberately, but you merely said, "Let's not talk about me."

"A person matures along with his loves, if he ever does," I said. "Good Lord, love itself is only a tiny drop of joy in the sea of despair that it creates around itself. It's terrible to love, because one always unwittingly hurts others.

"What of it if one hurts oneself?" I continued. "My suffering is my own and so is my guilt. I'm an impossible, a hopeless person. But believe me, I've never destroyed another person's life."

I stopped to consider whether that was true. "At least, not deliberately," I amended. "Except, of course, my wife's. And my own."

I raised my hand quickly to forestall your comment. "Don't misunderstand this, either. Naturally we have our happy days and will continue to have them. But every woman basically craves security. How can I give anyone a feeling of security when I continually surprise even myself?

"Believe me," I said, trembling, "if I've ever had happiness or luck or success, I've invariably destroyed it. Smashed it to bits. It's like a sickness in me, and I can't do anything about it. That's why it doesn't pay to envy me. But I've never deliberately ruined anyone else's life."

Having said that, I lightly touched your hand with my own. You were startled. You shifted in your chair, your neck became rigid and even your face stiffened.

"How strangely a person returns to his first love," I said quickly. "My childhood friend could serve as an example of that, too. But one could also cite it as an example of eroticism. How the first youthful erotic experience colors one's whole life, determining the erotic approach and the limits of ecstasy and gratification. One could tell it like that, too, touchingly."

I grew silent for a moment, then added quietly, "You see, she is dead, and has been for many years, But if I had never met her again after our youth, I would probably go to my grave knowing that something in me was eternally unfulfilled.

"I'm insatiable," I exclaimed. "Bottomless. I can't help it. I've hated myself for it, despised myself, until I've begun to understand that in order to develop, a person must learn to recognize himself. Not approve of, but recognize.

"Bitterness is the worst poison," I continued. "If it would corrode only the person himself, but in time it also corrodes his surroundings, and the person can do nothing about it. But love can melt bitterness, although only for a short while, and perhaps only now and then. Damn it, my surroundings ought to be grateful that I've been able to fall in love a few times and through love been liberated from my horrible self."

Then I hastened to contradict myself. "No, I don't want to be cynical because that isn't the truth, either. I'm selfish, glacially selfish. It's best for you to know that lest you expect too much of me. I do know how to talk, that I do. But words are always just an approximation. And usually how one says something means more than what one says. That's why lovers develop their own foolish language in which words are merely secret symbols of something that only the two of them know."

I recalled something and felt constrained to smile. "Once before the wars in my dark days—I'll tell you about them some other time— I met a couple who had sunk to the denatured alcohol stage. The woman was positively grimy. But you should have heard the man once say affectionately to his wife, 'Oh, you damn whore!' The way he said it, with brusque masculine gentleness, made it the finest declaration of love I've ever heard."

"How repulsive!" you breathed.

"No. Beautiful," I insisted.

"Why do you talk to me about such things?" you asked as though begging for mercy.

I didn't touch you. I didn't dare. "You should know. If you don't, it's useless telling you."

Just then I could have taken you in my arms and easily thrown everything overboard. I knew it and that's why I didn't try, although my whole being lusted for your lips, for you. I rose and thrust my hands into my jacket pockets.

"Let's go," I said.

The damp rain of midsummer night was soft as mist on my hot face. At the bottom of the hill a light shone from the window of the sauna chamber and the girls moved there as though on a lighted stage. As we approached I heard them laughing and talking animatedly. I calmed down.

At that very moment I heard a bird whistle, then warble and again change its song. A nightingale was singing in the reeds on the sauna shore. I could hardly believe my ears.

"A nightingale," I murmured, and the happiness of my youth welled up in me. This could no longer be a coincidence. Beyond the years, past death, the nightingale in the reeds sang of an old love on the threshold of a new.

We stood beside each other in the dusk, in the cold drizzle of a midsummer night. The nightingale whistled, warbled and changed its song ceaselessly. It sang near us, only a few steps away, but the gray bird was not visible in the dusk.

The warm light of life spilled from the sauna window into the damp evening. "My dead darling," I said, "why have you returned to sing to me? Is it an omen?"

I don't know why I said that. Certainly it wasn't pretense, for I felt Marvi's presence too strongly. It was as though her spirit had spread like a veil over the living scene and me.

I had the same feeling on many a night after you had left, when the sun had set and the moonlight touched the red walls of the house with a ghostly light. And the nightingale sang night after night in the reeds by the sauna shore.

During weekdays I often thought of taking out Marvi's few letters and reading them again. I knew that they were hidden somewhere among numerous other papers. I had not been able to destroy them. I should have sorted them all, but it was left undone for a long time. That usually happens when life flows along its familiar channel.

After all, nothing really had happened, although I knew that without a word or a touch, infinitely more had occurred between us than if I had slept with you. To you, too, and not only to me. Love is like that. Yes, that's what love is like.

2

Once, much later, we lay in bed together. The sun had circled the window to afternoon. You whispered in my ear, "Oh, my darling." Words, only words.

I asked, "Why do you act as though you had never loved anyone before? I know everything about you. Or perhaps not everything, since no one can know everything about another. But I do know a lot, more than you may think. So why are you like this to me?"

You pressed your fingers against my lips. "You always talk so much. Why talk unnecessarily?"

"I was born to play with words," I explained. "It's my profession. My calling, if you will, although I'm not usually so snobbish. But perhaps it's not even that. I just want to find out about myself, and you. So why?"

You thought hard, wrinkling your forehead. "I don't know. It's really silly, and they'd make fun of me if they knew. But don't laugh. I feel as though I had never been in love before. Perhaps there's something in me that no one else has been able to find."

Well, I certainly didn't love you because of your intellect. I reached for the bottle beside the bed. The sun had gone by the window, the ice cubes in the bucket had melted. "Do you want some?"

You merely shook your head on the pillow. "I don't either," I said. "I haven't the strength to lift the bottle. That's bad. I never thought I'd slip so far. But actually I've said many times that I surprise even myself. Well, you at least are not thinking of dear old England."

You looked at me inquiringly. Your eyes were blue-gray, and in the bright light the pupils had contracted again. You were tired. Your face was naked, for to me you dared reveal your naked face. That alone indicated that you really loved me, in your own way and with no false illusions.

I related the old tale about the English princess who married into the German court. Some time later her mother wrote to inquire how she was adapting herself to the unpleasant aspects of marriage. To which the girl replied, "I just shut my eyes tight and think of dear old England."

You laughed at the timeworn story, then stretched. "No, I'm not thinking of dear old England."

"Only of clothes and dressmakers," I said teasingly. But you didn't bother to reply. You only smiled knowingly.

"Try to remember that you're fifteen years younger than I," I warned you.

"You're not old," you reassured me, as a woman on the threshold of thirty reassures a man my age. "Don't imagine such a thing."

I didn't have the strength to argue. "Let's talk," I suggested. "Or are you asleep already?"

"No, no, I'm not asleep." You rubbed your eyes with your fists like a sleepy child. "Why should I waste a second in sleep when we can be together like this?"

"Let's talk, then," I said. "Let's steal time, we relentless thieves. But is it actually stealing to give another something that no one else has been able to accept? That's what you have done for me, and that's a lot. That's a tremendous lot, my darling. One has to mature to that through terrible years. I'm so glad that I didn't meet you when you were a young girl. I doubt whether you would have liked me. Perhaps I wouldn't have liked you, either."

Hands behind my head, I reminisced. "Do you remember the first time we really kissed? We were both drunk, of course, even you. It probably wouldn't have happened otherwise. My hand accidentally touched your bare skin. That's not like me. Believe me, that hasn't happened before. That touch burned me. Your skin was cool but it still burned me, and I knew that I would never be at peace until you were mine."

You looked reproachfully at me, but I shook my head stubbornly. "I'm not claiming that I can't live without you. That would be stupid. Naturally a person can go on living. Perhaps not as well, but living nevertheless. We mustn't exaggerate. We must try to say to each other only what we really mean."

I continued, "Then I knew that I would never be at peace until you were mine." I suddenly stroked your shoulder. "That's the worst part about me—it isn't enough that I possess the body, I must have everything—you, even your thoughts, so that I really know you. So that we alternately say just what the other has been thinking. That, too, is love."

You smiled. "Shall I pour you a drink?"

"That's too easy a thought transference," I said. "But go ahead and pour if you have the strength. I suppose I was thinking of it in passing."

You reached across me for the bottle. I felt you against my body. I knew your beauty. But beauty alone no longer sufficed for me. I took a drink from the glass and lighted a cigarette.

"I mentioned touching you," I continued. "I suppose that touch bound me to you. Well, shall I tell you some more about my child-hood friend Marvi? When the nightingale sang, she returned to my memory after many years. She returned from beyond the grave to tell me that she too had helped me to mature. Just as I released her from my touch and prepared her for another man.

"For another man," I repeated slowly. "You too are prettier than before, and your eyes are sparkling. Is it possible that I'm doomed to that same accursed task?"

"Never," you exclaimed in alarm. "Never. You mustn't think of it." You looked at me, just looked at me dreamily, then shook your head. "You don't want me to say never," she concluded, stroking my temples. "All right, I won't say it. I'll just urge you not to torment yourself, darling. Why do you always torment yourself needlessly? If you must talk, tell me about your childhood friend."

I thought back, and the memories no longer hurt. Neither was there any bitterness. They were only beautiful, those distant memories, even those of my boyhood. I scarcely recognized that boy anymore.

"I attended a boys' school," I began, "and didn't even have any sisters. It probably wasn't good for me. Undoubtedly it helped make my physical awakening so painful. To me girls were alarmingly tempting creatures when I first began to notice them. How pathetic boyhood timidity is! It compels one either to crawl into a shell, or to go overboard in talkativeness. I suppose my first kisses were just the clumsy games of puppyhood, groping and curious. I didn't love any particular girl. I was just in love with love and afraid that no one could ever love me. I was so round-cheeked and childish."

"You poor thing," you said, caressing my neck, as your eyes darkened.

"Don't," I begged, drawing away. "I spent the summer in a town where the heath was warm in the evenings and the pine trees were tall and copper-colored in the sunset. I was fifteen and terribly alone. I was working during vacation, and every morning before seven I would pass an endless line of women on the road making their way to the woolen mill. A thousand girls passed me every morning. It was a town of erotic hunger. I sensed it in the way I always sense things around me. But I won't talk about them. Besides, I had a friend, a girl whom I shyly kissed. But in a way it didn't mean anything, for she too was just curious. And a kiss, even the most unsuccessful, was like an incredible gift to me. Perhaps I wasn't so unpleasant after all. Perhaps someone actually could care for me."

"You poor thing," you said again, extending your glass. I filled it absentmindedly. In my memory I recalled the resinous fragrance of the heath and the bitter-damp evening smell of the cranberry tree in the yard. You swallowed the drink and your shoulders shook.

"Bad?" I asked and then continued. "It was a hot summer. The road exuded warmth in the evening. I sometimes saw Marvi on the road. Her hair was blond and she always walked with her chin in the air. She had an erect figure and the firm breasts of a girl. Her complexion was clear, and she was not as suntanned as many of the others that summer. My God, how I adored her before we had even exchanged a word! Much later she confessed that she had noticed me watching her on the road and had feared that I would speak to her, because she would have had to toss her head and snap at me. She wouldn't have dared do anything else. And how she tossed her head, haughtily, as though she were proud of being pretty. But actually it wasn't that. She was at least as uncertain of herself as I. It was just an indication of timidity, that habit of tossing her head.

"I knew her name," I went on. "I even knew something about her home. In a moment of daring I had walked through their courtyard. Several families lived there. It was an untidy yard and beside the steps grew a cranberry tree. I plucked a leaf and crumbled it in my fingers to catch its fragrance. It made me feel as though I owned something of her, although I didn't even know her then.

"Naturally my friend knew her," I continued. "They attended the same school, although Marvi was in a lower grade. My endless questioning annoyed her. 'You won't get anywhere with Marvi,' she teased me. 'Marvi's stuck-up. She doesn't go around with boys.' But I suppose every woman is a procuress at heart, or perhaps it was only the cruel curiosity of the teens, but once when she had joined me on the road she stopped to talk to Marvi. She disregarded my presence until Marvi's glance forced her to introduce us. Marvi shook my hand casually but her eyes were round with fear. As I suppose mine were. For the life of me I couldn't say anything that made sense, and so the opportunity passed. But at least I had met her. I had the right to tip my cap, stop and chat if I dared. It never went beyond the cap-tipping stage, however. I never dared even smile, and neither did she. We were both deadly serious when we greeted each other. She even paled in nodding to me. How amusing we must have been! A fifteen- and a fourteen-year-old. But perhaps it wasn't so laughable after all.

"Are you asleep," I asked, "or can you listen to some more?" Your hair shone disturbingly soft against the pillow. Your neck was slender and so was your face. You opened your eyes a little and said apathetically, "Go on."

I was telling it more to myself than to you. "This is probably boring, but it's essential if you're to know me. One Sunday toward the end of summer the building contractor with whom I was living took me along to inspect a large municipal building. There was a certain dark girl—a big girl compared to me. All of nineteen, I learned later. She remained behind to talk to me, showed me around the yard and then suggested, 'Let's go into the woods.' "

"Ahaa!" you exclaimed, raising yourself onto your elbow. I had to laugh.

"It wasn't quite so dangerous. We just went into the woods, she sat down on a hummock, sighed that it was hot and opened the top button of her blouse. I kissed her and she held me tightly, kissing me back in a way that was completely new to me. It was shocking and revolting, and I felt no desire for her moist lips. She smiled and raised my clumsy hand to her bosom and in confusion I opened still another button of her blouse. Again I felt as though I had been given a bounteous gift, although afterward I realized that I hadn't even liked her breast. It was big and soft. Still I felt humbly grateful that something like that could happen to me. Actually, this is quite a ridiculous tale."

"What then?" you asked. "Did the big girl hurt you?"

"Don't be silly," I retorted. "I probably would have run away in fright. Her eyes were dreamy for a moment, then she yawned, buttoned her blouse and said, 'We'll have to get back. It must be late.' Actually, it wasn't so late. On our way back, by the big barn, she casually asked how old I was. When I told her she lost all interest in me, and we never met again. But I still remember her warmly, for she gave me a priceless gift."

"I hate that girl!" you snapped.

"Why? It didn't mean anything," I assured you. "It was just experience, valuable experience for a timid fifteen-year-old. But surely you don't hate Marvi."

"I don't know," you said. "I don't know yet. I just hate the explorer in you, your cold-blooded curiosity. How can you do something like that unless you love the other?"

"Don't be childish, darling. There are men who never get beyond that stage. I mean, they only learn how to sleep with a woman, that's all. Perhaps they're satisfied. They experience lust, all right, but no gentleness, no beauty. I've been guilty of it myself, why deny it? But it leads only to the heart's death, and that to me is the worst that can happen to a person. Someone else, of course, might consider it happiness.

"There's no such thing as happiness," I went on. "There are only fluctuations, peaks and troughs of waves, the infinite rolling of the sea. There's joy and there's ecstasy, even though they're bought with lies and despair. But happiness there is not. Believe that, darling."

And so I again unwittingly brought tears into your eyes. I kissed your naked face, your nearness. "Don't," you pleaded. "I can't any longer. Don't."

"It is getting late," I conceded. "I see that the sun has already passed the window. But I'll finish the tale since I began it. I was going to tell you about physical contact. You see, my experience gave me courage, and the next time I met Marvi on the road I stopped to talk to her. I even smiled. I asked her to go with me to the dance, and after some hesitation she promised. I waited for her in the court-

yard by the cranberry tree. We both danced uncertainly and soon left
the floor. I didn't take her directly home. We walked to the other
side of the railroad yard, to a grove. There was moonlight, of course,
on that August night. No, the place is no longer there, but I remember
it clearly. I tried to make conversation about everything that interests
teen-agers, because I was afraid that she would get angry. I wouldn't
have hurt her for the world, but I had dreamed about her all summer
and so I timidly put my arms around her.

"I can still feel how she stiffened, but she didn't resist. She let me
kiss her lips, the lips that knew even less about kissing than mine.
Some fifteen years later she confessed that I was the first boy she
had ever allowed to kiss her. She was wearing a white dress that could
have been made over from her confirmation dress. I fumbled with it
until I had opened it and she, child that she was, thought that that
was the way it should be. My bashful hand found her white bosom,
and it was the most beautiful thing I had ever experienced. I didn't
dare kiss it, I didn't even dare move my hand. Both of us just stood
there, frightened. Suddenly she started, tore herself loose, and with
her back to me began fixing her dress.

"The moonlight dazzled my eyes, and my love dazzled me. That
moment I felt that nothing bad or wrong could ever happen to me.
'Marvi, dear Marvi,' I whispered. But she kept her back to me and
sniffled. Then I, who always manage to spoil everything, foolishly
stooped to pick up a small stone merely as an excuse to say something
to her. I circled around her and showed her the stone on my palm.
'Marvi,' I said, 'I'm taking this stone as a souvenir, so that I'll never
forget this moment.' At that she burst into tears and ran away. I
didn't dare call her by name, for the town was already asleep. I caught
up with her only by her front steps under the cranberry tree.

"She had calmed down by then. Tossing her head, she said with
such anger that I was horrified, 'I hate you! I hate you, and I'll never
let you speak to me again. Don't even try to greet me. If we happen
to meet I'll turn my head away.' That was the first time that my
world turned upside down because of a woman. Believe me, I didn't
have the slightest idea why she was so angry."

"You poor boy," you said, a woman's wisdom in your voice. "You
really believed what she said."

"Of course I did." Even decades later it made me angry. "I'm
basically a serious person. One of my shortcomings is that I believe
whatever is said to me. You know how easy it is to hurt me. But not
even you could guess why she was so disturbed. No, not because I
had touched her breast. Not at all. You see, as we kissed, she probably
felt something of what I myself did, and that's why she was so terribly hurt when she thought I needed a stone to remind me of something she could never forget. For the first time she had overcome her
timidity and pride. For the first time she had stiffly allowed someone

to touch her. It was as though she had been branded with a hot iron, she told me years later in a true confessions style. But to me it had seemed only a fleeting game that required a tangible reminder. So thoroughly can people misunderstand each other.

"I could only assume that I had unwittingly wronged or shamed her," I continued. "A terrible feeling of guilt came over me, and yet I didn't regret it. Even if she never wanted to see me again, I knew that I could never forget her. A blissful feeling still enveloped me, like a poem welling up in a person. I felt happy and unhappy simultaneously. It was the most beautiful experience of my youth. And as an erotic experience it was far more soul-stirring than anything that happened later.

"And so, darling, when I kissed you for the first time, it meant more to me than if I had possessed you. Actually, darling, I possessed you already when I accidentally touched your bare flesh for the first time. You understand, don't you—it was something I hadn't experienced before, something decisive, like the first embrace of my youth. It marked me, just as Marvi once marked me. Now do you understand why I've had to tell you this?"

You looked at me with smiling eyes and slowly shook your pretty head. "Oh, you! You always have to talk about things that are self-evident. Besides, it wasn't accidental, in case you still think that. After all, I am I. But now I'm hungry."

"Food, always food," I lamented. "The most trying thing about love is that one has to undress and dress at the most peculiar times. But of course you must have food."

We dressed. Leaning back in an easy chair, I watched you put on your face. Evening lipstick. Miss Dior fragrance. And silvery blue eye shadow on your lids. As you looked into the mirror you lifted your upper lip in a grimace and admired your teeth. Beautiful, even, gleaming white teeth. You were radiant.

As you rose to go out I said, "Listen."

You made a questioning sound. "You probably know that I love you terribly," I said.

"Silly," you murmured and ran your hand over my cheek. We went down to eat.

3

They were probably the heaviest steps of my life, the steps that led me to you. Undoubtedly you realized it. Much, much heavier than those that forced me away from you. Even though your smile was bright and my happiness limitless when we met, I realized that everything had its price. I was not meant to be a betrayer.

That's why agony and restlessness again seized me as they had so many previous times. Sleep fled and I lay awake nights with my only companion the burning oven that was my head. For me there was no home in the cold universe. I felt that the world itself was too small for human lust—merely a tight enclosure beyond which the distant stars flickered. I thought of time, too, and of flight in time. I thought of the furrowed gigantic pillar in the chapel of the Barcelona cathedral, and of Mount Eryx in Sicily and the well of Aphrodite. The marble mosaic floor that had come to light in the ruins of a Norman fortress, where the bodies of those who arrived from many lands to die for love were buried. Aphrodite of Eryx was the wealthiest Aphrodite of the Mediterranean. The earth in her yard is still layered with soot and ashes.

All these things came to my fevered mind in the early hours of the morning. On some nights restlessness compelled me to walk around. I moved carefully, lest I awaken someone. At my desk I leafed through books, searching for the faces of those long since dead who still lived in cloth, wood or stone. Their eyes stared restlessly into mine, their faces as vivid as when they were alive.

But of course a person doesn't awaken to the past with living eyes. Only for your sake would I have wanted to believe in return and immortality, to feel your lips once more in another life. To make love to you in another, because this world deemed it theft.

No, the vivid faces of the departed did not console me. I fingered the marble cube that I had picked up from Aphrodite's floor. The memory of your eyes, your lips, your limbs, scorched me.

What a horrible spell, I thought. Why did I have to meet just you? After all, I had been fairly happy. Or was it my own emptiness that had made me seek you out? I should have heeded the formidable bird with brown arrows on its back that followed me from bush to bush in the orchard on the last day of autumn.

I wondered, too, whether I was still only a child, once more greedily gulping down human life to nourish myself. For everything has an end, even lust. Especially lust. There is nothing more sickening than the death of passion. When even the dearest face becomes strange and ugly under a penetrating gaze. When one can count, in cold terror, every sign of deterioration, everything peculiar, distorted and calculating that one can find. In every face—even yours.

That is what I thought about during the murderous hours of early morning. And nothing in itself explained anything, because the reasons were twined like rope of many fibers. They could be fingered separately, each fiber could be cut, but together they were woven into a bond too strong for a mortal to cut. You were stronger than my will.

The piece of marble fell from my fingers and rolled onto the blue rug. As I stooped to retrieve it, I remembered how as a boy I had picked up the stone in memory of Marvi. Good Lord, it had been in my pocket the entire fall semester! I became sixteen. At that age a person lives and grows rapidly. Some time that winter I emptied my pockets and threw away the stone with other trash. It no longer meant anything to me, or so I thought. Whole new worlds were bubbling in my mind. If one girl didn't care for me, it didn't pay for me to waste my thoughts on her. Youth is an amazingly practical period. Its wounds heal quickly. If she felt contempt, perhaps hate, for me, why should it concern me? After all, I would never have to meet her again.

Instead of senselessly tormenting myself, I began to rearrange my desk drawers. Letters that for years had been tied into bundles came into my hand. But Marvi's few letters had to be somewhere apart. Finally I found them in a folder among some useless papers. I didn't even remember that her photograph was tucked in among the letters.

I recognized her restless handwriting on the envelopes, the handwriting of a lonely person. She had written them in pencil, at night after leaving me, or while waiting for me. Good Lord, had I wronged her, too? I didn't know. I knew only that apparently we were fated to meet, in order to free ourselves of each other.

I looked long at her picture. She was smiling, and there was none of the harsh, nervous stiffness that had marked her when I met her again. Only a gentle smile. She had had the picture taken at my request, so that I would have something to look at during her absence. Once I had been happy about that photograph. Now I merely looked at it quizzically and nothing stirred in me anymore. That was how Marvi looked during the weeks in which we loved each other.

She was then thirty. Presumably it is true that only when a woman approaches thirty can she accept love as well as give it. Before that everything is groping, excitement, blindness, uncertainty. And so many people never ripen to love. They probably don't realize it, however. At most they are aware of a vague dissatisfaction for which they compensate with such pastimes as color photography, card games or collecting. Or perhaps they do realize it but are trying to make the best of it, these dependable, conscientious, honest people. Fortunate people. Enviable people.

For love is a beast. Love is a siren. Love is worse than dope. One can die of love. A person can easily lose his nerve and sense of proportion because of it. The most scrupulous and stable person is in the greatest danger if love disastrously comes his way. Or must a person possess a basic flaw to attract love? Some gap, some mental decay? I thought of all this with Marvi's letters in my hand.

In my fevered and hypersensitive condition I could smell the acrid odor of the cranberry leaves in my fingers. I could not free myself of it although I had freed myself of Marvi.

No, I didn't read the letters then. Not yet. Some reluctance restrained me. I merely arranged them in chronological order according to their postmarks and tucked the photograph between them. I tossed them into the pile that I intended to take to the country for perusal, as though I needed to replenish myself with my former self. I knew full well that I was undergoing a change. Whether it was growth or decay I didn't know. I knew only that it hurt grievously.

I returned to my bed as quietly as I had left it. Cranberry tree. Backyard. Mental decay. I dozed off, my head full of smoldering ashes.

4

We were sitting in a restaurant, you and I. Only a few people were there, but even they disturbed me. You were sipping white wine. I wasn't drinking then. I just had to meet you, to see you again, even though among people and across a table. The white wine became you. Naturally you had done your utmost, but I intended to remain firm.

"Some night you'll crack," I said, "after you've sorrowed and lusted enough. I mean that I could never be happy anyway, no matter what happens."

A forlorn look came into your eyes. "Such long eyelashes," I said hastily. "By the way, I came across Marvi's letters recently. Remember?"

"Why do you always talk so?" you demanded. You were sullen and hurt.

"I haven't seen that dress before. It's attractive," I remarked placatingly. You touched the dress and smiled, looking into my eyes. I looked back smolderingly. "Nevertheless, you would be even lovelier if your only garment were the white wine."

You leaned toward me and smiled again. How you smiled! "You should know."

"Lead me not into temptation," I pleaded.

You shrugged and stiffened. "Thine is the power," you said submissively. I had wounded you. One always wounds when loving.

"Forgive me," I begged. "I'm impossible today. I'm impossible always. I suppose you know that by now."

It was true. Whatever we said, strangeness lay between us. The strangeness of people, of clothes, of the table. Only when two people are alone is it comfortable to love. That is why loving is so hopeless; the most hopeless thing there is. But in our case it wasn't that kind of strangeness. We both knew what it was; there was just no point in talking about it.

"May I have another glass of wine?" you asked.

"Of course. But let's return to Marvi's letters."

"Would you let me read them?" you broke in. "Since they seem to be so important to you."

"No, I wouldn't. Such things aren't done. I didn't even reread them. When I do, perhaps I'll burn them. Then I'll finally be free of Marvi. You see, a drop of her apparently still remains in my blood, otherwise I wouldn't think of her as often. For your sake, of course. Another glass of white wine, miss.

"I was in a mental institution when we met again after many years," I began, studying your expression. You didn't cringe. There was only a quiver in the corner of your eye.

"Didn't you know that?" I asked in feigned amazement. "How strange. You really don't know very much about me."

"What a shame," you said slowly, tilting your head. Your smile said that you knew at least as much about me as anyone else. Even more. That was most important to you: knowing something that no one else knew. I hadn't been able to hurt you, after all. You were too confident of your knowledge.

I regretted my confession. "I wasn't there very long. Only about six weeks. It was during the war, when I had exhausted myself to the breaking point. Or had been exhausted, however you want to put it. I wasn't as weary as I am now. In fact, I worked quite fast and I suppose they wanted to take advantage of it. At any rate, I had to take over an extra assignment that had to be done at night for security reasons. I completed the task, but lost my sleep. An unnerving trip that I had to undertake about the same time finished me.

"After that I couldn't sleep more than an hour or two each night, and then only with the aid of sleeping pills. The old momentum carried me forward for a few weeks, but no one can go on forever. Naturally, I began to drink. Stiff as a log, I could sleep several hours, but of course I suffered the consequences the next night. Finally the doctor sent me off to a mental institution and I went gladly. I wouldn't have had a vacation otherwise. Insomnia is a civilian complaint."

I thought back to those weeks. "That was my first real period of sleeplessness. It all started from that. I had always had spells of insomnia, but it became a sickness during the war, and since then it has struck almost every year. Sometimes in darkest winter, sometimes at the end of a hard assignment that leaves the brain grinding nothing. Nowadays I get over it in two or three weeks, for I know how to take care of myself. I used to take the insomniac's hypomanic excitement seriously, but now I know that it isn't normal; it's a sickness. The worst of it is that a person actually feels happy in that condition. The brain works faster, ideas fly, one has to be busy every moment. Or to prattle. But it's a sickness just the same."

I looked you in the eye. "Just as on those rare occasions when I feel happy I know that I'm sick. Unfortunately. I'm a melancholy person, so happiness for me spells sickness."

"Don't say that," you protested. "You mustn't say that." You glanced at the table.

"Another glass of white wine, miss," I ordered. "Go ahead and drink, sweetheart, if it helps matters. It probably won't hurt you. I'll take you home."

The waitress removed your lipstick-stained glass and bought a fresh drink. You had on your evening makeup with the silvery blue eye shadow. You were beautiful but shy, and the makeup allowed you to conceal your face from the world. Only to me did you dare show your naked face. I knew by that that you loved me. You submitted defenselessly to me, and I repaid you by hurting you. One should never belonged to another so completely, for it leads only to suffering and destruction.

" 'You mustn't say that,' " I mimicked you. "You women are crazy when you're in love. Marvi didn't find any flaws in me either, although the doctor gave me the old-fashioned Sulfonal cure that twisted my tongue and even my eyes but still didn't help my insomnia. When the head nurse was in a good mood she would make me some strong coffee at four or five in the morning just to pass the time.

"A stupid drug," I recalled. "It used to be used because it wasn't habit-forming. Actually, I suppose, a person could use anything as a narcotic if he wanted to. Even milk."

"Don't tease," you laughed. "You're just joking."

"Like hell I am. If you drink enough milk, the body's fluid balance is disturbed and you find yourself in a state of stupefaction similar to epilepsy. At least, when you drink white wine you know what you're getting. Sweetheart, you're not becoming tipsy before my very eyes, are you?"

You laughed at me, your eyes slits. Your mouth was that of a tiger. "You were going to tell me about Marvi." Then you became serious, opened your purse and studied your reflection. "Maybe I am getting drunk," you conceded and put on some more lipstick. You deliberately gave yourself a wider, more ruthless mouth.

"That two such drunkards had to meet," I marveled. "Perhaps that's all it is—the gratitude that one has found one's own kind. But don't be afraid. You're not so bad as I, and won't be even after fifteen years. But be careful."

"Only that," you said sadly. "Of course it's only that. What else did you drink?"

"Mumm Cordon Rouge," I said. "The champagne of melancholy, of tears. The driest champagne in the world—so dry that it squeaks between the teeth. Don't forget that. Let's not cry tonight."

"Tell me about Marvi," you urged. "You're always talking, anyway."

"It wouldn't work," I explained. "Believe me. If one of us were sober at times, the other would begin drinking, and that would be the end of it. We'd sail straight to hell, both of us."

"Darling, oh my darling," you pleaded. "In hell, could we be together, just the two of us?"

I shook my head. "Now you're being silly."

You leaned toward me, reaching out your hand. "I'd like to have a little girl by you," you said slyly. "I've always wanted a little girl. I'm a woman, don't forget."

"That's the damnable part of it. Fool that I was, I thought that you were grown up. Miss, another glass of white wine, please. Now in God's name don't start crying! You know how mascara smarts. People are looking at you. Now don't pretend."

I changed the subject. "About Marvi. I had heard about her over the years. I knew that she had left school and gone to the Institute of Social Sciences to study journalism. I suppose she had a flair for writing, but she was too shy to succeed in that field. Then she studied foreign languages and became a correspondent in a business firm. She was doing well at that when we met again.

"Actually, we had met briefly even before the war. Once on a train, I remember, when we talked easily and I noticed that she had the same erect figure and the same way of tossing her head. I also couldn't help noticing that she was brazenly wearing a brassiere. And why not? She had every reason to be proud of her figure. Although she made sure that I saw her engagement ring, I had a feeling that she wasn't completely oblivious to me."

You pinched my arm on the table and your eyes darkened. "Tell me about Marvi. Tell me what there is to tell, but don't gloat."

"Sorry, I was just getting into it. My mood was the basis for it, of course, and the fact that I was home with my family. No one can stand seeing another person deliberately driving himself toward a mental breakdown, much less understand it. That's why we were cruel to each other, my wife and I, wounding each other ceaselessly. The fault was mine, of course. Still it was as though sandpaper were being rubbed over bare skin. No woman can stand that, not even the most understanding. That knowledge in itself made me ill."

I stopped to ponder the matter. "Perhaps, after all, my insomnia represented a hysterical person's characteristic refuge in illness when the pressure has grown unbearable. However that may be, I happened to meet Marvi on the street one evening. Why just her? I would have greeted anyone who was kind just as enthusiastically. 'Marvi,' I must have shouted, 'for heaven's sake come and have a drink with me!' She tossed her head, smiled, and glanced at her watch. 'For five minutes,' she said. I don't think she even drank, just sat and watched me. And smiled as only Marvi could smile. She was no longer shy or afraid. But I just kept on drinking and babbling about everything, to keep her with me so that I wouldn't have to be alone. We sat there until closing time, when I suggested, 'Let's go to your place.' She looked frightened. Her landlady was a nervous elderly spinster who would throw her out. But in my condition, what did I care about disturbing other people?"

"Sometimes you can be very stubborn," you conceded.

"You see," I explained, "a person in such a nervous state generates electricity that catches others up in it. Marvi was swept along without even realizing it. And so we went to her room, she fearfully and on tiptoe. I still remember that room well. The wardrobe, the desk, the threadbare remnants of a once elegant bourgeois home. There was even an Oriental rug on the floor."

"And then?" you prompted.

"We kissed. We caressed each other. She was experienced, too, a grown woman. I must have told her that I had never been able to forget her. I suppose I cried, too, in my drunkenness. But then something inexplicable happened. My mind cleared suddenly, and I found myself kneeling before her. I had opened her blouse, and the beauty of her bosom made me speechless. Beauty so dazzling, so achingly fair that it permitted no impure thoughts. It stayed my drunken hand and halted my tongue. I couldn't even think of touching her, but only rested my forehead on her breast. It was as cool and inviolate as it had been when I had first placed my hand on it as a boy. 'Marvi,' I said, 'I don't deserve anything so beautiful.' I was drunk, of course. And then—"

"And then?" you probed.

"Then I fell into her bed and slept like a log. For the first time in weeks I slept until morning without waking once. Until at last her alarm clock rang and awakened her, lying beside me fully clothed and trembling wondering how she would get me out of the apartment without the knowledge of her landlady. That was impossible, of course. We heard her moving about and coughing in the vestibule. Besides, I had to go to the toilet. Seizing the bull by the horns, I straightened my tie, combed my hair and stepped into the vestibule to greet her with a smile. Then for the first time I mentioned that Marvi and I were childhood friends. She was an elegant old Swedish lady, and we became almost friendly. At least, she later told Marvi that she thought me very human. Well, I suppose that's one thing that can be said of me, don't you think, dear?"

"At the very least," you conceded generously. At any rate, I made you laugh in that fiendish situation.

"She didn't serve us coffee that first time, so we had some coffee substitute in a little café before she went to work. I had an interview that same morning, so it worked out well. I jotted down her telephone number—it was the least I could do. She was quite unhappy and ashamed of the whole affair. Everything could have ended there, with neither of us being obligated in any way, except perhaps to smile if we should meet on the street. Naturally I sent her flowers, and to the landlady also, along with a few humble words.

"But alas, already then there was a drop of Marvi's blood in me and I wanted to know everything about her—her aloof body, her thoughts, everything. No, I don't remember whether I was even in love with her. It's just that I was so desperately lonely, and her beauty glowed in me. Only a little. You don't have to be jealous. She was a spring, a clear spring, a muddy spring, a spring at the root of a cranberry tree. Dearest, am I getting drunk or are you? I guess talking so much is intoxicating. Normally I don't talk this much. Now I just have to, to you. It's better to talk than to cry.

"Tonight you're a brilliant listener," I praised her. "Miss, make it another one, please."

"Closing time," the waitress said amiably. She was tired but nevertheless tried to smile. It was good to have someone smile at us, even though she could not have understood.

"All right. The bill, then, please." You stared at me with unhappy eyes. "Don't be afraid, I'll take you home. I'll thrust you in through your front door. You won't be able to go anywhere else tonight."

"I've had enough," you said, shaking your head. "No more white wine for me."

"Don't lie. I know you. But I'll see you to your door. Once you get into bed, it'll pass. You always sleep so soundly."

"Bed," you drawled, as though savoring the word. You smiled, and once again your mouth was that of a tiger.

"I hate time," I said. "When I'm with you, I hate time. It flies by too fast, like a bullet straight to the heart. That's what it is to me. By the way, I've forgotten to tell you that I want you, terribly."

You looked at me, your mouth a bitter red. "Then why are you so merciless?" you demanded. "Thine is the power, thine is the power, thine is the power. How many times do I have to repeat it?"

The bill came. As we left, people stared at us. "Let's go," I said, and began reciting senselessly, "In bidding farewell to one's love. Tell me, do you love another? I have never loved another. *Felicità sta sempre all' altra riva.* Mind the rug, darling. Shall we walk? Your head will clear. Both our heads will clear."

You pressed against me as we went down the lobby stairs. "I'll never get over this. I don't want to."

"I only bring you misery," I thought aloud. "You were cheerful once, even happy. You had your work, your family, your friends, the whole world. I've brought you only misfortune."

"No, no, no." You sealed my lips with your hand. "You only bring happiness, nothing bad, nothing sordid. If only you allow me to meet you now and then.

The electric lanterns of night. The unnatural glow of neon lights. In the taxi no word was spoken. You merely squeezed my hand tightly in your bare hand. How naked a human hand can be! In the street outside your building I said, "Please wait a moment while I see the lady safely inside." The taxi driver sighed and twisted himself into a more comfortable position.

Before the elevator I said, "Wipe your lipstick off."

You clung to me as one drowning person clings to another. What am I? I thought. What do you think you see in me? What have I done to you? I saw mortal fear in your eyes.

"Sleep well," I said. The door separated us like the lid of a coffin.

In the taxi I sighed, "Let's go." Dark buildings. The unnatural glow of neon lights. My city. I took a handkerchief from my pocket and wiped my mouth. No stain. You were considerate, adorably considerate. Suddenly a ridiculous memory pushed its way through years of bitterness. Once somebody had wound her hairs carefully around my sleeve buttons to make sure that they were noticed. But who? For the life of me I couldn't remember who had done it. Was that what had happened with Marvi? Did I remember only the beautiful things? Had the unpleasant things sunk to the bottom of my mind into complete oblivion?

5

My work didn't progress. One siege of depression followed another at alarmingly brief intervals. Letters remained unopened for weeks. It was agonizing to answer the telephone. Time rumbled ahead like a tormented streetcar. Time pounded nerve-rackingly in my head. I was able once again to drop off into a dull sleep. I slept late, very late in the morning, because I had no desire to face another agonizing day. I thought, I have nothing to look forward to anymore. Why should I ruin your life? It would be better not to meet—better for you, perhaps for me as well, and certainly better for the other people.

But at night after turning off the light I lay awake, wide-eyed, staring into the darkness. It's dangerous to do that. I remembered the tingle of your touch too well, and so I fled to Marvi. Marvi was dead, but her gossamer being enveloped me and penetrated me. In the darkness her eyes mocked me and smiled at me, as though she now understood matters better than I. There was nothing evil or cloudy in her eyes, merely goodness as they smiled at me in the dark.

How her eyes radiated love on those dark December mornings! Soft snowflakes melted on her cheeks. Many mornings we would meet in a brightly lighted café before she went to work. I needed her. I needed her desperately, her warmth, her vitality. It was as though I were devouring her in order to replenish my own fading strength.

Years later I looked back on those weeks at the mental institution as the happiest period in my life. After the horrible pressure I was free, at least for a brief breathing spell. That meant a great deal during wartime. It was as though a giant machine had spewed me to one side temporarily. I needed human warmth, I wanted beauty to sustain me and help me live without cracking up.

Marvi, too, must have felt herself pathetically alone in a world of people. And when the tempest caught her up she probably didn't even want to resist. Not anymore. The tension of our first childhood contact drove us together. As I remember it, she wasn't even surprised when I called and told her that I was in a mental institution. She was merely happy that I called and promised to come and see me. She did come. I had a private room in which I could receive visitors undisturbed. That's how it began.

I remembered it all in the dark: the ancient wooden building, the slippery linoleum floors with their worn spots, the creaking rattan chairs, the off-key piano in the patients' recreation room, and the fat old head nurse who always smelled of camphor. There were the tall youth who sometimes came into my room to talk and borrow books, until one day he became restless, wandered from room to room with trembling mouth and tears of agitation in his eyes and finally collapsed in the dreadful unconsciousness of an epileptic fit.

There was also the black-haired boy with leechlike dark eyes and strangely flushed cheeks who begged matches of everyone, claiming that his night lamp had been disconnected and he couldn't read. But he wouldn't accept a flashlight. Only matches would do. No one gave him any but he got them somehow and one night tried to set fire to his mattress.

After the first few disturbed days and sleepless nights I remained secluded in my room. I needed no other companionship, for I had Marvi. She came every day to visit me.

My doctor was not opposed to it. He just gave me Sulfonal in increasingly larger doses. On his rounds he would sit opposite me at the table and ask questions aimlessly while watching me with shrewd eyes. He let me talk, the words tumbling over one another, my tongue thick from the drug. Hypomania, he diagnosed.

Seeing that whenever my wife came we only agitated each other, he freed her of the unpleasant duty. It was a relief to both of us when the doctor suggested that my wife discontinue her visits. In my condition I was a stranger to her, although in my hypersensitive state even that fact seemed an affront. I was alone, forsaken. No one cared for me. Disgusting self-pity is in itself an indication of sickness.

But Marvi swallowed it whole. Love is blind. She noticed nothing different or exceptional about me but accepted me as I was. Of course, extreme tension creates its own spell. My morbid fervor contaminated her, touching her with its unhealthiness.

I told the doctor that I had never been as happy as in the institution. He merely smiled knowingly and urged me to go out more and to cultivate other interests. I bought several paintings during those weeks. Somehow I needed their beauty, color and form. The doctor discussed them knowledgeably with me. He himself collected antique silver. Everyone has his own psychological compensation.

I had Marvi. Naturally I couldn't conceal her visits from the doctor. Not that they could have been concealed. He thought that she was good for me. One day I asked him whether I might visit Marvi that evening and stay out late. He smiled. "It's all right with me if you stay out late but you don't have to say where you'll go or what you'll do. In fact it's better if I don't know."

We had planned that visit for a long time, Marvi and I. We longed for each other. Hungered. Our passion welled up from the depths of our togetherness. A glance, a touch, an embrace no longer sufficed.

She had told me about her engagement. Some management trainee at the factory had begun taking her out evenings to the factory's social club. Invisible barriers separated the townspeople. Marvi's curiosity was satisfied by those parties at the club, by meeting the engineers' wives and being invited to homes that previously had been closed to her. She undoubtedly believed herself to be in love with the man since she accepted his proposal. But she was reluctant to have him touch her, and perhaps her very aloofness was a challenge.

After a while the man began to demand that she submit to him. After all, they would be married in a year when he had completed his training. Marvi finally consented, probably to convince herself that she actually loved him. She felt ill after the first time. The man talked her into sleeping with him a few more times, even though it was revolting. In fact, the man himself began to seem revolting. She was afraid that she might have a child and would be forced to marry a man whose very touch made her cringe. To her great relief she learned that she was not pregnant, and immediately thereafter broke her engagement. The feeling of relief was, however, accompanied by a feeling of incompetence. She feared that she might be abnormal, that she would never know how to love.

Not that she regretted submitting to her fiancé. Quite the contrary. Only then had she awakened to the direction her life was taking. If it hadn't happened, she might have married a man who was a stranger to her and committed herself to a life from which there was no escape. She shuddered to think that she might have had children by such a man.

But she wrapped herself tightly in her pride, began to work harder and to study languages. During the following years she gladly accepted invitations, learned to smoke and drink, and to kiss her escorts good night at the door. She even submitted to caresses to convince herself that she wasn't different from others, but once at home she had to wash her mouth, brush her teeth many times and clean the skin that a strange hand had touched.

"That's why your touch was like a revelation," she explained, her face pale, her hands pressed together. "I was prepared to force myself once more. After all, you were terribly drunk. I thought that I'd despise you afterward. But it wasn't anything like the other times. There was nothing cruel or greedy in your touch. No, it was beautiful. Really. I could never have believed that a touch could be beautiful."

That's how she explained it to me as we sat in my room in the institution, the air full of acrid cigarette smoke and the walls glowing with the paintings I had bought. Imagination. Infatuation. She was pale as she spoke, but she had to explain. She had to clarify for herself what it was and how it had happened to her.

"It was beautiful for me, too," I assured her. "So beautiful that it hurt, despite my drunkenness. I slept as though I had finally achieved peace of mind after years of waiting."

I thought back to our youth. "Marvi, do you remember when I was fifteen and touched you? What did you really think of me?"

"I suppose I thought you were terribly bold," she said slowly, "and that you were just toying with me. I was afraid of you. And insulted by the stone. But perhaps it was just pretense. At any rate, something happened to me, and it was as though I were locked up inside after that. I supposed I've remained locked up all these years."

That's what she said, as I remember it. She definitely did say "locked up." Perhaps a mere touch can do that to a shy person. Perhaps it can also set free. Again I remembered how my hand unwittingly touched your cool skin. Even though you yourself made it possible, as you later admitted. You were more experienced than I. A woman.

I lay awake in the dark with my eyes open. My body was tingling all over. I can't free myself of you, I thought, I simply can't. So why should I torture myself and you?

6

After lengthy temptation, I once again sat in an empty room in the middle of the night with the warmth of sherry in my veins, staring at a telephone. My inhibitions melted slowly in the sherry's glow. Only the click of a dial, a ring, and then your voice. No more was needed. I sat staring at the telephone for an hour or two, and somewhere deep within me I knew perfectly well that I would call you. I had known it when I ordered the first drink. A large glass, I told the waiter.

There's probably nothing bleaker than a strange room in which one sits in the middle of the night with a drink within reach staring at a telephone. A transients' room, the presence and breath of strangers still around one.

Then—your voice, your breathlessness over the phone. You came, in the middle of the night, at my first request, and disregarding the warnings that were shouted to you at home. You had no more pride than I. And when you were with me, and I felt the warmth of your neck under my lips, everything was incredibly simple and clear, as though nothing bad had ever happened. The spell returned. I loved the bleak room because of you.

Over my shoulder you glanced at the bottle on the table. "Dry Sack?" you asked.

"Dry Sack."

Your eyes were dark with emotion. "Bless Dry Sack for bringing you to me," you said. "Anything, anything at all if it brings you to me.

"If you only knew how terrible these weeks have been," you whispered. "I thought I'd never see you again."

"So did I," I admitted. "I'm a coward. But Dry Sack has more courage." I released your hand and poured myself another drink. The warmth of the sherry shimmered in my blood.

'Go ahead and drink if you must," you said. "I'm going to take a bath. Is there hot water at night? The telephone ringing so suddenly and so late and the sound of your voice made me break out in perspiration."

We didn't say much more than that then. Sometime much later you opened your eyes drowsily and asked, "What day and what century is this?"

"A little girl at the gates of heaven," I murmured. "She can afford to wait, a hundred, even a thousand years. She's had to wait before now. Time hasn't the same meaning there as it has on earth."

"Earth?" you asked. "Where's that? I'm sitting on top of a cloud."

"I was just dreaming," I explained. "She was wearing a little red skirt. I wonder if it was you or Marvi?"

"Don't. Your beard is scratchy."

I rubbed my chin. "I wonder what day this is. I know the year and the month, the country and the city. I think."

"What difference does it make?" you asked, beginning to cry. "It doesn't make any difference anymore." The tears rolled down your naked cheeks. You wept decorously and without sniffling. Your face became wet.

"No, it doesn't make any difference," I conceded. "We've spoiled everything again. Shall I ring for a razor? I'm sorry if it hurt you."

You clutched me with both hands. "No, don't. It doesn't scratch badly. In fact, it feels good."

I reached for the bottle again. It was empty. So be it. I leaned back, hands under my neck. "I suppose I could get some pajamas."

"No, don't," you pleaded. "It's just a waste of time."

"Just think," I said lazily, "there are people for whom time hangs heavy. Although that's nothing. Have you heard what a real dipsomaniac is? A man who drops into a tavern for a beer before bedtime and wakes up in Hong Kong three months later with a six-inch beard on his chin."

"Why couldn't we wake up in Hong Kong?" you suggested. "I'd love to wake up in Hong Kong with you."

"With empty pockets, dirty, ragged, and the hangover of the century?"

You put your arms around me and pressed your cheek against my shoulder. "If only you were poor, dirty and in the gutter, perhaps then I could keep you."

Suddenly you looked happy again. You began to study yourself and observed, "I have heavy arms. Can you really love me even though I have such heavy arms?"

"They're not heavy, they're very tempting," I assured her. "Besides, I'd love you even if you were so fat that I'd recognize you only by your eyes. But never fear, it'll pass in time. Everything always passes, and then I'll be rid of you. . . . If you only knew how your pupils dilate until your eyes are absolutely black. You're a terrible woman, really frightening. I'm not the lover for you."

"It's just difficult for you to begin," you said consolingly. I'm like that myself. If you only knew how afraid I am that I don't know how to make love.

"You! You were born to make love. That's a gift in itself. I've never met a woman with such a natural flair for it."

"That's not so; you're just saying it to please me," you sighed happily. "Once you slept with your head on my arm. A century ago, or was it two centuries? Your head was terribly heavy."

"Sometimes it weighs all of a ton," I said. Then I remembered something. "Once after I'd worked all day, straining my mind, my weight went up two whole pounds since morning, even though I didn't eat anything."

You looked dubious but ready to believe even that if I said it was so.

"That's not quite true," I amended hastily. "I wondered about it myself until I realized that the scales were out of order."

You were silent again. Your eyelashes were fantastically long, your cheeks had narrowed, your face was naked in my arms. How beautiful you were!

"No, I'm not a good lover," I repeated stubbornly. "Actually, people know very little about love. Like the doctor who took care of me at the mental institution. After I had been with Marvi that night he asked me if I'd had fun. I had to tell him that nothing had come of it. He nodded sympathetically and assured me that the Sulfonal was to blame. But I told him that I never succeed the first time. One has to familiarize oneself with the other first. Even a body has to familiarize itself with another body. This was something new to him. He removed his glasses and began wiping them in interest. I suppose even you were amused by me in the beginning, although you were very tactful. I like you because of that, too."

"Don't say that. I was so frightened that I trembled like gelatine," you said. "I was delighted that you were afraid, too."

"As a matter of fact," I remembered, "Marvi too was glad that nothing came of it."

"You're always talking about Marvi," you grumbled.

"We had anticipated it too long, that's why we were so tense. Actually, it could have been calamitous if everything had gone smoothly. As it was, Marvi had to overcome her inhibitions and stop thinking about herself. A woman loves with her whole body, and if she is responsive to love only a little is needed to bring her un-dreamed-of bliss. Good Lord, I felt myself completely inept, but Marvi literally blossomed. It was an even greater miracle to her than to me. She wept for joy, and there was nothing defensive or forbidding about her any longer. She herself said, 'My body is like water.' "

You stretched yourself graciously. "Fortunately your Marvi is dead, otherwise I might have to kill her. I feel as though I didn't have a bone in my body."

"What about your head?"

You touched it. "Not in my head, either. I wonder if I even have a head left. I love you."

"I can't understand why you do."

"Because you're just what you are. You move your hand thus and so. You turn your head a certain way. And when you speak or think you sometimes wrinkle your brow."

"So it's only physical," I said wistfully.

"Also physical," you corrected me. "Aren't you glad that you have a body?"

"Yes," I admitted. "For the first time I'm completely happy that I have a body. Even though it is only a poor miserable one."

'I love your poor miserable body," you said and kissed my cheek. "Besides, it isn't miserable. Don't insult it without cause."

"I've tried to be good to you. I have nothing more to give you, you know that."

"No one was ever good to me before you," you assured me in all seriousness. "I never even knew how good a person can be to an-other."

"You just think so. You're infatuated, you poor misguided woman. You don't know very much about me."

"I know enough," you whispered. "I know just enough. No matter what you did to me, you couldn't destroy that."

Perhaps it was true, perhaps only infatuation. "We're no different from the others," I said bitterly. "Many have experienced the same thing, in one way or another. Misunderstanding at home, too much alcohol, an illicit relationship. Contemptible. Unworthy. Looks ugly on the books. And still it's supposed to open up a new land, a sea of ecstasy into which no one ever has dived as we have, unconditionally and with no thought of tomorrow. No, don't think that we're any different from other people."

"Don't think of it, darling," you pleaded. "Don't think of it right now." You tried the bottle, reaching over me gracefully. It was still empty.

"Let it be," I said. "It wouldn't help anyway. Have some tea instead, with French bread and butter. You need it."

"No," you said and felt your waist. "I reduce beautifully when I'm with you. I feel so light, as though I actually were a little girl on top of a cloud."

"Two pounds a day," I calculated. "There could be worse ways of reducing. But it wouldn't work; you'd get nervous."

"I'm not cranky yet," you insisted. "Don't be afraid. Not until the third day." You began counting on your fingers. "Wait, what day is this?"

"I don't know." I was tired.

"Three plus twenty-seven," you counted. "How much is that?"

I honestly didn't have the strength to count. "Never mind," I said. "I don't know. It's exhausting me."

You touched my temples and chest with your fingertips. "Is that really you?" you said in wonder. "Can it be true? I thought that I'd never meet you again."

"Who did you think it was?" I demanded. "Although what does it matter? You yourself know what you're doing, adult that you are."

You pressed your palm to my mouth. "Again? It doesn't pay. There are no others, there never have been. You should know that. You're only torturing yourself."

"Infatuation," I said. "You're deceiving yourself but not me. You just think you are."

Hands under my head, your warmth against me, I thought back. "About Marvi and me, I don't even know whether we loved each other. She was just infatuated. As for myself, I don't know. I needed her, needed her desperately then. She healed me and gave me back my sleep. We needed each other. Perhaps she needed me even more than I needed her, for her life had reached a crucial point. It could have withered away like a flower without water.

"Both of us needed each other at that particular time, that's why it was easy to believe in fate. Or would I perhaps have devoured someone else who happened to come along? A fiery cloud compels me to it. Afterward I'm stolid and quenched. I submit to the daily grind, to recuperation, to waiting for the next time the spark is ignited. That's the only time I'm happy, when I'm sick or thoroughly immersed in my work. I suppose that's sickness of a sort, too. It takes so much of me—my will, my hopes, my nerves, my strength, until I'm like a wet rag that's been squeezed dry. Only my flaming brain continues grinding away at nothing."

I stared into your eyes with desire and desperation. My very look caused your pupils to dilate. You covered your eyes with your hands and pressed your face against my shoulder.

"Perhaps I'm like that," I continued, thinking aloud. "Perhaps I have to nourish my emptiness with living human flesh, like a vampire. Until you're drained and I take my leave, contented, able to return to my work. I suppose my work means everything to me, even more than you, or anyone. It just grows harder year by year. I've slowed down, but once I get started I frighten even myself. It's as though I were more than myself, more than this miserable body. Of course, that's only my imagination. Self-deception, to make me feel that life is worth while.

"One autumn a little bird persistently escorted me from bush to bush. It had brown arrowheads on its back. The Etruscans prophesied by lightning and birds. Perhaps the augur in me came to life, because since then I've been afraid of birds that spear their victims on hawthorn brambles. It was the dreaded bird of my childhood and it, too, had returned. It was a shrike."

"Darling," you begged, "don't torture yourself. Why do you always torture yourself so?"

"I'm like something that lives and grows in the dark and requires warm blood for nourishment," I went on relentlessly. "Human blood, human life. Perhaps that's why you were sucked into my whirlpool. And I once told you that I never deliberately destroy anyone's life!"

"But you've made me rich," you insisted. "I'm the richest woman in the world when I can be with you. When I can touch you like this. I didn't even know how beautiful life could be before now." That's what you said. Infatuation, lies. Lies, all lies. But you believed them yourself at the time.

"Marvi is dead," I said. "It happened years ago. I was abroad then, and didn't even know about it until I learned it quite by chance. The news stabbed me. Perhaps she still meant a lot to me. But I don't think she hated me. We needed each other so desperately then, for we had to free ourselves of that childhood memory that bound us. She probably believed she loved me, but I didn't want that. That's why I always called her my playmate. My dear playmate. Rubbish!"

"Don't torture yourself," you pleaded again. "You know how I am."

"I didn't mean that. Forgive me. That word 'playmate'—it was supposed to make everything so innocent, so fleeting. But it wasn't a game. Good Lord, how can one play with fire? Perhaps you and I are only children who accidentally have found a box of matches and from sheer curiosity light the first match. Until, sooty and singed, we drag ourselves out of the flames. Or perhaps perish. And irreplaceable values go up in smoke: duty, goodness, self-respect—everything that once seemed worth while. Darling, the bridges are already behind us."

"I don't care about anything, if only I can be with you," you declared stubbornly. "At least sometimes, even like this. Nothing else matters. Let them spit in my face. I can wait weeks, even months, if I know that one day the phone will ring and I'll hear your voice. And I'll come flying."

"You're absolutely mad," I said fondly, caressing your hair and forehead.

"We're not disturbing anyone," you continued. "We're not aggravating people. We don't even appear in public together. We're like mice that stay in a hole lest something bad happen."

"It's already happened," I told you. "You. I. Love itself aggravates people because so few know how to love. Because so few dare. In a way it's humiliating to lose one's pride and self-respect. Well, I don't have much to lose that way. Fortunately.

"The bridges are burning," I repeated, "but I know how to swim. I can always swim back. That's why I'm such a terrible person. Everything collapses, and still I always swim back to the familiar and the secure. Knowing what I am, how can you like me?"

"You're you."

"Fire and earth. I've never felt it so strongly as with you. I don't even know whether I'm lying when I say that, because of course it's never the same. But you were born to love. In another country, another time, kingdoms would have slumbered under your belt. Darling, because of you I'd like to believe in immortality. Am I still drunk? The bottle has been empty for a long time."

Again I thought of Marvi. "Snowflakes on her cheeks, the glow of her eyes on dark December mornings. How she thrived on love! And yet it was merely infatuation. She had found herself and been freed. In loving me she freed herself of me. And I still don't know whether I loved her at all, or whether then, too, it was just cold, cruel curiosity."

"Then, too?" you repeated, in your eyes the frightened look that I feared.

"Then, too," I repeated cold-bloodedly. "You know that. That's why I talk so much. I'm practicing, testing words, weighing them. Of course, the greatest art is in speaking between the lines. That's called style. It doesn't matter what is written, only what can be read between the lines. That's real skill, and that's why I keep on talking.

"The best time of all was when I was in the mental institution. But only until I began to improve. Then I wasn't happy there anymore. When I knew that I was well, everything somehow became more difficult. You know me—I'm no good at deceiving. Of course we still met occasionally, Marvi and I, but it wasn't the same. Something between us had fled. Oh, those dreary winter nights, the hard

snow, the air-raid sirens, the infrequent cheerless sunlight! I was relieved when she began telling me about another man. I didn't need
her any longer. Her presence disturbed me, and it was no longer
thrilling to touch her. Only sneaky. It couldn't continue like that.

"Although Marvi thought that she was unhappy about me, actually
she had already made her choice. 'Of course get married,' I urged her,
'but we mustn't meet anymore.' She exclaimed, 'Oh, I can't,' but
already there was a look in her eye. A home, social status. Certainly
being the wife of a company director was better than being an ordinary office worker. 'Is he repugnant to you?' I asked. She considered
the matter for a moment and said no. 'Then why are you hesitating?'

" 'You,' she replied. I told her that nothing would come of us
anyway, that this was the best way for us to part, when everything
was still beautiful. 'Shall I tell him about us?' she asked. I hesitated,
then suggested that she at least mention her engagement. If she
wanted to mention me, it might be better not to let him know that all
this happened recently. It was all over for her, anyway. I assured her
that I would never forget her, and so we parted. As I rode back into
town in the rumbling streetcar the wheels groaned, 'Marvi, oh Marvi!'
But actually I was relieved that I had gotten out of it so easily."

"Didn't you really ever meet again?" you asked in disbelief.

"I'm not quite that reprehensible," I said. "She called me a few
days before her wedding to tell me that all was well and that she had
become quite fond of the man. He had been unusually understanding
when she had told him about her past, and in turn had told her about
his own mistakes. Such things occur, although they don't mean anything when two people really love each other. It isn't wise to say too
much, however. It hurts, and might fester for years before breaking
out. After that I didn't see Marvi for a year and a half."

You raised yourself abruptly on your elbow, the sheet dropping
from your breast. "So you did meet again!"

"We separated as friends," I assured you. "Naturally I was curious
about her. She had a pile of my books she had borrowed and in moving had come across them. Marvi was very honest. Or perhaps she
just used the books as an excuse to see me. I visited her new home.
The man had been sent off somewhere. They had managed to put
together an attractive home despite wartime restrictions. And don't
stare at me like that, darling. Of course we kissed, but only casually.
Nothing happened to either of us. And so we sat sedately on opposite
sides of the table drinking the coffee Marvi had made. She was
prettier than ever. There was something strangely mellow about her,
and her eyes glowed with womanly gentleness. But not for me. Not
for me any longer. That really hurt. Only then I realized that I was
just a milepost in her life. She had continued far along the road that
I had opened up for her. After freeing herself of me she had ripened

into womanhood. I had meant no more to her than that. We had met only to liberate ourselves from each other."

"Oh, you men, how vain you are!" You sighed and reached for your purse. You examined yourself critically in the mirror. I halted your hand as you were about to put on some more lipstick.

"Not yet," I begged. You smiled, a human smile. Is there anything lovelier?

"Marvi was a stranger whom I no longer recognized," I continued. "I suppose that wounded my pride. She had developed according to her own capabilities and regardless of me. I had merely removed a barrier from the path of her growth. Something like that happened once when ice floes buried a silver birch and I waded out in rubber boots to pry away the ice with an iron bar. The tree was buried in mud, but when the weight was removed it rose by itself, slender and strong. By itself, with no help from me. It was like a miracle, even though I did catch pneumonia. I must have done something like that for Marvi.

"I never met her again after that," I went on. "But as we parted she looked into my eyes and said something that I didn't understand then. 'You taught me what love can be,' she said. 'Beautiful, and not merely selfish. I'll always be grateful to you for that. But now I know what passion is.' It was like a denial of all that had been between us. That's what I thought then. Now I understand what she meant, and I'm glad she said it. Marvi is dead, but because of you, darling, I feel a great tenderness toward her. She granted you to me, so that I might experience the same. Because without me she would never have been free to accept love."

"How did she die?" you asked with a woman's curiosity. I hadn't thought much about it. Only as I spoke something flashed into my mind like cannon fire. "I don't know. It's such a long time ago. She had weak lungs, but they weren't the cause. It might have been an infection, some internal infection. When I heard about it I could think only how much she loved life. But—"

"But what?" you asked.

"Nothing," I replied. "Absolutely nothing." I couldn't look you in the eye. "Let's not talk about her anymore."

I took your hand in mine and scrutinized your wrist. The wound had already healed. I kissed the wrist. "How could you do such a thing?" I whispered. "How could you? Such things aren't done."

You withdrew your hand quickly and looked away. "I was just drunk," you said defensively. "I was cruel and disgusting. But we've talked that out already. Let's not continue."

"One doesn't do such things," I repeated, "at least not when other people are present. I'm afraid the scar will remain. It was all just hysteria. Most unpleasant. And you didn't die, just soiled the rug and your dress and made an unfortunate scene."

You squeezed your eyes tight but tears forced their way between your lids. You put your arms around my neck. "I can't live without you," you sobbed.

"Nonsense," I said. "Don't be foolish. Don't ever say such things. We're both adults. We can always live if we must. You without me, I without you. We can live somehow. Don't say that again or I'll leave immediately."

"If we must," you repeated slowly and opened your eyes. There was no passion or gentleness in them now, just mortal terror. "One doesn't have to live. No one has to live if he doesn't want to."

"There you go again," I said. "Why the hell are we spoiling even these few moments? Why the hell do I have to talk so much?"

A strange room. An empty bottle of sherry, dying roses in a vase. A heaping ashtray, a rumpled sheet, a blanket that had covered strange people. Their presence lingered in the room.

No, we didn't talk anymore. It didn't change anything, and who cared what the surroundings were?

A century later we were drinking tea. You sat curled up with your feet in a chair, a lingering glow still in your limbs. You placed a saucer in front of me, poured the tea and put two lumps into my cup. You were a woman. It broke my heart. As I moved my hand I felt my nerves tensing from shoulder to fingertips, cramping my hand. My body still remembered the warmth of your limbs. I had only to move to feel you. It was frightening but also beautiful. Never before had I experienced anything like it. So I thought.

Even trite phrases can be significant. At that moment, in my infatuation, I thought that I knew how heartbreak felt.

7

It was spring already. We were eating Sunday dinner at home. Everything was as before, on the surface. But everything had been as before on numerous other occasions. And still nothing really was as it was. It never is, for everything changes. There are only good days and bad days, and the only thing to do is to enjoy the good ones without fearing the bad, even though one knows that they'll come again. Otherwise one hasn't the strength to live.

A hyacinth on the table spread its fragrance. Liisa had brought Heikki with her to dinner. We were speaking of the theater, as one does around the dinner table on Sundays. Enthusiastically. Naturally, Liisa had heard some gossip. When the conversation died down after that she glanced at me.

"Well, what have you been doing this spring?" she asked as one does when there is nothing better to say.

"I? Just drinking and whoring, that's all." That was one way of putting it.

It took a moment for Heikki to realize what I had said, then the piece of roast dropped from his mouth.

We laughed, although there really wasn't anything funny about it.

Marvi, I thought. I had to read her letters at long last. I had already talked myself free of her, but I had to read her letters to know what she thought, to know what really happened. I had been thinking of her only as I remembered her, and memory can play tricks.

After the guests had left I sat down at my desk. Outside, windows sparkled in the spring sunshine. On the wall opposite me hung a new painting of shadowy spruces. The evergreen fragrance of my life would end someday. Life comes to its conclusion with a scent of evergreens and a brown pillar of smoke. A copper urn full of oily ashes in a heath amidst copper-brown pines.

That's one way of saying it, a very good way.

No one can ever know, anyway. No one can understand what occurs between two people, not even they themselves. Too much remains between the lines.

I opened the box reluctantly and took out the slim packet of letters. Marvi still lived in her handwriting on the envelopes. Through death I touched her hand in touching her letters. It was unpleasant, and I was afraid. What reluctance kept me from opening the letters, although I had been thinking of her so much?

Finally I tore open the string. It cut my finger, like an omen. I spread the letters on the desk before me and leaned my head on my hand. It was an agonizingly heavy head.

I read:

> As though I were lost in a dark forest. Your hand so kind and secure. So glad if you remember me.

I read more:

> You asked me to write. How could I not write, when I am still so full of you? Perhaps I'm taking advantage of your nervous condition. Perhaps I'm hurting myself, too. It might be better if we didn't meet. Even a wise general retreats in time. But all these years I've unknowingly been searching for something. Now I know: goodness, tenderness, beauty. There were selfish, greedy hands that made me freeze to my depths. How can I explain it? I wouldn't visit you again if I could help it, but I can't. You called me playmate. Dear playmate, did it have to be you?

And again I read:

> You said something that hurt me. But then I tried to imagine how it would be without you, and only then realized that I can't go on like this. Dreary, gloomy years, nervous, prosaic years. That's not life, merely existence from day to day. What good is that kind of a life?

On a half-sheet of paper torn from a notebook she had written:

> I can't find any other paper. I worked late but I wanted to say
> good night to you. Tell me, darling, is it Christmas already?
> There's a festive spirit in the air and everybody is good to me
> and I'd like to be good to everybody. Or is this all just a dream
> from which I'll awaken in the morning when the alarm rings?
> But why should I pretend? I'll wake up when you leave the
> hospital. Even if it is a dream, it's the most beautiful dream of
> my life. Are you asleep already, darling? I'll kiss your eyes.
> There, you didn't wake up.

In another letter she confessed:

> My heart is so full. Please ask your doctor whether a heart
> can burst from joy. Dear playmate, I used to wonder so often
> what purpose my life had. Now I know. All these years I've just
> been waiting for you. How fortunate that you didn't come along
> sooner! I wasn't humble before but now I am, now I dare to be.
> And it's incredible to think that you were the first one ever to
> kiss me, even though I didn't understand that I was meant for
> you.

With a wrench in my heart I read:

> Thank you, thank you for everything wonderful that you have
> given me. Every time we meet I have the feeling that I'm not
> good enough for you. I don't have a will of my own anymore,
> or a life either. Everything is yours, and it makes me so happy.
> I don't understand how I could have lived at all before you came
> along. If you were to leave my life now, I couldn't go on living.
> Tell me, darling, what have you done to me? You only have to
> look at me. What have you done to me?

Three weeks had elapsed to the next letter. I had left the hospital,
and everything was becoming difficult. But Marvi wrote:

> I'm afraid that I'll just create problems for you. But I love you
> so terribly that I could even give you up if it would make you
> happier. Otherwise I won't let you go, though. All the other
> people are only shadows with whom I talk. Only you are reality.
> I can never see enough of you. Thank heaven that you exist and
> that I was allowed to meet you. What have I done to deserve
> such happiness?

The same words, still the same words. My fingertips were numb.
I spread the last letter before me. She had already had time to think,
but still she wrote:

> Actually, I wasn't alive before. Life was like a cold dream, and
> in that dream I performed the tasks that were allotted to me.
> But everything was purposeless. Only through you I learned to
> know myself. How can I repay you for everything you've given

me? There has never been anyone but you, not in the past, not now, and never will be. How many years I searched for you! They were agonizing, wretched years, but now I'm grateful even for them. I'll never be alone, I'll never be surrounded by emptiness. Darling, I'm so happy. Surely you'll at least let me see you some day?

That was the last letter. Only a few days later we met. She was very nervous and didn't even look me in the eye. She thought she was hurting me in telling me that she had found another man. She hadn't lied in her letters, it was just that she misinterpreted what had been between us. When she believed herself to be closest to me, actually she was drifting away. Everything happened only for the other man. I believe her marriage was a happy one.

So it was only infatuation. But a drop of Marvi's blood still remained in me. I felt her nearness and the touch of her hand as I touched her letters. If she hadn't written them, there would have been only my account of the affair. A secret feeling of guilt would have remained in me, a feeling that I had misused another person's life. But with her letters she freed me, even after death. I hadn't hurt her. I had only been good to her. Had I really?

But still, how and why did she die? And she so young and vital. I couldn't understand how it had happened. Then something in me trembled, as the earth trembles under the fire of heavy cannons. The cranberry tree. The will's decay. A crack through which decadence seeps in and destroys the tree. A white scar on a slender wrist. Blood on a rug. Blood on your pretty dress.

Blood on your pretty dress.

In that moment I drew apart from myself. The fragrance of hyacinths, the darkness of spruce trees. A vision appeared before me, and in a dazzling moment I experienced and saw everything that I had pondered, read and planned so agonizingly. Work had nothing to do with me or Marvi. It had developed within me knowingly and unknowingly. The realization swept away everything irrelevant, and I knew that even in my weakness and misery I was strong. I was still able to do something. I was not snuffed out yet. A long road lay before me—a year, perhaps even several years. But at this moment I was thirstless. This moment I was sated, and my emptiness was so filled to overflowing that tears smarted in my eyes.

The intoxicating discovery was followed by a relapse, a blissful relapse. I knew that I couldn't fulfill my vision as I had seen it briefly. I'm only human, after all. And everything human is only an approximation. I would be exasperated, I would flee. But work would compel me to return, the work for which I was born, for which everything else was only preparation and cold research. The fever in my body could never conquer the fever in my brain. I felt my face and it was hot. The spirit burned it, the spirit that was greater than I.

I smiled to myself in the realization that never again would I want to exchange places with anyone. Why couldn't I be satisfied with a calm and modest life? Why couldn't I be content with a safe, workaday happiness that only an external storm could threaten? Why did I myself destroy everything good that I had? My joy, happiness, success, everything—everything I would have to shatter in order to build anew.

My head was burning, and I felt a fiery, nerve-racking cloud spreading invisibly over me. It touched the walls of my study, made the paintings flame in strange colors and gave new life to the old familiar books. My head seemed to fill the entire room.

I knew that I would hopelessly torment those whom I loved, but I also knew that I would carefully put everything that had collapsed together, piece by piece. That had happened before, and each succeeding time it became more difficult. I was wearing out and so were the others. No, security was the thing I could give no one, whatever else I might be able to give.

But in that moment I didn't pity anyone. Pity was small compared to what lived and glowed in me. It was bigger than I, and if I lived on human blood I couldn't help it. The gods demand their sacrifices. Although I was unable to kill even a mouse, I could slowly drain everything good, gentle and beautiful. No, you didn't know me. You still didn't know me.

Miss Dior fragrance. Your eyes widening under my gaze. The warmth of your skin, your beauty.

I grew cold and numb thinking of you. You were only a distraction that prevented my concentrating on work and meditation. I had gotten everything from you that I wanted. I didn't need you anymore.

8

I met you once more. I had to. In a private room of a restaurant and cold sober. The waitress smiled understandingly. I did not; I was annoyed.

"Salmon?" I suggested. "Baked or broiled?" I couldn't meet your eyes.

"I don't know," you said wearily. "Don't ask such difficult questions."

We ate. You looked at me but I avoided your glance. "The trees outside the window are already green," I said. "Old, beautiful trees."

You asked, "Why are you like a stranger? What have I done? Have I hurt you somehow?"

I pushed my plate aside and lighted a cigarette. "That's what the others have said—like a stranger. It must be true, but I can't help it."

You reached across the table. "Please don't," I said, evading your touch.

You stiffened and grew cold. "So," you said.

I thrust my chair back to a more comfortable position. "I read Marvi's letters recently and they taught me a lot. Nothing is new. Everything has been experienced before. Perhaps not in the same way, but almost. Even to using the same words. It's frightening."

You stared at me. Your head was like a flower, a painted flower at the end of a slim, lovely neck. Your eyes were glacial and your pupils contracted.

"I can't talk as well as you," you said.

"In reading the letters I suddenly remembered all the unpleasant things," I explained. "How repulsive her room became, and how I hated the dirty rug and the smell of dust. The sheets weren't clean. As for her landlady, she was coquettish and sly. And Marvi. Once she had a cold, and there was a drop at the tip of her nose when I kissed her. Something like that spells the end of romance. Of course, if I had still loved her, I would have considered it enchanting. And when she undressed I no longer watched her, but her clothes. Her brassiere strap was broken and she had fastened it with a safety pin. The death of romance is terrible. I felt as though there were a coffin in the room when I tried to embrace her. But she didn't notice anything because she was still infatuated. I suppose I hated her already because she disturbed my orderly life."

"Do you hate me already?" you asked. "We said we'd speak only the truth to each other. There would be no sense in our lying."

I looked straight into your eyes and smiled. "How could I hate you?" I asked politely. "How can you even ask it? I love you."

You stared at me as though seeing me for the first time. "What kind of a monster are you, anyway?" you asked.

"Now don't get tragic," I pleaded. "You should know me by now. The flame ignites, burns brightly and then dies down. It always happens like that. It can't be helped."

You leaned over the table, your pupils again black. You were more sensitive than I had thought. "You don't mean what you're saying," you declared. "You're just lying to yourself. Don't try to make yourself worse than you are. I know you."

You rose from the table. "I know you." You touched my neck with your hand and pressed your cheek against mine. The fragrance of Miss Dior enveloped us. "Why are you torturing yourself again, darling?"

"Be careful, you'll smear me with lipstick," I tried to say harshly, but everything in me melted. I couldn't be cruel, not if I tried.

"Dearest, this is hopeless," I said and put my arm around your waist. "Don't love me. For God's sake don't love me, or something terrible will happen. We can't continue like this, not for your sake or mine. Passion has no place in the world. It brings disaster and death. Don't lead me to the death of my heart, dearest. Don't."

You smiled. "So this is how you are when you're sober. I love you this way, too. You don't know how I love you."

"It means war," I said. "Merciless war. Whoever loves more is always defeated, remember that. Watch out. I have my work and that keeps me going. You can't compete with it."

"You wouldn't be you otherwise," you replied stubbornly. "That's why I love you. Give me just a little hope that I can still see you. Otherwise I have nothing to wait for."

Your nearness, your warmth and touch. The power was stronger than I, stronger than goodness, honor, the world. My own helplessness made me sob. How could I have relinquished you? When we met, when we were alone, everything was so simple, so right.

"Let's drink, then," I suggested. "Bottoms up. Nothing matters any more."

"Don't drink unless you have to," you advised. "It'll make you feel bad."

"Bad!" I cried. My bitterness tasted acrid in my mouth. "It's bad enough that I'm alive, and that I had to meet you."

"Oh, you!" You sighed. "But I know how to be nice, too."

"Wipe your lipstick off," I ordered. "What the hell are we waiting for. Why the devil are you teasing me?"

You laughed, exquisitely. "Now which of us is teasing?" you asked triumphantly. "Why did you suggest that we meet here? Why so devious? Did you think that you could get rid of me so easily?"

"Then let's see it through," I said grimly. "Let's not drink or waste time. Let's go with clear heads for once. That's how desperate you've made me."

Your touch, your cool skin. You pressed your hands against your breast. "Soon you won't be desperate any longer," you whispered. "You'll be happy. You'll know how to laugh again. Don't think, darling. We don't have to drink. Don't. It'll only hurt you."

But your eyes closed and I again saw the long lashes, the silvery blue of your lids. How could I ever have given you up?

After an eon I awakened sharply from a deep sleep. At first I didn't know where I was, then imagined that I was safe in my own bed. I fumbled for a cigarette on the night table and only then really awakened.

I recognized the room and the walls. The same transients' room, the same invisible feel of strange steps. Disappointment stabbed through my body like a knife. With the salty taste of despair in my mouth I turned to look at you. You were sleeping soundly beside me in the strange bed. You were sleeping there. You.

Suddenly I remembered the dream from which I had awakened so abruptly. It wasn't an ordinary dream but a real dream, clearer and truer than life itself.

The door had opened without a knock and a woman stepped in

leading a black dog. Her face was covered with a veil that made her
a thousand times more fearsome than if her face were bare. The
dog's eyes were gleaming, and the veiled woman raised the three-
pronged spear in her hand and declared, "Now this room will be
emptied."

That's when I had awakened, trembling. I lighted a cigarette and
began coldly analyzing the dream. I knew the black dog; he was dead.
That meant that nothing could return to what it had been, as though
that were possible. Still, everything does return, at least superficially.

The veiled face I also knew, and the three-pronged spear. Amusing.
But I didn't smile, because it wasn't a mere dream, it was a vision.
And I realized with a feeling of horror that she was Hecate, the god-
dess of death. The characteristics fitted—the black dog, the trident.
My own body was the room that must be emptied.

Was it the piece of marble that I had picked up from Aphrodite's
floor on Mount Eryx that haunted me? But Aphrodite had had her
time. Now it was Hecate's turn.

Cigarette in my mouth, I propped myself up on one elbow to look
at you. Your face was naked and defenseless as you slept. It was a
strange, hateful face. Coldly, triumphantly, I noted every line, every
sign of wear. I had already worn you out. My passion had worn you
out.

I looked at your body and its beauty, and knew that I would conquer you because I was stronger. Always he who loves less is stronger.
Suddenly a great tenderness came over me, because you were weaker
and I could afford to be generous.

You opened your eyes under my gaze and a frightened expression
came into them. It was an expression that I feared.

"Darling, why are you crying?" you asked. You extended your arms
and buried my face in your bosom. I felt the lingering glow in my
limbs whenever I moved. I was beginning to hate that glow. I hated
my own body, the body of death.

"Why are you crying?" you repeated anxiously.

How could I tell you that I was crying because of you, because I
knew that it was all over between us and that I must get rid of you.

That's probably why I was crying. I knew that I would have to
exhaust you and torment you to the end so that you would flee to the
arms of another man. You were ripe for it, just as Marvi had been.

I didn't realize then how easy it would be. Only the look of a
wounded animal in your eyes. Only a street, and blood on your pretty
dress. Then everything was over.

At that moment I caught the fragrance of a cranberry tree, the
acrid smell of its crushed leaf in my fingers.

In The Seed *Pierre Gascar (pseudonym of Pierre Fournier) wrote: "No matter where I was sent, to the state school or elsewhere, I would not be alone. As long as a single human being suffers under others, there will never be too many of us to endure that suffering." Gascar spent five years as a Nazi prisoner of war in a disciplinary camp, and he draws material for much of his fiction from that experience. Notice the number of apparently casual references to war in "The Cat." How do they function in the story? Is it significant that darkness, the release of the cat, and the beginning of married life are related?*

Pierre Gascar was born in 1916 in Paris to parents of peasant origin. He published his first novel, The Furniture, *in 1949. Gascar's wierdly macabre fiction dramatizes the theme of desperation. His prose style is objective, documentary, and poetic. Further Reading:* The Seed *(1959),* Beasts and Men *(1960),* The Coral Barrier *(1961),* The Fugitive *(1964).*

FRANCE

The Cat

PIERRE GASCAR

The whole thing actually began with a rather trying scene, quite unlike anything they had hitherto experienced. It happened towards the end of June, during one of those difficult postwar years, a few weeks after Rose and Pierre Berthold were married.

They had just rented a furnished room in the apartment which the Pradiers, a successful business couple, had managed to secure at an exorbitant price but which was somewhat too big for them. The Pradiers were unpretentious people, with the free and easy manner that goes with

Copyright © 1956 by Little, Brown and Company (Inc.). From *Beasts and Men* by Pierre Gascar, by permission of Atlantic-Little, Brown and Co. Translated by Jean Stewart.

rapidly acquired wealth, and they were too much absorbed in their business to bother about formality in matters that were not directly connected with it. Instead of waiting till they were settled in their new apartment to receive their future tenants there and show them the room they proposed to let, they invited the Bertholds to take possession of the place before the owners were ready to occupy it. It was all decided quite suddenly over the telephone, one evening when the day's business had been concluded more expeditiously or more profitably than usual.

The new apartment took up the whole of one floor of a big old house in the center of town. The Pradiers had arranged to meet the young couple in front of Number 112, a number which, as evening drew on and the bustle of the busy streets died down, began to assume a cabalistic significance. This happens whenever you become conscious of the fact that Fate is there, with its golden numbers skillfully distributed amidst the *grisaille* of directories, registers, calendars, cadastral surveys or the migratory flight of birds. . . .

The sudden hush of evening, the somewhat oppressive atmosphere of the streets, which still retained the heat of the day, and above all the failure of the Pradiers to appear punctually at the rendezvous, increased Pierre's anxiety.

"If only they'd come, if only they'd come!" he kept repeating, twisting his fingers nervously.

Rose said nothing. Her husband's impatience was so disproportionate to the slight benefits they expected from their move that she did not even try to intervene. She would learn soon enough what it was that he hoped to find inside Number 112, and of which he himself was only obscurely aware.

Anxiety, indeed, seemed Pierre's natural condition. He was a man of thirty, rather short in stature, with a perpetually pensive air, and quite lacking in that subtle quality which is known nowadays as "presence"—a disturbing expression which, however, is used too lightly to allow those to whom it does not apply to enjoy the miraculous compensation of being actually out of the world without having given up life. A certain awkwardness resulting from his unimpressive physical appearance inhibited him, in daily life, from making any sort of expansive gesture. And his natural vitality, being constantly frustrated by fears and taboos, tended to dissipate itself in frequent indeterminate gestures and constrained attitudes that bore every appearance of anxiety; whereas really Pierre, who was accustomed to his own awkwardness and knew how to steer his way between snags, often enjoyed complete tranquillity.

That evening, however, his anxiety must have been authentic, for when the Pradiers at last emerged from a nearby street he seemed greatly relieved. A swarthy man in black was with the Pradiers. "I'm in on this deal too," he said to Pierre a few minutes later, using the curt business jargon which alone seemed likely to ensure fair play in future competition.

These words appeared to vex Pierre intensely. He knew that some of the rooms in the apartment were better arranged than others and, drawing Rose aside, he whispered to her that he was worried now lest he should not be able to secure the best of them.

The apartment was on the fourth floor. A wide uncarpeted staircase led to it, past doors on which gleamed the brass plates of business firms and professional men. They went up in almost total darkness and stopped on the fourth landing. Behind the door of the apartment a cat was mewing. M. Pradier, gnawing at his red mustache, hunted through his pockets for his keys; when at length he pushed open the door, the cat arched its back, purring with feverish excitement. It had probably eaten nothing since the departure of the last tenants, who had abandoned it two days before. The two women, Rose and Mme. Pradier, bent over it somewhat nervously, instinctively aware of the venomous power of hunger, of the demoniac transformations it could bring about. The cat fled and the two women tried in vain to catch it.

Pierre alone took no part in this display of cautious compassion. He was carefully examining the big hall, trying to guess at the layout of the apartment. He remembered hearing that there was only one dressing room with running water, and he cast a rapid glance along the walls looking for the pipes. To gain possession of the water supply seemed as imperative a task to Pierre as if he had been a general at the head of his army, entering a half-conquered city.

Guided by the water pipes, on which the paint was flaking off, he hurried ahead of his landlords and pushed open the door of the first room on his right. He found himself in a dressing room arranged in a recess at one end of a big room lighted by two French windows. He noticed that the blue cover of the sofa matched the material of the curtains screening the recess, that the furniture was almost new and yet in tolerably good taste, and that the oak floor was gleaming— or at least that over a large part of its surface the light was shimmering softly. It was still the light of day, scattering angular shadows, but failing fast and almost baffling his attempt to take stock. Already each floorboard, each piece of furniture was secretly a prey to night's weevils. And over it all there hung such a discreet glow, such stillness . . . Pierre opened the door on to the hall and called Rose; he had made his choice.

"No need to look any further," he told her when she stood by him. "We'll have this one and no other."

Rose ran her eyes around the room, without daring to step inside. Night was falling fast and it was a wonder now that she could carry on her scrutiny in such darkness. Something creaked, and she clutched Pierre's arm nervously.

"Yes, yes," she said, "you're quite right."

They closed the door again, and guided by the murmur of voices they joined the others, who had meanwhile disappeared into the depths of the apartment. None of the rooms through which they passed now—and they were unexpectedly numerous—was so pleasantly arranged as the blue room. Pierre took good care not to point this out to his landlords when he caught up with them. He took them along to show his choice: "We needn't bother seeing any others," he said, "since this one suits me perfectly."

"Suits me too," put in the other prospective lodger when Pierre opened the door.

They stood for a moment motionless in front of the great bare room, lonely in the evening light. It was one of those uncertain moments when twilight seems to linger although night has fallen, when everywhere else people are stumbling against furniture and groping for lamps, whereas you sit in your room, leaning your cheek on your hand, gazing at something in the window and in the sky that seems reluctant to die and perhaps will never die. . . . And they stood in silence, as though the threshold that they dared not cross marked the boundary of a forbidden zone.

Meanwhile, however, Pierre was scheming to draw M. Pradier to one side. He succeeded at last.

"Well, what d'you say about it?" he asked in a low voice.

"Why, I declare you've chosen the best room in the house. So I'll give you my terms," said Pradier. "It's a room quite unlike the rest; that must be taken into account. Besides, I realize it suits you. So I'll put my cards on the table: four thousand."

"I accept," Pierre said. "I can even pay you a month's rent in advance." He put his hand to his pocket, but the other stopped him.

"There's one thing more," went on Pierre, who mistrusted agreements made too quickly and wished Pradier had accepted his suggestion. "The hotel's costing me a lot. Could we sleep here tonight?"

"Of course," answered Pradier, "but I'll have to see my wife and ask her if everything's in order. Wait for me here. M. Viau will keep you company."

He stepped into the hall: "Why, my dear Viau, what are you doing there in the dark? Come along over here! Where's my wife got to?" he called.

"She's gone into the room," the other said, drawing near. Pradier went off.

"He's accepted," said Pierre to Rose, who had come up beside him. "I wonder why he doesn't give us some light," he remarked to Viau, whose figure he could now make out before him, a dark shape in which the face formed a lighter patch.

M. Viau shrugged his shoulders. "He must have his reasons. I've known him for a long time; he never does anything without good reason. I'm not implying that you need be mistrustful of him; nobody's more reliable than he is in business matters. It's a very fine room. Yes, you've really made a good choice."

"You don't mind my having done you out of it?" asked Pierre, who was at last beginning to relax.

"No, all things considered, no," answered Viau. "It might have suited me, but I've been thinking things over. I've got my reasons too. . . . But that doesn't mean I think you've made a mistake."

They stood for a moment in silence, in the darkness. At the far end of the hall a light shone out suddenly through the half-open door.

"I'd like to go and see what they're doing," said Pierre, who felt entitled now, as tenant, to take this liberty, especially as it was in "his" room that the light was shining.

He went along and stopped a yard from the door. Pradier and his wife were standing in the middle of the room.

"Well, there we are," Mme. Pradier was saying. "Everything's straight now. You must admit nobody would have guessed the floor was stained just there. . . ."

"You're right," Pradier answered, "and then, as I told you, I don't believe it was that at all. I've always heard that it happened in the little passage. They must have carried her in here afterwards, and she must have come to again. . . ."

"That's not the point!" cried Mme. Pradier. "I can't think why you go on worrying about exactly what happened. That's nothing to do with us. There was a big dark stain on this floor; I couldn't care less about how it got there. All that mattered was getting rid of it and being able to show a clean room. The other evening after washing it I couldn't be quite sure, because the wood hadn't dried. This evening when we got here I was afraid it might still show. But now I'm quite satisfied. Come on, let's go. . . ."

They opened the door and saw Pierre.

"Here you are," said Pradier, pointing to the room with an impressive gesture before switching off the light. "You are at home."

A few minutes later they were in the street, where they parted company.

Pierre and Rose hurried to their hotel. Half an hour afterwards they were bundling a few suitcases into a taxi. Pierre kept on touching his pocket to find, through the cloth, the key of the apartment, which Pradier had given him; this queer piece of metal, the like of which he had not possessed for a long time, now made him the equal of those men who were going home late through deserted streets, stepping firmly, indifferent to everything, self-confident, established in the world of property, and, as they clutched their smooth-surfaced keys, as unmindful of the terrors of night as though they were armed with knives.

"Well, what's up?" he asked Rose, who sat huddled in a corner of the cab. "You're very quiet!"

The passing gleam from a street lamp showed him his wife's face. She had closed her eyes, as she did whenever, overcome by the sadness of life, she took refuge in surrender and, as though envying the dead their peace, imitated their blindness and inertia. He groped for her hand and held it, like one long acquainted with her torments. The gesture brought solace chiefly to himself. Rose's unhappiness was liable to drag him deep into a sort of stormy darkness that had ceased to rage deafeningly but was present all around behind the illusion of daylight. But, if he held Rose's hand, he no longer feared the darkness of hell, and sometimes at night when they lay side by side he would excitedly imagine them walking together through eternity, amidst glistening rocks and crazy birds. . . . Rose gently withdrew her hand. The taxi was bowling along the black avenues.

"And then there's that wretched cat," said Rose, as though a long discussion had led up to this remark.

It was quite true! Pierre had completely forgotten about the cat. It had vanished so quickly that nobody had thought about it when they were leaving the apartment. No sooner had Rose uttered the words than Pierre imagined he could hear the cat's soft footfall running away from something unknown in the depths of a deserted house. It made him obscurely uneasy.

"We shall have to give it something to eat," he said, his brow puckered. "I wonder what, though—all the shops are shut."

He pressed his face against the windowpane in the hope of seeing some lighted shop or stall. But since the war the town went early to bed.

"Perhaps it's not even had anything to drink," suggested Rose, her interest reviving. "Why, none of us thought about that just now."

On trial again! Always something left undone or done unfairly, somebody hardly treated. . . .

"Listen to me! We're not going to worry our heads about a stray cat!" cried Pierre, annoyed by this fresh source of anxiety. "Is it our concern if it's hungry or thirsty? Is it our fault?"

"No, but it's beginning to be our fault," said Rose. "It always happens like this."

Pierre did not answer. Where will it be when I open the door? he was wondering. He remembered that the cat had come right up to the door when Pradier had unlocked it; it must be a domestic pet. But he imagined it, nevertheless, prowling about the depths of the huge dark rooms, at the far end of that mysterious domain they were about to possess, emaciated, sharp-clawed, sniffing at a dark stain on the floor. . . . The taxi had just stopped in front of the house, all the windows of which were dark.

"The best thing would be to kill it, obviously," said Rose as she got out of the cab. "Nobody'll want it. And I can't stand cats, particularly that cat."

Pierre was busy taking out their baggage and did not answer.

"I might say what all women say—it's something physical," Rose went on. "But it wouldn't be absolutely true. It's just on the border line."

She uttered the concluding words in a slow, hushed voice, as though striving, through narrowed eyes, to discern—under the faint mist rising from a rain-wet wood—the edge of the straight-plowed field of rational thought.

Exertion had brought back Pierre's good humor; carrying a heavy suitcase in each hand, he said with a smile: "On the border line of nonsense, in any case . . ."

Rose said nothing. She was climbing up the stair behind him, carrying a suitcase too, and leaning on the banisters, which shook a little.

"To kill it . . ." she went on after a moment. "But how could you kill it? Oh, I don't enjoy talking about it! I've thought of everything —throw it outside? But it would mew in the staircase and the neighbors would come and complain. . . . With a stick, perhaps. I've heard that if you give them a tiny tap on the nose they die. . . . The thought of it's making me ill. . . . And then you'd never have the courage. . . ."

Pierre had set down his cases on a landing to take breath. The light had been turned off automatically and he had to grope along the wall for a long time before finding the switch to turn it on.

"Stop talking nonsense!" he cried, his courage growing in the darkness. "You know quite well that we won't kill the poor creature!"

"Why not?" Rose replied. "It's getting on your nerves and you won't admit it. You were so pleased to have got this room and since you discovered that cat was there you've grown worried and glum again. Admit that you want to kill it; I'm only talking about it to make it easier for you."

"There's something worse than the cat," said Pierre, seizing his suitcases.

"Worse than the cat?" asked Rose timidly. All her curiosity was aroused and yet she was afraid of learning the secret.

But at that moment a mew sounded through the huge sleeping house and upset them again.

"How much higher have we got to climb?" cried Pierre angrily. "It's incredible; we're only on the third floor."

"I won't go in till you've put on the light in the hall," said Rose. "I'm frightened . . . everything's so sinister here."

"Sinister!" exclaimed Pierre. "Goodness, what grand words to use about a wretched cat!"

At last they were at the door. Pierre turned his key in the lock, went in and pressed the switch of the hall light.

"Where is it?" he could not help asking in a loud voice, before taking a step forward.

Rose followed him, looking carefully and distrustfully around her.

"Go and open the door of the room and turn on the light, for God's sake," she said, clearly on edge, to Pierre, who stood there motionless.

He obeyed. The cat was sitting in the middle of the room, quite still. Pierre did not wonder, at first, how it had found its way into the room, but he noticed that one corner of the sofa covered in blue repp, had been torn to shreds by its claws.

"Oh, so it's there," said Rose dreamily, as she followed Pierre into the room. She did not seem to be surprised by the mystery.

"There's nothing extraordinary about that; it must have slipped into the room while we were here, an hour ago," Pierre replied, to forestall his wife's panic. "Look what it's done."

He pointed to the damaged cover, but Rose only gave a fleeting glance to the disaster. She could not stop staring at the cat.

"Well, why don't you speak to it, call it, do something?" cried Pierre. "It's not sacrosanct!"

To set her an example he called out "Puss!" in a curt, imperious tone, feeling somewhat ridiculous. The cat had not moved, and went on looking at them, narrowing its green eyes.

"Are you going to kill it?" asked Rose with naïve anguish.

"We'll see, we'll see," answered Pierre, exasperated. "Please, Rose, let me bring in the luggage first. . . . If you knew how tired I am!"

He was about to leave the room, but changed his mind and went up to Rose. "Silly child, you mustn't be sad. . . ." Rose smiled, her heart heavier still, and kissed him. She leaned her head against his. Yes, thus they could face the storms of death, travel along the unending tunnels, run through the blackthorn bushes, walk down the steps to the pit. . . . If only there'd been birds crying, tossed by the wind, high up in the sky. . . . But no—there they sat, the two of them, side by side, their heads bowed over the same task—the old, daily task; and only the stain on the floor, over there in the corner, was stirring like an anthill.

"Come on!" said Rose, breaking away from his arms. "Let's get it over. . . ."

The cat had disappeared. Pierre brought in the luggage. Rose was sitting down, motionless, her hands clasped, under the feeble lamplight; thus would she appear one day, in some distant cell of time, before the pitiless judges of the last silence. She heard a faint cry from the neighboring house: "Sister Anne! Sister Anne!" She passed her hand over her brow; then everything was still. Pierre had just returned to the room. With his cases at his feet he stood there as motionless as she, his hands on his hips, like a workman prepared for fresh exertion. Rose watched him as he stood their quite humbly, ready to spare himself no trouble, and she felt the need to postpone what would inevitably happen.

"D'you really like this room?" she asked him.

Now she saw it in all its ugliness: the rust-spotted mirror above the gray marble mantelpiece, the Venetian table with its unsymmetrical twisted legs, the ferns patterned in monochrome on the blue wallpaper, ridiculously distorted where the strips of paper met. . . .

"Why, yes, for want of anything better," said Pierre with a shrug of his shoulders. "After all, it's our first room; the hotel wasn't *us*."

"And is this *us*?" said Rose, without any trace of indignation in her voice, as with a jerk of her chin she indicated the empty space before her, foursquare with just a dark shadow like an eye in each corner. "Pierre Berthold, pull yourself together! Don't you realize that we've been letting ourselves be led like children and that we were practically pushed into this room? Why is everybody against us— everybody without exception? Come on, Pierre! Tell me why they're all against us!"

"They're not against us," said Pierre, beginning to pace backwards and forwards. "They're just indifferent. It's quite natural. They've made it all seem quite natural! What right have we to expect them to be fond of us?"

"What right . . ." sighed Rose.

With her head still bowed, she was examining the floor, on which the pieces of furniture seemed to be set out as irrevocably as if their feet had been wedged. She caught herself thinking that she would have to polish the floor because of the dark stain she had just noticed.

"Where's that cat got to?" she asked suddenly, lifting her head. "You'd have done better to wring its neck."

Pierre shrugged his shoulders and left the room.

In the hall, the cat scurried off just under his feet. He followed it, calling softly. One after the other they darted down passages whose existence Pierre had had no notion, and through the remotest rooms in the apartment, where he had no time to put on the light and which were lit only by the dim night-glow of the city.

The cat still fled and Pierre now pursued it as doggedly as though his salvation depended on the success of this blind chase.

From the room, Rose heard the footsteps die away in the depths of the apartment. She suddenly thought: Suppose, when they returned, they brought a stranger to her? "Listen to those footsteps!" Now they were confirmed to a series of brief journeys to and fro among the furniture, now they calmly skirted an obstacle, now they stopped; the listener always has the feeling that a murderer is at work in the house. . . . Rose had got up, but the darkness that reigned in the neighboring rooms made her hesitate and she finally stood leaning against the frame of the door that led into the hall.

"Why, Pierre, what have you done with it!" she cried, solely in order to get an answer, as, seized with panic, she heard the steps drawing closer to her.

The stranger was crossing the last room with a heavy tread, taking an interminably devious route (probably to avoid a table), and now he was approaching sideways, like the dead, laboriously, so it seemed, and it was as though the hour had struck and here was the judge with his hollow-sounding step. . . . Rose could not make out his face yet, and this guessed-at presence assumed an importance which, in another minute, would make her howl with terror.

Pierre emerged into the light. He seemed to notice his wife's wild look. "You didn't really think I was going to kill it?" he said. "I've managed to shut it up in a sort of linen closet at the end of a little passage that leads into the rooms at the back. That part of the apartment is full of surprises—for instance, in the passage there's a little window with colored glass. The moon's shining through it now. Come and see. . . . Don't be afraid!"

He took Rose by the hand and she followed him through the rooms, which were lit up by the rising moon. He crossed them with the confident pride of previous experience, pointing out each obstacle in advance, making a careful inventory of this dead world. Thus, day by day, he would drag her a little farther into his wilderness: Why am I so docile? Rose wondered, and at the same time yielded to her love, which was deeper than love itself and bound irrevocably to a fate like Eurydice's.

She'd never expected the apartment to be so huge. At intervals, between empty spaces, her hand touched the polished surfaces of the pieces of furniture Pierre was identifying one by one. Suddenly the air was colder; Pierre had just opened the door into a passage.

"Just look!" he said. "It's as pretty as stained glass."

Little diamond-shaped panes of red and blue were half-hidden by an opaque curtain.

"It *is* stained glass," Rose answered. "It's only that there aren't any saints in it. . . ."

Pierre seemed not to hear. "The cat's shut up in there," he said, pointing to a door let into the paneling. "But I'm afraid of its suffocating. Just now it was scratching at the wood inside. It was making a hell of a noise!" he cried loudly, as though he wanted to tell the whole world about the creature's evildoing.

Roused by the sound of voices, the cat began to mew.

"Oh! Is it going to start up again?" cried Pierre angrily. "Are we going to have to stay up all night on account of it?"

"Well, let it out," Rose said. "It won't eat us."

"You're right, after all," replied Pierre. "But we'll have to be careful. Suppose it were to jump up at our faces? Eh, suppose it were to jump up at our faces? Id like to have a little light in here."

He examined the passage at some length, but found no switch. He came back to the little window and, standing on tiptoe, pulled back the black curtain — a relic of wartime — which half-covered it. The moon, which had meanwhile risen high into the sky, shone full on the closet door. It shone also on a large dark stain spreading out a little farther on, along the wall. Pierre drew closer to Rose; he could not take his eyes from it.

"Oh, they might at least have washed it off," he muttered, horror-stricken.

"Open the door, open the door," begged Rose, clutching his arm.

He obeyed. The cat sprang out and turned to face them, hissing. They drew back, but the cat had already fled towards the end of the passage. Pierre followed it as far as the hall, where the animal leaped out through an open window looking over a narrow courtyard. Pierre leaned out; from the black well there rose no cry, no sound of any fall. He came back to Rose. She had not stirred, and was shivering from head to foot. Then Pierre led her along, without a word, through the dark deserted apartment at the end of which lay waiting the room in which they were to begin their married life.

The technique of narration in "The Secret Room" is obviously objective. The description is, or seems to be, focused entirely on external detail, rendered as precisely and dispassionately as if viewed through the lens of a fine camera. Yet are we not aware of an observer who is something more than a camera eye? Are there not certain subjective reactions, certain value judgments, certain traces of interpretation present in the narrative? At first reading, this story may seem simply another example of what some have called the pornography of cruelty; but might it not have greater implications? What is the secret room? What relevance to contemporary life may be indicated by the story's precise rendition of surface and its near-total absence of conclusion?

Alain Robbe-Grillet was born in Brest in 1922 *and left a career in agronomic engineering to become a professional writer. His first novel,* The Erasers, *was published in* 1953; *since then he has concentrated on writing fiction, essays, and film scripts.* Further Reading: The Erasers (1964), For a New Novel (1965), La Maison de Rendez-Vous (1966).

FRANCE

The Secret Room

ALAIN ROBBE-GRILLET

To Gustave Moreau.

The first thing to be seen is a red stain, of a deep, dark, shiny red, with almost black shadows. It is in the form of an irregular rosette, sharply outlined, extending in several directions in wide outflows of unequal length, dividing and dwindling afterward into single sinuous streaks. The

"The Secret Room" from *Snapshots* and *Towards a New Novel* by Alain Robbe-Grillet, published by Calder & Boyars Ltd. at 30s., hardcover. To be published by Grove Press, Inc. Copyright © 1968 by Grove Press, Inc. Translated by Bruce Morrissette.

whole stands out against a smooth, pale surface, round in shape, at once dull and pearly, a hemisphere joined by gentle curves to an expanse of the same pale color—white darkened by the shadowy quality of the place: a dungeon, a sunken room, or a cathedral—glowing with a diffused brilliance in the semi-darkness.

Further back, the space is filled with the cylindrical trunks of columns, repeated with progressive vagueness in their retreat toward the beginning of a vast stone stairway, turning slightly as it rises, growing narrower and narrower as it approaches the high vaults where it disappears.

The whole setting is empty, stairway and colonnades. Alone, in the foreground, the stretched-out body gleams feebly, marked with the red stain—a white body whose full, supple flesh can be sensed, fragile, no doubt, and vulnerable. Alongside the bloody hemisphere another identical round. form, this one intact, is seen at almost the same angle of view; but the haloed point at its summit, of darker tint, is in this case quite recognizable, whereas the other one is entirely destroyed, or at least covered by the wound.

In the background, near the top of the stairway, a black silhouette is seen fleeing, a man wrapped in a long floating cape, ascending the last steps without turning around, his deed accomplished. A thin smoke rises in twisting scrolls from a sort of incense burner placed on a high stand of ironwork with a silvery glint. Nearby lies the milkwhite body, with wide streaks of blood running from the left breast, along the flank and on the hip.

It is a fully rounded woman's body, but not heavy, completely nude, lying on the back, the bust raised up somewhat by thick cushions thrown down on the floor, which is covered with oriental rugs. The waist is very narrow, the neck long and thin, curved to one side, the head thrown back into a darker area where, even so, may be discerned the facial features, the partly opened mouth, the wide-staring eyes, shining with a fixed brilliance, and the mass of long, black hair spread out in a complicated wavy disorder over a heavily folded cloth, of velvet perhaps, on which also rest the arm and shoulder.

It is a uniformly colored velvet of dark purple, or which seems so in this lighting. But purple, brown, blue also seem to dominate in the colors of the cushions—only a small portion of which is hidden beneath the velvet cloth, and which protrude noticeably, lower down, beneath the bust and waist—as well as in the oriental patterns of the rugs on the floor. Further on, these same colors are picked up again in the stone of the paving and the columns, the vaulted archways, the stairs, and the less discernible surfaces that disappear into the farthest reaches of the room.

The dimensions of this room are difficult to determine exactly; the body of the young sacrificial victim seems at first glance to occupy a substantial portion of it, but the vast size of the stairway leading down to it would imply rather that this is not the whole room, whose considerable space must in reality extend all around, right and left, as it does toward the far-away browns and blues among the columns standing in line, in every direction, perhaps toward other sofas, thick carpets, piles of cushions and fabrics, other tortured bodies, other incense burners.

It is also difficult to say where the light comes from. No clue, on the columns or on the floor, suggests the direction of the rays. Nor is any window or torch visible. The milkwhite body itself seems to light the scene, with its full breasts, the curve of its thighs, the rounded belly, the full buttocks, the stretched-out legs, widely spread, and the black tuft of the exposed sex, provocative, proffered, useless now.

The man has already moved several steps back. He is now on the first steps of the stairs, ready to go up. The bottom steps are wide and deep, like the steps leading up to some great building, a temple or theatre; they grow smaller as they ascend, and at the same time describe a wide helical curve, so gradually that the stairway has not yet made a halfturn by the time that it disappears near the top of the vaults, reduced then to a steep, narrow flight of steps without handrail, vaguely outlined, moreover, in the thickening darkness beyond.

But the man does not look in this direction, where his movement nonetheless carries him; his left foot on the second step and his right foot already touching the third, with his knee bent, he has turned around to look at the spectacle for one last time. The long, floating cape thrown hastily over his shoulders, clasped in one hand at his waist, has been whirled around by the rapid circular motion that has just caused his head and chest to turn in the opposite direction, and a corner of the cloth remains suspended in the air as if blown by a gust of wind; this corner, twisting around upon itself in the form of a loose S, reveals the red silk lining with its gold embroidery.

The man's features are impassive, but tense, as if in expectation— or perhaps fear—of some sudden event, or surveying with one last glance the total immobility of the scene. Though he is looking back-ward, his whole body is turned slightly forward, as if he were con-tinuing up the stairs. His right arm—not the one holding the edge of the cape—is bent sharply toward the left, toward a point in space where the balustrade should be, if this stairway had one, an inter-rupted gesture, almost incomprehensible, unless it arose from an instinctive movement to grasp the absent support.

As to the direction of his glance, it is certainly aimed at the body of the victim lying on the cushions, its extended members stretched out in the form of a cross, its bust raised up, its head thrown back. But the face is perhaps hidden from the man's eyes by one of the columns, standing at the foot of the stairs. The young woman's right hand touches the floor just at the foot of this column. The fragile wrist is encircled by an iron bracelet. The arm is almost in darkness, only the hand receiving enough light to make the thin, outspread fingers clearly visible against the circular protrusion at the base of the stone column. A black metal chain running around the column passes through a ring affixed to the bracelet, binding the wrist tightly to the column.

At the top of the arm a rounded shoulder, raised up by the cushions, also stands out well lighted, as well as the neck, the throat, and the other shoulder, the armpit with its soft hair, the left arm likewise pulled back with its wrist bound in the same manner to the base of another column, in the extreme foreground; here the iron bracelet and the chain are fully displayed, represented with perfect clarity down to the slightest details.

The same is true, still in the foreground but at the other side, for a similar chain, but not quite as thick, wound directly around the ankle, running twice around the column and terminating in a heavy iron ring embedded in the floor. About a yard further back, or perhaps slightly further, the right foot is identically chained. But it is the left foot, and its chain, that are the most minutely depicted.

The foot is small, delicate, finely molded. In several places the chain has broken the skin, causing noticeable if not extensive depressions in the flesh. The chain links are oval, thick, the size of an eye. The ring in the floor resembles those used to attach horses; it lies almost touching the stone pavement to which it is riveted by a massive iron peg. A few inches away is the edge of a rug; it is grossly wrinkled at this point, doubtless as a result of the convulsive, but necessarily very restricted, movements of the victim attempting to struggle.

The man is still standing about a yard away, half leaning over her. He looks at her face, seen upside down, her dark eyes made larger by their surrounding eye-shadow, her mouth wide open as if screaming. The man's posture allows his face to be seen only in a vague profile, but one senses in it a violent exaltation, despite the rigid attitude, the silence, the immobility. His back is slightly arched. His left hand, the only one visible, holds up at some distance from the body a piece of cloth, some dark colored piece of clothing, which drags on the carpet, and which must be the long cape with its gold embroidered lining.

This immense silhouette hides most of the bare flesh over which the red stain, spreading from the globe of the breast, runs in long rivulets that branch out, growing narrower, upon the pale background of the bust and the flank. One thread has reached the armpit and runs in an almost straight, thin line along the arm; others have run down toward the waist and traced out, along one side of the belly, the hip, the top of the thigh, a more random network already starting to congeal. Three or four tiny veins have reached the hollow between the legs, meeting in a sinuous line, touching the point of the V formed by the outspread legs, and disappearing into the black tuft.

Look, now the flesh is still intact: the black tuft and the white belly, the soft curve of the hips, the narrow waist, and, higher up, the pearly breasts rising and falling in time with the rapid breathing, whose rhythm grows more accelerated. The man, close to her, one knee on the floor, leans further over. The head, with its long, curly hair, and which is alone free to move somewhat, turns from side to side, struggling; finally the woman's mouth twists open, while the flesh is torn open, the blood spurts out over the tender skin, stretched tight, the carefully shadowed eyes grow abnormally larger, the mouth opens wider, the head twists violently, one last time, from right to left, then more gently, to fall back finally and become still, amid the mass of black hair spread out on the velvet.

At the very top of the stone stairway, the little door has opened, allowing a yellowish but sustained shaft of light to enter, against which stands out the dark silhouette of the man wrapped in his long cloak. He has but to climb a few more steps to reach the threshold.

Afterward, the whole setting is empty, the enormous room with its purple shadows and its stone columns proliferating in all directions, the monumental staircase with no handrail that twists upward, growing narrower and vaguer as it rises into the darkness, toward the top of the vaults where it disappears.

Near the body, whose wound has stiffened, whose brilliance is already growing dim, the thin smoke from the incense burner traces complicated scrolls in the still air: first a coil turned horizontally to the left, which then straightens out and rises slightly, then returns to the axis of its point of origin, which it crosses as it moves to the right, then turns back in the first direction, only to wind back again, thus forming an irregular sinusoidal curve, more and more flattened out, and rising, vertically, toward the top of the canvas.

Man, says Sartre, "is alone, abandoned on earth in the midst of his infinite responsibilities, without help, with no other aim than the one he sets himself, with no other destiny than the one he forges for himself on earth." This existential philosophy is dramatized in "The Room." Although Eve claims that she remains with Pierre because she loves him, the story suggests that her feelings for him are ambivalent. Why, then, does she stay with him? Why can't her father understand her resolution to stay, and what is the point of his concern (and hers) with normal behavior?

Jean-Paul Sartre was born in Paris in 1905. He studied philosophy in France, Egypt, Greece, Italy, and Germany. He then worked as a teacher in the secondary schools from 1929 until 1934 and was active in the Resistance movement during World War II. Sartre published La Nausée, *his first novel, in 1938;* The Wall, *a collection of short stories, in 1939; and* No Exit, *the play that began his widespread popularity in America, in 1944. In 1964 Jean-Paul Sartre refused the Nobel Prize. Further Reading:* Nausea *(1949),* No Exit *(1946),* Intimacy *(1949).*

The Room

JEAN-PAUL SARTRE

Mme. Darbedat held a *rahat-loukoum* between her fingers. She brought its carefully to her lips and held her breath, afraid that the fine dust of sugar that powdered it would blow away. "Just right," she told herself. She bit quickly into its glassy flesh and a scent of stagnation filled her mouth. "Odd how illness sharpens the sensations." She began to think of mosques, of obsequious Orien-

Jean-Paul Sartre, *Intimacy,* translated by Lloyd Alexander. Copyright 1948 by New Directions. Reprinted by permission of New Directions Publishing Corporation.

tals (she had been to Algeria for her honeymoon) and her pale lips started in a smile: the *rahat-loukoum* was obsequious too.

Several times she had to pass the palm of her hand over the pages of her book, for in spite of the precaution she had taken they were covered with a thin coat of white powder. Her hand made the little grains of sugar slide and roll, grating on the smooth paper: "That makes me think of Arcachon, when I used to read on the beach." She had spent the summer of 1907 at the seashore. Then she wore a big straw hat with a green ribbon; she sat close to the jetty, with a novel by Gyp or Colette Yver. The wind made swirls of sand rain down upon her knees, and from time to time she had to shake the book, holding it by the corners. It was the same sensation: only the grains of sand were dry while the small bits of sugar stuck a little to the ends of her fingers. Again she saw a band of pearl grey sky above a black sea. "Eve wasn't born yet." She felt herself all weighted down with memories and precious as a coffer of sandalwood. The name of the book she used to read suddenly came back to mind: it was called *Petite Madame*, not at all boring. But ever since an unknown illness had confined her to her room she preferred memories and historical works.

She hoped that suffering, heavy readings, a vigilant attention to her memories and the most exquisite sensations would ripen her as a lovely hothouse fruit.

She thought, with some annoyance, that her husband would soon be knocking at her door. On other days of the week he came only in the evening, kissed her brow in silence and read *Le Temps*, sitting in the armchair across from her. But Thursday was M. Darbedat's *day*: he spent an hour with his daughter, generally from three to four. Before going he stopped in to see his wife and both discussed their son-in-law with bitterness. These Thursday conversations, predictable to their slightest detail, exhausted Mme. Darbedat. M. Darbedat filled the quiet room with his presence. He never sat, but walked in circles about the room. Each of his outbursts wounded Mme. Darbedat like a glass splintering. This particular Thursday was worse than usual: at the thought that it would soon be necessary to repeat Eve's confessions to her husband, and to see his great terrifying body convulse with fury, Mme. Darbedat broke out in a sweat. She picked up a *loukoum* from the saucer, studied it for a while with hesitation, then sadly set it down: she did not like her husband to see her eating *loukoums*.

She heard a knock and started up. "Come in," she said weakly.

M. Darbedat entered on tiptoe. "I'm going to see Eve," he said, as he did every Thursday. Mme. Darbedat smiled at him. "Give her a kiss for me."

M. Darbedat did not answer and his forehead wrinkled worriedly: every Thursday at the same time, a muffled irritation mingled with the load of his digestion. "I'll stop in and see Franchot after leaving her, I wish he'd talk to her seriously and try to convince her."

He made frequent visits to Dr. Franchot. But in vain. Mme. Darbedat raised her eyebrows. Before, when she was well, she shrugged her shoulders. But since sickness had weighted down her body, she replaced the gestures which would have tired her by plays of emotion in the face: she said *yes* with her eyes, *no* with the corners of her mouth: she raised her eyebrows instead of her shoulders.

"There should be some way to take him away from her by force."

"I told you already it was impossible. And besides, the law is very poorly drawn up. Only the other day Franchot was telling me that they have a tremendous amount of trouble with the families: people who can't make up their mind, who want to keep the patient at home; the doctors' hands are tied. They can give their advice, period. That's all. He would," he went on, "have to make a public scandal or else she would have to ask to have him put away herself."

"And that," said Mme. Darbedat, "isn't going to happen tomorrow."

"No." He turned to the mirror and began to comb his fingers through his beard. Mme. Darbedat looked at the powerful red neck of her husband without affection.

"If she keeps on," said M. Darbedat, "she'll be crazier than he is. It's terribly unhealthy. She doesn't leave his side, she only goes out to see you. She has no visitors. The air in their room is simply unbreathable. She never opens the window because Pierre doesn't want it open. As if you should ask a sick man. I believe they burn incense, some rubbish in a little pan, you'd think it was a church. Really, sometimes I wonder . . . she's got a funny look in her eyes, you know."

"I haven't noticed," Mme. Darbedat said. "I find her quite normal. She looks sad, obviously."

"She has a face like an unburied corpse. Does she sleep? Does she eat? But we aren't supposed to ask her about those things. But I should think that with a fellow like Pierre next to her, she wouldn't sleep a wink all night." He shrugged his shoulders. "What I find amazing is that we, her parents, don't have the right to protect her against herself. Understand that Pierre would be much better cared for by Franchot. There's a big park. And besides, I think," he added, smiling a little, "he'd get along much better with people of his own type. People like that are children, you have to leave them alone with each other; they form a sort of freemasonry. That's where he should have been put the first day and for his own good, I'd say. Of course it's in his own best interest."

After a moment, he added, "I tell you I don't like to know she's alone with Pierre, especially at night. Suppose something happened. Pierre has a very sly way about him."

"I don't know," Mme. Darbedat said, "if there's any reason to worry. He always looked like that. He always seemed to be making fun of the world. Poor boy," she sighed, "to have had his pride and then come to that. He thought he was cleverer than all of us. He had a way of saying 'You're right' simply to end the argument . . . It's a blessing for him that he can't see the state he's in."

She recalled with displeasure the long, ironic face, always turned a little to the side. During the first days of Eve's marriage, Mme. Darbedat asked nothing more than a little intimacy with her son-in-law. But he had discouraged her: he almost never spoke, he always agreed quickly and absent-mindedly.

M. Darbedat pursued his idea. "Franchot let me visit his place," he said. "It was magnificent. The patients have private rooms with leather armchairs, if you please, and day-beds. You know, they have a tennis court and they're going to build a swimming pool."

He was planted before the window, looking out, rocking a little on his bent legs. Suddenly he turned lithely on his heel, shoulders lowered, hands in his pockets. Mme. Darbedat felt she was going to start perspiring: it was the same thing every time: now he was pacing back and forth like a bear in a cage and his shoes squeaked at every step.

"Please, please won't you sit down. You're tiring me." Hesitating, she added, "I have something important to tell you."

M. Darbedat sat in the armchair and put his hands on his knees; a slight chill ran up Mme. Darbedat's spine: the time had come, she had to speak.

"You know," she said with an embarrassed cough, "I saw Eve on Tuesday."

"Yes."

"We talked about a lot of things, she was very nice, she hasn't been so confiding for a long time. Then I questioned her a little, I got her to talk about Pierre. Well, I found out," she added, again embarrassed, "that she is *very* attached to him."

"I know that too damned well," said M. Darbedat.

He irritated Mme. Darbedat a little: she always had to explain things in such detail. Mme. Darbedat dreamed of living in the company of fine and sensitive people who would understand her slightest word.

"But I mean," she went on, "that she is attached to him *differently* than we imagined."

M. Darbedat rolled furious, anxious eyes, as he always did when he never completely grasped the sense of an allusion or something new.

"What does that all mean?"

"Charles," said Mme. Darbedat, "don't tire me. You should understand a mother has difficulty in telling certain things."

"I don't understand a damned word of anything you say," M. Darbedat said with irritation. "You can't mean . . ."

"Yes," she said.

"They're still . . . now, still . . . ?"

"Yes! Yes! Yes!" she said, in three annoyed and dry little jolts.

M. Darbedat spread his arms, lowered his head and was silent.

"Charles," his wife said, worriedly, "I shouldn't have told you. But I couldn't keep it to myself."

"Our child," he said slowly. "With this madman! He doesn't even recognize her any more. He calls her Agatha. She must have lost all sense of her own dignity."

He raised his head and looked at his wife severely. "You're sure you aren't mistaken?"

"No possible doubt. Like you," she added quickly, "I couldn't believe her and I still can't. The mere idea of being touched by that wretch . . . So . . ." she sighed, "I suppose that's how he holds on to her."

"Do you remember what I told you," M. Darbedat said, "when he came to ask for her hand? I told you I thought he pleased Eve *too much*. You wouldn't believe me." He struck the table suddenly, blushing violently. "It's perversity! He takes her in his arms, kisses her and calls her Agatha, selling her on a lot of nonsense about flying statues and God knows what else! Without a word from her! But what in heaven's name's between those two? Let her be sorry for him, let her put him in a sanitorium and see him every day,—fine. But I never thought . . . I considered her a widow. Listen, Jeannette," he said gravely, "I'm going to speak frankly to you; if she had any sense, I'd rather see her take a lover!"

"Be quiet, Charles!" Mme. Darbedat cried.

M. Darbedat wearily took his hat and the cane he had left on the stool. "After what you've just told me," he concluded, "I don't have much hope left. In any case, I'll have a talk with her because it's my duty."

Mme. Darbedat wished he would go quickly.

"You know," she said to encourage him, "I think Eve is more headstrong than . . . than anything. She knows he's incurable but she's obstinate, she doesn't want to be in the wrong."

M. Darbedat stroked his beard absently.

"Headstrong? Maybe so. If you're right, she'll finally get tired of it. He's not always pleasant and he doesn't have much to say. When I say hello to him he gives me a flabby handshake and doesn't say a word. As soon as they're alone, I think they go back to his obsessions: she tells me sometimes he screams as though his throat were being cut because of his hallucinations. He sees statues. They frighten him because they buzz. He says they fly around and make fishy eyes at him."

He put on his gloves and continued, "She'll get tired of it, I'm not saying she won't. But suppose she goes crazy before that? I wish she'd go out a little, see the world: she'd meet some nice young man —well, someone like Schroeder, an engineer with Simplon, somebody with a future, she could see him a little here and there and she'd get used to the idea of making a new life for herself."

Mme. Darbedat did not answer, afraid of starting the conversation up again. Her husband bent over her.

"So," he said, "I've got to be on my way."

"Goodbye, Papa," Mme. Darbedat said, lifting her forehead up to him. "Kiss her for me and tell her for me she's a poor dear."

Once her husband had gone, Mme. Darbedat let herself drift to the bottom of her armchair and closed her eyes, exhausted. "What vitality," she thought reproachfully. As soon as she got a little strength back, she quietly stretched out her pale hand and took a *loukoum* from the saucer, groping for it without opening her eyes.

Eve lived with her husband on the sixth floor of an old building on the Rue du Bac. M. Darbedat slowly climbed the 112 steps of the stairway. He was not even out of breath when he pushed the bell. He remembered with satisfaction the words of Mlle. Dormoy: "Charles, for your age, you're simply marvelous." Never did he feel himself stronger and healthier than on Thursday, especially after these invigorating climbs.

Eve opened the door: that's right, she doesn't have a maid. No girls *can* stay with her. I can put myself in their place. He kissed her. "Hello, poor darling."

Eve greeted him with a certain coldness.

"You look a little pale," M. Darbedat said, touching her cheek. "You don't get enough exercise."

There was a moment of silence.

"Is Mamma well?" Eve asked.

"Not good, not too bad. You saw her Tuesday? Well, she's just the same. Your Aunt Louise came to see her yesterday, that pleased her. She likes to have visitors, but they can't stay too long. Aunt Louise came to Paris for that mortgage business. I think I told you about it, a very odd sort of affair. She stopped in at the office to ask my advice. I told her there was only one thing to do: sell. She found a taker, by the way: Bretonnel. You remember Bretonnel. He's retired from business now."

He stopped suddenly: Eve was hardly listening. He thought sadly that nothing interested her any more. It's like the books. Before you had to tear them away from her. Now she doesn't even read any more.

"How is Pierre?"

"Well," Eve said. "Do you want to see him?"

"Of course," M. Darbedat said gaily, 'I'd like to pay him a little call."

He was full of compassion for this poor young man, but he could not see him without repugnance. *I detest unhealthy people.* Obviously, it was not Pierre's fault: his heredity was terribly loaded down. M. Darbedat sighed: *All the precautions are taken in vain, you find out those things too late.* No, Pierre was not responsible. But still he had always carried that fault in him; it formed the base of his character; it wasn't like cancer or tuberculosis, something you could always put aside when you wanted to judge a man as he is. His nervous grace, the subtlety which pleased Eve so much when he was courting her were the flowers of madness. He was already mad when he married her only you couldn't tell.

It makes you wonder, thought M. Darbedat, *where responsibility begins, or rather, where it ends.* In any case, he was always analysing himself too much, always turned in on himself. But was it the cause or effect of his sickness? He followed his daughter through a long, dim corridor.

"This apartment is too big for you," he said. "You ought to move out."

"You say that every time, Papa," Eve answered, "but I've already told you Pierre doesn't want to leave his room."

Eve was amazing. Enough to make you wonder if she realized her husband's state. He was insane enough to be in a strait-jacket and she respected his decisions and advice as if he still had good sense.

"What I'm saying is for your own good." M. Darbedat went on, somewhat annoyed, "It seems to me that if I were a woman I'd be afraid of these badly lighted old rooms. I'd like to see you in a bright apartment, the kind they're putting up near Auteuil, three airy little rooms. They lowered the rents because they couldn't find any tenants; this would be just the time."

Eve quietly turned the doorknob and they entered the room. M. Darbedat's throat tightened at the heavy odor of incense. The curtains were drawn. In the shadows he made out a thin neck above the back of an armchair: Pierre's back was turned. He was eating.

"Hello, Pierre," M. Darbedat said, raising his voice, "How are we today?" He drew near him: the sick man was seated in front of a small table; he looked sly.

"I see we had soft boiled eggs," M. Darbedat said, raising his voice higher. "That's good!"

"I'm not deaf," Pierre said quietly.

Irritated, M. Darbedat turned his eyes toward Eve as his witness. But Eve gave him a hard glance and was silent. M. Darbedat realized he had hurt her. Too bad for her. It was impossible to find just the right tone for this boy. He had less sense than a child of four and Eve wanted him treated like a man. M. Darbedat could not keep himself from waiting with impatience for the moment when all this ridiculous business would be finished. Sick people always annoyed him a little—especially madmen because they were wrong. Poor Pierre, for example, was wrong all along the line, he couldn't speak a reasonable word and yet it would be useless to expect the least humility from him, or even temporary recognition of his errors.

Eve cleared away the eggshells and the cup. She put a knife and fork in front of Pierre.

"What's he going to eat now," M. Darbedat said jovially.

"A steak."

Pierre had taken the fork and held it in the ends of his long, pale fingers. He inspected it minutely and then gave a slight laugh.

"I can't use it this time," he murmured, setting it down, "I was warned."

Eve came in and looked at the fork with passionate interest.

"Agatha," Pierre said, "give me another one."

Eve obeyed and Pierre began to eat. She had taken the suspect fork and held it tightly in her hands, her eyes never leaving it; she seemed to make a violent effort. How suspicious all their gestures and relationships are! thought M. Darbedat.

He was uneasy.

"Be careful, Pierre, take it by the middle because of the prongs."

Eve sighed and laid the fork on the serving table. M. Darbedat felt his gall rising. He did not think it well to give in to all this poor man's whims—even from Pierre's viewpoint it was pernicious. Franchot had said: "One must never enter the delirium of a madman." Instead of giving him another fork, it would have been better to have reasoned quietly and made him understand that the first was like all the others.

He went to the serving table, took the fork ostentatiously and tested the prongs with a light finger. Then he turned to Pierre. But the latter was cutting his meat peacefully: he gave his father-in-law a gentle, inexpressive glance.

"I'd like to have a little talk with you," M. Darbedat said to Eve.

She followed him docilely into the salon. Sitting on the couch, M. Darbedat realized he had kept the fork in his hand. He threw it on the table.

"It's much better here," he said.

"I never come here."

"All right to smoke?"

"Of course, Papa," Eve said hurriedly. "Do you want a cigar?"

M. Darbedat preferred to roll a cigarette. He thought eagerly of the discussion he was about to begin. Speaking to Pierre he felt as embarrassed about his reason as a giant about his strength when playing with a child. All his qualities of clarity, sharpness, precision, turned again him; *I must confess it's somewhat the same with my poor Jeannette.* Certainly Mme. Darbedat was not insane, but this illness had . . . stultified her. Eve, on the other hand, took after her father . . . a straight, logical nature; discussion with her was a pleasure; *that's why I don't want them to ruin her.* M. Darbedat raised his eyes. Once again he wanted to see the fine intelligent features of his daughter. He was disappointed with this face; once so reasonable and transparent, there was now something clouded and opaque in it. Eve had always been beautiful. M. Darbedat noticed she was made up with great care, almost with pomp. She had blued her eyelids and put mascara on her long lashes. This violent and perfect make-up made a painful impression on her father.

"You're green beneath your rouge," he told her. "I'm afraid you're getting sick. And the way you make yourself up now! You used to be so discreet."

Eve did not answer and for an embarrassed moment M. Darbedat considered this brilliant, wornout face beneath the heavy mass of black hair. He thought she looked like a tragedian. *I even know who she looks like. That woman . . . that Roumanian who played* Phèdre *in French at the Mur d'Orange.* He regretted having made so disagreeable a remark: *It escaped me! Better not worry her with little things.*

"Excuse me," he said smiling, "you know I'm an old purist. I don't like all these creams and paints women stick on their face today. But I'm in the wrong. You must live in your time."

Eve smiled amiably at him. M. Darbedat lit a cigarette and drew several puffs.

"My child," he began, "I wanted to talk with you: the two of us are going to talk the way we used to. Come, sit down and listen to me nicely; you must have confidence in your old Papa."

"I'd rather stand," Eve said. "What did you want to tell me?"

"I am going to ask you a single question," M. Darbedat said a little more dryly. "Where will all this lead you?"

"All this?" Eve asked astonished.

"Yes . . . all this whole life you've made for yourself. Listen," he went on, "don't think I don't understand you (he had a sudden illumination) but what you want to do is beyond human strength. You want to live solely by imagination, isn't that it? You don't want to admit he's sick. You don't want to see the Pierre of today, do you? You have eyes only for the Pierre of before. My dear, my darling little girl, it's an impossible bet to win," M. Darbedat continued. "Now I'm going to tell you a story which perhaps you don't know. When we were at Sables-d'Olonne—you were three years old—your mother made the acquaintance of a charming young woman with a superb little boy. You played on the beach with this little boy, you were thick as thieves, you were engaged to marry him. A while later, in Paris, your mother wanted to see this young woman again; she was told she had had a terrible accident. That fine little boy's head was cut off by a car. They told your mother, 'Go and see her, but above all don't talk to her about the death of her child, she *will not* believe he is dead.' Your mother went, she found a half-mad creature: she lived as though her boy was still alive; she spoke to him, she set his place at the table. She lived in such a state of nervous tension that after six months they had to take her away by force to a sanitorium where she was obliged to stay three years. No, my child," M. Darbedat said, shaking his head, "these things are impossble. It would have been better if she had recognized the truth courageously. She would have suffered once, then time would have erased with its sponge. There is nothing like looking things in the face, believe me."

"You're wrong," Eve said with effort. "I know very well that Pierre is . . ."

The word did not escape. She held herself very straight and put her hands on the back of the armchair: there was something dry and ugly in the lower part of her face.

"So . . . ?" asked M. Darbedat, astonished.

"So . . . ?"

"You . . . ?"

"I love him as he is," said Eve rapidly and with an irritated look.

"Not true," M. Darbedat said forcefully. "It isn't true: you don't love him, you can't love him. You can only feel that way about a healthy, normal person. You pity Pierre, I don't doubt it, and surely you have the memory of three years of happiness he gave you. But don't tell me you love him. I won't believe you."

Eve remained wordless, staring at the carpet absently.

"You could at least answer me," M. Darbedat said coldly. "Don't think this conversation has been any less painful for me than it has for you."

"More than you think."

"Well, then, if you love him," he cried, exasperated, "it is a great misfortune for you, for me and for your poor mother because I'm going to tell you something I would rather have hidden from you: before three years Pierre will be sunk in complete dementia, he'll be like a beast."

He watched his daughter with hard eyes: he was angry at her for having compelled him, by stubbornness, to make this painful revelation.

Eve was motionless; she did not so much as raise her eyes.

"I knew."

"Who told you?" he asked stupefied.

"Franchot. I knew six months ago."

"And I told him to be careful with you," said M. Darbedat with bitterness. "Maybe it's better. But under those circumstances you must understand that it would be unpardonable to keep Pierre with you. The struggle you have undertaken is doomed to failure, his illness won't spare him. If there were something to be done, if we could save him by care, I'd say yes. But look: you're pretty, intelligent, gay, you're destroying yourself willingly and without profit. I know you've been admirable, but now it's over . . . done, you've done your duty and more; now it would be immoral to continue. We also have duties to ourselves, child. And then you aren't thinking about us. You must," he repeated, hammering the words, "send Pierre to Franchot's clinic. Leave this apartment where you've had nothing but sorrow and come home to us. If you want to be useful and ease the sufferings of someone else, you have your mother. The poor woman is cared for by nurses, she needs someone closer to her, and *she*," he added, "can appreciate what you do for her and be grateful."

There was a long silence. M. Darbedat heard Pierre singing in the next room. It was hardly a song, rather a sort of sharp, hasty recitative. M. Darbedat raised his eyes to his daughter.

"It's no then?"

"Pierre will stay with me," she said quietly. "I get along well with him."

"By living like an animal all day long?"

Eve smiled and shot a glance at her father, strange, mocking and almost gay. *It's true*, M. Darbedat thought furiously, *that's not all they do; they sleep together.*

"You are completely mad," he said, rising.

Eve smiled sadly and murmured, as if to herself, "Not enough so."

"Not enough? I can only tell you one thing, my child. You frighten me."

He kissed her hastily and left. Going down the stairs he thought: *we should send out two strong-arm men who'd take the poor imbecile away and stick him under a shower without asking his advice on the matter.*

It was a fine autumn day, calm and without mystery; the sunlight gilded the faces of the passersby. M. Darbedat was struck with the simplicity of the faces; some weather-beaten, others smooth, but they reflected all the happiness and care with which he was so familiar.

I know exactly what I resent in Eve, he told himself, entering the Boulevard St. Germain. *I resent her living outside the limits of human nature. Pierre is no longer a human being: in all the care and all the love she gives him she deprives human beings of a little. We don't have the right to refuse ourselves to the world; no matter what, we live in society.*

He watched the faces of the passers-by with sympathy; he loved their clear, serious looks. In these sunlit streets, in the midst of mankind, one felt secure, as in the midst of a large family.

A woman stopped in front of an open-air display counter. She was holding a little girl by the hand.

"What's that?" the little girl asked, pointing to a radio set.

"Mustn't touch," her mother said. "It's a radio; it plays music."

They stood for a moment without speaking, in ecstasy. Touched, M. Darbedat bent down to the little girl and smiled.

II

"He's gone." The door closed with a dry snap. Eve was alone in the salon. *I wish he'd die.*

She twisted her hands around the back of the armchair: she had just remembered her father's eyes. M. Darbedat was bent over Pierre with a competent air; he had said "That's good!" the way someone says when they speak to invalids. He had looked and Pierre's face had been painted in the depths of his sharp, bulging eyes. *I hate him when he looks at him because I think he sees him.*

Eve's hands slid along the armchair and she turned to the window. She was dazzled. The room was filled with sunlight, it was everywhere, in pale splotches on the rug, in the air like a blinding dust. Eve was not accustomed to this diligent, indiscreet light which darted from everywhere, scouring all the corners, rubbing the furniture like a busy housewife and making it glisten. However, she went to the window and raised the muslin curtain which hung against the pane. Just at that moment M. Darbedat left the building; Eve suddenly caught sight of his broad shoulders. He raised his head and looked at the sky, blinking, then with the stride of a young man he walked away. *He's straining himself,* thought Eve, *soon he'll have a stitch in the side.* She hardly hated him any longer: there was so little in that head; only the tiny worry of appearing young. Yet rage took her again when she saw him turn the corner of the Boulevard St. Germain and disappear. *He's thinking about Pierre.* A little of their life had escaped from the closed room was being dragged through the streets, in the sun, among the people. *Can they never forget about us?*

The Rue du Bac was almost deserted. An old lady crossed the street with mincing steps; three girls passed, laughing. Then men, strong, serious men carrying briefcases and talking among themselves. *Normal people,* thought Eve, astonished at finding such a powerful hatred in herself. A handsome, fleshy woman ran heavily toward an elegant gentleman. He took her in his arms and kissed her on the mouth. Eve gave a hard laugh and let the curtain fall.

Pierre sang no more but the woman on the fourth floor was playing the piano; she played a Chopin Etude. Eve felt calmer; she took a step toward Pierre's room but stopped almost immediately and leaned against the wall in anguish; each time she left the room, she was panic-stricken at the thought of going back. Yet she knew she could live nowhere else: she loved the room. She looked around it with cold curiosity as if to gain a little time: this shadowless, odorless room where she waited for her courage to return. *You'd think it was a dentist's waiting room.* Armchairs of pink silk, the divan, the tabourets were somber and discreet, a little fatherly; man's best friends. Eve imagined those grave gentlemen dressed in light suits, all like the ones she saw at the window, entering the room, continuing a conversation already begun. They did not even take time to reconnoiter, but advanced with firm step to the middle of the room; one of them, letting his hand drag behind him like a wake in passing knocked over cushions, objects on the table, and was never disturbed by their contact. And when a piece of furniture was in their way, these poised men, far from making a detour to avoid it, quietly changed its place. Finally they sat down, still plunged in their conversation, without even glancing behind them. *A living-room for normal people*, thought Eve. She stared at the knob of the closed door and anguish clutched her throat: *I must go back. I never leave him alone so long.* She would have to open the door, then stand for a moment on the threshold, trying to accustom her eyes to the shadow and the room would push her back with all its strength. Eve would have to triumph over this resistance and enter all the way into the heart of the room. Suddenly she wanted violently to see Pierre; she would have liked to make fun of M. Darbedat with him. But Pierre had no need of her; Eve could not foresee the welcome he had in store for her. Suddenly she thought with a sort of pride that she had no place anywhere. *Normal people think I belong with them. But I couldn't stay an hour among them. I need to live out there, on the other side of the wall. But they don't want me out there.*

A profound change was taking place around her. The light had grown old and greying: it was heavy, like the water in a vase of flowers that hasn't been changed since the day before. In this aged light Eve found a melancholy she had long forgotten: the melancholy of an autumn afternoon that was ending. She looked around her, hesitant, almost timid: all that was so far away: there was neither day nor night nor season nor melancholy in the room. She vaguely recalled autumns long past, autumns of her childhood, then suddenly she stiffened: she was afraid of memories.

She heard Pierre's voice. "Agatha! Where are you?"

"Coming!" she cried.

She opened the door and entered the room.

The heavy odor of incense filled her mouth and nostrils as she opened her eyes and stretched out her hands—for a long time the perfume and the gloom had meant nothing more to her than a single element, acrid and heavy, as simple, as familiar as water, air or fire—and she prudently advanced toward a pale stain which seemed to float in the fog. It was Pierre's face: Pierre's clothing (he dressed in black ever since he had been sick) melted in obscurity. Pierre had thrown back his head and closed his eyes. He was handsome. Eve looked at his long, curved lashes, then sat close to him on the low chair. *He seems to be suffering,* she thought. Little by little her eyes grew used to the darkness. The bureau emerged first, then the bed, then Pierre's personal things: scissors, the pot of glue, books, the herbarium which shed its leaves onto the rug near the armchair.

"Agatha?"

Pierre had opened his eyes. He was watching her smiling. "You know, that fork?" he said. "I did it to frighten that fellow. There was *almost* nothing the matter with it."

Eve's apprehensions faded and she gave a light laugh. "You succeeded," she said, "You drove him completely out of his mind."

Pierre smiled. "Did you see? He played with it a long time, he held it right in his hands. The trouble is," he said, "they don't know how to take hold of things; they grab them."

"That's right," Eve said.

Pierre tapped the palm of his left hand lightly with the index of his right.

"They take with that. They reach out their fingers and when they catch hold of something they crack down on it to knock it out."

He spoke rapidly and hardly moving his lips; he looked puzzled.

"I wonder what they want," he said at last, "that fellow has already been here. Why did they send him to me? If they want to know what I'm doing all they have to do is read it on the screen, they don't even need to leave the house. They make mistakes. They have the power but they make mistakes. I never make any, that's my trump card. *Hoffka!*" he said. He shook his long hands before his forehead. "The bitch Hoffka! Paffka! Suffka! Do you want any more?"

"Is it the bell?" asked Eve.

"Yes. It's gone." He went on severely. "This fellow, he's just a subordinate. You know him, you went into the living-room with him."

Eve did not answer.

"What did he want?" asked Pierre. "He must have told you."

She hesitated an instant, then answered brutally. "He wanted you locked up."

When the truth was told quietly to Pierre he distrusted it. He had to be dealt with violently in order to daze and paralyze his suspicions. Eve preferred to brutalize him rather than lie: when she lied and he acted as if he believed it she could not avoid a very slight feeling of superiority which made her horrified at herself.

"Lock me up!" Pierre repeated ironically. "They're crazy. What can walls do to me. Maybe they think that's going to stop me. I sometimes wonder if there aren't two groups. The real one, the negro— and then a bunch of fools trying to stick their noses in and making mistake after mistake."

He made his hand jump up from the arm of the chair and looked at it happily.

"I can get through walls. What did you tell them?" he asked, turning to Eve with curiosity.

"Not to lock you up."

He shrugged. "You shouldn't have said that. You made a mistake too . . . unless you did it on purpose. You've got to call their bluff."

He was silent. Eve lowered her head sadly: *"They grab things!" How scornfully he said that—and he was right. Do I grab things too? It doesn't do any good to watch myself, I think most of my movements annoy him. But he doesn't say anything.* Suddenly she felt as miserable as when she was fourteen and Mme. Darbedat told her "You don't know what to do with your hands." She didn't dare make a move and just at that time she had an irresistible desire to change her position. Quietly she put her feet under the chair, barely touching the rug. She watched the lamp on the table—the lamp whose base Pierre had painted black—and the chess set. Pierre had left only the black pawns on the board. Sometimes he would get up, go to the table and take the pawns in his hands one by one. He spoke to them, called them Robots and they seemed to stir with a mute life under his fingers. When he set them down, Eve went and touched them in her turn (she always felt somewhat ridiculous about it). They had become little bits of dead wood again but something vague and incomprehensible stayed in them, something like understanding. *These are* his *things*, she thought. *There is nothing of mine in the room.* She had had a few pieces of furniture before; the mirror and the little inlaid dresser handed down from her grandmother and which Pierre jokingly called *"your* dresser." Pierre had carried them away with him; things showed their true face to Pierre alone. Eve could watch them for hours: they were unflaggingly stubborn and determined to deceive her, offering her nothing but their appearance—as they did to Dr. Franchot and M. Darbedat. *Yet,* she told herself with anguish, *I don't see them quite like my father. It isn't possible for me to see them exactly like him.*

She moved her knees a little: her legs felt as though they were crawling with ants. Her body was stiff and taut and hurt her; she felt it too alive, too demanding. *I would like to be invisible and stay here seeing him without his seeing me. He doesn't need me; I am useless in this room.* She turned her head slightly and looked at the wall above Pierre. Threats were written on the wall. Eve knew it but she could not read them. She often watched the big red roses on the wallpaper until they began to dance before her eyes. The roses flamed in shadow. Most of the time the threat was written near the ceiling, a little to the left of the bed; but sometimes it moved. *I must get up. I can't . . . I can't sit down any longer.* There were also white discs on the wall that looked like slices of onion. The discs spun and Eve's hands began to tremble: *Sometimes I think I'm going mad. But no,* she thought, *I can't go mad. I get nervous, that's all.*

Suddenly she felt Pierre's hand on her's.

"Agatha," Pierre said tenderly.

He smiled at her but he held her hand by the ends of his fingers with a sort of revulsion, as though he had picked up a crab by the back and wanted to avoid its claws.

"Agatha," he said, "I would so much like to have confidence in you."

She closed her eyes and her breast heaved. *I mustn't answer anything, if I do he'll get angry, he won't say anything more.*

Pierre had dropped her hand. "I like you, Agatha," he said, "but I can't understand you. Why do you stay in the room all the time?"

Eve did not answer.

"Tell my why."

"You know I love you," she said dryly.

"I don't believe you," Pierre said. "Why should you love me? I must frighten you: I'm haunted." He smiled but suddenly became serious. "There is a wall between you and me. I see you, I speak to you, but you're on the other side. What keeps us from loving? I think it was easier before. In Hamburg."

"Yes," Eve said sadly. Always Hamburg. He never spoke of their real past. Neither Eve nor he had ever been to Hamburg.

"We used to walk along the canal. There was a barge, remember? The barge was black; there was a dog on the deck."

He made it up as he went along; it sounded false.

"I held your hand. You had another skin. I believed all you told me. Be quiet!" he shouted.

He listened for a moment. "They're coming," he said mournfully.

Eve jumped up. "They're coming? I thought they wouldn't ever come again."

Pierre had been calmer for the past three days; the statues did not come. Pierre was terribly afraid of the statues even though he would never admit it. Eve was not afraid: but when they began to fly, buzzing, around the room, she was afraid of Pierre.

"Give me the ziuthre," Pierre said.

Eve got up and took the ziuthre: it was a collection of pieces of cardboard Pierre had glued together; he used it to conjure the statues. The ziuthre looked like a spider. On one of the cardboards Pierre had written "Power over ambush" and on the other, "Black." On a third he had drawn a laughing face with wrinkled eyes: it was Voltaire.

Pierre seized the ziuthre by one end and looked at it darkly.

"I can't use it any more," he said.

"Why?"

"They turned it upside down."

"Will you make another?"

He looked at her for a long while. 'You'd like me to, wouldn't you," he said between his teeth.

Eve was angry at Pierre. *He's warned every time they come: how does he do it? He's never wrong.*

The ziuthre dangled pitifully from the ends of Pierre's fingers. *He always finds a good reason not to use it. Sunday when they came he pretended he'd lost it but I saw it behind the paste pot and he couldn't fail to see it. I wonder if he isn't the one who brings them.* One could never tell if he were completely sincere. Sometimes Eve had the impression that despite himself Pierre was surrounded by a swarm of unhealthy thoughts and visions. But at other times Pierre seemed to invent them. *He suffers. But how much does he believe in the statues and the negro. Anyhow, I know he doesn't see the statues, he only hears them: when they pass he turns his head away; but he still says he sees them; he describes them.* She remembered the red face of Dr. Franchot: "But my dear madame, all mentally unbalanced persons are liars; you're wasting your time if you're trying to distinguish between what they really feel and what they pretend to feel." She gave a start. *What is Franchot doing here? I don't want to start thinking like him.*

Pierre had gotten up. He went to throw the ziuthre into the wastebasket: *I want to think like you,* she murmured. He walked with tiny steps, on tiptoe, pressing his elbows against his hips so as to take up the least possible space. He came back and sat down and looked at Eve with a closed expression.

"We'll have to put up black wallpaper," he said. "There isn't enough black in this room."

He was crouched in the armchair. Sadly Eve watched his meagre body, always ready to withdraw, to shrink: the arms, legs and head looked like retractable organs. The clock struck six. The piano downstairs was silent. Eve sighed: the statues would not come right away; they had to wait for them.

"Do you want me to turn on the light?"

She would rather not wait for them in darkness.

"Do as you please," Pierre said.

Eve lit the small lamp on the bureau and a red mist filled the room. Pierre was waiting too.

He did not speak but his lips were moving, making two dark stains in the red mist. Eve loved Pierre's lips. Before, they had been moving and sensual; but they had lost their sensuality. They were wide apart, trembling a little, coming together incessantly, crushing against each other only to separate again. They were the only living things in this blank face; they looked like two frightened animals. Pierre could mutter like that for hours without a sound leaving his mouth and Eve often let herself be fascinated by this tiny, obstinate movement.

I love his mouth. He never kissed her any more; he was horrified at contacts: at night they touched him—the hands of men, hard and dry, pinched him all over; the long-nailed hands of women caressed him. Often he went to bed with his clothes on but the hands slipped under the clothes and tugged at his shirt. Once he heard laughter and puffy lips were placed on his mouth. He never kissed Eve after that night.

"Agatha," Pierre said, "don't look at my mouth."

Eve lowered her eyes.

"I am not unaware that people can learn to read lips," he went on insolently.

His hand trembled on the arm of the chair. The index finger stretched out, tapped three times on the thumb and the other fingers curled: this was a spell. *It's going to start,* she thought. She wanted to take Pierre in her arms.

Pierre began to speak at the top of his voice in a very sophisticated tone.

"Do you remember Sao Paulo?"

No answer. Perhaps it was a trap.

"I met you there," he said, satisfied. "I took you away from a Danish sailor. We almost fought but I paid for a round of drinks and he let me take you away. All that was only a joke."

He's lying, he doesn't believe a word of what he says. He knows my name isn't Agatha. I hate him when he lies. But she saw his staring eyes and her rage melted. *He isn't lying,* she thought, *he can't stand it any more. He feels them coming; he's talking to keep from hearing them.* Pierre dug both hands into the arm of the chair. His face was pale; he was smiling.

"These meetings are often strange," he said, "but I don't believe it's by chance. I'm not asking who sent you. I know you wouldn't answer. Anyhow, you've been smart enough to bluff me."

He spoke with great difficulty, in a sharp, hurried voice. There were words he could not pronounce and which left his mouth like some soft and shapeless substance.

"You dragged me away right in the middle of the party, between the rows of black automobiles, but behind the cars there was an army with red eyes which glowed as soon as I turned my back. I think you made signs to them, all the time hanging on my arm, but I didn't see a thing. I was too absorbed by the great ceremonies of the Coronation."

He looked straight ahead, his eyes wide open. He passed his hand over his forehead very rapidly, in one spare gesture, without stopping his talking. He did not want to stop talking.

"It was the Coronation of the Republic," he said stridently, "an impressive spectacle of its kind because of all the species of animals that the colonies sent for the ceremony. You were afraid to get lost among the monkeys. I said among the monkeys," he repeated arrogantly, looking around him, "I could say *among the negroes!* The abortions sliding under the tables, trying to pass unseen, are discovered and nailed to the spot by my Look. The password is silence. To be silent. Everything in place and attention for the entrance of the statues, that's the countersign. Tralala . . ." he shrieked and cupped his hands to his mouth. "Tralalala, tralalalala!"

He was silent and Eve knew that the statues had come into the room. He was stiff, pale and distrustful. Eve stiffened too and both waited in silence. Someone was walking in the corridor: it was Marie the housecleaner, she had undoubtedly just arrived. Eve thought, *I have to give her money for the gas.* And then the statues began to fly; they passed between Eve and Pierre.

Pierre went "Ah!" and sank down in the armchair, folding his legs beneath him. He turned his face away; sometimes he grinned, but drops of sweat pearled his forehead. Eve could stand the sight no longer, this pale cheek, this mouth deformed by a trembling grimace; she closed her eyes. Gold threads began to dance on the red background of her eyelids; she felt old and heavy. Not far from her Pierre was breathing violently. *They're flying, they're buzzing, they're bending over him.* She felt a slight tickling, a pain in the shoulder and right side. Instinctively her body bent to the left as if to avoid some disagreeable contact, as if to let a heavy, awkward object pass. Suddenly the floor creaked and she had an insane desire to open her eyes, to look to her right, sweeping the air with her hand.

She did nothing; she kept her eyes closed and a bitter joy made her tremble: *I am afraid too,* she thought. Her entire life had taken refuge in her right side. She leaned towards Pierre without opening her eyes. The slightest effort would be enough and she would enter this tragic world for the first time. *I'm afraid of the statues,* she thought. It was a violent, blind affirmation, an incantation. She wanted to believe in their presence with all her strength. She tried to make a new sense, a sense of touch out of the anguish which paralysed her right side. She *felt* their passage in her arm, in her side and shoulder.

The statues flew low and gently; they buzzed. Eve knew that they had an evil look and that eyelashes stuck out from the stone around their eyes; but she pictured them badly. She knew, too, that they were not quite alive but that slabs of flesh, warm scales appeared on their great bodies; the stone peeled from the ends of their fingers and their palms were eaten away. Eve could not *see* all that: she simply thought of enormous women sliding against her, solemn and grotesque, with a human look and compact heads of stone. *They are bending over Pierre*—Eve made such a violent effort that her hands began trembling—*they are bending over me.* A horrible cry suddenly chilled her. They had touched him. She opened her eyes: Pierre's head was in his hands, he was breathing heavily. Eve felt exhausted: *a game*, she thought with remorse; *it was only a game. I didn't sincerely believe it for an instant. And all that time he suffered as if it were real.*

Pierre relaxed and breathed freely. But his pupils were strangely dilated and he was perspiring.

"Did you see them" he asked.

"I can't see them."

"Better for you. They'd frighten you," he said. "I am used to them."

Eve's hands were still shaking and the blood had rushed to her head. Pierre took a cigarette from his pocket and brought it up to his mouth. But he did not light it:

"I don't care whether I see them or not," he said, "but I don't want them to touch me: I'm afraid they'll give me pimples."

He thought for an instant, then asked, "Did you hear them?"

"Yes," Eve said, "it's like an airplane engine." (Pierre had told her this the previous Sunday.)

Pierre smiled with condescension. "You exaggerate," he said. But he was still pale. He looked at Eve's hands. "Your hands are trembling. That made quite an impression on you, my poor Agatha. But don't worry. They won't come back again before tomorrow." Eve could not speak. Her teeth were chattering and she was afraid Pierre would notice it. Pierre watched her for a long time.

"You're tremendously beautiful," he said, nodding his head. "It's too bad, too bad."

He put out his hand quickly and toyed with her ear. "My lovely devil-woman. You disturb me a little, you are too beautiful: that distracts me. If it weren't a question of recapitulation . . ."

He stopped and looked at Eve with surprise.

"That's not the word . . . it came . . . it came," he said, smiling vaguely. "I had another on the tip of my tongue . . . but this one . . . came in its place. I forget what I was telling you."

He thought for a moment, then shook his head.

"Come," he said, "I want to sleep." He added in a childish voice, "You know, Agatha, I'm tired. I can't collect my thoughts any more."

He threw away his cigarette and looked at the rug anxiously. Eve slipped a pillow under his head.

"You can sleep too," he told her, "they won't be back."

. . . Recapitulation . . .

Pierre was asleep, a candid, half-smile on his face; his head was turned to one side: one might have thought he wanted to caress his cheek with his shoulder. Eve was not sleepy, she was thoughtful: *Recapitulation*. Pierre had suddenly looked stupid and the word had slipped out of his mouth, long and whitish. Pierre had stared ahead of him in astonishment, as if he had seen the word and didn't recognize it; his mouth was open, soft: something seemed broken in it. He stammered. *That's the first time it ever happened to him: he noticed it, too. He said he couldn't collect his thoughts any more.* Pierre gave a voluptuous little whimper and his hand made a vague movement. Eve watched him harshly: *how is he going to wake up.* It gnawed at her. As soon as Pierre was asleep she had to think about it. She was afraid he would wake up wild-eyed and stammering. *I'm stupid,* she thought, *it can't start before a year; Franchot said so.* But the anguish did not leave her; a year: a winter, a springtime, a summer, the beginning of another autumn. One day his features would grow confused, his jaw would hang loose, he would half open his weeping eyes. Eve bent over Pierre's hand and pressed her lips against it: *I'll kill you before that.*

*Heinrich Böll was born in Cologne in 1917
and published his first novel,* The Train
Was on Time, *in 1956. Since then he has
written novels, short stories, essays, and
radio plays. While Böll's prose is popular in
Europe, his work has yet to receive widespread attention in the United States.*

*"Grown men, we tried to decipher the
misery but found no key; the sum of the
suffering was too big for the few whose guilt
was plain; there was still a remnant, and
this has not yet been allocated." How does
this statement relate to the soldier in "Pale
Anna"? What are the sources of the anxiety
dramatized in the story? Further Reading:*
The Train Was on Time (1956), Billiards
at Half-Past Nine (1962), The Clown
(1965).

GERMANY

Pale Anna

HEINRICH BÖLL

I didn't get home from the war till the
spring of 1950, and there was nobody left
in town whom I knew. Luckily for me,
my parents had left me some money. I
rented a room in town, and there I lay
on the bed, smoking and waiting and not
knowing what I was waiting for. The idea
of a job didn't appeal to me. I gave my
landlady money, and she bought what I
needed and cooked my meals. Whenever
she brought coffee or a meal to my room,
she stayed longer than I liked. Her son had
been killed at a place called Kalinovka,
and after coming into the room she
would set the tray down on the table and
come over to the darkish corner where my
bed was. That's where I dozed away my
time, stubbing out my cigarettes against
the wall so that the wallpaper around my
bed was covered with black smudges. My

Copyright © 1961 by Heinrich Böll. By permission of Joan Daves. Translated by Leila Ven-
newitz.

landlady was pale and skinny, and when her face hung there in the shadows over my bed I was scared of her. At first I thought she was queer in the head, for her eyes were very bright and large, and she kept on asking me about her son.

"Are you sure you didn't know him? The place was called Kalinovka —weren't you there?"

But I had never heard of a place called Kalinovka, and I would always turn toward the wall saying: "No, really, I can't remember him at all."

My landlady was not queer in the head, she was a very good soul, and I found her questioning painful. She questioned me very often, several times a day, and whenever I went into her kitchen I had to look at the photo of her son, a colored photo hanging over the sofa. He had been a laughing, fair-haired boy, and in the photo he was wearing an infantry dress-uniform.

"That was taken in the garrison town," said my landlady, "before they were sent to the front."

It was a half-length portrait: he was wearing his steel helmet, and behind him you could see some dummy castle ruins entwined with artificial creepers.

"He was a conductor," my landlady said, "a streetcar conductor. A good worker, my boy was." And then she would reach for the cardboard box of photographs that stood on her sewing table between the scraps of cloth for patching and the skeins of thread. And I had to go through piles of photos of her son: group pictures from his schooldays, each showing a boy seated in the middle with a slate between his knees, and on the slate a VI, a VII, and finally an VIII. In a separate packet, held together by a red rubber band, were the pictures of his first Communion: a smiling little boy in a formal black suit, holding an enormous candle and standing in front of a transparency painted with a golden chalice. Then came pictures of him as a mechanic's apprentice standing by a lathe, grimy-faced, his hands grasping a file.

"That wasn't the right kind of job for him," my landlady would say, "the work was too difficult." And she would show me the last photo taken before he was called up: he was wearing a streetcar conductor's uniform and standing beside a Number 9 streetcar at the terminus, where the tracks curve around in a loop, and I recognized the soda-pop stand where I had so often bought cigarettes, in the days before the war; I recognized the poplars, which are still there now, saw the villa, its gateway flanked by golden lions, which aren't there now, and I would remember the girl I used to think about so often during the war: she had been pretty, with a pale face and almond-shaped eyes, and she had always boarded the streetcar at the Number 9 terminus.

I would stare for a long time at the photo of my landlady's son at the Number 9 terminus and think of many things: of the girl, and

the soap factory where I was working in those days; I could hear the
screeching of the streetcar, see the pink soda-pop I used to drink at
the stand in summer, and the green cigarette ads, and again the girl.

"Maybe," the landlady would say, "you did know him after all."
I would shake my head and put the picture back in the box: it was a
shiny photo and looked like new, although by now it was eight years
old.

"No, no," I would say, "and I was never in Kalinovka—really I
wasn't."

I often had to go to the kitchen, and she often came to my room,
and all day I would think of the thing I wanted to forget: the war,
and I would toss my cigarette ash behind the bed and stub the glowing
tip out against the wall.

Sometimes, as I lay there in the evening, I could hear a girl's footsteps in the next room, or the Yugoslav who had the room next to the
kitchen; I could hear him swearing as he groped for the light switch
before going into his room.

It wasn't till I had been living there for three weeks and was holding Karl's picture for what must have been the fiftieth time that I
noticed that the streetcar he was standing beside, laughing, with his
leather pouch, wasn't empty. For the first time I looked closely at the
photo and saw that a girl sitting inside the streetcar, smiling, had got
into the snapshot. It was the pretty girl I used to think about so often
during the war. The landlady came up to me, studied the look on my
face, and said: "Now you recognize him, eh?" Then she stepped behind me and looked over my shoulder at the photo, and from close
behind me rose the smell of the fresh peas she was holding up in the
folds of her apron.

"No," I said quietly, "but the girl."

"The girl?" she said. "That was his fiancée, but maybe it's just as
well he never saw her again—."

"Why?" I asked.

She didn't answer, walked away, sat down on her chair by the
window, and went on shelling peas. Without looking at me she said:
"Did you know the girl?"

I kept a tight grip on the photo, looked at my landlady, and told
her about the soap factory, about the Number 9 terminus, and the
pretty girl that always got on there.

"Is that all?"

"Yes," I said. She tipped the peas into a sieve, turned on the
faucet, and I could see her thin back.

"When you see her you'll understand why it's a good thing he never
saw her again—."

"See her?" I asked.

She dried her hands on her apron, came over to me, and carefully
took away the photo. Her face seemed thinner than ever, her eyes

looked past me, but she gently laid her hand on my left arm. "She lives in the room next to yours, Anna does. We always call her our pale Anna because she's got such a white face. You really mean you haven't seen her yet?"

"No," I said, "I haven't, though I guess I've heard her a few times. What's wrong with her then?"

"I hate to tell you, but it's better for you to know. Her face has been completely destroyed, it's full of scars. She was thrown into a plate-glass window by a bomb blast. You won't recognize her."

That evening I waited a long while before hearing steps in the hall, but the first time I was wrong: it was the tall Yugoslav, who looked at me in astonishment when I dashed out into the hall. Embarrassed, I said "Good evening" and went back into my room.

I tried to imagine her face with scars, but I couldn't, and whenever I saw her face it was beautiful even with the scars. I thought about the soap factory, about my parents and about another girl I used to go out with often at that time. Her name was Elizabeth, but she was known as Puss, and when I kissed her she always laughed, and I felt like an idiot. I had written her post cards from the front, and she used to send me little parcels of homemade cookies that were always in crumbs by the time they arrived; she sent me cigarettes and newspapers, and in one of her letters she wrote: "Our boys will win the war all right, and I'm so proud you're one of them."

But I wasn't at all proud to be one of them, and when I was due for leave I didn't write and tell her, and I went out with the daughter of a tobacconist who lived in our apartment house. I gave the tobacconist's daughter soap sent me by my firm, and she gave me cigarettes, and we went to the movies together, and we went dancing, and once, when her parents were away, she took me up to her room, and I pressed her down onto the couch in the dark; but when I bent over her she switched on the light and smiled slyly up at me, and in the glare I saw Hitler on the wall, a colored photo, and all around Hitler's picture, arranged in the shape of a heart on the pink wallpaper, was a series of men wearing heroic expressions, post cards thumbtacked to the wall, and men in steel helmets cut out of illustrated weeklies. I left the girl lying there on the couch, lit a cigarette, and went away. Later on both girls wrote post cards to me at the front telling me I had behaved badly, but I didn't answer. . . .

I waited a long time for Anna, smoked one cigarette after another in the dark, thought of many things, and when the key was thrust into the lock I was too scared to get up and see her face. I heard her open the door to her room, move around in there humming softly to herself, and after a while I got up and waited in the hall. All of a sudden there was silence in her room, she wasn't moving about now, or humming, and I was afraid to knock. I could hear the tall Yugoslav walking up and down in his room, muttering to himself, could hear the water bubbling in my landlady's kitchen. But in Anna's room all was quiet, and through the open door of my own room I could see the black smudges from all those stubbed-out cigarettes on the wallpaper.

The tall Yugoslav was lying on his bed now, there were no more footsteps, I could just hear him muttering, the kettle in my landlady's kitchen had stopped bubbling, and I heard the sound of metal as the landlady put the lid on the coffeepot. Anna's room was still silent, and the thought struck me that later she would tell me everything she had been thinking about while I stood outside her door, and later on she did tell me everything.

I stared at a picture hanging beside the door: the silvery sheen of a lake and a naiad with wet fair hair emerging from it to smile at a young peasant hiding among some very green bushes. I could see part of the naiad's left breast, and her neck was very white and a little too long.

I don't know when it was, but some time later I took hold of the doorknob, and before I turned the knob and slowly pushed open the door I knew I had won Anna: her face was covered with little scars of a bluish sheen, the smell of mushrooms simmering in a pan came from her room, and I opened the door wide, laid my hand on Anna's shoulder, and tried to smile.

Stratis Myrivilis is often didactic. If he seems so in this story, what lesson is he trying to teach? Clearly the growth of the rose-tree is in some way emblematic of human growth. The tree embodied memories of the life of the house; when the rose-tree is cut down, and the house is gone, where may those memories be preserved? In what way is the rose-tree's struggle allegorical?

Myrivilis was born in Mytilini in 1892. He studied law and literature and took part in the Balkan War and World War I. A member of the Academy of Athens, he has published four novels and six collections of stories, as well as several volumes of nonfiction; his themes and subject matter are patriotically Greek. Further Reading: The Mermaid Madonna (1959).

GREECE

The Chronicle of an Old Rose-Tree

STRATIS MYRIVILIS

I want to write the story of a rose-tree. We lived together for sixteen long years, sixteen of the most significant years of my life, replete with harrowing events. I loved that rose-tree, for she was an old rose-tree with many branches and many roses. I feel she was fond of me, too. Such a feeling can blossom between a man and a tree.

I know a true, strange story, told me at Mytilini, a long time ago by some old convicts who were serving life-sentences at Castro. One of them had committed an appalling murder. He set fire to his house and burned up his wife and children —thinking the children weren't his. He

From *The Realm of Fiction: 61 Short Stories* [edited] by James B. Hall. Copyright © 1965 by McGraw-Hill, Inc. Used by permission of Mc-Graw-Hill Book Company. Translated by James B. Hall.

was the one who told me what happened, his eyes scalding in tears. Such a mystery is man.

During his long years behind bars, he was once acquainted with another convict, a lad who had come to prison fresh as a daisy, and had left as a man with gray hair. In the prison yard, the lad planted a walnut; it sprouted. All his thoughts and cares from that time on were for tending this plant. For fear that it might get hurt before it became strong he surrounded it with wire; he watered it with his ration of drinking water. Years passed, and the lad became a man; the walnut tree grew up, study and joyful.

One day the warden called the man into his office. He had been granted a pardon, and he could get his stuff and go. The prisoner stood speechless, amazed.

"And the walnut tree?" he stammered.

"What do you mean, the walnut tree?"

"I have no one in the world but that walnut tree," said the stunned prisoner.

The warden laughed.

"Well, what can we do? The walnut tree has to stay in its place."

The prisoner lowered his head; he could speak no more. He made a bundle of his rags. He sat on the horse-block facing the tree, and looked at it and shed bitter tears. Then a miracle happened, witnessed by all the prisoners who still tell of it. In the spring time of its life, all green with fresh, cool foliage, the tree began to wither. The leaves turned ragged and yellow; they crumpled completely, and fell. The trunk, too, dried down to its roots.

The old man's eyes were big with burning tears while he told me this story.

But my rose-tree did not commit suicide because of grief. A knife cut off her life.

But let me tell her story from the beginning.

When the Germans entered Athens, I received a telegram from my uncle who owned a house there. He was stranded on Lesbos, where he died a year later, at eighty-five. His telegram told me to move my wife and children immediately into his vacant home—before the Germans requisitioned it.

It was an old Athenian mansion, two stories, with eight large rooms, and a small garden in front. A beautiful trellis overarched the garden gate; each spring the fragrance of leaves and flowers filled all of Eresso Street. In the middle of the yard, in the middle of a white and gray marble patio, there stood the rose-tree: a grand rose-tree. How old was she? I seem to remember her from my student years when I went sometimes to visit my uncle. Three trunks grew upward for more than six feet, each trunk big as my arm. Higher, a multitude of branches were always loaded with roses, and gave off a strong scent, winter and summer, for the blossoms appeared the year round.

Around the courtyard was an iron fence, and the rose-tree hung over the spiked top, enticing the passers-by with her roses.

My uncle, the owner, was a strange old bachelor who spent most of his life in this house. As a student he came from the island, and he had rented one of its rooms from the first owner, an old French countess. Finally he bought the house and let her stay until she died of old age. She was a childless woman, alone, without anyone in the world. Alone, she idled her time reading old Parisian magazines, or she sometimes hummed Parisian songs of times past. She hummed them softly and heard them all alone. My uncle was like a parched reed; he lived alone there during and after his student years, an engineer by profession. He was slender, tall, austere, and always an elegant, meticulous dresser. He wore a fuzzed gray top hat, dangled a slim cane, and wrote in an impeccable *katharevousa*. He lived all alone beneath the gilded ceilings in those eight large rooms.

My uncle, it seemed, was also in love with the rose-tree; and she must have been the one and only love in his life, a life never adorned by a woman's grace. I say he must have been in love, for when the rose-tree grew tall above the iron spikes, the street urchins climbed the fence to gather the flowers. One day my uncle seized his pistol and chased them away—like a jealous lover. That day he called in workers to double the height of the iron fence so that no young rival could molest his tree.

In the sixteen years I lived there the rose-tree grew taller and taller, and put new branches over the second iron spikes.

My study was on the ground floor. It looked out a large window and into the yard. There the flowers of the rose-tree were abundant and rich in fragrance, for they were mayroses. To be sure the tree bloomed best in spring, but miraculously there were also blossoms in winter, in the fall, and all the year round. Even when Athens was covered with snow, she kept giving roses. If I opened my window, she spilled her branches into my room, soothing the bitter years of the occupation and the Communist reign of terror. She gave me great comfort. She was a symbol of hope. We were cold and hungry. We listened to the bullets ricochetting off the iron fence, but the rose-tree moved her blooming branches near us. No matter, we used to say. The sun will rise again, the grapes and peaches will bear fruit again, and love will come again to men who have become wild beasts, driven by a stupid, incomprehensible hate.

The streets had become deserted; no one dared show his face. One day a young woman passed by Exarcheia, hugging the walls. She held a bottle of milk. A rascal, on a rooftop, saw her, took aim and fired, killing her. Two or three neighbors rushed out to the rescue. Holding the bottle tight to her chest, she lived long enough to say:

"Give the milk to my child, neighbors . . ."

Then she died.

I cut a rose, put it in a vase on my desk, in memory of the unknown
mother. Later, peace gradually came and Greek ceased to fear Greek.
Spring came, and our rose-tree reddened from top to bottom. It was
so old, and yet so brimming with youth. Passers-by walked outside
and stopped on the sidewalk to look at it, as one looks at a beautiful
woman. They smiled at her and inhaled her strong fragrance. Couples
in love stopped and asked for a rose. My jealous uncle was no longer
alive, and those of us in the courtyard offered the blossoms. When we
were not at home, a young gallant clambered up the fence, and holding to an iron spike, reached out to steal a rose for his young, fair
Juliana.

Once I watched him from my desk, scampering down, jumping
back red of face, redder than his rose, looking all around for fear that
he might have been seen. The man behind the window saw him and
smiled, for he too had stolen roses and even now, on occasion, cannot
leave them alone. But the lad was not aware of that. The young man
was of heroic countenance, as if he had plucked an edelweiss from
the steepest peak of the Alps. For that, the man inside smiles at the
rose-tree whose pillaged branch is still moving. The two exchange an
understanding glance, so intended.

Then the good old days returned. Holy week came, churches
opened their doors, and the Athenians swallowed their tears and
waited for Easter. Then the maidens of the neighborhood came—and
Neapolis has many lovely maidens—knocked at our door and asked
that the rose-tree contribute to the decoration of the Epitaph. The
young myrrh-bearers left with their baskets full.

All this, and much more, belongs to the Annals of the Rose-tree. I
wonder how much more interesting the old rose-tree's own diary
would be, starting with the time when the hands of the young French
aristocrat first planted and watered the bush every evening from the
well of the yard. Those hands which aged year by year within the
eight empty rooms, withered, disfigured, died, and disintegrated many
years ago.

And so did that young islander, the student of the Polytechnic, for
forty years the only occupant of the house, who lived, grew, and
grayed near the rose-tree. That jealous lover of hers who once when
he saw a flock of urchins plundering its roses, chased them, waving his
pistol. At that time he was a high state official, with a white mustache
and a thin cane with a silver handle. He remained faithful to our rose-
tree till he died.

Our old rose-tree also had its heroic and tragic days. Every March
25 of our four-year occupation by the Germans, every October 28 of
our cruel occupation, my children and all young school children, cut
all the roses to take to the tomb of the Unknown Soldier. Schoolboys
and girls marched in procession with bouquets held high, and with
the National Anthem on their lips. All around, bullets from the
machine guns hissed; the armored car tracks chewed Athen's asphalt.

But our children advanced in formation, still singing. They looked hungry and gaunt, their legs emaciated, the bloom of youth gone from their faces.

But high in their hands, above their heads, the roses shone red. The conquerors grabbed the flowers, trampled them furiously. The children returned dusty, dirty, ragged, bruised, beaten by rifle butts. But their great eyes shone with the Greek flame that burned inside them day and night.

Then came the blackest December that ever hovered over Athens. For forty days mortars boomed and burst, shattering the branches of the rose-tree. Neapolis was stunned, silent in fear and horror. One day the old rose-tree stooped: below her branches the sidewalk by our gate was red. It was not the red paint with which the maniacs splashed walls with their slogans of fratricide. It was blood. Real, warm, oozing blood gushing from large wounds from a street that had known only the joyful shouts of children. Now the street echoed the moans of murdered men, six or seven innocent persons dying there.

After their homes had been blown up by the maniacs, these men had started from a corner of Athens, roving the streets, seeking shelter. A little bell hung from the top of our yard gate. My wife heard the bell ringing, ringing furiously. Germans, she thought, and was afraid to open the gate. When the row ceased, she found in front of our gate a heap of wretched, bloody corpses. These men had been ringing the little bell, seeking refuge.

But our old rose-tree was still there. Her roses spread and heartened us. Roses are everywhere, she said to us. It is enough to push aside the leaves and thorns, she kept telling us. Always there is a cool spring, delicate and pure, waiting, its hands filled with flowers. Even in the heartaches of men there is green in the heart of winter. Heave open your soul's windows, and they will find a way of placing their bouquets inside. Deep inside.

When I first occupied the house, the rose-tree filled the whole square of the yard, in the plot of ground at the center of the flagstone patio. Then two significant events occurred in that space. First, a new little plant sprung from the soil; no one knew what it was. Partaking of the water we gave the rose-tree, it kept growing under the rose's shade. When the new plant was about knee-high, a friend who knew about trees told us that by its leaves it looked like a plum-tree. Each year it grew fast, taking its water and nourishment from the same soil that fed the thick roots of the rose-tree. With the years, its slender trunk made its way through the branches that shaded it and popped out in full view of the sun it had been reaching for. It had become a grown tree, a strong, powerful tree that selfishly overwhelmed our rose-tree.

One spring, for the first time, its foliage filled with white blossoms, and then its branches bowed with red plums. It was bedecked with fruit like a Christmas tree. It covered the rose-tree, spread it branches triumphantly above the yard, and hung its plums invitingly over the iron fence. The street urchins no longer climbed the fence for roses. Suspended from the fence, they reached the tips of the plum branches and filled their pockets with unripe plums. The shady branches of the plum had shrouded the rose-tree which had accorded it hospitality for so many years, and the rose-tree began to wither. The other was a new life, rampant, straining for light and juices; under the earth its roots swelled strong and avid, clutched the roots of the rose-tree, hugging them, twining around them, and sucking their soil. I watched this drama day after day. Now the plum tree soared in full beauty and untrammeled youth, spread its branches everywhere, conquered air, and light, and also conquered the soil.

Our rose-tree began to wither. Most of the trunks began to rot, and I cut them to rid the space of dried up branches. Each spring a few new shoots sprang from the roots, but they made little progress. They were sickly and feeble. They grew a little, then they wilted and withered. The remaining stalk produced only a few flowers. There was no longer the abundance of past years. But the rose-tree persisted in giving forth some flowers, in revealing her presence even in this desperate battle. Finally she made the great decision. She imitated her adversary. From a large, thick bush, she became a climbing rose. She gathered all her remaining forces into upward growth and began to climb the plum tree, in two twining tresses, like two green snakes that twirled upward in search of the sun. To succeed in this, she used as support the very stout trunk of the plum tree. She clung to it and began to climb among its limbs. It was a relentless struggle to the end. Each time the two stalks gained growth, they stopped to rest at that step, on some node of the tree, and then sprang upward again.

We saw this metamorphosis and thought that that was the end, that we would no longer see roses. Then we stopped paying attention to what was happening. By now the rose was so entwined with the plum tree that we could no longer tell them apart.

Meanwhile, the plum tree grew taller, as high as our two-story house. On the second floor, above my study, was my son's study. I rarely went up there because I did not want to intrude while he worked. But one day, when he was away in the country, I entered the room and stood at the window. When I opened the outside shutters, suddenly a branch whisked in and a fragrance caressed my face. It was a large cluster of roses. They had bloomed in the crown of the plum tree, in the splendid sun, a trophy, and a shout of victory.

It was something thrilling.

From then on, high up in the branches of the plum tree, we saw more roses. The last roses kept blooming.

The plum tree was the first, most significant event in the life of the old rose-tree. The second event was something more modest, but quite pleasing.

In the enclosed square where the two trees stood, from the year that we moved into the house, there grew two night-blooming plants. They sprang up each year, on opposite sides of the square, one to the left, one to the right. Who knows where the seeds came from? Each year the two stems emerged. They were fragile, succulent, full of sap and vigor. When fall came, they put out red buds which opened at dusk and gave forth a strong aroma all through the night. It was a sweet aroma that one could almost taste. In bloom they stood on each side of the rose and the plum tree like two large lighted candlesticks. They withered with winter, and we raked them away with the leaves. In time the soil was trampled on, and the earth became hard as concrete. The plants poked up again, nevertheless, each late spring, all freshness anew, growing within a few days and becoming loaded with buds. We had these annuals all sixteen years that we had the house.

Now the old mansion has been torn down in order to raise a new building. Down came the double iron fence that protected the rose-tree from her passing lovers. And down came the plum tree, chopped down, falling with the rose-tree in its embrace. So were the two luminous night-blooming plants extinguished forever. And with them died the romantic memory of the old French countess, whose spirit till then only the flowers of the rose-tree evoked. And so remembrance of the tall, slender old bachelor died, too, he who guarded the roses with his loaded revolver.

In this short story I wanted to save some vestiges from the life of sixteen years, a life filled with fears and griefs, and with the joys and anguish of children and trees.

To what degree can freedom be granted, and to what degree must it be earned? Is freedom the absence of restraint? Does innocence lie in the judgment of others? Is justice a matter of an external and essentially uninvolved process? Are justice and innocence necessary ingredients of individual freedom? Agnar Thórdarson explores these questions in "If Your Sword Is Short." Does he provide satisfactory answers for the narrator? For the reader? Does the story justify the last sentence?

Although Thórdarson is well known in his native Iceland, only two of his stories have been translated into English. Thórdarson was born in Reykjavík in 1917 and studied in London, France, and the United States. He earned a degree in Icelandic language and literature from the University of Iceland and is now a librarian at the National Library, where he combines librarianship with play writing for the new Icelandic theater and radio. Further Reading: The Cock Crows Twice (1949), Atoms and Madams (1967).

If Your Sword Is Short

AGNAR THÓRDARSON

I was on my way to Keflavík. It was a lucky thing for me that I hadn't returned the car key. I would call Rikki up first thing in the morning. Jagged waves of barren lava rushed past me furiously— but now nothing should stop me. I moved back and forth in my seat as the car reached top speed.

There ahead of me I caught sight of a man coming toward me on a bicycle. A man on a bicycle looks ridiculous, like a monkey—or a spider . . . He had some-

Reprinted by permission of the author. Translated by Paul Schach.

thing tied on the fender behind him. A workingman with a weather-beaten face, grimy hands and stooped shoulders, he bent forward as he worked the pedals. Poor devil, he was unsteady on the bicycle. Odd that he should dismount from his bike to take off his hat, a brimless old thing, and bow to me as to the sun god. Or was he shaking his fist at me?

It really didn't matter. If he had been Markús, I would have steered straight at him at full speed. Or if I met Markús now in his expensive limousine, I would drive right into him, and Markús would be killed —an accident. Yes, obviously an accident. I would look down on his dead body, and then everything would be finished. This great man Markús, killed on a public highway—truly distressing, indeed . . .

And suddenly there were some horses coming out of a little depression—horses roaming about at night, electrifying creatures with a weird shyness in their eyes that can frighten people out of their senses. Do they have second sight? Can they see our wraiths?

Something crashed against the car. I was thrown forward over the steering wheel. For a second I must have lost consciousness, but I heard a cracking sound the moment the car overturned. Then there was silence. When I crawled out of the car, the man I had passed on the bicycle was standing over me, looking at me in amazement. He asked me whether I were injured. But I said that no bones were broken, and I was able to get to my feet without help. No, I wasn't hurt, just scratched a little bit, and I walked right around to the front of the car.

The man followed me and said, "That was a crime to drive like that."

His face was lean and stern-looking.

"You might just as well have hit me . . ."

I didn't answer him, but examined the horse in front of me. He was trying to get up on his feet, but his back was disabled and one hindleg was smashed. His forelegs were uninjured, and he was able to raise himself in front. He was a sorrel, with white spots on his forelegs and chest and a star on his forehead. I could see myself in his flashing eyes, and when I stroked his neck, he trembled and his skin quivered.

"You might just as well have hit me," the man repeated.

"And what if I had?" I snarled furiously.

I would have liked to challenge this stranger to single combat and kill him—for the sake of the horse. But the horse was doomed. His spine was obviously wrenched and twisted out of joint. The man walked back and forth in a semi-circle some distance away and glared at me stealthily: we were enemies.

I spoke softly to the horse, and he quieted down somewhat, but his neck was beginning to sweat profusely and his limp ears moved feebly back and forth.

An automobile stopped up on the highway, and a man and woman came running. They were dressed as though they had just come from a party, the woman with a fur stole over her shoulders.

"What happened?" they asked, stopping beside the man.

"You can see for yourself," he replied, pointing to the horse, broken and bloody.

"How did it happen?" asked the husband of the woman, and she screamed softly.

The workingman pointed to me.

"He was driving like crazy. I had to throw myself off my bike to keep from being killed, and a second later there was the horse—such reckless driving—completely insane, criminal . . ."

He pointed to his bicycle, which was lying a short distance away, muddy and half-rusted, with a bunch of rhubarb tied on the back fender. And he pointed to a strip of marsh on the other side of the road, where hoof tracks could still be seen glistening in the mudweeds in the brackish water. The other horses had drifted out into the heath and were grazing again. More people arrived, and someone suggested telephoning. They looked at me curiously, and I took a handkerchief out of my pocket and wiped away the blood which oozed from a small cut high on my cheek. I threw the handkerchief away angrily. The workingman had just finished telling his story about the bicycle for the second time, and now he pointed to the horse and said it would have to be shot to put it out of its misery.

"Don't you think it's possible to put the leg in a cast?" asked the woman with the stole.

I laughed. And the people stared at me in astonishment. All of a sudden I had become their common property. These people had nothing in common except me, the guilty culprit who mustn't escape. They had caught me, and they were rather proud of themselves for it. I mustn't get away. Their hostility toward me had joined them into a brotherhood.

Then I pulled the bottle out of my coat pocket and took a little swig in full view of my audience. For my sake and for their sake. To draw a clear line of demarcation between good and evil, so that these people would feel better when they went to bed and could say to themselves: "That fellow was a dirty dog!" (For they themselves were faultless and were always kind to dumb animals).

"He's dead drunk . . . he's still drinking . . . the pig . . . Why don't the police come?"

I looked the people right in the face and sneered. They had no idea how amusing I found them. I felt as though I could control their every action; I could cause them to talk or rebuke them to silence at will. It was just like being God, or a clever politician, who looks down upon the rabble and through the newspapers, the radio, and the moving pictures makes them think at all times exactly as he pleases . . .

I took the bottle, brandished it above my head in order to be as impressive as possible, and hurled it out into the marsh. I was interested in seeing which one would wade out to secure the evidence against me.

But just at that moment the police arrived. Two plump, red-cheeked, rustic-looking policemen climbed out of a jeep. They pushed the people back authoritatively, looked first at the horse, and then went over to the car.

The people, the audience, retired in a semi-circle from me as if to point out the one who was playing the chief role here, the villain.

One of the policemen took a black notebook from his pocket and began to write in it. He looked at the license number and said:

"Were you in this car?"

I nodded my head.

"Answer distinctly 'yes' or 'no'," said the policeman, touching the peak of his policeman's cap with his pencil.

"Yes," I said, "I was driving this car. I regard that as obvious."

"For the police nothing is obvious," he said in a bookish manner as though he had just completed a course in criminology, and wrote something in the book.

"Are you the owner of the car?"

"No," I replied, "I took it without the owner's leave."

"What do you mean by that?"

I said that it was a simple matter. I had taken the car without the owner's leave. Wasn't that perfectly good Icelandic?

"You mean by that, that you stole it?"

"I mean nothing except what I say," I answered.

I gazed around me with as much disdain as I could muster. But the policeman said that that would naturally come to light later, and looked with a self-important smirk at the people, who now stared at me with even greater curiosity than before.

The workingman had lifted up his bicycle.

He said, "The key is in the car."

The policeman abruptly stopped writing, and the one who meanwhile had been inspecting the automobile called that that was correct, the key was in the car.

But I remained silent and gave no explanations as to how I had obtained the key. That seemed to me all of a sudden to be a far too long and complicated matter.

Both the policemen examined the automobile carefully. One of them had a tape measure, with which he measured how far the automobile had gone off the road. I heard the people saying that I was drunk and that a blood test ought to be made.

The woman with the stole called out, "He threw a bottle over there," and she pointed out into the marsh near by.

The policeman who had questioned me said, "We ought to take the bottle along."

The husband of the woman fetched it for him.

Then I had to answer several more questions. They examined the cut on my temple and said that it was quite shallow, merely a scratch, but it was still bleeding a little, and so I tore a piece off my shirt-sleeve to stop the trickle of blood.

They also examined the horse, and the people said it was a shame to let it suffer so long unnecessarily. They checked its earmarks, and the horse was now very quiet and no longer struggled to get away, but its neck was dripping sweat.

And it was decided that one policeman should stay with the horse while the other one was to take me to the police station and send back a man with a gun.

The people began to leave one by one, and the policeman took me by the arm and led me to the jeep. I looked at the people through the window of the car, and I realized that they were happy that I had been apprehended. People always have a feeling of satisfaction when the guilty are apprehended. Yes, I understood that perfectly.

At the police station I sat before the desk-sergeant and listened to the policeman make his report. And when he came to the question of theft and the secrecy about the key, I became filled with suspense, just as though I didn't know the answer myself. Then followed some dry technical facts about the speed and condition of the car and about the circumstance that it had been thrown 3.42 meters off the road in spite of the fact that I had obviously applied the brakes the instant the collision occurred . . .

The policeman went on to tell about the workingman who had had to jump from his bicycle to save himself from being killed by the car going at breakneck speed. He stated the man's name and address, and he picked up the bottle and set it on the table before the desk-sergeant. The desk-sergeant looked up from his papers, pushed his glasses up on his forehead, and said in a firm voice:

"Hilmar Jóhannsson, do you admit that you were under the influence of alcohol?"

I replied that I didn't deny it.

The desk-sergeant said, "In that case I see no reason for making a blood test."

He looked at me again and said, "Well, there are many things we've got to clear up in this case, but perhaps you'll be more talkative tomorrow after a few hours in jail."

He picked up a silver snuffbox, tapped the cover lightly with his fingers, held it up to his nostrils, and inhaled deeply.

"That will be cell number seven," he said in a hollow nasal tone, staring into space with a rigid facial spasm while the nicotine took effect.

The policeman searched my pockets and emptied them of their contents. Everything was recorded and entered in the desk-sergeant's complaint book. I had left my topcoat lying in the automobile.

Then the policeman took me by the arm and led me out. He took me down a dark stone stairway, and the hot acrid stench of urine, putrefaction, and sweat which engulfed us choked and nauseated me.

Down below, the jailer took charge of me. I hadn't heard him coming until he was standing right beside us because he was wearing some sort of homemade rag shoes. He had on a collarless shirt with a gilt collar button at his neck, and he looked very tired. There was something about the appearance of his eyes which disturbed me. He was almost completely bald, and his skull-bones were quite prominent. I thought that most probably no other sun ever shone upon him than this electric prison-sun. His face was very white, and the wrinkles were filled with dirt.

He was having trouble with the knot in one of my shoes. I looked down at his fingers, which were stubby and fat like those of a child. And suddenly he stopped trying to untie the knot and jerked the shoe off.

He had laid his newspaper on the bench while he was working on my shoes. It was the weekly paper *Fálkinn*. I was just on the point of asking him to lend it to me when I remembered that I was a prisoner, and so I remained silent.

He also had me take off my coat and said, "And your belt too, my boy."

And then suddenly on of the inmates burst out laughing. "Let him hang himself. Let him hang himself. I dare you to—"

The jailer opened the door to cell number seven for me and motioned for me to enter. It was a very small cell, which contained only a narrow wooden bench fastened to the wall. One the bench lay a dark-red, folded blanket.

Standing in my stocking feet, I asked the jailer for a drink of water. I was very thirsty.

The jailer left the cell door open while he went to get some water in a plastic jug, and I took that as an indication that he didn't intend to treat me harshly.

When the jailer returned with the water, I remarked that it was quite cozy here.

"Cozy, cozy!" screamed the furious man on the other side of the partition. "I've asked Steingrímur a hundred times for an extra blanket, but that ox beats you and maims you and then lets you catch your death of cold to boot."

The jailer said, "I won't let you have any more covers to piss in. You can use the pot under the bench."

Then my cell door was locked from the outside, and I splashed what water I hadn't drunk in my face.

The prisoner in the cell next to mine demanded a drink of water too since I had got one, but the jailer absolutely refused to give him any water, and the other inmates shouted that he shouldn't give that devil a single drop. They demanded that he be thrown into the hole; he wasn't fit to be around other people.

The jailer scolded and cursed them. He said they were all branded with the same mark, as far as that was concerned. He said we weren't fit to live with normal, decent people; that's why we were here. He walked down the corridor, and then I heard him unfolding his paper.

I lay down and breathed the foul odor from the coarse blanket. I told myself that that was the smell I would have to get used to, the smell of prisoners.

My vehement neighbor on the other side of the partition had calmed down again, and now he wished to talk to me.

"Shut your mouth, shut your big mouth," screamed our fellow-inmates.

But my neighbor paid no attention to them. He said he had the backing of some influential people, and that he would take cruel revenge on the police.

"They'll pay plenty for this," he said.

He was a highly-regarded citizen in a responsible position, related by marriage to ministers of state and bank directors.

"My sister is married to the brother of Sigvaldi, the bank director," he said. "I'm going to take terrible vengeance."

"Be quiet, Lasi," called one of the prisoners. "Shut your big mouth and go to sleep."

And then suddenly the banging and screaming began anew. The prisoners cursed each other and pounded on the walls and doors so that it seemed as if the whole jail were shaking.

But that lasted just a short time, and soon afterwards I heard Lasi stretch out on his bench. I thought I heard him sobbing and muttering to himself that his wife was having a baby. But I paid no attention to him.

I tried to sleep, but the events of the evening gave me no peace. Again and again they penetrated into my consciousness, with all kinds of nightmarish twists. I thought I saw Frú Lilja coming to me in a nightgown, her face pale and tense, and she was terribly eager to keep me from being caught—she wanted to keep me hidden in a little closet under the stairway at her house. She said there were plots against my life, but that I would be out of danger in the closet under the stairs—and she came crawling to me with food where I lay on my straw mat. But then a large number of candles tumbled out of her lap—half-burned wax candles. Suddenly Markús came upon us. He put on thin rubber gloves and pointed a gun at me.

"Don't shoot, don't shoot," I screamed.

And then it was I who was holding the pistol and squeezing the trigger time after time. Markús just stood there and laughed. The gun was merely a cuspidor which Vera had kept as a keepsake and which she had used because the question of contagion had been uncertain for a long time after her operation: a tin receptacle as small and flat as a pint pocket flask and equipped with a spring lock . . .

I tossed restlessly and got awake on the hard bench, fell asleep once more, and was immediately back in this turmoil of dreams: Markús was choking in my arms, and I had a firm grip on his head and neck . . .

Everything became confused and jumbled together, and over everything shone a white light in a grating which penetrated my dreams with its unreal brightness.

Now and then I had the feeling that I was scattered far and wide in many pieces, just as though Killer-Jón had torn off my limbs . . .

The jailer was standing over me and shaking me. It was time for me to be taken before the examining magistrate.

I got to my feet, sweaty and disheveled, ran my hands through my hair several times, and felt the dried gore on my temple. One foot ached.

The jailer handed me my shoes, my belt, and my coat. And now for the first time I realized what it was I didn't like about this man's face: he was completely without eyebrows. He looked as though his face had been singed. I turned away from him.

I was led up the stairs again. The iron door closed behind me on screeching hinges. Down into the dungeon filtered the mild brightness of daylight. A June day, and outside the noise of traffic, the hustle and bustle of people, the shouts of the newspaper boys: an early morning in Reykjavík, when the day is still young and impersonal. No. now I had also become confused in the days. Was it Thursday or Friday morning?

I was taken away in a car.

And as I was walking up the path to the chambers of the judge, through the garden with birches and clumps of mountain ash, I happened to glance at the fountain, which I remembered from a long time ago when the house had been a private dwelling. It was a swan which spouted water in a glittering spray. But the swan was no longer spouting, and there was no rainbow surrounding it like splendid ornamental plumage. It had become rusty around the neck . . . Frú Karitas would no longer come out on the balcony and call: Pingó, Pingó . . . a fantastic name which stuck in my mind even though events of great importance slipped away from me: Pingó. I suddenly became quite distracted by this unexpected recollection. And even when I was sitting before the judge and mechanically answering questions about my name and address, my thoughts were out in the garden, which I could see through the window. I recalled how Frú Karitas used to take afternoon walks with Pingó, wearing his shiny dog-tag, on a leash. She was sway-backed and strutted like a peacock; her face was white and severe. She carried a walking stick which was inlaid with silver, and she always wore black because her children had all been born dead. We kids thought Pingó was only a half-grown pup and we wanted to pat him on the back, but Frú Karitas jerked the line and said harshly, "Pingó!"

I heard the judge saying, "We have secured a statement from Richard Hermannsson which establishes that your assertion is correct and that there is no question of theft involved here."

"Yes, of course," I said without giving a thought to what he was saying.

The window blinds were pulled halfway down because of the sun, and the light which was reflected from the large green-topped table before me made it difficult to see the faces of the judge and the court secretary clearly. The judge seemed to be wearing sun glasses, but I was deceived by the fact that the skin beneath his eyes was very dark. The dazzling green reflection was thrown against the white walls, and over by the door stood the policeman, black and silent.

I suddenly felt very warm.

Again I had to look out the window, out at the garden which had been an enchanted world to me in my childhood, the garden with its spouting swan and the clump of ash trees in a bed of white flowers which extended out from the house along the steps and the footpath.

I had once ventured into the garden on an expedition of exploration. I was stealing up the footpath strewn with snail and mussel shells and with tulips on both sides of it when I heard Pingó on the front lawn. I was frightened by his barking, and for safety's sake I bent down to pick up a small stone. Just at that moment Frú Karitas appeared between the Grecian pillars on the balcony.

"Are you throwing stones at my dog, you street brat?"

I squeezed the stone tightly in my hand and shouted, "I'm not a street brat. I just wanted to look at the swan."

But I slowly raised my arm, and in the next moment the stone flew from my hand. The dog let out a piteous yelp, and I took to my heels and fled, fled as fast as I could, over the tulip bed, down the shell-strewn footpath, and out of the garden. It seemed to me as though shouts and yells followed me like the clatter of horses' hoofs.

From a distance I heard the judge reading something about me. I asked him what he had said. He repeated that I was to be deprived of my driver's license for a period of several weeks in addition to the fine.

I merely nodded my head.

The secretary sat at an angle from me, and his pen scratched as he wrote.

I thought, "He ought to buy himself a new fountain pen."

I looked into the face of the judge and said, "I confess my guilt unconditionally."

For a moment the judge looked nonplussed, then he passed his hand over his hair and said with composure, "Yes, your case is about to be concluded."

I felt a sense of relief. I wanted as quickly as possible to get to the place where I was to atone for my guilt. And I smiled to myself as I thought that as a child I had fled from this garden, this very garden into which I had now been led to hear judgment pronounced upon me. In a certain sense that seemed symbolic. And I would not even have been surprised if Frú Karitas, risen from her bed of earth, had been sitting there and pointing with her stiff-jointed fingers to the letter of the law: "—You are guilty."

Yes, I was guilty in a far graver and more comprehensive sense than anyone could suspect. I had been mistaken about Markús; it was I and not he who was guilty. One day I would be led out into the bright sunlight, stood against a wall, and shot—

No appeal, no reprieve, nothing but a sentence hard and merciless in its justice . . .

I heard the judge ask me, Hilmar Jóhannsson, if the proceedings had been properly recorded; and I answered in the affirmative even though I had not followed the reading of the secretary.

Then he asked me to sign my name and called the policeman to witness it.

The judge arose and said, "Well, this case is concluded."

He went to the window and pulled up the blind. The secretary leaned back and began to pick his teeth with a pin. I could hear the shouting of the children playing in the street—

The policeman had opened the door wide.

I stood up and said, "Where am I to be taken?"

I saw immediately that they were amused at this question, and I choked back a sudden surge of rage.

The judge looked at me from the white window and said, "Taken? Nowhere. You're at liberty to go anywhere you want to as far as we're concerned. You're a free man."

"Free," I repeated. "Free?"

"This has all been a severe strain on your nerves," said the judge, "but for us it was just part of the day's work. Fortunately for you it was only a horse this time . . ."

"It could just as well have been a human being. I came within an inch of killing a human being."

"In this case an inch was as good as a mile," replied the judge, growing impatient.

The secretary with the pin in his hand looked at the policeman and laughed.

"I'm guilty," I said, "I'm guilty . . ."

"Take him out," said the judge with a motion toward the police-man, and then quickly looked down again at his fingernails.

"I demand—I demand justice," I shouted as the policeman took a firm grip on my shoulder and led me back out again.

The court clerk sprang to his feet with a laugh and slammed the door shut in my face. I was outside once more.

The sunshine poured down over the garden with its yellow laugh-ing dandelions. But there was no laughter in my heart. I was deeply hurt and depressed. I had been looking forward to the sight of the sky from behind prison walls, and to carving little figurines from the bones in the prisoners' soup. But now everything was taken away from me. Or stated more correctly: everything was given to me, but in such a way that I felt it wasn't mine, that I didn't deserve it.

I had wanted to earn the right to my freedom by working for it, by sacrificing myself. Then I would have been able to enjoy the sim-plest things of life.

I was overcome with melancholy and despair. I felt that wherever I stepped, everything would wither and die in my tracks.

I was free. I was utterly free, and that was like being dissolved into nothingness.

"Wedding Eve" is written almost entirely in dialogue. The setting has a cinematic quality, and the narrative voice interrupts only to qualify, to interpret. Despite the largely dramatic presentation, could we do without the narrative intrusion? At times it is difficult to distinguish which sister is speaking. Is there variation in their dialogue? Are their personalities distinctly individual? What effect is produced when the sisters offer alternate phrases in one continuous sentence?

Bryan MacMahon was born in the market town of Listowel in 1909. He was educated at St. Patrick's College and became a schoolmaster at Listowel Boys' National School. A novelist, poet, short story writer, dramatist, and folklorist, MacMahon published his first book, The Lion-Tamer, *in 1949. His play* Bugle in the Blood *was produced by the Abbey Theatre. Further Reading:* The Lion-Tamer and Other Stories *(1949),* The Red Petticoat and Other Stories *(1955).*

IRELAND

Wedding Eve

BRYAN MACMAHON

Softly: 'Freda, are you awake?'

The girl in the moonlit bed sat up gracefully. Quietly she said: 'Yes, Anna, I am awake.'

Her younger sister, Anna, came into the room. She had a heavy coat slung across her nightdress. Noiselessly she closed the door behind her. In mid-room she stopped. Her hands were joined prayerfully in front of her. She stood at a little distance from the end of the bed. Instinctively, her fingers reached out and

From the book *The Red Petticoat and Other Stories* by Bryan MacMahon. Copyright, ©, 1955 by Bryan MacMahon. Reprinted by permission of the author and E. P. Dutton & Co., Inc.

touched the wedding dress that was hanging on a shoulder on the great wardrobe door.

'What is it, Anna?'

'It's very quiet now, isn't it?'

Freda did not reply. Anna went to the window. She looked out to where the fall of grassy ground was. She looked at the lake and the island it contained. The moonlight had touched the castle in the island and was making a white mist on the mountains far away. Her standing there quenched a good deal of the moonlight. Over her shoulder she said: 'Do you think it will be all right?'

Thoughtfully: 'Yes!' Suddenly: 'Why do you ask?'

'This is the night to ask over and over again "Are you sure?"'

Freda did not reply.

Anna turned. Her fingers idled with some articles on an occasional table that lay in full moonlight. Half to herself she said: 'Old, new; borrowed, blue.' She lifted a trinket and dropped it heavily.

Freda said: 'I have reasoned it out. Insofar as a woman is able to reason things out'—she made a noise like laughter—'what with all the tides and winds of her body and mind. One day a week ago when I was at peace I walked to the lakeside where the branches were thickest. No wind blew. There was no sound, only the hollow pecking of the fish at the surface of the water. I asked myself: "Are you sure?" Just as you have asked me now. I answered myself: "Yes, I am sure!"'

'Things have happened since then, Freda. Trifles, I grant you! What about now?'

'*Now* is not so important. Of that I am certain. Now I am disorientated. Disorganized. What I reason out now is erroneous.'

Sharply: 'Is it because you are geared to him, Freda? Gearing is such an insidious process. A woman is open to be geared to a house, a dress or a string of pearls. If a woman is geared to the idea of a certain house, she makes every housing fact come congruent to that house and to none other. The whole world of her thought can revolve about its staircase.' She paused. 'Pity the hairdresser who is geared to hair.' A longer pause. 'Have you proof of his variety?'

Except for her peaceful breathing, Freda was silent.

Anna quoted: '"A strenuous virtue or a strenuous sin."' Then, with sham eagerness: 'I do not wish to say the things my tongue says. Tonight my mind is a galloping horse. If I do not speak as I am speaking now every cockcrow down the years will upbraid me, saying: "Her room was next to yours. You two had evolved a common language. All you had to do was to step out of bed when they had all gone, slip your feet into your mules, throw your heavy green coat across your shoulders, open the door of her room, come in and whisper: 'Freda, Freda, are you sure?', then stand in the moonlight" . . . as I am standing now.'

After a while, Freda said: 'It's the noise he makes with his pipe when he slams it into his palm, isn't it?'

'How stupid of us! And how sensible! What dimension are we in now, sister?'

The girl in the bed laughed richly. 'Such an absurdity!' she said. 'There is no one else in the world with whom I could discuss it but you.'

Anna said: 'To-day I watched him narrowly. Such a cocksure settled gesture! First his lips tighten. He breathes ponderously through his nose. Then, when you least expect it, he slams the pipe into his open palm, like this!' Anna slammed her right fist into the palm of her left hand. Exculpating herself, she said archly: 'Remember, we both put it into words together.' In a different tone: 'Do you still like the old man you can see so plainly in him?'

Freda was thoughtful. Anna returned to the window. She said in a sort of low chant: 'You must recall how much it cost us to crystallize it in words. The desire to be one! Jim and you will always be two.'

'I have given the matter much thought. It is conceivable that it does not exist. We are not sure that there is such a thing as one-ness. Have you experienced it?'

'Its existence argues God. I have not experienced it. With Peter I thought ... But no! It has been handed down from woman to woman through all the centuries. There is no alternative to its being true. It is a common factor of womankind. It is behind all singing. It is the Clue in us. Look how it ambushes us sometimes even with an utter stranger. Quite possibly a man physically repulsive. Women don't often put it into words. Times, lying awake beside snoring husbands, they stretch their hands up into the darkness in an effort to grasp this abstract something. The first woman in the world squatting on sand, sieving sand like time through her fingers and watching her husband move towards her over the sand must have puzzled prodigiously to express it. Then the other women: here and everywhere, borderless as to time and place—each had a skin which was one of the four colours. They sat beside countless fires idling with countless pokers. I see them sitting on cliff fences on sunny days. Some reached farther than others. But always a cross has marked the limit of their thrusting. Some were left inexplicably limp. But in the end they became resigned: they pushed their shoes before them and went forward to meet what they had to meet, saying: "What does it matter?" "Who am I?" "Let it drift!" "How inadequate I am!" and other similar verbal gestures of surrender. You and I, Freda, cannot hope to be exceptions. Pale shadows that we are, bred over-finely, educated unnecessarily, possessing leisure and a modicum of money, living as we do in this monstrous house, this ...'

'... ghastly castle in the most stagnant barony in Ireland.'

'... beside the lake on which lies the island on which there is a castle beyond which hang the imperturbable hills. Have we not won forward, sister, inch by inch? Have we not dispensed with several rungs of the mind's ladder until we have become superb leapers?' She turned. 'How will you like having to ascend and descend rung by wretched rung?'

Freda asked herself: 'How is that we made it go?' Then, in a low voice: 'If God made us in His own image . . .'

'. . . the virtues we possess are tiny micro- . . .'

'. . . micro-somethings of the virtues that pre-exist in the person of God . . .'

'. . . Who seeing, as it were, Himself, with illimitable wryness through the wrong end of His gigantic telescope . . .'

'. . . and flinging something akin to that image to instant flesh and blood. Bidding it exult . . .'

'. . . finitely. To love . . .'

'. . . finitely . . .'

'But always with the promise of the macro-somethings . . .'

'. . . of the fruition of that laughter that as yet is but the one-millionth part of the laughter of God . . .'

'. . . the fraction being arbitrary since the mind baulks at a smaller portion . . .'

'. . . there being times when it seems that God makes the promise factual in our transient flesh . . .'

'. . . when we swell and swing and sway and are exalted. . . . Music . . .'

'. . . and at the point when we dream ourselves to the very threshold of transfiguration . . .'

Anna said fiercely: 'Always there is the absurdity! The incongruity! The red moustache on the guinea hen! The brown cat sleeping on the cross of stone!'

Silence.

Freda chided softly: 'You broke it too soon! Just when it seemed that we had succeeded in expressing the inexpressible.'

Anna said: 'Believe me, sister, I am sorry. Please begin again.'

'It is little use. We had reached the end.'

'No! No! We can begin again . . . on a lower plane.'

Freda tried: 'A character we said that had streaks. Like a landscape that was worthy of being painted. Pitfalls and creeks and grassy hollows. Arid patches too. Glimpses of the river. Pegwood and the silver undersides of certain leaves.'

'Love begins in the head. The body of itself can only reach to thirty per cent of exultation.'

Freda's effort was discernible as effort: 'The question becomes heavy and hard. Sometimes it seems so easy.'

Anna seemed to surrender. 'Before I came in, while I was lying in the darkness, it seemed possessed of an unusual clarity.'

Shrewdly, Freda said: 'About Jim?' What followed came slow like a knife blade: 'There are times when his open right hand claws the air. Seeking an invisible tennis racquet.'

Very eagerly: 'Yes!'

'Yes!' Also very eagerly. 'You have noticed it! The sharpness of your "yes" betrays you. It has quizzed you too.' In a tired voice: 'Play square, Anna. You are not wholly altruistic.'

'You mean . . .'

Freda stiffened: 'I dare you to say I lie.'

After a pause, Anna said: 'You do not lie, Freda.'

Freda was merciless: 'The day as we rowed across to the island—you remember how the clasps of the boatman's braces caught the sun? And when we trampled the grass where the sheep had not been, so as to spread out our Foxford rug . . .'

'Go on!'

'When you cut your hand on the rose bush and Jim bound it. The riddle was not so easy as the blood came spurting and his hands were on yours. Was it, my sister? Why do you not answer? You must recall how the simple suddenly became the complex. Then we both saw the appalling futilities of our speakings here. As if, indeed, our united minds could cage or limn or trace or predict the mind of the meanest mortal on this earth. In all its magnificent variety! In all its astounding versatility! In all its glorious unpredictability! You saw it, Anna, didn't you? I tell you, you saw it! It lay there crystal clear between your hands and the rosehook that was coloured with your blood. Together, as on a handclap, we realized our limitations and our folly.'

Freda continued: 'You know that that is not all.'

'What more?'

'You saw the gesture, the tennis racquet gesture. You sensed the adventure that lay behind the staidness and the solidarity. Behind even the hollow sound of the pipe mouth on his palm.'

Vividly, Anna said: 'I saw it! Every part of me cried out for that adventure.'

'And that is why you are here, Anna. To see if I had seen that you had seen the adventure.'

Humbly: 'That is why I am here, Freda.'

The girl in the bed relaxed. She sighed and said: 'Now we are at peace again.'

Anna remained looking out of the window. Miles away on the hills an unexpected tongue of fire leaped up. Anna started reciting in a voice redolent of a bobbing ribbon on a girl's pigtail:

> Fire on the mountain, run, boys, run,
> You with the red coat, follow with the drum.
> The drums shall beat and we shall meet
> Fire on the thum thum thum thum thum . . .

The moonlight increased in brightness until it could be fairly said to imitate the day. It had the whiteness of fresh tin. Then as she looked out on it wonderingly, Anna saw the cigarette glow by the laurels. She saw the great form stalking on the grass beside the pathway's edge. She threw open one half of the casement and leaned out on the sill. Her lips were apart with eagerness. The cigarette glow had swung at the noise of the opening window.

'Father!' Anna called.

Freda sprang out of bed and shrugged into a dressing-gown. She opened the other half of the window. She too leaned forward. They straightened as they awaited his approach. Through the opes of the gown and coat they were seen to be slim and virginal. Their bodies were unbroken.

Bulky as The Liberator the father came stalking across the grass. For all his weight he moved like a cat. His pyjama-ends were white below the turn-ups of his trousers and were lapping over his shoes. He was wearing the enormous dressing-gown the sisters could not procure nearer than Dublin.

A Cairn terrier waddled after him.

'Hush, blast ye for petticoats!' their father said, with shallow bluster. 'D'you want to rouse all creation?'

'You'll catch your death!'

'Haven't I the right to walk where I like and when I like? Do I ask ye what ye're doing? Do I interfere when ye're at this jack-acting of dissection of motives, trends, causes and ridiculous phenomena? Answer me! Isn't someone bound to hold fast to the physical while ye're tampering with the metaphysical?'

'Rssst! Pooka! Pooka!' Anna called to the dog. The terrier, a miniature monument to resentment, was tempted to place his buttocks on the grass. He looked dismally up. He was tired of bizarre behaviour in the moonlight. Straw was warm. Grass was cold. Gravel was rough. Duty was duty. He owed women no allegiance.

The girls laughed. Freda said, provocatively: "Tomorrow, father, you must look your best when you're giving me to the man!'

'My best! Look, darlings, your dead mother—before her loveliness snared me, there was a time when I drank so much that I once saw a dairymaid hiding behind an ordinary green apple. Four nights in succession I slept in a hollow of the sandhills. The fifth night I straightened myself and passed gallant muster at a County Ball. A razor, a white shirt, the heels of your shoes shined, a leather bag and a constitution—they always get by.' He dragged on his cigarette. Slyly, he queried. 'At it again?'

'At it again!' they agreed.

He ground the cigarette into the grass. He became theatrical. 'Holy You Utter Divine Creator of Heaven, Hell, Purgatory, Earth, Stars and Planets we know not of! Are ye never going to give it a rest?'

'It ends here, father,' Anna said quietly.

He chose to ignore the importance of this statement. 'Ah, well, where would ye be got? Yeer mother was at the same game.' Wryly, half turning away: 'There isn't much of me in ye.' He turned around fully. Come now, admit it? Fair play is bonny play!'

'Divil a much, father,' they agreed.

He lifted his right arm to the horizontal and aimed an imaginary revolver at the shrubbery. 'Bang!' he said loudly. 'All my braggin' and carousin' and philanderin'. Bang! I never sired a son.' He stopped firing and looked up at them. 'Only the pair of ye!' He hullahooed with laughter. 'As if a church organ had a pair of pups and they turned out to be two small sweet fiddles.'

The young women straightened themselves at the open casement as they pealed laughter. Now more than ever before they were white, slim and virginal.

They became conscious of their father's hands. The uneasiness of them. He pulled up the sleeve from his left forearm, then slapped the flesh quickly with the palm of his right hand. 'Flesh!' he said. 'You can't whack it! Why did we get put into flesh,' he said, 'if not to break horses, caress woman and down upstarts? Three cheers for flesh!' Abruptly: 'I almost forgot.'

Simultaneously he thrust his hands into the pockets of his dressing-gown. He swung both arms fully at the same time. 'Catch!' he said.

The two large Jaffa oranges were lamps moving upwards through the night air. Now they were silver, now gold.

Standing quite still, Freda caught her orange and trapped it firmly against her body. Anna, over-eager, leaned forward and fumbled hers out into the night. Twice her fingers dribbled it hopefully. Then the orange fell heavily to the gravel below.

'Just how you muffed Peter!' her father said. He glanced at the orange. 'Catch a man or an orange as Freda caught hers. By standing quite still and clutching firmly what comes to you.'

'I could have caught Peter, father,' Anna said furiously. 'You at least know that.'

'You could have caught the orange, too,' he said. 'Here!' He recovered the fruit and flung it up into the room. Anna refused to try for it: it padded away unheeded into the recesses of the bedroom. Pouting, Anna watched the orange flame her sister was holding in her hand.

'To hell with ye!' their father shouted. 'To hell with all women! Sometimes! Now, for instance. To the bright belly of hell with them to-night.' His voice was clotted with loss. As he walked away he laughed richly over his shoulder. His postscript came: 'To-morrow, it will be different.'

Despite her anger, Anna laughed. She watched the terrier plod philosophically after the hillock that was her father.

When her sister had gone, Freda closed the casement, then set a match to the candle on the dressing-table. Sitting on the mahogany stool before the mirror she began to preen and flirt and twist herself

for her own delectation. Now and again she made her nostrils widen
in a way she had long practised. She opened her dressing-gown and
lifted her head high from her body. In the background of her reflection the candlelight barely stroked the wedding dress. Suddenly she
stopped, and putting her face close against her own image, asked:
'Are you sure? Are you sure?' Leaning away from the mirror, she said
with vehemence. 'I'm certain! Absolutely certain!' Then with a shrug
of her shoulders and a shrivelled laugh: 'At least, I think I am!'

Drawing back the left sleeve of her dressing-gown she smacked the
flesh of her forearm with the open palm of her right hand. When the
laughter came it was her father's, but the unpractised smack was her
own. She grimaced. A gesture saved from his rakish days, she thought.

She looked around her sharply. The orange was on the dressing-
table. Of a sudden she snatched it up and catching it as she had
caught it when it had come flying in the open casement, pressed it
to her, true and steady against the valley of her breasts.

Frank O'Connor (pseudonym of Michael O'Donovan) was born in Cork in 1903. At the age of twelve he compiled a "collected edition" of his prose and poetry, written in Gaelic. His formal education ended when he was fourteen. Later, he became a professional librarian and then a director of the famous Abbey Theatre, where he acquired "a lasting passion for techniques." O'Connor's first collection of stories, Guests of the Nation, *appeared in 1931; since then he has published twenty-six volumes of stories, poetry, criticism, and nonfiction.*

"Story telling," writes Frank O'Connor, "is the nearest thing one can get to the quality of a pure lyric poem. It doesn't deal with problems; it doesn't have any solutions to offer; it just states the human condition." Is this true of "The Man of the World?" Why did Larry feel that the woman's image would be impressed upon his mind until the day he died? What is the effect of having the story narrated by a grown man remembering his youth? Further Reading: The Stories of Frank O'Connor (1952), More Stories of Frank O'Connor (1954), Stories by Frank O'Connor (1956).

The Man of the World

FRANK O'CONNOR

When I was a kid there were no such things as holidays for me and my likes, and I have no feeling of grievance about it because, in the way of kids, I simply invented them, which was much more satisfactory. One year, my summer holiday was a couple of nights I spent at the house of a friend called Jimmy Leary, who lived at the other side of the road from us. His parents sometimes went

© Copyright 1956 by Frank O'Connor. Reprinted from *Domestic Relations*, by Frank O'Connor by permission of Alfred A. Knopf, Inc.

away for a couple of days to visit a sick relative in Bantry, and he was given permission to have a friend in to keep him company. I took my holiday with the greatest seriousness, insisted on the loan of Father's old travelling bag and dragged it myself down our lane past the neighbors standing at their doors.

"Are you off somewhere, Larry?" asked one.

"Yes, Mrs. Rooney," I said with great pride. "Off for my holidays to the Learys'."

"Wisha, aren't you very lucky?" she said with amusement.

"Lucky" seemed an absurd description of my good fortune. The Learys' house was a big one with a high flight of steps up to the front door, which was always kept shut. They had a piano in the front room, a pair of binoculars on a table near the window, and a toilet on the stairs that seemed to me to be the last word in elegance and immodesty. We brought the binoculars up to the bedroom with us. From the window you could see the whole road up and down, from the quarry at its foot with the tiny houses perched on top of it to the open fields at the other end, where the last gas lamp rose against the sky. Each morning I was up with the first light, leaning out the window in my nightshirt and watching through the glasses all the mysterious figures you never saw from our lane: policemen, railwaymen, and farmers on their way to market.

I admired Jimmy almost as much as I admired his house, and for much the same reasons. He was a year older than I, was well-mannered and well-dressed, and would not associate with most of the kids on the road at all. He had a way when any of them joined us of resting against a wall with his hands in his trousers pockets and listening to them with a sort of well-bred smile, a knowing smile that seemed to me the height of elegance. And it was not that he was a softy, because he was an excellent boxer and wrestler and could easily have held his own with them any time, but he did not wish to. He was superior to them. He was—there is only one word that still describes it for me—sophisticated.

I attributed his sophistication to the piano, the binoculars, and the indoor john, and felt that if only I had the same advantages I could have been sophisticated, too. I knew I wasn't, because I was always being deceived by the world of appearances. I would take a sudden violent liking to some boy, and when I went to his house, my admiration would spread to his parents and sisters, and I would think how wonderful it must be to have such a home; but when I told Jimmy he would smile in that knowing way of his and say quietly: "I believe they had the bailiffs in a few weeks ago," and, even though I didn't know what bailiffs were, bang would go the whole world of appearances, and I would realize that once again I had been deceived.

It was the same with fellows and girls. Seeing some bigger chap we knew walking out with a girl for the first time, Jimmy would say casually: "He'd better mind himself: that one is dynamite." And, even though I knew as little of girls who were dynamite as I did of bailiffs, his tone would be sufficient to indicate that I had been taken in by sweet voices and broad-brimmed hats, gaslight and evening smells from gardens.

Forty years later I can still measure the extent of my obsession, for, though my own handwriting is almost illegible, I sometimes find myself scribbling idly on a pad in a small, stiff, perfectly legible hand that I recognize with amusement as a reasonably good forgery of Jimmy's. My admiration still lies there somewhere, a fossil in my memory, but Jimmy's knowing smile is something I have never managed to acquire.

And it all goes back to my curiosity about fellows and girls. As I say, I only imagined things about them, but Jimmy knew. I was excluded from knowledge by the world of appearances that blinded and deafened me with emotion. The least thing could excite or depress me: the trees in the morning when I went to early Mass, the stained-glass windows in the church, the blue hilly streets at evening with the green flare of the gas lamps, the smells of cooking and perfume—even the smell of a cigarette packet that I had picked up from the gutter and crushed to my nose—all kept me at this side of the world of appearances, while Jimmy, by right of birth or breeding, was always at the other. I wanted him to tell me what it was like, but he didn't seem to be able.

Then one evening he was listening to me talk while he leant against the pillar of his gate, his pale neat hair framing his pale, good-humored face. My excitability seemed to rouse in him a mixture of amusement and pity.

"Why don't you come over some night the family is away and I'll show you a few things?" he asked lightly.

"What'll you show me, Jimmy?" I asked eagerly.

"Noticed the new couple that's come to live next door?" he asked with a nod in the direction of the house above his own.

"No," I admitted in disappointment. It wasn't only that I never knew anything, but I never noticed anything either. And when he described the new family that was lodging there, I realized with chagrin that I didn't even know Mrs. MacCarthy, who owned the house.

"Oh, they're just a newly married couple," he said. "They don't know that they can be seen from our house."

"But how, Jimmy?"

"Don't look up now," he said with a dreamy smile while his eyes strayed over my shoulder in the direction of the lane. "Wait till you're going away. Their end wall is only a couple of feet from ours. You can see right into the bedroom from our attic."

"And what do they do, Jimmy?"

"Oh," he said with a pleasant laugh, "everything. You really should come."

"You bet I'll come," I said, trying to sound tougher than I felt. It wasn't that I saw anything wrong in it. It was rather that, for all my desire to become like Jimmy, I was afraid of what it might do to me.

But it wasn't enough for me to get behind the world of appearances. I had to study the appearances themselves, and for three evenings I stood under the gas lamp at the foot of our lane, across the road from the MacCarthys', till I had identified the new lodgers. The husband was the first I spotted, because he came from his work at a regular hour. He was tall, with stiff jet-black hair and a big black guardsman's moustache that somehow failed to conceal the youthfulness and in-genuousness of his face, which was long and lean. Usually, he came accompanied by an older man, and stood chatting for a few minutes outside his door— a black-coated, bowler-hatted figure who made large, sweeping gestures with his evening paper and sometimes doubled up in an explosion of loud laughter.

On the third evening I saw his wife—for she had obviously been waiting for him, looking from behind the parlor curtains, and when she saw him she scurried down the steps to join in the conversation. She had thrown an old jacket about her shoulders and stood there, her arms folded as though to protect herself further from the cold wind that blew down the hill from the open country, while her hus-band rested one hand fondly on her shoulder.

For the first time, I began to feel qualms about what I proposed to do. It was one thing to do it to people you didn't know or care about, but, for me, even to recognize people was to adopt an emo-tional attitude towards them, and my attitude to this pair was already one of approval. They looked like people who might approve of me, too. That night I remained awake, thinking out the terms of an anony-mous letter that would put them on their guard, till I had worked myself up into a fever of eloquence and indignation.

But I knew only too well that they would recognize the villain of the letter and that the villain would recognize me, so I did not write it. Instead, I gave way to fits of anger and moodiness against my par-ents. Yet even these were unreal, because on Saturday night when Mother made a parcel of my nightshirt—I had now become suffi-ciently self-conscious not to take a bag—I nearly broke down. There was something about my own house that night that upset me all over again. Father, with his cap over his eyes, was sitting under the wall lamp, reading the paper, and Mother, a shawl about her shoulders, was crouched over the fire from her little wickerwork chair, listening; and I realized that they, too, were part of the world of appearances I was planning to destroy, and as I said good-night, I almost felt that I was saying good-bye to them as well.

But once inside Jimmy's house I did not care so much. It always had that effect on me, of blowing me up to twice the size, as though I were expanding to greet the piano, the binoculars, and the indoor toilet. I tried to pick out a tune on the piano with one hand, and Jimmy, having listened with amusement for some time, sat down, and played it himself as I felt it should be played, and this, too, seemed to be part of his superiority.

"I suppose we'd better put in an appearance of going to bed," he said disdainfully. "Someone across the road might notice and tell. *They*'re in town, so I don't suppose they'll be back till late."

We had a glass of milk in the kitchen, went upstairs, undressed, and lay down, though we put our overcoats beside the bed. Jimmy had a packet of sweets but insisted on keeping them till later. "We may need these before we're done," he said with his knowing smile, and again I admired his orderliness and restraint. We talked in bed for a quarter of an hour; then put out the light, got up again, donned our overcoats and socks, and tiptoed upstairs to the attic. Jimmy led the way with an electric torch. He was a fellow who thought of everything. The attic had been arranged for our vigil. Two trunks had been drawn up to the little window to act as seats, and there were even cushions on them. Looking out, you could at first see nothing but an expanse of blank wall topped with chimney stacks, but gradually you could make out the outline of a single window, eight or ten feet below. Jimmy sat beside me and opened his packet of sweets, which he laid between us.

"Of course, we could have stayed in bed till we heard them come in," he whispered. "Usually you can hear them at the front door, but they might have come in quietly or we might have fallen asleep. It's always best to make sure."

"But why don't they draw the blind?" I asked as my heart began to beat uncomfortably.

"Because there isn't a blind," he said with a quiet chuckle. "Old Mrs. MacCarthy never had one, and she's not going to put one in for lodgers who may be gone tomorrow. People like that never rest till they get a house of their own."

I envied him his nonchalance as he sat back with his legs crossed, sucking a sweet just as though he were waiting in the cinema for the show to begin. I was scared by the darkness and the mystery, and by the sounds that came to us from the road with such extraordinary clarity. Besides, of course, it wasn't my house and I didn't feel at home there. At any moment I expected the front door to open and his parents to come in and catch us.

We must have been waiting for half an hour before we heard voices in the roadway, the sound of a key in the latch and, then, of a door opening and closing softly. Jimmy reached out and touched my arm lightly. "This is probably our pair," he whispered. "We'd better not speak any more in case they might hear us." I nodded, wishing I had never come. At that moment a faint light became visible in the great expanse of black wall, a faint, yellow stairlight that was just sufficient to silhouette the window frame beneath us. Suddenly the whole room lit up. The man I had seen in the street stood by the doorway, his hand still on the switch. I could see it all plainly now, an ordinary small, suburban bedroom with flowery wallpaper, a colored picture of the Sacred Heart over the double bed with the big brass knobs, a wardrobe, and a dressing table.

The man stood there till the woman came in, removing her hat in a single wide gesture and tossing it from her into a corner of the room. He still stood by the door, taking off his tie. Then he struggled with the collar, his head raised and his face set in an agonized expression. His wife kicked off her shoes, sat on a chair by the bed, and began to take off her stockings. All the time she seemed to be talking because her head was raised, looking at him, though you couldn't hear a word she said. I glanced at Jimmy. The light from the window below softly illuminated his face as he sucked with tranquil enjoyment.

The woman rose as her husband sat on the bed with his back to us and began to take off his shoes and socks in the same slow, agonized way. At one point he held up his left foot and looked at it with what might have been concern. His wife looked at it, too, for a moment and then swung halfway around as she unbuttoned her skirt. She undressed in swift, jerky movements, twisting and turning and apparently talking all the time. At one moment she looked into the mirror on the dressing table and touched her cheek lightly. She crouched as she took off her slip, and then pulled her nightdress over her head and finished her undressing beneath it. As she removed her underclothes she seemed to throw them anywhere at all, and I had a strong impression that there was something haphazard and disorderly about her. Her husband was different. Everything he removed seemed to be removed in order and then put carefully where he could find it most readily in the morning. I watched him take out his watch, look at it carefully, wind it, and then hang it neatly over the bed.

Then, to my surprise, she knelt by the bed, facing towards the window, glanced up at the picture of the Sacred Heart, made a large hasty Sign of the Cross, and, covering her face with her hands, buried her head in the bedclothes. I looked at Jimmy in dismay, but he did not seem to be embarrassed by the sight. The husband, his folded trousers in his hand, moved about the room slowly and carefully, as though he did not wish to disturb his wife's devotions, and when he pulled on the trousers of his pyjamas he turned away. After that he put on his pyjama jacket, buttoned it carefully, and knelt beside her. He, too, glanced respectfully at the picture and crossed himself slowly and reverently, but he did not bury his face and head as she had done. He knelt upright with nothing of the abandonment suggested by her pose, and with an expression that combined reverence and self-respect. It was the expression of an employee who, while admitting that he might have a few little weaknesses like the rest of the staff, prided himself on having deserved well of the management. Women, his slightly complacent air seemed to indicate, had to adopt these emotional attitudes, but he spoke to God as one man to another. He finished his prayers before his wife; again he crossed himself slowly, rose, and climbed into bed, glancing again at his watch as he did so.

Several minutes passed before she put her hands out before her on the bed, blessed herself in her wide, sweeping way, and rose. She crossed the room in a swift movement that almost escaped me, and next moment the light went out—it was as if the window through which we had watched the scene had disappeared with it by magic, till nothing was left but a blank black wall mounting to the chimney pots.

Jimmy rose slowly and pointed the way out to me with his flashlight. When we got downstairs we put on the bedroom light, and I saw on his face the virtuous and sophisticated air of a collector who has shown you all his treasures in the best possible light. Faced with that look, I could not bring myself to mention the woman at prayer, though I felt her image would be impressed on my memory till the day I died. I could not have explained to him how at that moment everything had changed for me, how, beyond us watching the young married couple from ambush, I had felt someone else watching us, so that at once we ceased to be the observers and became the observed. And the observed in such a humiliating position that nothing I could imagine our victims doing would have been so degrading.

I wanted to pray myself but found I couldn't. Instead, I lay in bed in the darkness, covering my eyes with my hand, and I think that even then I knew that I should never be sophisticated like Jimmy, never be able to put on a knowing smile, because always beyond the world of appearances I would see only eternity watching.

"Sometimes, of course, it's better than that," Jimmy's drowsy voice said from the darkness. "You shouldn't judge it by tonight."

In "Gogol's Wife" Landolfi satirizes scholarly and genteel biographers. The effect of the story depends heavily on the method of presentation. Why do you suppose Landolfi chose to narrate in the first person? What kind of man is the narrator? How does our judgment of his character affect our response to the story? One technique of writing fantasy is recounting the fantastic in credible, concrete terms. Does Landolfi do so?

Tommaso Landolfi was born at Pico in 1908 and attended the University of Lorience, earning a degree in Russian literature. His first book of stories, Dialogue on the Greater Harmonies, *was published in 1937, and since then he has authored novels and many more short stories and has published several Russian translations. Landolfi is sometimes referred to as "the Italian Kafka." His intellectually balanced fiction (the following story is a typical example) blends surrealism, fantasy, humor, and irony. Further Reading:* Dialogue on the Greater Harmonies (1937), Gogol's Wife and Other Stories (1963).

ITALY

Gogol's Wife

TOMMASO LANDOLFI

At this point, confronted with the whole complicated affair of Nikolai Vassilevitch's wife, I am overcome by hesitation. Have I any right to disclose something which is unknown to the whole world, which my unforgettable friend himself kept hidden from the world (and he had his reasons), and which I am sure will give rise to all sorts of malicious and stupid misunderstandings? Something, moreover, which will very probably of-

Tommaso Landolfi, *Gogol's Wife & Other Stories.* © 1961 & © 1963 by New Directions. Reprinted by permission of New Directions Publishing Corporation. Translated by Wayland Young.

fend the sensibilities of all sorts of base, hypocritical people, and possibly of some honest people too, if there are any left? And finally, have I any right to disclose something before which my own spirit recoils, and even tends toward a more or less open disapproval?

But the fact remains that, as a biographer, I have certain firm obligations. Believing as I do that every bit of information about so lofty a genius will turn out to be of value to us and to future generations, I cannot conceal something which in any case has no hope of being judged fairly and wisely until the end of time. Moreover, what right have we to condemn? Is it given to us to know, not only what intimate needs, but even what higher and wider ends may have been served by those very deeds of a lofty genius which perchance may appear to us vile? No indeed, for we understand so little of these privileged natures. "It is true," a great man once said, "that I also have to pee, but for quite different reasons."

But without more ado I will come to what I know beyond doubt, and can prove beyond question, about this controversial matter, which will now—I dare to hope—no longer be so. I will not trouble to recapitulate what is already known of it, since I do not think this should be necessary at the present stage of development of Gogol studies.

Let me say it at once: Nikolai Vassilevitch's wife was not a woman. Nor was she any sort of human being, nor any sort of living creature at all, whether animal or vegetable (although something of the sort has sometimes been hinted). She was quite simply a balloon. Yes, a balloon; and this will explain the perplexity, or even indignation, of certain biographers who were also the personal friends of the Master, and who complained that, although they often went to his house, they never saw her and "never even heard her voice." From this they deduced all sorts of dark and disgraceful complications—yes, and criminal ones too. No, gentlemen, everything is always simpler than it appears. You did not hear her voice simply because she could not speak, or to be more exact, she could only speak in certain conditions, as we shall see. And it was always, except once, in tête-à-tête with Nikolai Vassilevitch. So let us not waste time with any cheap or empty refutations but come at once to as exact and complete a description as possible of the being or object in question.

Gogol's so-called wife was an ordinary dummy made of thick rubber, naked at all seasons, buff in tint, or as is more commonly said, flesh-colored. But since women's skins are not all of the same color, I should specify that hers was a light-colored, polished skin, like that of certain brunettes. It, or she, was, it is hardly necessary to add, of feminine sex. Perhaps I should say at once that she was capable of very wide alterations of her attributes without, of course, being able to alter her sex itself. She could sometimes appear to be thin, with hardly any breasts and with narrow hips more like a young

lad than a woman, and at other times to be excessively well-endowed
or—let us not mince matters—fat. And she often changed the color
of her hair, both on her head and elsewhere on her body, though not
necessarily at the same time. She could also seem to change in all
sorts of other tiny particulars, such as the position of moles, the
vitality of the mucous membranes and so forth. She could even to a
certain extent change the very color of her skin. One is faced with the
necessity of asking oneself who she really was, or whether it would be
proper to speak of a single "person"—and in fact we shall see that
it would be imprudent to press this point.

The cause of these changes, as my readers will already have understood, was nothing else but the will of Nikolai Vassilevitch himself.
He would inflate her to a greater or lesser degree, would change her
wig and her other tufts of hair, would grease her with ointments and
touch her up in various ways so as to obtain more or less the type of
woman which suited him at that moment. Following the natural
inclinations of his fancy, he even amused himself sometimes by producing grotesque or monstrous forms; as will be readily understood,
she became deformed when inflated beyond a certain point or if she
remained below a certain pressure.

But Gogol soon tired of these experiments, which he held to be
"after all, not very respectful" to his wife, whom he loved in his own
way—however inscrutable it may remain to us. He loved her, but
which of these incarnations, we may ask ourselves, did he love? Alas,
I have already indicated that the end of the present account will fur-
nish some sort of an answer. And how can I have stated above that it
was Nikolai Vassilevitch's will which ruled that woman? In a certain
sense, yes, it is true; but it is equally certain that she soon became no
longer his slave but his tyrant. And here yawns the abyss, or if you
prefer it, the Jaws of Tartarus. But let us not anticipate.

I have said that Gogol obtained with his manipulations *more or
less* the type of woman which he needed from time to time. I should
add that when, in rare cases, the form he obtained perfectly incarnated
his desire, Nikolai Vassilevitch fell in love with it "exclusively," as
he said in his own words, and that this was enough to render "her"
stable for a certain time—until he fell out of love with "her." I
counted no more than three or four of these violent passions—or, as
I suppose they would be called today, infatuations—in the life (dare
I say in the conjugal life?) of the great writer. It will be convenient
to add here that a few years after what one may call his marriage.
Gogol had even given a name to his wife. It was Caracas, which is,
unless I am mistaken, the capital of Venezuela. I have never been
able to discover the reason for this choice: great minds are so
capricious!

Speaking only of her normal appearance, Caracas was what is
called a fine woman—well built and proportioned in every part. She

had every smallest attribute of her sex properly disposed in the proper location. Particularly worthy of attention were her genital organs (if the adjective is permissible in such a context). They were formed by means of ingenious folds in the rubber. Nothing was forgotten, and their operation was rendered easy by various devices, as well as by the internal pressure of the air.

Caracas also had a skeleton, even though a rudimentary one. Perhaps it was made of whalebone. Special care had been devoted to the construction of the thoracic cage, of the pelvic basin and of the cranium. The first two systems were more or less visible in accordance with the thickness of the fatty layer, if I may so describe it, which covered them. It is a great pity that Gogol never let me know the name of the creator of such a fine piece of work. There was an obstinacy in his refusal which was never quite clear to me.

Nikolai Vassilevitch blew his wife up through the anal sphincter with a pump of his own invention, rather like those which you hold down with your two feet and which are used today in all sorts of mechanical workshops. Situated in the anus was a little one-way valve, or whatever the correct technical description would be, like the mitral valve of the heart, which, once the body was inflated, allowed more air to come in but none to go out. To deflate, one unscrewed a stopper in the mouth, at the back of the throat.

And that, I think, exhausts the description of the most noteworthy peculiarities of this being. Unless perhaps I should mention the splendid rows of white teeth which adorned her mouth and the dark eyes which, in spite of their immobility, perfectly simulated life. Did I say simulate? Good heavens, simulate is not the word! Nothing seems to be the word, when one is speaking of Caracas! Even these eyes could undergo a change of color, by means of a special process to which, since it was long and tiresome, Gogol seldom had recourse. Finally, I should speak of her voice, which it was only once given to me to hear. But I cannot do that without going more fully into the relationship between husband and wife, and in this I shall no longer be able to answer to the truth of everything with absolute certitude. On my conscience I could not—so confused, both in itself and in my memory, is that which I now have to tell.

Here, then, as they occur to me, are some of my memories.

The first and, as I said, the last time I ever heard Caracas speak to Nikolai Vassilevitch was one evening when we were absolutely alone. We were in the room where the woman, if I may be allowed the expression, lived. Entrance to this room was strictly forbidden to everybody. It was furnished more or less in the Oriental manner, had no windows and was situated in the most inaccessible part of the house. I did know that she could talk, but Gogol had never explained to me the circumstances under which this happened. There were only the two of us, or three, in there. Nikolai Vassilevitch and I were drinking vodka and discussing Butkov's novel. I remember that we left this topic, and he was maintaining the necessity for radical reforms in the laws of inheritance. We had almost forgotten her. It was then that, with a husky and submissive voice, like Venus on the nuptial couch, she said point-blank: "I want to go poo poo."

I jumped, thinking I had misheard, and looked across at her. She was sitting on a pile of cushions against the wall; that evening she was a soft, blonde beauty, rather well-covered. Her expression seemed commingled of shrewdness and slyness, childishness and irresponsibility. As for Gogol, he blushed violently and, leaping on her, stuck two fingers down her throat. She immediately began to shrink and to turn pale; she took on once again that lost and astonished air which was especially hers, and was in the end reduced to no more than a flabby skin on a perfunctory bony armature. Since, for practical reasons which will readily be divined, she had an extraordinarily flexible backbone, she folded up almost in two, and for the rest of the evening she looked up at us from where she had slithered to the floor, in utter abjection.

All Gogol said was: "She only does it for a joke, or to annoy me, because as a matter of fact she does not have such needs." In the presence of other people, that is to say of me, he generally made a point of treating her with a certain disdain.

We went on drinking and talking, but Nikolai Vassilevitch seemed very much disturbed and absent in spirit. Once he suddenly interrupted what he was saying, seized my hand in his and burst into tears. "What can I do now?" he exclaimed. "You understand, Foma Paskalovitch, that I loved her?"

It is necessary to point out that it was impossible, except by a miracle, ever to repeat any of Caracas' forms. She was a fresh creation every time, and it would have been wasted effort to seek to find again the exact proportions, the exact pressure, and so forth, of a former Caracas. Therefore the plumpish blonde of that evening was lost to Gogol from that time forth forever; this was in fact the tragic end of one of those few loves of Nikolai Vassilevitch, which I described above. He gave me no explanation; he sadly rejected my proffered comfort, and that evening we parted early. But his heart had been laid bare to me in that outburst. He was no longer so reticent with me, and soon had hardly any secrets left. And this, I may say in parenthesis, caused me very great pride.

It seems that things had gone well for the "couple" at the beginning of their life together. Nikolai Vassilevitch had been content with Caracas and slept regularly with her in the same bed. He continued to observe this custom till the end, saying with a timid smile that no companion could be quieter or less importunate than she. But I soon began to doubt this, especially judging by the state he was sometimes in when he woke up. Then, after several years, their relationship began strangely to deteriorate.

All this, let it be said once and for all, is no more than a schematic attempt at an explanation. About that time the woman actually began to show signs of independence or, as one might say, of autonomy. Nikolai Vassilevitch had the extraordinary impression that she was acquiring a personality of her own, indecipherable perhaps, but still distinct from his, and one which slipped through his fingers. It is certain that some sort of continuity was established between each of her appearances—between all those brunettes, those blondes, those redheads and auburn-headed girls, between those plump, those slim, those dusky or snowy or golden beauties, there was a certain something in common. At the beginning of this chapter I cast some doubt on the propriety of considering Caracas as a unitary personality; nevertheless I myself could not quite, whenever I saw her, free myself of the impression that, however unheard of it may seem, this was fundamentally the same woman. And it may be that this was why Gogol felt he had to give her a name.

An attempt to establish in what precisely subsisted the common attributes of the different forms would be quite another thing. Perhaps it was no more and no less than the creative afflatus of Nikolai Vassilevitch himself. But no, it would have been too singular and strange if he had been so much divided off from himself, so much averse to himself. Because whoever she was, Caracas was a disturbing presence and even—it is better to be quite clear—a hostile one. Yet neither Gogol nor I ever succeeded in formulating a remotely tenable hypothesis as to her true nature; when I say formulate, I mean in terms which would be at once rational and accessible to all. But I cannot pass over an extraordinary event which took place at this time.

Caracas fell ill of a shameful disease—or rather Gogol did—though he was not then having, nor had he ever had, any contact with other women. I will not even try to describe how this happened, or where the filthy complaint came from; all I know is that it happened. And that my great, unhappy friend would say to me: "So, Foma Paskalovitch, you see what lay at the heart of Caracas; it was the spirit of syphilis."

Sometimes he would even blame himself in a quite absurd manner; he was always prone to self-accusation. This incident was a real catastrophe as far as the already obscure relationship between husband and wife, and the hostile feelings of Nikolai Vassilevitch himself, were concerned. He was compelled to undergo long-drawn-out and painful treatment—the treatment of those days—and the situation was aggravated by the fact that the disease in the woman did not seem to be easily curable. Gogol deluded himself for some time that, by blowing his wife up and down and furnishing her with the most widely divergent aspects, he could obtain a woman immune from the contagion, but he was forced to desist when no results were forthcoming.

I shall be brief, seeking not to tire my readers, and also because what I remember seems to become more and more confused. I shall therefore hasten to the tragic conclusion. As to this last, however, let there be no mistake. I must once again make it clear that I am very sure of my ground. I was an eyewitness. Would that I had not been!

The years went by. Nikolai Vassilevitch's distaste for his wife became stronger, though his love for her did not show any signs of diminishing. Toward the end, aversion and attachment struggled so fiercely with each other in his heart that he became quite stricken, almost broken up. His restless eyes, which habitually assumed so many different expressions and sometimes spoke so sweetly to the heart of his interlocutor, now almost always shone with a fevered light, as if he were under the effect of a drug. The strangest impulses arose in him, accompanied by the most senseless fears. He spoke to me of Caracas more and more often, accusing her of unthinkable and amazing things. In these regions I could not follow him, since I had but a sketchy acquaintance with his wife, and hardly any intimacy— and above all since my sensibility was so limited compared with his. I shall accordingly restrict myself to reporting some of his accusations, without reference to my personal impressions.

"Believe it or not, Foma Paskalovitch," he would, for example, often say to me: "Believe it or not, *she's aging!*" Then, unspeakably moved, he would, as was his way, take my hands in his. He also accused Caracas of giving herself up to solitary pleasures, which he had expressly forbidden. He even went so far as to charge her with betraying him, but the things he said became so extremely obscure that I must excuse myself from any further account of them.

One thing that appears certain is that toward the end Caracas, whether aged or not, had turned into a bitter creature, querulous, hypocritical and subject to religious excess. I do not exclude the possibility that she may have had an influence on Gogol's moral position during the last period of his life, a position which is sufficiently well known. The tragic climax came one night quite unexpectedly when Nikolai Vassilevitch and I were celebrating his silver wedding—one of the last evenings we were to spend together. I neither can nor should attempt to set down what it was that led to his decision, at a time when to all appearances he was resigned to tolerating his consort. I know not what new events had taken place that day. I shall confine myself to the facts; my readers must make what they can of them.

That evening Nikolai Vassilevitch was unusually agitated. His distaste for Caracas seemed to have reached an unprecedented intensity. The famous "pyre of vanities"—the burning of his manuscripts

—had already taken place; I should not like to say whether or not at the instigation of his wife. His state of mind had been further inflamed by other causes. As to his physical condition, this was ever more pitiful, and strengthened my impression that he took drugs. All the same, he began to talk in a more or less normal way about Belinsky, who was giving him some trouble with his attacks on the *Selected Correspondence*. Then suddenly, tears rising to his eyes, he interrupted himself and cried out: "No. No. It's too much, too much. I can't go on any longer," as well as other obscure and disconnected phrases which he would not clarify. He seemed to be talking to himself. He wrung his hands, shook his head, got up and sat down again after having taken four or five anxious steps round the room. When Caracas appeared, or rather when we went in to her later in the evening in her Oriental chamber, he controlled himself no longer and began to behave like an old man, if I may so express myself, in his second childhood, quite giving way to his absurd impulses. For instance, he kept nudging me and winking and senselessly repeating: "There she is, Foma Paskalovitch; there she is!" Meanwhile she seemed to look up at us with a disdainful attention. But behind these "mannerisms" one could feel in him a real repugnance, a repugnance which had, I suppose, now reached the limits of the endurable. Indeed . . .

After a certain time Nikolai Vassilevitch seemed to pluck up courage. He burst into tears, but somehow they were more manly tears. He wrung his hands again, seized mine in his, and walked up and down, muttering: "That's enough! We can't have any more of this. This is an unheard of thing. How can such a thing be happening to me? How can a man be expected to put up with *this?*"

He then leapt furiously upon the pump, the existence of which he seemed just to have remembered, and, with it in his hand, dashed like a whirlwind to Caracas. He inserted the tube in her anus and began to inflate her. . . . Weeping the while, he shouted like one possessed: "Oh, how I love her, how I love her, my poor, poor darling! . . . But she's going to burst! Unhappy Caracas, most pitiable of God's creatures! But die she must!"

Caracas was swelling up. Nikolai Vassilevitch sweated, wept and pumped. I wished to stop him but, I know not why, I had not the courage. She began to become deformed and shortly assumed the most monstrous aspect; and yet she had not given any signs of alarm —she was used to these jokes. But when she began to feel unbearably full, or perhaps when Nikolai Vassilevitch's intentions became plain to her, she took on an expression of bestial amazement, even a little beseeching, but still without losing that disdainful look. She was afraid, she was even committing herself to his mercy, but still she could not believe in the immediate approach of her fate; she could not believe in the frightful audacity of her husband. He could not see her face because he was behind her. But I looked at her with fascination, and did not move a finger.

At last the internal pressure came through the fragile bones at the base of her skull, and printed on her face an indescribable rictus. Her belly, her thighs, her lips, her breasts and what I could see of her buttocks had swollen to incredible proportions. All of a sudden she belched, and gave a long hissing groan; both these phenomena one could explain by the increase in pressure, which had suddenly forced a way out through the valve in her throat. Then her eyes bulged frantically, threatening to jump out of their sockets. Her ribs flared wide apart and were no longer attached to the sternum, and she resembled a python digesting a donkey. A donkey, did I say? An ox! An elephant! At this point I believed her already dead, but Nikolai Vassilevitch, sweating, weeping and repeating: "My dearest! My beloved! My best!" continued to pump.

She went off unexpectedly and, as it were, all of a piece. It was not one part of her skin which gave way and the rest which followed, but her whole surface at the same instant. She scattered in the air. The pieces fell more or less slowly, according to their size, which was in no case above a very restricted one. I distinctly remember a piece of her cheek, with some lip attached, hanging on the corner of the mantelpiece. Nikolai Vassilevitch stared at me like a madman. Then he pulled himself together and, once more with furious determination, he began carefully to collect those poor rags which once had been the shining skin of Caracas, and all of her.

"Good-by, Caracas," I thought I heard him murmur, "Good-by! You were too pitiable!" And then suddenly and quite audibly: "The fire! The fire! She too must end up in the fire." He crossed himself— with his left hand, of course. Then, when he had picked up all those shriveled rags, even climbing on the furniture so as not to miss any, he threw them straight on the fire in the hearth, where they began to burn slowly and with an excessively unpleasant smell. Nikolai Vassilevitch, like all Russians, had a passion for throwing important things in the fire.

Red in the face, with an inexpressible look of despair, and yet of sinister triumph too, he gazed on the pyre of those miserable remains. He had seized my arm and was squeezing it convulsively. But those traces of what had once been a being were hardly well alight when he seemed yet again to pull himself together, as if he were suddenly remembering something or taking a painful decision. In one bound he was out of the room.

A few seconds later I heard him speaking to me through the door in a broken, plaintive voice: "Foma Paskalovitch, I want you to promise not to look. *Golubchik*, promise not to look at me when I come in."

I don't know what I answered, or whether I tried to reassure him in any way. But he insisted, and I had to promise him, as if he were a child, to hide my face against the wall and only turn round when he said I might. The door then opened violently and Nikolai Vassilevitch burst into the room and ran to the fireplace.

And here I must confess my weakness, though I consider it justified by the extraordinary circumstances. I looked round before Nikolai Vassilevitch told me I could; it was stronger than me. I was just in time to see him carrying something in his arms, something which he threw on the fire with all the rest, so that it suddenly flared up. At that, since the desire to *see* had entirely mastered every other thought in me, I dashed to the fireplace. But Nikolai Vassilevitch placed himself between me and it and pushed me back with a strength of which I had not believed him capable. Meanwhile the object was burning and giving off clouds of smoke. And before he showed any sign of calming down there was nothing left but a heap of silent ashes.

The true reason why I wished to see was because I had already glimpsed. But it was only a glimpse, and perhaps I should not allow myself to introduce even the slightest element of uncertainty into this true story. And yet, an eyewitness account is not complete without a mention of that which the witness knows with less than complete certainty. To cut a long story short, that something was a baby. Not a flesh and blood baby, of course, but more something in the line of a rubber doll or a model. Something, which, to judge by its appearance, could have been called *Caracas' son*.

Was I mad too? That I do not know, but I do know that this was what I saw, not clearly, but with my own eyes. And I wonder why it was that when I was writing this just now I didn't mention that when Nikolai Vassilevitch came back into the room he was muttering between his clenched teeth: "Him too! Him too!"

And that is the sum of my knowledge of Nikolai Vassilevitch's wife. In the next chapter I shall tell what happened to him afterwards, and that will be the last chapter of his life. But to give an interpretation of his feelings for his wife, or indeed for anything, is quite another and more difficult matter, though I have attempted it elsewhere in this volume, and refer the reader to that modest effort. I hope I have thrown sufficient light on a most controversial question and that I have unveiled the mystery, if not of Gogol, then at least of his wife. In the course of this I have implicitly given the lie to the insensate accusation that he ill-treated or even beat his wife, as well as other like absurdities. And what else can be the goal of a humble biographer such as the present writer but to serve the memory of that lofty genius who is the object of his study?

Alberto Moravia (pseudonym of Alberto Pincherle) was born in Rome in 1907. At the age of nine he contracted tuberculosis of the bone and spent most of the next eight years in bed. It was during this period of convalescence that Moravia first became obsessed with boredom, "a frightful thing, yet a great creative force. A necessary poison. No one who is not bored can create anything." He began to write stories and poems and published his first novel, The Indifferent Ones, *in 1929. Moravia is now one of Italy's most prolific novelists as well as a short story writer, essayist, and literary critic.*

An existential preoccupation with boredom, absurdity, and reality is found in most of Moravia's work. In "Bitter Honeymoon" isolation slowly gives way to human contact and to an intimacy, both sexual and spiritual, which in an absurd and largely meaningless world serves, if only temporarily, as a stay against despair. Moravia's description of place functions as a powerful element in the effect of the story. How does external environment reflect the internal states of the characters? Does the characters' movement through terrain and climate parallel their movement toward spiritual rapport? Why does Simona finally give herself to Giacomo? Further Reading: The Wayward Wife and Other Stories *(1960),* The Empty Canvas *(1961),* More Roman Tales *(1964).*

ITALY

Bitter Honeymoon

ALBERTO MORAVIA

They had chosen Anacapri for their honeymoon because Giacomo had been there a few months before and wanted to

Reprinted with permission of Farrar, Straus & Giroux, Inc. from *Bitter Honeymoon* by Alberto Moravia. Copyright © 1952, 1956 by Valentino Bompiani & Co. Also by permission of Martin Secker & Warburg Limited, London.

go back, taking his bride with him. His previous visit had been in the spring, and he remembered the clear, crisp air and the flowers alive with the hum of thousands of insects in the golden glow of the sun. But this time, immediately upon their arrival, everything seemed very different. The sultry dog-days of mid-August were upon them and steaming humidity overclouded the sky. Even on the heights of Anacapri, there was no trace of the crisp air, of flowers or the violent sea whose praises Giacomo had sung. The paths winding through the fields were covered with a layer of yellow dust, accumulated in the course of four months without rain, in which even gliding lizards left traces of their passage. Long before autumn was due, the leaves had begun to turn red and brown, and occasional whole trees had withered away for lack of water. Dust particles filled the motionless air and made the nostrils quiver, and the odors of meadows and sea had given way to those of scorched stones and dried dung. The water, which in the spring had taken its color from what seemed to be banks of violets floating just below the surface, was now a gray mass reflecting the melancholy, dazzling light brought by the *scirocco* which infested the sky.

"I don't think it's the least bit beautiful," Simona said on the day after their arrival, as they started along the path to the lighthouse. "I don't like it—no, not at all."

Giacomo, following several steps behind, did not answer. She had spoken in this plaintive and discontented tone of voice ever since they had emerged from their civil marriage in Rome, and he suspected that her prolonged ill-humor, mingled with an apparent physical repulsion, was not connected so much with the place as with his own person. She was complaining about Anacapri because she was not aware that her fundamental dissatisfaction was with her husband. Theirs was a love match to be sure, but one based rather on the will to love than on genuine feeling. There was good reason for his presentiment of trouble when, as he slipped the ring on her finger, he had read a flicker of regret and embarrassment on her face; for on their first night at Anacapri she had begged off, on the plea of fatigue and seasickness, from giving herself to him. On this, the second day of their marriage, she was just as much of a virgin as she had been before.

As she trudged wearily along, with a bag slung over one shoulder, between the dusty hedges, Giacomo looked at her with almost sorrowful intensity, hoping to take possession of her with a single piercing glance, as he had so often done with other women. But, as he realized right away, the piercing quality was lacking; his eyes fell with analytical affection upon her, but there was in them none of the transfiguring power of real passion. Although Simona was not tall, she had childishly long legs with slender thighs, rising to an indentation, almost a cleft at either side, visible under her shorts, where they were joined to the body. The whiteness of her legs was chaste, shiny and cold, she had a narrow waist and hips, and her only womanly feature, revealed when she turned around to speak to him, was the fullness of her low-swung breasts, which seemed like extraneous and burdensome weights, unsuited to her delicate frame. Similarly her thick, blond hair, although it was cut short, hung heavily over her neck. All of a sudden, as if she felt that she was being watched, she wheeled around and asked: "Why do you make me walk ahead of you?"

Giacomo saw the childishly innocent expression of her big blue eyes, her small, tilted nose and equally childishly rolled-back upper lip. Her face, too, he thought to himself, was a stranger to him, untouched by love.

"I'll go ahead, if you like," he said with resignation.

And he went by her, deliberately brushing her breast with his elbow to test his own desire. Then they went on walking, he ahead and she behind. The path wound about the summit of Monte Solaro, running along a wall of mossy stones with no masonry to hold them together and rows of vines strung out above them. On the other side there was a sheer descent, through uninhabited stretches of vineyard and olive grove, to the mist-covered gray sea. Only a solitary pine tree, halfway down the mountain, with its green crest floating in the air, recalled the idyllic purity of the landscape in its better days. Simona walked very slowly, lagging farther behind at every step. Finally she came to a halt and asked: "Have we far to go?"

"We've only just started," Giacomo said lightly. "At least an hour more."

"I can't bear it," she said ill-humoredly, looking at him as if she hoped he would propose giving up the walk altogether. He went back to her and put his arm around her waist.

"You can't bear the exertion or you can't bear me?"

"What do you mean, silly?" she countered with unexpected feeling. "I can't bear to go on walking, of course."

"Give me a kiss."

She administered a rapid peck on his cheek.

"It's so hot . . ." she murmured. "I wish we could go home."

"We must get to the lighthouse," Giacomo answered. "What's the point of going back? . . . We'll have a swim as soon as we arrive. It's a wonderful place, and the lighthouse is all pink and white. . . . Don't you want to see it?"

"Yes; but I'd like to fly there instead of walking."

"Let's talk," he suggested. "That way you won't notice the distance."

"But I have nothing to say," she protested, almost with tears in her voice.

Giacomo hesitated for a moment before replying:

"You know so much poetry by heart. Recite a poem and I'll listen; then before you know it, we'll be there."

He could see that he had hit home, for she had a truly extraordinary memory for verse.

"What shall I recite?" she asked with childish vanity.

"A canto from Dante."

"Which one?"

"The third canto of the *Inferno*," Giacomo said at random.

Somewhat consoled, Simona walked on, once more ahead of him, beginning to recite:

> "*Per me si va nella città dolente:*
> *per me si va nell'eterno dolore:*
> *per me si va tra la perduta gente . . .*"

She recited mechanically and with as little expression as a schoolgirl, breathing hard because of the double effort required of her. As she walked doggedly along, she paused at the end of every line, without paying any attention to syntax or meaning, like a schoolgirl endowed with zeal rather than intelligence. Every now and then she turned appealingly around and shot him a fleeting look, yes, exactly like a schoolgirl, with the blue-and-white cap perched on her blond hair. After they had gone some way they reached a wall built all around a large villa. The wall was covered with ivy, and leafy oak branches grew out over it.

"*'E caddi, come l'uom, cui sonno piglia,*" Simona said, winding up the third canto; then she turned around and asked: "Whose place is this?"

"It belonged to Axel Munthe," Giacomo answered; "but he's dead now."

"And what sort of a fellow was he?"

"A very shrewd sort indeed," said Giacomo. And, in order to amuse her, he added: "He was a doctor very fashionable in Rome at the turn of the century. If you'd like to know more about him, there's a story I've been told is absolutely true. . . . Would you like to hear it?"

"Yes; do tell me."

"Once a beautiful and frivolous society woman came to him with all sorts of imaginary ailments. Munthe listened patiently, examined her, and when he saw that there was nothing wrong, said: 'I know a sure cure, but you must do exactly what I say. . . . Go and look out of the open window and lean your elbows on the sill.' She obeyed, and Munthe went after her and gave her a terrific kick in the rear. Then he escorted her to the door and said: 'Three times a week, and in a few months you'll be quite all right.'"

Simona failed to laugh, and after a moment she said bitterly, looking at the wall: "That would be the cure for me."

Giacomo was struck by her mournful tone of voice.

"Why do you say that?" he asked, coming up to her. "What's come into your head?"

"It's true. . . . I'm slightly mad, and you ought to treat me exactly that way."

"What are you talking about?"

"About what happened last night," she said with startling frankness.

"But last night you were tired and seasick."

"That wasn't it at all. I'm never seasick, and I wasn't tired, either. I was afraid, that's all."

"Afraid of me?"

"No; afraid of the whole idea."

They walked on in silence. The wall curved, following the path and hanging slightly over, as if it could hardly contain the oak trees behind it. Then it came to an end, and in front of them lay a grassy plateau, below which the mountainside fell abruptly down to the arid and lonely promontories of Rio. The plateau was covered with asphodels, whose pyramidal flowers were of a dusty rose, almost gray in color. Giacomo picked some and handed them to his wife, saying: "Look. How beautiful . . ."

She raised them to her nose, like a young girl on her way to the altar, inhaling the fragrance of a lily. Perhaps she was conscious of her virginal air, for she pressed close to him, in something like an embrace, and whispered into one ear: "Don't believe what I just told you. . . . I wasn't afraid. . . . I'll just have to get used to the idea. . . . Tonight . . ."

"Tonight?" he repeated.

"You're so very dear to me," she murmured painfully, adding a strictly conventional phrase, which she seemed to have learned for the occasion, "Tonight I'll be yours."

She said these last two words hurriedly, as if she were afraid of the conventionality rather than the substance of them, and planted a hasty kiss on his cheek. It was the first time that she had ever told Giacomo that he was dear to her or anything like it, and he was tempted to take her in his arms. But she said in a loud voice: "Look! What's that down there on the sea?" And at the same time she eluded his grasp.

Giacomo looked in the direction at which she was pointing and saw a solitary sail emerging from the mist that hung over the water.

"A boat," he said testily.

She started walking again, at a quickened pace, as if she were afraid that he might try once more to embrace her. And as he saw her escape him he had a recurrent feeling of impotence, because he could not take immediate possession of his beloved.

"You won't do that to me tonight," he muttered between clenched teeth as he caught up with her.

And she answered, lowering her head without looking around: "It will be different tonight. . . ."

It was really hot—there was no doubt about that—and in the heavy air all round them there seemed to Giacomo to reside the same obstacle, the same impossibility that bogged down his relationship with his wife: the impossibility of a rainfall that would clear the air, the impossibility of love. He had a sensation of something like panic, when looking at her again he felt that his will to love was purely intellectual and did not involve his senses. Her figure was outlined quite precisely before him, but there was none of the halo around it in which love usually envelops the loved one's person. Impulsively he said: "Perhaps you shouldn't have married me."

Simona seemed to accept this statement as a basis for discussion, as if she had had the same thought without daring to come out with it.

"Why?" she asked.

Giacomo wanted to answer, "Because we don't really love each other," but although this was the thought in his mind, he expressed it in an entirely different manner. Simona was a Communist and had a job at Party headquarters. Giacomo was not a Communist at all; he claimed to attach no importance to his wife's political ideas, but they had a way of cropping up at the most unexpected moments as underlying motives for disagreement. And now he was astonished to hear himself say: "Because there is too great a difference of ideas between us."

"What sort of ideas do you mean?"

"Political ideas."

He realized, then, why her standoffishness had caused him to bring politics into the picture; it was with the hope of arousing a reaction to a point on which he knew her to be sensitive. And indeed she answered immediately: "That's not so. The truth is that I have certain ideas and you have none at all."

As soon as politics came up she assumed a self-sufficient, pedantic manner, quite the opposite of childish, which always threatened to infuriate him. He asked himself in all conscience whether his irritation stemmed from some latent anti-Communist feeling within himself, but quickly set his mind at rest on this score. He had no interest in politics whatsoever, and the only thing that bothered him was the fact that his wife did have such an interest.

"Well, whether or not it's a question of ideas," he said dryly, "there is *something* between us."

"What is it, then?"

"I don't know, but I can feel it."

After a second she said in the same irritating tone of voice: "I know quite well. It *is* a question of ideas. But I hope that some day you'll see things the way I do."

"Never."

"Why never?"

"I've told you so many times before. . . . First, because I don't want to be involved in politics of any kind, and second, because I'm too much of an individualist."

Simona made no reply, but in such cases her silence was direr than spoken disapproval. Giacomo was overcome by a wave of sudden anger. He overtook her and seized her arm.

"All this is going to have very serious consequences some day," he shouted. "For instance, if a Communist government comes to power, and I say something against it, you'll inform on me."

"Why should you say anything against it?" she retorted. "You just said that you don't want to be involved in politics of any kind."

"Anything can happen."

"And then the Communists aren't in power. . . . Why worry about a situation that doesn't exist?"

It was true then, he thought to himself, since she didn't deny it, that she would inform on him. He gripped her arm tighter, almost wishing to hurt her.

"The truth is that you don't love me," he said.

"I wouldn't have married you except for love," she said clearly, and she looked straight at him, with her lower lip trembling. Her voice filled Giacomo with tenderness, and he drew her to him and kissed her. Simona was visibly affected by the kiss; her nostrils stiffened and she breathed hard, and although her arms hung down at her sides, she pressed her body against his.

"My spy," he said, drawing away and stroking her face. "My little spy."

"Why do you call me spy?" she asked, taking immediate offense.

"I was joking."

They walked on, but as he followed her Giacomo wondered whether he had meant the word as a joke after all. And what about his anger? Was that a joke too? He didn't know how he could have given way to such unreasonable anger and have made such even more unreasonable accusations, and yet he dimly understood that they were justified by Simona's behavior. Meanwhile, they had come to the other side of the mountain, and from the highest point of the path they looked down at an immense expanse of air, like a bottomless well. Five minutes later they had a view of all one side of the island, a long, green slope covered with scattered vines and prickly pears, and at the bottom, stretching out into the sea, the chalky promontory on which stood the lighthouse. The sweep of the view was tremendous, and the pink-and-white checked lighthouse, hung between sky and sea, seemed far away and no larger than a man's hand. Simona clapped her hands in delight.

"How perfectly lovely!" she exclaimed.

"I told you it was beautiful, and you wouldn't believe me."

"Forgive me," she said, patting his cheek. "You always know best and I'm very silly."

Before he could control himself, Giacomo said: "Does that go for politics too?"

"No; not for politics. But don't let's talk about that just now."

He was annoyed with himself for having fallen back into an argument, but at the same time he suffered a return of the left-out and jealous feeling that overcame him every time she made a dogmatic, almost religious reference to her political ideas.

"Why shouldn't we talk about it?" he said as gently as he could. "Perhaps if we talked about it, we might understand one another better."

Simona did not reply, and Giacomo walked on after her, in an extremely bad humor. Now he was the one to feel the heaviness and heat of the day, while Simona, intoxicated by the sight of the distant sea, shouted: "Let's run down the rest of the way. I can't wait to get into the water."

With her sling bag bobbing about on her shoulder, she began to run down the path, emitting shrill cries of joy. Giacomo saw that she was throwing her legs in all directions like an untrained colt. Suddenly the thought, "Tonight she'll be mine" floated through his head and quieted him. What could be the importance of belonging to a political party in comparison to that of the act of love, so ageless and so very human? Men had possessed women long before the existence of political parties or religions. And he was sure that in the moment when he possessed Simona he would drive out of her every allegiance except that of her love for him. Strengthened by this thought he ran after her, shouting in his turn: "Wait for me, Simona!"

She stopped to wait, flushed, quivering and bright-eyed. As he caught up with her he said pantingly: "Just now I began to feel very happy. I know that we're going to love one another."

"I know it too," she said, looking at him out of her innocent blue eyes.

Giacomo put one arm around her waist, catching her hand in his and compelling her to throw it over his shoulders. They walked on in this fashion, but Simona's eyes remained set on the water below. Giacomo, on the other hand, could not tear his thoughts away from the body he was holding so tightly. Simona was wearing a skimpy boy's jersey with a patch in the front. And her head was boyish in outline as well, with the unruly short hair falling over her cheeks. Yet her slender waist fitted into the curve of his arm with a womanly softness which seemed to foreshadow the complete surrender promised for the coming night. Suddenly he breathed into her ear: "You'll always be my little friend and comrade."

Simona's mind must have been on the lighthouse, and the word "comrade" came through to her alone, out of context, without the sentimental intonation that gave it Giacoma's intended meaning. For she answered with a smile: "We can't be comrades . . . at least, not until you see things the way I do. . . . But I'll be your wife."

So she was still thinking of the Party, Giacomo said to himself with excusable jealousy. The word "comrade" had for her no tender connotations, but only political significance. The Party continued to have a prior claim to her loyalty.

"I didn't mean it that way," he said disappointedly.

"I'm sorry," she said, hastening to correct herself. "That's what we call each other in the Party."

"I only meant that you'd be my lifelong companion."

"That's true," she said, lowering her head in embarrassment, as if she couldn't really accept the word except politically.

They dropped their arms and walked down the path with no link between them. As they proceeded, the lighthouse seemed to approach them, revealing its tower shape. The water beyond it had a metallic sheen, derived from the direct rays of the sun, while behind them the mountain seemed to grow higher, with a wall of red rock rising above the lower slope which they were now traversing. At the top was a summerhouse with a railing around it, in which they could distinguish two tiny human figures enjoying the view.

"That vantage-point is called La Migliara," Giacomo explained. "A few years ago an Anacapri girl threw herself down the mountain from it, but first she wound her braids around her head and over her eyes so as not to see what she was doing."

Simona tossed a look over her shoulder at the top of the mountain. "Suicide is all wrong," she said.

Giacomo felt jealousy sting him again.

"Why?" he asked. "Does the Party forbid it?"

"Never mind about the Party." She looked out over the sea and thrust her face and chest forward as if to breathe in the breeze blowing in their direction. "Suicide's all wrong because life is beautiful and it's a joy to be alive."

Again Giacomo didn't really want to get into a political argument; he wanted to make a show of the serenity and detachment which he thoroughly believed were his. But again his annoyance carried him away.

"But T——" (this was the name of a Communist friend they had in common) "committed suicide, didn't he?"

"He did wrong," she said succinctly.

"Why so? He must have had some reason. What do you know?"

"I do know, though," she said obstinately. "He did wrong. It's our duty to live."

"Our duty?"

"Yes; duty."

"Who says so?"

"Nobody. It just is."

"I might just as well say that it's our duty to take our life if we feel it's not worth living. . . . Nobody says so. It just is."

"That's not true," she answered inflexibly. "We were made to live and not to die. . . . Only someone that's sick or in a morbid state of mind can think that life's not worth living."

"So you think that T—— was either sick or in a morbid state of mind, do you?"

"At the moment when he killed himself, yes, I do."

Giacomo was tempted to ask her if this was the Party line, as seemed to him evident from that stubborn note in her voice which annoyed him so greatly, but this time he managed to restrain himself. By now they had reached the bottom of the slope and were crossing a dry, flat area, covered with wood-spurge and prickly pears. Then the land turned into rock and they found themselves before the lighthouse, at the end of the path, which seemed like the end of all human habitation and the beginning of a new and lonely world of colorless chalk and stone. The lighthouse soared up above them as they plunged down among the boulders toward the sea. At a bend, they suddenly came upon a basin of green water, surrounded by rocky black cliffs, eroded by salt. Simona ran down to the cement landing and exclaimed: "Wonderful! Just what I was hoping for! Now we can swim. And we have it all to ourselves. We're quite alone."

She had no sooner spoken these words than a man's voice came out of the rocks: "Simona! What a pleasant surprise."

They turned around, and when a face followed the voice, Simona shouted: "Livio! Hello! Are you here too? What are you doing?"

The young man who emerged from the rocks was short and powerfully built, with broad shoulders. His head contrasted with this athletic body, for it was bald, with only a fringe of hair around the neck, and his flat face had a scholarly expression. The face of a ferret, Giacomo thought, taking an instant dislike to it, not exactly intelligent, but keen and treacherous. He knew the fellow by sight and was aware that he worked in Simona's office. Now Livio came into full view, pulling up his tight, faded red trunks.

"I'm doing the same thing you are, I suppose," he said by way of an answer.

Then Simona said something which gave Giacomo considerable satisfaction.

"That's not very likely. . . . Unless you've just got yourself married. . . . I'm here on my honeymoon. . . . Do you know my husband?"

"Yes; we know each other," Livio said easily, jumping down on to a big square stone and shaking Giacomo's hand so hard that the latter winced with pain as he echoed: "Yes, we've met in Rome." Livio then turned to Simona and added: "I'd heard something to the effect that you were about to marry. But you should have told the comrades. They want to share your joys."

He said all this in a colorless, businesslike voice, but one which was not necessarily devoid of feeling. Giacomo noticed that Simona was smiling and seemed to be waiting for Livio to go on, while Livio stood like a bronze statue on a stone pedestal, with his trunks pulled tightly over his voluminous pubis and all the muscles of his body standing out, and talked down to them. Giacomo felt as if he were somehow left out of their conversation, and drew away, all the while listening intently. They conversed for several minutes without moving, asking one another about various Party workers and where they had spent their vacations.

But Giacomo was struck less by what they said than by the tone in which they said it. What was this tone exactly, and why did it rub him the wrong way? There was a note of complicity in it, he concluded, a reference to some secret bond different from that of either friendship or family. For a moment he wondered if it weren't just what one would find between fellow employees in a bank or government office. But upon reflection, he realized that it was entirely different. It was . . . he searched for some time, groping for an exact definition . . . it was the tone of voice of two monks or two nuns meeting one another. And why then did it rub him the wrong way? Not because he disapproved of Livio's and Simona's political ideas; in the course of a rational discussion he might very well allow that these had some basis. No; there was nothing rational about his hostility; its cause was obscure even to himself and at times it seemed to be one with his jealousy, as if he were afraid that Simona would escape him through her Party connections. As these thoughts ran through his mind, his face grew dark and discontented, so that when Simona joined him, all smiles, a moment later, she exclaimed in surprise: "What's wrong? Why are you unhappy?"

"Nothing . . . It's just the heat."

"Let's go in the water. . . . But first, where can we undress?"

"Just follow me. . . . This way."

He knew the place well, and now led Simona through a narrow passage among the rocks. Behind these rocks they stepped across some other lower ones and then went around a huge mass which sealed off a tiny beach of very fine, black sand at the foot of glistening, black rocky walls around a pool of shallow water filled with black seaweed. The effect was that of a room, with the sky for a ceiling, a watery floor and walls of stone.

"No swimming-bath can match this," Giacomo observed, looking around him.

"At last I can shed my clothes," said Simona with a sigh of relief.

She put her bag down on the sand and bent over to take out her bathing-suit, while, leaning against the rocks, Giacomo stripped himself in a second of his shirt and trousers. The sight of him stark naked caused her to give a nervous laugh.

"This is the sort of place to go swimming with no suits on, isn't it?" she said.

"Unfortunately, one can never manage to be alone," Giacomo replied, thinking of Livio.

He walked, still naked, with bare feet, over the cold sand in her direction, but she did not see him coming because she was pulling her jersey over her head. Her nakedness, he reflected, made her seem more virginal than ever. Her low-swung, round breasts had large rosy nipples, and a look of purity about them, as if they had never been offered to a masculine caress. Indeed, her virginal quality was so overwhelming that Giacomo did not dare press her to him as he had intended, but stood close by while she pulled her head out of the jersey. She shook back her ruffled hair and said in surprise: "What are you doing? Why don't you put on your trunks?"

"I'd like to make love right here and now," said Giacomo.

"On these rocks? Are you mad?"

"No. I'm not mad."

They were facing each other now, he entirely naked and she naked down to the waist. She crossed her arms over her breasts as if to support and protect them and said entreatingly: "Let's wait till tonight. . . . And meanwhile let's go swimming . . . please. . . ."

"Tonight you'll put me off again."

"No; it will be different tonight."

Giacomo walked silently away and proceeded to put on his trunks, while Simona, obviously relieved, hastily donned her two-piece suit. She shouted gaily: "I'm off for a swim! If you love me, you'll follow."

"Let's go in right here," Giacomo suggested.

Simona paused and stuck her white foot into the green and brown seaweed that choked the black water.

"This pool is too murky. . . . It's no more than a puddle. Let's go where we just came from."

"But we shan't be alone."

"Oh, we have plenty of time for that."

They went back to the basin, where Livio was taking a sun-bath on the cement landing, lying as still as if he were dead. Somehow this increased Giacomo's dislike of him. Yes; he was the sort of fellow that goes in for purposeful tanning, and then wanders about showing it off, wearing skimpy trunks designed to exhibit his virility as well. When Livio heard them coming he leaped to his feet and said: "Come on, Simona. Let's dive in and race over to that rock."

"You'll have to give me a handicap of at least a length," she said joyfully, forgetful of her husband.

"I'll give you three lengths, if you say so."

There it was, Giacomo could not help thinking, the same intimate, conspiratorial, clubby, Party manner, that tone of voice in which, despite their marriage, she had never spoken to him, and perhaps never would speak either. Sitting on a flat rock, just above the landing, he watched his wife plunge awkwardly in and then swim like a dark shadow under the green water until she came out, with her blond head drippnig.

"That was a real belly-flop," Livio shouted, making a perfect dive to join her. He too swam underwater, but for a longer distance than Simona, so that he came out farther away. Giacomo wondered if this "Party manner" weren't all a product of his imagination, and if there hadn't been in the past some more intimate personal relationship between them. And he realized that this second hypothesis was, on the whole, less disagreeable than the first. Then he said to himself that if he were to mention any such suspicion to Simona she would be outraged and brand it as utterly "bourgeois," not to say "evil-minded and filthy." The moment after he dismissed it as out of the question. No, they were comrades, as she had said, and nothing more. What still puzzled him was why he objected more to their being Party comrades than to their being lovers. With a wavering effort of goodwill, he said to himself that his jealousy was absurd, and he must drive it out of his mind. . . . And all the while he watched the two of them race across the dazzling green water in the direction of a round rock which emerged at the far end of the basin. Livio got there first, and, hoisting himself up on a protruding spur, shouted back at Simona: "I win! You're all washed up!"

"Speak for yourself!" Simona retorted.

This was the sort of joking insult he and Simona should have batted back and forth between them, Giacomo reflected. If they didn't joke that way on their honeymoon, when would they ever do it? He got up decisively, ran several steps along the landing and went in after them. He landed square on his stomach and was infuriated by the pain. After swimming several strokes under water he came up and started toward the rock where Livio and Simona were sitting. They were close together, talking uninterruptedly, with their legs dangling. He didn't relish the sight; in fact, it took away all the pleasure he should have felt from plunging hot and dusty into the cool water. He swam angrily ahead, arrived at the rock breathless and said, hanging on to a ledge: "Do you know, this water's very, very cold."

"It seemed warm to me," said Simona, momentarily interrupting the conversation to shoot him a glance.

"I swam here in April," Livio put in; "it was cold then, I can tell you."

With a curiosity that seemed to Giacomo somewhat flirtatious, Simona asked him: "Were you all alone?"

"No. I came with Nella," Livio answered.

Giacomo was trying to clamber up on the rock, but the only place where he could get a solid grip was the one where Livio and Simona were sitting. They seemed to be oblivious of his struggles, and he preferred not to ask them to move over. Finally, he caught hold of a jutting piece of rock studded with jagged points, one of which left a pain in the palm of his hand as if it had dug deep into the flesh. Just as he got himself into a sitting position, the other two, with a shout of "Let's race back!" dived into the water, showering him with spray. He looked furiously after them as they raced toward the shore. Only when he had regained his self-control did he plunge in and follow. Simona and Livio were sitting in the shelter of a cliff and Simona was opening a lunch-box that she had taken out of her bag.

"Let's have something to eat," she said to Giacomo as he approached them. "But we must share it with Livio. He says he meant to go back up the mountain, but in this heat it would be too ridiculous."

Without saying a word, Giacomo sat down in the rocks beside them. The contents of the lunch-box turned out to be scanty: some meat sandwiches, two hard-boiled eggs and a bottle of wine.

"Livio will have to be content with very little," Giacomo said gruffly.

"Don't worry," Livio answered gaily. "I'm a very abstemious fellow."

Simona seemed extremely happy as she sat with crossed legs, dividing the lunch. She gave a sandwich to each one of them, bit into her own, and asked Livio:

"Where did you get your tan?"

"On the Tiber," he replied.

"Your whole group is very river-minded, isn't it, Livio?" she asked between one bite and another.

"All except Regina. She scorns the river completely; says it isn't aristocratic enough for her."

The things they talked about were trivial and childish enough, Giacomo reflected. And yet there was a greater intimacy between them than between husband and wife.

"No matter how hard she tries, Regina will never be able to put her background behind her," Simona observed.

"Who is Regina?" asked Giacomo.

"Someone in our outfit . . . the daughter of a wealthy landowner . . . a very fine girl, really," Livio told him. "But wiping out an old trade-mark is no easy matter."

"And in this case, what trade-mark do you mean?"

"The bourgeois trade-mark."

"If you people ever get into power," Giacomo said impulsively, "you'll have to wipe that trade-mark out of millions of people."

"That's exactly what we'll do," Livio said with complete self-confidence. "That's our job, isn't it, Simona?"

Simona's mouth was full, but she nodded assent.

"The Italian bourgeoisie will be a tough nut to crack," Livio went on, "but we'll crack it, even if we have to kill off a large proportion in the process."

"There's a chance you may be killed off yourselves," said Giacomo.

"That's the risk we have to run in our profession," Livio retorted.

Giacomo noticed that Simona did not seem to go along with Livio's ruthlessness; at this last remark she frowned and uttered no word of approval. Livio must have been aware of this, for he brusquely changed the subject.

"Simona, you really should have told us you were getting married, you know. There are some things it's not fair to hide!"

There was a note of tenderness toward Giacomo in Simona's reply.

"We decided from one day to the next. . . . Only the legal witnesses were present. Even our own parents weren't in on it."

"You mean you didn't want them?"

"We didn't want them, and anyhow they might not have come. . . . Giacomo's father and mother didn't want him to marry me."

"Because you're too far to the left, is that it?"

"No," Giacomo interposed. "My people don't go in for politics at all. But my mother had her eye on a certain girl. . . ."

"They may not go in for politics, as you say," Livio said, after another mouthful, "but there are always political implications. How could it be otherwise? Politics gets into everything these days."

True enough, Giacomo thought to himself. Even into honeymoons and a newly-married couple's first embrace. Then, annoyed at his own train of thought, he held out the hard-boiled eggs to his companions.

"You two eat them," he said. "I'm not hungry."

"Be honest now," Livio said with a look of surprise on his face.

"Why aren't you hungry?" Simona asked him.

"That damned *scirocco*, I imagine."

Livio looked up at the cloudy sky.

"There'll be a storm before night. I can promise you that," he said.

Livio's conversation was made up of commonplaces and clichés, Giacomo reflected. But Simona seemed to like them. They conveyed more to her than his own attempts to express emotions that were difficult if not impossible to put into words. Meanwhile Simona, having finished her lunch, said: "Let's lie down for a sun-bath now."

"Will you be my pillow, Simona?" Livio asked, sliding toward her with the plain intention of putting his head on her lap.

For the first time Simona took her husband's presence into account.

"It's too hot for that, and you're too heavy."

And she looked at Giacomo out of the corner of her eyes as if to say: From now on, I won't let anyone do that but you. Giacomo's spirits soared, and he once more felt that there was a possibility of love between them. He got up and said: "Shall we go for a walk among the rocks?"

"Yes," she said promptly, following his example. And she added, to Livio: "See you later. . . . We're going to explore."

"Have a good time," Livio threw after them.

Simona led the way through the passage which her husband had shown her before. She made straight for the black beach, sat down at the foot of a rock and said: "Stretch out and put your head on my legs. . . . You'll be more comfortable that way."

Overcome by joy, Giacomo threw his arms around her and drew her to him. He gave her a kiss, and Simona returned it, blowing hard through her nose, almost as if she were suffering. When they had drawn apart, she repeated: "Stretch out, and we'll snatch a bit of sleep together."

She leaned her back against the rock, and Giacomo, his heart overflowing with love, lay down and put his head on her lap. He closed his eyes, and Simona began to stroke his face. With a hesitant and timid motion, she passed her hand over his cheeks, under his chin and up to the top of his head, where she ran her fingers through his hair. When Giacomo opened his eyes for a split second he saw that she was looking at him with childish intentness and curiosity. Meeting his glance, she bent over, placed a quick kiss on each of his eyes and told him to go to sleep. Giacomo closed his eyes again and gave himself up to enjoyment of the light touch of her tireless little hand until finally he dozed off. He slept for an indefinable length of time and woke up feeling chilled. Simona was sitting in the same position, with his head on her lap. Looking up, he saw the reason for his feeling so cold. The sky was filled with heavy, black storm clouds.

"How long have I been asleep?" he asked her.

"About an hour."

"And what about you?"

"I didn't sleep. I was looking at you."

"The sun's disappeared."

"Yes."

"There's going to be quite a rainstorm."

"Livio's gone," she said by way of an answer.

"Who is that Livio, anyhow?" Giacomo asked without moving.

"A Party comrade, a friend."

"I don't care for him."

"I know that," she said with a smile. "You made it pretty plain. As he was going away he pointed to you as you lay there asleep and said: "What's the matter? Has he got in for me?'"

"I haven't got it in for him. . . . But he has no manners. I'm on my honeymoon, and he acts as if it were his."

"He's a good fellow."

"You used to be in love with him. Admit it!"

She came out with a peal of innocent, silvery laughter.

"You must be crazy. I couldn't possibly fall in love with him. He doesn't appeal to me in the least."

"But the way you talked to one another . . ."

"He's a Party comrade," she repeated, "and that's the way we talk." She was silent, for a moment, and then said with unexpected bitterness: "He's unintelligent. That's why he doesn't appeal to me."

"He doesn't seem to me much more stupid than the next man."

"He said a lot of foolish things," she went on angrily. "That we'd kill people off, for instance. . . . He knows better and spoke that way just to show off. . . . but such loose talk is harmful to the Party."

"You're the one that's got it in for him now."

"No. I haven't got it in for him; but he had no business to talk that way." Then she added, more coolly, "As a matter of fact, he's of value to the Party, even if he isn't too bright. He's absolutely loyal; you could ask him to do anything."

"And what value have I?" Giacomo was bold enough to ask jokingly.

"You can't have any value, since you're not one of us."

Giacomo was displeased by this answer. He got up and looked at the lowering sky.

"We'd better get back home before it rains. What do you say?"

"Yes. I think we had better."

Giacomo hesitated for a moment, put his arm around her waist and asked softly: "When we get there, will you be mine . . . at last?"

She nodded, turning her head away in order not to meet his eyes. Feeling easier in his mind, Giacomo quickly got dressed. A few steps away, Simona pulled on her shorts and jersey and started to adjust her bag over her shoulder. But with a tender protectiveness such as he had not displayed on the way down, Giacomo said: "I'll carry that for you."

They started off. First they crossed the flatland, where the pale green branches of the prickly pears seemed to gleam discordantly against the dark sky. As they reached the beginning of the slope they turned around to look behind them. The pink-and-white lighthouse stood out against a majestic mass of black storm clouds rising from the horizon to invade that part of the sky which was still empty. These clouds, shaped like great rampant beasts, had smoking underbellies, and irregular fringes hung down from them over the sea, which was spottily darkening in some places, while in others it still shone like burnished lead in the sun. The fringes were gusts of rain, just beginning to comb the surface of the water. Meanwhile, a turbulent wind covered the prickly pears with yellow dust and a blinding stroke of lightning zigzagged diagonally across the sky from one point to another. After a long silence they heard the thunder—no clap, but rather a dull rumble within the clouds. Giacomo saw his wife pale and instinctively shrink toward him.

"Lightning scares me to death," she said, looking at him.

Giacomo raised his eyes to the half-clear, half-stormy sky.

"The storm isn't here yet," he said. "It's still over the sea. If we hurry, we may get home without a wetting."

"Let's hurry, then," she said, continuing to climb up the path.

The clouds, apparently driven by an increasingly powerful wind, were spreading out over the sky with startling rapidity. Simona quickened her pace to almost a run, and Giacomo could not help teasing her.

"Afraid of lightning? What would the comrades say to that? A good Marxist like yourself shouldn't have any such fear."

"It's stronger than I am," she said in a childish voice, without turning around.

There were steps, first narrow and then wide, to facilitate the ascent of the lower part of the path, and higher up it rose in wide curves through groves of olive trees. Simona was a long way ahead; Giacomo could see her striding along fifty or sixty feet in front of him. At the top they paused to catch their breath and look around. Anacapri, momentarily at their backs, stood reassuringly behind a barrier of green, looking like an Arab city, with its terraces, campanile and gray-domed church. Giacomo pointed to the shrunken lighthouse on the promontory below, profiled against the threatening storm.

"Just think, we were right down there!" he murmured.

"I can't wait to be home," said Simona, perhaps with the thunder and lightning in mind. Then, meeting Giacomo's eyes, she added with hesitant coquetry: "What about you?"

"I agree," he answered in a low voice, with emotion.

The climb was over, and all they had to do now was follow the level path to their rented house, which was well this side of Anacapri. They walked by the wall around the Munthe villa, along a meadow planted with oak trees, and there, just round a bend, was the white wall of their house and the rusty iron gate in the shade of a carob tree with pods hanging all over it. The clouds were straight above them now, and it was as dark as evening. Simona hurriedly pushed open the gate and went on ahead without waiting for her husband to follow. Giacomo walked more slowly down the marble steps among the cactus plants. As he went, there was another rumble of thunder, louder this time, like an overturned wagon-load of stones rolling down a hill. From inside the house Simona called back: "Shut the door tight!"

The house was on a hillside, set back among the trees, and consisted of four roughly furnished rooms. Giacomo made his way in amid almost complete darkness. There was no electric light, but oil lamps of various shapes and colors were lined up on the hall table. He lifted the glass off one of these, lit a match, touched it to the wick, put back the glass and entered the dining room. No one was there, but he could hear Simona moving in the room next to it. He did not wish to join her immediately, and, feeling thirsty, he poured himself out a glass of white wine. Finally, he picked up the lamp and went to the bedroom door. The bedroom, too, was almost dark. The window giving on to the garden was open, and through it, in what light was left among the shadows, he could make out the terrace surrounded by lemon trees planted in big pots. Simona, in a dressing gown, was tidying the still unmade bed. He set the lamp down on the bedside table and said: "Are you still afraid of the lightning?"

She was leaning over the bed, with one leg slightly raised, smoothing the sheet. Pulling herself up, she answered: "No. Now that I'm in the house I feel safer."

"And are you afraid of me?"

"I never was afraid of you."

Giacomo walked around the bed and took her into his arms. Standing beside the head of the bed, they exchanged a kiss. Giacomo undid the sash of Simona's dressing gown and it slipped down over her shoulders and hips to the floor. But Simona did not interrupt the kiss; indeed she prolonged it with an awkward eagerness, betrayed by her characteristic way of blowing through her nose. With sudden decisiveness, Giacomo let her go.

"Lie down, will you?" he said, hurriedly taking off his clothes.

Simona hesitated and then lay down on the bed. Giacomo was aware of being impelled by strictly animal feelings, as if he were not in a house, but in a dark cave—yes, as if he were a primitive man, moved by carnal appetite alone. Yet it was with a certain tenderness that he lay down beside his wife. She was facing the wall, but brusquely she turned around and pressed herself against him, snuggling into his arms. For a few minutes they lay there, motionless, then Giacomo began chastely and gently to caress her. He wanted to possess her on her own virginal terms, without bringing any of his masculine experience into play. His light caresses and the words he whispered through her hair into one ear were intended to calm her fears and lead her almost insensibly to give herself to him. He was not in a hurry and it seemed to him that his new policy of consideration and patience would win for him what his haste of the previous evening had failed to obtain. And by degrees he had the impression that, in response to his words and caresses, she was yielding not only her body, but also that inward part of her which had resisted him heretofore. Simona did not speak, but her breathing grew gradually heavier. All of a sudden, almost involuntarily, he gave way to a natural impulse and attempted to take her. Under the impact of his body, Simona seemed at first to surrender, then brusquely she rebelled and struggled to free herself. With a mixture of anger and submission she whispered: "I can't do it! I can't!"

Giacomo refused to heed her change of heart and tried to prevail over her by force. She defended herself with her feet and knees and hands, while he did everything to overcome her. In the combat their naked bodies were bathed in perspiration. Finally Giacomo lost his patience, leaped out of bed, and went into the bathroom, saying: "I'll be back in a minute."

Guided by a furious inspiration, he groped his way to the wash basin, took the razor blade he had used for shaving that morning and plunged it into the cushion of his thumb. He felt the cold blade cut through his skin, but had no pain. Then he put the blade back on the shelf and squeezed his thumb, which gave out an abundant flow of blood. He went back to the bedroom and threw himself upon his wife, rubbing his bloody thumb on the sheet between her legs. Then he shouted angrily: "You may not realize it, but you're no longer a virgin!"

Tremblingly she asked: "How do you know?"

"Just look!"

He took the lamp from the table and threw its light upon the bed. Simona was hunched up on the pillow, with her knees against her chin and her arms crossed over her breasts. She looked down at the place where Giacomo had thrown the light and saw a long streak of red blood. Batting her eyelids in disgust, she said: "Are you sure?"

"Positive!"

But just at that moment her eyes traveled to the hand in which Giacomo was holding the lamp. Blood was streaming out of the cut in the cushion of his thumb. In a plaintive voice she cried out: "It's not my blood. It's yours! . . . You cut yourself on purpose."

Giacomo put the lamp back on the table and shouted in a rage: "That the only blood I'll see tonight or any night to come. You're still a virgin and you always will be!"

"Why do you say that? What makes you so unkind?"

"That's the way it is," he answered. "You'll never be mine. Some part of you is hostile to me, and hostile it will remain."

"What part do you mean?"

"You're closer to that fool, Livio, than you are to me," he said, coming out with his jealousy at last. "That part of you which is close to Livio is hostile to me."

"That's not true."

"Yes; it is true. And it's equally true that if your Party came to power you'd inform on me. . . ."

"Who says so?"

"You said so yourself this morning, on the way to the lighthouse."

"I said nothing at all."

"Well, what would you do, then?"

She hesitated for a moment and then said:

"Why do you bring up such things at a time like this?"

"Because they prevent you from loving me and becoming my wife."

"I wouldn't inform on you," she said at last. "I'd leave you, that's all."

"But you're supposed to inform on your enemies," he shouted, angrier than ever. "It's your duty."

Still huddled up at the head of the bed, she burst into tears.

"Giacomo, why are you so unkind? . . . I'd kill myself. That's what I'd do."

Giacomo did not have the courage to remind her that on the way to the lighthouse she had branded suicide as morbid and absolutely inadmissible. After all, this contradiction was more flattering to him than an open declaration of love. Meanwhile, still in tears, she had got down from the bed and gone over to the open window. Giacomo lay on the bed, watching. She stood straight, with her head bent to the side and one arm raised against the frame. Suddenly the room was lit up, and every object in it, her naked, white body, the garden and the potted lemon trees around the terrace. There followed a metallic crack and a violent tremor which made the window and the walls of the room tremble. Simona gave a terrified cry, left the window and threw herself sobbing into her husband's arms. Giacomo pressed her to him, and almost immediately, while still weeping, she sought his embrace, he penetrated her body without any difficulty whatsoever. He had the feeling that a hidden flower, composed of only two petals, had opened—although still remaining invisible—to something that in the dark night of the flesh played the role of the sun. Nothing was settled, he reflected later on, but for the time being it was enough to know that she would kill herself for him.

From the first to the final page of "Death in Midsummer," events unfold against a carefully delineated pattern of seasonal change. The story begins and ends in summer, and it begins and ends at the edge of the sea. The unity between what happens, and where and when it happens, is not mere stylistic felicity; it is the story's meaning. Why does Yukio Mishima dwell so carefully on Yasue's maidenhood at the beginning of the story? Does the birth of another child toward the end of the story serve only to provide a kind of compensatory happy ending? Yukio Mishima is a writer who creates significant moments from which significant truths emerge. What significant truth emerges here?

Yukio Mishima is one of the most prolific serious writers in the world and perhaps the greatest living master of the short story form. In the past twenty years he has published sixteen novels, more than fifty short stories, seven volumes of essays, more than twenty plays, and two travel books. He was graduated from the Peer's School in 1944 (at the age of nineteen) with a citation from the Emperor as most brilliant student; in the same year he completed his first book, A Forest in Full Flower. *Further Reading:* The Sound of Waves (1956), Madame de Sade (1967).

JAPAN

Death in Midsummer

YUKIO MISHIMA

La mort . . . nous affecte plus profondément sous le regne pompeux de l'été.

BAUDELAIRE—LES PARADIS ARTIFICIELS

A. Beach, near the southern tip of the Izu Peninsula, is still unspoiled for sea bathing. The sea bottom is pitted and uneven,

Yukio Mishima, *Death in Midsummer.* © 1966 by New Directions. Reprinted by permission of New Directions Publishing Corporation. Translated by Edward G. Seindensticker.

it is true, and the surf is a little rough; but the water is clean, the slope of to sea is gentle, and conditions are on the whole good for swimming. Largely because it is so out of the way, A. Beach has none of the noise and dirt of resorts nearer Tokyo. It is a two hour bus ride from Itō.

Almost the only inn is the Eirakusō, which also has cottages to rent. There are only one or two of the shabby refreshment stands that clutter most beaches in summer. The sand is rich and white, and halfway down the beach a rock, surmounted by pines, crouches over the sea almost as if it were the work of a landscape gardener. At high tide it lies half under water.

And the view is beautiful. When the west wind blows the mists from the sea, the islands off shore come in sight, Ōshima near at hand and Toshima farther off, and between them a little triangular island called Utoneshima. Beyond the headland of Nanago lies Cape Sakai, a part of the same mountain mass, throwing its roots deep into the sea; and beyond that the cape known as the Dragon Palace of Yatsu, and Cape Tsumeki, on the southern tip of which a lighthouse beam revolves each night.

In her room at the Eirakusō Tomoko Ikuta was taking a nap. She was the mother of three children, though one would never have suspected it to look at the sleeping figure. The knees showed under the one-piece dress, just a little short, of light salmon-pink linen. The plump arms, the unworn face, and the slightly curled lips gave off a girl-like freshness. Perspiration had come out on the forehead and in the hollows beside the nose. Flies buzzed dully, and the air was like the inside of a heated metal dome. The salmon linen rose and fell so slightly that it seemed the embodiment of the heavy, windless afternoon.

Most of the other guests were down on the beach. Tomoko's room was on the second floor. Below her window was a white swing for children. There were chairs on the lawn, nearly a half acre wide, as well as tables and a peg for quoits. The quoits lay scattered over the lawn. No one was in sight, and the buzzing of an occasional bee was drowned out by the waves beyond the hedge. The pines came immediately up to the hedge, and gave way beyond to the sand and the surf. A stream passed under the inn. It formed a pool before spilling into the ocean, and fourteen or fifteen geese would splash and honk most indelicately as they fed there every afternoon.

Tomoko had two sons, Kiyoo and Katsuo, who were six and three, and a daughter, Keiko, who was five. All three were down on the beach with Yasue, Tomoko's sister-in-law. Tomoko felt no qualms about asking Yasue to take care of the children while she had a nap herself.

Yasue was an old maid. In need of help after Kiyoo was born, Tomoko had consulted with her husband and decided to invite Yasue in from the provinces. There was no real reason why Yasue had gone unmarried. She was not particularly alluring, indeed, but then neither was she homely. She had declined proposal after proposal, until she was past the age for marrying. Much taken with the idea of following her brother to Tokyo, she leaped at Tomoko's invitation. Her family had plans for marrying her off to a provincial notable.

Yasue was far from quick, but she was very good-natured. She addressed Tomoko, younger than she, as an older sister, and was always careful to defer to her. The Kanazawa accent had almost disappeared. Besides helping with the children and the housework, Yasue went to sewing school and made clothes for herself, of course, and for Tomoko and the children too. She would take out her notebook and sketch new fashions in downtown store windows, and sometimes she would find a shopgirl glaring at her and even reprimanding her.

She was down on the beach in a stylish green bathing suit. This alone she had not made—it was from a department store. Very proud of her fair north-country skin, she showed hardly a trace of sunburn. She always hurried from the water back to her umbrella. The children were at the edge of the water building a sand castle, and Yasue amused herself by dripping the watery sand on her white leg. The sand, immediately dry, fell into a dark pattern, sparkling with tiny shell fragments. Yasue hastily brushed at it, as if from a sudden fear that it would not wash off. A half-transparent little insect jumped from the sand and scurried away.

Stretching her legs and leaning back on her hands, Yasue looked out to sea. Great cloud masses boiled up, immense in their quiet majesty. They seemed to drink up all the noise below, even the sound of the sea.

It was the height of summer, and there was anger in the rays of the sun.

The children were tired of the sand castle. They ran off kicking up the water in the shallows. Startled from the safe little private world into which she had slipped, Yasue ran after them.

But they did nothing dangerous. They were afraid of the roar of the waves. There was a gentle eddy beyond the line where the waves fell back. Kiyoo and Keiko, hand in hand, stood waist-deep in the water, their eyes sparkling as they braced against the water and felt the sand at the soles of their feet.

"Like someone's pulling," said Kiyoo to his sister.

Yasue came up beside them and warned them not to go in any deeper. She pointed at Katsuo. They shouldn't leave him there alone, they should go up and play with him. But they paid no attention to her. They stood hand in hand, smiling happily at each other. They had a secret all their own, the feel of the sand as it pulled away from their feet.

Yasue was afraid of the sun. She looked at her shoulder and her breasts, and she thought of the snow in Kanazawa. She gave herself a little pinch high on the breasts. She smiled at the warmth. The nails were a little long and there was dark sand under them—she would have to cut them when she got back to her room.

She no longer saw Kiyoo and Keiko. They must have gone back up on the beach.

But Katsuo was alone. His face was strangely twisted, and he was pointing toward her.

Her heart beat violently. She looked into the water at her feet. It was receding again, and in the foam some two yards away a little brown body was rolling over and over. She caught a glimpse of Kiyoo's dark-blue swimming trunks.

Her heart beat still more violently. She moved toward the body as if she were fighting her way out of a corner. A wave came farther in than usual, loomed over her, broke before her eyes. It struck her square in the breast. She fell back into the water. She had had a heart attack.

Katsuo began crying, and a youth ran up from near by. Several others ran out through the shallows. The water leaped up around their naked black bodies.

Two or three saw the fall. They thought nothing about it. She would get up again. But at such times there is always a premonition, and as they ran up it half seemed to them that there had been something wrong with that fall.

Yasue was carried up to the scorching sand. Her eyes were open and her teeth clenched, and she seemed to be gazing in horror at something planted squarely in front of her. One of the men felt her pulse. There was none.

"She's staying at the Eirakusō." Someone recognized her.

The manager of the inn must be called. A boy from the village, determined not to let anyone steal this proud work from him, ran over the hot sand at top speed.

The manager came. He was about forty. He had on shorts and a sagging T-shirt, and, worn through here and there, a woolen band over his stomach. He argued that Yasue should be given first aid at the inn. Someone objected. Without waiting for the argument to be settled, two young men picked Yasue up and started to carry her off. The wet sand where she had lain showed the outlines of a human form.

Katsuo followed wailing after them. Someone noticed and picked him up.

Tomoko was aroused from her nap. The manager, well trained for his work, shook her gently. She lifted her head and asked what was wrong.

"The lady named Yasue . . ."

"Has something happened to Yasue?"

"We've given her first aid, and the doctor will be here in no time."

Tomoko jumped up and hurried out with the manager. Yasue lay on the lawn beside the swing, and a near-naked man knelt straddling her. He was giving her artificial respiration. To one side was a heap of straw and broken-up orange crates, and two men were doing their best to start a fire. The flames would immediately give way to smoke. The wood was still wet from a storm the night before. A third man fanned away the smoke as it curled toward Yasue's face.

Her head thrown back, Yasue looked for all the world as if she were breathing. In the sunlight that filtered through the trees, sweat glistened on the dark back of the man astride her. The white legs, stretched out on the grass, were plump and chalky. They seemed apathetic, quite divorced from the struggle going on above.

Tomoko knelt in the grass.

"Yasue! Yasue!"

Would they save Yasue? Why had it happened? What could she say to her husband? Weeping and incoherent, she jumped from question to question. Presently she turned sharply to the men around her. Where were the children?

"Look. Your mother's here." A middle-aged fisherman held a frightened Katsuo in his arms. Tomoko glanced at the boy, and nodded her thanks to the fisherman.

The doctor came and continued the artificial respiration. Her cheeks burning in the firelight, Tomoko hardly knew what she was thinking. An ant crawled across Yasue's face. Tomoko crushed it and flicked it away. Another ant crawled from the shaking hair up toward the ear. Tomoko crushed it too. Crushing ants became her job.

The artificial respiration went on for four hours. There were finally signs that *rigor mortis* was setting in, and the doctor gave up. The body was covered with a sheet and carried to the second floor. The room was dark. A man left the body and ran ahead to switch on the light.

Exhausted, Tomoko felt a sort of sweet emptiness come over her. She was not sad. She thought of the children.

"The children?"

"Down in the play room with Gengo."

"All three of them?"

"All three?" The men looked at each other.

Tomoko pushed them aside and ran downstairs. The fisherman, Gengo, in a cotton kimono, sat on the sofa going over a picture book with Katsuo, who had on an adult's shirt over his swimming trunks. Katsuo's mind was on something else. He was not looking at the book.

As Tomoko came in, the guests who knew of the tragedy stopped fanning themselves and looked at her.

She almost threw herself on Katsuo.

"Kiyoo and Keiko?" she asked harshly.

Katsuo looked up at her timidly. "Kiyoo . . . Keiko . . . all bubbles." He began sobbing.

Tomoko ran down to the beach in her bare feet. The pine needles stabbed at her as she went through the grove. The tide had come in, and she had to climb over the rock to the bathing beach. The sand stretched out white below her. She could see far into the dusk. One umbrella, checkered yellow and white, had been left behind. It was her own.

The others overtook her on the beach. She was running recklessly through the surf. When they tried to stop her, she brushed them irritably away.

"Don't you see? There are two children out there."

Many had not heard what Gengo had had to say. They thought Tomoko was mad.

It hardly seemed possible that no one had thought of the other two children in the whole four hours they were looking after Yasue. The people at the inn were used to seeing the three children together. And however upset their mother might be, it was strange that no warning came to her of the death of her two children.

Sometimes, however, such an incident sets in motion a sort of group psychology that lets only the same simple thoughts come to everyone. It is not easy to stand outside. It is not easy to register a dissent. Aroused from her afternoon nap, Tomoko had simply taken over what the others passed on to her, and had not thought to question.

All that night there were bonfires some yards apart up and down the beach. Every thirty minutes the young men would dive to look for the bodies. Tomoko was on the beach with them. She could not sleep, partly no doubt because she had slept too long that afternoon.

On the advice of the constabulary, the nets were not set out the following morning.

The sun came up over the headland to the left of the beach, and the morning breeze struck Tomoko's face. She had dreaded the daylight. It seemed to her that with the daylight the whole of the truth must come out, and the tragedy would for the first time become real.

"Don't you think you should get some rest?" said one of the older men. "We'll call you if we find anything. You can leave everything to us."

"Please do, please do," said the inn manager, red-eyed from lack of sleep. "You've had enough bad luck. What will your husband do if you take sick yourself?"

Tomoko was afraid to see her husband. Seeing him would be like meeting a trial judge. But she would have to see him. The time was coming near—yet another disaster was coming near, it seemed to her.

Presently she summoned up her courage to send a telegram. It gave her an excuse to leave the beach. She had begun to feel that the direction of all the divers had been turned over to her.

She looked back as she walked off. The sea was quiet. A silvery light flashed in near the shore. Fish were jumping. They seemed quite intoxicated with delight. It was unfair that Tomoko should be so unhappy.

Her husband, Masaru Ikuta, was thirty-five. A graduate of the Tokyo University of Foreign Studies, he had gone to work for an American company before the war. His English was good, and he knew his business—he was abler than his silent manner suggested. Now the manager of the Japanese office of an American automobile company, he had the use of a company automobile, half as advertising, and he made 150,000 yen a month. He also had ways of appropriating certain secret funds for himself, and Tomoko and Yasue, with a maid to take care of the children, lived in comfort and security. There was no pressing need to cut the family down by three.

Tomoko sent a telegram because she did not want to talk to Masaru over the telephone. As was the custom in the suburbs, the post office telephoned the message when it arrived, and the call came just as Masaru was about to leave for work. Thinking it a routine business call, he calmly picked up the telephone.

"We have a rush telegram from A. Beach," said the woman in the post office. Masaru began to feel uneasy. "I'll read it to you. Are you ready? 'YASUE DEAD. KIYOO AND KEIKO MISSING. TOMOKO.' "

"Would you read it again, please?"

It sounded the same the second time: "YASUE DEAD. KIYOO AND KEIKO MISSING. TOMOKO." Masaru was angry. It was as though, for no reason he could think of, he had suddenly received notice of his dismissal.

He immediately telephoned the office and said he would not be in. He thought he might drive to A. Beach. But the road was long and dangerous, and he had no confidence that he could drive it, upset as he was. As a matter of fact he had recently had an accident. He decided to take a train to Itō, and a taxi from there.

The process by which the unforeseen event works its way into a man's consciousness is a strange and subtle one. Masaru, who set out without even knowing the nature of the incident, was careful to take a good supply of money with him. Incidents required money.

He took a taxi to Tokyo station. He felt nothing he could really call emotion. He felt rather what a detective might feel on his way to the scene of a crime. Plunged less in speculation than in deduction, he quivered with curiosity to know more about the incident that involved him so deeply.

She could have telephoned. She was afraid to talk to me. With a

husband's intuition, he sensed the truth. But in any case the first
problem is to go see for myself.

He looked out the window as they came near the heart of the city.
The sun of the midsummer morning was even more blinding because
of the white-shirted crowds. The trees along the road cast deep
shadows directly downward, and at the entrance to a hotel the gaudy
red-and-white awning was taut, as if the sunlight were a heavy metal.
The newly dug earth where the street was being repaired was already
dry and dusty.

The world around him was quite as it had always been. Nothing
had happened, and if he tried he could believe that nothing had
happened even to him. A childish annoyance came over him. In an
unknown place, an incident with which he had had nothing to do
had cut him off from the world.

Among all these passengers none was so unfortunate as he. The
thought seemed to put him on a level above or a level below the
ordinary Masaru, he did not know which. He was someone special.
Someone apart.

No doubt a man with a large birthmark on his back sometimes
feels the urge to call out: "Listen, everyone. You don't know it, but
I have a big, purple birthmark on my back."

And Masaru wanted to shout at the other passengers: "Listen,
everybody. You don't know it, but I have just lost my sister and two
of my three children."

His courage left him. If only the children were safe . . . He began
trying to think of other ways to interpret the telegram. Possibly
Tomoko, distraught over Yasue's death, had assumed that the children were dead when they had only lost their way. Might not a second telegram be waiting at the house even now? Masaru was quite
taken up with his own feelings, as if the incident itself were less important than his reaction to it. He regretted that he had not called
the Eirakusō immediately.

The plaza in front of Itō station was brilliant in the midsummer
sun. Beside the taxi stand was a little office, no bigger than a police
box. The sunlight inside it was merciless, and the edges of the dis-
patch sheets on the walls were brown and curled.

"How much to A. Beach?"

"Two thousand yen." The man wore a driver's cap, and had a
towel around his neck. "If you're in no hurry, you can save money
going by bus. It leaves in five minutes," he added, either out of kindness or because the trip seemed too much of an effort.

"I'm in a hurry. Someone in my family has just died there."

"Oh? You're related to the people who drowned at A. Beach?
That's too bad. Two children and a woman all at once, they say."

Masaru felt dizzy under the blazing sun. He did not say another
word to the driver until the taxi reached A. Beach.

There was no particularly distinguished scenery along the way. At first the taxi climbed up one dusty mountain and down the next, and the sea was rarely in sight. When they passed another car along a narrow stretch of road, branches slapped at the half-open window like startled birds, and dropped dirt and sand rudely on Masaru's carefully pressed trousers.

Masaru could not decide how to face his wife. He was not sure that there was such a thing as a "natural approach" when none of the emotions he had ready seemed to fit. Perhaps the unnatural was in fact natural.

The taxi pulled through the darkened old gate of the Eirakusō. As it came up the driveway, the manager ran out with a clattering of wooden sandals. Masaru automatically reached for his wallet.

"I'm Ikuta."

"A terrible thing," said the manager, bowing deeply. After paying the driver, Masaru thanked the manager and gave him a thousand-yen bill.

Tomoko and Katsuo were in a room adjoining the room where Yasue's coffin lay. The body was packed in dry ice ordered from Itō, and would be cremated now that Masaru had arrived.

Masaru stepped ahead of the manager and opened the door. Tomoko, who had lain down for a nap, jumped up at the sound. She had not been asleep.

Her hair was tangled and she had on a wrinkled cotton kimono. Like a convicted criminal, she pulled the kimono together and knelt meekly before him. Her motions were astonishingly quick, as though she had planned them in advance. She stole a glance at her husband and collapsed in tears.

He did not want the manager to see him lay a comforting hand on her shoulder. That would be worse than having the most intimate bedroom secrets spied on. Masaru took off his coat and looked for a place to hang it.

Tomoko noticed. Taking a blue hanger from the lintel, she hung up the sweaty coat for him. Masaru sat down beside Katsuo, who had been awakened by his mother's weeping and lay looking up at them. The child, on his knee, was as unresisting as a doll. How can children be so small? he wondered. It was almost as if he were holding a toy.

Tomoko knelt weeping in a corner of the room.

"It was all my fault," she said. Those were the words Masaru most wanted to hear.

Behind them, the manager too was in tears. "I know it's no business of mine, sir, but please don't blame Mrs. Ikuta. It happened while she was taking a nap, and through no fault of hers."

Masaru felt as if he had heard or read of all this somewhere.

"I understand, I understand."

Obeying the rules, he stood up with the child in his arms, and, going over to his wife, laid his hand gently on her shoulder. The gesture came easily.

Tomoko wept even more bitterly.

The two bodies were found the next day. The constabulary, diving all up and down the beach, finally found them under the headland. Sea bugs had nibbled at them, and there were two or three bugs up each little nostril.

Such incidents of course go far beyond the dictates of custom, and yet at no time are people more bound to follow custom. Tomoko and Masaru forgot none of the responses and the return gifts custom demanded.

A death is always a problem in administration. They were frantically busy administering. One might say that Masaru in particular, as head of the family, had almost no time for sorrow. As for Katsuo, it seemed to him that one festival day succeeded another, with the adults all playing parts.

In any case, they steered their way through the whole complex affair. The funeral offerings came to a considerable sum. Funeral offerings are always larger when the head of the family, who can still provide, is a survivor than when it is his funeral.

Both Masaru and Tomoko were somehow braced for what had to be done. Tomoko did not understand how this almost insane grief and this careful attention to detail could exist side by side. And it was surprising too that she could eat so heavily without even noticing the taste.

What she dreaded most was having to see Masaru's parents. They arrived from Kanazawa in time for the funeral. "It was all my fault," she forced herself to say again, and by way of compensation she turned to her own parents.

"But who should they feel sorriest for? Haven't I just lost two children? There they all are, accusing me. They put the whole blame on me, and I have to apologize to them. They all look at me as if I were the absent-minded maid who dropped the baby in the river. But wasn't it Yasue? Yasue is lucky she's dead. Why can't they see who's been hurt? I'm a mother who has just lost two children.

"You're being unfair. Who is accusing you? Wasn't his mother in tears when she said she felt sorrier for you than anyone?"

"She was just saying so."

Tomoko was thoroughly dissatisfied. She felt like one demoted and condemned to obscurity, one whose real merit went unnoticed. It seemed to her that such intense sorrows should bring special privileges with them, extraordinary privileges. Some of the dissatisfaction was with herself, apologizing thus abjectly to her mother-in-law. It was to her mother that she went running when her irritation, like an itching rash all over her body, got the better of her.

She did not know it, but she was actually in despair at the poverty of human emotions. Was it not irrational that there was nothing to do except weep when ten people died, just as one wept for but a single person?

Tomoko wondered why she did not collapse. It seemed strange that she did not collapse, standing there in mourning for more than an hour in the midsummer heat. Sometimes she felt a little faint, and what saved her each time was a fresh start of horror at death. "I'm a stronger person than I thought," she said, turning a tearful face to her mother.

Talking with his parents of Yasue, Masaru shed tears for the sister who had thus died an old maid, and Tomoko felt a touch of resentment toward him too.

"Who is more important to him, Yasue or the children?" she wanted to ask.

There was no doubt that she was tense and ready. She could not sleep on the night of the wake, even though she knew she should. And yet she had not even a suggestion of a headache. Her mind was clear and taut.

Callers would worry over her, and sometimes she answered them roughly: "You needn't think about me. It makes no difference whether I am alive or dead."

Thoughts of suicide and insanity left her. Katsuo would be for a time the best reason why she should go on living. But sometimes she thought that it was only a failure of courage, or perhaps passion gone limp, whatever it was that made her think, as she looked at Katsuo being read to by the mourning women, how good it was that she had not killed herself. On such nights she would lie in her husband's arms and, turning eyes as wide as a rabbit's on the circle of light from the bed lamp, repeat over and over again, like one pleading a case: "I was wrong. It was my fault. I should have known from the start that it was a mistake to leave the three children with Yasue."

The voice was as hollow as a voice testing a mountain echo.

Masaru knew what this obsessive sense of responsibility meant. She was waiting for some sort of punishment. She was greedy for it, one might say.

After the fourteenth-day services, life returned to normal. People urged them to go off somewhere for a rest, but mountain and seashore both terrified Tomoko. She was convinced that misfortunes never came alone.

One evening late in summer, Tomoko went into the city with Katsuo. She was to meet her husband for dinner when he finished work.

There was nothing Katsuo could not have. Both his mother and his father were almost uncomfortably gentle. They handled him as they would a glass doll, and it was a great undertaking even to see him across a street. His mother would glare at the automobiles and trucks stopped for a light, and dash across with his hand clutched in hers.

The last of the swimming suits in the store windows assailed her. She had to turn her eyes from a green bathing suit like Yasue's. Afterward she wondered whether the mannequin had had a head. It seemed that it had not—and again that it had, and a face exactly like Yasue's dead face, the eyes closed in the wet, tangled hair. All the mannequins became drowned corpses.

If only summer would end. The very word "summer" carried with it festering thoughts of death. And in the evening sun she felt a festering warmth.

Since it was still a little early, she took Katsuo into a department store. It was only a half-hour or so before closing time. Katsuo wanted to look at toys, and they went up to the third floor. They hurried past the beach playthings. Mothers were frantically going through a heap of marked-down bathing suits for children. One woman held a pair of dark-blue trunks high to the window, and the afternoon sun reflected from the buckle. Enthusiastically looking for a shroud, thought Tomoko.

When he had bought his blocks, Katsuo wanted to go up to the roof. The roof playground was cool. A fairly strong breeze from the harbor flapped at the awnings.

Tomoko looked through the wire netting at Kachidoki Bridge beyond the city, and at the Tsukishima docks and the cargo ships anchored in the bay.

Taking his hand from hers, Katsuo went over to the monkey cage. Tomoko stood over him. Possibly because of the wind, the monkey smell was strong. The monkey gazed at them with wrinkled forehead. As it moved from one branch to another, a hand carefully pressed to its hips, Tomoko could see at the side of the oldish little face a dirty ear with red veins showing through. She had never looked so carefully at an animal before.

Beside the cage was a pond. The fountain in the middle was turned off. There were beds of portulaca around the brick rim, on which a child about Katsuo's age was teetering precariously. His parents were nowhere in sight.

I hope he falls in. I hope he falls in and drowns.

Tomoko watched the uncertain legs. The child did not fall. When he had been once around, he noticed Tomoko's gaze and laughed proudly. Tomoko did not laugh. It was as if the child were making fun of her.

She took Katsuo by the hand and hurried down from the roof.

At dinner, Tomoko spoke after rather too long a silence: "Aren't you quiet, though. And you don't seem the least bit sad."

Startled, Masaru looked to see whether anyone had heard. "You don't see? I'm only trying to cheer you up."

"There's no need to do that."

"So you say. But what about the effect on Katsuo?"

"I don't deserve to be a mother, anyway."

And so the dinner was ruined.

Masaru tended more and more to retreat before his wife's sorrow. A man has work to do. He can distract himself with his work. Meanwhile Tomoko nursed the sorrow. Masaru had to face this monotonous sorrow when he came home, and so he began coming home later at night.

Tomoko called a maid who had worked for her long before and gave away all of Kiyoo's and Keiko's clothes and toys. The maid had children about the same ages.

One morning Tomoko awoke a little later than usual. Masaru, who had been drinking again the night before, lay curled up on his side of the double bed. There was still a dank smell of liquor. The springs squeaked as he turned over in his sleep. Now that Katsuo was alone, she let him sleep in their second-floor bedroom, though she knew of course that it would be better not to. Through the white mosquito net over their own bed and the net over Katsuo's she looked at the child's sleeping face. He always wore a sort of pout when he slept.

Tomoko reached out of the mosquito net for the curtain cord. The roughness of the stiff cord in its hempen cover was pleasant against her sweaty hand. The curtain parted a little. The light struck the sandalwood tree from below, so that the shadows piled on each other, and the wide clusters of leaves were even softer than usual. Sparrows were chirping noisily. Every morning they would wake up and start chattering to one another, and apparently they would then form a line and run up and down the eaves trough. The confused patter of little feet would go from one end of the trough to the other and back again. Tomoko smiled as she listened.

It was a blessed morning. She had to feel that it was, for no reason at all. She lay quietly with her head still on the pillow. A feeling of happiness diffused itself through her whole body.

Suddenly she gasped. She knew why she was so happy. Last night for the first time she had not dreamed of the children. Every night she had dreamed of them, and last night she had not. She had had instead some pleasant, foolish little dream.

She had forgotten so soon, then—her heartlessness struck her as fearful. She wept tears of apology to the children's spirits. Masaru opened his eyes and looked at her. But he saw a sort of peace in the weeping, and not the usual anguish.

"You thought of them again?"

"Yes." It seemed too much trouble to tell the truth.

But now that she had told a lie, she was annoyed that her husband did not weep with her. If she had seen tears in his eyes, she might have been able to believe her lie.

The forty-ninth-day services were over. Masaru bought a lot in the Tama Cemetery. These were the first deaths in his branch of the family, and the first graves. Yasue was charged with watching over the children on the Far Shore too: by conference with the main family, her ashes were to be buried in the same lot.

Tomoko's fears came to seem groundless as the sadness only grew deeper. She went with Masaru and Katsuo to see the new cemetery lot. Already it was early autumn.

It was a beautiful day. The heat was leaving the high, clear sky.

Memory sometimes makes hours run side by side for us, or pile one on another. It played this strange trick on Tomoko twice in the course of the day. Perhaps, with the sky and the sunlight almost too clear, the edges of her subconscious too were somehow made half transparent.

Two months before the drownings, there had been that automobile accident. Masaru had not been hurt, of course, but after the drownings Tomoko never rode with him in the car when she took Katsuo out. Today Masaru too had to go by train.

They changed at M. for the little branch line to the cemetery. Masaru got off the train first with Katsuo. Held back in the crowd, Tomoko was able to get off only a second or two before the door closed. She heard a shrill whistle as the door slid shut behind her, and, almost screaming, she turned and tried to force it open again. She thought she had left Kiyoo and Keiko inside.

Masaru led her off by the arm. She looked at him defiantly, as if he were a detective arresting her. Coming to herself an instant later, she tried to explain what had happened—she must explain somehow. But the explanation only made Masaru uncomfortable. He thought she was acting.

Young Katsuo was delighted at the old-fashioned locomotive that took them to the cemetery. It had a high smokestack, and it was wonderfully tall, as though on stilts. The wooden sill on which the engineer leaned his elbow might have been made of coal. The locomotive groaned and sighed and gnashed its teeth, and finally started off through the unexciting suburban market gardens.

Tomoko, who had never been to the Tama Cemetery before, was astonished at its brightness. So wide a space, then, was given to the dead? The green lawns, the wide tree-lined avenues, the blue sky above, clear far into the distance. The city of the dead was cleaner and better ordered than the city of the living. She and her husband had had no cause to learn of cemeteries, but it did not seem unfortunate that they had now become qualified visitors. While neither of them especially thought about the matter, it seemed that the period of mourning, an unrelieved parade of the dark and the sinister, had brought them a sort of security, something stable, easy, pleasant even. They had become conditioned to death, and, as when people are conditioned to depravity, they had come to feel that life held nothing they need fear.

The lot was on the far side of the cemetery. Perspiring freely as they walked in from the gate, they looked curiously at Admiral T's grave, and laughed at a large, tasteless tombstone decorated with mirrors.

Tomoko listened to the subdued humming of the autumn cicadas, and smelled the incense and the cool, shady grass. "What a nice place. They'll have room to play, and they won't be bored. I can't help thinking it will be good for them. Strange, isn't it?"

Katsuo was thirsty. There was a high brown tower at the crossroads. The circular steps at the base were stained from the leaking fountain in the center. Several children, tired of chasing dragonflies, were noisily drinking water and squirting water at each other. Now and then a spray of water traced a thin rainbow through the air.

Katsuo was a child of action. He wanted a drink, and there was no help for it. Taking advantage of the fact that his mother was not holding his hand, he ran toward the steps. Where was he going? she called sharply. For a drink of water, he answered over his shoulder. She ran after him and took both his arms firmly from behind. "That hurt," he protested. He was frightened. Some terrible creature had pounced upon him from behind.

Tomoko knelt in the coarse gravel and turned him toward her. He looked at his father, gazing in astonishment from beside a hedge some distant off.

"You are not to drink that water. We have some here."

She began to unscrew the lid of the thermos bottle on her knee.

They reached their bit of property. It was in a newly opened section of the cemetery, behind rows of tombstones. Frail young box trees were planted here and there, after a definite pattern, one could see if one looked carefully. The ashes had not yet been moved from the family temple, and there was no grave marker. There was only a roped-off bit of level land.

"And all three of them will be here together," said Masaru.

The remark did little to Tomoko. How, she wondered, could facts be so completely improbable? For one child to drown in the ocean— that could happen, and no doubt anyone would accept it as a fact. But for three people to drown; that was ridiculous. And yet ten thousand was different again. There was something ridiculous about the excessive, and yet there was nothing ridiculous about a great natural catastrophe, or war. One death was somehow grave and solemn, as were a million deaths. The slightly excessive was different.

"Three of them! What nonsense! Three of them," she said.

It was too large a number for one family, too small a number for society. And there were none of the social implications of death in battle or death at one's post. Selfish in her womanly way, she turned over and over again the riddle of this number. Masaru, the social being, had in the course of time come to note that it was convenient to see the matter as society saw it: they were in fact lucky that there were no social implications.

Back at the station, Tomoko fell victim again to that doubling up of time. They had to wait twenty minutes for the train. Katsuo wanted one of the toy badgers on sale in front of the station. The badgers, dangling from sticks, were of cotton wadding scorched a badger color, to which were added eyes, ears, and tails.

"You can still buy these badgers!" exclaimed Tomoko.

"And children seem to like them as much as ever."

"I had one when I was a child."

Tomoko bought a badger from the old woman at the stall and gave it to Katsuo. And a moment later she caught herself looking around at the other stalls. She would have to buy something for Kiyoo and Kieko, who had been left at home.

"What is it?" asked Masaru.

"I wonder what's the matter with me. I was thinking I had to buy something for the others." Tomoko raised her plump white arms and rubbed roughly with clenched fists at her eyes and temples. Her nostrils trembled as though she were about to weep.

"Go ahead and buy something. Buy something for them." Masaru's tone was tense and almost pleading. "We can put it on the altar."

"No. They have to be alive." Tomoko pressed her handkerchief to her nose. She was living, the others were dead. That was the great evil. How cruel it was to have to be alive.

She looked around her again: at the red flags hanging from the bars and restaurants in front of the station, at the gleaming white sections of granite piled high before the tombstone shops, at the yellowing paper-paneled doors on the second floors, at the roof tiles, at the blue sky, now darkening toward evening clear as porcelain. It was all so clear, so well defined. In the very cruelty of life was a deep peace, as of falling into a faint.

Autumn wore on, and the life of the family became day by day more tranquil. Not of course that grief was quite discarded. As Masaru saw his wife growing calmer, however, the joys of home and affection for Katsuo began to bring him back early from work; and even if, after Katsuo was in bed, the talk turned to what they both wanted not to talk of, they were able to find a sort of consolation in it.

The process by which so fearful an event could melt back into everyday life brought on a new sort of fear, mixed with shame, as if they had committed a crime that was finally to go undetected. The knowledge, always with them, that three people were missing from the family seemed at times to give a strange sense of fulfillment.

No one went mad, no one committed suicide. No one was even ill. The terrible event had passed and left scarcely a shadow. Tomoko came to feel bored. It was as if she were waiting for something.

They had long forbidden themselves plays and concerts, but Tomoko presently found excuses: such pleasures were in fact meant to comfort the grieving. A famous violinist from America was on a concert tour, and they had tickets. Katsuo was forced to stay at home, partly at least because Tomoko wanted to drive to the concert with her husband.

She was a long time getting ready. It took long to redo hair that had for months been left untended. Here face in the mirror, when she was ready, was enough to bring back memories of long-forgotten pleasures. How to describe the pleasure of quite losing oneself in a mirror? She had forgotten what a delight a mirror could be—no doubt grief, with its stubborn insistence on the self, drew one away from such ecstasies.

She tried on kimono after kimono, finally choosing a lavish purple one and a brocade obi. Masaru, waiting behind the wheel of the car, was astonished at his beautiful wife.

People turned to look at her all up and down the lobby. Masaru was immensely pleased. It seemed to Tomoko herself, however, that no matter how beautiful people thought her, something would be lacking. There had been a time when she would have gone home quite satisfied after having attracted so much attention. This gnawing dissatisfaction, she told herself, must be the product of a liveliness and gaiety that only emphasized how far from healed her grief was. But as a matter of fact it was only a recurrence of the vague dissatisfaction she had felt at not being treated as became a woman of sorrows.

The music had its effect on her, and she walked through the lobby with a sad expression on her face. She spoke to a friend. The expression seemed quite to suit the words of consolation the friend murmured. The friend introduced the young man with her. The young man knew nothing of Tomoko's sorrows and said nothing by way of consolation. His talk was of the most ordinary, including one or two lightly critical remarks about the music.

What a rude young man, thought Tomoko, looking at the shining head as it moved off through the crowd. He said nothing. And he must have see how sad I was.

The young man was tall and stood out in the crowd. As he turned to one side, Tomoko saw the eyebrows and the laughing eyes, and a lock of hair straying down over the forehead. Only the top of the woman's head was visible.

Tomoko felt a stab of jealousy. Had she hoped to have from the young man something besides consolation, then—had she wanted other, rather special words? Her whole moral being quaked at the thought. She had to tell herself that this new suspicion was quite at odds with reason. She who had never once been dissatisfied with her husband.

"Are you thirsty?" asked Masaru, who had been speaking to a friend. "There's an orangeade stand over there."

People were sucking the orange liquid from tilted bottles. Tomoko looked over with the puzzled squint one so often sees on the nearsighted. She was not in the least thirsty. She remembered the day she had kept Katsuo from the fountain and had made him drink boiled water instead. Katsuo was not the only one in danger. There must be all sorts of little germs milling about in the orangeade.

She went slightly insane in her pursuit of pleasure. There was something vengeful in this feeling that she must have pleasure.

Not of course that she was tempted to be unfaithful to her husband. Wherever she went, she was with him or wanted to be.

Her conscience dwelt rather on the dead. Back from some amusement, she would look at the sleeping face of Katsuo, who had been put to bed early by the maid, and as she thought of the two dead children she would be quite overcome with remorse. Indeed the pursuit of pleasure became a sure way to stir up a pang of conscience.

Tomoko remarked suddenly that she wanted to take up sewing. This was not the first time Masaru had found it hard to follow the twists and jumps in a woman's thinking.

Tomoko began her sewing. Her pursuit of pleasure became less strenuous. She quietly looked about her, meaning to become the complete family woman. She felt that she was "looking life square in the face."

There were clear traces of neglect in her reappraised surroundings. She felt as if she had come back from a long trip. She would spend a whole day washing and a whole day putting things in order. The middle-aged maid had all her work snatched away from her.

Tomoko came on a pair of Kiyoo's shoes, and a little pair of light-blue felt slippers that had belonged to Keiko. Such relics would plunge her into meditation, and make her weep pleasant tears; but they all seemed tainted with bad luck. She called a friend who was immersed in charities, and, feeling most elevated, gave everything to an orphanage, even clothes that might fit Katsuo.

As she sat at her sewing machine, Tomoko accumulated a wardrobe. She thought of making herself some fashionable new hats, but she had no time for that. At the machine, she forgot her sorrows. The hum and the mechanical movements cut off that other erratic melody, her emotional ups and downs.

Why had she not tried this mechanical cutting off of the emotions earlier? But then of course it came at a time when her heart no longer put up the resistance it would once have. One day she pricked her finger, and a drop of blood oozed out. She was frightened. Pain was associated with death.

But the fear was followed by a different emotion: if such a trivial accident should indeed bring death, that would be an answer to a prayer. She spent more and more time at the machine. It was the safest of machines, however. It did not even touch her.

Even now, she was dissatisfied, waiting for something. Masaru would turn away from this vague seeking, and they would go for a whole day without speaking to each other.

Winter approached. The tomb was ready, and the ashes were buried.

In the loneliness of winter, one thinks longingly of summer. Memories of summer threw an even sharper shadow across their lives. And yet the memories had come to seem like something out of a storybook. There was no avoiding the fact that, around the winter fire, everything took on an air of fiction.

In midwinter, there were signs that Tomoko was pregnant. For the first time, forgetfulness came as a natural right. Never before had they been quite so careful—it seemed strange that the child might be born safely, and only natural that they should lose it.

Everything was going well. A line was drawn between them and old memories. Borrowing strength from the child she was carrying, Tomoko for the first time had the courage to admit that the pain was gone. She had only to recognize that fact.

Tomoko tried to understand. It is difficult to understand while an incident is before one's eyes, however. Understanding comes later. One analyzes the emotions, and deduces, and explains to oneself. On looking back, Tomoko could not but feel dissatisfied with her inadequate emotions. There could be no doubt that the dissatisfaction would stay longer, a drag on her heart, than the sorrow itself. But there could be no going back for another try.

She refused to admit any incorrectness in her responses. She was a mother. And at the same time she could not leave off doubting.

While true forgetfulness had not yet come, something covered Tomoko's sorrow as a thin coating of ice covers a lake. Occasionally it would break, but overnight it would form again.

Forgetfulness began to show its real strength when they were not watching for it. It filtered in. It found the tiniest opening, and filtered in. It attacked the organism like an invisible germ, it worked slowly but steadily. Tomoko was going through unconscious motions as when one resists a dream. She was most uneasy, resisting forgetfulness.

She told herself that forgetfulness came through the strength of the child inside her. But it was only helped by the child. The outlines of the incident were slowly giving way, dimming, blurring, weathering, disintegrating.

There had appeared in the summer sky a fearsome marble image, white and stark. It had dissolved into a cloud—the arms had dropped off, the head was gone, the long sword in the hand had fallen. The expression on the stone face had been enough to raise the hair, but slowly it had blurred and softened.

One day she switched off a radio drama about a mother who had lost a child. She was a little astonished at the promptness with which she thus disposed of the burden of memory. A mother awaiting her fourth child, she felt, had a moral obligation to resist the almost dissolute pleasure of losing herself in grief. Tomoko had changed in these last few months.

For the sake of the child, she must hold off dark waves of emotion. She must keep her inward balance. She was far more pleased with the dictates of mental hygiene than she could be with insidious forgetfulness. Above all, she felt free. With all the injunctions, she felt free. Forgetfulness was of course demonstrating its power. Tomoko was astonished at how easily managed her heart was.

She lost the habit of remembering, and it no longer seemed strange that the tears failed to come at memorial services or visits to the cemetery. She believed that she had become magnanimous, that she could forgive anything. When for instance spring came and she took Katsuo walking in a near-by park, she was no longer able to feel, even if she tried, the spite that would have swept over her immediately after the tragedy had she come upon children playing in the sand. Because she had forgiven them, all these children were living in peace. So it seemed to her.

While forgetfulness came to Masaru sooner than to his wife, that was no sign of coldness on his part. It was rather Masaru who had wallowed in sentimental grief. A man even in his fickleness is generally more sentimental than a woman. Unable to stretch out the emotion, and conscious of the fact that grief was not particularly stubborn in following him about, Masaru suddenly felt alone, and he allowed himself a trifling infidelity. He quickly tired of it. Tomoko became pregnant. He hurried back to her like a child hurrying to its mother.

The tragedy left them as a castaway leaves a sinking ship. Soon they were able to view it as it must have seemed to people who noticed it in a corner of the newspapers that day. Tomoko and Masaru even wondered if they had had a part in it. Had they not been but the spectators who happened to be nearest? All who had actually participated in the incident had died, and would participate forever. For us to have a part in a historical incident, our very existence must somehow be at stake. And what had Masaru and his wife had at stake? In the first place, had they had time to put anything at stake?

The incident shone far away, a lighthouse on a distant headland. It flashed on and off, like the revolving light on Cape Tsumeki, south of A. Beach. Rather than an injury it became a moral lesson, and it changed from a concrete fact to a metaphor. It was no longer the property of the Ikuta family, it was public. As the lighthouse shines on beach wastes, and on waves baring their white fangs at lonely rocks all through the night, and on the groves around it, so the incident shone on the complex everyday life around them. People should read the lesson. An old, simple lesson that parents may be expected to have engraved on their minds: You have to watch children constantly when you take them to the beach. People drown where you would never think it possible.

Not that Masaru and his wife had sacrificed two children and a sister to teach a lesson. The loss of the three had served no other purpose, however; and many a heroic death produces as little.

Tomoko's fourth child was a girl, born late in the summer. Their happiness was unbounded. Masaru's parents came from Kanazawa to see the new grandchild, and while they were in Tokyo Masaru took them to the cemetery.

The named the child Momoko. Mother and child did well—Tomoko knew how to take care of a baby. And Katsuo was delighted to have a sister again.

It was the following summer—two years after the drowning, a year after Momoko's birth. Tomoko startled Masaru by saying she wanted to go to A. Beach.

"Didn't you say you would never go there again?"

"But I want to."

"Aren't you strange? I don't want to at all, myself."

"Oh? Let's forget about it, then."

She was silent for two or three days. Then she said: "I *would* like to go."

"Go by yourself."

"I couldn't."

"Why?"

"I'd be afraid."

"Why do you want to go to a place you're afraid of?"

"I want all of us to go. We would have been all right if you'd been along. I want you to go too."

"You can't tell what might happen if you stay too long. And I can't take much time off."

"One night will be enough."

"But it's such an out-of-the-way place."

He asked her again what had made her want to go. She only answered that she did not know. Then he remembered one of the rules in the detective stories he was so fond of: the murderer always wants to go back to the scene of the crime, whatever the risks. Tomoko was taken by a strange impulse to revisit the place where the children died.

Tomoko asked a third time—with no particular urgency, in the same monotonous way as before—and Masaru determined to take two days off, avoiding the weekend crowds. The Eirakusō was the only inn at A. Beach. They reserved rooms as far as possible from that unhappy room. Tomoko as always refused to drive with her husband when the children were along. The four of them, husband and wife and Katsuo and Momoko, took a taxi from Itō.

It was the height of the summer. Behind the houses along the way were sunflowers, shaggy as lions' manes. The taxi scattered dust on the open, honest faces, but the sunflowers seemed quite undisturbed.

As the sea came in sight to the left, Katsuo gave a squeal of delight. He was five now, and it was two years since he had last been to the coast.

They talked little in the taxi. It was shaking too violently to be the best place for conversation. Momoko now and then said something they understood. Katsuo taught her the word "sea," and she pointed out the other window at the bald red mountain and said: "Sea." To Masaru it was as if Katsuo were teaching the baby an unlucky word.

They arrived at the Eirakusō, and the same manager came out. Masaru tipped him. He remembered only too clearly how his hand had trembled with that other thousand-yen note.

The inn was quiet. It was a bad year. Masaru began remembering things and became irritable. He scolded his wife in front of the children.

"Why the devil did we come here? We only remember things we don't want to. Things we had finally forgotten. There are any number of decent places we could have gone on our first trip with Momoko. And I'm too busy to be taking foolish trips."

"But you agreed to, didn't you?"

"You kept at me."

The grass was baking in the afternoon sun. Everything was exactly as two years before. A blue-green-and-red swimming suit was drying on the white swing. Two or three quoits lay around the peg, half hidden in the grass. The lawn was shady where Yasue's body had lain. The sun, leaking through the trees to the bare grass, seemed suddenly to dapple the undulations of Yasue's green bathing suit—it was the way the flecks of light moved with the wind. Masaru did not know that the body had lain there. Only Tomoko had the illusion. Just as for Masaru the incident itself had not happened while he did not know of it, so that patch of grass would be forever only a quiet, shady corner. For him, and still more for the other guests, thought Tomoko.

His wife was silent, and Masaru tired of scolding her. Katsuo went down into the garden and rolled a quoit across the grass. He squatted down and watched intently to see where it would go. It bounced awkwardly through the shadows, took a sudden jump, and fell. Katsuo watched, motionless. He thought it should get up again.

The cicadas were humming. Masaru, now silent, felt the sweat come out around his collar. He remembered his duty as a father. "Let's go down to the beach, Katsuo."

Tomoko carried Momoko. The four of them went through the gate in the hedge and out under the pine trees. The waves came in swiftly and spread shining over the beach.

It was low tide, and they could make their way around the rock to the beach. Taking Katsuo by the hand, Masaru walked across the hot sand in pattens borrowed from the inn.

There was not a single beach umbrella. They could see no more than twenty people the whole length of the bathing beach, which began from just beyond the rock.

They stood silently at the edge of the water.

There were grand clusters of clouds again today, piled one upon another. It seemed strange that a mass so heavy with light could be borne in the air. Above the packed clouds at the horizon, light clouds trailed away as though left behind in the blue by a broom. The clouds below seemed to be enduring something, holding out against something. Excesses of light and shade cloaked in form, a dark, inchoate passion shaped by a will radiant and architectural, as in music.

From beneath the clouds, the sea came toward them, far wider and more changeless than the land. The land never seems to take the sea, even its inlets. Particularly along a wide bow of coast, the sea sweeps in from everywhere.

The waves came up, broke, fell back. Their thunder was like the intense quiet of the summer sun, hardly a noise at all. Rather an earsplitting silence. A lyrical transformation of the waves, not waves, but rather ripples one might call the light, derisive laughter of the waves at themselves—ripples came up to their feet, and retreated again.

Masaru glanced sideways at his wife.

She was gazing out to sea. Her hair blew in the sea breeze, and she seemed undismayed at the sun. Her eyes were moist and almost regal. Her mouth was closed tight. In her arms she held one-year-old Momoko, who wore a little straw hat.

Masaru had seen that face before. Since the tragedy, Tomoko's face had often worn that expression, as if she had forgotten herself, and as if she were waiting for something.

"What are you waiting for?" he wanted to ask lightly.

But the words did not come. He thought he knew without asking. He clutched tighter at Katsuo's hand.

Dazai Osamu was born in 1909 to a rich and influential family and because of his dissipation and excesses became a modern Japanese legend before his death in 1948. During 1930 he studied French literature at Tokyo University but did not graduate. Although his literary career was short, he produced numerous short stories, novels, essays, and plays. His fiction is simply rendered, rhythmic, and detailed.

Many of Dazai Osamu's stories are autobiographical reflections, dealing with the dissolute and disillusioned. His characters may not be especially admirable, but because of the author's personal involvement with them and his profound understanding of their thoughts and actions, his people do not become "monsters." Is this statement true of the characters in "Villon's Wife"? Is the concluding line of dialogue in this story spoken ironically? How does it relate to the story's theme? Further Reading: The Setting Sun (1947), No Longer Human (1958).

JAPAN

Villon's Wife

DAZAI OSAMU

I was awakened by the sound of the front door being flung open, but I did not get out of bed. I knew it could only be my husband returning dead drunk in the middle of the night.

He switched on the light in the next room and, breathing very heavily, began to rummage through the drawers of the table and the bookcase, searching for something. After a few minutes there was a noise that sounded as if he had flopped down on the floor. Then I could hear only his panting. Wondering what he might be up to, I called to him from where I lay. "Have you had supper yet? There's some cold rice in the cupboard."

Reprinted by permission of Grove Press, Inc. Copyright © 1956 by Grove Press. Translated by Donald Keene.

"Thank you," he answered in an unwontedly gentle tone. "How is the boy? Does he still have a fever?"

This was also unusual. The boy is four this year, but whether because of malnutrition, or his father's alcoholism, or sickness, he is actually smaller than most two-year-olds. He is not even sure on his feet, and as for talking, it's all he can do to say "yum-yum" or "ugh." Sometimes I wonder if he is not feeble-minded. Once, when I took him to the public bath and held him in my arms after undressing him, he looked so small and pitifully scrawny that my heart sank, and I burst into tears in front of everybody. The boy is always having upset stomachs or fevers, but my husband almost never spends any time at home, and I wonder what if anything he thinks about the child. If I mention to him that the boy has a fever, he says, "You ought to take him to a doctor." Then he throws on his coat and goes off somewhere. I would like to take the boy to the doctor, but I haven't the money. There is nothing I can do but lie beside him and stroke his head.

But that night, for whatever reason, my husband was strangely gentle, and for once asked me about the boy's fever. It didn't make me happy. I felt instead a kind of premonition of something terrible, and cold chills ran up and down my spine. I couldn't think of anything to say, so I lay there in silence. For a while there was no other sound but my husband's furious panting.

Then there came from the front entrance the thin voice of a woman, "Is anyone at home?" I shuddered all over as if icy water had been poured over me.

"Are you at home, Mr. Otani?" This time there was a somewhat sharp inflection to her voice. She slid the door open and called in a definitely angry voice, "Mr. Otani. Why don't you answer?"

My husband at last went to the door. "Well, what is it?" he asked in a frightened, stupid tone.

"You know perfectly well what it is," the woman said, lowering her voice. "What makes you steal other people's money when you've got a nice home like this? Stop your cruel joking and give it back. If you don't, I'm going straight to the police."

"I don't know what you're talking about. I won't stand for your insults. You've got no business coming here. Get out! If you don't get out, I'll be the one to call the police."

There came the voice of another man. "I must say, you've got your nerve, Mr. Otani. What do you mean we have no business coming here? You amaze me. This time it is serious. It's more than a joke when you steal other people's money. Heaven only knows all my wife and I have suffered on account of you. And on top of everything else you do something as low as you did tonight. Mr. Otani, I misjudged you."

"It's blackmail," my husband angrily exclaimed in a shaking voice.

"It's extortion. Get out! If you've got any complaints I'll listen to them tomorrow."

"What a revolting thing to say. You really are a scoundrel. I have no alternative but to call the police."

In his words was a hatred so terrible that I went goose flesh all over.

"Go to hell," my husband shouted, but his voice had already weakened and sounded hollow.

I got up, threw a wrap over my nightgown, and went to the front hall. I bowed to the two visitors. A round-faced man of about fifty wearing a knee-length overcoat asked, "Is this your wife?", and, without a trace of a smile, faintly inclined his head in my direction as if he were nodding.

The woman was a thin, small person of about forty, neatly dressed. She loosened her shawl and, also unsmiling, returned my bow with the words, "Excuse us for breaking in this way in the middle of the night."

My husband suddenly slipped on his sandals and made for the door. The man grabbed his arm and the two of them struggled for a moment. "Let go or I'll stab you!" my husband shouted, and a jacknife flashed in his right hand. The knife was a pet possession of his, and I remembered that he usually kept it in his desk drawer. When he got home he must have been expecting trouble, and the knife was what he had been searching for.

The man shrank back and in the interval my husband, flapping the sleeves of his coat like a huge crow, bolted outside.

"Thief!" the man shouted and started to pursue him, but I ran to the front gate in my bare feet and clung to him.

"Please don't. It won't help for either of you to get hurt. I will take the responsibility for everything."

The woman said, "Yes, she's right. You can never tell what a lunatic will do."

"Swine! It's the police this time! I can't stand any more." The man stood there staring emptily at the darkness outside and muttering, as if to himself. But the force had gone out of his body.

"Please come in and tell me what has happened. I may be able to settle whatever the matter is. The place is a mess, but please come in."

The two visitors exchanged glances and nodded slightly to one another. The man said, with a changed expression, "I'm afraid that whatever you may say, our minds are already made up. But it might be a good idea to tell you, Mrs. Otani, all that has happened."

"Please do come in and tell me about it."

"I'm afraid we won't be able to stay long." So saying the man started to remove his overcoat.

"Please keep your coat on. It's very cold here, and there's no heating in the house."

"Well then, if you will forgive me."

"Please, both of you."

The man and the woman entered my husband's room. They seemed appalled by the desolation they saw. The mats looked as though they were rotting, the paper doors were in shreds, the walls were beginning to fall in, and the paper had peeled away from the storage closet, revealing the framework. In a corner were a desk and a bookcase—an empty bookcase.

I offered the two visitors some torn cushions from which the stuffing was leaking, and said, "Please sit on the cushions—the mats are so dirty." And I bowed to them again. "I must apologize for all the trouble my husband seems to have been causing you, and for the terrible exhibition he put on tonight, for whatever reason it was. He has such a peculiar disposition." I choked in the middle of my words and burst into tears.

"Excuse me for asking, Mrs. Otani, but how old are you?" the man asked. He was sitting cross-legged on the torn cushion, with his elbows on his knees, propping his chin on his fists. As he asked the question he leaned forward toward me.

"I am twenty-six."

"Is that all you are? I suppose that's only natural, considering your husband's about thirty, but it amazes me all the same."

The woman, showing her face from behind the man's back, said, "I couldn't help wondering, when I came in and saw what a fine wife he has, why Mr. Otani behaves the way he does."

"He's sick. That's what it is. He didn't used to be that way, but he keeps getting worse." He gave a great sigh, then continued, "Mrs. Otani, my wife and I run a little restaurant near the Nakano Station. We both originally came from the country, but I got fed up dealing with penny-pinching farmers, and came to Tokyo with my wife. After the usual hardships and breaks, we managed to save up a little and, along about 1936, opened a cheap little restaurant catering to customers with at most a yen or two to spend at a time on entertainment. By not going in for luxuries and working like slaves, we managed to lay in quite a stock of whisky and gin. When liquor got short and plenty of other drinking establishments went out of business, we were able to keep going.

"The war with America and England broke out, but even after the bombings got pretty severe, we didn't want to be evacuated to the country, not having any children to tie us down. We figured that we might as well stick to our business until the place got burnt down. Your husband first started coming to our place in the spring of 1944, as I recall. We were not yet losing the war, or if we were we didn't know how things actually stood, and we thought that if we could just hold out for another two or three years we could somehow get peace on terms of equality. When Mr. Otani first appeared in our shop, he was not alone. It's a little embarrassing to tell you about it, but I might as well come out with the whole story and not keep anything from you. Your husband sneaked in by the kitchen door along with an older woman. I forgot to say that about that time the front door of our place was shut, and only a few regular customers got in by the back.

"This older woman lived in the neighborhood, and when the bar where she worked was closed and she lost her job, she often came to our place with her men friends. That's why we weren't particularly surprised when your husband crept in with this woman, whose name was Akichan. I took them to the back room and brought out some gin. Mr. Otani drank his liquor very quietly that evening. Akichan paid the bill and the two of them left together. It's odd, but I can't forget how strangely gentle and refined he seemed that night. I wonder if when the devil makes his first appearance in somebody's house he acts in such a lonely and melancholy way.

"From that night on Mr. Otani was a steady customer. Ten days later he came alone and all of a sudden produced a hundred-yen note. At that time a hundred yen was a lot of money, more than two or three thousand yen today. He pressed the money into my hand and wouldn't take no for an answer. 'Take care of it please,' he said, smiling timidly. That night he seemed to have drunk quite a bit before he came, and at my place he downed ten glasses of gin as fast as I could set them up. All this was almost entirely without a word. My wife and I tried to start a conversation, but he only smiled rather shamefacedly and nodded vaguely. Suddenly he asked the time and got up. 'What about the change?' I called after him. 'That's all right,' he said. 'I don't know what to do with it,' I insisted. He answered with a sardonic smile, 'Please save it until the next time. I'll be coming back.' He went out. Mrs. Otani, that was the one and only time that we ever got any money from him. Since then he has always put us off with one excuse or another, and for three years he has managed without paying a penny to drink up all our liquor almost singlehanded."

Before I knew what I was doing I burst out laughing. It all seemed so funny to me, although I can't explain why. I covered my mouth in confusion, but when I looked at the lady I saw that she was also laughing unaccountably, and then her husband could not help but laugh too.

"No, it's certainly no laughing matter, but I'm so fed up that I feel like laughing, too. Really, if he used all his ability in some other direction, he could become a cabinet minister or a Ph.D. or anything else he wanted. When Akichan was still friends with Mr. Otani she used to brag about him all the time. First of all, she said, he came from a terrific family. He was the younger son of Baron Otani. It is true that he had been disinherited because of his conduct, but when his father, the present baron, died, he and his elder brother were to divide the estate. He was brilliant, a genius in fact. In spite of his youth he was the best poet in Japan. What's more, he was a great scholar, and a perfect demon at German and French. To hear Aki-chan talk, he was a kind of god, and the funny thing was that she didn't make it all up. Other people also said that he was the younger son of Baron Otani and a famous poet. Even my wife, who's getting along in years, was as enthusiastic about him as Akichan. She used to tell me what a difference it makes when people have been well brought up. And the way she pined for him to come was quite unbearable. They say the day of the nobility is over, but until the war ended I can tell you that nobody had his way with the women like that disin-herited son of the aristocracy. It is unbelievable how they fell for him. I suppose it was what people would nowadays call 'slave mentality.'

"For my part, I'm a man, and at that a very cool sort of man, and I don't think that some little peer—if you will pardon the expression —some member of the country gentry who is only a younger son, is all that different from myself. I never for a moment got worked up about him in so sickening a way. But all the same, that gentleman was my weak spot. No matter how firmly I resolved not to give him any liquor the next time, when he suddenly appeared at some unex-pected hour, looking like a hunted man, and I saw how relieved he was at last to have reached our place, my resolution weakened, and I ended up by giving him the liquor. Even when he got drunk, he never made any special nuisance of himself, and if only he had paid the bill he would have been a good customer. He never advertised himself and didn't take any silly pride in being a genius or anything of the sort. When Akichan or somebody else would sit beside him and sound off to us about his greatness, he would either change the subject completely or say, 'I want some money so I can pay the bill,' throwing a wet blanket over everything.

"The war finally ended. We started doing business openly in black-market liquor and put new curtains in front of the place. For all its seediness the shop looked rather lively, and we hired a girl to lend a little charm. Then who should show up again but that damned gentleman. He no longer brought women with him, but always came in the company of two or three writers for newspapers and magazines. He was drinking even more than before, and used to get very wild-looking. He began to come out with really vulgar jokes, which he had never done before, and sometimes for no good reason he would hit one of the reporters he brought with him or start a fist fight. What's more, he seduced the twenty-year-old girl who was working in our place. We were shocked, but there was nothing we could do about it at that stage, and we had no choice but to let the matter drop. We advised the girl to resign herself to bearing the child, and quietly sent her back to her parents. I begged Mr. Otani not to come any more, but he answered in a threatening tone, 'People who make money on the black market have no business criticizing others. I know all about you.' The next night he showed up as if nothing had happened.

"Maybe it was by way of punishment for the black-market business we had been doing that we had to put up with such a monster. But what he did tonight can't be passed over just because he's a poet or a gentleman. It was plain robbery. He stole five thousand yen from us. Nowadays all our money goes for stock, and we are lucky if we have five hundred or one thousand yen in the place. The reason why we had as much as five thousand tonight was that I had made an end-of-the-year round of our regular customers and managed to collect that much. If I don't hand the money over to the wholesalers immediately we won't be able to stay in business. That's how much it means to us. Well, my wife was going over the accounts in the back room and had put the money in the cupboard drawer. He was drinking by himself out in front but seems to have noticed what she did. Suddenly he got up, went straight to the back room, and without a word pushed my wife aside and opened the drawer. He grabbed the bills and stuffed them in his pocket.

"We rushed into the shop, still speechless with amazement, and then out into the street. I shouted for him to stop, and the two of us ran after him. For a minute I felt like screaming 'Thief!' and getting the people in the street to join us, but after all, Mr. Otani is an old acquaintance, and I couldn't be too harsh on him. I made up my mind that I would not let him out of my sight. I would follow him wherever he went, and when I saw that he had quieted down, I would calmly ask for money. We are only small business people, and when we finally caught up with him here, we had no choice but to suppress our feelings and politely ask him to return the money. And then what happened? He took out a knife and threatened to stab me! What a way to behave!"

Again the whole thing seemed so funny to me, for reasons I can't explain, that I burst out laughing. The lady turned red, and smiled a little. I couldn't stop laughing. Even though I knew that it would have a bad effect on the proprietor, it all seemed so strangely funny that I laughed until the tears came. I suddenly wondered if the phrase "the great laugh at the end of the world," that occurs in one of my husband's poems, didn't mean something of the sort.

And yet it was not a matter that could be settled just by laughing about it. I thought for a minute and said, "Somehow or other I will make things good, if you will only wait one more day before you report to the police. I'll call on you tomorrow without fail." I carefully inquired where the restaurant was, and begged them to consent. They agreed to let things stand for the time being, and left. Then

I sat by myself in the middle of the cold room trying to think of a plan. Nothing came to me. I stood up, took off my wrap, and crept in among the covers where my boy was sleeping. As I stroked his head I thought how wonderful it would be if the night never never ended.

My father used to keep a stall in Asakusa Park. My mother died when I was young, and my father and I lived by ourselves in a tenement. We ran the stall together. My husband used to come now and then, and before long I was meeting him at other places without my father's knowing it. When I became pregnant I persuaded him to treat me as his wife, although it wasn't officially registered, of course. Now the boy is growing up fatherless, while my husband goes off for three or four nights or even for a whole month at a time. I don't know where he goes or what he does. When he comes back he is always drunk; and he sits there, deathly pale, breathing heavily and staring at my face. Sometimes he cries and the tears stream down his face, or without warning he crawls into my bed and holds me tightly. "Oh, it can't go on. I'm afraid. I'm afraid. Help me!"

Sometimes he trembles all over, and even after he falls asleep he talks deliriously and moans. The next morning he is absent-minded, like a man with the soul taken out of him. Then he disappears and doesn't return for three or four nights. A couple of my husband's publisher friends have been looking after the boy and myself for some time, and they bring money once in a while, enough to keep us from starving.

I dozed off, then before I knew it opened my eyes to see the morning light pouring in through the cracks in the shutters. I got up, dressed, strapped the boy to my back and went outside. I felt as if I couldn't stand being in the silent house another minute.

I set out aimlessly and found myself walking in the direction of the station. I bought a bun at an outdoor stand and fed it to the boy. On a sudden impulse I bought a ticket for Kichijoji and got on the streetcar. While I stood hanging from a strap I happened to notice a poster with my husband's name on it. It was an advertisement for a magazine in which he had published a story called "François Villon." While I stared at the title "François Villon" and at my husband's name, painful tears sprang from my eyes, why I can't say, and the poster clouded over so I couldn't see it.

I got off at Kichijoji and for the first time in I don't know how many years I walked in the park. The cypresses around the pond had all been cut down, and the place looked like the site of a construction. It was strangely bare and cold, not at all as it used to be.

I took the boy off my back and the two of us sat on a broken bench next to the pond. I fed the boy a sweet potato I had brought from home. "It's a pretty pond, isn't it? There used to be many carp and goldfish, but now there aren't any left. It's too bad, isn't it?"

I don't know what he thought. He just laughed oddly with his mouth full of sweet potato. Even if he is my own child, he did give me the feeling almost of an idiot.

I couldn't settle anything by sitting there on the bench, so I put the boy on my back and returned slowly to the station. I bought a ticket for Nakano. Without thought or plan, I boarded the streetcar as though I were being sucked into a horrible whirlpool. I got off at Nakano and followed the directions to the restaurant.

The front door would not open. I went around to the back and entered by the kitchen door. The owner was away, and his wife was cleaning the shop by herself. As soon as I saw her I began to pour out lies of which I did not imagine myself capable.

"It looks as if I'll be able to pay you back every bit of the money tomorrow, if not tonight. There's nothing for you to worry about."

"Oh, how wonderful. Thank you so much." She looked almost happy, but still there remained on her face a shadow of uneasiness, as if she was not yet satisfied.

"It's true. Someone will bring the money here without fail. Until he comes I'm to stay here as your hostage. Is that guarantee enough for you? Until the money comes I'll be glad to help around the shop."

I took the boy off my back and let him play by himself. He is accustomed to playing alone and doesn't get in the way at all. Perhaps because he's stupid, he's not afraid of strangers, and he smiled happily at the madam. While I was away getting the rationed goods for her, she gave him some empty American cans to play with, and when I got back he was in a corner of the room, banging the cans and rolling them on the floor.

About noon the boss returned from his marketing. As soon as I caught sight of him I burst out with the same lies I had told the madam. He looked amazed. "Is that a fact? All the same, Mrs. Otani, you can't be sure of money until you've got it in your hands." He spoke in a surprisingly calm, almost explanatory tone.

"But it's really true. Please have confidence in me and wait just this one day before you make it public. In the meantime I'll help in the restaurant."

"If the money is returned, that's all I ask," the boss said, almost to himself. "There are five or six days left to the end of the year, aren't there?"

"Yes, and so, you see, I mean—oh, some customers have come. Welcome!" I smiled at the three customers—they looked like workmen—who had entered the shop, and whispered to the madam, "Please lend me an apron."

One of the customers called out, "Say, you've hired a beauty. She's terrific."

"Don't lead her astray," the boss said, in a tone which wasn't altogether joking, "she cost a lot of money."

"A million-dollar thoroughbred?" another customer coarsely joked.

"They say that even in thoroughbreds the female costs only half-price," I answered in the same coarse way, while putting the sake on to warm.

"Don't be modest! From now on in Japan there's equality of the sexes, even for horses and dogs," the youngest customer roared. "Sweetheart, I've fallen in love. It's love at first sight. But is that your kid over there?"

"No," said the madam, carrying the boy from the back room in her arms. "We got this child from our relatives. At last we have an heir."

"What'll you leave him beside your money?" a customer teased.

The boss, with a dark expression, muttered, "A love affair and debts." Then, changing his tone, "What'll you have? How about a mixed grill?"

It was Christmas Eve. That must have been why there was such a steady stream of customers. I had scarcely eaten a thing since morning, but I was so upset that I refused even when the madam urged me to have a bite. I just went on flitting around the restaurant as lightly as a ballerina. Maybe it is only conceit, but the shop seemed exceptionally lively that night, and there were quite a few customers who wanted to know my name or tried to shake my hand.

But I didn't have the slightest idea how it would all end. I went on smiling and answering the customers' dirty jokes with even dirtier jokes in the same vein, slipping from customer to customer, pouring the drinks. Before long I got to thinking that I would just as soon my body melted and flowed away like ice cream.

It seems as if miracles sometimes do happen even in this world. A little after nine a man entered, wearing a Christmas tricornered paper hat and a black mask which covered the upper part of his face. He was followed by an attractive woman of slender build who looked thirty-four or thirty-five. The man sat on a chair in the corner with his back to me, but as soon as he came in I knew who it was. It was my thief of a husband.

He sat there without seeming to pay any attention to me. I also pretended not to recognize him, and went on joking with the other customers. The lady seated opposite my husband called me to their table. My husband stared at me from beneath his mask, as if he were surprised in spite of himself. I lightly patted his shoulder and asked, "Aren't you going to wish me a merry Christmas? What do you say? You look as if you've already put away a quart or two."

The lady ignored this. She said, "I have something to discuss with the proprietor. Would you mind calling him here for a moment?"

I went to the kitchen, where the boss was frying fish. "Otani has come back. Please go and see him, but don't tell the woman he's with anything about me. I don't want to embarrass him."

"If that's the way you want it, it's all right with me," he consented easily, and went out front. After a quick look around the restaurant, the boss walked straight to the table where my husband sat. The beautiful lady exchanged two or three words with him, and the three of them left the shop.

It was all over. Everything had been settled. Somehow I had believed all along that it would be, and I felt exhilarated. I seized the wrist of a young customer in a dark-blue suit, a boy not more than twenty, and I cried, "Drink up! Drink up! It's Christmas!"

In just thirty minutes—no, it was even sooner than that, so soon it startled me, the boss returned alone. "Mrs. Otani, I want to thank you. I've got the money back."

"I'm so glad. All of it?"

He answered with a funny smile, "All he took yesterday."

"And how much does his debt come to altogether? Roughly—the absolute minimum."

"Twenty thousand yen."

"Does that cover it?"

"It's a minimum."

"I'll make it good. Will you employ me starting tomorrow? I'll pay it back by working."

"What! You're joking!" And we laughed together.

Tonight I left the restaurant after ten and returned to the house with the boy. As I expected, my husband was not at home, but that didn't bother me. Tomorrow when I go to the restaurant I may see him again, for all I know. Why has such a good plan never occurred to me before? All the suffering I have gone through has been because of my own stupidity. I was always quite a success at entertaining the customers at my father's stall, and I'll certainly get to be pretty skillful at the restaurant. As a matter of fact, I received about five hundred yen in tips tonight.

From the following day on my life changed completely. I became lighthearted and gay. The first thing I did was to go to a beauty parlor and have a permanent. I bought cosmetics and mended my dresses. I felt as though the worries that had weighed so heavily on me had been completely wiped away.

In the morning I get up and eat breakfast with the boy. Then I put him on my back and leave for work. New Year's is the big season at the restaurant, and I've been so busy my eyes swim. My husband comes in for a drink once every few days. He lets me pay the bill and then disappears again. Quite often he looks in on the shop late at night and asks if it isn't time for me to be going home. Then we return pleasantly together.

"Why didn't I do this from the start? It's brought me such happiness."

"Women don't know anything about happiness or unhappiness."

"Perhaps not. What about men?"

"Men only have unhappiness. They are always fighting fear."

"I don't understand. I only know I wish this life could go on forever. The boss and the madam are such nice people."

"Don't be silly. They're grasping country bumpkins. They make me drink because they think they'll make money out of it in the end."

"That's their business. You can't blame them for it. But that's not the whole story is it? You had an affair with the madam, didn't you?"

"A long time ago. Does the old guy realize it?"

"I'm sure he does. I heard him say with a sigh that you had brought him a seduction and debts."

"I must seem a horrible character to you, but the fact is that I want to die so badly I can't stand it. Ever since I was born I have been thinking of nothing but dying. It would be better for everyone concerned if I were dead, that's certain. And yet I can't seem to die. There's something strange and frightening, like God, which won't let me die."

"That's because you have your work."

"My work doesn't mean a thing. I don't write either masterpieces or failures. If people say something is good, it becomes good. If they say it's bad, it becomes bad. But what frightens me is that somewhere in the world there is a God. There is, isn't there?"

"I haven't any idea."

Now that I have worked twenty days at the restaurant I realize that every last one of the customers is a criminal. I have come to think that my husband is very much on the mild side compared to them. And I see now that not only the customers but everyone you meet walking in the streets is hiding some crime. A beautifully dressed lady came to the door selling sake at three hundred yen the quart. That was cheap, considering what prices are nowadays, and the madam snapped it up. It turned out to be watered. I thought that in a world where even such an aristocratic-looking lady is forced to resort to such tricks, it is impossible for anyone alive to have a clear conscience.

God, if you exist, show yourself to me! Toward the end of the New Year season I was raped by a customer. It was raining that night, and it didn't seem likely that my husband would appear. I got ready to go, even though one customer was still left. I picked up the boy, who was sleeping in a corner of the back room, and put him on my back. "I'd like to borrow your umbrella again," I said to the madam.

"I've got an umbrella. I'll take you home," said the last customer, getting up as if he meant it. He was a short, thin man about twenty-five, who looked like a factory worker. It was the first time he had come to the restaurant since I started working there.

"It's very kind of you, but I am used to walking by myself."

"You live a long way off, I know. I come from the same neighborhood. I'll take you back. Bill, please." He had only had three glasses and didn't seem particularly drunk.

We boarded the streetcar together and got off at my stop. Then we walked in the falling rain side by side under the same umbrella through the pitch-black streets. The young man, who up to this point hadn't said a word, began to talk in a lively way. "I know all about you. You see, I'm a fan of Mr. Otani's and I write poetry myself. I was hoping to show him some of my work before long, but he intimidates me so."

We had reached the house. "Thank you very much," I said. "I'll see you again at the restaurant."

"Good-bye," the young man said, going off into the rain.

I was wakened in the middle of the night by the noise of the front gate being opened. I thought that it was my husband returning, drunk as usual, so I lay there without saying anything.

A man's voice called, "Mrs. Otani, excuse me for bothering you."

I got up, put on the light, and went to the front entrance. The young man was there, staggering so badly he could scarcely stand.

"Excuse me, Mrs. Otani. On the way back I stopped for another drink, and, to tell the truth, I live at the other end of town, and when I got to the station the last streetcar had already left. Mrs. Otani, would you please let me spend the night here? I don't need any blankets or anything else. I'll be glad to sleep here in the front hall until the first streetcar leaves tomorrow morning. If it wasn't raining I'd sleep outdoors somewhere in the neighborhood, but it's hopeless with this rain. Please let me stay."

"My husband isn't at home, but if the front hall will do, please stay." I got the two torn cushions and gave them to him.

"Thanks very much. I've had too much to drink," he said with a groan. He lay down just as he was in the front hall, and by the time I got back to bed I could already hear his snores.

The next morning at dawn without ceremony he took me.

That day I went to the restaurant with my boy as usual, acting as if nothing had happened. My husband was sitting at a table reading a newspaper, a glass of liquor beside him. I thought how pretty the morning sunshine looked, sparkling on the glass.

"Isn't anybody here?" I asked. He looked up from his paper. "The boss hasn't come back yet from marketing. The madam was in the kitchen just a minute ago. Isn't she there now?"

"You didn't come last night, did you?"

"I did come. It's got so that I can't get to sleep without a look at my favorite waitress's face. I dropped in after ten but they said you had just left."

"And then?"

"I spent the night here. It was raining so hard."

"I may be sleeping here from now on."

"That's a good idea, I suppose."

"Yes, that's what I'll do. There's no sense in renting the house forever."

My husband didn't say anything but turned back to his paper. "Well, what do you know. They're writing bad things about me again. They call me a fake aristocrat with Epicurean leanings. That's not true. It would be more correct to refer to me as an Epicurean in terror of God. Look! It says here that I'm a monster. That's not true, is it? It's a little late, but I'll tell you now why I took the five thousand yen. It was so that I might give you and the boy the first happy New Year in a long time. That proves I'm not a monster, doesn't it?"

His words didn't make me especially glad. I said, "There's nothing wrong with being a monster, is there? As long as we can stay alive."

Sometimes known as "The Poet of the Rain," Kim Yong Ik writes fiction in his third language, English. Born in a small fishing village in Korea, Kim was imprisoned in Japan during the Second World War because of his criticism of that government's political policies. After the Korean conflict (1950–1953) he migrated to America, where he wrote short stories, juvenile fiction, and a novel. Reflected in most of Kim's fiction is a resentment toward the uprooting and alienating force of war and a compassion for the "little people" who labor all their lives for a handful of rice.

In this story the backwash of war causes the structure of the family to disintegrate. What is the effect of the boy's devotion to the dog? What has the dog "revealed" to him? What is implied by the dog's death? The last paragraph of the story, despite its apparent simplicity, is densely packed with implication. What has happened to the boy? Further Reading: The Diving Gourd *(1958),* The Happy Days *(1960),* Blue in the Seed *(1964).*

KOREA

From below the Bridge

KIM YONG IK

At last they were leaving their shelter below the bridge in Pusan to go by train to the valley home from which they had fled when the war came. The Father was already on the low, sagging bridge whose railing had long ago disappeared, waiting for his family. Again and again he was repeating to himself: If we had walked home ten days ago we would have been drinking our village water by now.

As he stepped nearer the edge of the wooden structure he saw in the water the broken shadows of his restless figure with his tall horsehair hat, wavering to

---

Reprinted by permission of the author.

and fro across the river's surface, often scattered by the floating ice patches. The Boy came out from under the bridge to the sunny spot at the stream's edge to leash his dozing dog for the day's trip. He moved a few steps in his squatting position like a river crab to avoid the icicles that hung from the rim of the bridge, their falling drops like melting shadows of frozen tears of the people who had passed over long seasons ago.

At the sight of the hempen cord in the Boy's hand, the cord by which he had carried his shoe-shine box across his shoulders until yesterday, the old yellow dog got up, growled disapprovingly and wrinkled his black nose. The Boy commanded in a tone of playful seriousness: "No gettaway, Bo! No! Gook!"

As the Boy kept on shouting the words he vaguely understood, the gaunt-looking dog raised his long ears, yet did not attempt to slip away. The Father came to the bridge entrance post. "In the home valley, don't repeat that 'dog' language. What will the village people think of me, your father?" he said.

Tying the cord around his dog's neck, the Boy retorted sulkily: "Don't you have earholes? I have told you it's the big-nose soldier's language."

He could not understand why his father could not tell the soldier from the dog language, for the Father sometimes seemed to have more sensitive ears than his dog's. At the slightest foot sound on the bridge above their temporary home, his father's face always became painfully distorted. Whenever the sounds were prolonged the Father would raise both hands aloft as if someone were about to step on his head. Mumbling the same words over and over again to his dog, the Boy put his fingers between the cord and the throat to see if the loop was too tight.

The Father shouted angrily: "You must stop from today! The dog-words your father does not understand." He looked down at his be-wildered mirrored face in the water. The needle spots of the sun through the hat crowded upon the deep furrows on the forehead of this man who had just crossed the peak of forty years.

The Mother came from under the bridge, carrying a shapeless cloth bundle on her head. Her lips protruded when she said: "I have never seen anyone who speaks the language starve." She talked as if she knew her son understood the fortuneteller's charm words that invite prosperity into their doorway. "It is the money-language Pusan people nowadays break each other's heads to learn."

With a shoebrush the Boy removed the dirt from around the ribs that jutted out harshly from the thin, ill-fed body of his dog, then placed the brush back in his pocket, which looked like any one of the many patches on his drab coat. The Mother, putting her un-occupied hands together awkwardly before her, sighed: "Is this all I carry back home after one year and one winter?" She turned and looked long at the square-framed structure of cardboard, burlap and straw matting that had been their protection from the winter wind.

The Father hurried his wife impatiently. "Come! You didn't forget anything. There is nothing worth a straw to take back home."

The Mother sneered through her nose, "Hm-m," as she began to climb up the riverbank. The Boy, pulling his dog by the leash, dragged upward his ill-fitting shoes, the castoffs of a soldier.

A faint smile at his son smoothed the Father's sunken cheek as he said: "Not one in my family was hurt, not even the dog. Your grandfather used to say that as long as the head of a household does not lower himself, no blow of quarrel or war would reach his family."

The Mother said to her son: "Oh, he chatters like a ditch stone after the spring rain." As though he were too old to believe his father's remarks, the Boy, with a superior air, smiled at his mother as she came up the bank and onto the bridge.

Speaking bitterly, the Mother said to her husband: "In this world upside down, when every man holds his hat upside down at others' doors, what are you trying to put into your son's head? You already talked as much as Jesus' people about your head part but not a word about stomach."

Hurrying as if she thought she would no longer be able to speak like this in her home valley, the Mother sputtered on. "Such a mountain boasting from a man who lived off his eleven-year-old son."

The Father, pretending not to hear, lifted his straw shoes quietly, stepping on the noon shadow of his horsehair hat. The salty, warm waves of the sea wind moved across the yellow dust, making the winding path wiggle and blinding the road ahead. The Boy, leading the dog, walked bent over, ahead of his mother, sometimes spitting the dust off his tongue.

There passed oxen, puffing, pulling the wagons: then bicycles, and honking cars. The Boy often pulled his father's sleeve to remind him not to walk too close to the middle of the road. The Mother behind grumbled: "Are you having a dream inside your horsehair hat that you own the road?" She clicked her lips with the tip of her tongue, "Tsk, tsk," and said to herself, as she had often before: "If I had not borne my son, I would have crushed those hats flat and left him long ago."

For the first few months after the war came the Mother had told her husband time and time again not to wear his horsehair hat when he went out to try to get a job at the docks. Whenever the Father, his lips apart, had replied in any way at all, his remark had always been the same: "I am meeting those people for the first time," he would remind her, then would go out wearing his outer gown and hat. Sometimes he would turn to his son with a shadowy chagrin on his face to say: "The hatless people are vulgar and low and fight over a small straw matter."

At the market corner the shoeshine boys near their stools were calling to big-nose soldiers passing by: "Hi, Joe! Me shoeshine presento; you, cigaretto presento!"

"Aren't you going to say good-by to your friends?" asked his mother.

Instead of crossing the road to meet them, the Boy walked faster. The dog lifted his ears marketward but followed the boy in short paces.

For the Boy had enjoyed the work of shining shoes after he had learned the trade from the older ones. He had soon learned the trick of saving his expensive shoe polish by pouring only one-third into a can, then adding resin, candle wax and gasoline, which gave the same shine. He liked to bargain with the big-nose soldiers, who sometimes gave him "cigaretto" or "chocoletto" after his "presento shoeshine."

When he had earned cigarettes, he would look in the market crowd for his mother, who was there selling the Western things he had earned from his soldier customers. Often the dog had found her for him, barking at the sight of her. The Father, having seen him in the market corner, would remark later: "My son is taking dirt off strangers' shoes." The Boy in turn had wished his father would not come to the market because the other boys giggled at the sight of the high hat.

Later the Boy had joined the shoeshine group before the church beyond the market and did not tell his father where he worked. Just since the evenings after the winter cold, after the shoeshine hour, the Boy had stood in the church street, offering to take the big-nose soldiers to the "Shibi-Shibi girls" lurking at the foot of the hill behind the church. When he had given the money to his mother without telling her what he had done to earn it at night, she had said proudly: "My nose is getting bigger at having my son who supports a whole family."

The salty, peppery wind blew with no dust now as they walked along the barbed-wire fence beyond which were scattered the barracks. Farther away lay the patches of sea amid the crowding vessels. The dog began to zigzag, lowering his nose and pausing to sniff. The Boy, pulling on the leash, shouted: "No, Bo! No! Son of bitchee! Gettaway! No! Gook!" But near the tin barracks the dog began to whimper pleadingly, arching his back, then pushed his head through the strand of wire at the bottom of the fence.

The Father, taking the leash by the middle, pulled the dog. This raised the foreleg with which he was trying to hug a fence post. Pulling harder, the Father said: "We must leave the town today."

The neck cord was being pulled too hard against the animal's throat and now, stiff like a stone, he was being dragged, whimpering chokingly. The Boy hit his father on the hand, crying: "You are strangling him." In a whirling motion the Boy pushed his father and made him stagger so that he dropped the leash. The dog, flattening his back and diving under the fence, fled toward the tin houses.

The Father's face turned mushroom pale as he lifted his trembling fist toward his son. The Mother came between, saying: "Hungry men even crawl into others' fences and women give themselves to other men to feed their families."

The Father looked at his wife hard for a while as if he were actually crying, "Say that again!" then dropped his fist weakly.

A soldier with a tattoo on his chest and clad only in pants held out a bone toward the dog and whistled. As the Father walked away, the Mother said: "Wait! Your anger has no root. You can't keep such starch always."

Several other soldiers came out of the barracks to empty their dishes and playfully competed, letting the dog lick their plates. The dog was confusedly in a hurry, moving from one dish to another. When the dog later came out slowly through the sentinel gate with his stomach distended and his nose held contentedly high, the Father was no longer in sight. Picking up the leash again, the Boy hurried with his mother toward the station, keeping his eyes above the crowd.

The railroad station inside was stuffy with choking dust, the smell of sweat and bottom-scraping, high-pitched noises. The people moved like fish that are caught but making a last attempt to jump out of the boat. The Boy and his mother moved, bumping into women with their babies, and into venders with their trays, until they saw the tall hat near the platform entrance. Two men in buttoned-up uniforms were examining the tickets before passengers could enter the gate to go aboard the train.

The Boy stepped first inside the fence, passing by a small railroad officer, but the hand that held the leash was pulled back. As the dog made a slight whimper, the short officer said, barring the dog: "No dog. There is not enough room for even two-legged passengers."

"I'll put him on my lap," said the Boy promptly, "and he won't take up any room."

Another officer, lanky and stooped, pushed the Boy back from the entrance, commanding, "Step aside!" and gestured with his hand for others to hurry in. Behind them the Father stammered: "That— is—my son." Then, pointing to his wife in front of him, he explained: "We are one family—three of us and one dog." The stooped man pushed the three aside with his arms stretched out so that other passengers could enter.

When the Father refused to step aside, the officer said: "You cannot talk all day here as at your country market, horsehair man. The dog needs a ticket."

The Father bent over slightly, pleading: "Just close your eyes when we pass through with the dog." The creature growled at the angry faces of the station men and the hangers-on who had gathered round. One of them said: "Give me the dog. I'll take care of the shabby thing."

The Father picked up the animal in his arms and, with his face reddening even back behind his ears, said to his son weakly: "We have to lose one dog, to go back. He does not have many days ahead for the day to be buried."

The Boy looked at the hungry mouths of the hangers-on and knew that they would even eat his dog. He cried: "I won't go without my dog. If he should die they would not bury him."

The Father looked around for a moment and then rapidly walked toward the fence with the dog. As he passed the entrance the stooped railroad man caught him by the sleeve. The Father struggled to pull loose. The throng behind them shouted impatiently: "Let us go in!"

As the Father pulled himself free the stooped officer reached for the tall hat and snatched it off. In the wind-passing moment the horsehair hat was thrown to the floor. The dog jumped out of his master's arms and the Father quickly covered his head with both hands, looking like a cock that had lost its comb.

The short railroad man said, very loud: "You! You! Not even half old enough, trying to put on the old hat and act like an old country-man."

The Father walked out of the entrance crabwise and reached his hat before the boy could pick it up, tapped the dust from it and, by putting his hand inside, tried to round out the crushed top again.

The Mother said cautiously: "We will put off our leaving until we can earn the ticket for our dog and some extra to spend when we get there."

The Father shouted: "I won't go back to that bridge to hear the tramp-crash sound above my head! I won't stay at the bridge all day alone, just to keep away men who might take the shelter for a toilet!" The white saliva oozed out of the corner of his mouth even after he had stopped talking and his jaw was thrust out by his clenched teeth.

The Mother, looking at the crowd that had begun to pour in onto the platform, said: "These people rush home to make rice seed beds in the coming rain, but you don't even have land there."

The Father stopped the Mother's talk by raising his voice very loud, louder than the Boy had ever heard it before. "From now, today, you are to listen to the head of the household," he commanded. Handing his tickets to the Boy, he continued: "The dog can have my ticket. I'll walk home on my two feet." In a shivering tone he spoke to his wife and son: "Go! Hurry back to the train!" When his family did not move, he gave a hurt look and, holding his hat high, swam out through the crowd with the other hand.

For a moment the two stood looking at each other, then made their way to follow him. Outside, the Father had now crossed the

street, tipping to one side, it seemed, as though the hat in his hand
hurt his foot. He crossed another street, unmindful of the impatient
honking of cars.

An uninterrupted stream of automobiles passed by endlessly and,
when the two at last were able to cross and then hasten on to the next
intersection, the Father was out of sight. They stood looking, trying
to catch sight of his head above the crowd on the northbound road
that led to their home.

"Didn't he always say he would walk home, but won't we find him
at the bridge hovel? He will change his mind and turn back," said
the Mother. "Let's go back there."

"But," the Boy remonstrated, "he knows we are leaving. We should
follow him onto the northbound road."

"The bridge shelter will be occupied by someone else if we don't
go there now," the Mother insisted. "Even if your father does walk,
we can catch a train tomorrow, or two or three days later, and yet
arrive there before he does."

The sun was about to drown in the evening dusk, but it broke at the
bridge rim, its pieces scattered with the smoke streak in the windy
air. A woman wearing the trousers of a soldier squatted with her two
children, fanning a brazier before their former shelter. As the boy
and his mother approached, the shadow of the smoke began to wiggle
on the patched matting wall. The dog hastened down the bank ahead
of them and disappeared.

Finding the shelter already occupied by a woman refugee, the Boy
stood out in the road below the bridge, looking to see if his father
might be coming back. For a long while his eyes trailed the gray
path and the road that led to the bridge but he saw no one. Noticing
that his mother was talking with the woman, who painted her lips
as strong as red pepper, he walked away hurt, along the bank, throwing stones into the fog settling over the river. Suddenly he saw his
dog lying near the broom sedge at the bend. As he whistled to him,
Bo stood half up on his forepaws, but soon became wobbly and lay
down again. Bo was breathing with his tongue out. The tongue was
slightly discolored and the Boy caught a whiff of a cloying smell. In
a small patch of oats behind him there was the wet mixture his dog
had thrown up. He tapped the dog's back gently for a while, hoping
the too sudden fullness of the long-starved stomach would go down.
When it did not the Boy turned and went slowly toward the shelter.

The woman in soldier pants and his mother were still talking. She
was saying to his mother, "For just one night I get—" but at his approach she began to speak in whispers. The foot sounds above were
now intensified by the gathering dusky dampness.

"The dog is sick, Oma," he interrupted. "He must have eaten the
chicken bones."

"That dog has been living on borrowed time. Nowadays very few men live out their own ages," said the Mother casually. Slowly she moved about, then handed her son some canned food that the other woman had brought out for them.

The Boy took a mouthful of the beef stew and said to his mother: "Oma, I'll go out tonight."

"For what?" she asked in a surprised tone. "You no longer have your shoeshine equipment. You can sleep here."

But the Boy, already scrambling up the bank, promised: "I won't be late, Oma."

The bridge looked adrift tonight, like a tipped-over boat on the darkening water. The Boy could not remember a single night when his dog had not gone with him. Again the eerie impression of the town at night, when he had entered it for the first time with his parents, stirred in him. The spinning car lights chopped the town into pieces. Figures walked close to others' walls and windows as though they had come out of a crowded graveyard and sought entrance into open windows to dance in others' dreams.

Soon the paper-rustling market lay like a torn quilt under which men in winter still pulled at the ends to keep warm. After passing the market on the upward road, he heard the sound of the church bell that had recently been gathering more and more of Jesus' people every night. He missed Bo's howling at the church step right after the bell's ringing.

As the Boy turned he saw the dim yellow light in front of the church. A flock of small figures darted out of the alley near the church and followed three big-nose soldiers. As one of the men picked up a stone the small boys scattered like a hide-and-seek group. One figure away down in the darkest part of the alley was crying angrily aloud as if he had made a poor bargain or had found himself completely outwitted by a big-nose soldier.

The Boy walked on down the street, looking for a passing soldier. The street down the curve was brightened and made the shadows of the small figures look like ghosts on stilts.

"M.P.!" suddenly pierced the sky and the street. The Boy, with others, ran into the sanctuary of the church. A white patrol jeep moved up slowly, followed by a Korean police car, and slowly went away. Soon the older boys ran out of the door and began to pipe their hungry cries after two big-nose passing soldiers, one eating an ice cream cone, the other popcorn. The Boy still stayed inside for fear the patrol jeep might suddenly turn and come back.

Then the Boy was startled to see his cold, lusterless yellow dog turning his tail to the glow at the church steps. Pushing the door open, he dashed out, calling, "Bo! Bo!" The dog lifted his black muzzle that still gave out a foul odor. After the Boy had hugged his pet, he ordered, "Bo, getta 'ell outa 'ere," and pointed down the alley beside the church so that the dog would stay there until he was ready to go. The animal wobbled away.

The Boy turned back toward the street and followed two big-nosed soldiers. As the church hymn floated out on the evening sea wind he raised his voice loud enough to be heard: "Shibi-Shibi girl have yes. Presento price." But soon he saw it was of no use, for the soldier guard came near the lighted area of the recreation center. Disappointed, the Boy came slowly back to the corner of the church building and called Bo to come play with him, looking hard into the alley until another soldier should pass by. The dog did not leap up as he usually did. The Boy walked into the alley under the church windows, calling repeatedly. "Bo! Bo! Bo!" As he stepped into the darker alley behind the building, he shouted still, "Bo-o!"

He heard his dog whimper from the foot of the hill. "Maybe a Shibi-Shibi girl or her big-nose is kicking my dog out of their way while they bargain." He started to run toward the whimpering sounds. Suddenly from the rear window of the church a light was flashed. In the alley Shibi-Shibi girls and soldiers turned their backs and scattered like spiders. Someone inside shouted: I'll have to call the police if you disturb services." At the stone steps that led to the winding road to the hilltop his dog came down with his eyes shining in the light from the window.

Quickly the Boy went over and held the dog, looking up to see the one who might be harming his pet. There, halfway between the foot of the hill and the steps, stood the woman wearing the soldier pants. Just below her was another figure, one that looked familiar to him, a woman with a muffler close to her mouth. She hunched herself down as small as possible. The Boy stepped up a few steps, and cried in hoarse dismay: "Oma!"

Her paper white face looked down. She covered the front part of her jacket with her hands as if she were naked. She gasped haltingly and muttered: "S-o-n, what are you doing here?" The light from the rear window went out and he stood unable to see for a moment.

The Boy turned and hurried out of the alley, where a song from the church echoed, and away from the piping cries of the night boys. He walked away from the car lights into the night. From behind he heard the occasional whimper of his dog and his mother crying his name as she followed him. He walked fast out of the deserted town so that he would not be seen by his mother.

As he ran rapidly on he could no longer hear the cries of his dog but only the loud croakings of the rain frogs near the river. When he reached the northbound road he realized that he was alone. He turned and walked back, but stopped when he found his mother stooped over the dog that was lying on the edge of the road. The frogs croaked louder and the sickle moon moved into a cloud over the mountain.

An oxcart came rattling by and passed on, then stopped a few wagon lengths beyond as the cartman called out: "Is anyone sick? Do you want to use my empty cart?"

Hearing no answer, the man scratched a match and revealed his old, bearded face. The Mother, putting her hand on the dog, nodded to the oxcart man. He used the match to light his short-stemmed pipe and said after a long puff: "There is no use carrying a dying dog."

When the Boy and his mother did not speak or move, the man lifted the dog in his arms and placed him in the cart. Pulling the reins gently he urged his ox on and invited them: "Come along with me, now, but I'm not going far."

The Boy walked beside the old man and the Mother behind the cart.

After a long silence the old man broke into speech. "Where is your home?"

"Sang Po." The Boy cleared his throat.

"Why did you start on such a long journey in this rain-buried night?" When he had received no answer he asked: "What is your father doing?"

"He is a horsehair hat weaver," the Boy replied promptly.

Then the old one raised his voice: "And what is he doing now to feed you and your mother?"

Again there was no answer. The old man apologized. "I did not mean to hurt you. It is a pity that so few wear the hats nowadays." After a short pause he reminisced. "On my wedding day I was riding on a pony back, and wearing the tall hat. It was the happy days when I wore the hat. I know how the custom was started in this country. Would you like to hear about it, my boy?"

Again when there was no answer the older one continued: "In the ancient times, as in these days, the people would fight over a small straw matter. The scholars invented the moon-brimmed hats and encouraged the people to wear them, so they could not so easily fight for fear of smashing their delicately woven hats."

When the frogs began to croak again the old man spoke louder. "Yes; there was a time when every man longed to wear the moon-large hats."

The cart went down a grade on the cobbled road between the rice fields and halted at the branch road under the dark grove. The old man went behind his cart and lit a match near the Mother. The Boy went back to help unload his dog, which lay on scattered straw. Raindrops began to fall as the old man, looking up into the sultry darkness, said to the Boy: "Just leave this sick dog where he is now. I'll keep him and bury him for you. You can see he has not long to live."

Some time after the cart had crawled off into the wet darkness the

Boy turned at last to go back toward the northbound road. He walked fast to keep ahead of his mother. At each step the tight feeling in his throat tried to come out of his mouth, which was shut against the rain. When he realized that there was no one to whom he could talk, no one to whom he could tell what had happened that night or what his dog had revealed, the Boy began to weep aloud between the hoarse croakings of the rain frogs in the rice fields.

*Juan Rulfo was born in 1918 in Jalisco.
His small output of fiction is focused on
Mexican life, but his work is in no way
regional. Mexico serves merely as the setting
from which his fiction expands outward in
its implications.*

*"Talpa" is a story of love and guilt. The
normal sequence of time is shuffled about to
suggest the reliving of the central event of
the story. This event begins and ends in
linear time, but it continues to exist as the
vertex of the lives of the survivors. Did the
brother and wife love Tanilo or hate him?
Did they deliberately lead him to his death
or hope to get him cured? The narrator in-
sists on his own and Natalia's guilt. Must
we believe him? Can we decide objectively?
What is the effect of Rulfo's unrelentingly
graphic description of Tanilo's condition?
Further Reading: The Burning Plain and
Other Stories (1967).*

MEXICO

Talpa

JUAN RULFO

Natalia threw herself into her mother's
arms, crying on and on with a quiet sobbing. She'd bottled it up for many days,
until we got back to Zenzontla today and
she saw her mother and began feeling like
she needed consolation.

But during those days when we had so
many difficult things to do—when we
had to bury Tanilo in a grave at Talpa
without anyone to help us, when she and
I, just the two of us alone, joined forces
and began to dig the grave, pulling out
the clods of earth with our hands, hurrying to hide Tanilo in the grave so he
wouldn't keep on scaring people with his
smell so full of death—then she didn't
cry.

By Juan Rulfo, from *The Burning Plain* (*El
llano en llamas*), translated by George Schade,
University of Texas Press, 1967. Reprinted by
permission of the publisher.

Not afterward either, on the way back, when we were traveling at night without getting any rest, groping our way as if asleep and trudging along the steps that seemed like blows on Tanilo's grave. At that time Natalia seemed to have hardened and steeled her heart so she wouldn't feel it boiling inside her. Not a single tear did she shed.

She came here, near her mother, to cry, just to upset her, so she'd know she was suffering, upsetting all the rest of us besides. I felt that weeping of hers inside me too as if she was wringing out the cloth of our sins.

Because what happened is that Natalia and I killed Tanilo Santos between the two of us. We got him to go with us to Talpa so he'd die. And he died. We knew he couldn't stand all that traveling; but just the same, we pushed him along between us, thinking we'd finished him off forever. That's what we did.

The idea of going to Talpa came from my brother Tanilo. It was his idea before anyone else's. For years he'd been asking us to take him. For years. From the day when he woke up with some purple blisters scattered about on his arms and legs. And later on the blisters became wounds that didn't bleed—just a yellow gummy thing like thick distilled water came out of them. From that time I remember very well he told us how afraid he was that there was no cure for him any more. That's why he wanted to go see the Virgin of Talpa, so she'd cure him with her look. Although he knew Talpa was far away and we'd have to walk a lot under the sun in the daytime and in the cold March nights, he wanted to go anyway. The blessed Virgin would give him the cure to get rid of that stuff that never dried up. She knew how to do that, by washing them, making everything fresh and new like a recently rained-on field. Once he was there before Her, his troubles would be over; nothing would hurt him then or hurt him ever again. That's what he thought.

And that's what Natalia and I latched on to so we could take him. I had to go with Tanilo because he was my brother. Natalia would have to go too, of course, because she was his wife. She had to help him, taking him by the arm, bearing his weight on her shoulders on the trip there and perhaps on the way back, while he dragged along on his hope.

I already knew what Natalia was feeling inside. I knew something about her. I knew, for example, that her round legs, firm and hot like stones in the noonday sun, had been alone for a long time. I knew that. We'd been together many times, but always Tanilo's shadow separated us; we felt that his scabby hands got between us and took Natalia away so she'd go on taking care of him. And that's the way it'd be as long as he was alive.

I know now that Natalia is sorry for what happened. And I am too; but that won't save us from feeling guilty or give us any peace ever again. It won't make us feel any better to know that Tanilo would've died anyway because his time was coming, and that it hadn't done any good to go to Talpa, so far away, for it's almost sure he would've died just as well here as there, maybe a little afterward, because of all he suffered on the road, and the blood he lost besides, and the anger and everything—all those things together were what killed him off quicker. What's bad about it is that Natalia and I pushed him when he didn't want to go on anymore, when he felt it was useless to go on and he asked us to take him back. We jerked him up from the ground so he'd keep on walking, telling him we couldn't go back now.

"Talpa is closer now than Zenzontla." That's what we told him.

But Talpa was still far away then, many days away.

We wanted him to die. It's no exaggeration to say that's what we wanted before we left Zenzontla and each night that we spent on the road to Talpa. It's something we can't understand now, but it was what we wanted. I remember very well.

I remember those nights very well. First we had some light from a wood fire. Afterward we'd let the fire die down, then Natalia and I would search out the shadows to hide from the light of the sky, taking shelter in the loneliness of the countryside, away from Tanilo's eyes, and we disappeared into the night. And that loneliness pushed us toward each other, thrusting Natalia's body into my arms, giving her a release. She felt as if she was resting; she forgot many things and then she'd go to sleep with her body feeling a great relief.

It always happened that the ground on which we slept was hot. And Natalia's flesh, the flesh of my brother Tanilo's wife, immediately became hot with the heat of the earth. Then those two heats burned together and made one wake up from one's dreams. Then my hands groped for her; they ran over her red-hot body, first lightly, but then they tightened on her as if they wanted to squeeze her blood out. This happened again and again, night after night, until dawn came and the cold wind put out the fire of our bodies. That's what Natalia and I did along the roadside to Talpa when we took Tanilo so the Virgin would relieve his suffering.

Now it's all over. Even from the pain of living Tanilo found relief. He won't talk any more about how hard it was for him to keep on living, with his body poisoned like it was, full of rotting water inside that came out in each crack of his legs or arms. Wounds this big, that opened up slow, real slow, and then let out bubbles of stinking air that had us all scared.

But now that he's dead things are different. Now Natalia weeps for him, maybe so he'll see, from where he is, how full of remorse her soul is. She says she's seen Tanilo's face these last days. It was the only part of him that she cared about—Tanilo's face, always wet with the sweat which the effort to bear his pain left him in. She felt it approaching her mouth, hiding in her hair, begging her, in a voice she could scarcely hear, to help him. She says he told her that he was finally cured, that he no longer had any pain. "Now I can be with you, Natalia. Help me to be with you," she says he said to her.

We'd just left Talpa, just left him buried there deep down in that ditch we dug to bury him.

Since then Natalia has forgotten about me. I know how her eyes used to shine like pools lit up by the moon. But suddenly they faded, that look of hers was wiped away as if it'd been stamped into the earth. And she didn't seem to see anything any more. All that existed for her was her Tanilo, whom she'd taken care of while he was alive and had buried when his time came to die.

It took us twenty days to get to the main road to Talpa. Up to then the three of us had been alone. At that point people coming from all over began to join us, people like us who turned onto that wide road, like the current of a river, making us fall behind, pushed from all sides as if we were tied to them by threads of dust. Because from the ground a white dust rose up with the swarm of people like corn fuzz that swirled up high and then came down again; all the feet scuffling against it made it rise again, so that dust was above and below us all the time. And above this land was the empty sky, without any clouds, just the dust, and the dust didn't give any shade.

We had to wait until nighttime to rest from the sun and that white light from the road.

Then the days began to get longer. We'd left Zenzontla about the middle of February, and now that we were in the first part of March it got light very early. We hardly got our eyes closed at night when the sun woke us up again, the same sun that'd gone down just a little while ago.

I'd never felt life so slow and violent as when we were trudging along with so many people, just like we were a swarm of worms all balled together under the sun, wriggling through the cloud of dust that closed us all in on the same path and had us corralled. Our eyes followed the dust cloud and struck the dust as if stumbling against something they could not pass through. And the sky was always gray, like a heavy gray spot crushing us all from above. Only at times, when we crossed a river, did the dust clear up a bit. We'd plunge our feverish and blackened heads into the green water, and for a moment a blue smoke, like the steam that comes out of your mouth when it's cold, would come from all of us. But a little while afterward we'd disappear again, mixed in with the dust, sheltering each other from the sun, from that heat of the sun we all had to endure.

Eventually night will come. That's what we thought about. Night will come and we'll get some rest. Now we have to get through the day, get through it somehow to escape from the heat and the sun. Then we'll stop—afterward. What we've got to do now is keep plugging right along behind so many others just like us and in front of many others. That's what we have to do. We'll really only rest well when we're dead.

That's what Natalia and I thought about, and maybe Tanilo too, when we were walking along the main road to Talpa among the procession, wanting to be the first to reach the Virgin, before she ran out of miracles.

But Tanilo began to get worse. The time came when he didn't want to go any farther. The flesh on his feet had burst open and begun to bleed. We took care of him until he got better. But, he'd decided not to go any farther.

"I'll sit here for a day or two and then I'll go back to Zenzontla." That's what he said to us.

But Natalia and I didn't want him to. Something inside us wouldn't let us feel any pity for Tanilo. We wanted to get to Talpa with him, for at that point he still had life left in him. That's why Natalia encouraged him while she rubbed his feet with alcohol so the swelling would go down. She told him that only the Virgin of Talpa would cure him. She was the only one who could make him well forever. She and no one else. There were lots of other Virgins, but none like the Virgin of Talpa. That's what Natalia told him.

Then Tanilo began to cry, and his tears made streaks down his sweaty face, and he cursed himself for having been bad. Natalia wiped away the streaky tears with her shawl, and between us we lifted him off the ground so he'd walk on a little further before night fell.

So, dragging him along was how we got to Talpa with him.

The last few days we started getting tired too. Natalia and I felt that our bodies were being bent double. It was as if something was holding us and placing a heavy load on top of us. Tanilo fell down more often and we had to pick him up and sometimes carry him on our backs. Maybe that's why we felt the way we did, with our bodies slack and with no desire to keep on walking. But the people who were going along by us made us walk faster.

At night that frantic world calmed down. Scattered everywhere the bonfires shone, and around the fire the pilgrims said their rosaries, with their arms crossed, gazing toward the sky in the direction of Talpa. And you could hear how the wind picked up and carried that noise, mixing it together until it was all one roaring sound. A little bit afterward everything would get quiet. About midnight you could hear someone singing far away. Then you closed your eyes and waited for the dawn to come without getting any sleep.

We entered Talpa singing the hymn praising Our Lord.

We'd left around the middle of February and we got to Talpa the last days of March, when a lot of people were already on their way back. All because Tanilo took it into his head to do penance. As soon

as he saw himself surrounded by men wearing cactus leaves hanging
down like scapularies, he decided to do something like that too. He
tied his feet together with his shirt sleeves so his steps became more
desperate. Then he wanted to wear a crown of thorns. A little later he
bandaged his eyes, and still later, during the last part of the way, he
knelt on the ground and shuffled along on his knees with his hands
crossed behind him; so that thing that was my brother Tanilo Santos
reached Talpa, that thing so covered with plasters and dried streaks
of blood that it left in the air a sour smell like a dead animal when
he passed by.

When we least expected it we saw him there among the dancers.
We hardly realized it and there he was with a long rattle in his hand,
stomping hard on the ground with his bare bruised feet. He seemed
to be in a fury, as if he was shaking out all the anger he'd been carrying inside him for such a long time, or making a last effort to try to
live a little longer.

Maybe when he saw the dances he remembered going every year
to Tolimán during the novena of Our Lord and dancing all night
long until his bones limbered up without getting tired. Maybe that's
what he remembered and he wanted to get back the strength he used
to have.

Natalia and I saw him like that for a moment. Right afterward we
saw him raise his arms and slump to the ground with the rattle still
sounding in his bloodspecked hands. We dragged him out so he
wouldn't be tromped on by the dancers, away from the fury of those
feet that slipped on stones and leaped about stomping the earth without knowing that something had fallen among them.

Holding him up between us as if he was crippled, we went into
the church with him. Natalia had him kneel down next to her before
that little golden figure of the Virgin of Talpa. And Tanilo started
to pray and let a huge tear fall, from way down inside him, snuffing
out the candle Natalia had placed in his hands. But he didn't realize
this; the light from so many lit candles kept him from realizing what
was happening right there. He went on praying with his candle
snuffed out. Shouting his prayers so he could hear himself praying.

But it didn't do him any good. He died just the same.

"*. . . from our hearts filled with pain we all send her the same plea.
Many laments mixed with hope. Her tenderness is not deaf to
laments nor tears, for She suffers with us. She knows how to take
away that stain and to leave the heart soft and pure to receive her
mercy and charity. Our Virgin, our mother, who wants to know
nothing of our sins, who blames herself for our sins, who wanted to
bear us in her arms so life wouldn't hurt us, is right here by us, re-
lieving our tiredness and the sicknesses of our souls and our bodies
filled with thorns, wounded and supplicant. She knows that each
day our faith is greater because it is made up of sacrifices . . .*"

That's what the priest said from up in the pulpit. And after he quit talking the people started praying all at once with a noise just like a lot of wasps frightened by smoke.

But Tanilo no longer heard what the priest was saying. He'd become still, with his head resting on his knees. And when Natalia moved him so he'd get up he was already dead.

Outside you could hear the noise of the dancing, the drums and the hornpipes, the ringing of bells. That's when I got sad. To see so many living things, to see the Virgin there, right in front of us with a smile on her face, and to see Tanilo on the other hand as if he was in the way. It made me sad.

But we took him there so he'd die, and that's what I can't forget.

Now the two of us are in Zenzontla. We've come back without him. And Natalia's mother hasn't asked me anything, what I did with my brother Tanilo, or anything. Natalia started crying on her shoulder and poured out the whole story to her.

I'm beginning to feel as if we hadn't reached any place; that we're only here in passing, just to rest, and that then we'll keep on traveling. I don't know where to, but we'll have to go on, because here we're very close to our guilt and the memory of Tanilo.

Maybe until we begin to be afraid of each other. Not saying anything to each other since we left Talpa may mean that. Maybe Tanilo's body is too close to us, the way it was stretched out on the rolled petate, filled inside and out with a swarm of blue flies that buzzed like a big snore coming from his mouth, that mouth we couldn't shut in spite of everything we did and that seemed to want to go on breathing without finding any breath. That Tanilo, who didn't feel pain any more but who looked like he was still in pain with his hands and feet twisted and his eyes wide open like he was looking at his own death. And here and there all his wounds dripping a yellow water, full of that smell that spread everywhere and that you could taste in your mouth, like it was a thick and bitter honey melting into your blood with each mouthful of air you took.

I guess that's what we remember here most often—that Tanilo we buried in the Talpa graveyard, that Tanilo Natalia and I threw earth and stones on so the wild animals wouldn't come dig him up.

In Mulisch's stories thought becomes action, imagination shapes nature, and humans and inanimate objects converge; the master plan is beyond the comprehension of man. Perhaps we cannot decide what the story means, and perhaps that indecision is integral to the meaning. But the details which Mulisch provides may not be irrelevant. Why is the story set in New Guinea? What attitudes are implied by the obscene names which the troops assign to native villages? Why is the rape of a native girl introduced? Why are we told of Masuro's fondness for hunting? Why is narrative time spent on the school days of Lonestein and Masuro? What is the point of Lonestein's vision during Masuro's scream? What is gained by relating the story in the form of a letter?

Harry Mulisch—novelist, playwright, essayist, and short story author—was born in Haarlein in 1927. His first book, Archibald Strohalm, *was published in 1952. Since then Mulisch has incorporated into his fiction a sense of improvisation: myth, humor, and hallucination are blended with both detached objectivity and a subjectivity which is serious and sour. His description is detailed and concrete, and his several styles are imaginatively bizarre. Further Reading:* Blackmailing Life (1953), The Black Light (1956), The Stone Bridal Bed (1963).

NETHERLANDS

What Happened to Sergeant Masuro ?

HARRY MULISCH

Reprinted by permission from *The Hudson Review*, Vol. XIV, No. 1 (Spring, 1961). Copyright © 1961 by The Hudson Review, Inc. Translated from the Dutch by Roy Edwards.

ON HER NETHERLANDS
MAJESTY'S SERVICE
Ministry of War

To: Bureau O.Z.,
Section A, Room 3,
The Hague,
Holland.

Gentlemen,

It is a calm man who is writing this to you—a man with the calm that comes to the surface when hope has fled.

I suppose you know this tone. I do not know who you are, or under what Ministry you come, or what the initials of your name mean. I have never heard of your Bureau before. I should not be surprised if you also came under a Ministry I had never heard of before. Lieutenant-Colonel Stratema, Commanding Officer of the Fifth Battalion, 124th Regiment of Infantry, in New Guinea, gave me your address and told me I had to notify you of the affair of Sergeant Masuro "as if I was telling it to a friend."

Right . . . so you are my friend, Gentlemen. You shall hear what I know about it. I know *nothing* about it. I only know that it happened and that I was there. Incidentally, I have the impression that you have also received a report from the Colonel, and from Dr. Mondrian —and that they do not know anything about your Bureau either, except that, as I assume, it collects information about cases like Sergeant Masuro's.

There are other cases of the kind, are there, Gentlemen? I am not surprised. Only too many? Is that why I had to swear on the Bible to keep it secret? They also occur in Holland? I should not be surprised at that either. When Dr. Mondrian, at Kaukenau, had looked at Masuro till he could look no more, he began to interrogate me, with a drawn face, about our life in the interior. "God above, Lieutenant, it stands to reason, all that inhumanity round about you is more than human nature can endure."

I knew what he was thinking. He thought it had come of fear. Fear is capable of anything. It is a magician like Apollonius of Tyana, a prophet like Isaiah, a political mass-murderer, and a greater lover than Don Juan. But what happened to Masuro cannot have had anything to do with fear.

"I know the interior better than you do, Doctor. It could have happened just as easily in Amsterdam, in an office, or on a warm summer evening as he sat behind his paper near the open window, with the radio tuned in to Hilversum."

My panic, even then, was different from his—paler, more restrained, but not less violent. I told him that, in my opinion, it hardly had anything to do with *Masuro*, even. That it could happen to *any-one*, to him, Mondrian, as easily as to me—at any moment.

"Perhaps it's already at work in one of us, Doctor."

I saw that he could not take it. With a haggard face he looked at what was left of Masuro. He wanted a *reason*—otherwise, where was he? And the only thing that could pass for a reason, with a great deal of good (and occult) will, was fear. But there was no fear. Masuro hadn't known what fear was.

I knew Masuro well, in a manner of speaking. So I shall tell it to you as if you were a friend, Gentlemen, although it's a mystery to me what you will do with the information when you have it.

Two years ago, when he was posted to my section at Potapègo, I happened to be standing jabbering to the village headman. The truck from Kaukenau arrived, and out of the cab stepped a swarthy, heavily built fellow with a big head, round eyes and thick lips. Then, suddenly, I saw his name in the Major's letter before me again.

"Harry Masuro!"

He came towards me grinning.

"Afternoon, sir. Who'd have thought you'd be boss over me one day, down on the planet's backside?"

I had met him for the first time in the dressing-room of the gymnasium, when I was eleven years old. He was in the sixth class of the elementary school; I was in the fifth. I came to fetch something I had forgotten. Masuro was sitting alone in the sweaty atmosphere of the poky room, immobile as an image among the dingy little heaps of clothes. From the gym came the sound of pupils exercising, and a voice of command counting up to four, over and over again.

"Aren't you allowed to join in?"

"I'm being punished."

"What for?"

He looked at me with his big brown eyes.

"For nothing."

Even then, he had that same appearance of something that was both heavy and sharply outlined. I felt he was not lying. I should have liked to become friends with him, but that was hardly possible with someone in a class lower or higher than one's own. Nowhere in the world is there such class consciousness as in schools; it is enough to turn communists green with envy. Occasionally I had a talk with him, and he came one evening to peer at the moons of Jupiter through my telescope.

"The universe is a great sack full of stones and light."

Two years later I went to secondary school, and sat in the same form with him; he had failed to pass up at the end of the year. But by then it was too late, the time for becoming friends was gone. Things like that often depend on a month or a week; perhaps even on a day or a minute. If I had met my wife a year later than I did our marriage would have been the happiest in the world, and I should not be here now, at Kaukenau in New Guinea.

We hardly ever talked to each other; a feeling of something like shame had come between us. He had few interests; and in those days broad rivers of biology and history were flowing through my head. But if I got to know one thing about him, it was that he was not afraid. And yet he was no braggart either. I never heard him say: "Dare you to do this!" or "Dare you to do that!"—and then perform some heroic stunt or other. That was only done by boys who were actually afraid of doing what they did, and, above all, afraid of being thought to be afraid. And that kind of fear, too, was lacking in Masuro. But when it came to doing something which really called for courage, we saw Masuro do it while we shat in our trousers. (As, for instance, when someone had to break into the headmaster's study in order to find out what was in the examination papers.) But in his case it was not courage, but the absence of fear. And it seemed as if that gave him a certain invulnerability. When he was punished, it was always for nothing—never for anything he *had* done.

Otherwise, he was a perfectly ordinary boy, Harry Masuro, cool as a cucumber and cheeky as the devil. If it should now appear otherwise, Gentlemen, it is because I am trying, perhaps rather too hard, to refute that fear theory of Dr. Mondrian's; and perhaps because, in spite of myself, I too am looking for a reason for what happened to him—a reason which is not there.

Another two years passed, and, shortly before the war, I lost sight of him. He left school and I heard that he had gone to the East Indies with his parents.

"Just so as to be shoved into a camp by the Japs," he told me at Potapègo, where we celebrated our reunion after fifteen years: I, a National-Service Lieutenant, he a regular Sergeant posted to my section.

By then, he had already seen eight years of tropical service. Once out of the internment camp he had immediately volunteered for the army. His father and mother had both died in camp. He had trodden the whole length of the Indonesian "Via Dolorosa": the defeat of the Japanese; the breakdown of the Linggajati agreement between the Dutch and the Republic; the police actions; punitive expeditions in Java and Sumatra . . . he also appeared to have had something to do with "Turk" Westerling's attempt at counter-revolution. Naturally, I did not ask further questions. It was all rather obscure and difficult to piece together. No doubt you have at your disposal better channels than I have, to help you to find out more about it.

You can, of course, search in that direction, but you will find nothing. That is to say, nothing *directly* bound up with what happened. I don't know . . . perhaps there are such things as "hidden connections"—it's quite possible; but if so, they are very subterranean, round-the-back, underhand, not to be found. Over the whole planet something indescribable is under way, a sort of process . . . even the sun shines differently now from before the war. I wouldn't know how to express it more clearly. Innumerable totally new, incomprehensible powers have come into play; a new kind of people . . . in Singapore, Prague, Amsterdam, Alamogordo, Jakarta (and The Hague), gentlemen of an entirely new kind sit round tables in cafés and government buildings; *they* are the powers. Two tables or rooms farther off, and nobody knows who they are. It has ceased to have anything to do with politics. A party of men drives through Borneo in a column of motor vehicles. What language do they speak? Nobody understands it. But it has *something to do with it.* Above Ceram a small, drab aircraft without distinguishing marks is shot down by an Indonesian battery. It is empty. Nor are there any cameras on board. Only radio apparatus for remote control; or was it a living creature? Everything has something to do with it. No one has got the hang of it as yet; no one understands what is going on, what is possible, where it will end; and anyone who may think that at home in Holland things are different, lives in a world which no longer exists, and is making a terrible mistake.

But Masuro was not afraid. In that unnamable process he had played his part—undoubtedly a small part, but a part that could not bear the light of day, a part played behind a lowered curtain, in a play that no one knows, and with nobody in the prompter's box. I could see that he looked upon service with me as a kind of holiday. He was right—so it was. So it *was!* I ask myself whether it still is, after what happened to him.

In any case, with my unit there was less reason for fear than anywhere else in the Archipelago. I am responsible for law and order in an area about as big as London. But the powers that beset us do not sit ensconced in the mountains or the jungles. Those poor Papuans . . . they wave our flag, and they build bungalows for us, what do they know? New Guinea is way back in the Pleistocene, 100,000 B.C. Only when one of my men shoots a cassowary or a cockatoo is a shot heard; otherwise never. Sometimes, between the lianas or on or in a stinking swamp, we discover Dutch subjects four feet six inches high, who have never seen a white man. Such a kraal we then christen Nieuw Emmercompascuum, just as British soldiers might christen it New Middle Wallop; or we give it a name derived from the metabolic processes: Cocksuckington, or Fuckshot. We have to do something. Provided there is law and order.

For the rest, wherever we come, law and order is at an end; then the air rings with shouts and curses in Dutch, with shots—and sometimes with blows, when I am not looking. We drive around in three jeeps and a truck full of food, petrol and ammunition. Often we are on the road for weeks at a stretch, in touch with Kaukenau by radio.

It was right up Masuro's street; he was mad on hunting and shot the monkeys out of the trees from where he sat in the moving jeep. Naturally, I had more to do with him than with the other seven men; but also, in a way, less. Between us there was still something of that shamefacedness which we had had at secondary school on account of our neglected friendship. To him I talked about other things than to the others: about the past, about Holland, about nothing. Once he told me he had four children, two in Java, one in Celebes, and one in Halmahera.

When he was on guard duty at night, he hummed to himself between the tents, or on the verandas of the log huts which we had had built for us here and there by the Papuans. He liked keeping guard; he often let the next on duty sleep on, and he took his watch as well. It gave him a rest from something. His music was a great, gleaming, throbbing ball, which floated through the night between the tents. Hour after hour he hummed with a throat like an organ, and gazed at the mountains or at the black jungle, where everything rustled and murmured and screeched. Sometimes the Stone Age squatted down at a respectful distance from him, and listened absorbedly.

Everything went well for two years.

On the day that things went wrong, we were camping in Shitorbust, a hamlet of twenty huts full of dwarfs. That was Sunday a week ago, 19th July 1955. It was in May that we discovered it. It lies at the edge of the jungle, on the bank of the Titimuka river. We had not been able to make ourselves understood.

When I was about eighteen years old, Gentlemen—during the war —I wanted to become a Magus. I held my breath, tried to tie my legs in a knot, concentrated my attention on the patch made on the wall by a squashed mosquito, gazed at the bridge of people's noses and read books on "Personal Magnetism" and "Thought Power." From these I learned the exercise of recalling the events of the past day before going to sleep, and quickly running through them again, from the moment of waking onwards. That has since become a habit of mine. I am astonishingly clever at it. When I am not too tired I see the tiniest details again before me, and even such as had escaped my notice during the day. In a certain sense I live twice, and the second time more intensely than the first.

Gentlemen at The Hague, I have passed in review that day at Shitorbust, and the journey thither, not once but a dozen times. I remember every branch under which we drove, every stone in the foaming Titimuka, every cry from the black gnomes. I know that on that day, except for a spot of trouble with Private Steiger, *nothing* remarkable happened, *nothing* that made it different from the other days, and in any case *nothing* that had anything to do with Masuro.

Because it was pouring rain, we had been rather late in leaving our last camping-place, a hole called Umigapa. It was a shower from the mountains; when it stopped, we had half an hour of lovely weather, and at twelve o'clock the sun was beating down on our heads again. The troop was a bit browned off; we had been on the road for a fort-night, and I had promised that Shitorbust would be our last port of call. After that, it would be still another three or four days before we were back at Kaukenau. I sat in the second jeep, next to Private Elsemoor. Masuro was in the back, lounging across the seat with his carbine between his legs, and staring up at the tree tops. We didn't say much. I remember every word of what we said, but it was of no importance.

At about two o'clock I allowed Elsemoor to break column and drive off the road, to have a talk with a group of kapaukos who were dragging a dead kangaroo behind them to the swamps. At four o'clock we reached the Titimuka, and drove upstream on the narrow, shady strip of ground between the tropical forest and the water, half stupefied by the stench of rotting plants and leaves. Corporal Persin, in the first jeep, espied footprints in the mud, and five of us went for a short distance into the pitch-black jungle, but in vain. It was as dense and impenetrable as a city.

Otherwise, nothing happened. When we were bumping and jolting along the road again, Masuro turned once quickly on to his stomach and shot a crocodile to the bottom of the river. At half past six we drove into Shitorbust.

The Herr Geheimrat was already waiting to receive us, at the head of the whole tribe. He was the village chief, a naked little man hardly higher than my waist, with a civilized Mormon beard and wild eyes; to cover his privates he had a magnificent pointed calabash, which stood up as far as his nipples. He was growing bald at the temples, like an intellectual; I had told my men that the Germans call those patches of thinning hair "Geheimratsecken" ("Privy Councillor's corners"), and from then on he had his name. I suspect him of being the head of a gang of cannibals. "Manowe?" I had asked him the previous time, "Manowe?" His whole face lit up; it proved to be the only word he understood. With us, in any case, he had to make do with corned beef. He ate his fill at our welcoming banquet, together with two other village bigwigs; the representatives of our side were Masuro and I. The others were busy putting up the tents, while the village looked thoughtfully on.

During that meal, *nothing* happened that was out of the ordinary.

After eating, some of the men got their heads down under the mosquito curtains, while I made contact with Kaukenau and re-ported. Later, we went and lay in front of our tents, smoking and listening to the radio. Jakarta was broadcasting a lecture on Malayan poetry, but there was dance music on Sydney. Behind us and on the other side of the plashing river everything grew steadily taller and blacker and the darkness turned into millions of crickets. When it had become almost entirely dark, we lit the lamps, and saw that we were surrounded by motionless squatting dwarfs, listening to the music. Persin shouted at them, but they did not go away. When he fired his Sten gun off, they scattered into the night in all directions.

From now on I shall just report it verbatim, Gentlemen, then you'll be able to judge for yourselves.

"Where's Steiger?" I asked Masuro. During dinner I had seen him laughing and leering at a girl of about sixteen, with fine breasts and a belly as round as a ball.

"He's in love."

"Is he gone?"

"Yes."

"Did you *know*?"

"Yes."

"It was your duty to tell me so, god damn. Call him."

"Steiger!" Masuro bellowed.

A few seconds passed. Then an answering shout came from somewhere behind the vehicles.

"Stick it back in your stinking pants and come here! Double!" Excuse me, Gentlemen, but that was what he said, and that was how I would tell it to a friend. He shouted quite good-humouredly, though. He was on holiday.

I began to get very worried. A moment later Steiger stood before me, sweating.

"At it again, Steiger?"

"Yes, sir. Thought you wouldn't notice it, sir."

"Where is that kid?"

"Run off, sir."

"Did anyone in the village see you go away with her?"

"No, sir. She was sitting by herself under the truck, listening to the music."

That was a load off my mind. But I was still seething.

"You kept your hand over her mouth, I suppose?"

"No sir. She wanted it."

"Hold your hands out."

He held out his hands. In the left one there were deep marks of teeth.

"I've . . . always had that, sir."

"From sucking your thumb, I suppose? Just stand like that for a while, and keep your hands out."

I let Steiger stand with his hands held out for a full quarter of an hour. No one said anything more. The music sounded softly through the rushing of the river. The insects clotted in a thick, crackling, dying layer round the lamps, so that the light was only half as strong.

In the jungle on the other side something began to scream and abruptly stopped.

After a quarter of an hour had passed, I rubbed my thumb over Steiger's palm. The imprints were as good as gone.

"Double the guard tonight, Sergeant," I said to Masuro.

"Right, sir."

"Get to your wank-pit, Steiger, and report to the Captain when you get to Kaukenau. You knew what you were letting yourself in for?"

"Yes, sir."

"Then bugger off."

I could do that sort of thing to Steiger—no one liked him much, except perhaps Masuro. When he had disappeared, and the others had turned to minding their own business again, Masuro came and sat down beside me, and smoked a fat cigar in silence.

"I know more or less what you're thinking," I said, after a while. "But you should have told me, all the same."

"Never done anything of the kind yourself, Lonestein?"

That was something new. For the first time in fifteen years he called me by my name; throughout the last two years I had been "sir" to him. It mollified me—probably I had greatly admired him formerly; and I suddenly started getting confidential.

"If I hadn't, I might perhaps have given him his head."

I could feel Masuro looking at me.

"You're used to the islands, Masuro," I said. "There they eat rice."

He continued to look at me. I stared at the other side of the river. A rustling noise came from the forest, followed by a soft rumble. A tree falling, after a thousand years.

"It happened to me somewhere on the Mimika; when I had just arrived here. A bit of stuff just like Steiger's. I hadn't had a nibble for three months. What did it matter—a kapauko bint right from the middle of the wilderness of a hundred thousand years ago . . . I held my hand over her mouth, but when I'd got halfway she bit into it, began to yell, and I had to let her go. When we came back a month later, she was no longer in the village." I looked into his eyes. "They had killed and eaten her."

You may as well know it, Gentlemen of Bureau O.Z. After what has happened to Masuro, I have no further interest in keeping secrets of that kind . . . if it comes to that (it suddenly occurs to me) perhaps your Bureau's job is not so much to investigate cases like Masuro's —which are not to be investigated—as to keep an eye on those who witnessed them. You're quite welcome to discharge me from the Service, Gentlemen. I'm no longer interested in that either.

But, to go on. Masuro asked: "How do you know that?"

I shrugged my shoulders and looked straight in front of me again.

"They were manowes."

"She can just as easily have been ill, or married off to someone in another tribe, or simply dead."

"Maybe," I nodded. "But Steiger's going to pay for it."

The rustling and rumbling in the forest still went on—trees that collapsed under the burden that had come to hang on them, and dragged other trees down with them in a panic of breaking nests and crushed animals.

I did not know whether they had eaten her. In any case, it was possible. But it had never been possible for me to grasp that idea in all its implications, and to figure out what it would mean to me. (Slaughtering, cutting in pieces, cooking, spicing . . . .)

I looked at my watch. If I shut my eyes now, I can see the dial again: three minutes past nine. On the roof of the truck glowed the cigarette of Persin, who was on guard. From behind us came, once or twice, a clear sound that was like a tick and a sob at the same time. Masuro sat puffing at his cigar like a farmer after the day's work.

Nothing happened that was out of the ordinary.

I had the wireless switched off, Masuro posted the double guard, and gradually everyone went to sleep. Only Elsemoor was still about, sitting a little farther up the river bank with his feet in the water. Masuro was no talker, and I was in need of distraction.

"Be careful of the sand fleas, Elsemoor, or you'll be dancing tomorrow."

"I'm not touching the bottom, sir."

"He's thinking about his girl," said Masuro. "Perhaps at this moment she's being dragged behind the cars in Rotterdam."

"Care to come and sit with us, Elsemoor?"

"Thanks, sir."

Always that "sir." He came and sat down beside Masuro like a little boy shaking hands with the Queen.

"I suppose you were thinking about your girl?"

"No, sir, I haven't got a girl. I was thinking about school."

"About school? Did you know that the Sergeant and I sat together in the same form once?"

He looked at us reverently. I began to laugh, and offered him a cigarette.

"And school, then? *What* were you thinking about it?"

"Nothing in particular," he said shyly. "As it happens . . . about country-conquering."

"Country-conquering?"

When he described it, I remembered it again. A game with knives. Each player gets a piece of a square of trodden-down sand. The players take it in turn to throw the knife into a neighbouring "country," and the part cut off from it in that way has been conquered, provided it adjoins the attacker's country. The player whose territory is no longer big enough to stand on has lost.

"What's the odds?" I said to Masuro. "Shall we go country-conquering, the three of us?"

Although, in various respects, I had an ascendancy over him (and not only because of my rank), in a way Masuro was always the boss: from the tone in which he said something, or did not say something, from a look in his eye, from the manner in which he now stood up and opened his pocket-knife. He had seen more of life than I had, and past experiences play a part in the slightest word and gesture. They are always weightier than innate powers of intelligence or character. Sometimes I felt diffident about giving him an order, and then I was amazed, and almost embarrassed, by the meticulousness with which he carried it out.

Like a conscientious lackey suffering somewhat under the whims of his masters, Elsemoor cut the plants out of the ground and prepared an immaculate arena. He must have been the sort of lad who couldn't make love if one corner of the carpet was turned up. In the meantime it had become pitch-black; the lamp shone like a planet and evoked against the edge of the forest a super-ghastly phantasmagoria of caverns, animals' heads, grottoes and enchantments of which none of us, with the best will in the world, could be frightened any more. (So much for Dr. Mondrian's theory.)

And now, Gentlemen, I have to treat you to a little-report on a competition. After all, it's *data* you want, isn't it?

Masuro threw first, and cut off three quarters of my country at one stroke. Elsemoor gave the impression of being faced with a difficult dilemma. If he annexed territory from Masuro, extra guards might result; if he annexed any from me, cancellation of leave hung above his head. He confined himself to taking a small bite from the piece that Masuro had robbed from me, looking at me like an Italian as he did so. I had bad luck; my knife repeatedly fell flat on the ground, which mishap Elsemoor never failed to follow up with a sporting, sympathetic "Oh." Masuro planted his knife in the earth like a toreador, ate away everything round about us, and challenged us over and over again to prove that we were able to stand on our plots. But, blenching with fright, Elsemoor suddenly conquered almost all of his, so that Masuro had a job to maintain himself even on the toes of one foot.

I enjoyed myself enormously. Once Masuro nodded in the direction of the village, and I saw the shape of Herr Geheimrat. Quite alone, he squatted on the bank of the river and watched the white men stabbing his ground to death with knives and jollity. It put me off, and I called to Persin, ordering him to do something about it. Two shots rang out, and the headman was gone at once.

Masuro won again. Tacitly, Elsemoor and I ganged up against him, but suddenly Elsemoor fell out: after a brilliant throw on the part of Masuro, he suddenly had not a square centimetre left. With a gesture by which he acknowledged his master, and a sigh of relief, he went and sat down. I robbed Masuro of another small piece, and then he lifted his hand, holding his knife far behind his back, in order to eliminate me too in one throw.

But his arm remained immobile, and the knife dropped behind him with its point in the ground, outside the "country." His eyes grew bigger and bigger.

"I can't get my arm down," he said.

I stared at him. Above us I heard the deep buzzing of a hornbill as it flew over.

I thought I was dreaming. I went up to him and felt his right arm. There seemed no longer to be a joint in it.

"Sit down," I said.

Submissively, Masuro went and sat down on the countries right across all frontiers, with his arm in the air. Carefully I began to pull on it, and slowly he yielded to my pulling, as if he was keeping all his muscles tense. He had to support himself on the ground with his other arm.

"Pain?"

"No."

Elsemoor sat looking on, open-mouthed. At last the arm was down.

"Can you move it?"

He moved it, arm and fingers; I saw that he had to make a tremendous effort to do so. Panickily he looked at it.

"Are you ever bothered by rheumatism in that arm?"

"No—never."

He was upset, so very upset that it astonished me. Suddenly he shouted at Elsemoor: "Why don't you try wearing another bloody mug on your head?"

I heard a note in his voice I had never heard before. It was no longer a holiday voice. Alarmed, Elsemoor sprang to his feet, saluted and made off.

"Go and kip down yourself," I said, Heaven knows why. "I'll do your guard for you."

I was surprised that he took it from me. (Yes, that was the silliest part about it: that he took it!) Without saying anything, he stood up and walked woodenly to our tent. His right arm hung stiffly down, but I saw that his left arm did not move either, and that his knees were as rigid as a cavalry officer's.

"It'll be gone by tomorrow," I added.

I may as well tell you, I write with little or no conviction. With that conviction can one write about an avalanche? One can talk with conviction about the *causes*: how it could have happened, what was done to prevent it. The avalanche itself is merely *brute*, insensate,

something which is not our concern because we can't defend ourselves against it. And if we perceive that there were no causes, even?
Then there is absolutely nothing left of us, Gentlemen in Room 3,
absolutely nothing.

Masuro slept like a log all night, with his clothes on. I shared the
last watch with Kranenburg, and we talked about the stars, but at the
back of my mind I never stopped worrying about Masuro. In spite
of Steiger everything remained quiet in the village.

When I shook Masuro awake at half past six, I was suddenly seized
by something like a feeling of panic in my hands: *no human being
was as heavy as that!* I pulled him up, I pulled a horse up, a rhinoc-
eros, but the realization did not get any farther than my hands. With
eyes as round as billiard balls he stood in the tent, tottering, like a
robot, from one leg to the other. It was as if he did not see me. With
stiff legs he tottered out to where the men stood washing, and blinked
at the sun. The ground under my feet shook with the weight of his
body. He raised his hand to his face as if it were a dumb-bell weighing a ton, belched and shut his eyes.

I felt as if my feet were in my head and my head was in my boots.
For several long seconds I stared at his back. Suddenly it came home
to me—how heavy he had been. *Impossibly* heavy. I began to swallow
hard, a dozen times at least, and at last managed to get the words
out:

"Sergeant . . . come into the tent a moment, will you, please."

He looked at me and tottered back. In the tent I stood and faced
him; my hands were trembling.

"Listen, Masuro, you're ill, do you hear, you're ill. We're striking
camp immediately and getting back to Kaukenau as quickly as possible."

He looked at me and said nothing.

"Do you understand me, Masuro?"

"Yes."

"We'll strike camp immediately."

I eyed him for a moment, and then left him standing there. Outside, I called the men together, and said as calmly as I could:

"Lads . . . the Sergeant's ill. Something wrong with his joints . . .
and with his weight . . . I don't know what it is, but it's something
pretty bad. If we manage to reach the valley before dark, we can
drive through the night and be at Kaukenau tomorrow afternoon.
We'll leave the whole mess as it is, and take the route via Ugei. We're
leaving at once."

They ran to the tents and I remained where I was. I dared not go
back to Masuro. I went to the wireless operator and quickly called
up Kaukenau, and briefly told them that Masuro had been attacked
by an unknown disease, and that we were on our way. I got the
Captain; he was rather sceptical, and asked for further details, but

I made the wireless op produce interference, and switched the transmitter off.

I knew it was not a disease. Growing heavier is no disease. I wanted to get to Kaukenau in order to be among people, as if I believed that such a thing could not subsist among people.

Ten minutes later we drove away. I had no more time to spare for Herr Geheimrat, and waved goodbye to him from my jeep. The entire tribe was present again, with children on backs and breasts. Herr Geheimrat nodded, holding on to his calabash with a grin.

I sat in the back; Masuro was in the front, next to Elsemoor. Masuro bolt upright, not turning his head a centimetre to left or right; Elsemoor at the steering-wheel with an expression on his face as if he were having to pass his driving-test. We did not speak. I dared not utter a word. All the time, I had to look at the back of Masuro's head; I was afraid as I had never been before, and nevertheless . . . nevertheless, I still could not take it in. I could not take in a hundredth part of it. Nor will that ever be possible. Just imagine, in Amsterdam, the statue of General Van Heutsz stepping down off his pedestal and starting to talk to you about the colonial war in Achin. You would never manage to take it in.

At noon I called a halt, so that we could eat something. While everyone was getting out, I walked sweating round to the front of the jeep, to look at Masuro. Small patches had appeared under his skin, all over his face.

"How do you feel now, Masuro?"

Glassily he looked into my eyes.

"I don't feel."

"Have you pain anywhere?"

He shook his head almost imperceptibly.

"Wouldn't you like to get out and stretch your legs?"

He closed his eyes.

"Just leave me alone."

Suddenly I seized him and shook him by the shoulders—an elephant, a three-ton truck.

"*Masuro, what's the matter with you?*"

He panted, and his teeth began to chatter.

My head spun. He did not want to eat either. I went and fetched something for myself from the truck, where the men were sitting on the ground among empty tins. They looked at me, but asked no questions. I got my ration and walked a short distance into the barren plain, where I sat down to eat. Empty and silent, the vehicles stood behind each other, looking as if they would stand like that for ever. In the second vehicle, the motionless body of Masuro. I tried to realize that something impossible was taking place, but I did not succeed, any more than I could imagine that the girl beside the Mimika had been eaten—while *that* was nevertheless within the realm of possibility. I looked at the sky. Something incomprehensible was busy about its evil work in Masuro.

We drove on, hour after hour, endlessly. I never took my eyes off Masuro: a massive neck, covered with black hair; a square head. I had taken his carbine and put it beside me. Was I afraid he might start shooting? We drove fast, and his body bounced up and down like a tree trunk on a lorry. I decided to go on to Fuckshot, where we had a bungalow and could cook a hot meal. It was a journey to the moon; my brain had long ceased to ponder on it, it wasn't a subject for brains, it was brute, brute, brute and impenetrable as a stone. We arrived at half past seven, and then it seemed as if the time had flown.

Cackling exuberantly, the village headman came up to our jeep, smacking his lips at the prospect of the welcoming feast. I got rid of him, saying that we had a case of serious illness with us. He edged away, walking backwards in fear; the whole tribe began to walk backwards.

I gritted my teeth and began to help Masuro out of the jeep. As soon as I touched him, I knew he had become a great deal heavier. The men looked on in silence. Slowly, very slowly we walked to the log hut. The steps of the little stair cracked and sagged under his weight. I pushed the door open; a fat toad scrambled away. With both my arms around him, I let him down on to one of the rude wooden chairs. It was quite impossible for him to bend his knees any more. When he sat down he fell through the chair, and hit the ground with a crash that made the whole place shake.

He began to cry.

"*Masuro. . . .*" I whispered.

I was at my wits' end. I ran to the still open door and began to shout that we had to go on at once, that there was no time for cooking. The men must have heard the crash; motionless they sat, half in and half out of the vehicles.

I knelt beside Masuro. He was sobbing like a child. Except for those specks on his face there was nothing out of the ordinary to be seen on him, but he must have weighed at least a quarter of a ton.

"What's happening to me?" he blubbered.

"Oh Jesus Christ, Masuro, Jesus Christ, Masuro!"

I held him tight with both hands. Big tears trickled down his cheeks.

"What *is* happening to me, Lonestein? I'm getting stiffer and heavier all the time. What have I done?"

"Perhaps we'll be at Kaukenau by tomorrow morning, and then they'll give you treatment at once! In the hospital they're sure to. . . ." I could say no more. "Keep your pecker up, Masuro," I whispered. "Lie down."

He was done for, and he knew it, and I knew it. Docilely he let me lay him over backwards. I took him by his shoulders and began to push. It was like manhandling a railway truck along the rails. A sweet woody smell hung in the twilight of the hut. When I pushed too quickly his legs shot into the air with the weight of a piano. Suddenly I began to cry myself. Masuro looked up at me with big eyes.

"Surely it's impossible that such a thing should happen . . . ?" he said.

In despair, I shook my head.

"No, Masuro, it's impossible."

"I'm so tired."

He closed his eyes, his chest rose and fell laboriously. The patches on his face were more distinct than they had been in the afternoon; they were coming up everywhere under the skin, as if something was going to break through it. His hands were covered with them too . . . . To Kaukenau! To human beings!

"I can hardly get my breath any more," he groaned. "It's just as if there's a Roman sitting on my chest."

God in Heaven, I thought, help Masuro. He has done nothing. He has grown so heavy that he falls through his chair. There's a Roman sitting on his chest.

But I would sooner have shot him, and buried him on the spot, as deep as I could. Persin, Elsemoor, Steiger, Kranenburg—they would all have kept as quiet as the grave, that much is certain. They would have let him disappear from their thoughts like a splinter from their flesh.

And now you're licking your lips and settling yourselves back in your chairs, aren't you, Gentlemen of Section A? Now for the revelations, you think. Whispered between sobs, into my ear! They didn't come. No admissions. No confession. Nothing. He only lay crying on the floor, getting heavier and heavier, and didn't know what was happening to him. Nor did his spirit go forth from him, winging up into the blue in stately flight—anything but! What is the spirit? Sometimes a Napoleon, whose dream externalizes itself and floods all Europe, and, when it slowly retreats, leaves behind it tangible tokens over the entire continent: palaces, obelisks, triumphal arches, corpses, legal systems, Holy Alliances and, in Holland, surnames— Jan Pieter's son becomes Jan Lonestein, and so forth. But generally the spirit is a hat we wear on our heads against the draught; when we meet a woman, we politely take it off.

Kranenburg came timidly in with one or two tins in his hands. Masuro still did not want to eat anything; and I knew that I should not be able to get anything down my throat either. I had the tins put in the jeep, and called Corporal Persin. When he appeared in the doorway and looked into my eyes, I knew that *he* would have made sure no one said anything if I had killed Masuro.

"Give me a hand with the Sergeant, will you, Persin. Then we'll go on."

For a second or two he did not move; then he came. Neither of us was a milksop, but this was too much. With trembling lips Masuro looked at our faces, growing red with exertion. Gasping, out of breath, we finally succeeded in getting him upright. Then he fell through the floor, between us, with an ear-splitting crash. From down by our knees, he began to scream, with a sound such as the jungle had never heard before—smaller than a pygmy, he was, with the splintered planks round his waist. A moment later Persin brought the butt of his revolver down on the crown of the screaming head. Suddenly all was still; the head did not fall over.

Beside myself, I looked at Persin. God, Gentlemen! It was as if I had made an endless journey through France, Burgundy, Trèves, Cluny, in the few seconds that the screaming lasted. A vision, a fantastic vision that had nothing whatsoever to do with the case, unless it was via the Lord alone knew what subterranean connections! I saw a vast crowd in the square of Rheims, at the foot of the Cathedral, exulting in the execution of a tall fair-haired man in a violet mantle embroidered with gold, while trumpeters with gaudy emblems on their breasts blew the azure air infinitely high and empty. I saw a Pope amid a small retinue traveling over the Alps to Germany, and in the north a king, with his family, was stumbling through the snow to meet him, on bare feet—and above the head of the Pope hovered his voice and said: "Thou, Hildebrand, Pope no more, but recreant monk! I, Henry, King by the Grace of God, with all my Bishops I say unto you: descend from the throne, descend from the throne, Thou accursed through all the ages!" And at Loches I saw how a French king, weeping and wringing his hands, had the forest cut down in which the news of his little son's death had reached him. Kings, kings, narrow streets tapering to a point, full of the clang of iron on iron, iron on copper, bronze on silver; the churches full of rotting and moaning beggars; trumpets, and mounted knights with pieces of meat between their teeth, in dense russet-brown crowds of the common people. I saw that the entire land of Europe looked different from now, more fairy-tale-like, warmer, olive-green, with bizarre mouse-gray rocks which sprouted out of the ground between the houses, waxed larger and shriveled up; slight trees grew, slender and delicately feathered, heathen gods with bows in their hands toppled from their pedestals, and sometimes a gray-headed man walked the same road, three times, always a dozen yards at a time, without seeing himself. The third time he met Jesus. I constantly saw the backs of cripples, bent between their crutches, disappearing behind a hill on their way to the city. And everywhere, everywhere had been built over; behind an olive-green forest eight deserted skyscrapers towered up. There was not only another time but another *dimension* in Masuro's screaming—impossible to regain. There were rocks which are no more, without a geological reason for it.

The vision must have arisen from the very marrow of my bones. I felt as if I had died. New Guinea. I looked from Persin back to Masuro. With two more men to help us we pulled him out of the floor and carried him in silence to the truck. Fifty yards away the kapaukos stood huddled together, jumping and barking like monkeys. They must have heard the screaming—but perhaps they had got wind of something else, something for which they had an organ of reception that made them jump and bark in panic in an unknown world.

Friend, we know as little about life as a new-born baby knows about a woman. If we happen to turn around and glimpse a little more of it, our knees turn to water.

That night I sat in the pitch-black truck beside Masuro—a looming block of darkness in a world of roaring engines. I could have made a light, but something kept me from doing so. (What? Paracelsus' fur cap. The sum of Austerlitz.) Masuro grew so heavy that his body no longer bounced as we rode over a stone or through a rut; I heard nothing more. I sat on my haunches against the back of the cab and was slung to and fro. My eyes had glided from their sockets and hung in all the corners, and themselves became darkness.

Masuro spoke once more, for the last time; perhaps he had long been conscious.

"Lonestein? . . . are you there? . . . just lay me down in the open, and they can break their teeth on me."

It was the darkness that spoke, with a voice as if through a telephone, without depth, one-dimensional. I made no answer. It was all over with him—and with me too. Or was it perhaps only just beginning? A new kind of human being. . . . For the future: calm without hope, prepared for anything. I was in the utter darkness of the truck; I thought of nothing; that night the darkness became my body.

The rest you know. The following morning, when Dr. Mondrian tried to stick his lancet into Masuro for the post-mortem (on the floor: the operating-table would not have supported him), the point broke off. What was left of the skin he scratched away—a dry, leathery membrane. Masuro had turned to stone. From top to toe, inside and out. A sort of granite, pale gray to pink, with black specks and streaks that looked like letters. He was sawn apart in a native stone quarry; a grain of grit flew into my eye, so that the tears ran down my cheeks for hours. Everyone, officers, doctors, crowded round the two halves of Masuro. The fresh section shone with a blue sheen. His entrails had been preserved in the stone like rare fossils.

"Atrocities?" Dr. Mondrian asked me, with dry lips.

How well I understood the man!

"Not under my command."

"But earlier perhaps? In '48 . . . in Celebes?"

"Turned to stone from cruelty, Doctor? Which of us would still be of flesh?"

"Not from cruelty—from remorse. A kind of process . . . a remorse which has remained below the threshold of consciousness. A certain secretion which has arisen, chemical conversions, a kind of petrifying exudation. . . ."

"Is that scientifically feasible, Dr. Mondrian?"

It was as if he grew a pointed beard; I could smell the plush of the Viennese couch:

"Everything is possible! Science knows nothing, absolutely nothing, of the region in which spirit and body communicate! A no man's land. A region as big as . . . as the whole of New Guinea! We know nothing about it, nothing."

But he was wrong. Four has long ceased to be twice two. Out in the street, the traffic rolls by. A woman finds her husband fallen through his chair at the window, changed into a stone image. In the towns the jungle becomes more and more dense, and the air is emptier than ever. Here and there, the prints of human feet are to be seen in the earth, but in the void above, the wind blows.

I canceled the charge against Steiger.

Lieutenant K. Lonestein, No. 121370,
Section G III, 5th Battalion,
124th Regiment of Infantry

Kaukenau
New Guinea.
26th July 1955.

Mrozek transforms everyday events into bizarre, yet simply rendered, parables of the modern world. Through a blend of fantasy, wit, and poetic sensibility, his buoyant, mysterious sketches expose whatever political and social practices the author finds false. What is satirized in "From the Darkness"?

Born in Poland in 1930, Slawomir Mrozek studied architecture and painting before becoming a professional journalist, caricaturist, stort story author, playwright, and creator of children's stories. Further Reading: The Policeman (1956), The Elephant (1963), Tango (1967).

POLAND

From the Darkness

SLAWOMIR MROZEK

In this remote village of ours we are in the grip of terrible ignorance and superstition. Here I am, wanting to go outside to relieve myself, but at this moment hordes of bats are flying about, like leaves blown by an October wind, their wings knocking against the window panes, and I am afraid that one of them will get into my hair and I will never be able to get it out. So I am sitting here, comrades, instead of going out, repressing my need, and writing this report for you.

Well, as far as the purchase of grain is concerned, this has been falling ever since the devil appeared at the mill and took off his cap in an elegant greeting. His cap was in three colours: red, white and blue, and on it was embroidered *Tour de la Paix.* The peasants have been avoiding

"From the Darkness" by Slawomir Mrozek, from *The Elephant,* published by Macdonald & Co. (Publishers) Ltd., London, and reprinted with their permission. Reprinted also by permission of Grove Press, Inc. Copyright © 1962 by Macdonald & Co. (Publishers) Ltd. Translated from the Polish by Konrad Syrop.

the mill, and the manager and his wife were driven by worry to drink until one day he splashed her with vodka and set her on fire. Then he left for the People's University, where he is going to read Marxism so that, as he says, he has something to put against those irrational elements.

And the manager's wife died in the flames and we have one more ghost.

I have to tell you that at night something howls here; howls so terribly that your heart almost stops beating. Some say that it is the spirit of poor Karas, who never had a bean, cursing the rich kulaks; others say that it is wealthy Krywon complaining after death about the compulsory deliveries. A proper class war.

My cabin stands on the edge of the forest, alone. The night is black, the forest is black and my thoughts are like ravens. One day my neighbour, Jusienga, was sitting on a tree stump by the forest, reading *Horizons of Technology*, when something got at him from the back so that for three days he never stopped staring vacantly.

We need your advice, comrades, because we are alone here, miles from anywhere, surrounded only by distance and graves.

A forester has told me that at full moon in the clearings heads without bodies roll about, chase each other, knock at each other's cold foreheads as if they wanted something, but come dawn they all disappear and there are only trees left to murmur, not too loudly because they are afraid. Oh my God, nothing will make me go outside, not even the greatest need.

And it is the same with everything. You talk about Europe, comrades, but here. . . . No sooner do we pour our milk into jugs than hunchback dwarfs appear from somewhere and spit into it.

One night old Mrs. Glus woke up swimming in sweat. She looked at her eiderdown and what did she see? The small credit, that had been given to us before the elections (so that we could build a bridge here) and died suddenly without Extreme Unction, that credit was sitting on her eiderdown, all green and choking with laughter. The old woman started to scream but nobody came to see what was the matter. Can one be sure who is screaming and from what ideological position?

And at the spot where we were to have the bridge an artist got drowned. He was only two years old, but already a genius. Had he grown up he would have understood and described everything. But now all he can do is to fly about and fluoresce.

Of course, all those happenings have changed our psychology. People believe in sorcery and superstition. Only yesterday they found a skeleton behind Mocza's barn. The priest says that it is a political skeleton. They believe in ghosts and things, and even in witches. True, we have one woman who takes milk away from the cows and gives them fever, but we want to get her to join the Party and in this way deprive the enemies of progress of at least one argument.

How those bats flap their wings. Christ! how they fly and squeak "pee-pee" and again "pee-pee." There is nothing like those big houses where everything must be inside and there is no need to go into the bushes.

But there are even worse things than that. As I am writing this the door has opened and a pig's snout has appeared. It is looking at me very queerly, it is staring at me . . .

Have I not told you that things are different here?

Relying on Jewish folklore and history, Isaac Bashevis Singer frequently dramatizes Hasidic Jews. Many of his stories are set in the Eastern Europe of centuries past, and many include an element of the supernatural. "Gimpel the Fool" is a simple yet imaginative rendering of the age-old tale of the not-so-foolish fool. Wherein lies Gimpel's wisdom? How is this story relevant to the cynical world of the twentieth century?

Isaac Singer was born in Radzymiu in 1894 but has lived in the United States since 1935. During the twenties he was a journalist for the Yiddish press in Warsaw and since that time has occupied himself as a novelist, essayist, and short story writer. He has produced a large volume of work, most of which has yet to be translated. In the worlds of Isaac Bashevis Singer, spiritual joy and the positive human spirit triumph over evil. Is this true in "Gimpel the Fool"? Further Reading: Gimpel the Fool and Other Stories (1957), The Magician of Lublin (1960), Short Friday and Other Stories (1964).

POLAND

Gimpel the Fool

ISAAC BASHEVIS SINGER

I am Gimpel the Fool. I don't think myself a fool. On the contrary. But that's what folks call me. They gave me the name while I was still in school. I had seven names in all: imbecile, donkey, flaxhead, dope, glump, ninny, and fool. The last name stuck. What did my foolishness consist of? I was easy to take in. They said, "Gimpel, you know the rabbi's wife has been brought to childbed?" So I skipped school. Well, it turned out to

From A Treasury of Yiddish Stories edited by Irving Howe and Eliezer Greenberg. Copyright 1953 by Isaac Bashevis Singer. Reprinted by permission of The Viking Press, Inc. Translated by Saul Bellow.

be a lie. How was I supposed to know? She hadn't had a big belly. But I never looked at her belly. Was that really so foolish? The gang laughed and hee-hawed, stomped and danced and chanted a good-night prayer. And instead of the raisins they give when a woman's lying in, they stuffed my hand full of goat turds. I was no weakling. If I slapped someone he'd see all the way to Cracow. But I'm really not a slugger by nature. I think to myself: Let it pass. So they take advantage of me.

I was coming home from school and heard a dog barking. I'm not afraid of dogs, but of course I never want to start up with them. One of them may be mad, and if he bites there's not a Tartar in the world who can help you. So I made tracks. Then I looked around and saw the whole market place wild with laughter. It was no dog at all but Wolf-Leib the Thief. How was I supposed to know it was he? It sounded like a howling bitch.

When the pranksters and leg-pullers found that I was easy to fool, every one of them tried his luck with me. "Gimpel, the Czar is coming to Frampol; Gimpel, the moon fell down in Turbeen; Gimpel, little Hodel Furpiece found a treasure behind the bathhouse." And I like a golem believed everyone. In the first place, everything is possible, as it is written in the Wisdom of the Fathers, I've forgotten just how. Second, I had to believe when the whole town came down on me! If I ever dared to say, "Ah, you're kidding!" there was trouble. People got angry, "What do you mean! You want to call everyone a liar?" What was I to do? I believed them, and I hope at least that did them some good.

I was an orphan. My grandfather who brought me up was already bent toward the grave. So they turned me over to a baker, and what a time they gave me there! Every woman or girl who came to bake a batch of noodles had to fool me at least once. "Gimpel, there's a fair in heaven; Gimpel, the rabbi gave birth to a calf in the seventh month; Gimpel, a cow flew over the roof and laid brass eggs." A student from the yeshiva came once to buy a roll, and he said, "You, Gimpel, while you stand here scraping with your baker's shovel the Messiah has come. The dead have arisen." "What do you mean?" I said. "I heard no one blowing the ram's horn!" He said, "Are you deaf?" And all began to cry, "We heard it, we heard!" Then in came Rietze the Candle-dipper and called out in her hoarse voice, "Gimpel, your father and mother have stood up from the grave. They're looking for you."

To tell the truth, I knew very well that nothing of the sort had happened, but all the same, as folks were talking, I threw on my wool vest and went out. Maybe something had happened. What did I stand to lose by looking? Well, what a cat music went up! And then I took a vow to believe nothing more. But that was no go either. They confused me so that I didn't know the big end from the small.

I went to the rabbi to get some advice. He said, "It is written, better to be a fool all your days than for one hour to be evil. You are not a fool. They are the fools. For he who causes his neighbor to feel shame loses Paradise himself." Nevertheless the rabbi's daughter took me in. As I left the rabbinical court she said, "Have you kissed the wall yet?" I said, "No; what for?" she answered, "It's the law; you've got to do it after every visit." Well, there didn't seem to be any harm in it. And she burst out laughing. It was a fine trick. She put one over on me, all right.

I wanted to go off to another town, but then everyone got busy matchmaking, and they were after me so they nearly tore my coat tails off. They talked at me and talked until I got water on the ear. She was no chaste maiden, but they told me she was virgin pure. She had a limp, and they said it was deliberate, from coyness. She had a bastard, and they told me the child was her little brother. I cried, "You're wasting your time. I'll never marry that whore." But they said indignantly, "What a way to talk! Aren't you ashamed of yourself? We can take you to the rabbi and have you fined for giving her a bad name." I saw then that I wouldn't escape them so easily and I thought: They're set on making me their butt. But when you're married the husband's the master, and if that's all right with her it's agreeable to me too. Besides, you can't pass through life unscathed, nor expect to.

I went to her clay house, which was built on the sand, and the whole gang, hollering and chorusing, came after me. They acted like bear-baiters. When we came to the well they stopped all the same. They were afraid to start anything with Elka. Her mouth would open as if it were on a hinge, and she had a fierce tongue. I entered the house. Lines were strung from wall to wall and clothes were drying. Barefoot she stood by the tub, doing the wash. She was dressed in a worn hand-me-down gown of plush. She had her hair put in braids and pinned across her head. It took my breath away, almost, the reek of it all.

Evidently she knew who I was. She took a look at me and said, "Look who's here! He's come, the drip. Grab a seat."

I told her all; I denied nothing. "Tell me the truth," I said, "are you really a virgin, and is that mischievous Yechiel actually your little brother? Don't be deceitful with me, for I'm an orphan."

"I'm an orphan myself," she answered, "and whoever tries to twist you up, may the end of his nose take a twist. But don't let them think they can take advantage of me. I want a dowry of fifty guilders, and let them take up a collection besides. Otherwise they can kiss my you-know-what." She was very plainspoken. I said, "It's the bride and not the groom who gives a dowry." Then she said, "Don't bargain with me. Either a flat 'yes' or a flat 'no'—Go back where you came from."

I thought: No bread will ever be baked from *this* dough. But ours is not a poor town. They consented to everything and proceeded with the wedding. It so happened that there was a dysentery epidemic at the time. The ceremony was held at the cemetery gates, near the little corpse-washing hut. The fellows got drunk. While the marriage contract was being drawn up I heard the most pious high rabbi ask, "Is the bride a widow or a divorced woman?" And the sexton's wife answered for her, "Both a widow and divorced." It was a black moment for me. But what was I to do, run away from under the marriage canopy?

There was singing and dancing. An old granny danced opposite me, hugging a braided white *chalah*. The master of revels made a "God 'a mercy" in memory of the bride's parents. The schoolboys threw burrs, as on Tishe b'Av fast day. There were a lot of gifts after the sermon: a noodle board, a kneading trough, a bucket, brooms, ladles, household articles galore. Then I took a look and saw two strapping young men carrying a crib. "What do we need this for?" I asked. So they said, "Don't rack your brains about it. It's all right, it'll come in handy." I realized I was going to be rooked. Take it another way though, what did I stand to lose? I reflected: I'll see what comes of it. A whole town can't go altogether crazy.

II

At night I came where my wife lay, but she wouldn't let me in. "Say, look here, is this what they married us for?" I said. And she said, "My monthly has come." "But yesterday they took you to the ritual bath, and that's afterward, isn't it supposed to be?" "Today isn't yesterday," said she, "and yesterday's not today. You can beat it if you don't like it." In short, I waited.

Not four months later she was in childbed. The townsfolk hid their laughter with their knuckles. But what could I do? She suffered intolerable pains and clawed at the walls. "Gimpel," she said, "I'm going. Forgive me!" The house filled with women. They were boiling pans of water. The screams rose to the welkin.

The thing to do was to go to the House of Prayer to repeat Psalms, and that was what I did.

The townsfolk liked that, all right. I stood in a corner saying Psalms and prayers, and they shook their heads at me. "Pray, pray!" they told me. "Prayer never made any woman pregnant." One of the congregation put a straw to my mouth and said, "Hay for the cows." There was something to that too, by God!

She gave birth to a boy. Friday at the synagogue the sexton stood up before the Ark, pounded on the reading table, and announced, "The wealthy Reb Gimpel invites the congregation to a feast in honor of the birth of a son." The whole House of Prayer rang with laughter.

My face was flaming. But there was nothing I could do. After all, I *was* the one responsible for the circumcision honors and rituals.

Half the town came running. You couldn't wedge another soul in. Women brought peppered chick-peas, and there was a keg of beer from the tavern. I ate and drank as much as anyone, and they all congratulated me. Then there was a circumcision, and I named the boy after my father, may he rest in peace. When all were gone and I was left with my wife alone, she thrust her head through the bed-curtain and called me to her.

"Gimpel," said she, "why are you silent? Has your ship gone and sunk?"

"What shall I say?" I answered. "A fine thing you've done to me! If my mother had known of it she'd have died a second time."

She said, "Are you crazy, or what?"

"How can you make such a fool," I said, "of one who should be the lord and master?"

"What's the matter with you?" she said. "What have you taken it into your head to imagine?"

I saw that I must speak bluntly and openly. "Do you think this is the way to use an orphan?" I said. "You have borne a bastard."

She answered, "Drive this foolishness out of your head. The child is yours."

"How can he be mine?" I argued. "He was born seventeen weeks after the wedding."

She told me then that he was premature. I said, "Isn't he a little too premature?" She said, she had had a grandmother who carried just as short a time and she resembled this grandmother of hers as one drop of water does another. She swore to it with such oaths that you would have believed a peasant at the fair if he had used them. To tell the plain truth, I didn't believe her; but when I talked it over next day with the schoolmaster he told he that the very same thing had happened to Adam and Eve. Two they went up to bed, and four they descended.

"There isn't a woman in the world who is not the granddaughter of Eve," he said.

That was how it was; they argued me dumb. But then, who really knows how such things are?

I began to forget my sorrow. I loved the child madly, and he loved me too. As soon as he saw me he'd wave his little hands and want me to pick him up, and when he was colicky I was the only one who could pacify him. I bought him a little bone teething ring and a little gilded cap. He was forever catching the evil eye from someone, and then I had to run to get one of those abracadabras for him that would get him out of it. I worked like an ox. You know how expenses go up when there's an infant in the house. I don't want to lie about it; I didn't dislike Elka either, for that matter. She swore at me and cursed,

and I couldn't get enough of her. What strength she had! One of her
looks could rob you of the power of speech. And her orations! Pitch
and sulphur, that's what they were full of, and yet somehow also full
of charm. I adored her every word. She gave me bloody wounds
though.

In the evening I brought her a white loaf as well as a dark one,
and also poppyseed rolls I baked myself. I thieved because of her and
swiped everything I could lay hands on: macaroons, raisins, almonds,
cakes. I hope I may be forgiven for stealing from the Saturday pots
the women left to warm in the baker's oven. I would take out scraps
of meat, a chunk of pudding, a chicken leg or head, a piece of tripe,
whatever I could nip quickly. She ate and became fat and handsome.

I had to sleep away from home all during the week, at the bakery.
On Friday nights when I got home she always made an excuse of
some sort. Either she had heartburn, or a stitch in the side, or hiccups,
or headaches. You know what women's excuses are. I had a bitter
time of it. It was rough. To add to it, this little brother of hers, the
bastard, was growing bigger. He'd put lumps on me, and when I
wanted to hit back she'd open her mouth and curse so powerfully I
saw a green haze floating before my eyes. Ten times a day she threatened to divorce me. Another man in my place would have taken
French leave and disappeared. But I'm the type that bears it and
says nothing. What's one to do? Shoulders are from God, and burdens
too.

One night there was a calamity in the bakery; the oven burst, and
we almost had a fire. There was nothing to do but go home, so I
went home. Let me, I thought, also taste the joy of sleeping in bed
in mid-week. I didn't want to wake the sleeping mite and tiptoed into
the house. Coming in, it seemed to me that I heard not the snoring
of one but, as it were, a double snore, one a thin enough snore and
the other like the snoring of a slaughtered ox. Oh, I didn't like that!
I didn't like it at all. I went up to the bed, and things suddenly turned
black. Next to Elka lay a man's form. Another in my place would
have made an uproar, and enough noise to rouse the whole town, but
the thought occurred to me that I might wake the child. A little
thing like that—why frighten a little swallow, I thought. All right
then, I went back to the bakery and stretched out on a sack of flour
and till morning I never shut an eye. I shivered as if I had had malaria.
"Enough of being a donkey," I said to myself. "Gimpel isn't going to
be a sucker all his life. There's a limit even to the foolishness of a fool
like Gimpel."

In the morning I went to the rabbi to get advice, and it made a
great commotion in the town. They sent the beadle for Elka right
away. She came, carrying the child. And what do you think she did?
She denied it, denied everything, bone and stone! "He's out of his
head," she said. "I know nothing of dreams or divinations." They

yelled at her, warned her, hammered on the table, but she stuck to her guns: it was a false accusation, she said.

The butchers and the horse-traders took her part. One of the lads from the slaughterhouse came by and said to me, "We've got our eye on you, you're a marked man." Meanwhile the child started to bear down and soiled itself. In the rabbinical court there was an Ark of the Covenant, and they couldn't allow that, so they sent Elka away.

I said to the rabbi, "What shall I do?"

"You must divorce her at once," said he.

"And what if she refuses?" I asked.

He said, "You must serve the divorce. That's all you'll have to do."

I said, "Well, all right, Rabbi. Let me think about it."

"There's nothing to think about," said he. "You mustn't remain under the same roof with her."

"And if I want to see the child?" I asked.

"Let her go, the harlot," said he, "and her brood of bastards with her."

The verdict he gave was that I mustn't even cross her threshold—never again, as long as I should live.

During the day it didn't bother me so much. I thought: It was bound to happen, the abscess had to burst. But at night when I stretched out upon the sacks I felt it all very bitterly. A longing took me, for her and for the child. I wanted to be angry, but that's my misfortune exactly, I don't have it in me to be really angry. In the first place—this was how my thoughts went—there's bound to be a slip sometimes. You can't live without errors. Probably that lad who was with her led her on and gave her presents and what not, and women are often long on hair and short on sense, and so he got around her. And then since she denies it so, maybe I was only seeing things? Hallucinations do happen. You see a figure or a mannikin or something, but when you come up closer it's nothing, there's not a thing there. And if that's so, I'm doing her an injustice. And when I got so far in my thoughts I started to weep. I sobbed so that I wet the flour where I lay. In the morning I went to the rabbi and told him that I had made a mistake. The rabbi wrote on with his quill, and he said that if that were so he would have to reconsider the whole case. Until he had finished I wasn't to go near my wife, but I might send her bread and money by messenger.

III

Nine months passed before all the rabbis could come to an agreement. Letters went back and forth. I hadn't realized that there could be so much erudition about a matter like this.

Meanwhile Elka gave birth to still another child, a girl this time. On the Sabbath I went to the synagogue and invoked a blessing on her. They called me up to the Torah, and I named the child for my mother-in-law—may she rest in peace. The louts and loudmouths of the town who came into the bakery gave me a going over. All Frampol refreshed in spirits because of my trouble and grief. However, I resolved that I would always believe what I was told. What's the good of *not* believing? Today it's your wife you don't believe; tomorrow it's God Himself you won't take stock in.

By an apprentice who was her neighbor I sent her daily a corn or a wheat loaf, or a piece of pastry, rolls or bagels, or, when I got the chance, a slab of pudding, a slice of honeycake, or wedding strudel—whatever came my way. The apprentice was a goodhearted lad, and more than once he added something on his own. He had formerly annoyed me a lot, plucking my nose and digging me in the ribs, but when he started to be a visitor to my house he became kind and friendly. "Hey, you, Gimpel," he said to me, "you have a very decent little wife and two fine kids. You don't deserve them."

"But the things people say about her," I said.

"Well, they have long tongues," he said, "and nothing to do with them but babble. Ignore it as you ignore the cold of last winter."

One day the rabbi sent for me and said, "Are you certain, Gimpel, that you were wrong about your wife?"

I said, "I'm certain."

"Why, but look here! You yourself saw it."

"It must have been a shadow," I said.

"The shadow of what?"

"Just one of the beams, I think."

"You can go home then. You owe thanks to the Yanover rabbi. He found an obscure reference in Maimonides that favored you."

I seized the rabbi's hand and kissed it.

I wanted to run home immediately. It's no small thing to be separated for so long a time from wife and child. Then I reflected: I'd better go back to work now, and go home in the evening. I said nothing to anyone, although as far as my heart was concerned it was like one of the Holy Days. The women teased and twitted me as they did every day, but my thought was: Go on, with your loose talk. The truth is out, like the oil upon the water. Maimonides says it's right, and therefore it is right!

At night, when I had covered the dough to let it rise, I took my share of bread and a little sack of flour and started homeward. The moon was full and the stars were glistening, something to terrify the soul. I hurried onward, and before me darted a long shadow. It was winter, and a fresh snow had fallen. I had a mind to sing, but it was growing late and I didn't want to wake the householders. Then I felt like whistling, but I remembered that you don't whistle at night because it brings the demons out. So I was silent and walked as fast as I could.

Dogs in the Christian yards barked at me when I passed, but I
thought: Bark your teeth out! What are you but mere dogs? Whereas
I am a man, the husband of a fine wife, the father of promising
children.

As I approached the house my heart started to pound as though it
were the heart of a criminal. I felt no fear, but my heart went thump!
thump! Well, no drawing back. I quietly lifted the latch and went
in. Elka was asleep. I looked at the infant's cradle. The shutter
was closed, but the moon forced its way through the cracks. I saw the
newborn child's face and loved it as soon as I saw it—immediately—
each tiny bone.

Then I came nearer to the bed. And what did I see but the apprentice lying there beside Elka. The moon went out all at once. It was
utterly black, and I trembled. My teeth chattered. The bread fell from
my hands, and my wife waked and said, "Who is that, ah?"

I muttered, "It's me."

"Gimpel?" she asked. "How come you're here? I thought it was
forbidden."

"The rabbi said," I answered and shook as with a fever.

"Listen to me, Gimpel," she said, "go out to the shed and see if
the goat's all right. It seems she's been sick." I have forgotten to say
that we had a goat. When I heard she was unwell I went into the
yard. The nannygoat was a good little creature. I had a nearly human
feeling for her.

With hesitant steps I went up to the shed and opened the door.
The goat stood there on her four feet. I felt her everywhere, drew her
by the horns, examined her udders, and found nothing wrong. She
had probably eaten to much bark. "Good night, little goat," I said.
"Keep well." And the little beast answered with a "Maa" as though
to thank me for the good will.

I went back. The apprentice had vanished.

"Where," I asked, "is the lad?"

"What lad?" my wife answered.

"What do you mean?" I said. "The apprentice. You were sleeping
with him."

"The things I have dreamed this night and the night before," she
said, "may they come true and lay you low, body and soul! An evil
spirit has taken root in you and dazzles your sight." She screamed out,
"You hateful creature! You moon calf! You spook! You uncouth
man! Get out, or I'll scream all Frampol out of bed!"

Before I could move, her brother sprang out from behind the oven
and struck me a blow on the back of the head. I thought he had
broken my neck. I felt that something about me was deeply wrong,
and I said, "Don't make a scandal. All that's needed now is that
people should accuse me of raising spooks and *dybbuks*." For that

was what she had meant. "No one will touch bread of my baking."

In short, I somehow calmed her.

"Well," she said, "that's enough. Lie down, and be shattered by wheels."

Next morning I called the apprentice aside. "Listen here, brother!" I said. And so on and so forth. "What do you say?" He stared at me as though I had dropped from the roof or something.

"I swear," he said, "you'd better go to an herb doctor or some healer. I'm afraid you have a screw loose, but I'll hush it up for you." And that's how the thing stood.

To make a long story short, I lived twenty years with my wife. She bore me six children, four daughters and two sons. All kinds of things happened, but I neither saw nor heard. I believed, and that's all. The rabbi recently said to me, "Belief in itself is beneficial. It is written that a good man lives by his faith."

Suddenly my wife took sick. It began with a trifle, a little growth upon the breast. But she evidently was not destined to live long; she had no years. I spent a fortune on her. I have forgotten to say that by this time I had a bakery of my own and in Frampol was considered to be something of a rich man. Daily the healer came, and every witch doctor in the neighborhood was brought. They decided to use leeches, and after that to try cupping. They even called a doctor from Lublin, but it was too late. Before she died she called me to her bed and said, "Forgive me, Gimpel."

I said, "What is there to forgive? You have been a good and faithful wife."

"Woe, Gimpel!" she said. "It was ugly how I deceived you all these years. I want to go clean to my Maker, and so I have to tell you that the children are not yours."

If I had been clouted on the head with a piece of wood it couldn't have bewildered me more.

"Whose are they?" I asked.

"I don't know," she said. "There were a lot . . . but they're not yours." And as she spoke she tossed her head to the side, her eyes turned glassy, and it was all up with Elka. On her whitened lips there remained a smile.

I imagined that, dead as she was, she was saying, "I deceived Gimpel. That was the meaning of my brief life."

IV

One night when the period of mourning was done, as I lay dreaming on the flour sacks, there came the Spirit of Evil himself and said to me, "Gimpel, why do you sleep?"

I said, "What should I be doing? Eating *kreplach?*"

"The whole world deceives you," he said, "and you ought to deceive the world in your turn."

"How can I deceive all the world?" I asked him.

He answered, "You might accumulate a bucket of urine every day and at night pour it into the dough. Let the sages of Frampol eat filth."

"What about the judgment in the world to come?" I said.

"There is no world to come," he said. "They've sold you a bill of goods and talked you into believing you carried a cat in your belly. What nonsense!"

"Well then," I said, "and is there a God?"

He answered, "There is no God either."

"What," I said, "*is* there, then?"

"A thick mire."

He stood before my eyes with a goatish beard and horn, long-toothed, and with a tail. Hearing such words, I wanted to snatch him by the tail, but I tumbled from the flour sacks and nearly broke a rib. Then it happened that I had to answer the call of nature, and, passing, I saw the risen dough, which seemed to say to me, "Do it!" In brief, I let myself be persuaded.

At dawn the apprentice came. We kneaded the bread, scattered caraway seeds on it, and set it to bake. Then the apprentice went away, and I was left sitting in the little trench by the oven, on a pile of rags. Well, Gimpel, I thought, you've revenged yourself on them for all the shame they've put on you. Outside the frost glittered, but it was warm beside the oven. The flames heated my face. I bent my head and fell into a doze.

I saw in a dream, at once, Elka in her shroud. She called to me, "What have you done, Gimpel?"

I said to her, "It's all your fault," and started to cry.

"You fool!" she said. "You fool! Because I was false is everything false too? I never deceived anyone but myself. I'm paying for it all, Gimpel. They spare you nothing here."

I looked at her face. It was black; I was startled and waked, and remained sitting dumb. I sensed that everything hung in the balance. A false step now and I'd lose Eternal Life. But God gave me His help. I seized the long shovel and took out the loaves, carried them into the yard, and started to dig a hole in the frozen earth.

My apprentice came back as I was doing it. "What are you doing boss?" he said, and grew pale as a corpse.

"I know what I'm doing," I said, and I buried it all before his very eyes.

Then I went home, took my hoard from its hiding place, and divided it among the children. "I saw your mother tonight," I said. "She's turning black, poor thing."

They were so astounded they couldn't speak a word.

"Be well," I said, "and forget that such a one as Gimpel ever existed." I put on my short coat, a pair of boots, took the bag that held my prayer shawl in one hand, my stock in the other, and kissed the *mezzuzah*. When people saw me in the street they were greatly surprised.

"Where are you going?" they said.

I answered, "Into the world." And so I departed from Frampol.

I wandered over the land, and good people did not neglect me. After many years I became old and white; I heard a great deal, many lies and falsehoods, but the longer I lived the more I understood that there were really no lies. Whatever doesn't really happen is dreamed at night. It happens to one if it doesn't happen to another, tomorrow if not today, or a century hence if not next year. What difference can it make? Often I heard tales of which I said, "Now this is a thing that cannot happen." But before a year had elapsed I heard that it actually had come to pass somewhere.

Going from place to place, eating at strange tables, it often happens that I spin yarns—improbable things that could never have happened—about devils, magicians, windmills, and the like. The children run after me, calling, "Grandfather, tell us a story." Sometimes they ask for particular stories, and I try to please them. A fat young boy once said to me, "Grandfather, it's the same story you told us before." The little rouge, he was right.

So it is with dreams too. It is many years since I left Frampol, but as soon as I shut my eyes I am there again. And whom do you think I see? Elka. She is standing by the washtub, as at our first encounter, but her face is shining and her eyes are as radiant as the eyes of a saint, and she speaks outlandish words to me, strange things. When I wake I have forgotten it all. But while the dream lasts I am comforted. She answers all my queries, and what comes out is that all is right. I weep and implore, "Let me be with you." And she consoles me and tells me to be patient. The time is nearer than it is far. Sometimes she strokes and kisses me and weeps upon my face. When I awaken I feel her lips and taste the salt of her tears.

No doubt the world is entirely an imaginary world, but it is only once removed from the true world. At the door of the hovel where I lie, there stands the plank on which the dead are taken away. The gravedigger Jew has his spade ready. The grave waits and the worms are hungry; the shrouds are prepared—I carry them in my beggar's sack. Another *shnorrer* is waiting to inherit my bed of straw. When the time comes I will go joyfully. Whatever may be there, it will be real, without complication, without ridicule, without deception. God be praised: there even Gimpel cannot be deceived.

In "The Defeated," Nadine Gordimer presents a richly detailed description of the
home and family of Miriam's childhood but
makes only generalized allusion to the narrator's "clean, pleasant little home." She
describes Miriam's parents concretely and
at length, but we learn almost nothing of
the narrator's parents. There is much in the
story to indicate that Miriam's rise in fortune is paralleled by a decline in human
validity. The title also suggests this ambig-
uity. Just who are the defeated? What are
the terms of their defeat?

Nadine Gordimer was born in South
Africa in 1923 and was educated in convent
schools and the University of Witwaters-
rand in Johannesburg. Her first novel,
The Lying Days, appeared in 1954 and
helped establish her international reputa-
tion as a novelist and short story writer.
Miss Gordimer's stories express her love for
mankind, despite his savagery, and a sad
soul-cry for the displacement of the human
spirit. Further Reading: The Soft Voice of
the Serpent and Other Stories (1952), A
World of Strangers (1958), Friday's Foot-
print and Other Stories (1960).

UNION OF
SOUTH AFRICA

The Defeated

NADINE GORDIMER

My mother did not want me to go near
the Concession stores because they
smelled, and were dirty, and the natives
spat tuberculosis germs into the dust. She
said it was no place for little girls.

But I used to go down there sometimes,
in the afternoon, when static four o'clock
held the houses of our Mine, and the sun
washed over them like the waves of the
sea over sand castles. I felt that life was
going on down there at the Concession

Reprinted from the author's collection *The Soft
Voice of the Serpent and Other Stories.* Copyright 1952 by Nadine Gordimer.

stores: noise, and movement and—yes, bad smells, even—and so I
would wander down the naked road, with the hot sun comfortably
drying the membrane inside my nose, seeing the irregular line of
narrow white shops lying away ahead like a jumble of shoes boxes.

The signs of life that I craved were very soon evident: rich and careless of its vitality, it overflowed from the crowded pavement of the
stores, and the surrounding veld was littered with sucked-out oranges
and tatters of dirty paper, and worn into the shabby barrenness
peculiar to earth much trampled upon by the feet of men. A fat, one-
legged native, with the patient detachment of the businessman who
knows himself indispensable, sat on the bald veld beside the path that
led from the Compound, his stock of walking sticks standing up,
handles tied together, points splayed out fanwise, his pyramids of
bright, thin-skinned oranges waiting. Sometimes he had mealies as
well—those big, hard, full-grown ears with rows of yellowish tombstones instead of little pearly teeth—and a brazier made from a
paraffin tin to roast them by. Propped against the chipped pillars of
the pavement, there were always other vendors, making their small
way in lucky beans, herbs, bracelets beaten from copper wire, knitted
caps in wonderful colors—blooming like great hairy petunias, or
bursting suns, from the needles of old, old native women—and, of
course, oranges. Everywhere there were oranges; the pushing, ambling
crowds filling the pavement ate them as they stared at the windows,
the gossips, sitting with their blankets drawn close and their feet in
the gutter, sucked at them, the Concession store cats sniffed at the
skins where they lay, hollow-cheeked, discarded in every doorway.

Quite often I had to flick the white pith from where it had landed,
on my shoe or even my dress, spat negligently by some absorbed
orange-eater contemplating a shirt through breath-smudged plate
glass. The wild, wondering dirty men came up from the darkness of
the mine and they lay themselves out to the sun on the veld, and to
their mouths they put the round fruit of the sun; and it was the
expression of their need.

I would saunter along the shopwindows amongst them, and for
me there was a quickening of glamour about the place: the air was
thicker with their incense-like body smell, and the sudden rank
shock of their stronger sweat, as a bare armpit lifted over my head.
The clamor of their voices—always shouting, but so merry, so angry!
—and the size of their laughter, and the open-mouthed startle with
which they greeted every fresh sight: I felt vaguely the spell of the
books I had read, returning; markets in Persia, bazaars in Cairo. . . .
Nevertheless, I was careful not to let them brush too closely past me,
lest some unnamable *something* crawl from their dusty blankets or
torn cotton trousers onto my clean self, and I did not like the way
they spat, with that terrible gurgle in the throat, into the gutter, or,
worse still, blew their noses loudly between finger and thumb, and
flung the excrement horribly to the air.

And neither did I like the heavy, sickening, greasy carrion-breath that poured from the mouth of the Hotela la Bantu, where the natives hunched intent at zinc-topped forms, eating steaming no-color chunks of horror that bore no relation to meat as I knew it. The down on my arms prickled in revulsion from the pulpy entrails hanging in dreadful enticement at the window, and the blood-embroidered sawdust spilling out of the doorway.

I know that I wondered how the storekeepers' wives, who sat on soap boxes outside the doorways of the shops on either side of the eating house, could stand the breath of that maw. How they could sit, like lizards in the sun; and all the time they breathed in the breath of the eating house: took it deep into the recesses of their beings, whilst my throat closed against it in disgust.

It was down there one burning afternoon that I met Mrs. Saiyeto-vitz. She was one of the storekeepers' wives, and I had seen her many times before, sitting before the deep, blanket-hung cave of her husband's store, where a pile of tinsel-covered wooden trunks shimmered and flashed a pink or green eye out of the gloom into the outside—wearing her creased alpaca apron, her fat insteps leaning over her down-at-heel shoes. Sometimes she knitted, and sometimes she just sat. On this day there was a small girl hanging about her, drawing on the shopwindow with a sticky forefinger. When the child turned to look at me, I recognized her as one of the girls from "our school"; a girl from my class, as a matter of fact, called Miriam Saiyetovitz. Yes, that was her name: I remembered it because it was ugly—I was always sorry for girls with ugly names.

Miriam was a tousled, black-haired little girl, who wore a red bow in her hair. Now she recognized me, and we stood looking at one another; all at once the spare line of the name "Miriam Saiyetovitz," that was like the scrolled pattern of an iron gate with only the sky behind it, shifted its perspective in my mind, so that now between the cold curly M's and the implacable A's of that gate's framework, I saw a house, a complication of buildings and flowers and figures walking, where before there was nothing but the sky. Miriam Saiyeto-vitz—and this: behind her name and her school self, the hot and buzzing world of the stores. And I smiled at her, very friendly.

So she knew we had decided to recognize one another and she sauntered over to talk to me. I stood with her in the doorway of her father's store, and I, too, wrote my name and drew cats composed of two capital O's and a sausage tail, with the point of my hot and sticky finger on the window. Of course, she did not exactly introduce me to her mother—children never do introduce their mothers; they merely let it be known, by referring to the woman in question off-hand, in the course of play, or going up to speak to her in such a way that the relationship becomes obvious. Miriam went up to her mother and said diffidently: "Ma, I know this girl from school—she's in class with me, can we have some red lemonade?"

And the woman lifted her head from where she sat, widelegged, so that you couldn't help seeing the knee-elastic of her striped pink bloomers holding over the cotton tops of her stockings, and said, peering, "Take it! Take it! Go, have it!"

Because I did not then know her, I thought that she was angry, she spoke with such impatience; but soon I knew that it was only her eager generosity that made her fling permission almost fiercely at Miriam whenever the child made some request. Mrs. Saiyetovitz's glance wavered over to me, but she did not seem to be seeing me very clearly: indeed, she could not, for her small, pale, pale eyes narrowed into her big, simple, heavy face were half-blind, and she had always to peer at everything, and never quite see.

I saw that she was very ugly.

Ugly, with blunt ugliness of a toad; the ugliness of seeming not entirely at home in any element—as if the earth were the wrong place, too heavy and magnetic for a creature already so blunt; and the water would be no better: too subtle and contour-swayed for a creature so graceless. And yet her ugliness was without repellence. When I grew older I often wondered why; she should have been repellent, one should have turned from her, but one did not. She was only ugly. She had the short, stunted yet heavy bones of generations of oppression in the Ghettos of Europe; breasts, stomach, hips crowded sadly, no height, wide strong shoulders and a round back. Her head settled right down between her shoulders without even the grace of a neck, and her dun flat hair was cut at the level of her ears. Her features were not essentially Semitic; there was nothing so *definite* as that about her: she had no distinction whatever.

Miriam reappeared from the shades of the store, carrying two bottles of red lemonade. A Shangaan emerged at the same time, clutching a newspaper parcel and puzzling over his handful of change, not looking where he was going. Miriam swept past him, the dusty African with his odd, troglodyte unsureness, and his hair plastered into savage whorls with red clay. With one swift movement she knocked the tin caps of the bottles against the scratched frame of the shopwindow, and handed my lemonade to me. "Where did you get it so quickly?" I asked, surprised. She jerked her head back towards the store: "In the kitchen," she said—and applied herself to the bottle.

And so I knew that the Saiyetovitzes lived there, behind the Concession store.

Saturday afternoons were the busiest. Mrs. Saiyetovitz's box stood vacant outside and she helped her husband in the shop. Saturday afternoon was usually my afternoon for going down there, too; my mother and father went out to golf, and I was left with the tick of the clock, the purring monologue of our cat, and the doves gurgling in the empty garden.

On Saturdays every doorway was crowded; a continual shifting stream snaked up and down the pavements; flies tangled overhead, the air smelled hotter, and from the doorway of every store the high, wailing blare and repetition of native songs, played on the gramophone, swung out upon the air and met in discord with the tune of the record being played next door.

Miriam's mother's brother was the proprietor of the Hotela la Bantu, and another uncle had the bicycle shop two doors down. Sometimes she had a message to deliver at the bicycle shop, and I would go in with her. Spare wheels hung across the ceiling, there was a battered wooden counter with a pile of puncture repair outfits, a sewing machine or two for sale, and, in the window, bells and pumps and mascots cut out of tin, painted yellow and red for the adornment of handle bars. We were invariably offered a lemonade by the uncle, and we invariably accepted. At home I was not allowed to drink lemonades unlimited; they might "spoil my dinner"; but Miriam drank them whenever she pleased.

Wriggling in and out amongst the gray-dusty bodies of the natives —their silky brown skin dies in the damp fug underground: after a few months down the mine, it reflects only weariness—Miriam looked with her own calm, quick self-possession upon the setting in which she found herself. Like someone sitting in a swarm of ants; and letting them swarm, letting them crawl all over and about her. Not lifting a hand to flick them off. Not crying out against them in disgust; nor explaining, saying, well, I *like* ants. Just sitting there and letting them swarm, and looking out of herself as if to say: What ants? What ants are you talking about? I giggled and shuddered in excitement at the sight of the dried bats and cobwebby snakeskins rotting in the bleary little window of the medicine shop, but Miriam tugged at my dress and said, "Oh, come on—" I exclaimed at the purple and red shirts lying amongst the dead flies in the wonderful confusion of Saiyetovitz's store window, but Miriam was telling me about her music exam in September, and only frowned at the interruption. I was approaching the confusion of adolescence, and sometimes an uncomfortable, terrible, fascinating curiosity—like a headless worm which lay shamefully hidden in the earth of my soul— crawled out into my consciousness at the sight of the animal obviousness of the natives' male bodies in their scanty covering; but the flash of my guilt at these moments met no answer in Miriam, although she was the same age as I.

If the sight of a boy interrupting his conversation to step out a yard or two onto the veld to relieve himself filled me with embarrassment and real disgust, so that I wanted to go and look at flowers—it seemed that Miriam did not see.

It was quite a long time before she took me into her father's store. For months it remained a vague, dark, dust-moted world beyond the blanket-hung doorway, into which she was swallowed up and appeared again, whilst I waited outside, with the boys who looked and looked and looked at the windows. Then one day, as she was entering, she paused, and said suddenly and calmly: "Aren't you coming . . . ?" Without a word, I followed her in.

It was cool in the store; and the coolness was a surprise. Out of the sun-baked pavement—and into the store that was cool, like a cellar! Light danced only furtively along the folds of the blankets that hung from the ceiling: crackling silent and secret little fires in the curly woolen furze. The blankets were dark somber hangings, in proud colors, bold and primal. They hung like dark stalactites in the cave, still and heavy, communing only their own colors back to themselves. They brooded over the shop; and over Mr. Saiyetovitz there beneath, treading the worn cement with his disgruntled, dispossessed air of doing his best, but . . . I had glimpsed him before. He lurked within the depths of his store like a beast in its lair, and now and then I had seen the glimmer of his pale, pasty face with the wide upper lip under which the lower closed glumly and puffily.

John Saiyetovitz (his name wasn't John at all, really—it was Yanka, but when he arrived at Cape Town, long ago, the Immigration authorities were tired of attempting to understand and spell the unfamiliar names of the immigrants pouring off the boat, and by the time they'd got the "Saiyetovitz" spelt right, they couldn't be bothered puzzling over the "Yanka," so they scrawled "John" on his papers, and John he was)—John Saiyetovitz was a gentle man, with an almost hangdog gentleness, but when he was trading with the natives, strange blasts of power seemed to blow up in his soul. Africans are the slowest buyers in the world; to them, buying is a ritual, a slow and solemn undertaking. They must go carefully; they nervously scent pitfalls on every side. And confronted with a selection of different kinds of the one thing they want, they are as confused as a child before a plate of pastries; fingering, hesitating, this or that . . . ? On a busy Saturday they must be allowed to stand about the shop endlessly, looking up and about, pausing to shake their heads and give a profound "OW!"; sauntering off; going to press their noses against the window again; coming back. And Mr. Saiyetovitz—always the same, unshaven and collarless—lugging a blanket down from the shelves, flinging it upon the counter—and another, and then another, and standing, arms hanging, sullen and smoldering before the blank-faced purchaser. The boy with his helpless stance, and his eyes rolling up in the agony of decision, filling the shop with the sickly odor of his anxious sweat, and clutching his precious guitar.

Waiting, waiting.

And then Mr. Saiyetovitz swooping away in a gesture of rage and denial; don't care, sick-to-death. And the boy anxious, edging forward to feel the cloth again, and the whole business starting up all over again; more blankets, different colors, down from the shelf and hooked from the ceiling—stalactites crumpled to woolen heaps to wonder over. Mr. Saiyetovitz throwing them down, moving in jerks of rage now, and then roughly bullying the boy into a decision. Shouting at him, bundling his purchase into his arms, snatching the money, gesturing him cowed out of the store.

Mr. Saiyetovitz treated the natives honestly, but with bad grace. He forced them to feel their ignorance, their inadequacy, and their submission to the white man's world of money. He spiritually maltreated them, and bitterly drove his nail into the coffin of their confidence.

With me, he was shy, he smiled widely and his hand went to the stud swinging loose at the neck of his half-buttoned shirt, and drew as if in apology over the stubbled landscape of his jaw. He always called me "little girl" and he liked to talk to me in the way that he thought children like to be talked to, but I found it very difficult to make a show of reply, because his English was so broken and fragmentary. So I used to stand there, and say yes, Mr. Saiyetovitz, and smile back and say thank you! to anything that sounded like a question, because the question usually was did I want a lemonade?, and of course, I usually did.

The first time Miriam ever came to my home was the day of my birthday party.

Our relationship at school had continued unchanged, just as before; she had her friends and I had mine, but outside of school there was the curious plane of intimacy on which we had, as it were, surprised one another wandering, and so which was shared peculiarly by us.

I had put Miriam's name down on my guest list; she was invited; and she came. She wore a blue taffeta dress which Mrs. Saiyetovitz had made for her (on the old Singer on the counter in the shop, I guessed) and it was quite nice if a bit too frilly. My home was pretty and well-furnished and full of flowers and personal touches of my mother's hands; there was space, and everything shone. Miriam did not open her eyes at it; I saw her finger a bowl of baby-skinned pink roses in the passing, but all afternoon she looked out indifferently as she did at home.

The following Saturday at the store we were discussing the party. Miriam was telling Mrs. Saiyetovitz about my presents, and I was standing by in pleasurable embarrassment at my own importance.

"Well, please God, Miri," said Mrs. Saiyetovitz at the finish, "you'll also have a party for your birday in April. . . . Ve'll be in d'house, and everything'll be nice, just like you want."—They were leaving the rooms behind the shop—the mournful green plush curtains glooming the archway between the bedroom and the living room; the tarnished samovar; the black beetles in the little kitchen;

Miriam's old black piano with the candlesticks, wheezing in the drafty passage; the damp puddly yard piled with empty packing cases and eggshells and banana skins; the hovering smell of fish frying. They were going to live in a little house in the township nearby.

But when April came, Miriam took ten of her friends to the Saturday afternoon bioscope in celebration of her birthday. "And to Costas Café afterwards for ice cream," she stated to her mother, looking out over her head. I think Mrs. Saiyetovitz was disappointed about the party, but she reasoned then, as always, that as her daughter went to school and was educated and could speak English, whilst she herself knew nothing, wasn't clever at all, the little daughter must know best what was right and what was nice.

I know now what of course I did not know then: that Miriam Saiyetovitz and I were intelligent little girls into whose brains there never had, and never would, come the freak and wonderful flash that is brilliance. Our were alabaster intellects: clear, perfect, light; no streaks of dark, unknown granite splitting to reveal secret veins of brightness, like thin gold, between stratum and stratum. We were fitted to be good schoolteachers, secretaries, organizers; we did everything well, nothing badly, and nothing remarkably. But to the Saiyetovitzes, Miriam's brain blazed like the sun, warming their humbleness.

In the year-by-year passage through school, our classmates thinned out one by one; the way seedlings come up in a bunch to a certain stage in their development, and then by some inexplicable process of natural selection, one or two continue to grow and branch up into the air, whilst the others wither or remain small and weedy. The other girls left to go and learn shorthand-and-typewriting: weeded out by the necessity of earning a living. Or moved, and went to other schools: transplanted to some ground of their own. Miriam and I remained, growing straight and steadily. . . .

During our matriculation year a sense of wonder and impending change came upon us both; the excitement of coming to an end that is also a beginning. We felt this in one another, and so were drawn together in new earnestness. Miriam came to study with me in the garden at my house, and oftener than ever, I slipped down to the Concession stores to exchange a book or discuss work with her. For although they now had a house, the Saiyetovitzes still lived, in the wider sense of the word, at the store. When Miriam and I discussed our schoolwork, the Saiyetovitzes crept about, very quiet, talking to one another only in hoarse, respectful whispers.

It was during this year, when the wonder of our own capacity to learn was reaching out and catching into light like a veld fire within us, that we began to talk of the University. And, all at once, we talked of nothing else. I spoke to my father of it, and he was agreeable, although my mother thought a girl could do better with her time. But so long as my father was willing to send me, I knew I should go. Ah yes, said Miriam. She liked my father very much; I knew that. In fact she said to me once—it was a strange thing to say, and almost emotionally, she said it, and at a strange time, because we were on the bus going into the town to buy a new winter coat which she had wanted very badly and talked about longingly for days, and her father had just given her the money to get it—she said to me: You know, I think your father's just right.—I mean, if you had to choose somebody, a certain kind of person for a father, well, your father'd be just the kind you'd want.

When she broached the subject of University to her parents, they were agreeable for her to go, too. Indeed, they wanted her to go almost more than she herself did. But they worried a great deal about the money side of it; every time I went down to the store there'd be a discussion of ways and means, Saiyetovitz slowly munching his bread and garlic polony lunch, and worrying. Miriam didn't worry about it; they'll find the money, she said. She was a tall girl, now, with beautiful breasts, and a large, dark-featured face that had a certain capable elegance, although her father's glum mouth was unmistakable and on her upper lip faint dark down foreshadowed a heavy middle-age. Her parents were peasants; but she was the powerful young Jewess. Beside her, I felt pale in my Scotch gingery-fairness: lightly drawn upon the mind's eye, whilst she was painted in oils.

We both matriculated; not so well as we thought we should, but well enough; and we went to the University. And there too, we did well enough. We had both decided upon the same course: teaching. In the end, it had seemed the only thing to do. Neither of us had any particular bent.

It must have been a hard struggle for the Saiyetovitzes to keep Miriam at the University, buy her clothes, and pay for her board and lodging in Johannesburg. There is a great deal of money to be made out of native trade concessions purchased from the government; and it doesn't require education or trained commercial astuteness to make it—in fact, trading of this sort seems to flourish in response to something very different: what is needed is instinctive peasant craftiness such as can only be found in the uneducated, in those who have scratched up their own resources. Storekeepers with this quality of peasant craft made money all about Mr. Saiyetovitz, bought houses and motorcars and banded their wives' retired hands with diamonds in mark of their new idleness. But Mr. Saiyetovitz was a peasant without the peasant's craft; without that flaw in his simplicity that might have given him checks and deeds of transfer to sign, even if he were unable to read the print on the documents. . . . Without this craft, the peasant has only one thing left to him: hard work, dirty work, with the sweet, sickly body-smell of the black men about him all day.

Saiyetovitz made no money: only worked hard and long, standing in his damp shirt amidst the clamor of the stores and the death-smell from the eating house always in his nose.

Meanwhile, Miriam fined down into a lady. She developed a half-bored, half-intolerant shrug of the shoulders in place of the childish sharpness that had been filed jagged by the rub-rub of rough life and harsh contrast. She became soft-voiced, where she had been loud and gay. She watched and conformed; and soon took on the attitude of liberal-mindedness that sets the doors of the mind slackly open, so that any idea may walk in and out again, leaving very little impression: she could appreciate Bach and Stravinsky, and spend a long evening listening to swing music in the dark of somebody's flat.

Race and creed had never meant very much to Miriam and me, but at the University she sifted naturally towards the young Jews who were passing easily and enthusiastically, with their people's extraordinary aptitude for creative and scientific work, through Medical School. They liked her; she was invited to their homes for tennis parties, swimming on Sundays, and dances, and she seemed as unimpressed by the luxury of their ten-thousand-pound houses as she had been by the contrast of our clean, pleasant little home, long ago, when she herself was living behind the Concession store.

She usually spent part of the vacations with friends in Johannesburg; I missed her—wandering about the Mine on my own, out of touch, now, with the girls I had left behind in the backwater of the small town. During the second half of one July vacation—she had spent the first two weeks in Johannesburg—she asked me if she could come and spend Sunday at my home, and in the afternoon, one of the Medical students arrived at our house in his small car. He had come from Johannesburg; Miriam had evidently told him she would be with us. I gathered her parents did not know of the young man's visit, and I did not speak of it before them.

So the four years of our training passed. Miriam Saiyetovitz and I had dropped like two leaves, side by side into the same current, and been carried downstream together: now the current met a swirl of dead logs, reeds, and the force of other waters, and broke up, divided its drive and its one direction. The leaves floated clear; divergent from one another. Miriam got a teaching post in Johannesburg, but I was sent to a small school in the Northern Transvaal. We met seldom during the first six months of our adult life: Miriam went to Capetown during the vacation, and I flew to Rhodesia with the first profits of my independence. Then came the war, and I, glad to escape so soon the profession I had once anticipated with such enthusiasm, joined the nursing service and went away for the long, strange interlude of four years. Whilst I was with a field hospital in Italy, I heard that Miriam had married—a Doctor Somebody-or-other: my informant wasn't sure of the name. I guessed it must be one of the boys whom she had known as students. I sent a cable of congratulation, to the Saiyetovitzes' address.

And then, one day I came back to the small mining town and found it there, the same; like a face that has been waiting a long time. My Mother, and my Dad, the big wheels of the shaft turning, the trees folding their wings about the Mine houses; and our house, with the green, square lawn and the cat watching the doves. For the first few weeks I faltered about the old life, feeling my way in a dream so like the old reality that it hurt.

There was a feel about an afternoon that made my limbs tingle with familiarity. . . . What . . . ? And then, lying on our lawn under the hot sky, I knew: just the sort of glaring summer afternoon that used to send me down to the Concession stores, feeling isolated in the heat. Instantly, I thought of the Saiyetovitzes, and I wanted to go and see them, see if they were still there; what Miriam was doing; where she was, now.

Down at the stores it was the same as ever, only dirtier, smaller, more chipped and smeared—the way reality often is in contrast with the image carried long in the mind. As I stepped so strangely on that old pocked pavement, with the skeleton cats and the orange peel and the gobs of spit, my heart tightened with the thought of the Saiyetovitzes. I was in a kind of excitement to see the store again. And there it was; and excitement sank out at the evidence of the monotony of "things." Blankets swung a little in the doorway. Flies crawled amongst the shirts and shoes posed in the window, the hot, wet, sickening fatty smell came over from the eating house. I met it with the old revulsion: it was like breathing inside someone's stomach. And in the store, amongst the wicked glitter of the tin trunks, beneath the secret whispering of the blankets, the old Saiyetovitzes sat glumly, with patience, waiting. . . . As animals wait in a cage; for nothing.

In their delight at seeing me again, I saw that they were older, sadder; that they had somehow given themselves into the weight of their own humbleness, they were without a pinnacle on which to fix their eyes. Whatever place it was that they looked upon now, it was flat.

Mr. Saiyetovitz's mouth had creased in further to the dead folds of his chin; his hair straggled to the rims of his ears. As he spoke to me, I noticed that his hands lay, with a curious helpless indifference, curled on the counter. Mrs. Saiyetovitz shuffled off at once to the back of the shop to make a cup of tea for me, and carried it in, slopping over into the saucer. She was uglier than ever, now, her back hunched up to meet her head, her old thick legs spiraled in crêpe bandages because of varicose veins. And blinder too, I could see: that enquiring look of the blind or deaf smiling unsure at you from her face.

The talk turned almost at once to Miriam, and as they answered my questions about her, I saw them go inert. Yes, she was married; had married a doctor—a flicker of pride in the old man at this. She lived in Johannesburg. Her husband was doing very well. There was a photograph of her home, in one of the more expensive suburbs; a large, white modern house, with flower borders and a fishpond. And there was Miri's little boy, sitting on his swing; and a studio portrait of him, taken with his mother.

There was the face of Miriam Saiyetovitz, confident, carefully made-up and framed in a good hairdresser's version of her dark hair, smiling queenly over the face of her child. One hand lay on the child's shoulder, a smooth hand, wearing large, plain, expensive diamond rings. Her bosom was proud and rounded now—a little too heavy, a little overripe in the climate of ease.

I could see in her face that she had forgotten a lot of things.

When his wife had gone into the back of the shop to refill my teacup, old Saiyetovitz went silent, looking at the hand that lay before him on the counter, the fingers twitching a little under the gaze.

It doesn't come out like you think, he said, it doesn't come out like you think.

He looked up at me with a comforting smile.

And then he told me that they had seen Miriam's little boy only three times since he was born. Miriam they saw hardly at all; her husband never. Once or twice a year she came out from Johannesburg to visit them, staying an hour on a Sunday afternoon, and then driving herself back to Town again. She had not invited her parents to her home at any time; they had been there only once, on the occasion of the birth of their grandson.

Mrs. Saiyetovitz came back into the store: she seemed to know of what we had been speaking. She sat down on a shot-purple tin trunk and folded her arms over her breast. Ah yes, she breathed, ah yes. . . .

I stood there in Miriam's guilt before the Saiyetovitzes, and they were silent, in the accusation of the humble.

But in a little while a Swazi in a tobacco-colored blanket sauntered dreamily into the shop, and Mr. Saiyetovitz rose heavy with defeat.

Through the eddy of dust in the lonely interior and the wavering fear round the head of the native and the bright hot dance of the jazz blankets and the dreadful submission of Mrs. Saiyetovitz's conquered voice in my ear, I heard his voice strike like a snake at my faith: angry and brow-beating, sullen and final, lashing weakness at the weak.

Mr. Saiyetovitz and the native.

Defeated, and without understanding in their defeat.

Sergei Antonov was born in Leningrad in 1915 and was educated at the Highways Institute. He began writing and publishing verse in 1944 and has produced several novels (including The Trucks on the Road Are Ours, *which won a Stalin Prize in 1950), as well as short stories and motion picture scripts.*

Antonov's writing is laced with the flavor of rural Russia. His semi-didactic, metaphorical fiction often protests the arrogance of the old guard which, through narrowmindedness and ineptitude, thwarts social progress. Does the theme of "The Application Form" emerge naturally from the confrontation of characters? Is Antonov using the short story form as a vehicle for presenting propaganda? Further Reading: It Happened in Penkovo (1953), The Elder (1963).

UNION OF SOVIET
SOCIALIST REPUBLICS

The Application Form

SERGEI ANTONOV

Semyon Yeremeyevich, chief of the regional communications administration, was an ordinary sort of man, who always arrived on time for work, greeted his secretary with a handshake, and sometimes even wrote comments for the wall newspaper under the pen-name of 'Fly'. The visitors in his waiting-room began arriving to see him in the morning. Some of them came on important business, while others came with matters that could easily have been settled at a lower level, without bothering Semyon Yeremeyevich. But his way of working was to receive all applicants and attend to the matter troubling them personally.

"The Application Form" by Sergi Antonov published by Penguin Books Ltd. Translated by John Richardson.

The waiting-room was furnished simply, though efficiently. By the door was the secretary's desk and on it stood a typewriter with a wide carriage. There was a loudspeaker hanging in one corner and the radio used to be turned on both to entertain the visitors as well as to drown the chief's voice filtering through from the office, since there could easily be outsiders among those who had come to see him.

Semyon Yeremeyevich's office was marked by the simplicity of the man himself. At the far end was a wide desk with some bronze ink-wells and in front of it were two leather armchairs. On the right was a long conference table covered with a green cloth and neatly lined on either side with chairs. Semyon Yeremeyevich hated anyone sitting at this table and whenever he saw that one of the chairs had been moved, he always pushed it back into place himself, so that their backs formed a straight and even line.

On the day on which our story begins, life in the waiting-room was taking its normal course. The secretary was putting wax seals on a package, the visitors were awaiting their turn, and the radio was playing a sentimental waltz. At exactly ten o'clock there came a brief ring.

The nimble secretary disappeared for a moment into the office, then came back and said:
'Comrade Yefimova, this way please.'
The young woman in the stylish hat entered the office. She seemed to be nervous since she forgot to shut both black oilcloth-covered doors behind her.

Semyon Yeremeyevich was writing slowly, with his head on one side, as was his custom.
'Please take a seat,' he said without raising his eyes.

Yefimova sat down on the edge of the cold chair and looked across the bronze inkstand barrier at Semyon Yeremeyevich. He had the nice, plump face of a non-smoker and completely white hair.

'Yes, what can I do for you?' he asked, continuing to write.
The woman gave a slight cough and began the sentence she had prepared and polished in her mind some time before.
'My name's Yefimova. I came here a week ago about getting a job. You took my record and application form and told me to come today....'
The chief was writing in silence. She glanced at him as though not realizing that the done thing was just to sit and wait.

'Yes?' responded Semyon Yeremeyevich.

He found it difficult to shift his attention. In front of him lay a copy of a complaint from the villagers of Vesyoloye regarding the inefficiency of their relay broadcasting network. The complaint had somehow reached Moscow, and it was from there that the copy had arrived, accompanied by an order to deal with the hitch straight away, punish the culprits, and report action taken on the matter by such and such a date. The date had expired the day before. The order was sharply worded and contained some insulting insinuations—offensive to Semyon Yeremeyevich—regarding poor management. Letters like that were always answered by the chief personally.

The first thing he did, as was the form, was to stamp the word 'Secret' in the corner at the top. Then he noted down that during the summer the relay network in certain parts of the region had not been operating properly as a result of the transformers burning out along the line. And the transformers had burned out as a result of the excessive storms during the summer. It had not been possible to repair the damage in good time for the following reasons: firstly, only ten per cent of the specialists requested in application number such-and-such had been supplied and the teams of linesmen had not yet been drawn up; secondly, work was hampered by inclement weather; thirdly . . .

'Yes, what can I do for you?' repeated Semyon Yeremeyevich, somewhat peeved that the third reason had gone right out of his head. There wasn't anything surprising about that, really, as anyone occupying a more or less official post knows how one's attention wanders when there are outsiders in the office. Julius Caesar was the only person who could read, write, and speak without notes all at the same time. But that was in Ancient Rome and the requirements were quite different.

'My name's Yefimova,' began the persistent woman. 'I've come about work.'

'You'll have to go to the personnel department and fill in an application form,' replied Semyon Yeremeyevich gently.

'You already have my form and record.'

'What's your name?'

'Yefimova.'

Rummaging about in the bottom drawer of his desk, Semyon Yeremeyevich brought out a file marked 'Personnel'. Yefimova's papers were indeed with him.

The form stated that Yevgenia Vasilevna Yefimova, female, born 1922, of working-class origin, had entered a Leningrad institute in 1940, had graduated with honours, and had qualified as an electrical engineer specializing in radio. Specialists in that line were always desperately needed and Semyon Yeremeyevich began to read more carefully. The record further specified that Yefimova had discontinued her studies at the institute on account of the war, but had gained her diploma in 1950. It then said that she had married in 1952 and had been divorced in 1953.

All the d's in the short, one-page record had little tails sticking up. Noticing these funny tails, Semyon Yeremeyevich recalled that he had recently handled both the record and the application form, and having recalled the documents, recalled the face of the timid, frail woman and the unpleasant story involved.

Tearing himself away from the papers, he looked at Yefimova. Her lips were inexpertly painted, especially for the occasion it appeared, and such frivolity could only make an unfavourable impression on the chief.

'What people I have in the personnel department,' he thought. 'They're dead scared of responsibility.'

The difficulty was that during the war Yefimova had remained in occupied territory.

That was the reason why her papers had made their way from the safe in the personnel department to Semyon Yeremeyevich's desk. That was the reason why the Wednesday before Semyon Yeremeyevich had asked her to come back in a week's time.

After graduating from the institute, Yefimova had been employed as a line engineer for two years at a radio station, under a man named Savelyev, but had left in 1952, as stated in the application form, 'for family reasons'. The whole of that week the chief of the administration had been going to ring up Savelyev, who now occupied a similar post to Semyon Yeremeyevich in a neighbouring region, and make inquiries about Yefimova's fitness report.

Unless Savelyev praised her, she could be turned down with a clear conscience and that would be the end of the tricky business.

But being bogged down in current matters, he had not got round to this. He asked Yevgenia Vasilevna to wait another week, and as soon as she had left the room, put through a long-distance call.

Savelyev took the matter lightly, however. He said that Yefimova was an honest, highly skilled worker, and expressed his willingness to give her a reference.

'But don't you think she'll have a hard time in the network?' asked Semyon Yeremeyevich. 'She's sort of weak-willed and spineless. Sort of timid.'

Savelyev didn't think so. To his mind Yefimova had always been pertinacious and exacting.

'And what about her private life?' asked Semyon Yeremeyevich. 'First she gets married, then she gets divorced. It's too casual. . . .'

Savelyev explained that she had married a district radio announcer. Her husband had insisted that she give up work. Soon afterwards it turned out that the announcer had left a wife and children somewhere in the country, and Yefimova had got a divorce. 'And quite rightly, too, in my opinion,' added Savelyev.

'But did you know she hasn't had a job now for six months?'

Savelyev didn't know that.

'There you are,' said Semyon Yeremeyevich, 'one's got to get to know one's employees.'

'Go on, take her on!' cried Savelyev. 'You won't regret it.'

The conversation ended with that. It was easy for Savelyev to talk, of course, since Yefimova had been sent to him from the Chief Administration, while Semyon Yeremeyevich would have to take her on himself, on his own responsibility. On the face of it, of course, there was no objection to employing Yefimova, but, if you looked at the matter more closely, the application form wasn't quite in order. If she were given work, there'd be no end of difficulties. A revision committee might arrive and look into personal backgrounds, for instance —then there'd be trouble. Among the technical staff one man was of upper-class origin, while another had been God knows what before the Revolution—apparently a deacon—but anyway not our sort. And now there'd be this woman as well. It's quite clear, they'd say, why your transformers burn out. You've surrounded yourself with unsuitable people; your vigilance has been lulled. And they'd charge you with bungling, to boot. . . .

A week later Yefimova was in the office again.

'How's your family situation?' asked the chief.

'I live with my Mum and Dad," began Yevgenia Vasilevna, 'at No. 10 Brick Street.'

'Is that the street near Mayday Park?'

'Yes, near the Park; it's a tiny house. The two end windows are ours and the others belong to the neighbours. Mum has a job at the brick works. Dad's very old and disabled. He has to be taken about in a chair.'

'What does he have, a push-chair?'

'Yes, a simple sort of chair . . . with levers. But he's on the feeble side and can't work the levers.'

'He ought to have a motor-chair. Our industry's now producing them.'

'We applied, but they wouldn't give us one. They require a whole heap of information.'

This state of affairs outraged Semyon Yeremeyevich.

'What a disgrace,' he said. 'You must be more insistent. Write to the newspapers. To Moscow, if need be.'

'Thank you. You know, it's because of Dad that I live here. Otherwise I'd have gone to Savelyev long ago. He'd have taken me on.'

'So you can't work out of town.'

'You see yourself how difficult it would be.'

'Yes, a pity. I had already chosen you a job out of town.'

'Where?'

'In Vesyoloye village. They badly need a line engineer there.'

'Is it far from here?'

'About a hundred kilometres. A hundred and twenty, I believe.'

'I couldn't possibly go there,' said Yefimova with the reluctance natural in most of the visitors. 'Isn't there anywhere a bit nearer? I don't mind commuting so long as I can be home in the evenings.'

'Yes, of course, I understand,' said Semyon Yeremeyevich with a gentle smile. 'I can see the situation. At one time I had trouble with my father, too.'

'Why, no, there's no question of trouble. . . . But perhaps something will turn up a bit nearer."

'Difficult to say. Why don't you look again in a week's time?'

Yefimova came back a week later. This time she was in a state of great agitation and kept crumbling a lace handkerchief in her hand.

'How's my application, Comrade Chief?' she asked, deliberately not addressing him by his name and patronymic.

'Nothing yet for the moment. Nothing except Vesyoloye village,' replied the chief, tactfully ignoring her tone. 'They badly need a line engineer in Vesyoloye.'

'Your secretary was just typing out in front of me an order appointing a technician to an urban radio station. So you must have had some vacancies. And you probably have some others. You've simply been telling lies.'

Any other head of an establishment would have promptly called a visitor to order for an attack like that, but Semyon Yeremeyevich did not begin shouting or arguing. He merely stood up from his chair and said with restraint:

'Comrade Yefimova!'

'I can guess what the trouble is.' Yefimova also stood up. Her pale cheeks were covered with red blotches. 'You're afraid of the fact that I stayed in occupied territory.'

'What do you mean? What has the Occupation got to do with it?' Semyon Yeremeyevich sat down and straightened a heap of files. He always liked order, one might even say perfect order, on his desk. And if he came across an unsharpened pencil or an unfilled inkwell, he always calls his secretary and reprimanded her accordingly.

'Wait, let me explain, anyway,' Yefimova kept on. 'At the very beginning of the war our institute was evacuated to Pyatigorsk from Leningrad under siege. Then, when the front moved up, they kept promising to move us to Central Asia. But they didn't have time. The more adventurous folk got away on train roofs and footboards, but I couldn't do that. . . . You couldn't get any tickets at the station. . . . And they wouldn't let you in convoys from other parts. . . . Then we started off on foot. . . . Then we were surrounded. . . . It was a very hard time. . . .'

'I remember the time,' sighed Semyon Yeremeyevich. 'They got me out of the Crimea just at the last moment,' and he straightened the files on his desk.

'You had to be got out, of course.'

'Yes, an order came from Moscow to leave immediately. Though I was hoping to join the partisans—I've been a partisan at heart since childhood. But nothing came of it. Orders are orders.'

'I wanted to join the partisans, too. Except that I didn't know where they were to be found.'

'A fine partisan you'd make! Were you long under the Germans?'

Five months. I had to work as a teacher. You had to live as best you could. I'm to blame, of course, for not joining the partisans. . . . Now I'd take work in any network, as a simple technician. Even so, they won't take me on.'

'Responsibility shirkers!'

'No, they're not shirkers. There's a regulation that people with higher education do not have the right to stay in lower-grade jobs. Don't smile, the regulation is right. We were trained and money was spent on us. So we must work at full capacity. Incidentally, I completed my education after the war even though the directorate of the institute knew I'd been in occupied territory.'

'Yes,' sighed Semyon Yeremeyevich, 'they gave you a narrow field of specialization.'

'I've tried to change it. I recently applied to the Foreign Languages Institute. But they said I already had higher education and that my application would not be considered until last. If there were any places left.'

'Responsibility shirkers,' repeated Semyon Yeremeyevich.

'I think they're right. Other people want higher education, too.

But I just don't know what to do. It's better to live without hands and feet than without work.'

She stared into space in front of her, and asked:

'And how do I get there? To this Vesyoloye village?'

Semyon Yeremeyevich patiently explained that she would first have to take the train, then the bus. It was about three kilometres from the bus station, not more. But she had to remember that in winter the buses didn't run regularly, especially when there were snow-drifts. And the train fares would be at her own expense. But the transport situation was usually normal. As regards accommodation in Vesyoloye, there was nothing encouraging to be said. The only possibility was sent to rent a private flat.

Semyon Yeremeyevich got up from his desk, shook Yefimova's hand, and suggested she should come back again in a fortnight's time, just in case.

A fortnight later Yefimova arrived in a delighted mood. This time she had no lipstick on.

'Everything's been arranged, Semyon Yeremeyevich!' she began without even greeting him. 'The director of the brickworks has transferred Mum to the second shift at my request. And a girl, a distant relation of the neighbours, is going to come to us in the mornings. She's recently arrived from the country. She'll do the cooking and tidying up. And on Sundays I'll come home. That's all right, isn't it?'

'Why where have you got a job?' asked Semyon Yeremeyevich.

'What do you mean, where? I'm going to Vesyoloye.'

'Oh, I see. . . .' Semyon Yeremeyevich lowered his eyes and straightened the files. 'You see, we couldn't delay so long. The vacancies in Vesyoloye have been filled.'

Yefimova slowly stood up from the chair and began looking round her.

'But you said . . .' she began. 'You said . . . in a fortnight's time. You . . .'

She suddenly turned away, covered her face with her hands and ran out of the office. And, incidentally, both doors had to be shut behind her.

Yefimova didn't come again, Semyon Yeremeyevich seemed to pay little attention to the fact and gradually forgot all about the troublesome visitor. But one day, while setting his desk in order, he came across the brief record. Running his eyes along the lines with the d's with funny little tails, he recalled the woman in the feathered hat, and began wondering. What had happened to her? Where was she now? Perhaps she had got a job somewhere? Unlikely. All her papers and references were there. And anyway she could only work in radio communications and her speciality was very narrow. Perhaps she had gone to Moscow to complain and had got as far as the Minister? If so, he could expect a stern inquiry from people who knew nothing about the truth of the matter. On what grounds had Engineer Yefimova not been given work? You tell us, they'd say, that you lack specialists, yet there are specialists crying out to be employed. What could be said in reply to that?

Semyon Yeremeyevich summoned his secretary and, sorting out the files, asked if by any chance a thinnish woman called Yefimova had put her name down for an interview.

Yefimova was not on any of the lists.

Semyon Yeremeyevich began wondering again. He may have called to mind the distant case of a woman who had been unable to get a job for some time because her husband had been mixed up in some murky affair and had been arrested. The woman had written about her trials and tribulations to the relevant quarter and then thrown herself in the river. Although this had occurred in another network and many years before, it had naturally left a mark on Semyon Yeremeyevich's sensitive make-up.

He began to have nerves. Red spots appeared on his hands, just as the year before when representatives of the Chief Administration had paid him a visit.

Three weeks later Semyon Yeremeyevich was about to order a trustworthy member of his staff to go to Yefimova's flat and put an end to the uncertainty, but after a consultation with him, decided against it and left the order unissued. A visit of that kind would have looked odd under any circumstances and was not good form, to say the least.

Finally Semyon Yeremeyevich decided to let the matter drop and patiently wait for peace of mind. But every day the vague apprehension in his responsive heart grew stronger and more persistent. He began shouting and banging his desk with his fist, and on one occasion forgot to mark an important file 'Secret', which had never happened before.

One day, while returning from a meeting, he drove as far as Brick Street, ordered the driver to wait round the corner, and went over to No. 10. It was a dark September evening. A lamp-post lit up the beamed walls of a single-storey house, the pitted brick foundations, the shutters with old, peeling paint, the iron porch-top creaking in the wind, two uneven doorposts, and a letter-box stuffed with rags. The pieces of string dangling by the walls had once been entwined with hops. Thick beds of nettles grew round the porch in summer, and now the yellowish, faded stems pushed their way through the porch steps. The front door was obviously boarded up and the tenants went in through the back door across the yard.

Three of the windows in the house were brightly lit, but there was no light in the two end ones which Yefimova had described. The black glass panes stared gloomily at Semyon Yeremeyevich.

For some time he stood alone in the deserted street in the wind and cold, thinking of the number of chance happenings which interfere with normal work, how difficult it was to run a large staff, and how much endurance an administrator needed. Then he shivered with cold and went back to the car.

The next morning he woke up with a headache and went to work without having breakfast.

To his surprise he found Yefimova in the waiting-room. She had asked the secretary to put her name on the list for that day. This time Yefimova looked determined, and there was a fresh young blush on her cheeks.

'Don't worry about the list, Yevgenia Vasilevna,' exclaimed Semyon Yeremeyevich, who could not stand ceremony. 'Come along with me,' and taking her by the arm, he led her into his office.

'I've come for my documents, Comrade Chief,' said Yefimova, breaking away from him.

'Have you got a job?'

'Yes, I have.'

'Where, if it's not a secret?'

'With Savelyev. He heard about my situation and wrote me a letter. He promised me a room in a hostel for a start, and a flat in a year's time.'

'Well, good luck to you,' said Semyon Yeremeyevich, genuinely delighted. 'I kept a job for you, too, but you haven't been here for such a long time.'

'I was out of town. I went digging potatoes.'

'What on earth induced you to do that?'

'Mum was sent from the brickworks, but the work was too hard for her, so I went instead. By the way, Vesyoloye is seventy-two kilometres from here, not a hundred.'

'Have you been there?'

'Yes, and I saw what was going on there at the radio station.'

'What was that?'

'The electricians are selling government wire. They tell the gullible subscribers that there are no supplies in the storehouse. Then they pretend to procure the installation wire themselves. And take money for it.'

'Scandalous!' said Semyon Yeremeyevich. 'Why doesn't the chief look into it?'

'There isn't anyone there to look into it. There's been no line engineer there for six months. It's a complete shambles there, while you . . . while you just read your bits of paper.'

Yefimova turned round and left without saying good-bye.

'What neurotic, ill-mannered visitors!' thought Semyon Yeremeyevich. He shook his head condescendingly and reached out for a file marked 'Correspondence with Higher Levels'.

"Its life in history has long ago ended for always. There is only the past, the songs and legends about it—a kind of timelessness. This delights me most of all." So the Ukraine is described by Ivan Bunin, an author whose fiction deals with the world of the old gentry in rural Russia. His themes mirror the horrors of peasant life and of inward desolation of the spirit. His stories are stark in detail, frequently linking images frozen in time. What images are linked in "Sunstroke"? What effect does Bunin achieve by contrasting nature with the transitory quality of man?

Ivan Bunin won the Nobel Prize in 1931, the first Russian writer to be so honored. Born in 1870 in Vororneh, the son of an aristocratic family, Bunin was forced into exile in Western Europe after the Revolution. He lived in Paris, writing fiction, essays, and poetry, until his death in 1953. Further Reading: The Gentleman from San Francisco and Other Stories (1915), The Dreams of Chang, and Other Stories (1923), The Grammar of Love (1934).

UNION OF SOVIET
SOCIALIST REPUBLICS

Sunstroke

IVAN BUNIN

They had had their dinner, and they left the brilliantly lighted dining room and went on deck, where they paused by the rail. She closed her eyes and, palm turned outward, pressing her hand to her cheek, laughed with unaffected charm. Everything was charming about this little woman. She said:

"I'm quite intoxicated . . . Or I've gone wholly out of my mind. Where did you drop down from? But three hours ago I scarcely suspected your existence. I don't even know where you came on

Translated by Teka Matheson.

board. Was it Samara? Well, it doesn't matter, my dear. Really, my head's in a whirl, or is it the boat turning?"

Before them was darkness—and lights. Out of the darkness a strong breeze blew in their faces, while the light glided past them: with Volga friskiness the steam cut a sharp curve, as it approached the small pier.

The lieutenant took her hand, lifting it to his lips. The strong small hand smelt of sunburn. Bliss and anguish caused his heart to grow tremulous at the thought that underneath this light linen dress she was doubtless all strong and tanned after a whole month's lying under the southern sun upon the hot sea sands (she had said she was coming from Anapu). The lieutenant murmured: "Let's get off here...."

"Where?" she asked in astonishment.

"Here, on this pier."

"Why?"

He was silent. Again she laid the back of her hand upon her hot cheek.

"You're mad...."

"Let's get off," he repeated dully. "I implore you...."

"*Akh*, do as you like," she said, turning away.

The moving steamer crashed with a dull thud against the dimly lighted pier, and the pair almost fell upon each other. The end of a cable came flying above their heads, then the ship reeled and the water clamorously seethed, the gangplank rattled.... The lieutenant ran for the luggage.

Presently, they passed through the tiny drowsy pier shed and, once out of doors, found themselves ankle-deep in sand; in silence they seated themselves in the dust-covered hackney cab. The ascent of the steep road, soft with dust, punctuated with infrequent lamp posts standing awry, seemed endless. At last they emerged on top, the carriage rattled along a paved street; here was a square, some administrative buildings, a belfry, the warmth and the smells of a summer night in a provincial town.... The cabby stopped before a lighted entrance; through the open doors could be seen the steep wooden stairway. An old unshaven servant in a pink shirt and frock coat reluctantly took their bags and went forward on his tired feet. They entered a large but terribly stuffy room still hot from the day's sun, its windows hung with white curtains, its mirror-topped mantelpiece decorated with two unused candles—and no sooner had they entered and the servant closed the door upon them than the lieutenant impetuously flung himself upon her and they both lost themselves in a kiss of such agonizing rapture that the moment was long to be remembered by them: nothing like it had ever been experienced by either one or the other.

At ten o'clock the next morning, a morning hot and sunny and gay with the ringing of church bells, with the humming in the market-place facing the hotel, with the smell of hay and tar and all those complex odors with which every provincial Russian town reeks, she, this nameless little woman, for she refused to reveal her name, jestingly called herself the lovely stranger, left him, resuming her journey. They had slept little, but when she emerged from behind the screen near the bed, within five minutes all washed and dressed, she looked as fresh as a seventeen-year-old girl. Was she embarrassed? Very little. As before, she was simple, gay and—quite rational.

"No, no my dear," she said in response to his suggestion that they pursue the journey together. "No, you must remain here until the next boat. If we go on together, everything will be spoiled. I wouldn't like that. Please believe me, I'm not at all the sort of woman I may have led you to think. All that happened here never happened before and never will again. It's as if I suffered an eclipse . . . Or, to be more precise, it's as if we both experienced something in the nature of a sunstroke."

The lieutenant rather lightly agreed with her. In gay happy spirits he escorted her in a carriage to the pier, which they reached just as the rose-tinted steamer was on the point of departure, and, on deck, in the presence of other passengers, he kissed her, and barely managed to jump on to the already receding gangplank.

With the same lightness of spirit he returned to the hotel. Yet something had changed. Their room without her seemed quite different. It was still full of her—and empty. That was strange! It still smelt of her excellent English eau-de-cologne, her unfinished cup was still on the tray, but she was no longer there. . . . And the lieutenant's heart suddenly felt such tremors of tenderness that he made haste to smoke, and slapping his boot-leg with a crop, he paced up and down the room.

"A strange occurrence!" he said aloud, laughing, yet conscious of tears in his eyes. " 'Please believe me, I'm not at all the sort of woman I may have led you to think. . . .' And now she's gone. . . . An absurd woman!"

The screen was pushed to one side, the bed had not yet been made. And he felt that now he simply hadn't the courage to look upon this bed. He arranged the screen around it, closed the window that he might void hearing the market hum and the creaking of cart wheels, lowered the blown-out white curtains, and sat down on the divan. . . . Well, so that was the end to the "chance encounter!" She was gone— and was now far away, doubtless sitting in the glassed-in white salon or on the deck, gazing at the immense sun-glinting river, at the passing barges, the yellow sand-banks, the distant radiance of water and sky, at the whole immeasurable expanse of the Volga. . . . And farewell, for ever, for eternity. . . . For how could they ever meet again? "I can't, after all," he mused, "for one reason or another, visit the town where her husband is, and her three-year-old daughter, and the rest of her family, the place where she leads her everyday life!"—And that town suddenly appeared to him as a most exceptional, a forbidden town, and the thought that she would go on living in it her lonely life, perhaps frequently remembering him, remembering their chance transient encounter, while he would never see her again, this thought stunned and unmanned him. No, this could not be! It was wholly absurd, unnatural, incredible! And he felt such anguish, such futility of existence in the years to come, that he was seized with terror, with despair.

"What the devil!" he thought, rising, and, again pacing up and down the room, he tried to avoid the sight of the bed behind the screen. "What's the matter with me? Who'd have thought it possible that the first time—and there. . . . What is there about her, and what exactly has happened? Really, it is as if there were some sort of sunstroke! But the main thing is, how am I to spend the whole day without her in this God-forsaken place?"

He vividly remembered her as she was, with all of her most intimate traits; he remembered the smell of her sunburn and of her linen dress, of her strong body, the live, simple, gay sound of her voice. . . . The mood of but lately experienced delights of her feminine loveliness, was still singularly strong upon him; nevertheless, the main thing was another altogether new mood—that strange, incomprehensible mood, non-existent while they were still together, a mood which he could not have even imagined yesterday, when he first made this new, merely diverting, as he had thought, acquaintance, and concerning which he could no longer speak to anyone, no, not to anyone! "Yes, the main thing," he went on thinking, "is that you'll never be able to talk about it! And what is one to do, how is one to pass this endless day, with these memories, with this intolerable anguish, in this God-forsaken little town by the same radiant Volga, upon whose waters this rose-tinted steamer has borne her away!"

It was necessary to save himself, to occupy himself with something, to find amusement, to go somewhere. He resolutely put his cap on; strode vigorously, clinking his spurs, down the empty corridors; ran down the steep stairway toward the entrance . . . Well, where should he go? At the entrance was a young cabby in a smart peasant's coat, calmly smoking a tiny cigar, apparently waiting for someone. The lieutenant glanced at him in distraught wonder: how was it possible for anyone to sit so calmly on a coachbox, and smoke, and seem so unconcerned, so indifferent? "Evidently, in this whole town I alone am so terribly unhappy," he thought, turning in the direction of the market place.

The market was dispersing. Unwittingly he trod upon the fresh manure among the wagons, among the cart loads of cucumbers, among the new pots and pans, and the women, who sat on the ground, vied with one another in trying to call his attention to their pots, which they took in their hands and made ring with their fingers, demonstrating their quality, while the peasants dinned in his ears: "Here are first-class cucumbers, Your Honor!" All this was stupid, absurd, and he ran from the place. He entered the church, where chanting was going on; it was loud and cheerful and determined, as if the chanters were conscious of the fulfillment of a duty; then he strode on through the streets, and in the heat of the sun wandered along the paths of a tiny neglected garden on the slope of a hill, over-looking the broad river with its splendor as of glinting steel. The shoulder straps and buttons of his white summer uniform grew so hot that it was impossible to touch them. The inner band of his cap was wet with perspiration, his face flamed. . . .

On returning to the hotel he found delicious relief in the shelter of the large, empty, cool dining room; he removed his cap, sat down at a little table before an open window, through which the heat blew —a breeze for all that—and ordered an iced soup of pot herbs. Every-thing was good, in everything there was immeasurable happiness, in-tense joy, even in this sultriness and in these market smells; in the whole unfamiliar little town and in this old provincial hotel it was present, this happiness, and with it all, his heart was simply being rent into shreds. He drank several small glasses of vodka, and made a snack of pickled cucumbers, and he felt that without the least falter-ing he would choose to die tomorrow, if only by some miracle he could return here and spend but this one day with her—if only to have a chance to tell her and somehow prove to her, persuade her of his harrowing and marvelous love . . . But why prove it to her? Why persuade her? He could not tell why, yet it seemed more necessary than life itself.

"My nerves are playing me pranks," he thought, as he poured him-self a fifth glass of vodka.

He considered an entire small decanter, hoping in intoxication to forget, to bring to an end his agonized exultation. But, no, it only grew more intense.

He pushed away the cold herb soup, asked for black coffee, and began to smoke and resolutely to deliberate upon ways and means of freeing himself from this unexpected, sudden love. But to free him-self—he felt this acutely—was impossible. And, suddenly, with a rapid movement, he rose, picked up his cap and crop, and, asking where the post office was, quickly went in the direction indicated, with the phrasing of a telegram already in his head: "Henceforth my life is wholly yours, unto death, to do with what you will." On reaching the thick-walled house, which sheltered the post and telegraph office, he paused in horror: he knew the town where she lived, he knew that she had a husband and a three-year-old daughter, but he knew neither her first name nor her surname! Several times in the course of the evening he had asked her, and each time she laughed and said:

"Why must you know who I am? I am Maria Green, Fairyland Queen. . . . Or simply the lovely stranger. . . . Isn't that enough for you?"

On the corner, near the post office, was a photographic showcase. He looked steadily at a large portrait of a military man with elaborate epaulettes, with bulging eyes and low forehead, with surprisingly magnificent whiskers and expansive chest, all decorated with orders. . . . How absurdly ridiculous, how horribly ordinary it all was, because his heart had been vanquished, he understood it now—by this terrible "sunstroke," this intense love, this intense happiness. He glanced at a bridal couple—a young man in a long frock coat and white necktie, his hair cut in hedge-hog style; on his arm, in bridal veil—but he then diverted his gaze to the portrait of a good-looking, spirited girl in a student's cap perched awry. . . . Then, tormented by a harrowing envy toward all these strangers, *non-suffering* human beings, he began to look fixedly down the street.

"Where can I go? What can I do?" the insoluble, oppressive question persisted in his mind and soul.

The street was deserted. The houses were all alike, white two-storied, middle class, with large gardens, and they gave the appearance of being uninhabited; a thick white dust covered the pavement; all this dazzled; everything was drenched with the hot, flaming, joyous, seemingly aimless sunshine. In the distance the street rose, humped and pressed against the pure, cloudless, grayish horizon, reflecting lilac. There was something southern in this, reminiscent of Sebastopol, Kertch . . . Anapu. The thought of the last was particularly unbearable. And the lieutenant, with lowered head, screwing up his eyes against the light, with fixed gaze on the ground, reeling, stumbling, spur catching on spur, retraced his footsteps.

He returned to the hotel, shattered with fatigue, as if he had performed a long journey in Turkestan or the Sahara. Gathering his last strength, he entered his large, desolate room. The room had already been cleaned, and her last traces removed—only a solitary hairpin, forgotten by her, lay on the tiny table by the bed! He took off his jacket and glanced in the mirror: his face—the ordinary face of an officer, swarthy from sunburn, with whitish sun-bleached mustaches and bluish-white eyes, seeming against the sunburn whiter than they were—now showed a disraught, insane expression, and in his thin white shirt with standing starched collar there was something youthful and infinitely pathetic. He lay down on the bed, on his back, and rested his dust-covered boots on the footboard. The windows were open, the curtains lowered, and from time to time the light breeze filled them, blowing into the room sultriness and the odor of hot roofs and of all that luminous, now quite desolate, mute, unpeopled world of the Volga. He lay with his arms under his head and gazed fixedly into space. His head held the dim picture of the remote south, of the sun, the sea, Anapu, and it was something fabulous—as if the town to which she had gone, the town in which she had doubtless arrived, was like no other town—and with it all their ripened the persistent thought of pungent, hot tears—and at last fell asleep. When he again opened his eyes there was already visible, through the curtains, the darkening reddish evening sun. The breeze had died down, the room was stuffy and dry, as in a wind furnace. . . . And he remembered yesterday and this morning precisely as if they had been ten years ago.

In no great haste he rose, in no great haste he washed himself; then he pulled the curtains aside, rang for the servant, asked for a samovar and his bill, and for a long time he drank tea with lemon. Then he ordered a cab and had his luggage taken out, and, seating himself in the reddish, burnt-out seat of the carriage, he gave the servant a whole five rubles as a tip.

"It looks, Your Honor, as though I brought you here last night!" said the cabby cheerfully, as he seized the reins.

When they reached the pier, the blue summer night already darkened above the Volga and many varicolored flames were scattered upon the river and flames hung in the mast of the approaching steamer.

"Got you here just in time!" said the cabby ingratiatingly.

The lieutenant also gave him five rubles, then with ticket in hand went to the pier. . . . Even as yesterday there was the soft sound of the hawsers, and the light dizziness from the vacillation under foot; then came the flying end of the cable, the clamor of the seething waters under the wheels of the steamer receding from the impact. . . . And the sight of the much-peopled steamer, ablaze with light, and the smells of its kitchens, seemed to extend a warm welcome.

Another minute, and the steamer was under way, going up the river, in the direction in which it had borne her away that same morning.

Ahead of it, the dark summer sunset was rapidly fading; gloomily, dreamily and iridescently, it was reflected in the river, showing patches glimmering with tremulous ripples in the distance under the sunset, and the flames scattered in the darkness round the steamer went on receding and receding.

The lieutenant sat under cover on deck, conscious of having aged by ten years.

Yuri Kazakov is a writer who describes but does not judge. His approach is objective, his prose unadorned. The tone of his work is often bitter, nearly always melancholy. Solitude and defeat form his central themes. In what ways are Ageyev and Vika defeated in this story?

Yuri Kazakov was born in 1928 and was trained as a musician (double bass). In 1953 he entered the Gorky Literary Institute, where he began to write serious fiction. The characters he creates are often anti-heroes—weakly passive people who are alienated from Soviet society and from each other. Further Reading: Selected Short Stories (1964), Going to Town and Other Stories (1964).

UNION OF SOVIET
SOCIALIST REPUBLICS

Adam and Eve

YURI KAZAKOV

The painter Ageyev was staying at a hotel in a northern town where he had come to paint the fishermen. The town was spaciously laid out; it had broad squares, streets, and avenues, and because of this it looked empty.

It was autumn. Low, ragged clouds came scudding from the west over the grey-brown woods misted with hoar-frost, it rained a dozen times a day, and the lake loomed over the town like a leaden wall. Ageyev stayed late in bed, smoked on an empty stomach, and stared at the window lined and streaming with rain. Below it the roofs of the houses gleamed sullenly, reflecting the sky; the room reeked of tobacco smoke and of some-

"Adam and Eve" by Yuri Kazakov, translated by Manya Harari, from *Half-Way to the Moon* edited by Patricia Blake and Max Hayward. Copyright © 1963 by Encounter Ltd. Reprinted by permission of Holt, Rinehart and Winston, Inc., and Weidenfeld & Nicolson Ltd., London.

thing else peculiar to hotel rooms. His head ached, he had a ceaseless buzzing in his ears and an occasional twinge of pain in his heart.

Ageyev had been talented from his childhood up, and now, at twenty-five, his expression was scornful: there was a disdain, a weariness about the drooping brown eyelids and the lower lip, and his dark eyes were languid and arrogant. He wore a velvet jacket and a beret, and walked with a slouch, his hands in his pockets, hardly seeming to give an inattentive glance to people in the street or indeed to anything he came across in general, but retaining of everything a memory so indestructibly sharp that his breast actually ached with it.

There was nothing for him to do in the town itself and he spent the morning sitting at the table in his room holding his head, or lying down, waiting for 12 o'clock when the bar would open downstairs. When at last it came he walked down unsteadily, and each time looked with hatred at the picture in the hall. The picture showed the the near-by lake with its inlets, and an unnaturally orange growth of stunted birches on the ledges of unnaturally purple rocks. It was autumn in the picture as well.

In the bar he ordered a brandy and squinting inwards with the effort of not spilling it slowly drank it down. Having drunk, he lit a cigarette, and looked round at whoever might be there as he waited impatiently for the first jolting warmth which he knew would at once make him feel well, and lovingly disposed to everything—life, people, the town, and even the rain.

After that he would go out and walk about the streets, wondering where to go with Vika, and what to do in general and how to go on living. A couple of hours later he was back in the hotel; by then he was sleepy and he went to bed and slept.

And when he woke up he went down again, to the restaurant. Now the day was nearly over, it was dusk outside the windows, and when evening came the jazz band in the restaurant struck up. Girls with made-up faces came in, sat in pairs at little tables, chewed wax-like chops, drank vermouth, danced with anyone who asked them, and wore an expression of happiness and of intoxication with high life. Ageyev gazed in misery round the large, familiar, smoke-filled hall. He hated the girls, and their boyfriends, and the wretched band with its piercing pipes and thumping drums, and the awful food, and the local vodka which the waitress invariably served short.

At midnight the restaurant closed. Ageyev staggered back to his third floor, wheezed as he fumbled at the keyhole, undressed, made mooing noises, ground his teeth, and pitched headlong into blackness until morning.

That day was like all the others, but on the next at 2 o'clock he went to meet Vika's train. He arrived early and, with only a brief glance at the platform and the passengers with their luggage, went straight into the refreshment room. Yet there had been a time when the mere sight of a railway platform excited him and filled him with wander-lust.

A tall waitress with red hair brought him his vodka.

'What a girl,' Ageyev muttered, his eyes following her with greedy pleasure, and when she came up to him again he said: 'Hello, baby. You're just what I've been looking for all my life.'

The waitress smiled unmoved. She was used to hearing this sort of thing from almost everyone. People would drop in for half an hour and sit muttering—usually vulgarities—never to come back and see the station or the red-haired waitress again.

'I must paint you,' said Ageyev, getting tipsy. 'I'm an artist.'

She shifted the glasses on his table and smiled: she liked hearing it all the same.

'You listen to me, I'm a genius, I'm known in the West! What about it?'

'It is not us the artists come to paint.' She spoke with a slightly un-Russian accent.

'How do you know?' He looked at her breast.

'Oh! They always want fishermen. And workmen—signalmen. Or else there's a little island with a wooden church—they all go there, they come . . . from Moscow, from Leningrad. And they're all like you—with berets—that what you call them?'

'They're all idiots. Well, we'll meet again, eh?' he added hurriedly as he heard the sound of the approaching train. 'What's your name?'

'Zhanna, if you must know.'

'You're not Russian, are you?'

'No, I'm a Finn. Yuonaleinen.'

'Hell of a name,' Ageyev mumbled, finishing his vodka and coughing.

He paid, gave Zhanna's shoulder a squeeze, and walked out on to the platform in high spirits. 'What a waste of a woman!' he thought, screwing up his eyes at the light-blue express as its coaches flashed past him. The eyestrain made him feel giddy and he turned away. 'Shouldn't have had that drink,' he thought absentmindedly and, in a sudden fright at the thought of Vika's arrival, lit a cigarette.

The passengers were already moving from the train to the exit. He sighed, threw the cigarette away, and went to look for Vika. She saw him first and shouted to him. He turned and watched her as she came towards him in her fleecy black coat. The coat swung unfastened and her knees pushing at the hem of her skirt made it billow out.

She shyly gave him her net-gloved hand. Her hair, bleached by the sun, short and ruffled, fell over her forehead. From under it her slanted Tartar eyes looked up at him alarmed, while her mouth was crimson and taut, with dry cracked lips half open like a child's.

'Hello,' she said a little breathlessly, and wanted to go on, perhaps to say something gay and clever, prepared in advance, but faltered into silence.

Ageyev unaccountably fixed his eyes on the transparent scarf round her neck, then with a scared schoolboy expression snatched her shiny suitcase from her, and together they walked down the wide street from the station.

'Your face is a bit puffy somehow . . .' she said. 'How are you getting on?' She looked around her. 'I like it here.'

'Ugh!' He made the unpleasant guttural sound he always used to express contempt.

'Have you been drinking?' She pushed her hands into her pockets and bent her head. Her hair fell forward.

'Ugh!' he said again, with a side-glance at Vika.

Vika was very pretty and about her clothes, her ruffled hair, her way of speaking, there was something elusively Muscovite to which he had become unused in the north. In Moscow they had only met a couple of times, they didn't know each other properly, and her arrival, the leave he knew she had wangled with difficulty, and the fact—which he also sensed—that she was ready for anything, all struck him as somehow unexpected and strange.

'I'm lucky with women,' he thought with pleased surprise, and deliberately stopped as if to put on his gloves, but really to look at Vika from the back. She slowed down, half-turning and looking at him questioningly, then glanced round absentmindedly at the shops and the passers-by.

She was pretty from the back as well, and the fact that she had not walked on but slowed down with that interrogative glance which seemed in itself to express her dependence on him—all this pleased him enormously, even though a moment ago he had felt embarrassed and confused by her arrival. He vaguely realized that he had only had that drink to get rid of his embarrassment.

'I've brought you your press cuttings,' said Vika when he had caught up with her. 'You know they're giving you hell? There was a terrific row going on at the exhibition the day I went.'

'Ugh!' he said again, though with profound satisfaction, adding in immediate alarm: 'They haven't taken down the "Kolkhoz Girl"?'

'No, it's still up,' Vika laughed. 'Nobody can make head or tail of it, they're all shouting and arguing—the boys with the beards and the jeans, they don't know where they are, they're going round in circles.'

'And you, do you like it?'

Vika smiled vaguely, and Ageyev, suddenly furious, frowned and snorted, pouting his lower lip, his dark eyes listless and sullen. 'I'll get drunk,' he decided.

And all that day he walked about the town with Vika like a stranger, yawned, mumbled indistinguishable answers to her questions, waited at the pier while she found out the times of the steamers, and in the evening got drunk, hard as she begged him not to, locked himself in his room, and, while knowing with deep, acute pain that she was alone in hers, upset and bewildered, only smoked and sniggered to himself. And thought about red-haired Zhanna.

The telephone rang a couple of times. He knew it was Vika, but let it ring. 'Go chase yourself, you silly goose,' he thought furiously.

The next day Vika woke Ageyev early and made him wash and dress while she packed his rucksack herself, dragged his paintbox, easel, and fishing tackle from under the bed, looked in the desk drawers, clinked empty bottles, and was generally aloof and businesslike, paying him no attention whatever.

'Just like a wife,' thought Ageyev, watching her in amazement. He scowled and thought how quickly a woman could get used to a man and become as cold and masterful as if they had been living together for ages.

He had a headache and wanted to go down to the bar but, remembering it wouldn't yet be open, coughed, grunted, lit a cigarette on an empty stomach, and felt still worse. Meanwhile, Vika had been down and paid the bill and called a taxi. 'Oh hell, let her,' he thought dully, going out and getting into it. He sat back and closed his eyes. The early morning rain meant that it would rain all day. It even began to snow, the heavy, wet flakes falling fast and turning black almost before the first touch of the wet roofs and pavements.

At the pier Ageyev felt worse than ever. Overcome with misery, half asleep and without an idea of why or where he was going, he listened drowsily to the wind hooting and whistling, water smacking the landing steps, motor-boats starting up on a high note, spluttering and dying down. Vika too had quite lost her spirits and was sad and cold as she sat beside him looking round helplessly, wilting in her short tight trousers and still bareheaded. The wind ruffled her hair and blew it over her forehead, and she looked as if she had just received a telegram and was going to a funeral.

'She would wear trousers,' Ageyev thought spitefully, closing his eyes and trying to make himself comfortable against the wooden partition. 'Where the devil am I off to? God, I feel awful!'

They could hardly wait for their boat and watched impatiently as it pulled alongside, hissing, steaming, pounding, creaking against the pier and scraping white shavings off its timber stanchions.

Even when they went aboard Ageyev felt no better. Somewhere down below, where everything blissfully seethed and rumbled, and yellow pistons went up and down in hot oil, it was warm, but the forward cabin was gloomy, cold, and had a musty smell. The wind

howled, the waves splashed against the sides of the ship, and glasses
tinkled nervously as it gently lurched. Brown, thinned-out woods,
villages darkened by the rain, buoys and battered markers drifted
slowly past the bleary portholes. Ageyev shivered feverishly and went
out.

After wandering about on the ribbed metal flooring of the lower
deck, he found shelter next to the engine room and close to the
restaurant. The restaurant was not yet open, although an evil smell
came from the salt cod cooking in the galley. Ageyev climbed on to
the warm top of a metal bunker, leaned against a stack of birch logs
glossy in their satin bark, and listened to the measured sighing of the
engine, the splashing of the paddles and the discordant voices of the
passengers. As usual those who were still excited by their send-off
were gabbling noisily and cracking jokes, while from the stern came
the sounds of a concertina, shouts, and the loud tapping of heels on
the iron deck.

Near the hot water tap tea was being brewed in mugs and teapots,
and people sat on bundles and suitcases, drinking it and breaking
pieces off French rolls, glancing out, warm and cosy, at the dark dis-
hevelled waves which the wind chased across the lake. Women were
taking off their kerchiefs and doing their hair, children had already
settled down to play and were running and bustling about.

The lights went on, yellow through frosted glass, and at once it
became still more dark and cold outside. Ageyev idly shifted his gaze.
The gangways were cluttered up with sacks of potatoes, hampers,
barrels of gherkins and bales of other stuff. The passengers were all
people from the neighbourhood, making their way to some place or
other up the coast, and their talk was all of local things: cattle, new
regulations, mothers-in-law, fishing, the lumber camps, and the
weather.

'It doesn't matter!' thought Ageyev. 'It's only one day—then the
island, a cottage, silence and solitude . . . It doesn't matter!'

The restaurant opened at last, and immediately Vika pushed her
way towards him through the crowd. She gave him a sad look and a
smile.

'Want a drink, you poor dear?' she said. 'Well go along and get it!'

Ageyev went and came back with a small bottle and some bread
and gherkins. Vika, who had climbed on to the bunker, met him with
a look of attentive concern. He sat down next to her, worked the cork
out of the bottle, took a pull at it and munched a gherkin. Feeling
better, he turned to her with a certain animation.

'Eat!' he mumbled, and Vika too began to eat.

'Tell me, what's the matter with you?' she asked after a while.

Ageyev had another drink and thought a while. Then he lit a
cigarette and looked down at the suede shoe dangling from Vika's
foot.

'Just fed up, old girl,' he said quietly. 'I expect I'm just no good as
an artist and a fool as well. Here I am painting on and on with everybody telling me it's no good, it's all wrong . . .

'What do they say? "Ideological immaturity!" "On a slippery slope!"
"A spirit alien to our people!" . . . As if the whole nation were behind
them nodding in agreement. You know?'

You're silly!' Vika said gently. She suddenly laughed and put her
head on his shoulder. Her hair had a strange, bitter smell. Ageyev
rubbed his cheek against it and shut his eyes.

Suddenly she was close and dear to him. He remembered the first
time he kissed her in Moscow, in the passage at the flat of an artist
friend. He had arrived a little drunk and gay, Vika was quiet and
looked bewildered; they had had a long talk in the kitchen, or rather
he had talked to her, telling her he was a genius and no one else was
any good. Then they went to join the others and in the passage he
kissed her and told her he was terribly in love with her.

She didn't believe him but she caught her breath and blushed, her
eyes dark and her lips dry, and began to chatter and laugh with some
other girls who were there without looking at him again. He too stuck
to the men, arguing about some drawings or other, and he and Vika
sat in different rooms.

Vika talked and giggled with her girl-friends and with someone
who kept coming in and going out, feeling happy because he was in
the next room sitting in an arm-chair and, like her, making conversation with someone. She told him so afterwards.

It was good now, in this out-of-the-way place in the north, suddenly to remember that recent yet for ever vanished evening. It meant
that they had a past. They did not yet really love each other, nothing
bound them together, they were still seeing other people who had
been in their lives before, they had never spent a night together, they
still didn't know one another. But they already had a past, and this
was good.

'Seriously,' said Ageyev, 'out here I've kept on thinking about my
life. You know it was horrid here without you, pouring with rain and
nowhere to go. I sat in my room or downstairs, drunk, and kept
brooding . . . I've just about had enough. When I was at art school
I used to imagine I'd turn everything upside down, I'd knock them
all sideways with my painting. I'd travel, I'd live in a cave—like a
sort of Rockwell Kent, you know. Then I got my diploma and at once
they started on me—'You bastard, you so-and-so!'—preaching at me.
They haven't stopped hounding me ever since, the swine. And the
longer it goes on the worse it gets. "You abstractionist, you neo-real-
ist, you formalist, you've got this and that deviation—just you wait,
we'll get you!" . . .'

He moved a little aside from her and had another drink. His head-

ache had stopped, and he felt like sitting and talking and thinking
on and on, because Vika was sitting next to him and listening. He
looked at her out of the corner of his eyes—her face was alive and
grave, the eyes under their shadow of lashes long and black. He looked
closer—they really were black, and her lips were rough, and Ageyev's
heart began to thump. As for Vika, she had tucked up her feet on
the bunker, unfastened her coat, propped her chin on her knees and
was gazing into his face.

'You're not looking well,' she said, touching his chin. 'You haven't
shaved, you're so rough.'

'I'm kind of stale,' he grinned and looked away at the lake. 'I keep
on thinking about myself and Van Gogh . . . Do I really have to
kick the bucket too before they take me seriously? As if my colours,
my drawing, my figures weren't as good as theirs. All those opportunists—I'm sick of the whole business!'

'You don't expect time-servers to admit you're any good,' she said
quickly, as though by the way.

'Why not?'

'I just don't know . . . For them to recognize you they'd have to
recognize they've been wrong all their lives.'

'Oh!' Ageyev lit a cigarette and smoked it in silence, looking at his
feet and rubbing his face; the stubble on his shallow cheeks scraped
against his fingers. 'Three years!' he said. 'And I'm still doing illustra-
tions to earn my keep. Three years since I finished art school, and
there are good-for-nothings who envy me: "Ah, he's famous! Ah, he's
known in the West . . ." Idiots. If they only knew. Every picture I
do . . . And I still haven't a studio. You paint a spring landscape—it's
the wrong spring! It isn't nature, it's biology! they say. What do you
think of that? You can't get into a show, the selection committees
make your life a misery, and if you do get in with something unim-
portant it's still worse. And the reviewers! They rave about being
modern, but what they understand by it is beneath contempt. And
the lies they tell, and if they do say a word of truth it's only for a
demagogic end!'

'And has there never been a word of truth said about you?' She
broke off a sliver of birch and nibbled it thoughtfully.

'Oh you!' Ageyev went pale. 'You little college girl! You're still on
the sidelines, you haven't run foul of them, you've got your books,
your dialectical materialism, your field-work . . . If they say "man", it
has to be with a capital M. Their enlightened gaze sees nothing but
Man as a Whole—the country, whole millennia, the cosmos! One
individual is no good to them. They don't think about him. You have
to give them millions. They hide behind the millions, and we, those
of us who are something we're beatniks . . . Spiritual teddy boys,
that's what we are! We haven't a heroic style!' He laughed unpleas-
antly. 'We don't portray the masses! There they are, the masses,'

Ageyev nodded at the passengers. 'And I love them, and it makes me sick to drool over them in ecstasy. I love them in the flesh—their eyes, their hands—see? Because it's they who hold up the earth. That's the whole point. If everyone is good, then society is good as well, that's what I'm telling you! I think about it day and night. I'm in a bad way, I've no commissions, no money. To hell with it, I don't mind. What matters is that I'm right all the same, and let nobody try to teach me. It's life that teaches me—and as for being optimistic and believing in the future and in those masses they go on about—I can give 100 yards start to any one of those critics.'

He snorted, his nostrils flared, and his eyes clouded.

'It's bad for you to drink . . .' Vika said softly, looking up at him with pity.

'Wait a second!' Ageyev said hoarsely. 'I've got something the matter with me . . . asthma or something. Can't breathe properly.'

His cigarette had gone out, he lit it and inhaled but had a fit of coughing and threw it down, putting one foot on the floor to stamp it out. He looked at Vika and made a face.

'Get out of the way, I'm going to bed!' He blinked angrily, got off the bunker and went below.

While they were talking the heating had been turned on, the cabin was warm and the porthole had steamed over. Sitting beside it, Ageyev rubbed the glass with his sleeve; his left eyelid was twitching. He knew that Vika was now his salvation. But there was something about her that infuriated him. She had come to him . . . fresh, pretty, in love—oh hell! Why, why did he always have to be arguing and proving something or other? And to her of all people! To Vika, who had come all that way, her heart turning over and her knees weak at the thought of their first night together, of him, of holding him close to her, and he the drunken devil . . . Oh God! And it would all have been all right, perfect—if only she had agreed with him at once, if she had said, 'Yes, you're right!' He would have gone out of his mind with joy, he would have carried her off to the lake, to a cottage, he would have sat her by the window and rushed to his canvas. Her tiny face, her slanted eyes and sun-bleached hair, her chin propped on her fist . . . He might never paint anything better in his life! Oh God!

He began to take off his clothes, feeling lonely and sorry for himself to the point of tears. 'What the hell,' he thought, 'it doesn't matter! It isn't the first time!' He shuddered at the things he had said to her. He must work, not talk.

When he was undressed he climbed on to the upper bunk and turned to the wall, but even then went on moving his head about restlessly on the shiny pillow-case, unable to settle down.

It was evening by the time the steamer neared the island. A brief
sunset, dim and remote, burnt itself out, and dusk was falling as the
boat nosed its way through countless reefs. They could now see the
church with its many domes; as they drew closer to the island it
shifted on the horizon, now right, now left, and at one moment was
behind them.

Vika had a stubborn, hurt face. Ageyev whistled between his teeth,
glancing indifferently from side to side at the flat islands and the
villages, and inspecting with some interest the splendid boats which
looked like Viking sailing ships.

When they came right up to the island, they saw a windmill and a
beautiful ancient farmhouse with its outbuildings and barns—all
empty and without a sign of life, like pieces in a museum. Ageyev
grinned.

'Just the right thing for me,' he muttered, looking at Vika with
rage. 'Right in the forefront of the seven-year plan as you might say—
no?'

Vika said nothing. Her expression was now withdrawn as if she had
planned it all in advance and come on her own and found everything
as expected.

No one except the two of them landed on the island. And there
was no one on the open wooden landing-stage except an old woman
with a lantern shining, although it was still daylight.

'Well, here we are, you and I, like Adam and Eve.' Ageyev grinned
again, stepping down on the damp planks of the jetty.

Vika again made no reply.

A woman in a wadded coat and boots appeared on the bank,
smiling in welcome while she was still far off.

'Only the two of you?' she shouted gaily as she hurried towards
them, shifting her eyes from one to the other. When she came up to
them she took Vika's suitcase from her and talked to them as if they
were long-expected guests.

'Well, thank goodness,' she rattled on in her friendly voice, climbing up the bank. 'I was beginning to think no one else would come
this year, the season was over, time to dig in for the winter, and now
you've come. I'll take you to our hotel.'

'Hotel?' Ageyev asked in his disagreeable voice.

The woman laughed.

'They all say that, they're all surprised, though it's more than a year
since I came. Had my old man with me but he died. Now I'm alone.
Certainly there's a hotel! For tourists and artists and people like that.
There's a lot of them come in the summer and stay on and paint.'

Thinking of his misery at the hotel, Ageyev sighed and screwed up
his face. He had been looking forward to a cottage, a small farmhouse
with a smell of cows and a porch and an attic.

But the hotel turned out to be attractive. There was a big stove in the kitchen, and three bedrooms—all empty, and another very odd room with slender pillars down the middle, carved and painted in old-Russian style, supporting the ceiling, and big modern windows reaching to the floor on three sides, as in a glassed-in hall.

In every bedroom there were bare beds showing their webbing and bare bedside tables of rough wood.

Ageyev and Vika chose a room with a stove and a window to the south. Framed water-colours hung on the walls. Ageyev glanced at them and twitched his lip. They were painstaking student sketches of either the church or the windmill.

The landlady kept going in and out carrying sheets, pillows, and pillow-cases, and with them came a good smell of clean linen.

'Well, now you can settle down,' she said, pleased. 'That's nice. I get bored all by myself. It's nice in summer with all those jolly painters, but now there's hardly another soul on the island.'

'How do we manage about food?' asked Vika.

'Oh, you won't starve,' she shouted cheerfully from somewhere down the passage. 'There's a village at the other end of the island, you can get milk and things, or there's a shop on Pog Island, you can go by boat. Are you from Leningrad?'

'No, Moscow,' said Vika.

'Well, that's nice, we always get Leningraders. I've plenty of logs and kindling—they were restoring the church last summer, a lot of stuff was left over. And I've got the keys of the church. When you want to go just tell me and I'll open it up.'

The landlady went away and Vika, happy and tired, flopped on her bed.

'It's too good to be true!' she said. 'It really is! It's brilliant of you, my darling Adam. Do you like baked potatoes?'

Ageyev smirked, twitched his lip and went out. He walked quietly past the graveyard round the church. It had grown dark and, as he walked towards it from the east, the church towered above him with its magnificent silhouette, luminous in the spaces between its onion domes and in the open arches of its belfry. Two birds were calling to each other from different places in measured, monotonous voices, and there was a strong smell of grass and of autumn cold.

'It's the end of the world,' thought Ageyev as he passed the church and came to the lake. He went down to the landing-stage and sat on a bollard, looking at the west. A couple of hundred yards away there was another island, flat and bare except for willow bushes. Beyond it lay still another, and there seemed to be a village: a lone light shone far off through the trees. Soon a motor-boat started up on a high thin note somewhere over there, and went on and on, then suddenly spluttered out.

Ageyev felt lonely, but he sat on smoking, getting used to the silence and the clean smell of the autumn freshness and the water, thinking about himself, about his pictures, thinking that he was a messiah, a great artist, and that here he was, all alone at the end of the world, while various critics who lived in Gorky Street in Moscow were at this moment sitting with girls in restaurants, drinking brandy, eating roast chicken, wiping their greasy lips with their napkins and uttering various fine and lofty words, and that everything they said was a lie, because they weren't thinking about lofty things but only about getting the girls into bed. And in the mornings they would take coffee for their hangover and drops for their heart condition, and write articles about him, and again tell lies, because not one of them believed in what he wrote but only thought of how much he would get for it, and not one of them had ever sat in solitude on a damp pier, looking at a dark, uninhabited island and preparing for creative achievement.

These thoughts were both sad and comforting: there was a bitter sweetness in them. He enjoyed thinking such thoughts and he often did.

At one moment he found himself mentally humming the tune, remembered out of the blue, of the old Countess's solo in *The Queen of Spades*. And this ghostly music—which he heard somewhere deep inside him with all its orchestral accompaniment including the sinister note of the clarinets and the bassoons and the painful suspense of the pauses—began to terrify him because it was death.

Then, as suddenly and sharply, to the point of pain, like the longing for air, he felt a longing for the smell of tea—not brewed tea, not tea in a glass, but dry tea leaves. At once there came to him straight out of his childhood, the memory of a milky glass teapot with a touching landscape painted on it, and his dream of living in the little house with the red roof, and the dry rustling sound as his mother took the lid off the teapot and poured the tea leaves in, and the smell as the cloudy-opal teapot filled with darkness.

This immediately made him remember his mother, her love for him, her life lived in him and for him. And himself, so quick and lively, with moments of such unaccountable joy and vitality that he could hardly believe that this could ever have been himself.

With belated pain he thought of how often he had been rude, inconsiderate, and unfeeling towards his mother, how rarely, while he had the chance, he had been willing to listen to her childhood stories of a remote, long-vanished past. Of how little, in his childish selfishness, he had appreciated the constancy of her love, a love such as he had never since experienced from anyone in all his life.

And remembering all this, he at once began to doubt himself and to think that perhaps his critics were right and he was wrong and was doing nothing as it should be done. He thought that all his life some basic idea—an idea in the highest sense—must have been lacking in him. That he had all too often, talented as he was, looked down with lazy indifference on everything except his talent and his life—and this at such a time!

With helpless rage he remembered all the arguments he had had, ever since his student days, with painters, with art experts, with whoever would not accept his view of painting, colour, design. He thought now that the reason he could not convince them, rout them, prove to them his messianic role, was that he lacked the inspiration of an idea. How indeed could you have a prophet without an idea?

So he sat for a long time. Vika came out of the house, walked a little way along the wooden boards towards the shore, stood looking around her and called him in a low voice. He heard her but neither moved nor spoke. And yet he loved her, his heart quickened at the thought of her. And the two of them were like Adam and Eve, alone with the stars and the water on this dark uninhabited island—and it was not for nothing that she had come to him, and how miserable she must have been in that hotel room when he had drunk himself into a stupor and gone away, deserting her!

A bitter alienation, an estrangement from the world came over him and he wanted nothing and no one. He remembered that wild animals when they are sick go off and hide in some far-away place in the forest, there to cure themselves by means of some mysterious herb or else to die. He regretted that it was the fall and the weather was so chilly, that he was in boots and a sweater—how nice, if it were summer, to find a corner of this or some other island, with rocks, sand, and clear water, and to lie all day in the sun and to think of nothing. And to walk barefoot. And fish. And watch sunsets. He realized that he was boundlessly weary—of himself, his thoughts, his corroding doubts, of getting drunk—and that altogether he was ill.

'Nice to go to the south, somewhere by the sea . . .' he thought nostalgically as he got up. Leaving the pier and turning his back on the lake, he again came face to face with the enormous ancient church and the small hotel sheltering beside it. The windows of the hotel shone brightly while the church was dark, locked up, and strange to him. Yet there was something masterful and commanding about the church, something which aroused thoughts of history and of the greatness of the people—and also of quietness and solitude.

'Seg-Pogost,'* he recalled the name of the island and the church. 'Seg-Pogost.'

He walked up to the house and stood on the steps, peering into the darkness, trying to guess at what for so many centuries without him

---

* *Seg*: a Finnish corruption of St Serge; *Pogost*: churchyard.

had lived its own life—the genuine life of the earth, the water, and the people. But he could make out nothing except the dim radiance of the surrounding waters and the few cosmically gleaming tatters of sky in the rifts between the clouds, and so he went inside.

The room was brightly lit by a paraffin lamp. The stove roared and crackled and there was a smell of baked potatoes. Vika was flushed and busy, the whole place had acquired a friendly, lived-in air, and everything in it—the blouses and dresses hanging up or flung on the bed, the black gloves on the bedside table, the powder compact with a zip—told of the presence of a young woman and gave off a smell of scent.

'Where were you?' Vika asked with a quiver of her eyebrows. 'I looked for you.'

Ageyev said nothing and went into the kitchen to wash. There he spent some time inspecting his stubble in the mirror but decided not to shave and only washed, cheerfully clattering the things on the washstand and drying himself on the warm rough towel; then he came back, lay down, put his boots on the headboard, stretched, and lit a cigarette.

'Come and eat,' said Vika.

They ate in silence. Clearly Vika was delighted with her surroundings and her only trouble was Ageyev. The kettle purred and whistled on the stove.

'How long is your leave?' Ageyev asked abruptly.

'Ten days,' Vika sighed. 'Why?'

'Nothing . . .'

'Three days gone,' thought Ageyev.

Again there was a long silence. When they had their tea it was time for bed. Vika blushed hotly and looked in desperation at Ageyev. He looked away and frowned, then got up, lit a cigarette, and walked over to the window. He too was blushing and glad that Vika could not see it. There was rustling sounds behind him; finally Vika couldn't stand it and begged him:

'Do put out the light!'

Without looking at her, Ageyev blew out the flame of the oil lamp, quickly undressed, got into his bed and turned to the wall. 'Just try and come to me,' he thought. But Vika didn't come. She lay so still that he couldn't even hear her breathing.

Some twenty minutes went by; neither of them was asleep and they both knew it. It was dark in the room and the sky outside the window was black. The wind rose and buffeted the walls. Suddenly the window curtain was lit up for a brief moment. Ageyev thought at first that someone had walked past and shone a torch on the wall and the window, but a few seconds later there came a low rumble of thunder.

'There's a storm,' Vika said softly, sitting up in bed and looking at the dark window. 'An autumn storm.'

After another flash and rumble, the wind died down and it began at once to pelt with rain, water gurgled in the rainpipe.

'It's raining,' said Vika. 'I like it when it rains. I like thinking when it rains.'

'You couldn't keep quiet, could you?' Ageyev lit a cigarette and blinked: his eyes were smarting.

'You know what? I'm leaving,' said Vika, and Ageyev felt her hating him. 'I'm going by the first boat. You're nothing but an egoist. I've been thinking and thinking these past two days—what are you? What's the matter with you? Well, I know now—you're just selfish. You talk about the people, about art, but all you think about is yourself and absolutely no one else . . . You don't need anyone. It's revolting! Why on earth did you ask me to come, why? I know why—to pat you on the back and say, "yes, darling," isn't that it? Well, my lad, you can look for another victim. I'm ashamed to think how I pestered the Dean of the Faculty and told lies about my father being ill . . .'

She burst into loud sobs.

'Shut up, you fool!' Ageyev said miserably, realizing it was all over. 'And get out of here, go away, the sooner the better!'

He got up and sat in front of the window, leaning his elbows on the bedside table. It was still raining and there was something large, dark and quivering on the ground outside—he looked at it for a long time before he realized it was a puddle. He wanted to cry, to blink his eyes and rub them with his sleeve as he did when he was a child, but it was many years since he'd been able to cry.

Vika had buried her head in her pillow and lay sobbing and catching her breath, while Ageyev sat still, breaking matchsticks and crumbling cigarette ends in the ash-tray. At first he had felt sick and cold with misery and disgust. Now this had passed, he had somehow risen above it, aloof, detached from pettiness, and feeling sorry for everyone, quiet and saddened by the insurmountable resistance of the human mass. And yet everything deep inside him was boiling, seething, hurt, and he could not be silent, he could no longer smile his condescending smile or get out of things with his loathsome 'Ugh!' He had to say something.

But he said nothing, he only thought, though he wasn't really thinking about anything, only keeping quiet and glancing through the window at the dark, quivering puddle outside. There was a singing, a jangling in his head as if he was ill and had a temperature, and he saw before him an endless procession of people walking silently through the halls of a gallery, their expressions enigmatic, elusive, and sorrowful. 'Why sorrowful?" he was held up by the thought; 'I've got it wrong somehow.' But he was at once distracted and began to think of higher things, of the highest, the loftiest of all, as it seemed to him.

He was thinking that whatever happened he would do what he must. And that no one would stop him. And that in the end this would be to his credit.

He stood up, and without dressing, with swollen veins in his temples, went out on to the porch. There he stood and spat—for some reason his mouth was full of sweetish saliva, it kept filling with it and he kept spitting it out, and there was a lump in his throat, choking him.

'It's all over!' he muttered softly. 'To hell with it. It's all over.'

All next day Ageyev slumped on his bed with his face to the wall. He would go to sleep and wake up and hear Vika walk about the room and round the house. She called him to lunch and to dinner but he lay with his teeth angrily clenched and not opening his eyes, in a kind of stupor, until he fell asleep again.

By the evening his muscles were aching and he was forced to get up. Vika was out; Ageyev went to find the landlady.

'Would you give me the key of the boat,' he begged her. 'I have to go to the shop for some cigarettes.'

The landlady gave him the key of the padlock, told him where to find the oars, and showed him the direction in which to row.

There was a headwind, the oars were heavy and awkward, the boat was heavy too, though so fine to look at, and Ageyev had blisters on his hands by the time he reached the other island.

He bought cigarettes, a bottle of vodka, and some snacks, and walked back to the mooring-stage.

On the way he was overtaken by a stocky, bow-legged fisherman in a winter hat and with a red face.

'Hello, there,' said the fisherman, drawing level with him and looking him over. 'You an artist? From Seg-Pogost?'

He had parcels wrapped in newspaper which he held carefully in both hands and two bottles of vodka stuffed in the pockets of his jacket.

'We've got a party on today! After our steam bath,' he gave the news joyfully as to an old friend. 'Shall we have one for the road?'

The fisherman clumped across into his boat which had an outboard-motor with a bright-green casing, produced four bottles (two out of his trouser pockets), and carefully put three of them down on the tarpaulin in the prow; the fourth he opened at once and after fumbling for an empty jam jar and rinsing it in the lake poured Ageyev a drink. Ageyev drank it down and chewed a biscuit. The fisherman poured one out for himself and climbed ashore.

'Glad to know you,' he said cheerfully. 'Been here long?'

'Only since yesterday,' said Ageyev, inspecting him deliberately.

'Painting the church?' he winked.

'Whatever I find.'

'You should come over and visit our work-gang,' the fisherman offered, the vodka rushing to his head. 'Got a woman with you? We've got women,' he spread his hands, 'like that! See? You'll want to paint the lot, see?'

He went back to the boat for the bottle they had started and poured Ageyev another drink.

'Let's finish it up, shall we?'

'Actually, I've got my own,' said Ageyev, also getting out a bottle.

'We'll drink yours when you come to us,' said the fisherman. 'It's not far; you just say when you want to come and we'll fetch you by motor-boat. We like artists, they're all right. We had a professor from Leningrad staying a while back. He said, never in my life, he said, have I seen people like you!' The fisherman roared with laughter. 'We'll give you fish soup. You'll have a good time, when the girls start making a row it goes on all night. It's a fine life.'

'Where do you fish?' asked Ageyev smiling.

'Off Kizhm Island, but don't worry, we'll fetch you. Or if you think of coming over by yourself just ask for Stepan's gang—that's me, Stepan, get it? Soon as you're out of the reefs, turn left, past the lighthouse, and you'll see the island. You can't miss it. There they'll tell you.'

'I'll certainly come!' Ageyev said happily.

'That's right! You come along! You respect me, right? You treat me like a human being, right? Well, that's all there is to it! That's the lot . . . That's settled then. Right? Well, that's all. Good-bye for now, I've got to run, the boys are waiting . . .'

He climbed over into his boat, unmoored it, pushed off, and started the engine. It set up a thin buzzing. He threw himself into the bows but they reared up all the same; using the tiller the fisherman steered the boat into deep water and skimmed away, leaving a white frothing arc on the water behind him.

Smiling to himself, Ageyev got into his boat and started back. He now sat facing the sunset and he couldn't help stopping and resting on his oars from time to time, to watch the colours of the sky and the lake. Half-way to Seg-Pogost there was a small island, and when he rounded it the wind died down and the water lay still and heavy like molten gold.

In the perfect silence and the calm Ageyev shipped his oars and turned round to look at the church. A rain-cloud, almost like a black wall, rose in the east, while from the west the sun was shedding its last rays, and everything they lit—the island, the church, the windmill, the old farm—seemed, against the cloud, to glow with a particularly ominous red. Far away on the side of the horizon from which the cloud was moving, hung tattered drapes of rain and a huge rainbow shone funereally.

Ageyev settled himself more comfortably in the boat, had another drink, and nibbling a biscuit sat looking at the church. The sun was setting, the cloud was drawing nearer, it already overshadowed almost everything in sight, the rain had by now reached Seg-Pogost. The boat was drifting slightly with the current.

But around Ageyev all was as yet calm and still, while in the west the sky burned with a wide band of misty red flung around the setting sun.

Ageyev sat examining the church and felt like painting it. He was thinking that it was not, of course, only three centuries old, but immeasurably older; it was as old as the earth and the stones. The other thing he couldn't get out of his mind was the image of the jolly fisherman, and he felt like painting him as well.

When he turned to the west the sun had set. The rain had come at last. He pulled his hood over his head and picked up the oars. The heavy rain was for some reason warm and gay, and fish jumped all around him as he rowed.

Coming up to the landing-stage at full tilt, Ageyev saw Vika. She stood motionless in the rain, a plastic raincoat thrown over her shoulders, and watched him as he moored and padlocked the boat, took out the oars and the rucksack with his purchases and stuffed the half-empty bottle into his pocket.

'You can look!' Ageyev thought cheerfully as he walked in silence to the house.

Vika stayed at the pier. Without turning to look at him she continued to watch the lake in the afterglow and the rain.

Coming into the warm room Ageyev saw that her things were no longer around and her suitcase stood by the door. 'Ah!' he said, and lay down. The rain drummed on the roof. Calm and comfortable after his vodka, he shut his eyes and dozed off. He soon woke up; it was not yet dark but the rain had stopped and the sky had cleared and had a cold, high radiance.

Ageyev yawned and went to find the landlady. Taking from her the keys of the church, he went inside the fence which surrounded the churchyard, crossed it, stepping between old tombs, unlocked the door of the bell tower, and started up the dark, narrow, creaking stairs.

There was a smell of jackdaw droppings and of dry wood, and it was dark, but the higher he climbed the more light there was and the cleaner the air. At last he reached the platform of the belfry, his heart wobbly and his legs weak from the sensation of height.

At first, as he climbed on to the platform through the trap-door, he saw only the sky through the arches—high up, with a few fleecy clouds in it and the first large stars, and with light in its depth from the blue rays of the long extinguished sun.

Then as he looked down he saw another sky, as enormous and as light as the one above. Stretching to the horizon on all sides, the whole immeasurable mass of the surrounding water was luminous with reflected light, and the small islands on it were like clouds.

From the moment Ageyev sat down on the balustrade, his arm hooked round a pillar, he never moved again until it was quite dark and Cassiopeia stood out in all its pearly brilliance, and later, after he came down, he walked round and round the church along the path, peering at it this way and that and sighing.

When he came home, the stove was crackling once again. Vika was cooking supper, but she was quiet and already far away.

'Is the boat coming soon? Did you find out?' asked Ageyev.

'At 11 o'clock, I think,' Vika said, after a silence.

Ageyev's heart lurched, he wanted to say something, to ask her some question, but he said nothing and only dragged his paintbox from under the bed, set out paint tubes and small bottles of turpentine on the window-sill and the bed, sorted his brushes, and began to knock at a set of stretchers. Vika kept glancing at him in amazement.

They sat down to supper in silence like the first time, and looked each other in the eyes. Ageyev saw Vika's dry lips, her face suddenly so dear to him. His heart gave another lurch and he realized that the time to say good-bye had come.

He got a bottle of vodka from under the bed and poured out for Vika and himself.

'Well . . .' he said huskily, and cleared his throat. 'Here's to our parting!'

Vika put down her glass without drinking, leaned back in her chair and thus, with her head thrown back, looked at him from under lowered eyelids. Her face was quivering, a vein was throbbing in her neck, her lips moved, it was more than Ageyev could bear to see. He felt hot. Getting up, he opened the window and leaned out for a breath of the strong night air.

'It's stopped raining,' he said, coming back to the table and taking another drink. 'It isn't raining any more.'

'You don't need any money?' asked Vika. 'I've got too much. I brought a lot, you know, thinking . . .' She bit her lip and smiled pitifully.

'No, I don't,' said Ageyev. 'I'll stop drinking now.'

'I still think you're wrong,' Vika said sadly. 'You're just ill. If you gave up drinking everything would go right.'

'Oh, would it,' he grinned. 'I'd have a one-man show at once, would I? Cheers!' He drank again. 'And the opportunists would realize they're no artists, right?'

'Where were you this evening?' Vika asked, after a silence.

'Over there,' he gestured vaguely. 'Upstairs. Calling on God.'

'You won't be coming to Moscow soon?' she asked again, looking at the paints, brushes, and easels scattered round the room.

'Not yet, no,' he said, seeing in his imagination the fisherwomen he would get to know, their legs, their breasts. Their eyes. Seeing them at their work, with clenched teeth and red arms as they hauled the nets. 'In about a month, I should think. Or later still. I'll have a go at painting the fisherfolk. And the water.' He paused. 'And the sky. That's how it is, old girl.'

Vika went outside to listen for the boat.

'It's too early,' she said, coming back. After looking at herself thoughtfully in the mirror she got her scarf out of her suitcase, put it on her head and tied the ends under her chin. Then she sat down and clenched her hands between her knees. She sat in silence, her head bowed low, as if she were sitting at a station, as if Ageyev were unknown to her; her thoughts were far away. Her hair had golden lights under the chiffon scarf. Ageyev lay on the bed, squinting, examining her with curiosity and smoking nervously.

'I can't stand it,' said Vika with a sigh. I'll go to the pier.'

She got up, sighing again, stared for a few seconds fixedly, unblinking, at the lamp, and put on her coat. Ageyev swung his legs to the floor and sat up.

'Well, all right,' he said. 'Good-bye,* old girl! Like me to see you off? . . .'

Vika went to get her identity card from the landlady. Ageyev took a quick drink, snorted, pulled a face and began to dress, looking attentively at his shaking hands and hearing Vika's and the landlady's voices behind the partition. He picked up the suitcase and went out on to the porch. The steps, the handrail, the plankway to the pier, were still damp from the recent rain. He waited for Vika to come out and walked down. She followed him, her heels tapping on the planks.

When they came to the pier Ageyev put the suitcase on the ground and Vika immediately sat down on it, shrank into herself, and froze into stillness. Ageyev shivered with cold and turned up his collar. Suddenly, out of the dead, unnatural silence of the night there came the high, robust sound of a plane. As it approached, it grew louder, stronger, but at the same time lower in tone, more velvety, muffled, as if someone were ceaselessly drawing a bow over the strings of a cello, gradually lowering the peg, until at last it receded, dying down to a low belly rumble.

Once again there was dead silence. After stamping about next to Vika, Ageyev moved away and climbed the bank. He paused at the

---

* *Good-bye* in English in the text.

top, then walked a few steps towards the southern tip of the island and looked round.

The stars were burning steadily overhead, while all over the reefs on the water below were small red and white lights gleaming and blinking on buoys and markers. Suddenly it was as if a breath rushed through the sky; the stars blinked and shuddered. The sky grew black, shuddered again and rose, filling with blue trembling light. Ageyev turned to look at the north and immediately saw its origin. From behind the church—from behind its silent blackness—there came, spreading its beams and swaying, billowing, folding in and swelling out, the faint, pale-blue-golden radiance of the Northern Lights. Whenever they flared out everything—the lake, the shore, the stones, and the wet grass—shone, and the church stood out in firm silhouette; when it faded everything became diminished, and obscure, and vanished.

The earth was turning. Ageyev suddenly felt it with his legs and his heart as it turned and flew, together with its lakes, cities, people and their hopes—turned and flew, ringed with light, into frightening infinity. And here he stood upon this earth, this island, in the silent light of the night, and Vika was leaving him. Adam was being left by Eve—and not at some uncertain future time but now, at once. And it was like death, which you can laugh at from a distance but cannot even bear to think about when it is close beside you.

He couldn't bear it and walked quickly back to the landing-stage, feeling his boots getting soaked through in the wet grass, seeing nothing in the darkness but knowing that now they were black and shiny.

When he came back to the pier the lantern was already shining on a post, the old woman stood yawning on the steps below, while from beyond a low hill in the north came a new beam, trembling like the Aurora but warmer in tone. The beam shifted, there came the quick noises of paddles, and suddenly, high and resonant, the ship's siren, echoing on and on from island to island.

'Did you see the Northern Lights? It was that, wasn't it?' Vika asked in a quick and low voice. She was excited and no longer sitting on her suitcase but standing by the railings.

'Yes, I saw,' Ageyev cleared his throat.

The ship wheeled into sight round a bend and could now be heard more clearly. The small star of its searchlight shone brightly in the bow. Now the light reached the landingstage and the lamp glistened on the planks. The engines stopped and the ship drifted on of its own momentum towards the pier. The old woman shielded her eyes with her hand from the brilliant light, peering at something on board. Turning his back on the searchlight Ageyev saw its beam tremble smokily on the beautiful old farm as if spotlighting an antique.

As the steamer pulled alongside the searchlight turned and flooded the pier with a dazzling milky brightness. Vika and Ageyev watched silently as the ship was moored. A sailor on deck flung the end of the cable to the old woman. The old woman unhurriedly slipped the loop over a bollard. The sailor bent down and wound the cable in. The cable tautened and creaked and the pier shuddered. The steamer softly bumped against it. The sailor let down the gangway and stood under the lamp, checking the ticket of some passenger who was getting off. At last he let him through and turned to Vika and Ageyev.

'Coming aboard?' he asked uncertainly.

'Well, off with you,' said Ageyev, giving Vika's shoulder a careless pat. 'All the best!'

Her lips trembled.

'Good-bye,' she said, and climbed on deck, her shoes tapping on the gangway.

The boat was almost empty, the lower deck dimly lit and the cabin portholes dark. Either there was no one in the cabins or the passengers were asleep. Steam hissed between the ship's side and the pier and floated up in transparent puffs.

Vika went below without looking back and vanished in the ship's bowels. The siren shrieked hurriedly—one long and three short blasts, the old woman slipped the noose off the bollard, the gangway was pulled up, the ventilators clanged shut on deck—and the boat, a warm, familiar, breathing creature, the only thing alive in the cold night, was pulling out, gurgling with its paddles and whirling sharply right.

The old woman yawned again, muttered that the Northern Lights were early this year and this meant a hard winter, picked up her lantern and walked up the bank, throwing a patch of light in front of her, smearing yellow light over her boots and carrying on her side a big unsteady shadow which, as she swung the lantern, leapt from the bank over the pier into the lake.

Ageyev stood still smoking a cigarette, and walked back to the warm hotel. The Northern Lights were still flashing but were now faint and all of the same colour—white.

Clifton Fadiman once described Ernest Hemingway as "the hero who distrusts heroism; the prophet of those who are without faith." Does this quotation apply to the following story? Why is the abortion in "Hills like White Elephants" not openly discussed? What is thus implied about the central characters? How does Hemingway's clipped and bare prose reinforce the story's theme?

Hemingway was born in Illinois in 1899 and died of self-inflicted shotgun wounds in 1961. A world-wanderer and expatriate writer, Hemingway was a war correspondent and soldier, a big game hunter and aficionado of bullfighting. His first book, Three Stories and Ten Poems, *was published in 1923. In 1954 he was awarded both the Pulitzer Prize and the Nobel Prize for his novel* The Old Man and the Sea. *Further Reading:* The Sun Also Rises (1926), Men without Women (1927), A Farewell to Arms (1929).

UNITED STATES
OF AMERICA

Hills like White Elephants

ERNEST HEMINGWAY

The hills across the valley of the Ebro were long and white. On this side there was no shade and no trees and the station was between two lines of rails in the sun. Close against the side of the station there was the warm shadow of the building and a curtain, made of strings of bamboo beads, hung across the open door into the bar, to keep out flies. The American and the girl with him sat at a table in the shade, outside the building. It was very hot and the express from Barcelona would come in forty minutes. It stopped at this junction for two minutes and went on to Madrid.

"What should we drink?" the girl asked. She had taken off her hat and put it on the table.

"It's pretty hot," the man said.

"Let's drink beer."

"Dos cervezas," the man said into the curtain.

"Big ones?" a woman asked from the doorway.

"Yes. Two big ones."

The woman brought two glasses of beer and two felt pads. She put the felt pads and the beer glasses on the table and looked at the man and the girl. The girl was looking off at the line of hills. They were white in the sun and the country was brown and dry.

"They look like white elephants," she said.

"I've never seen one," the man drank his beer.

"No, you wouldn't have."

"I might have," the man said. "Just because you say I wouldn't have doesn't prove anything."

The girl looked at the bead curtain. "They've painted something on it," she said. "What does it say?"

"Anis del Toro. It's a drink."

"Could we try it?"

The man called "Listen" through the curtain. The woman came out from the bar.

"Four reales."

"We want two Anis del Toro."

"With water?"

"Do you want it with water?"

"I don't know," the girl said. "Is it good with water?"

"It's all right."

"You want them with water?" asked the woman.

"Yes, with water."

"It tastes like licorice," the girl said and put the glass down.

"That's the way with everything."

"Yes," said the girl. "Everything tastes of licorice. Especially all the things you've waited so long for, like absinthe."

"Oh, cut it out."

"You started it," the girl said. "I was being amused. I was having a fine time."

"Well, let's try and have a fine time."

"All right. I was trying. I said the mountains looked like white elephants. Wasn't that bright?"

"That was bright."

"I wanted to try this new drink. That's all we do, isn't it—look at things and try new drinks?"

"I guess so."

The girl looked across at the hills.

"They're lovely hills," she said. "They don't really look like white elephants. I just meant the coloring of their skin through the trees."

"Should we have another drink?"

"All right."

The warm wind blew the bead curtain against the table.

"The beer's nice and cool," the man said.

"It's lovely," the girl said.

"It's really an awfully simple operation, Jig," the man said. "It's not really an operation at all."

The girl looked at the ground the table legs rested on.

"I know you wouldn't mind it, Jig, It's really not anything. It's just to let the air in."

The girl did not say anything.

"I'll go with you and I'll stay with you all the time. They just let the air in and then it's all perfectly natural."

"Then what will we do afterward?"

"We'll be fine afterward. Just like we were before."

"What makes you think so?"

"That's the only thing that bothers us. It's the only thing that's made us happy."

The girl looked at the bead curtain, put her hand out and took hold of two of the strings of beads.

"And you think then we'll be all right and be happy."

"I know we will. You don't have to be afraid. I've known lots of people that have done it."

"So have I," said the girl. "And afterward they were all so happy."

"Well," the man said, "if you don't want to you don't have to. I wouldn't have you do it if you didn't want to. But I know it's perfectly simple."

"And you really want to?"

"I think it's the best thing to do. But I don't want you to do it if you don't really want to."

"And if I do it you'll be happy and things will be like they were and you'll love me?"

"I love you now. You know I love you."

"I know. But if I do it, then it will be nice again if I say things are like white elephants, and you'll like it?"

"I'll love it. I love it now but I just can't think about it. You know how I get when I worry."

"If I do it you won't ever worry?"

"I won't worry about that because it's perfectly simple."

"Then I'll do it. Because I don't care about me."

"What do you mean?"

"I don't care about me."

"Well, I care about you."

"Oh, yes. But I don't care about me. And I'll do it and then everything will be fine."

"I don't want you to do it if you feel that way."

The girl stood up and walked to the end of the station. Across, on the other side, were fields of grain and trees along the banks of the Ebro. Far away, beyond the river, were mountains. The shadow of a cloud moved across the field of grain and she saw the river through the trees.

"And we could have all this," she said. "And we could have everything and every day we make it more impossible."

"What did you say?"

"I said we could have everything."

"We can have everything."

"No, we can't."

"We can have the whole world."

"No, we can't."

"We can go everywhere."

"No, we can't. It isn't ours any more."

"It's ours."

"No, it isn't. And once they take it away, you never get it back."

"But they haven't taken it away."

"We'll wait and see."

"Come on back in the shade," he said. "You mustn't feel that way."

"I don't feel any way," the girl said. "I just know things."

"I don't want you to do anything that you don't want to do——"

"Nor that isn't good for me," she said. "I know. Could we have another beer?"

"All right. But you've got to realize——"

"I realize," the girl said. "Can't we maybe stop talking?"

They sat down at the table and the girl looked across at the hills on the dry side of the valley and the man looked at her and at the table.

"You've got to realize," he said, "that I don't want you to do it if you don't want to. I'm perfectly willing to go through with it if it means anything to you."

"Doesn't it mean anything to you? We could get along."

"Of course it does. But I don't want anybody but you. I don't want any one else. And I know it's perfectly simple."

"Yes, you know it's perfectly simple."

"It's all right for you to say that, but I do know it."

"Would you do something for me now?"

"I'd do anything for you."

"Would you please please please please please please please stop talking?"

He did not say anything but looked at the bags against the wall of the station. There were labels on them from all the hotels where they had spent nights.

"But I don't want you to," he said, "I don't care anything about it."

"I'll scream," the girl said.

The woman came out through the curtains with two glasses of beer and put them down on the damp felt pads. "The train comes in five minutes," she said.

"What did she say?" asked the girl.

"That the train is coming in five minutes."

The girl smiled brightly at the woman, to thank her.

"I'd better take the bags over to the other side of the station," the man said. She smiled at him.

"All right. Then come back and we'll finish the beer."

He picked up the two heavy bags and carried them around the station to the other tracks. He looked up the tracks but could not see the train. Coming back, he walked through the barroom, where people waiting for the train were drinking. He drank an Anis at the bar and looked at the people. They were all waiting reasonably for the train. He went out through the bead curtain. She was sitting at the table and smiled at him.

"Do you feel better?" he asked.

"I feel fine," she said. "There's nothing wrong with me. I feel fine."

From Bernard Malamud's novel The Assistant *emerges a constant theme: to live is to suffer; to live life fully is to learn from suffering. This theme also permeates "The Magic Barrel" and is even more fully developed here. How does it include the significance of Leo's encounter with Stella? Both Leo's attitudes and his search for self-realization seem highly relevant to many of the youth movements of today. Where can parallels be drawn, and how does the resolution of the story (if, indeed, there is a resolution) fit into this pattern of resemblance?*

In 1952, at the age of thirty-eight, Bernard Malamud published his first novel, The Natural. *He was born in Brooklyn, was educated at City College and Columbia University, and has published four novels and two collections of stories. His fiction is characteristically compassionate and tragic, yet not without humor. Further Reading:* The Assistant (1957), The Magic Barrel (1958), Idiots First (1963).

UNITED STATES
OF AMERICA

The Magic Barrel

BERNARD MALAMUD

Not long ago there lived in uptown New York, in a small, almost meager room, though crowded with books, Leo Finkle, a rabbinical student in the Yeshivah University. Finkle, after six years of study, was to be ordained in June and had been advised by an acquaintance that he might find it easier to win himself a congregation if he were married. Since he had no present prospects of marriage, after two tormented days of turning it over in his mind, he called in Pinye Salzman, a marriage broker whose two-line advertisement he had read in the *Forward*.

Reprinted with permission of Farrar, Straus & Giroux, Inc. from *The Magic Barrel* by Bernard Malamud. Copyright © 1954, 1958 by Bernard Malamud.

The matchmaker appeared one night out of the dark fourth-floor hallway of the graystone rooming house where Finkle lived, grasping a black, strapped portfolio that had been worn thin with use. Salzman, who had been long in the business, was of slight but dignified build, wearing an old hat, and an overcoat too short and tight for him. He smelled frankly of fish, which he loved to eat, and although he was missing a few teeth, his presence was not displeasing, because of an amiable manner curiously contrasted with mournful eyes. His voice, his lips, his wisp of beard, his bony fingers were animated, but give him a moment of repose and his mild blue eyes revealed a depth of sadness, a characteristic that put Leo a little at ease although the situation, for him, was inherently tense.

He at once informed Salzman why he had asked him to come, explaining that his home was in Cleveland, and that but for his parents, who had married comparatively late in life, he was alone in the world. He had for six years devoted himself almost entirely to his studies, as a result of which, understandably, he had found himself without time for a social life and the company of young women. Therefore he thought it the better part of trial and error—of embarrassing fumbling—to call in an experienced person to advise him on these matters. He remarked in passing that the function of the marriage broker was ancient and honorable, highly approved in the Jewish community, because it made practical the necessary without hindering joy. Moreover, his own parents had been brought together by a matchmaker. They had made, if not a financially profitable marriage —since neither had possessed any worldly goods to speak of—at least a successful one in the sense of their everlasting devotion to each other. Salzman listened in embarrassed surprise, sensing a sort of apology. Later, however, he experienced a glow of pride in his work, an emotion that had left him years ago, and he heartily approved of Finkle.

The two went to their business. Leo had led Salzman to the only clear place in the room, a table near a window that overlooked the lamp-lit city. He seated himself at the matchmaker's side but facing him, attempting by an act of will to suppress the unpleasant tickle in his throat. Salzman eagerly unstrapped his portfolio and removed a loose rubber band from a thin packet of much-handled cards. As he flipped through them, a gesture and sound that physically hurt Leo, the student pretended not to see and gazed steadfastly out the window. Although it was still February, winter was on its last legs, signs of which he had for the first time in years begun to notice. He now observed the round white moon, moving high in the sky through a cloud menagerie, and watched with half-open mouth as it penetrated a huge hen, and dropped out of her like an egg laying itself. Salzman, though pretending through eyeglasses he had just slipped on, to be engaged in scanning the writing on the cards, stole occasional glances at the young man's distinguished face, noting with pleasure the long, severe scholar's nose, brown eyes heavy with learning, sensitive yet ascetic lips, and a certain, almost hollow quality of the dark cheeks. He gazed around at shelves upon shelves of books and let out a soft, contented sigh.

When Leo's eyes fell upon the cards, he counted six spread out in Salzman's hand.

"So few?" he asked in disappointment.

"You wouldn't believe me how much cards I got in my office," Salzman replied. "The drawers are already filled to the top, so I keep them now in a barrel, but is every girl good for a new rabbi?"

Leo blushed at this, regretting all he had revealed of himself in a curriculum vitae he had sent to Salzman. He had thought it best to acquaint him with his strict standards and specifications, but in having done so, felt he had told the marriage broker more than was absolutely necessary.

He hesitantly inquired, "Do you keep photographs of your clients on file?"

"First comes family, amount of dowry, also what kind promises," Salzman replied, unbuttoning his tight coat and settling himself in the chair. "After comes pictures, rabbi."

"Call me Mr. Finkle. I'm not yet a rabbi."

Salzman said he would, but instead called him doctor, which he changed to rabbi when Leo was not listening too attentively.

Salzman adjusted his horn-rimmed spectacles, gently cleared his throat and read in an eager voice the contents of the top card:

"Sophie P. Twenty four years. Widow one year. No children. Educated high school and two years college. Father promises eight thousand dollars. Has wonderful wholesale business. Also real estate. On the mother's side comes teachers, also one actor. Well known on Second Avenue."

Leo gazed up in surprise. "Did you say a widow?"

"A widow don't mean spoiled, rabbi. She lived with her husband maybe four months. He was a sick boy she made a mistake to marry him."

"Marrying a widow has never entered my mind."

"This is because you have no experience. A widow, especially if she is young and healthy like this girl, is a wonderful person to marry. She will be thankful to you the rest of her life. Believe me, if I was looking now for a bride, I would marry a widow."

Leo reflected, then shook his head.

Salzman hunched his shoulders in an almost imperceptible gesture of disappointment. He placed the card down on the wooden table and began to read another:

"Lily H. High school teacher. Regular. Not a substitute. Has savings and new Dodge car. Lived in Paris one year. Father is successful dentist thirty-five years. Interested in professional man. Well Americanized family. Wonderful opportunity."

"I knew her personally," said Salzman. "I wish you could see this girl. She is a doll. Also very intelligent. All day you could talk to her about books and theyater and what not. She also knows current events."

"I don't believe you mentioned her age?"

"Her age?" Salzman said, raising his brows. "Her age is thirty-two years."

Leo said after a while, "I'm afraid that seems a little too old."

Salzman let out a laugh. "So how old are you, rabbi?"

"Twenty-seven."

"So what is the difference, tell me, between twenty-seven and thirty-two? My own wife is seven years older than me. So what did I suffer? —Nothing. If Rothschild's a daughter wants to marry you, would you say on account her age, no?"

"Yes," Leo said dryly.

Salzman shook off the no in the yes. "Five years don't mean a thing. I give you my word that when you will live with her for one week you will forget her age. What does it mean five years—that she lived more and knows more than somebody who is younger? On this girl, God bless her, years are not wasted. Each one that it comes makes better the bargain."

"What subject does she teach in high school?"

"Languages. If you heard the way she speaks French, you will think it is music. I am in the business twenty-five years, and I recommend her with my whole heart. Believe me, I know what I'm talking, rabbi."

"What's on the next card?" Leo said abruptly.

Salzman reluctantly turned up the third card:

"Ruth K. Nineteen years. Honor student. Father offers thirteen thousand cash to the right bridegroom. He is a medical doctor. Stomach specialist with marvelous practice. Brother in law owns own garment business. Particular people."

Salzman looked as if he had read his trump card.

"Did you say nineteen?" Leo asked with interest.

"On the dot."

"Is she attractive?" He blushed. "Pretty?"

Salzman kissed his finger tips. "A little doll. On this I give you my word. Let me call the father tonight and you will see what means pretty."

But Leo was troubled. "You're sure she's that young?"

"This I am positive. The father will show you the birth certificate."

"Are you positive there isn't something wrong with her?" Leo insisted.

"Who says there is wrong?"

"I don't understand why an American girl her age should go to a marriage broker."

A smile spread over Salzman's face.

"So for the same reason you went, she comes."

Leo flushed. "I am pressed for time."

Salzman, realizing he had been tactless, quickly explained. "The father came, not her. He wants she should have the best, so he looks around himself. When we will locate the right boy he will introduce him and encourage. This makes a better marriage than if a young girl without experience takes for herself. I don't have to tell you this."

"But don't you think this young girl believes in love?" Leo spoke uneasily.

Salzman was about to guffaw but caught himself and said soberly, "Love comes with the right person, not before."

Leo parted dry lips but did not speak. Noticing that Salzman had snatched a glance at the next card, he cleverly asked, "How is her health?"

"Perfect," Salzman said, breathing with difficulty. "Of course, she is a little lame on her right foot from an auto accident that it happened to her when she was twelve years, but nobody notices on account she is so brilliant and also beautiful."

Leo got up heavily and went to the window. He felt curiously bitter and upbraided himself for having called in the marriage broker. Finally, he shook his head.

"Why not?" Salzman persisted, the pitch of his voice rising.

"Because I detest stomach specialists."

"So what do you care what is his business? After you marry her do you need him? Who says he must come every Friday night in your house?"

Ashamed of the way the talk was going, Leo dismissed Salzman, who went home with heavy, melancholy eyes.

Though he had felt only relief at the marriage broker's departure, Leo was in low spirits the next day. He explained it as arising from Salzman's failure to produce a suitable bride for him. He did not care for his type of clientele. But when Leo found himself hesitating whether to seek out another matchmaker, one more polished than Pinye, he wondered if it could be—his protestations to the contrary, and although he honored his father and mother—that he did not, in essence, care for the matchmaking institution? This thought he quickly put out of mind yet found himself still upset. All day he ran around in the woods—missed an important appointment, forgot to give out his laundry, walked out of a Broadway cafeteria without paying and had to run back with the ticket in his hand; had even not recognized his landlady in the street when she passed with a friend

and courteously called out, "A good evening to you, Doctor Finkle."
By nightfall, however, he had regained sufficient calm to sink his nose
into a book and there found peace from his thoughts.

Almost at once there came a knock on the door. Before Leo could
say enter, Salzman, commercial cupid, was standing in the room. His
face was gray and meager, his expression hungry, and he looked as if
he would expire on his feet. Yet the marriage broker managed, by
some trick of the muscles, to display a broad smile.

"So good evening. I am invited?"

Leo nodded, disturbed to see him again, yet unwilling to ask the
man to leave.

Beaming still, Salzman laid his portfolio on the table. "Rabbi, I
got for you tonight good news."

"I've asked you not to call me rabbi. I'm still a student."

"Your worries are finished. I have for you a first-class bride."

"Leave me in peace concerning this subject." Leo pretended lack
of interest.

"The world will dance at your wedding."

"Please, Mr. Salzman, no more."

"But first must come back my strength," Salzman said weakly. He
fumbled with the portfolio straps and took out of the leather case an
oily paper bag, from which he extracted a hard, seeded roll and a
small, smoked white fish. With a quick motion of his hand he stripped
the fish out of its skin and began ravenously to chew. "All day in a
rush," he muttered.

Leo watched him eat.

"A sliced tomato you have maybe?" Salzman hesitantly inquired.
"No."

The marriage broker shut his eyes and ate. When he had finished
he carefully cleaned up the crumbs and rolled up the remains of the
fish, in the paper bag. His spectacled eyes roamed the room until he
discovered, amid some piles of books, a one-burner gas stove. Lifting
his hat he humbly asked, "A glass tea you got, rabbi?"

Conscience-stricken, Leo rose and brewed the tea. He served it with
a chunk of lemon and two cubes of lump sugar, delighting Salzman.

After he had drunk his tea, Salzman's strength and good spirits
were restored.

"So tell me, rabbi," he said amiably, "you considered some more
the three clients I mentioned yesterday?"

"There was no need to consider."

"Why not?"

"None of them suits me."

"What then suits you?"

Leo let it pass because he could give only a confused answer.

Without waiting for a reply, Salzman asked, "You remember this
girl I talked to you—the high school teacher?"

"Age thirty-two?"

But, surprisingly, Salzman's face lit in a smile. "Age twenty-nine."

Leo shot him a look. "Reduced from thirty-two?"

"A mistake," Salzman avowed. "I talked today with the dentist. He took me to his safety deposit box and showed me the birth certificate. She was twenty-nine years last August. They made her a party in the mountains where she went for her vacation. When her father spoke to me the first time I forgot to write the age and I told you thirty-two, but now I remember this was a different client, a widow."

"The same one you told me about? I thought she was twenty-four?"

"A different. Am I responsible that the world is filled with widows?"

"No, but I'm not interested in them, nor for that matter, in school teachers."

Salzman pulled his clasped hands to his breast. Looking at the ceiling he devoutly exclaimed, "Yiddishe kinder, what can I say to somebody that he is not interested in high school teachers? So what then you are interested?"

Leo flushed but controlled himself.

"In what else will you be interested," Salzman went on, "if you not interested in this fine girl that she speaks four languages and has personally in the bank ten thousand dollars? Also her father guarantees further twelve thousand. Also she has a new car, wonderful clothes, talks on all subjects, and she will give you a first-class home and children. How near do we come in our life to paradise?"

"If she's so wonderful, why wasn't she married ten years ago?"

"Why?" said Salzman with a heavy laugh. "—Why? Because she is *partikiler*. That is why. She wants the *best*."

Leo was silent, amused at how he had entangled himself. But Salzman had aroused his interest in Lily H., and he began seriously to consider calling on her. When the marriage broker observed how intently Leo's mind was at work on the facts he had supplied, he felt certain they would soon come to an agreement.

Late Saturday afternoon, conscious of Salzman, Leo Finkle walked with Lily Hirschorn along Riverside Drive. He walked briskly and erectly, wearing with distinction the black fedora he had that morning taken with trepidation out of the dusty hat box on his closet shelf, and the heavy black Saturday coat he had thoroughly whisked clean. Leo also owned a walking stick, a present from a distant relative, but quickly put temptation aside and did not use it. Lily, petite and not unpretty, had on something signifying the approach of spring. She was au courant, animatedly, with all sorts of subjects, and he weighed her words and found her surprisingly sound—score another for Salzman, whom he uneasily sensed to be somewhere around, hiding perhaps high in a tree along the street, flashing the lady signals with a pocket mirror; or perhaps a cloven-hoofed Pan, piping nuptial ditties as he danced his invisible way before them, strewing wild buds on the walk and purple grapes in their path, symbolizing fruit of a union, though there was of course still none.

Lily startled Leo by remarking, "I was thinking of Mr. Salzman, a curious figure, wouldn't you say?"

Not certain what to answer, he nodded.

She bravely went on, blushing, "I for one am grateful for his introducing us. Aren't you?"

He courteously replied, "I am."

"I mean," she said with a little laugh—and it was all in good taste, or at least gave the effect of being not in bad—"do you mind that we came together so?"

He was not displeased with her honesty, recognizing that she meant to set the relationship aright, and understanding that it took a certain amount of experience in life, and courage, to want to do it quite that way. One had to have some sort of past to make that kind of beginning.

He said that he did not mind. Salzman's function was traditional and honorable—valuable for what it might achieve, which, he pointed out, was frequently nothing.

Lily agreed with a sigh. They walked on for a while and she said after a long silence, again with a nervous laugh, "Would you mind if I asked you something a little bit personal? Frankly, I find the subject fascinating." Although Leo shrugged, she went on half embarrassedly, "How was it that you came to your calling? I mean was it a sudden passionate inspiration?"

Leo, after a time, slowly replied, "I was always interested in the Law."

"You saw revealed in it the presence of the Highest?"

He nodded and changed the subject. "I understand that you spent a little time in Paris, Miss Hirschorn?"

"Oh, did Mr. Salzman tell you, Rabbi Finkle?" Leo winced but she went on, "It was ages ago and almost forgotten. I remember I had to return for my sister's wedding."

And Lily would not be put off. "When," she asked in a trembly voice, "did you become enamored of God?"

He stared at her. Then it came to him that she was talking not about Leo Finkle, but of a total stranger, some mystical figure, perhaps even passionate prophet that Salzman had dreamed up for her —no relation to the living or dead. Leo trembled with rage and weakness. The trickster had obviously sold her a bill of goods, just as he had him, who'd expected to become acquainted with a young lady of twenty-nine, only to behold, the moment he laid eyes upon her strained and anxious face, a woman past thirty-five and aging rapidly. Only his self control had kept him this long in her presence.

"I am not," he said gravely, "a talented religious person," and in seeking words to go on, found himself possessed by shame and fear. "I think," he said in a strained manner, "that I came to God not because I loved Him, but because I did not."

This confession he spoke harshly because its unexpectedness shook him.

Lily wilted. Leo saw a profusion of loaves of bread go flying like ducks high over his head, not unlike the winged loaves by which he had counted himself to sleep last night. Mercifully, then, it snowed, which he would not put past Salzman's machinations.

He was infuriated with the marriage broker and swore he would throw him out of the room the minute he reappeared. But Salzman did not come that night, and when Leo's anger had subsided, an unaccountable despair grew in its place. At first he thought this was caused by his disappointment in Lily, but before long it became evident that he had involved himself with Salzman without a true knowledge of his own intent. He gradually realized—with an emptiness that seized him with six hands—that he had called in the broker to find him a bride because he was incapable of doing it himself. This terrifying insight he had derived as a result of his meeting and conversation with Lily Hirschorn. Her probing questions had somehow irritated him into revealing—to himself more than her—the true nature of his relationship to God, and from that it had come upon him, with shocking force, that apart from his parents, he had never loved anyone. Or perhaps it went the other way, that he did not love God so well as he might, because he had not loved man. It seemed to Leo that his whole life stood starkly revealed and he saw himself for the first time as he truly was—unloved and loveless. This bitter but somehow not fully unexpected revelation brought him to a point of panic, controlled only by extraordinary effort. He covered his face with his hands and cried.

The week that followed was the worst of his life. He did not eat and loss weight. His beard darkened and grew ragged. He stopped attending seminars and almost never opened a book. He seriously considered leaving the Yeshivah, although he was deeply troubled at the thought of the loss of all his years of study—saw them like pages torn from a book, strewn over the city—and at the devastating effect of this decision upon his parents. But he had lived without knowledge of himself, and never in the Five Books and all the Commentaries— mea culpa—had the truth been revealed to him. He did not know where to turn, and in all this desolating loneliness there was no *to whom*, although he often thought of Lily but not once could bring himself to go downstairs and make the call. He became touchy and irritable, especially with his landlady, who asked him all manner of

personal questions; on the other hand, sensing his own disagreeable-
ness, he waylaid her on the stairs and apologized abjectly, until
mortified, she ran from him. Out of this, however, he drew the consolation that he was a Jew and that a Jew suffered. But gradually, as
the long and terrible week drew to a close, he regained his composure
and some idea of purpose in life: to go on as planned. Although he
was imperfect, the ideal was not. As for his quest of a bride, the
thought of continuing afflicted him with anxiety and heartburn, yet
perhaps with this new knowledge of himself he would be more successful than in the past. Perhaps love would now come to him and a
bride to that love. And for this sanctified seeking who needed a
Salzman?

The marriage broker, a skeleton with haunted eyes, returned that
very night. He looked, withal, the picture of frustrated expectancy—
as if he had steadfastly waited the week at Miss Lily Hirschorn's side
for a telephone call that never came.

Casually coughing, Salzman came immediately to the point: "So
how did you like her?"

Leo's anger rose and he could not refrain from chiding the matchmaker: "Why did you lie to me, Salzman?"

Salzman's pale face went dead white, the world had snowed on
him.

"Did you not state that she was twenty-nine?" Leo insisted.

"I give you my word—"

"She was thirty-five, if a day. At *least* thirty-five."

"Of this don't be too sure. Her father told me—"

"Never mind. The worst of it was that you lied to her."

"How did I lie to her, tell me?"

"You told her things about me that weren't true. You made me
out to be more, consequently less than I am. She had in mind a totally
different person, a sort of semi-mystical Wonder Rabbi."

"All I said, you was a religious man."

"I can imagine."

Salzman sighed. "This is my weakness that I have," he confessed.
"My wife says to me I shouldn't be a salesman, but when I have two
fine people that they would be wonderful to be married, I am so happy
that I talk too much." He smiled wanly. "This is why Salzman is a
poor man."

Leo's anger left him. "Well, Salzman, I'm afraid that's all."

The marriage broker fastened hungry eyes on him.

"You don't want any more a bride?"

"I do," said Leo, "but I have decided to seek her in a different way.
I am no longer interested in an arranged marriage. To be frank, I
now admit the necessity of premarital love. That is, I want to be in
love with the one I marry."

"Love?" said Salzman, astounded. After a moment he remarked, "For us, our love is our life, not for the ladies. In the ghetto they—"

"I know, I know," said Leo. "I've thought of it often. Love, I have said to myself, should be a by-product of living and worship rather than its own end. Yet for myself I find it necessary to establish the level of my need and fulfill it."

Salzman shrugged but answered, "Listen, rabbi, if you want love, this I can find for you also. I have such beautiful clients that you will love them the minute your eyes will see them."

Leo smiled unhappily. "I'm afraid you don't understand."

But Salzman hastily unstrapped his portfolio and withdrew a manila packet from it.

"Pictures," he said, quickly laying the envelope on the table.

Leo called after him to take the pictures away, but as if on the wings of the wind, Salzman had disappeared.

March came. Leo had returned to his regular routine. Although he felt not quite himself yet—lacked energy—he was making plans for a more active social life. Of course it would cost something, but he was an expert in cutting corners; and when there were no corners left he would make circles rounder. All the while Salzman's pictures had lain on the table, gathering dust. Occasionally as Leo sat studying, or enjoying a cup of tea, his eyes fell on the manila envelope, but he never opened it.

The days went by and no social life to speak of developed with a member of the opposite sex—it was difficult, given the circumstances of his situation. One morning Leo toiled up the stairs to his room and stared out the window at the city. Although the day was bright his view of it was dark. For some time he watched the people in the street below hurrying along and then turned with a heavy heart to his little room. On the table was the packet. With a sudden relentless gesture he tore it open. For a half-hour he stood by the table in a state of excitement, examining the photographs of the ladies Salzman had included. Finally, with a deep sigh he put them down. There were six, of varying degrees of attractiveness, but look at them long enough and they all became Lily Hirschorn: all past their prime, all starved behind bright smiles, not a true personality in the lot. Life, despite their frantic yoohooings, had passed them by; they were pictures in a brief case that stank of fish. After a while, however, as Leo attempted to return the photographs into the envelope, he found in it another, a snapshot of the type taken by a machine for a quarter. He gazed at it a moment and let out a cry.

Her face deeply moved him. Why, he could at first not say. It gave him the impression of youth—spring flowers, yet age—a sense of having been used to the bone, wasted; this came from the eyes, which were hauntingly familiar, yet absolutely strange. He had a vivid impression that he had met her before, but try as he might he could not place her although he could almost recall her name, as if he had read it in her own handwriting. No, this couldn't be; he would have remembered her. It was not, he affirmed, that she had an extraordinary beauty—no, though her face was attractive enough; it was that *something* about her moved him. Feature for feature, even some of the ladies of the photographs could do better; but she leaped forth to his heart—had *lived*, or wanted to—more than just wanted, perhaps regretted how she had lived—had somehow deeply suffered: it could be seen in the depths of those reluctant eyes, and from the way the light enclosed and shone from her, and within her, opening realms of possibility: this was her own. Her he desired. His head ached and eyes narrowed with the intensity of his gazing, then as if an obscure fog had blown up in the mind, he experienced fear of her and was aware that he had received an impression, somehow, of evil. He shuddered, saying softly, it is thus with us all. Leo brewed some tea in a small pot and sat sipping it without sugar, to calm himself. But before he had finished drinking, again with excitement he examined the face and found it good: good for Leo Finkle. Only such a one could understand him and help him seek whatever he was seeking. She might, perhaps, love him. How she had happened to be among the discards in Salzman's barrel he could never guess, but he knew he must urgently go find her.

Leo rushed downstairs, grabbed up the Bronx telephone book, and searched for Salzman's home address. He was not listed, nor was his office. Neither was he in the Manhattan book. But Leo remembered having written down the address on a slip of paper he had read Salzman's advertisement in the "personals" column of the *Forward*. He ran up to his room and tore through his papers, without luck. It was exasperating. Just when he needed the matchmaker he was nowhere to be found. Fortunately Leo remembered to look in his wallet. There on a card he found his name written and a Bronx address. No phone number was listed, the reason—Leo now recalled—he had originally communicated with Salzman by letter. He got on his coat, put a hat on over his skull cap and hurried to the subway station. All the way to the far end of the Bronx he sat on the edge of his seat. He was more than once tempted to take out the picture and see if the girl's face was as he remembered it, but he refrained, allowing the snapshot to remain in his inside coat pocket, content to have her so close. When the train pulled into the station he was waiting at the door and bolted out. He quickly located the street Salzman had advertised.

The building he sought was less than a block from the subway, but it was not an office building, nor even a loft, nor a store in which one could rent office space. It was a very old tenement house. Leo found Salzman's name in pencil on a soiled tag under the bell and climbed three dark flights to his apartment. When he knocked, the door was opened by a thin, asthmatic, gray-haired woman, in felt slippers.

"Yes?" she said, expecting nothing. She listened without listening. He could have sworn he had seen her, too, before but knew it was an illusion.

"Salzman—does he live here? Pinye Salzman," he said, "the match-maker?"

She stared at him a long minute. "Of course."

He felt embarrassed. "Is he in?"

"No." Her mouth, though left open, offered nothing more.

"The matter is urgent. Can you tell me where his office is?"

"In the air." She pointed upward.

"You mean he has no office?" Leo asked.

"In his socks."

He peered into the apartment. It was sunless and dingy, one large room divided by a half-open curtain, beyond which he could see a sagging metal bed. The near side of a room was crowded with rickety chairs, old bureaus, a three-legged table, racks of cooking utensils, and all the apparatus of a kitchen. But there was no sign of Salzman or his magic barrel, probably also a figment of the imagination. An odor of frying fish made Leo weak to the knees.

"Where is he?" he insisted. "I've got to see your husband."

At length she answered, "So who knows where he is? Every time he thinks a new thought he runs to a different place. Go home, he will find you."

"Tell him Leo Finkle."

She gave no sign she had heard.

He walked downstairs, depressed.

But Salzman, breathless, stood waiting at his door.

Leo was astounded and overjoyed. "How did you get here before me?"

"I rushed."

"Come inside."

They entered, Leo fixed tea, and a sardine sandwich for Salzman. As they were drinking he reached behind him for the packet of pictures and handed them to the marriage broker.

Salzman put down his glass and said expectantly, "You found somebody you like?"

"Not among these."

The marriage broker turned away.

"Here is the one I want." Leo held forth the snapshot.

Salzman slipped on his glasses and took the picture into his trembling hand. He turned ghastly and let out a groan.

"What's the matter?" cried Leo.

"Excuse me. Was an accident this picture. She isn't for you."

Salzman frantically shoved the manila packet into his portfolio. He thrust the snapshop into his pocket and fled down the stairs.

Leo, after momentary paralysis, gave chase and cornered the marriage broker in the vestibule. The landlady made hysterical outcries but neither of them listened.

"Give me back the picture, Salzman."

"No." The pain in his eyes was terrible.

"Tell me who she is then."

"This I can't tell you. Excuse me."

He made to depart, but Leo, forgetting himself, seized the matchmaker by his tight coat and shook him frenziedly.

"Please," signed Salzman. "*Please.*"

Leo ashamedly let him go. "Tell me who she is," he begged. "It's very important for me to know."

"She is not for you. She is a wild one—wild, without shame. This is not a bride for a rabbi."

"What do you mean wild?"

"Like an animal. Like a dog. For her to be poor was a sin. This is why to me she is dead now."

"In God's name, what do you mean?"

"Her I can't introduce to you," Salzman cried.

"Why are you so excited?"

"Why, he asks," Salzman said, bursting into tears. "This is my baby, my Stella, she should burn in hell."

Leo hurried up to bed and hid under the covers. Under the covers he thought his life through. Although he soon fell asleep he could not sleep her out of his mind. He woke, beating his breast. Though he prayed to be rid of her, his prayers went unanswered. Through days of torment he endlessly struggled not to love her; fearing success, he escaped it. He then concluded to convert her to goodness, himself to God. The idea alternately nauseated and exalted him.

He perhaps did not know that he had come to a final decision until he encountered Salzman in a Broadway cafeteria. He was sitting alone at a rear table, sucking the bony remains of a fish. The marriage broker appeared haggard, and transparent to the point of vanishing.

Salzman looked up at first without recognizing him. Leo had grown a pointed beard and his eyes were weighted with wisdom.

"Salzman," he said, "love has at last come to my heart."

"Who can love from a picture?" mocked the marriage broker.

"It is not impossible."

"If you can love her, then you can love anybody. Let me show you some new clients that they just sent me their photographs. One is a little doll."

"Just her I want," Leo murmured.

"Don't be a fool, doctor. Don't bother with her."

"Put me in touch with her, Salzman," Leo said humbly. "Perhaps I can be of service."

Salzman had stopped eating and Leo understood with emotion that it was now arranged.

Leaving the cafeteria, he was, however, afflicted by a tormenting suspicion that Salzman had planned it all to happen this way.

Leo was informed by letter that she would meet him on a certain corner, and she was there one spring night, waiting under a street lamp. He appeared, carrying a small bouquet of violets and rosebuds. Stella stood by the lamp post, smoking. She wore white with red shoes, which fitted his expectations, although in a troubled moment he had imagined the dress red, and only the shoes white. She waited uneasily and shyly. From afar he saw that her eyes—clearly her father's —were filled with desperate innocence. He pictured, in her, his own redemption. Violins and lit candles revolved in the sky. Leo ran forward with flowers outthrust.

Around the corner, Salzman, leaning against a wall, chanted prayers for the dead.

"Intelligent, thinking people could take things like this in their stride, just as they took the larger absurdities of deadly dull jobs in the city and deadly dull homes in the suburbs." In this way Richard Yates' characters rationalize their deadly dull lot in American culture. The author of "Builders" writes about men and women who are chained to a society which is undergoing mechanistic, cookie-cutter transition. They are people who are alienated from each other and from themselves —unable to love, to communicate, to act, or to find internal meaning. The climax of the following story jars the reader; but why? Does the story justify the intense, emotional conclusion? Does the abrupt shift in tone of the last paragraph cause you to re-think the story? What, if any, is the significance of frequent references to Hemingway? How does the narrator's attitude toward Bernie change?

Richard Yates was born in Yonkers, New York, in 1926. He served in the infantry in World War II, contracted tuberculosis, and, during the time that he was convalescing in a sanatorium, began his first novel, Revolutionary Road. *Further Reading:* Revolutionary Road (1961), Eleven Kinds of Loneliness (1962).

UNITED STATES
OF AMERICA

Builders

RICHARD YATES

Writers who write about writers can easily bring on the worst kind of literary miscarriage; everybody knows that. Start a story off with "Craig crushed out his cigarette and lunged for the typewriter," and there isn't an editor in the United States who'll feel like reading your next sentence.

Copyright © 1957, 1961, 1962 by Richard Yates. From *Eleven Kinds of Loneliness* by Richard Yates, by permission of Atlantic-Little, Brown and Co.

So don't worry: this is going to be a straight, no-nonsense piece of fiction about a cab driver, a movie star, and an eminent child psychologist, and that's a promise. But you'll have to be patient for a minute, because there's going to be a writer in it too. I won't call him "Craig," and I can guarantee that he won't get away with being the only Sensitive Person among the characters, but we're going to be stuck with him right along and you'd better count on his being as awkward and obtrusive as writers nearly always are, in fiction or in life.

Thirteen years ago, in 1948, I was twenty-two and employed as a rewrite man on the financial news desk of the United Press, in New York. The salary was fifty-four dollars a week and it wasn't much of a job, but it did give me two good things. One was that whenever anybody asked me what I did I could say, "Work for the UP," which had a jaunty sound; the other was that every morning I could turn up at the *Daily News* building wearing a jaded look, a cheap trench coat that had shrunk a size too small for me, and a much-handled brown fedora ("Battered" is the way I would have described it then, and I'm grateful that I know a little more now about honesty in the use of words. It was a handled hat, handled by endless nervous pinchings and shapings and reshapings; it wasn't battered at all). What I'm getting at is that just for those few minutes each day, walking up the slight hill of the last hundred yards between the subway exit and the *News* building, I was Ernest Hemingway reporting for work at the *Kansas City Star*.

Had Hemingway been to the war and back before his twentieth birthday? Well, so had I; and all right, maybe there were no wounds or medals for valor in my case, but the basic fact of the matter was there. Had Hemingway bothered about anything as time-wasting and career-delaying as going to college? Hell, no; and me neither. Could Hemingway ever really have cared very much about the newspaper business? Of course not; so there was only a marginal difference, you see, between his lucky break at the *Star* and my own dismal stint on the financial desk. The important thing, as I knew Hemingway would be the first to agree, was that a writer had to begin somewhere.

"Domestic corporate bonds moved irregularly higher in moderately active trading today . . ." That was the kind of prose I wrote all day long for the UP wire, and "Rising oil shares paced a lively curb market," and "Directors of Timken Roller Bearing today declared"— hundreds on hundreds of words that I never fully understood (What in the name of God are puts and calls, and what is a sinking fund debenture? I'm still damned if I know), while the teletypes chugged and rang and the Wall Street tickers ticked and everybody around me argued baseball, until it was mercifully time to go home.

It always pleased me to reflect that Hemingway had married young; I could go right along with him there. My wife Joan and I lived as far west as you can get on West Twelfth Street, in a big three-window room on the third floor, and if it wasn't the Left Bank it certainly wasn't our fault. Every evening after dinner, while Joan washed the dishes, there would be a respectful, almost reverent hush in the room, and this was the time for me to retire behind a three-fold screen in the corner where a table, a student lamp and a portable typewriter were set up. But it was here, of course, under the white stare of that lamp, that the tenuous parallel between Hemingway and me endured its heaviest strain. Because it wasn't any "Up in Michigan" that came out of my machine; it wasn't any "Three Day Blow," or "The Killers"; very often, in fact, it wasn't really anything at all, and even when it was something Joan called "marvelous," I knew deep down that it was always, always something bad.

There were evenings too when all I did behind the screen was goof off—read every word of the printing on the inside of a matchbook, say, or all the ads in the back of the *Saturday Review of Literature*— and it was during one of those times, in the fall of the year, that I came across these lines:

> Unusual free-lance opportunity for talented writer. Must have imagination. Bernard Silver.

—and then a phone number with what looked like a Bronx exchange.

I won't bother giving you the dry, witty, Hemingway dialogue that took place when I came out from behind the screen that night and Joan turned around from the sink, with her hands dripping soapsuds on the open magazine, and we can also skip my cordial, unenlightening chat with Bernard Silver on the phone. I'll just move on ahead to a couple of nights later, when I rode the subway for an hour and found my way at last to his apartment.

"Mr. Prentice?" he inquired. "What's your first name again? Bob? Good, Bob, I'm Bernie. Come on in, make yourself comfortable."

And I think both Bernie and his home deserve a little description here. He was in his middle or late forties, a good deal shorter than me and much stockier, wearing an expensive-looking pale blue sport shirt with the tails out. His head must have been half again the size of mine, with thinning black hair washed straight back, as if he'd stood face-up in the shower; and his face was one of the most guileless and self-confident faces I've ever seen.

The apartment was very clean, spacious and cream-colored, full of carpeting and archways. In the narrow alcove near the coat closet ("Take your coat and hat; good. Let's put this on a hanger there and we'll be all set; good"), I saw a cluster of framed photographs showing World War I soldiers in various groupings, but on the walls of the living room there were no pictures of any kind, only a few wrought-iron lamp brackets and a couple of mirrors. Once inside the room you weren't apt to notice the lack of pictures, though, because all your attention was drawn to a single, amazing piece of furniture. I don't know what you'd call it—a credenza?—but whatever it was it seemed to go on forever, chest-high in some places and waist-high in others, made of at least three different shades of polished brown veneer. Part of it was a television set, part of it was a radio-phonograph; part of it thinned out into shelves that held potted plants and little figurines; part of it, full of chromium knobs and tricky sliding panels, was a bar.

"Ginger ale?" he asked. "My wife and I don't drink, but I can offer you a glass of ginger ale."

I think Bernie's wife must always have gone out to the movies on nights when he interviewed his writing applicants; I did meet her later, though, and we'll come to that. Anyway, there were just the two of us that first evening, settling down in slippery leatherette chairs with our ginger ale, and it was strictly business.

"First of all," he said, "tell me, Bob. Do you know *My Flag Is Down?*" And before I could ask what he was talking about he pulled it out of some recess in the credenza and handed it over—a paperback book that you still see around the drugstores, purporting to be the memoirs of a New York taxicab driver. Then he began to fill me in, while I looked at the book and nodded and wished I'd never left home.

Bernard Silver was a cab driver, too. He had been one for twenty-two years, as long as the span of my life, and in the last two or three of these years he had begun to see no reason why a slightly fictionalized version of his own experiences shouldn't be worth a fortune. "I'd like you to take a look at this," he said, and this time the credenza yielded up a neat little box of three-by-five-inch file cards. Hundreds of experiences, he told me; all different; and while he gave me to understand that they might not all be strictly true, he could assure me there was at least a kernel of truth in every last one of them. Could I imagine what a really good ghost-writer might do with a wealth of material like that? Or how much that same writer might expect to salt away when his own fat share of the magazine sales, the book royalties and the movie rights came in?

"Well, I don't know, Mr. Silver. It's a thing I'd have to think over. I guess I'd have to read this other book first, and see if I thought there was any—"

"No, wait a while. You're getting way ahead of me here, Bob. In the first place I wouldn't want you to read that book because you wouldn't learn anything. That guy's all gangsters and dames and sex and drinking and that stuff. I'm completely different." And I sat swilling ginger ale as if to slake a gargantuan thirst, in order to be able to leave as soon as possible after he'd finished explaining how completely different he was. Bernie Silver was a warm person, he told me; an ordinary, everyday guy with a heart as big as all outdoors and a real philosophy of life; did I know what he meant?

I have a trick of tuning out on people (it's easy; all you do is fix your eyes on the speaker's mouth and watch the rhythmic, endlessly changing shapes of lips and tongue, and the first thing you know you can't hear a word), and I was about to start doing that when he said:

"And don't misunderstand me, Bob. I never yet asked a writer to do a single word for me on spec. You write for me, you'll be paid for everything you do. Naturally it can't be very big dough at this stage of the game, but you'll be paid. Fair enough? Here, let me fill up your glass."

This was the proposition. He'd give me an idea out of the file; I'd develop it into a first-person short story by Bernie Silver, between one and two thousand words in length, for which immediate payment was guaranteed. If he liked the job I did, there would be plenty of others where it came from—an assignment a week, if I could handle that much—and in addition to my initial payment, of course, I could look forward to a generous percentage of whatever subsequent income the material might bring. He chose to be winkingly mysterious about his plans for marketing the stories, though he did manage to hint that the *Reader's Digest* might be interested, and he was frank to admit he didn't yet have a publisher lined up for the ultimate book they would comprise, but he said he could give me a couple of names that would knock my eye out. Had I ever heard, for example, of Manny Weidman?

"Or maybe," he said, breaking into his all-out smile, "maybe you know him better as Wade Manley." And this was the shining name of a movie star, a man about as famous in the thirties and forties as Kirk Douglas or Burt Lancaster today. Wade Manley had been a grammar-school friend of Bernie's right here in the Bronx. Through mutual friends they had managed to remain sentimentally close ever since, and one of the things that kept their friendship green was Wade Manley's oft-repeated desire to play the role of rough, lovable Bernie Silver, New York Hackie, in any film or television series based on his colorful life. "Now I'll give you another name," he said, and this time he squinted cannily at me while pronouncing it, as if my recognizing it or not would be an index of my general educational level. "Dr. Alexander Corvo."

And luckily I was able not to look too blank. It wasn't a celebrity name, exactly, but it was far from obscure. It was one of those *New York Times* names, the kind of which tens of thousands of people are dimly aware because they've been coming across respectful mentions of them in the *Times* for years. Oh, it might have lacked the impact of "Lionel Trilling" or "Reinhold Niebuhr," but it was along that line; you could probably have put it in the same class with "Huntington Hartford" or "Leslie R. Groves," and a good cut or two above "Newbold Morris."

"The whaddyacallit man, you mean?" I said. "The childhood-tensions man?"

Bernie gave me a solemn nod, forgiving this vulgarity, and spoke the name again with its proper identification. "I mean Dr. Alexander Corvo, the eminent child psychologist."

Early in his rise to eminence, you see, Dr. Corvo had been a teacher at the very same grammar school in the Bronx, and two of the most unruly, dearly loved little rascals in his charge there had been Bernie Silver and Manny What's-his-name, the movie star. He still retained an incurable soft-spot for both youngsters, and nothing would please him more today than to lend whatever influence he might have in the publishing world to furthering their project. All the three of them needed now, it seemed, was to find that final element, that elusive catalyst, the perfect writer for the job.

"Bob," said Bernie, "I'm telling you the truth. I've had one writer after another working on this, and none of them's been right. Sometimes I don't trust my own judgment; I take their stuff to Dr. Corvo and he shakes his head. He says, 'Bernie, try again.' "

"Look, Bob." He came earnestly forward in his chair. "This isn't any fly-by-night idea here; I'm not stringing anybody along. This thing is building. Manny, Dr. Corvo and myself—we're *building* this thing. Oh, don't worry, Bob, I *know*—what, do I look that stupid?—I know they're not building the way *I'm* building. And why should they? A big movie star? A distinguished scholar and author? You think they haven't got plenty of things of their own to build? A lot more important things than this? Naturally. But Bob, I'm telling you the truth: they're interested. I can show you letters, I can tell you times they've sat around this apartment with their wives, or Manny has anyway, and we've talked about it hours on end. They're interested, nobody has to worry about that. So do you see what I'm telling you, Bob? I'm telling you the truth. This thing is building." And he began a slow, two-handed building gesture, starting from the carpet, setting invisible blocks into place until they'd made a structure of money and fame for him, money and freedom for both of us, that rose to the level of our eyes.

I said it certainly did sound fine, but that if he didn't mind I'd like to know a little more about the immediate payment for the individual stories.

"And now I'll give you the answer to that one," he said. He went to the credenza again—part of it seemed to be a kind of desk—and after sorting out some papers he came up with a personal check. "I won't just tell you," he said. "I'll show you. Fair enough? This was my last writer. Take it and read it."

It was a canceled check, and it said that Bernard Silver had paid, to the order of some name, the sum of twenty-five dollars and no cents. "Read it!" he insisted, as if the check were a prose work of uncommon merit in its own right, and he watched me while I turned it over to read the man's endorsement, which had been signed under some semi-legible words of Bernie's own about this being advance payment in full, and the bank's rubber stamp. "Look all right to you?" he inquired. "So that's the arrangement. All clear now?"

I guessed it was as clear as it would ever be, so I gave him back the check and said that if he'd show me one of the file cards now, or whatever, we might as well get going.

"Way-*hait* a minute, now! Hold your *horses* a minute here." His smile was enormous. "You're a pretty fast guy, you know that, Bob? I mean I like you, but don't you think I'd have to be a little bit of a dope to go around making out checks to everybody walked in here saying they're a writer? I know you're a newspaperman. Fine. Do I know you're a writer yet? Why don't you let me see what you got there in your lap?"

It was a manila envelope containing carbon copies of the only two halfway presentable short stories I had ever managed to produce in my life.

"Well," I said. "Sure. Here. Of course these are a very different kind of thing than what *you're*—"

"Never mind, never mind; naturally they're different," he said, opening the envelope. "You just relax a minute, and let me take a look."

"What I mean is, they're both very kind of—well, literary, I guess you'd say. I don't quite see how they'll give you any real idea of my—"

"Relax, I said."

Rimless glasses were withdrawn from the pocket of his sport shirt and placed laboriously into position as he settled back, frowning, to read. It took him a long time to get through the first page of the first story, and I watched him, wondering if this might turn out to be the very lowest point in my literary career. A *cab* driver, for Christ's sake. At last the first page turned, and the second page followed so closely after it that I could tell he was skipping. Then the third and the fourth—it was a twelve- or fourteen-page story—while I gripped my empty, warming ginger ale glass as if in readiness to haul off and throw it at his head.

A very slight, hesitant, then more and more judicial nodding set in as he made his way toward the end. He finished it, looked puzzled, went back to read over the last page again; then he laid it aside and picked up the second story—not to read it, but only to check it for length. He had clearly had enough reading for one night. Off came the glasses and on came the smile.

"Well, very nice," he said. "I won't take time to read this other one now, but this first one's very nice. Course, naturally, as you said, this is a very different kind of material you got here, so it's a little hard for me to—*you* know—" and he dismissed the rest of this difficult sentence with a wave of the hand. "I'll tell you what, though, Bob. Instead of just reading here, let me ask you a couple of questions about writing. For example." He closed his eyes and delicately touched their lids with his fingers, thinking, or more likely pretending to think, in order to give added weight to his next words. "For example, let me ask you this. Supposing somebody writes you a letter and says, 'Bob, I didn't have time to write you a short letter today, so I had to write you a long one instead.' Would you know what they meant by that?"

Don't worry, I played this part of the evening pretty cool. I wasn't going to let twenty-five bucks get away from me without some kind of struggle; and my answer, whatever sober-sided nonsense it was, could have left no doubt in his mind that this particular writing candidate knew something of the difficulty and the value of compression in prose. He seemed gratified by it, anyway.

"Good. Now let's try a different angle. I mentioned about 'building' a while back; well, look. Do you see where writing a story is building something too? Like building a house?" And he was so pleased with his own creation of this image that he didn't even wait to take in the careful, congratulatory nod I awarded him for it. "I mean a house has got to have a roof, but you're going to be in trouble if you build your roof first, right? Before you build your roof you got to build your walls. Before you build your walls you got to lay your foundation—and I mean all the way down the line. Before you lay your foundation you got to bulldoze and dig yourself the right kind of hole in the ground. Am I right?

I couldn't have agreed with him more, but he was still ignoring my rapt, toadying gaze. He rubbed the flange of his nose with one wide knuckle; then he turned on me triumphantly again.

"So all right, supposing you build yourself a house like that. Then what? What's the first question you got to ask yourself about it when it's done?"

But I could tell he didn't care if I muffed this one or not. *He* knew what the question was, and he could hardly wait to tell me.

"Where are the windows?" he demanded, spreading his hands. "That's the question. Where does the light come in? Because do you see what I mean about the light coming in, Bob? I mean the—the *philosophy* of, your story; the *truth* of it; the—"

"The illumination of it, sort of," I said, and he quit groping for his third noun with a profound and happy snap of the fingers.

"That's it. That's it, Bob. You got it."

It was a deal, and we had another ginger ale to clinch it as he thumbed through the idea file for my trial assignment. The "experience" he chose was the time Bernie Silver had saved a neurotic couple's marriage, right there in the cab, simply by sizing them up in his rear-view mirror as they quarreled and putting in a few well-chosen words of his own. Or at least, that was the general drift of it. All it actually said on the card was something like:

> High class man & wife (Park Ave.) start
> fighting in cab, very upset, lady starts
> yelling divorce. I watch them in rear
> view and put my 2 cents worth in & soon
> we are all laughing. Story about marriage, etc.

But Bernie expressed full confidence in my ability to work the thing out.

In the alcove, as he went through the elaborate business of getting my trench coat out of the closet and helping me on with it, I had time for a better look at the World War I photographs—a long company line-up, a number of framed yellow snapshots showing laughing men with their arms around each other, and one central picture of a lone bugler on a parade ground, with dusty barracks and a flag high in the distance. It could have been on the cover of an old American Legion magazine, with a caption like "Duty"—the perfect soldier, slim and straight at attention, and Gold Star Mothers would have wept over the way his fine young profile was pressed in manly reverence against the mouth of his simple, eloquent horn.

"I see you like my boy there," Bernie said fondly. "I bet you'd never guess who that boy is today?"

Wade Manley? Dr. Alexander Corvo? Lionel Trilling? But I suppose I really did know, even before I glanced around at his blushing, beaming presence, that the boy was Bernie himself. And whether it sounds silly or not, I'll have to tell you that I felt a small but honest-to-God admiration for him. "Well, I'll be damned, Bernie. You look—you look pretty great there."

"Lot skinnier in those days, anyway," he said, slapping his silken paunch as he walked me to the door, and I remember looking down into his big, dumb, flabby face and trying to find the bugler's features somewhere inside it.

On my way home, rocking on the subway and faintly belching and tasting ginger ale, I grew increasingly aware that a writer could do a hell of a lot worse than to pull down twenty-five dollars for a couple of thousand words. It was very nearly half what I earned in forty miserable hours among the domestic corporate bonds and the sinking fund debentures; and if Bernie like this first one, if I could go on doing one a week for him, it would be practically the same as getting a 50 per cent raise. Seventy-nine a week! With that kind of dough coming in, as well as the forty-six Joan brought home from her secretarial job, it would be no time at all before we had enough for Paris (and maybe we wouldn't meet any Gertrude Steins or Ezra Pounds there, maybe I wouldn't produce any *Sun Also Rises*, but the earliest possible expatriation was nothing less than essential to my Heming-

way plans). Besides, it might even be fun—or at least, it might be fun
to tell people about: I would be the hackie's hack, the builders'
builder.

In any case I ran all the way down to West Twelfth Street that
night, and if I didn't burst in on her, laughing and shouting and
clowning around, it was only because I forced myself to stand leaning
against the mailboxes downstairs until I'd caught my breath and
arranged my face into the urbane, amused expression I planned to
use for telling her about it.

"Well, but who do you suppose is putting up all the money?" she
asked. "It can't be out of his own pocket, can it? A cab driver couldn't
afford to pay out twenty-five a week for any length of time, could he?"

It was one aspect of the thing that hadn't occurred to me—and it
was just like her to come up with so dead-logical a question—but I
did my best to override her with my own kind of cynical romanticism.
"Who knows? Who the hell cares? Maybe Wade Manley's putting
up the money. Maybe Dr. Whaddyacallit's putting it up. The point
is, it's there."

"Well," she said, "good, then. How long do you think it'll take you
to do the story?"

"Oh, hell, no time at all. I'll knock it off in a couple hours over the
weekend."

But I didn't. I spent all Saturday afternoon and evening on one
false start after another; I kept getting hung up in the dialogue of
the quarreling couple, and in technical uncertainties about how much
Bernie could really see of them in his rear-view mirror, and in doubts
about what any cab driver could possibly say at such a time without
the man's telling him to shut up and keep his eyes on the road.

By Sunday afternoon I was walking around breaking pencils in half
and throwing them into the wastebasket and saying the hell with it;
the hell with everything; apparently I couldn't even be a God damn
ghost writer for a God damn ignorant slob of a driver of a God damn
taxi-cab.

"You're *trying* too hard," Joan said. "Oh, I knew this would happen. You're being so insufferably *literary* about it, Bob; it's ridiculous.
All you have to do is think of every corny, tear-jerking thing you've
ever read or heard. Think of Irving Berlin."

And I told her I'd give her Irving Berlin right in the mouth in
about a minute, if she didn't lay off me and mind her own God damn
business.

But late that night, as Irving Berlin himself might say, something
kind of wonderful happened. I took that little bastard of a story and
I built the hell out of it. First I bulldozed and dug and laid myself
a real good foundation; then I got the lumber and bang, bang, bang—
up went the walls and on went the roof and up went the cute little
chimney top. Oh, I put plenty of windows in it too—big, square ones
—and when the light comes pouring in it left no earthly shadow of

a doubt that Bernie Silver was the wisest, gentlest, bravest and most lovable man who ever said "folks."

"It's perfect," Joan told me at breakfast, after she'd read the thing. "Oh, it's just perfect, Bob. I'm sure that's just exactly what he wants."

And it was. I'll never forget the way Bernie sat with his ginger ale in one hand and my trembling manuscript in the other, reading as I'd still be willing to bet he'd never read before, exploring all the snug and tidy wonders of the little home I'd built for him. I watched him discovering each of those windows, one after another, and saw his face made holy with their light. When he was finished he got up— we both got up—and he shook my hand.

"Beautiful," he said. "Bob, I had a feeling you'd do a good one, but I'll tell you the truth, I didn't know you'd do as good a one as this. Now you want your check, and I'll tell you something. You're not getting any check. For this you get cash."

Out came his trusty black cab driver's wallet. He thumbed through its contents, picked out a five-dollar bill and laid it in my hand. He evidently wanted to make a ceremony out of presenting me with one bill after another, so I stood smiling down at it and waiting for the next one; and I was still standing there with my hand out when I looked up and saw him putting the wallet away.

Five bucks! And even now I wish I could say that I shouted this, or at least that I said it with some suggestion of the outrage that gripped my bowels—it might have saved an awful amount of trouble later—but the truth is that it came out as a very small, meek question: "Five bucks?"

"Right!" He was rocking happily back on his heels in the carpet.

"Well, but Bernie, I mean what's the deal?" I mean, you showed me that check, and I—"

As his smile dwindled, his face looked as shocked and hurt as if I'd spat into it. "Oh, Bob," he said. "Bob, what is this? Look, let's not play any games here. I know I showed you that check; I'll show you that check again." And the folds of his sport shirt quivered in righteous indignation as he rummaged in the credenza and brought it out.

It was the same check, all right. It still read twenty-five dollars and no cents; but Bernie's cramped scribbling on the other side, above the other man's signature and all mixed up with the bank's rubber stamp, was now legible as hell. What it said, of course, was: "In full advance payment, five write-ups."

So I hadn't really been robbed—conned a little, maybe, that's all— and therefore my main problem now, the sick, ginger-ale-flavored feeling that I was certain Ernest Hemingway could never in his life have known, was my own sense of being a fool.

"Am I right or wrong, Bob?" he was asking. "Am I right or wrong?" And then he sat me down again and did his smiling best to set me straight. How could I possibly have thought he meant twenty-five a time? Did I have any idea what kind of money a hackie took home? Oh, some of your owner-drivers, maybe it was a different story; but your average hackie? Your fleet hackie? Forty, forty-five, maybe sometimes fifty a week if they were lucky. Even for a man like himself, with no kids and a wife working full time at the telephone company, it was no picnic. I could ask any hacks if I didn't believe him; it was no picnic. "And I mean you don't think anybody *else* is picking up the tab for these write-ups, do you? Do you?" He looked at me incredulously, almost ready to laugh, as if the very idea of my thinking such a thing would remove all reasonable doubt about my having been born yesterday.

"Bob, I'm sorry there was any misunderstanding here," he said, walking me to the door, "but I'm glad we're straight on it now. Because I mean it, that's a beautiful piece you wrote, and I've got a feeling it's going to go places. Tell you what, Bob, I'll be in touch with you later this week, okay?"

And I remember despising myself because I didn't have the guts to tell him not to bother, any more than I could shake off the heavy, fatherly hand that rode on my neck as he walked. In the alcove, out in front of the young bugler again, I had a sudden, disturbing notion that I could foretell an exchange of dialogue that was about to take place. I would say, "Bernie, were you really a bugler in the army, or was that just for the picture?"

And with no trace of embarrassment, without the faintest flickering change in his guileless smile, he would say, "Just for the picture."

Worse still: I knew that the campaign-hatted head of the bugler himself would turn then, that the fine tense profile in the photograph would slowly loosen and turn away from the mouthpiece of a horn through which its dumb, no-talent lips could never have blown a fart, and that it would wink at me. So I didn't risk it. I just said, "See you, Bernie," and got the hell out of there and went home.

Joan's reaction to the news was surprisingly gentle. I don't mean she was "kind" to me about it, which would have damn near killed me in the shape I was in that night; it was more that she was kind to Bernie.

Poor, lost, brave little man, dreaming his huge and unlikely dream —that kind of thing. And could I imagine what it must have cost him over the years? How many of these miserably hard-earned five-dollar payments he must have dropped down the bottomless maw of second- and third- and tenth-rate amateur writers' needs? How lucky for him, then, through whatever dissemblings with his canceled check, to have made contact with a first-rate professional at last. And how touching, and how "sweet," that he had recognized the difference by saying, "For this you get cash."

"Well, but for Christ's sake," I told her, grateful that it could for once be me instead of her who thought in terms of the deadly practicalities, "For Christ's sake, you know *why* he gave me cash, don't you? Because he's going to sell that story to the *Reader's* God damn *Digest* next week for a hundred and fifty thousand dollars, and because I had a photostated check to prove I wrote it he'd be in trouble, that's why."

"Would you like to bet?" she inquired, looking at me with her lovely, truly unforgettable mixture of pity and pride. "Would you like to bet that if he does sell it, to the *Reader's Digest* or anywhere else, he'll insist on giving you half?"

"Bob Prentice?" said a happy voice on the telephone, three nights later. "Bernie Silver. Bob, I've just come from Dr. Alexander Corvo's home, and listen. I'm not going to tell you *what* he told me, but I'll tell you this. Dr. Alexander Corvo thinks you're pretty good."

Whatever reply I made to this—"Does he really?" or "You mean he really likes it?"—it was something bashful and telling enough to bring Joan instantly to my side, all smiles. I remember the way she plucked at my shirtsleeve as if to say, There—what did I tell you? And I had to brush her away and wag my hand to keep her quiet during the rest of the talk.

"He wants to show it to a couple of his connections in the publishing field," Bernie was saying, "and he wants me to get another copy made up to send out to Manny on the Coast. So listen, Bob, while we're waiting to see what happens on this one, I want to give you some more assignments. Or wait—listen." And his voice became enriched with the dawning of a new idea. "Listen. Maybe you'd be more comfortable working on your own. Would you rather do that? Would you rather just skip the card file, and use your own imagination?"

Late one rainy night, deep in the upper West Side, two thugs got into Bernie's cab. To the casual eye they might have looked like ordinary customers, but Bernie had them spotted right away because "Take it from me, a man doesn't hack the streets of Manhattan for twenty-two years without a little specialized education rubbing off."

One was a hardened-criminal type, of course, and the other was little more than a frightened boy, or rather "just a punk."

"I didn't like the way they were talking," Bernie told his readers through me, "and I didn't like the address they gave me—the lowest dive in town—and most of all I didn't like the fact that they were riding in my automobile."

So do you know what he did? Oh, don't worry, he didn't stop the cab and step around and pull them out of the back seat and kick them one after the other in the groin—none of that *My-Flag-Is-Down* nonsense. For one thing, he could tell from their talk that they weren't making a getaway; not tonight, at least. All they'd done tonight was case the joint (a small liquor store near the corner where he'd picked them up); the job was set for tomorrow night at eleven. Anyway, when they got to the lowest dive in town the hardened criminal gave the punk some money and said, "Here, kid; you keep the cab, go on home and get some sleep. I'll see you tomorrow." And that was when Bernie knew what he had to do.

"That punk lived way out in Queens, which gave us plenty of time for conversation, so I asked him who he liked for the National League pennant." And from there on, with deep folk wisdom and consummate skill, Bernie kept up such a steady flow of talk about healthy, clean-living, milk-and-sunshine topics that he'd begun to draw the boy out of his hard delinquent shell even before they hit the Queensboro Bridge. They barreled along Queens Boulevard chattering like a pair of Police Athletic League enthusiasts, and by the time the ride was over, Bernie's fare was practically in tears.

"I saw him swallow a couple of times when he paid me off" was the way I had Bernie put it, "and I had a feeling something had changed in that kid. I had a hope of it, anyway, or maybe just a wish. But I knew I'd done all I could for him." Back in town, Bernie called the police and suggested they put a couple of men around the liquor store the following night.

Sure enough, a job was attempted on that liquor store, only to be foiled by two tough, lovable cops. And sure enough, there was only one thug for them to carry off to the pokey—the hardened-criminal one. "I don't know where the kid was that night," Bernie concluded, "but I like to think he was home in bed with a glass of milk, reading the sports page."

There was the roof and there was the chimney top of it; there were all the windows with the light coming in; there was another approving chuckle from Dr. Alexander Corvo and another submission to the *Reader's Digest*; there was another whisper of a chance for a Simon and Schuster contract and a three-million-dollar production starring Wade Manley; and there was another five in the mail for me.

A small, fragile old gentleman started crying in the cab one day, up around Fifty-ninth and Third, and when Bernie said, "Anything I can help with, sir?" there followed two and a half pages of the most heart-tearing hard-luck story I could imagine. He was a widower; his only daughter had long since married and moved away to Flint, Michigan; his life had been an agony of loneliness for twenty-two years, but he'd always been brave enough about it until now because he'd had a job he loved—tending the geraniums in a big commercial greenhouse. And now this morning the management had told him he would have to go: too old for that kind of work.

"And only then," according to Bernie Silver, "did I make the connection between all this and the address he'd given me—a corner near the Manhattan side of the Brooklyn Bridge."

Bernie couldn't be sure, of course, that his fare planned to hobble right on out to the middle of the bridge and ease his old bones over the railing; but he couldn't take any chances, either. "I figured it was time for me to do some talking" (and he was right about that: another heavy half-page of that tiresome old man's lament and the story would have ruptured the hell out of its foundation). What came next was a brisk page and a half of dialogue in which Bernie discreetly inquired why the old man didn't go and live with his daughter in Michigan, or at least write her a letter so that maybe she'd invite him; but oh, no, he only keened that he couldn't possibly be a burden on his daughter and her family.

" 'Burden?' I said, acting like I didn't know what he meant. 'Burden? How could a nice old gentleman like you be a burden on anybody?"

" 'But what else would I be? What can *I* offer them?' "

"Luckily we were stopped at a red light when he asked me that, so I turned around and looked him straight in the eye. 'Mister,' I said, 'don't you think that family'd like having somebody around the place that knows a thing or two about growing geraniums?' "

Well, by the time they got to the bridge the old man had decided to have Bernie let him off at a nearby Automat instead, because he said he felt like having a cup of tea, and so much for the walls of the damn thing. This was the roof: Six months later, Bernie received a small, heavy package with a Flint, Michigan, postmark, addressed to his taxi fleet garage. And do you know what was in that package? Of course you do. A potted geranium. And here's your chimney top: There was also a little note, written in what I'm afraid I really did describe as a fine old spidery hand, and it read, simply, "Thank you."

Personally, I thought this one was loathsome, and Joan wasn't sure about it either; but we mailed it off anyway and Bernie loved it. And so, he told me over the phone, did his wife Rose.

"Which reminds me, Bob, the other reason I called; Rose wants me to find out what evening you and your wife could come up for a little get-together here. Nothing fancy, just the four of us, have a little drink and a chat. You think you might enjoy that?"

"Well, that's very nice of you, Bernie, and of course we'd enjoy it very much. It's just that offhand I don't quite know when we could arrange to—hold on a second." And I covered the mouthpiece and had an urgent conference about it with Joan in the hope that she'd supply me with a graceful excuse.

But she wanted to go, and she had just the right evening in mind, so all four of us were hooked.

"Oh, good," she said when I'd hung up. "I'm glad we're going. They sound sweet."

"Now, *look*." And I aimed my index finger straight at her face. "We're not going at all if you plan to sit around up there making them both aware of how 'sweet' they are. I'm not spending any evenings as gracious Lady Bountiful's consort among the lower classes, and that's final. If you want to turn this thing into some goddam Bennington girls' garden party for the servants, you can forget about it right now. You hear me?"

Then she asked me if I wanted to know something, and without waiting to find out whether I did or not, she told me. She told me I was just about the biggest snob and biggest bully and biggest all-around loud-mouthed jerk she'd ever come across in her life.

One thing led to another after that; by the time we were on the subway for our enjoyable get-together with the Silvers we were only barely on speaking terms, and I can't tell you how grateful I was to find that the Silvers, while staying on ginger ale themselves, had broken out a bottle of rye for their guests.

Bernie's wife turned out to be a quick, spike-heeled, girdled and bobby-pinned woman whose telephone operator's voice was chillingly expert at the social graces ("How do you do? So nice to meet you; do come in; please sit down; Bernie, help her, she can't get her coat off"); and God knows who started it, or why, but the evening began uncomfortably with a discussion of politics. Joan and I were torn between Truman, Wallace, and not voting at all that year; the Silvers were Dewey people. And what made it all the worse, for our tender liberal sensibilities, was that Rose sought common ground by telling us one bleak tale after another, each with a more elaborate shudder, about the inexorable, menacing encroachment of colored and Puerto Rican elements in this part of the Bronx.

But things got jollier after a while. For one thing they were both delighted with Joan—and I'll have to admit I never met anyone who wasn't—and for another the talk soon turned to the marvelous fact of their knowing Wade Manley, which gave rise to a series of proud reminiscences. "Bernie never takes nothing off him, though, don't worry," Rose assured us. "Bernie, tell them what you did that time he was here and you told him to sit down and shut up. He did! He did! He kind of gave him a push in the chest—this *movie* star!—and he said, 'Ah, siddown and sheddep, Manny. *We* know who you are!' Tell them, Bernie."

And Bernie, convulsed with pleasure, got up to reenact the scene. "Oh, we were just kind of kidding around, you understand," he said, "but anyway, that's what I did. I gave him a shove like this, and I said, 'Ah, siddown and sheddep, Manny. *We* know who you are!'"

"He did! That's the God's truth! Pushed him right down in that chair over there! Wade Manley!"

A little later, when Bernie and I had paired off for a man-to-man talk over the freshening of drinks, and Rose and Joan were cozily settled in the love seat, Rose directed a roguish glance at me. "I wouldn't want to give this husband of yours a swelled head, Joanie, but do you know what Dr. Corvo told Bernie? Shall I tell her, Bernie?"

"Sure, tell her! Tell her!" And Bernie waved the bottle of ginger ale in one hand and the bottle of rye in the other, to show how openly all secrets could be bared tonight.

"Well," she said, "Dr. Corvo said your husband is the finest writer Bernie's ever had."

Later still, when Bernie and I were in the love seat and the ladies were at the credenza, I began to see that Rose was a builder too. Maybe she hadn't built that credenza with her own hands, but she'd clearly done more than her share of building whatever heartfelt convictions were needed to sustain the hundreds on hundreds of dollars its purchases must be costing them on the installment plan. A piece of furniture like that was an investment in the future; and now, as she stood fussing over it and wiping off little parts of it while she talked to Joan, I could have sworn I saw her arranging a future party in her mind. Joan and I would be among those present, that much was certain ("This is Mr. Robert Prentice, my husband's assistant. and Mrs. Prentice"), and the rest of the guest list was almost a foregone conclusion too: Wade Manley and his wife, of course, along with a careful selection of their Hollywood friends; Walter Winchell would be there, and Earl Wilson and Toots Shor and all that crowd; but far more important, for any person of refinement, would be the presence of Dr. and Mrs. Alexander Corvo and some of the people who comprised their set. People like the Lionel Trillings and the Reinhold Niebuhrs, the Huntington Hartfords and the Leslie R. Groveses—and if anybody on the order of Mr. and Mrs. Newbold Morris wanted to come, you could be damn sure they'd have to do some pretty fancy jockeying for an invitation.

It was, as Joan admitted later, stifling hot in the Silver's apartment that night; and I cite this as a presentable excuse for the fact that what I did next—and it took me a hell of a lot less time to do it in 1948 than it does now, believe me—was to get roaring drunk. Soon I was not only the most vociferous but the only talker in the room; I was explaining that, by Jesus God, we'd all four of us be millionaires yet.

And wouldn't we have a ball? Oh, we'd be slapping Lionel Trilling around and pushing him down into every chair in this room and telling him to shut up—"And you too, Reinhold Niebuhr, you pompous, sanctimonious old fool! Where's *your* money? Why don't you put your money where your mouth is?"

Bernie was chuckling and looking sleepy, and Joan was looking humiliated for me, and Rose was smiling in cool but infinite understanding of how tiresome husbands could sometimes be. Then we were all out in the alcove trying on at least a half a dozen coats apiece, and I was looking at the bugler's photograph again wondering if I dared to ask my burning question about it. But this time I wasn't sure which I feared more: that Bernie might say, "Just for the picture," or that he might say, "Sure I was!" and go rummaging in the closet or in some part of the credenza until he'd come up with the tarnished old bugle itself, and we'd all have to go back and sit down again while Bernie put his heels together, drew himself erect, and sounded the pure, sad melody of Taps for us all.

That was in October. I'm a little vague on how many "By Bernie Silver" stories I turned out during the rest of the fall. I do remember a comic-relief one about a fat tourist who got stuck at the waist when he tried to clumb up through the skyview window of the cab for better sightseeing, and a very solemn one in which Bernie delivered a lecture on racial tolerance (which struck a sour note with me, considering the way he'd chimed in with Rose's views on the brown hordes advancing over the Bronx); but mostly what I remember about him during that period is that Joan and I could never seem to mention him without getting into some kind of an argument.

When she said we really ought to return his and Rose's invitation, for example, I told her not to be silly. I said I was sure they wouldn't expect it, and when she said "Why?" I gave her a crisp, impatient briefing on the hopelessness of trying to ignore class barriers, of pretending that the Silvers could ever really become our friends, or that they'd ever really want to.

Another time, toward the end of a curiously dull evening when we'd gone to our favorite premarital restaurant and failed for an hour to find anything to talk about, she tried to get the conversation going by leaning romantically toward me across the table and holding up her wineglass. "Here's to Bernie's selling your last one to the *Reader's Digest!*"

"Yeah," I said. "Sure. Big deal."

"Oh, don't be so gruff. You know perfectly well it could happen any day. We might make a lot of money and go to Europe and everything."

"Are you kidding?" It suddenly annoyed me that any intelligent, well-educated girl in the twentieth century could be so gullible; and that such a girl should actually be my wife, that I would be expected to go on playing along with this kind of simple-minded innocence for years and years to come, seemed, for the moment, an intolerable situation. "Why don't you grow up a little? You don't really think there's ever been a chance of his selling that junk, do you?" And I looked at her in a way that must have been very much like Bernie's own way of looking at me, the night he asked if I'd really thought he meant twenty-five a time. "Do you?"

"Yes, I do," she said, putting her glass down. "Or at least, I did. I thought you did too. If you don't, it seems sort of cynical and dishonest to go on working for him, doesn't it?" And she wouldn't talk to me all the way home.

The real trouble, I guess, was that we were both preoccupied with two far more serious matters by this time. One was our recent discovery that Joan was pregnant, and the other was that my position at the United Press had begun to sink as steadily as any sinking fund debenture.

My time on the financial desk had become a slow ordeal of waiting for my superiors to discover more and more of how little I knew about what I was doing; and now however pathetically willing I might be to learn all the things I was supposed to know, it had become much too ludicrously late to ask. I was hunching lower and lower over my clattering typewriter there all day and sweating out the ax—the kind, sad dropping of the assistant financial editor's hand on my shoulder ("Can I speak to you inside a minute, Bob?")—and each day that it didn't happen was a kind of shabby victory.

Early in December I was walking home from the subway after one of those days, dragging myself down West Twelfth Street like a seventy-year-old, when I discovered that a taxicab had been moving beside me at a snail's pace for a block and a half. It was one of the green-and-white kind, and behind its windshield flashed an enormous smile.

"Bob! What's the matter, there, Bob? You lost in thought or something? This where you live?"

When he parked the cab at the curb and got out, it was the first time I'd ever seen him in his working clothes: a twill cap, a buttoned sweater and one of those columnar change-making gadgets strapped to his waist; and when we shook hands it was the first time I'd seen his fingertips stained a shiny gray from handling other people's coins and dollar bills all day. Close up, smiling or not, he looked as worn out as I felt.

"Come on in, Bernie." He seemed surprised by the crumbling doorway and dirty stairs of the house, and also by the white-washed, poster-decorated austerity of our big single room, whose rent was probably less than half of what he and Rose were paying uptown, and I remember taking a dim Bohemian's pride in letting him notice these things; I guess I had some snobbish notion that it wouldn't do Bernie Silver any harm to learn that people could be smart and poor at the same time.

We couldn't offer him any ginger ale and he said a glass of plain water would be fine, so it wasn't much of a social occasion. It troubled me afterwards to remember how constrained he was with Joan—I don't think he looked her full in the face once during the whole visit —and I wondered if this was because of our failure to return that invitation. Why is it that wives are nearly always blamed for what must at least as often as not be their husbands' fault in matters like that? But maybe it was just that he was more conscious of his cab driver's costume in her presence than in mine. Or maybe he had never imagined that such a pretty and cultivated girl could live in such stark surroundings, and was embarrassed for her.

"I'll tell you what I dropped by about, Bob. I'm trying a new angle." And as he talked I began to suspect, more from his eyes than his words, that something had gone very wrong with the long-range building program. Maybe a publishing friend of Dr. Corvo's had laid it on the line at last about the poor possibilities of our material; maybe Dr. Corvo himself had grown snappish; maybe there had been some crushing final communication from Wade Manley, or, more crushingly, from Wade Manley's agency representative. Or it might have been simply that Bernie was tired after his day's work in a way that no glass of plain water would help; in any case he was trying a new angle.

Had I ever heard of Vincent J. Poletti? But he gave me this name as if he knew perfectly well it wouldn't knock my eye out, and he followed it right up with the information that Vincent J. Poletti was a Democratic State Assemblyman from Bernie's own district in the Bronx.

"Now, this man," he said, "is a man that goes out of his way to help people. Believe me, Bob, he's not just one of your cheap vote-getters. He's a real public servant. What's more, he's a comer in the Party. He's going to be our next Congressman. So here's the idea, Bob. We get a photograph of me—I have this friend of mine'll do it for nothing—we get it taken from the back seat of the cab, with me at the wheel kind of turning around and smiling like this, get it?" He turned his body away from his smiling head to show me how it would look. "And we print this picture on the cover of a booklet. The title of the booklet—" and here he sketched a suggestion of block lettering in the air—"the title of the booklet is 'Take It from Bernie.' Okay? Now. Inside the booklet we have a story—just exactly like the others you wrote except this time it's a little different. This time I'm telling a story about why Vincent J. Poletti is the man we need for Congress. I don't mean just a bunch of political talk, either, Bob. I mean a real little story."

"Bernie, I don't see how this is going to work. You can't have a 'story' about why anybody is the man we need for Congress."

"Who says you can't?"

"And anyway I thought you and Rose were Republicans."

"On the national level, yes. On the local level, no."

"Well, but hell, Bernie, we just had an election. There won't be another election for two years."

But he only tapped his temple and made a faraway gesture to show that in politics it paid a man to think ahead.

Joan was over in the kitchen area of the room, cleaning up the breakfast dishes and getting the dinner started, and I looked to her for help, but her back was turned.

"It just doesn't sound right, Bernie. I don't know anything about politics."

"So? Know, schmow. What's to know? Do you know anything about driving a cab?"

No; and I sure as hell didn't know anything about Wall Street, either—Wall Street, Schmall Street!—but that was another depressing little story. "I don't know, Bernie; things are very unsettled right now. I don't think I'd better take on any more assignments for the time being. I mean for one thing I may be about to—" but I couldn't bring myself to tell him about my UP problem, so I said, "For one thing Joan's having a baby now, and everything's sort of—"

"Wow! Well, isn't that something!" He was on his feet and shaking my hand. "Isn't—that—something! Congratulations, Bob, I think this is—I think this is really wonderful. Congratulations, there, Joanie!" And it seemed a little excessive to me at the time, but maybe that's the way such news will always strike a middle-aged, childless man.

"Oh, listen, Bob," he said when we settled down again. "This Poletti thing'll be duck soup for you; and I'll tell you what. Seeing as this is just a one-shot and there won't be any royalties, we'll make it ten instead of five. Is that a deal?"

"Well, but wait a second, Bernie. I'm going to need some more information. I mean what exactly does this guy do for people?"

And it soon became clear that Bernie knew very little more about Vincent J. Poletti than I did. He was a real public servant, that was all; he went out of his way to help people. "Oh, Bob, listen. What's the difference? Where's your imagination? You never needed any help before. Listen. What you just told me gives me one idea right off the bat. I'm driving along; these two kids hail me out in front of the maternity hospital, this young veteran and his wife. They got this little-biddy baby, three days old, and they're happy as larks. Only here's the trouble. This boy's got no job or anything. They only just moved here, they don't know anybody, maybe they're Puerto Ricans or something, they got a week's rent on their room and that's it. Then they're broke. So I'm taking them home, they live right in my neighborhood, and we're chatting away, and I say, 'Listen, kids. I think I'll take you to see a friend of mine.' "

"Assemblyman Vincent J. Poletti."

"Naturally. Only I don't tell them his name yet. I just say, 'this friend of mine.' So we get there and I go in and tell Poletti about it and he comes out and talks to the kids and gives them money or something. See? You got a good share of your story right there."

"Hey, yeah, and wait a minute, Bernie." I got up and began dramatically pacing the floor, the way people in Hollywood story conferences are supposed to do. "Wait a minute. After he gives them money, he gets into your cab and you take off with him down the Grand Concourse, and those two Puerto Rican kids are standing there on the sidewalk kind of looking at each other, and the girl says, 'Who *was* that man?' And the boy looks very serious and he says, 'Honey, don't you know? Didn't you notice he was wearing a mask?' And she says, 'Oh no, it couldn't be the—' And he says 'Yes, yes, it was. Honey, that was the Lone Assemblyman.' And then listen! You know what happens next? Listen! Way off down the block they hear this voice, and you know what the voice is calling?" I sank to the floor on one trembling knee to deliver the punch line. "It's calling 'Hi-yo, Bernie *Silver*—away!' "

And it may not look very funny written down, but it almost killed me. I must have laughed for at least a minute, until I went into a coughing fit and Joan had to come and pound me on the back; only very gradually, coming out of it, did I realize that Bernie was not amused. He had chuckled in bewildered politeness during my seizure, but now he was looking down at his hands and there were embarrassing blotches of pink in his sober cheeks. I had hurt his feelings. I remember resenting it that his feelings could be hurt so easily, and resenting it that Joan had gone back to the kitchen instead of staying to help me out of this awkward situation, and then beginning to feel very guilty and sorry, as the silence continued, until I finally decided that the only decent way of making it up to him was to accept the assignment. And sure enough, he brightened instantly when I told him I'd give it a try.

"I mean you don't necessarily have to use that about the Puerto Rican kids," he assured me. "That's just one idea. Or maybe you could start it off that way and then go on to other things, the more the better. You work it out any way you like."

At the door, shaking hands again (and it seemed that we'd been shaking hands all afternoon), I said, "So that's ten for this one, right Bernie?"

"Right, Bob."

"Do you really think you should have told him you'd do it?" Joan asked me the minute he'd gone.

"Why not?"

"Well, because it *is* going to be practically impossible, isn't it?"

"Look, will you do me a favor? Will you please get off my back?"

She put her hands on her hips. "I just don't understand you, Bob. Why *did* you say you'd do it?"

"Why the hell do you think? Because we're going to need the ten bucks, that's why."

In the end I built—oh, built, schmilt. I put page one and then page two and then page three into the old machine and I *wrote* the son of a bitch. It did start off with the Puerto Rican kids, but for some reason I couldn't get more than a couple of pages out of them; then I had to find other ways for Vincent J. Poletti to demonstrate his giant goodness.

What does a public servant do when he really wants to go out of his

way to help people? Gives them money, that's what he does; and
pretty soon I had Poletti forking over more than he could count. It
got so that anybody in the Bronx who was even faintly up against it
had only to climb into Bernie Silver's cab and say, "The Poletti
place," and their troubles were over. And the worst part of it was my
own grim conviction that it was the best I could do.

Joan never saw the thing, because she was asleep when I finally
managed to get it into an envelope and into the mail. And there
was no word from Bernie—or about him, between the two of us—
for nearly a week. Then, at the same hour as his last visit, the frayed-
out end of the day, our doorbell rang. I knew there was going to be
trouble as soon as I opened the door and found him smiling there,
with spatters of rain on his sweater, and I knew I wasn't going to stand
for any nonsense.

"Bob," he said, sitting down, "I hate to say it, but I'm disappointed
in you this time." He pulled my folded manuscript out of his
sweater. "This thing is—Bob, this is nothing."

"It's six and a half pages. That's not nothing, Bernie."

"Bob, please don't give me six and a half pages. I know it's six and
a half pages, but it's nothing. You made this man into a fool, Bob.
You got him giving his dough away all the time."

"You told me he gave dough, Bernie."

"To the Puerto Rican kids I said yes, sure, maybe he could give a
little, fine. And now you come along and you got him going around
spending here like some kind of—some kind of drunken sailor or
somehing."

I thought I might be going to cry, but my voice came out very low
and controlled. "Bernie, I did ask you what else he could do. I did tell
you I didn't know what the hell else he could do. If you wanted him
to do something else, you should've made that clear."

"But *Bob*," he said, standing up for emphasis, and his next words
have often come back to me as the final, despairing everlasting cry of
the Philistine, "Bob, *you're* the one with the imagination!"

I stood up too, so that I could look down at him. *I* knew I was the
one with the imagination. I also knew I was twenty-two years old and
as tired as an old man, that I was about to lose my job, that I had a
baby on the way and wasn't even getting along very well with my
wife; and now every cab driver, every two-bit politician's pimp and
phony bugler in the city of New York was walking into my house and
trying to steal my money.

"Ten bucks, Bernie."

He made a helpless gesture, smiling. Then he looked over into the
kitchen area, where Joan was, and although I meant to keep my eyes
on him, I must have looked there too, because I remember what she
was doing. She was twisting a dish towel in her hands and looking
down at it.

"Listen, Bob," he said. "I shouldn't of said it was nothing. You're right! Who could take a thing six and a half pages long and say it's nothing? Probably a lot of good stuff in this thing, Bob. You want your ten bucks; all right, fine, you'll get your ten bucks. All I'm asking is this. First take this thing back and change it a little, that's all. Then we can—"

"Ten bucks, Bernie. Now."

His smile had lost its life, but it stayed right there on his face while he took the bill out of his wallet and handed it over, and while I went through a miserable little show of examining it to make God damn sure it was a ten.

"Okay, Bob," he said. "We're all square, then. Right?"

"Right."

Then he was gone, and Joan went swiftly to the door and opened it and called, "Goodnight, Bernie!"

I thought I heard his footsteps pause on the stairs, but I didn't hear any answering "Goodnight" from him, so I guessed that all he'd done was to turn around and wave to her, or blow her a kiss. Then from the window I saw him move out across the sidewalk and get into his taxicab and drive away. All this time I was folding and refolding his money, and I don't believe I've ever held anything in my hand that I wanted less.

The room was very quiet with only the two of us moving around in it, while the kitchen area steamed and crackled with the savory smells of a dinner that I don't think either of us felt like eating. "Well," I said. "That's that."

"Was it really necessary," she inquired, "to be so dreadfully unpleasant to him?"

And this, at the time, seemed clearly to be the last loyal possible thing she could have said, the unkindest cut of all. "Un*pleasant* to him! Un*pleasant* to him! Would you mind telling me just what the hell I'm supposed to do? Am I supposed to sit around being 'pleasant' while some cheap, lying little parasitic leech of a *cab* driver comes in here and bleeds me *white*? Is that what you want? Huh? Is *that* what you want?"

Then she did what she often used to do at moments like that, what I sometimes think I'd give anything in life never to have seen her do: she turned away from me and closed her eyes and covered her ears with both hands.

Less than a week later the assistant financial editor's hand did fall on my shoulder at last, right in the middle of a paragraph about domestic corporate bonds in moderately active trading.

It was still well before Christmas, and I got a job to tide us over as a demonstrator of mechanical toys in a Fifth Avenue dimestore. And I think it must have been during that dimestore period—possibly while winding up a little tin-and-cotton kitten that went "Mew!" and rolled over, "Mew!" and rolled over, "Mew!" and rolled over—it was along in there sometime, anyway, that I gave up whatever was left of the idea of building my life on the pattern of Ernest Hemingway's. Some construction projects are just plain out of the question.

After New Year's I got some other idiot job; then in April, with all the abruptness and surprise of spring, I was hired for eighty dollars a week as a writer in an industrial public-relations office, where the question of whether or not I knew what I was doing never mattered very much because hardly any of the other employees knew what they were doing either.

It was a remarkably easy job, and it allowed me to save a remarkable amount of energy each day for my own work, which all at once began to go well. With Hemingway safely abandoned, I had moved on to an F. Scott Fitzgerald phase; then, the best of all, I had begun to find what seemed to give every indication of being my own style. The winter was over, and things seemed to be growing easier between Joan and me too, and in the early summer our first daughter was born.

She caused a one- or two-month interruption in my writing schedule, but before long I was back at work and convinced that I was going from strength to strength: I had begun to bulldoze and dig and lay the foundation for a big, ambitious, tragic novel. I never did finish the book—it was the first in a series of more unfinished novels than I like to think about now—but in those early stages it was fascinating work, and the fact that it went slowly seemed only to add to its promise of eventual magnificence. I was spending more and more time each night behind my writing screen, emerging only to pace the floor with a headful of serene and majestic daydreams. And it was late in the year, all the way around to fall again, one evening when Joan had gone out to the movies, leaving me as baby-sitter, when I came out from behind the screen to pick up a ringing phone and heard: "Bob Prentice? Bernie Silver."

I won't pretend that I'd forgotten who he was, but it's not too much to say that for a second or two I did have trouble realizing that I'd ever really worked for him—that I could ever really have been involved, at first hand, in the pathetic delusions of a taxicab driver. It gave me pause, which is to say that it caused me to wince and then to sheepishly grin at the phone, to duck my head and smooth my hair with my free hand in a bashful demonstration of *noblesse oblige* —this accompanied by a silent, humble vow that whatever Bernie Silver might want from me now, I would go out of my way to avoid any chance of hurting his feelings. I remember wishing Joan were home, so that she could witness my kindness.

But the first thing he wanted to know about was the baby. Was it a boy or a girl? Wonderful! And who did she look like? Well, of course, naturally, they never did look like anybody much at that age.

And how did it feel to be a father? Huh? Feel pretty good? Good! Then he took on what struck me as a strangely formal, cap-holding tone, like that of a long-discharged servant inquiring after the lady of the house. "And how's Mrs. Prentice?"

She had been "Joan" and "Joanie" and "Sweetheart" to him in his own home, and I somehow couldn't believe he'd forgotten her name; I could only guess that he hadn't heard her call out to him on the stairs that night after all—that maybe, remembering only the way she'd stood there with her dish towel, he had even blamed her as the instigator of my own intransigence over the damned ten bucks. But all I could do now was tell him she was fine. "And how've you people been, Bernie?"

"Well," he said, "*I've* been all right," and here his voice fell to the shocked sobriety of hospital-room conferences. "But I almost lost Rose, a couple of months back."

Oh, it was okay now, he assured me, she was much better and home from the hospital and feeling well; but when he started talking about "tests" and "radiology" I had the awful sense of doom that comes when the unmentionable name of cancer hangs in the air.

"Well, Bernie," I said, "I'm terribly sorry she's been ill, and please be sure to give her our—"

Give her our what? Regards? Best wishes? Either one, it suddenly seemed to me, would carry the unforgivable taint of condescension. "Give her our love," I said, and immediately chewed my lip in fear that his might sound the most condescending of all.

"I will! I will! I'll certainly do that for you, Bob," he said, and so I was glad I'd put it that way. "And now, what I called you about is this." And he chuckled. "Oh, don't worry, no politics. Here's the thing. I've got this really terrifically talented boy working for me now, Bob. This boy's an artist."

And great God, what a sickly, intricate thing a writer's heart is! Because do you know what I felt when he said that? I felt a twinge of jealousy. "Artist," was he? I'd show them who the hell the artist was around *this* little writing establishment.

But right away Bernie started talking about "strips" and "layouts," so I was able to retire my competitive zeal in favor of the old, reliable ironic detachment. What a relief!

"Oh, an *artist*, you mean. A *comic*-strip artist."

"Right. Bob, you ought to see the way this boy can draw. You know what he does? He makes me look like me, but he makes me look a little bit like Wade Manley too. Do you get the picture?"

"It sounds fine, Bernie." And now that the old detachment was working again, I could see that I'd have to be on my guard. Maybe he wouldn't be needing any more stories—by now he probably had a whole credenza full of manuscripts for the artist to work from—but he'd still be needing a writer to do the "continuity," or whatever it's

called, and the words for the artist's speech balloons, and I would now
have to tell him, as gently and gracefully as possible, that it wasn't
going to be me.

"Bob," he said, "this thing is really building. Dr. Corvo took one
look at these strips and he said to me, 'Bernie, forget the magazine
business, forget the book business. You've found the solution.'"

"Well. It certainly does sound good, Bernie."

"And Bob, here's why I called. I know they keep you pretty busy
down there at the UP, but I was wondering if you might have time to
do a little—"

"I'm not working for the UP any more, Bernie." And I told him
about the publicity job.

"Well," he said. "That sounds like you're really coming up in the
world there, Bob. Congratulations."

"Thanks. Anyway, Bernie, the point is I really don't think I'd have
time to do any writing for you just now. I mean I'd certainly like to,
it isn't that; it's just that the baby does take up a lot of time here,
and then I've got my own work going—I'm doing a novel now, you
see—and I really don't think I'd better take on anything else."

"Oh, Well, okay, then, Bob; don't worry about it. All I meant,
you see, is that it really would've been a break for us if we could of
made use of your—*you* know, your writing talent in this thing."

"I'm sorry too, Bernie, and I certainly do wish you luck with it."

You may well have guessed by now what didn't occur to me, I
swear, until at least an hour after I'd said goodbye to him: that this
Bernie hadn't wanted me as a writer at all. He'd thought I was still
at the UP, and might therefore be a valuable contact close to the
heart of the syndicated comic-strip business.

I can remember exactly what I was doing when this knowledge
came over me. I was changing the baby's diaper, looking down into
her round, beautiful eyes as if I expected her to congratulate me,
or thank me, for having once more managed to avoid the terrible
possibility of touching her skin with the point of the safety pin—I was
doing that, when I thought of the way his voice had paused in saying,
"We could of made use of your—"

During that pause he must have abandoned whatever elaborate
building plans might still have lain in saying, "your connections there
at the UP" (and he didn't know I'd been fired; for all he knew I
might still have as many solid connections in the newspaper business
as Dr. Corvo had in the child psychology field or Wade Manley had
in the movies), and had chosen to finish it off with "your writing
talent" instead. And so I knew that for all my finicking concern over
the sparing of Bernie's feelings in that telephone conversation, it was
Bernie, in the end, who had gone out of his way to spare mine.

Reading all this over, I can see now that it hasn't been built very
well. Its beams and joists, its very walls are somehow out of kilter;

its foundation feels weak; possibly I failed to dig the right kind of hole in the ground in the first place. But I can see too that there's no point in worrying about such things now, because it's time to put the roof on it—to bring you up to date on what happened to all of us builders.

I don't know what happened to Bernie, and I can't honestly say that I've thought very much about him over the years. It might be a nice touch to tell you that I never get into a taxicab without taking a close look at the driver's neck and profile, but it wouldn't be true. One thing that is true, though, and it's just now occurred to me, is that very often in trying to hit on the right wording for some touchy personal letter, I've thought of: "I didn't have time to write you a short letter today, so I had to write you a long one instead."

Whether I meant it or not when I wished him luck with his comic strip, I think I started meaning it an hour later. I mean it now, whole-heartedly, and the funny part is that he might still be able to build it into something, connections or not. Sillier things than that have built empires in America. At any rate I hope he hasn't lost his interest in the project, in one form or another; but more than anything I hope to God—and I'm not swearing this time—I hope to whatever God there might be that he hasn't lost Rose.

Everybody knows what happened to Wade Manley. He died un-expectedly a few years later, in bed; and the fact that it was the bed of a young woman not his wife was considered racy enough to keep the tabloids busy for weeks. You can still see reruns of his old movies on television, and whenever I see one I'm surprised all over again to find that he was a good actor—much too good, I expect, ever to have gotten caught in any cornball role as a cab driver with a heart as big as all outdoors.

As for Dr. Corvo, there was a time when everybody knew what happened to him, too. It happened in the very early fifties, whichever year it was that the television companies built and launched their most massive advertising campaigns. One of the most massive of all was built around a signed statement by Dr. Alexander Corvo, eminent child psychologist, to the effect that any boy or girl in our time whose home lacked a televison set would quite possibly grow up emotionally deprived. Every other child psychologist, every articulate liberal, and very nearly every parent in the United States came down on Alexander Corvo like a plague of locusts, and when they were done with him there wasn't an awful lot of eminence left. Since then, I'd say offhand that the *New York Times* would give you half a dozen Alexander Corvos for a single Newbold Morris any day of the week.

That takes the story right on up to Joan and me, and now I'll have to give you the chimney top. I'll have to tell you that what she and I were building collapsed too, a couple of years ago. Oh, we're still friendly—no legal battles over alimony, or custody, or anything like that—but there you are.

And where are the windows? Where does the light come in?

Bernie, old friend, forgive me, but I haven't got the answer to that one. I'm not even sure if there *are* any windows in this particular house. Maybe the light is just going to have to come in as best it can, through whatever chinks and cracks have been left in the builder's faulty craftsmanship, and if that's the case you can be sure that nobody feels worse about it than I do. God knows, Bernie; God knows there certainly ought to be a window around here somewhere, for all of us.